1,000,000 Books

are available to read at

www.ForgottenBooks.com

Read online
Download PDF
Purchase in print

ISBN 978-1-330-87873-6
PIBN 10116155

THE
MISTRESS OF BRAE FARM

A Novel

BY

ROSA NOUCHETTE CAREY

AUTHOR OF 'NELLIE'S MEMORIES,' 'BARBARA HEATHCOTE'S TRIAL,'
'NOT LIKE OTHER GIRLS,' ETC.

London
MACMILLAN AND CO., Limited
NEW YORK: THE MACMILLAN COMPANY
1906

First Edition (1 vol. Crown 8vo) 1897
Reprinted 1897, 1898, 1899, 1900, 1901, 1902, 1906

CONTENTS

THE MISTRESS OF BRAE FARM

CHAPTER I

THE MISTRESS OF BRAE FARM

'Tranquillity is a good thing.'—PERIANDER.
'Misfortunes are common to all.'—PHOCYLIDES.

THE young mistress of Brae Farm was looking over the little green gate that divided the garden from the big farmyard.

It was still early in the afternoon, and there was a hush and stillness over the whole place as though a universal siesta prevailed. Presently from the long green meadow the cows would come slowly in single file to the milking-shed, and later on the cart-horses clattering heavily down the lane on their way to the pond.

The turkeys and geese and even the cocks and hens were all afield, only the pigeons sat in rows on the red roof of the granary sunning themselves in the sweet May sunshine; and the sole occupants of the farmyard below were an old grey pony with paniers, dozing peacefully with his feet embedded in the clean yellow straw, and an infant asleep in one of the paniers.

'Mattie Renshawe come for some more new-laid eggs,' observed Ellison to herself, but she spoke aloud, for the fine collie sitting erect beside her uttered a low whine of pleasure at his mistress's voice.

'Hush, Bairn, we must not wake the baby!' and the dog was at once silent, as though he understood her, and then he and his mistress resumed their quiet watching.

Some one once remarked that if he were asked who was the most contented woman he had ever known, he should name Ellison Lee. 'Of course,' he went on, 'in this sorry old world of ours there is no such thing as perfect contentment ; the thing is impossible, an anomaly—altogether absurd ; but if you wish me to name a person who is in thorough harmony with her environment, who has the three greatest blessings ever vouchsafed to humanity — good sense, good temper, and a good digestion—that person is my cousin once removed, Ellison Lee.'

Colonel Trevor was not alone in this opinion ; most people admired and envied the young mistress of Brae Farm, and, indeed, if one were to add up her numerous advantages, the list would be a fairly large one.

Young, for surely seven-and-twenty may be called young, with easy means, good health, and no encumbrances in the shape of idle brothers to be settled in the world, or troublesome young sisters ; with a moderate share of good looks and sufficient cleverness to enable her to hold her own even in these days of multitudinous examinations and high culture ; and, above all, with a natural aptitude for doing the right thing at the right moment, without selfish reserves or morbid dread of consequences ; surely, with all these qualifications, Ellison Lee might be called a fortunate person. No, whatever were her faults—and most certainly she had her share of them in common with other true daughters of Eve—there was nothing morbid about her.   One might wish perhaps that she had more imagination, that she were a little less satisfied with her own decisions ; but these were merely specks and flaws, to be smiled over and forgiven, for few unmarried women in her solitary independent circumstances could have given less occasion for the enemy to blaspheme.

'Yes ; she is a bit proud, and she does not like to be contradicted,' Mrs. Drake, the blacksmith's wife, would say to her gossips, 'and when she has made up her mind there is no turning her ; but at the bottom she is sound and sweet as the kernel of a nut, and there is no nonsense about her.   I like a woman who has a head on her shoulders, and who can put down her foot when the right time comes.   How do you suppose she would manage with that young bailiff, Sam Brattle, and all those men if she was afraid of opening her mouth and putting down her foot ?—and it is a solid foot too !'

The mistress of Brae Farm was an authority in Highlands, although that favoured little place, set so snugly in its cup-like hollow amid heather-covered hills and climbing fir-woods, had half a dozen big houses scattered here and there—Brae House to wit, and Redlands, and Price's Folly, not to mention Ferncliffe, where old Mrs. Langton lived ; but, nevertheless, Miss Lee at Brae Farm could hold her own even with her wealthier neighbours.

Ellison Lee was certainly no beauty, but her face was a pleasant one. She was a tall, strong young woman, somewhat heavily moulded, but she carried herself well ; she had calm, serious blue eyes, that always looked straight at one, and the smooth coils of light brown hair set off a well-shaped head. People always called her a fine woman, and somehow the term suited her. She had matured early, and never thought or spoke of herself as a girl.

'I always envy Ellison her repose of manner,' Mrs. Trevor would say ; 'she is the most restful person I know ; nothing ever flurries her ; my pet name for her is "Fairy Order," and as I often tell you, Gavin could not do better,' and here a glance of mutual understanding would pass between the ladies. Highlands, in spite of its being an earthly paradise, was not free from the gossip and tittle-tattle and small babblement common to a village.

Highlands had long ago made up its mind that Colonel Trevor would one day marry Ellison Lee. His wife had been dead more than eight years. He was forty at least ; very young ladies were not to his taste—he never knew how to say pretty things to them— and the friendship between him and his cousin was a deep and true one.

When Mrs. Earnshaw of Price's Folly walked up to Brae House Mrs. Trevor would speak quite openly, for, being old schoolfellows, they were great cronies. 'You see, Hermione,' she would say, 'now Gavin has retired from active service he ought to marry again and settle down. A man wants more than a mother and sister. Ellison suits him down to the ground, every one can see what he thinks of her.'

'Yes, and their lands march together,' returned her companion sympathetically. 'It would be a fine thing for the Colonel to have the Brae-lands united ; he would leave a grand estate to his children.'

'Aren't we counting our chickens before they are hatched ?' observed Mrs. Trevor, smiling, and then she sighed ; her infant grandson lay with his young mother in an Indian grave.

While the two ladies sat and gossiped softly over the Colonel's future in the pleasant Brae drawing-room, Colonel Trevor was revolving the same thoughts as he rode up the long meadow, with his face set as usual in the direction of the Brae Farm, where Ellison was waiting for him at the green gate.

Gavin Trevor was a thin soldierly-looking man ; he had a brown weather-beaten face and a dark moustache ; but the hair on his temples was already turning grey ; he had keen searching eyes that could soften pleasantly at times, and the slight brusquerie of manner that strangers noticed at first, soon wore off when people knew him better. To a close observer his face bore traces of past troubles. He had married early, and his choice had been a fortunate one, and for two years he considered himself the happiest of men. He loved his profession, he was respected and liked in the regiment, and he and his wife were looked upon as a model couple.

When she died, and he stood beside the bed and looked at her with the dark downy head of their new-born child nestled close to her cold breast, the springs of happiness seemed to dry up within him, and he went out of that death-chamber a stricken man.

But he struggled on bravely, and in a year or two people began to say that Major Trevor would marry again, but he only frowned when any such hint reached his ears.

Death had been rife in the regiment, and he got his promotion early ; but soon afterwards he had an attack of the deadly Indian fever, and though he fought it gallantly, and stuck to his post, there were recurring attacks, and his doctor began to look grave ; sorrow had undermined the fine constitution, and he was no longer fit for his work.

'You must go back to England, Colonel, and be sharp about it too, if you do not want to be buried here,' for Doctor Morton could speak the truth brutally when he chose, and he chose to do so now.

'Do you mean that I shall never be fit for active service again ?' asked Trevor sharply ; 'speak plainly, man, for heaven's sake.'

'I mean that India has played the deuce with you, and it will be years before you are quite to rights again ; take my advice, Colonel, you are young yet, go back to England and settle down quietly for a year or two,' he was going to say 'get a wife,' but a look in his patient's eyes checked him ; 'take life easily and you will make an old man yet,' and though Colonel Trevor pooh-poohed him as an alarmist, he took his advice in the end.

During his long absence in India, his father had died ; he was now the owner of the Brae, and there, on his return, he found his widowed mother and his sister Muriel. When the first few months had passed, and the sweet country air had already told favourably on him, and he looked less hollow-eyed and emaciated, Mrs. Trevor suggested that the Dower House, as it was called, a comfortable, unpretentious house about a mile away, should be put in order for her and Muriel.

'I do not mean that we should go and live there now, and leave you alone in this great house, Gavin,' she continued, somewhat alarmed by the same stony look in his dark eyes that Dr. Morton had noticed. 'But the Dower House is in such a dilapidated state—-Robinson was saying so when he came over here—it will take months to make it really habitable.'

'Yes, mother, I am well aware of that. I meant to speak to Robinson myself, and have it done up next spring for letting, that is, if you will give me permission to do so. Ellison agreed with me that it would be a good investment.'

'But if you let it, Gavin, what is to become of me and Muriel? The poor girl is not likely to marry—you must see that for yourself; and if you ever—— Don't frown so, Gavin! poor dear Helen has been dead over five years now, and she would be the first to wish you to be happy.'

'Mother!' returned Gavin, hoarsely, 'you mean it well, of course, I know that, and I am not going to be such a fool as to quarrel with you; but if you love me, you will never drop this sort of hint again. A man knows best how to manage his own affairs; we will leave the question of the Dower House for you and Muriel until I seriously make up my mind to marry again; to the best of my belief that day will never come.'

And so the Dower House was done up and decorated from garret to basement, and re-christened Ferncliffe, and in due course of time a tenant for it was found; and though three years more had elapsed since that conversation, Mrs. Trevor still remained mistress of Brae House, and still gossiped gently to her crony, Mrs. Earnshaw, of the time when Gavin would at last make up his mind to marry again, and she and Muriel would have to turn out and live in the Dower House. Colonel Trevor was reviewing the last three years as he rode slowly up the Darley Road; his reins had dropped on the mare's neck; on the whole, the review was a satisfactory one. He had grown stronger, and had almost attained his normal condition of health. Though the old energy and pluck were wanting, he no longer fretted for his work, but he still kept up his interest in his old regiment; he had grown reconciled to his quiet, country life; it suited him, and he found plenty of occupation; and then it was so near town, he could run up to his club whenever he wished, and be in touch with the last new question of the day; when he was to be met so often in St. James's and Piccadilly, no one could accuse him of being buried alive.

And then he had developed a new talent, or, to speak properly, revived an old taste; he had taken to sketching and painting, and during his visits to town he had begun to haunt sundry studios.

'There is nothing like having a hobby!' Mrs. Trevor would say briskly to her pale daughter. 'Look at Gavin, how busy he is from morning to night; this new craze of his for painting is so good for him, that is why Ellison encourages him so, she wants him to turn the octagon room into a studio, and we could surely spare it. You might take some lessons yourself, Muriel, and then you could go out sketching with him.'

'You forget, mother, that I have no taste for drawing, and that I could not draw a straight line to save my life.' Muriel spoke in a tone of quiet exasperation ; when would her mother understand that an artist could not be made to order ? But Mrs. Trevor only sighed and shrugged her shoulders—was there any possible thing in which Muriel would consent to interest 'herself' ?

'I have jogged on pretty comfortably all these years,' thought Colonel Trevor, passing his hand lightly over the mare's mane. 'Don't go to sleep, Miss Alice, for I can see Ellison at the gate.' It was evident that Miss Alice saw her too, for she pricked up her dainty ears and quickened her pace.

'Yes, I have not had a bad time,' thought Gavin, thinking, as he had often done before, how much comfort of mind and hours of pleasant, kindly companionship he owed to Ellison. From the first she had been his trusty comrade and friend ; her tact and strong common-sense had often helped him over the rough places of daily life.

It was rather difficult to avoid friction with his mother. Mrs. Trevor was a warm-hearted, affectionate woman, but she was over-sensitive and excitable, and Muriel 'was a thing of moods and tenses,' as her cousin once observed. Gavin never professed to understand his sister, though he was very kind to her ; but he could talk freely on all subjects to Ellison.

He waved his hand to her gaily, and then lifted his hat, and Ellison leaned over the gate to pat Miss Alice's glossy brown neck, while Bairn leapt up against the bars with joyous barks of welcome.

'She is in splendid condition, Gavin,' observed Ellison, looking at the mare with critical approving eyes. 'Sam Brattle was right when he advised you to buy her ; it is sometimes cheapest to pay a long figure for a thing you want.'

'I paid a precious long figure for Miss Alice,' laughed Colonel Trevor ; 'but in spite of her skittishness, I would not part with her for double her price ; she is like the rest of her sex, full of tricks, and with plenty of virtues. Well, Ellison, how long are you going to keep that gate shut ? Is not the mistress of Brae Farm at home this afternoon ?'

Ellison drew back slowly, but there was a slight blush on her fair sedate face.

'I am always at home to my friends, Gavin, and I have so much to tell you ; will you take Miss Alice round to the stable ? you will find some one about—and I will go in and make tea.'

CHAPTER II

'Teach me to feel another's woe,
To hide the fault I see;
The mercy I to others show,
That mercy show to me.'

POPE.

As Colonel Trevor led his mare away, Ellison walked quickly back to the house.

It was an irregular low grey house, without any pretension; but in summer-time its weather-beaten old walls were smothered in creepers. Glorious *Gloire de Dijon* roses peeped in at the bedroom windows; honeysuckle and starry clematis draped the stone porch, and clusters of blue-grey wisteria festooned the dairy window.

All round the house lay a delightful old garden, for it was one of Ellison's peculiarities that she would cultivate none but old-fashioned flowers.

Rows of white and orange lilies and gorgeous hollyhocks lined the border, with deep blue delphiniums and the humbler larkspur; heart-shaped beds of small yellow and purple pansies studded the lawn, and straggling masses of London pride and sweet-smelling pinks were everywhere. All the summer long it was a garden of delights. The air would be fragrant with the heavy scent of syringa and the spicy fragrance of the deep red carnations. How the bees and birds loved that garden; there were nests by the score in the shrubbery that led to the kitchen garden, and the row of bee-hives under the south wall—where the peaches grew—brought in a goodly amount of honey. All round the house and gardens lay a ring of sloping meadows, and from her bedroom window Ellison could catch a glimpse of the chimneys of the Brae House, and beyond that the dark foliage of the Brae Woods.

From early spring to late autumn the front door always stood open. Through the porch one passed into a small square hall, somewhat dark from its heavy wainscoting. In winter a glorious fire burnt in the big open grate, but in summer it was filled with honesty, or branches of may and rhododendron ; an oak settle, black with age, a grandfather's clock, and a chest big enough to hold the unfortunate bride in the 'The Mistletoe Bough,' gave it an air of comfort. On one side of the hall was the dining-room, on the other Ellison's sitting-room ; two red-baized doors shut off the staircase and the other offices.

Ellison's sitting-room—for she always sternly refused to call it her drawing-room—was a long handsome room, extending from the front to the back of the house. One could not look round it without recognising at once that it was the heart and nucleus of the home, that it was the living room of its mistress ; every corner had traces of her taste and various occupations. One wall was lined with bookcases, chiefly filled with standard works of a solid description ; fiction, except in the shape of Dickens and Thackeray and Sir Walter Scott, was not largely represented ; clearly utility, not sentiment or imagination, was the salient characteristic of the young mistress of Brae Farm.

A writing-table and a business-like looking bureau, bristling with papers, stood at one end. This was where Ellison wrote her letters and kept her weekly accounts. A Japanese screen shut off this part of the room. A couch, a round table, and two or three comfortable-looking chairs filled up the centre, and the deep front bay-window, with its cushioned seat and small square tea-table, was evidently where Ellison entertained her friends. There were no useless nicknacks to be seen anywhere, only the shelves of fine old china near the fireplace, and one or two good pictures gave it the colouring it needed. It was in this room that Ellison lived her busy useful life—except for meals she never entered her dining-room, unless it was to interview her bailiff, Sam Brattle ; her humbler visitors and pensioners were always received in a small room leading out of the kitchen, called the still-room. There stood the great presses and cupboards where Ellison kept her groceries and jams and wonderful syrups, and the small stock of drugs that were always at her neighbours' service.

The nearest doctor lived at Bramfield, two miles away ; even when his services were urgently needed, it might be hours before he returned from his rounds to receive the message. The villagers in Highlands doctored themselves and their children a great deal with Miss Lee's help. It was through her exertions that the National Health Committee sent down a lecturer to deliver a course on 'First Aid to the Injured and Sick,' in the Iron room below the vicarage, which was called the Institute, that had been built by the late Mr. Trevor as a thank-offering for his wife's recovery from a dangerous illness.

When Ellison's small stock of drugs were exhausted, they could always be procured at Tom Brattle's, or 'Brattle's' as it was called. Tom was Sam Brattle's elder brother, and drove a thriving trade in Highlands. You might buy anything at Brattle's—from a straw hat and a cambric dress to moist sugar and onions, or a pennyworth of sweets. Books, photographs, music, bacon, and fat pork ; ginger-beer and every kind of children's toys, beads, soap, and ribbons were all in this wholesale depôt for the village.

Although it was May, a small bright fire was burning cheerily in the sitting-room, and a kettle was singing lustily on its trivet. When Ellison had made the tea out of the old-fashioned tea-caddy that stood ready to hand, she rang for the hot cakes, of which there was always a liberal supply at Brae Farm, then she took her usual seat and began rinsing the cups in a careful methodical way, and every now and then glancing towards the gate. 'Gavin was a long time,' she thought ; 'surely Joe Brand must be in the yard'; then a smile came to her lips as she saw the Colonel's tall spare figure approaching the house.

'Well, this is pleasant,' he said, looking round him contentedly as he threw himself down on the cushioned seat opposite Ellison. 'I never knew any room to beat this for comfort. I often make my mother cross by telling her so. You know you love it yourself, Ellison. Would you change it for one of ours at the Brae ? No ; I thought so '—as she shook her head ; 'the drawing-rooms are too big for comfort, and the library too dark ; the morning-room is so-so, but the billiard-room is a barrack ; as for my sanctum——'

'Now, Gavin,' interrupted his cousin, 'how can you have the baseness to find fault with all those beautiful rooms ? The drawing-rooms are charming ! they beat Redlands, and as for Price's Folly, they could put two of their rooms into one of yours. It is simply blarney to be praising up my poor sitting-room at their expense ; let me give you some more milk—that tea is too strong—but you kept me so long waiting.'

'I suppose people's ideas of comfort differ,' he returned, as he held out his cup, 'but you always seem so snug, I suppose because you live here from morning to night ; now my mother spends her mornings in the octagon room, or in her big dressing-room, and her afternoons and evenings in the inner drawing-room, only sometimes she takes a fancy to use the other one ; in fact, you never know where to find her.'

'I see what you mean,' replied Ellison, as she unrolled a large piece of knitting. This was one of her habits, never to let her fingers be idle while she talked ; countless were the socks and cross-overs and comforters she knitted during stray quarters-of-an-hour. 'Yes, I know I do love my sitting-room, but I have never enjoyed it more than during the last six weeks.'

'For shame, Ellison—poor Miss Lockwood ; after all, she was a good-natured, harmless creature.'

'Ah, you may call her that if you like. Letitia was not without her good points. She certainly made herself extremely useful, and her needlework was beautiful ; but how was one to endure her endless chatter and trivialities ? You know very well, Gavin, that Cousin Louise often declared it would have driven her wild to be in my place.'

'Yes, I know, from morning to night—

"It was Letty's delight
To chatter and talk without stopping," etc. etc.'

'No, but seriously, Gavin, I never knew I had nerves before ; but I understand now what you mean when you say you feel quite jumpy. I was prickly all over. If it had only been sensible talk, but it was everlasting chit-chat ; the droning of a wasp, or the buzzing of a blue-bottle against the glass, would have conveyed as much sense to my mind. No, no, Letitia Lockwood is a good creature and an excellent Christian ; but she has the smallest amount of brain-power that I ever knew in any woman. I was obliged to tell her, at last, that we did not suit each other. Poor soul, she had a good cry over what she called my hard-heartedness and want of feeling ; but if you knew how delicious my first solitary evening was to me.'

'But, Ellison,' looking at her keenly, 'has not my mother convinced you yet that you are too young to live alone ?'

'No one would ever convince me of that,' returned Ellison obstinately, 'but I am willing to give in for the sake of peace ; besides,' her decided tone faltering a little, 'my dear father always wished me to have a companion ; he told me the night he was taken ill, that at my age it was better not to brave conventionality. Poor old dad ! I daresay he was right.'

'And you are looking out for some one to replace Miss Lockwood ?'

'No,' she returned quietly, 'there is no need for me to look out. My cousin, Lorraine Herbert, needs help ; her husband died about a year and a half ago. She is in sadly straitened circumstances, and I have offered a home to her and her child.'

To dear Joan
in loving memory of
Aunt Carrie who
passed away April 9th '25.

Colonel Trevor looked extremely surprised. He was well aware that Ellison never asked advice, and that she seldom mentioned any fresh arrangement until she had made up her mind that it was feasible and desirable. She had too much backbone and decision of character to talk over pros and cons in the usual feminine fashion ; nevertheless, in his masculine judgment, this was rather a serious step to take ; surely it would have been better to have spoken to his mother first.

For the moment he felt hurt ; but not wishing to show this he said quickly—

'Lorraine Herbert—have I ever heard the name ? She must be a cousin on your mother's side, then ? '

'She is my first cousin, and therefore my nearest relative ; her name was Broughton before she married ; surely you have heard me mention Uncle Philip, who was so unfortunate and died abroad ? ' But Colonel Trevor shook his head.

'You forget how many years I have been in India—possibly my mother may have heard the name of Broughton ; but since I have been home, there has been no mention of them.'

'It is rather inconceivable, but the fact is, Lorraine and I are perfect strangers to each other. Uncle Philip lived abroad, partly on account of his health and partly because of reduced circumstances —he was always Murad the Unlucky of the family—then Lorraine married and settled in Ireland, and until three weeks ago we never met.'

'You know nothing of her, and yet you are offering her a home ; is this your usual prudence, Ellison ? ' Colonel Trevor's voice had a note of anxiety in it.

'At least I know that she is Uncle Philip's daughter, and my next of kin, and that she and her child are in danger of starving,' she replied quietly. 'I see you are put out, Gavin, because I have not spoken to you or Cousin Louise, but you know what I have often said to you—unless one is lame one does not need crutches ; and as long as I have reason and judgment I can manage my own business.'

The words might have sounded brusque, if they had not been accompanied by a bright smile ; but Colonel Trevor was not to be propitiated by a smile ; he was tenacious, perhaps a trifle obstinate by nature—his mother always said so—and he was determined to get to the bottom of the matter. To be sure, his opinion had not been asked, but his friendship for Ellison made him anxious to protect her if possible from taking a wrong line of action.

On her side Ellison was secretly amused, and yet touched by Gavin's evident anxiety, but at the same time she thought he might have trusted her judgment. Was she the sort of person to do an impulsive thing? It was not to please herself that she was offering this home to her widowed cousin; for in her heart she knew that it was a self-sacrificing action, and one that she had been reluctant to perform. Altruism does not flourish naturally in some soils, and Ellison by no means desired her cousin to live with her; but, as she said to Colonel Trevor later on, how was she to engage a stranger when poor Lorraine needed a home? when duty was staring her in the face, how was she to refuse it and yet call herself a Christian?

'I could not have eaten my bread in comfort if I had not done it,' she went on. 'I could not have slept peacefully after seeing her and the child in that miserable garret; but I did not act impulsively, I came home, and thought over it for a week,'—she might have added truly, 'and prayed over it,' for Ellison was deeply religious, though she was too reserved to express her deeper feeling—'but it was no good shirking the question, it was a plain duty and I could not turn my back on it.'

'What put it in your head to go and see her, Ellison?'

'She wrote to me. She had wanted to write for months, but she could not find my address. She had never seen me or my home; but of course she knew that she had a cousin. She found the address at last on an old letter father had written to Uncle Philip, and then she wrote at once. I liked the letter, there was no humbug about it; it was quite simple and direct to the point. Her husband was dead, and she and her little boy were in great distress; and she was utterly without friends. The address was Beaumont Street, Camden Town.'

'And you went to her at once?'

'Yes—the very next day. I telegraphed that I was coming. You were in town, Gavin, so you knew nothing about it. Am I wearying you, or do you want to hear everything?'

'Everything,' was his terse answer. 'You know all your affairs interest me.'

'You are very good to me,' she returned gently. 'Do you know Camden Town?' and as he nodded, 'ah, but you are not well acquainted with Beaumont Street. How can people live their lives in such places? how can they be good and patient and love their children, and not hate the day they were born? Oh, I am speaking strongly, I know,' as he merely elevated his eyebrows at this; 'but if you had only seen the street, the black railway-arch at one end, and the unkempt children playing in the road, and the draggled women, and the dingy homes with their dismal areas and windows that looked as though they were never cleaned, you would not wonder at my disgust. The very sunshine was less bright in Beaumont Street.'

'And Mrs. Herbert was living in this desirable neighbour-hood ?'

'Yes, she had been lodging there for five months—such a lodging—a bedroom at the top of the house, with a view of the opposite chimney-pots. And here I found Lorraine and her baby boy, and a miserable little tabby kitten that she had rescued from starvation and the cruel mercies of the street. By the bye,' interrupting herself, 'I have promised to give the kitten a home too.'

'You are a good woman, Ellison ; I always said so. But go on. Your story is deeply interesting, and you are telling it very well. I want you to describe your cousin.'

'Let me say a word about the room first. Shabby little place as it was, it was so neat—you could tell at once that a lady lived in it—and Lorraine's appearance was as neat, too. She has left off her widow's dress—white collars and cuffs were luxuries that could be dispensed with—but her gown was black of course.'

'Is she younger or older than you, Ellison ?'

'Older by three years. Lorraine is thirty, but she does not look her age. She is not exactly good-looking, but her face is pleasing. I should call her interesting. She is tall and rather thin and pale ; but she has nice eyes and lovely hair—that red-brown hair that looks auburn in the sunshine. Her boy is like her. He is rather a delicate little fellow, not pretty, but very engaging. Of course Lorraine dotes on him. He was only about fifteen months old when his father died.'

'I suppose she talked a great deal about her husband ?'

'Yes, she told me everything in the frankest possible way. She is like her letter — very simple and direct. She did not wait for me to ask her questions, but told me all I wanted to know.

'She has had a hard life, Gavin. When her father died—he died at Lausanne—she went to Ireland with a family, who had been staying in a *pension* near them, as governess to the two girls.

'The O'Briens were kind-hearted people, and she was fairly comfortable with them, and might have remained so ; but in an evil day she made the acquaintance of a young artist—Ralph Herbert—and, after a few months, was induced to marry him.

'It was a rash and most imprudent marriage. Lorraine frankly owned this at once. She was not in love with Ralph Herbert ; still at that time she believed in him. She knew that he was poor, but he told her that he had some orders coming in, and that, as he was utterly free from debt, they could live comfortably in a quiet way. Lorraine had no wish to leave the O'Briens, and she pleaded for a longer engagement; but Ralph told her that his love for her was impeding his work, that he was too restless to paint, and that, after they were once married, he would settle down and make a name for himself.

'When I asked her how she could bring herself to marry a man of whose antecedents she was nearly ignorant, and whom she confessed she did not really love, she told me that he seemed so lonely and unhappy that she longed to comfort him. "I belonged to no one, and Ralph needed me; and then he had such a way with him," she finished.

'Poor Lorraine! Before many months were over she had reason to rue her imprudence. Ralph Herbert was a man who did not know how to speak the truth; when he told her he had no debts he had lied to her freely. Before they had been married six months there was an execution in the house, and their furniture was seized. They led a wandering Bohemian life after this, never staying long in any place, and always, as she feared, leaving debts behind them.

'Nothing she could say to him seemed of any avail; he had simply no sense of honour; she hinted to me in a guarded sort of way that he had other vices. "I know he cared for me to the last," she said mournfully, "but I never really influenced him; if he had not died we should have gone from bad to worse, for how was I to leave him, the father of my boy." It went to my heart to hear her, Gavin.

'Just before he died a small windfall came to him in the shape of a couple of hundred pounds; this enabled her to bury him decently and pay a few of the most pressing debts. Her health had suffered from the strain of nursing him, and for some months she was unable to do anything. There were doctor's bills to pay and other expenses, and her money began to dwindle.

'It was impossible to resume her teaching, for she could not leave her boy. Soon after Christmas she was obliged to give up her comfortable rooms for the attic I found her in when she wrote to me. Things were at their lowest ebb, and she was keeping herself and the boy by taking in plain work; a shop in Camden Town employed her, and she was thankful to be enabled in this way to keep a respectable roof over her head.'

'Poor soul,' returned Colonel Trevor, 'what a tragic story; but I fear there are many similar cases. There are no end of improvident marriages, even in other ranks of life; many a respectable young couple, who have taken their responsibilities too early, without counting the cost, have laid up a heritage of poverty and misery for their children. I know many such stories.'

'So do I, but the grimness of the reality never strikes us so forcibly as when we hear it from the person's own lips. When Lorraine told me that she had tasted nothing but bread and weak tea since the previous morning, I could not keep the tears out of my eyes, and yet I am not an imaginative woman. I think I never enjoyed anything more than watching her eat a mutton chop. It really did me good.'

Colonel Trevor's eyes lingered on Ellison's face with quiet tenderness; it always rested him to look at her and hear her talk. Her calmness and absence of all excitability or exaggeration pleased and satisfied him, but at this moment he had a glimpse of a deeper underlying goodness. How quietly she was telling her story; she was making so little of her own sacrifice. It was her duty to shelter her next-of-kin, that was how she had put it, but she had said nothing at all of her own trouble and inconvenience.

'And when does your cousin come to you?' he asked, after a moment's silence.

'Next week—Wednesday, I think. I could not fix an earlier date, as I had to re-paint and re-paper the rooms I have set apart for her and the boy. She has begged me to keep my spare room intact for chance guests, for of course I talked things over with her on my second visit, but the room she will have is a very pleasant one, and has the same outlook as mine. Why are you looking at me so solemnly, Gavin?'

'I am only thinking what a good woman you are,' he returned quietly, as he put his hand over hers, 'and God bless all such women, I say.' And then he rose as though to take his leave.

CHAPTER III

LORRAINE

'Who ne'er his bread in sorrow ate,
Who ne'er the mournful midnight hours,
Weeping upon his bed has sate,
He knows ye not—ye Heavenly Powers.'
From GOETHE'S *Wilhelm Meister.*

It was on a fresh lovely afternoon in May, when Lorraine
Herbert sat in the railway compartment, with her boy in her
lap, looking out dreamily at the flying hedgerows, and counting
the milestones as she passed them.

In another quarter of an hour they would reach Bramfield,
where her cousin would be waiting for her on the platform.
Lorraine felt as though she were in some dream ; could it be true
that those months of misery were over ; that Beaumont Street
with its sordid surroundings was already a thing of the past,
and that she was entering on another chapter of her strange
life history ?

What a chequered and changeful life hers had been ; those
years of girlhood spent in foreign cities, picking up a desultory
education—much as the birds pick up their crumbs of sustenance.
Now she was learning embroidery and French at a convent, under
the tutelage of placid meek-eyed nuns ; or studying German
with a stout, placid, little Frau Hoffman, who lived in the flat
above them ; or adding up sums, and listening to fragments of
Kant's philosophy, from the lips of old Professor Schreiber, who
took snuff and used a huge red handkerchief, and who was
exceedingly kind and patient, with 'dem Englishen Mädchen.'
It was a desultory and aimless life for a girl to lead ; but it was
not without its pleasures. Those summer evenings, for example,
when they sat in the park at Brussels, listening to the music of

the band, while the stars came out above their heads ; or had ices and coffee in the Place, and watched the children dancing under the trees, and she had longed to dance too.

Then there were the friends who had been so good to her, the pastor and his wife at Lausanne, and the little French widow, and the Englishman and his tall daughters whom they had met at the *pension;* but indeed it would have been impossible to enumerate all her friends. Lorraine, who was sociable by nature, had pleasant acquaintances in every town or village that she visited. 'Thou wilt never want for friends, dear child,' an old Quaker lady had once said to her, 'for thy loving nature will draw affection to thee, as the honey in the flower draws the bee.'

Lorraine always told herself that she had been happier than most girls ; she loved her father dearly, and their free wandering life had suited her. 'When I was a wee child, I always thought I should like to be a gipsy, and live in a caravan,' she would say to her friends ; 'but going about with father is just as nice, if we only had a little more money ; but there, it is no use crying for the moon,' she would finish merrily, for she had a light heart, and made the best of everything. To her joyous nature, it was intense pleasure only to be alive and feel the sunshine ; and all things, sunshine and rain, hail and snow, winter and summer, and night and day, were to her the good gifts of God, and after a different fashion she enjoyed them all.

With her father's death, her bright, unthinking girlhood had come to an end ; but after a time her buoyant nature asserted itself. 'I can never be sad long,' she would sometimes say, and, indeed, sadness was at all times foreign to her. It never became habitual, as in some morbid natures. For a time the cruel pressure of circumstances might crush her as a daisy is crushed under foot, but when the footstep has passed on, the daisy raises its head again, and Lorraine's nature was singularly elastic.

The one great mistake of her life was marrying Ralph Herbert ; but she was pliant and sympathetic, and his passion had dominated her. He had given her no peace, and in a weak moment she had yielded to his urgency. 'Only marry me, and you shall never repent it, my darling,' he had said to her. She had married him, and every hour some fresh humiliation, some soul-degrading necessity, made repentance more poignant and bitter.

Lorraine, who had a sturdy honesty of her own, who would rather have starved than feasted on delicacies for which she was unable to pay, had to stand by and witness her husband's crooked dealings ; it was a wonder that she escaped from his influence uncontaminated, but he could never bring her round to his views. 'Owe no man anything, but to love one another,' was her creed ; and, even in her worst days, she remained loyal to it.

'If we cannot afford it, we must go without it, Ralph,' she had said to him about a week after their marriage ; but he had merely laughed, and ordered the shopman to send the goods home.

'Don't be such a little goose, Lorrie darling,' he said as she remonstrated, 'every other fellow does it, and of course I shall pay for it when I have painted that picture'; but he never did, and by and by she understood him better, and her young heart grew sick within her.

Lorraine did not quite lose hope. She expected to be a mother ; but her first confinement was a terrible one ; the child, a girl, died, and it was feared that Lorraine would die too, but her constitution triumphed. She got better, and her husband behaved well to her; and as he was working hard at a large picture, and it was likely to be a success, she had a few months' peace ; then things began to go wrong again, and by and by her little Theodore was born.

Lorraine had been perfectly frank with her cousin, but instinctive generosity made her say as little as possible about her husband's vices. 'My married life was just a gloomy tunnel,' she said to Ellison later on, 'but one could at times see the sunshine. I never quite lost courage, though I suffered horribly at times. I was sorry for Ralph, but he killed the little love I had for him. I came to the conclusion that he was warped in some way, poor fellow, he did not seem to see things as I saw them, and when he did a mean thing, he was never ashamed of it.' But neither then nor afterwards did she enlarge on this dark portion of her life, though she would talk for an hour together of those months in Beaumont Street, and of her hardships and struggles.

'Weariness may endure for a night, but joy cometh in the morning,' thought Lorraine, as her glistening eyes rested on the green meadows, where the lambs were frolicking about their woolly mothers. 'How can I ever be grateful enough to my cousin ?'

Ellison's fair serious face and quiet blue eyes had seemed almost angelic to her that day as they sat together by the window overlooking the sooty chimney-pots, with Waif and the boy playing at their feet, but there had been no impulsive offer of help at first.

'You are my cousin, Lorraine, I have no nearer relative, it was right that you should send for me in your trouble ; we must see what is to be done,' and then food had been sent for, and when Lorraine had finished her meal, Ellison had placed a five-pound note in her hand, and had promised to come again in a week's time.

Lorraine tried not to feel disappointed when Ellison had left her—'She was a dear woman,' she said to herself, 'a ministering angel; but she wished she had kissed her at parting.' Lorraine, lonely and unnerved, longed to throw her arms round Ellison's neck. 'She is good, she is true, she will not fail me, but she is undemonstrative,' she thought as she took up her work again, but every day she counted the hours until Ellison came again.

'I have thought things over,' observed Ellison, in her quiet leisurely way, as soon as she had seated herself on her second visit. 'I live alone, and the house is roomy. Will you come to me, Lorraine, and bring your boy, and make Brae Farm your home?'

'My home! For always, do you mean? A home for me and baby boy?' And when Ellison said 'Yes,' Lorraine had utterly broken down, and wept passionately. At that moment Ellison felt that she had done well.

'On Wednesday, the sixteenth, I shall expect you,' were her parting words. 'I will write all my directions about the journey; and, Lorraine, if you want any more money for yourself or the boy, I can spare you some.' But Lorraine shook her head.

'You have given me plenty. We will not disgrace you, Ellison. I will set about a new frock for my boy at once.' And then a warm kiss had passed between them, for, with all Ellison's reserve, it was impossible not to thaw under Lorraine's loving expressions of gratitude. 'You are my good angel, Ellison!'

'I would rather be your good friend, Lorraine; angels are not in my line at all.' And then she lifted Theodore in her arms, and, as she kissed the thin, pale little face, she suddenly remembered a baby brother who had died. Poor wee Willie! How she had grieved for him! 'This little fellow will look all the better for country air,' she said kindly; 'he is not half heavy enough for his age.' And it was then that Lorraine put in a petition for the kitten, to which Ellison had graciously acceded.

Lorraine's vivid imagination was taking a bird's-eye view of her past life; but, as the train slackened speed, she was recalled to the present again, and, putting down her boy, she rose and looked eagerly out of the window.

Yes, there was Ellison, in her closely-fitting blue serge and little black hat, looking as serene and cheerful as ever, with a splendid brown-and-white collie beside her. She nodded and smiled as she met Lorraine's eyes.

'You are in capital time,' she said, as she lifted out Theodore ;
'I have not been waiting more than five minutes. Will you point
out your luggage, Lorraine ?' And then they went together to the
luggage van.

'There are all mine and Tedo's earthly belongings,' observed
Lorraine, in a whispered aside to her cousin, as the porter dragged
out a large shabby trunk and a smaller tin box ; but Ellison took
no notice of this speech.

'Take them up in the cart, Joe,' she observed to a grey-haired
groom in undress livery, who was waiting on the platform. And
then Lorraine gave up her ticket and they went out of the station.

There was a small open waggonette standing before the door,
with a strong, handsome brown mare in the shafts. Ellison assisted
her cousin and lifted in the boy, then she mounted the driving-seat.

'Let the mare go and jump in, Daniel !' she said to a small
apple-cheeked boy in a grey suit ; and Daniel seated himself bash-
fully at the extreme edge of the waggonette. For some time
Lorraine watched him anxiously ; she felt so sure that he would
fall out. But Daniel was used to balancing himself in perilous
positions, and he was perpetually clambering in and out of the
waggonette to open and shut gates.

Ellison drove on rapidly ; but now and then she pointed with
her whip to some interesting landmark. 'There is Price's Folly,'
she said suddenly, when they had passed through three or four
open gates, and had driven through some long park-like meadows.
'The Earnshawes live there ; they are very pleasant people —
Admiral Earnshawe and his wife ; they have four sons, but they
are all abroad. Do you see the house, Lorraine ?'

Lorraine answered in the affirmative ; she had good eyes, and
could well discern the old-fashioned irregular house lying in the
wooded hollow.

'You never told me how beautiful it was !' exclaimed Lorraine
in almost an injured voice. But Ellison only laughed.

'I wanted you to find out the beauties for yourself ; and I was
never good at description. Steady, Mollie, old girl ! It is not
nearly tea-time yet, and we are in no hurry. I hope you are not
nervous, Lorraine ; Mollie is a little fresh this afternoon.' But
Lorraine returned truly that she loved going fast.

They had left the meadows now, and were driving down lovely
wooded lanes. Now and then they passed a comfortable-looking
cottage, or a bit of broken land wooded with Scotch fir, larch, and
pine ; then came another gate.

'This is Highlands,' observed Ellison ; and Lorraine stood up
in the waggonette and silently gazed over her cousin's shoulder.

Below them lay the village—the cottages with their brown roofs and red tilings nestling among grassy slopes and fir woods— a range of low hills closed the horizon, later on they would be purple with heather. On one side the pine woods seemed to climb the hill rather steeply, and on their left hand were the church and vicarage and another and less sombre wood. A broken common with cattle feeding upon it lay directly before them and seemed to stretch from one end of the village to the other.

'Do you like it, Lorraine; is it not a charming view? I am so fond of our dear little Highlands. Do you see that gate yonder with two or three cottages beside it? Our nearest way to the farm would be through that gate and down Fernleigh Lane; but if you are not tired we will drive through the Brae Woods, there they are behind the vicarage, you can see the Lodge and the gate from here.'

'Ah, yes, do let us go there!' exclaimed Lorraine. 'I have never seen a village like this in England—it looks like an earthly paradise. Oh, how good people ought to be who live here.'

'People are much the same everywhere,' returned Ellison prosaically. 'Human nature has its faults in Highlands as well as Camden Town.' Then, as Lorraine shivered slightly as though a cold wind had suddenly passed over her, Daniel opened the gate and Ellison drove slowly up the steep broken path, talking all the time. 'Strangers are always rather surprised when they first see Highlands,' she remarked. 'One or two have asked me where the village really is, because they can see only a few scattered houses, but in reality there are thirty or forty cottages, and we have at least nine or ten good private houses within two miles of the church, though Brae House and Redlands carry off the palm; and there are two or three comfortable farmhouses besides—in fact, Highlands is an exceptionally favoured little place.'

'It must be very healthy.'

'Yes, indeed; and however hot the summer is we have always a breeze. As nothing is ever perfect in this life, I am bound to tell you that in the late autumn we occasionally get a good deal of mist, for the place is high and catches the clouds; but often Highlands is in sunshine when the weald below is in fog. There, I will pull up a moment and you can just look down what I suppose I must call the main street—though street properly there is none. There is Brattle's our Universal Provider, the Whiteley of Highlands; that white cottage with the red double-peaked roof belongs to Drake the blacksmith. Mrs. Drake is a great friend of mine, I will tell you about her by and by; it is a good-sized cottage and they let lodgings. Just below is the *Waggon and Horses*, our one inn, and then comes our cobbler, and a few more cottages. The door of the *Waggon and Horses* and those white palings before the forge are the favourite resorts of the rustic youth of Highlands, and on Sunday afternoons you may see them thick as crows lining the palings ; they do absolutely nothing as far as I know, neither talk nor smoke ; but they look perfectly happy.'

'And you have lived in this lovely place all your life, Ellison !'

'Yes, my dear ; and one day I hope to be buried in that pretty churchyard. Ah, I see baby boy is asleep, and I must drive on ; but there seems so much to show you ; there is our institute, Lorraine, the iron room standing alone ; now we are going to turn into the Brae Woods. An old servant of my father's lives at the lodge—my cousin Colonel Trevor gave her the place.'

Lorraine uttered a little cry of irrepressible delight at the sight of the charming woodland road, that wound through the chase, bordered with spruce firs and other coniferous and ornamental trees and shrubs. Clumps of rhododendrons were here and there, then came a group of cedars, every now and then there were snug copses and a view of tangled undergrowth ; the right side was closed in by the same range of hills that bounded the village ; but on the left there were winding walks, sedulously cultivated, leading to a broad expanse of open meadowland.

'That is Brae House, through those iron gates we are passing,' observed Ellison. 'I think I told you about my cousins the Trevors of Brae ; all this part of Highlands belongs to my cousin Colonel Trevor. Brae Farm was always the property of one branch of the family, and is now in my possession ; you cannot see it just yet, the trees hide it, but in a moment we shall come to it.'

But Lorraine did not answer her, she leaned back in her seat almost wearily, and pressed her sleeping boy closer to her breast ; in her grateful heart she was saying to herself, 'He had "led me by paths that I have not known." Theo, my precious baby, to think that this is to be our home.'

CHAPTER IV

'A creature not too bright or good
For human nature's daily food ;
For transient sorrows, simple wiles,
Praise, blame, love, kisses, tears, and smiles.'
WORDSWORTH.

'WELCOME home, Lorraine,' and Ellison's warm friendly grasp seemed to accentuate her words. The kisses and smooth caresses of other women never came readily to her ; she often said herself that she preferred as little demonstration as possible. 'There is so much in a hand-shake,' she would add ; 'there is nothing more characteristic, a warm heart and a cold, loose shake of the hand so seldom go together.' There was no lack of feeling in Ellison's firm pressure of her cousin's hand, and a great deal of kindness in her voice, as she said simply, 'I will do my best to make you happy, dear ; and I am sure that when we know each other better that we shall be good friends.'

'Thank you,' returned Lorraine in a low voice, but her lips trembled and she could say no more ; she instinctively felt that any emotional speech would jar on Ellison. Her own heart-beats warned her that she was growing agitated, so she walked to the window and looked out for a moment, until she had swallowed the lump in her throat and the dimness had passed from her eyes, then she said quietly, 'What a dear room, Ellison !'

'So every one says ; but I am glad you like it. Look, that is your corner, Lorraine, and there is where I always sit in the evening. I am a regular old maid, and am terribly conservative in my habits. Now shall we go upstairs, and I will show you your room and Theodore's nursery—his playroom, I mean,' as Lorraine looked at her a little anxiously ; 'a child wants a room where he can keep his toys and make a mess. I thought when he got older we could put him a little bed in there.'

'You think of everything,' returned Lorraine gratefully; and then they passed through one of the red-baized doors, and up a broad, low staircase with quaintly carved balustrades, the landing-place being furnished with another dark oak chest and some fine blue dragon china. The bedrooms opened on a wide airy passage, but what at once arrested Lorraine's attention was an illuminated name over every door. Ellison paused as she noticed her cousin's surprise.

'All our rooms have names; it is an old custom at Brae Farm, and I have grown fond of it. "Good rest," that is your room, Lorraine; mine has always been "Peace," the spare room "Hospitality." The servants have some of the cardinal virtues inscribed over their doors: "Charity," "Prudence," "Content," "Cheerfulness." I was rather at a loss how to christen the nursery, but I have called it the "Dovecote," because the doves have a habit of sitting on that particular window-sill; they have taken a fancy to it, and there is no good trying to drive them away. You can alter the name if you like, Lorraine; remember, my dear,' laying her hand on her cousin's arm impressively, 'you are absolutely mistress of these two rooms—you can change any arrangement that does not suit you without referring to me at all.'

'There is no fear of my wanting to change anything,' returned Lorraine impulsively, as she looked round the cheerful room. All the furniture at the Brae Farm was old-fashioned. Lorraine's wardrobe, chest of drawers, and washstand were all of dark Spanish mahogany, and the dressing-table was covered with spotted muslin in the style of twenty years ago; only the brass bedstead and the cot beside it were recent purchases. But it was a charming room, nevertheless: a wide bay-window overlooked the lawn and the meadows, with a side glimpse of the granary and straw-stacks; an easy chair and a writing-table stood within the bay. 'Good rest,' how well the name suited it, and again the young widow's heart swelled almost painfully within her.

Theodore had been sleeping heavily in his mother's arms all this time, but at this moment he woke up and, rubbing his eyes, began clamouring for his tea.

'Bread and butter, mammie,' he said fretfully, taking hold of his mother's chin to get her attention. 'Boy vants his tea.'

'Yes, Tedo, darling; but you must see your playroom first. May I take him in, Ellison?'

The 'Dovecote' was flooded with the afternoon sunshine as they entered it, and through the open window the cooing of the doves was distinctly audible. It was a small room, but Ellison had taken great pains to fit it up for a child's use; there was a low table and chair, a high guard, a toy-cupboard with a box of bricks already on the shelf, and a wooden horse, at the sight of which Tedo burst into a perfect shout of delight.

'See mine horse!' he exclaimed, trotting up to it at once, and in a moment he was astride it and almost beside himself with joy; 'mine beauty horse. Boy's very own,' he kept saying over and over again.

'Tedo, my sweet, you must kiss Cousin Ellison, and thank her for all these beautiful things.' But Tedo shook his head, and only gee-geed louder. He had not opened his baby heart yet to Ellison; to Tedo the world consisted of his mother and himself and Waif—poor Waif, who was just then mewing piteously in his hamper.

'No, don't force him,' replied Ellison, who was far too sensible to be wounded by a child's repulse. 'Dorcas will bring you some warm water, Lorraine; and when you and Tedo are ready you will find tea ready too. We shall have it in the dining-room this evening on account of Tedo. By the bye, I forgot to tell you, Dorcas, that rosy-cheeked little damsel who brought me my letters is the one to wait on you and Tedo; Ruth is my private attendant. I tell you these little things, Lorraine, that you may feel yourself at home'; and then she nodded and withdrew.

How Lorraine longed for a quiet half-hour just to adjust her confused thoughts and to take stock, as it were, of this new strange feeling of happiness; but Tedo was tired and hungry, so she made haste to get rid of the dust, and then carried him downstairs, and a few minutes later he was sitting in his high chair between his mother and Ellison, eating bread and jam with great gusto.

'I hope we shall not put you out of your usual habits,' observed Lorraine, as she looked across the liberally spread tea-table at her cousin. The different sorts of bread, the cakes, and preserves filled her with amazement; there were new-laid eggs, too, and some slices of delicate pink ham. Never had Lorraine tasted such cream, and such butter, but she was extremely hungry, and did justice to the various delicacies.

'I thought you would like a square meal after your journey,' replied Ellison; 'but our five o'clock tea is generally in the sitting-room, and is quite a movable feast; at Brae Farm we have it at all hours. When Tedo gets more used to us,' she went on, 'Dorcas shall give him his tea in here. It is not my habit to dine late, Lorraine; I always make my dinner at luncheon; but we have supper at eight, and prayers at a quarter to ten. We are early risers here, and breakfast is always served at eight. When we are alone, I should think Tedo might have his breakfast and dinner with us.'

'That is for you to decide, Ellison. I want to meet your wishes in everything.'

'But you would like Tedo with us as much as possible,' returned Ellison, smiling kindly at her ; and again the troublesome tears rushed to Lorraine's eyes.

'He has never been away from me a single hour since he was born—have you, my bonnie boy ?' and she kissed his fair curls passionately. Tedo was not a pretty child, except to his mother's eyes ; he was pale and thin, and there was a solemnity about him that was almost unchildlike ; but he had Lorraine's soft brown eyes, and when he smiled or roused into animation he was a most engaging little creature ; but in Beaumont Street he had certainly failed to thrive.

'He is very like you, Lorraine ; but his hair is lighter.'

'So was mine when I was a tiny child,' returned Lorraine eagerly. 'Tedo's hair has begun to darken ; he is not like Ralph, except in the shape of the mouth. Ralph had a good mouth, though his moustache hid it.'

Tedo was growing decidedly sleepy after his tea, so Lorraine suggested that she should put him to bed and unpack her things, and Ellison assented to this so promptly that Lorraine for one moment felt as though her absence would be a relief to her cousin ; but she dismissed this thought as quickly as it came, and was soon hard at work, settling her few belongings in the spacious wardrobe. But here a pleasant surprise awaited her, for she discovered a dressing-gown in two soft shades of grey hanging from one of the pegs, and on the toilet-table were some ivory brushes. Ellison, who knew her cousin's scanty resources, and whose own belongings would not have disgraced any fine lady, had provided a few necessary articles for Ellison's use.

'I thought you would not be offended,' she observed, blushing slightly as Lorraine thanked her gratefully. 'Those brushes were lying in my wardrobe unused, but I got the dressing-gown in town. You must let me treat you as though you were my sister. I do not pretend to be rich, but I have more than I need. I want to make you a good allowance for your dress, and you shall repay me if you like by helping me with my sewing, or,' smilingly, 'there is the poultry-yard, you might take that off my hands ; but all this is for future consideration at present. I only want you to be happy and amuse yourself.'

'I should not be happy unless you allowed me to help you,'

returned Lorraine gravely; 'in saying this, you have taken a load from me. I was so afraid when I entered the house and saw all those servants that there would be nothing for me to do.'

'All those servants,' laughed Ellison; 'you could not have counted more than four. That tall stout woman was Sarah Tucker, my factotum and cook. Mrs. Tucker is a widow, and has lived at Brae Farm ever since she lost her husband, twenty-two years ago; she is a good-looking woman, and when she is in one of her tantrums she always declares she will marry Job Masters, one of our carters, but I never believe her. I would rather part with my right hand than Sarah; she is simply invaluable. I always put her into good humour by telling her I should forbid the banns.'

'But there are three others,' observed Lorraine.

'Yes. Eunice, the dairymaid, and Dorcas and Ruth. Ruth is a very superior young woman; she is parlour-maid and ladies'-maid, not that I need much of her help; did you notice her, Lorraine? an interesting-looking girl with fine hazel eyes. Ruth is terribly good-looking, and I am afraid my bailiff, Sam Brattle, thinks so.'

Ellison went on chatting cheerfully about her household as they sat together in the twilight after supper; she had noticed the sup-pressed wistful look in Lorraine's eyes, and guessed intuitively that she needed the relief of expression. 'She is longing to pour out her heart to me,' she said to herself. 'Lorraine is terribly emotional, but to-night it is safer to talk on commonplaces; when she has had a night's sleep she will realise her position more soberly. How strange,' she continued musingly.

'She is thirty, a widow, and a mother, and has lived through the whole gamut of a woman's experience, and beside her I am only a big ignorant child—and yet, while I take even this change in my domestic routine calmly, Lorraine's brown eyes seemed as though they were looking into a magnificent fairyland. She is on the verge of tears every moment from sheer happiness, but she has the self-control not to shed them. I shall help her best, and myself too, by talking about trifles; she is far too tired to-night to launch into any painful experiences.'

Some one has justly said that we can only act truly if we act according to our own nature, but for once Ellison's calm wisdom was at fault. If Lorraine could have put down her head on her cousin's shoulder and told her how she felt she would not have shed those hysterical tears later on in her own room. No two natures were ever more dissimilar. Ellison, in spite of her good-ness, was self-centred, and in an ordinary way could live without sympathy; her affections were strong and tenacious; change was impossible to her, and she was extremely loyal to those she loved, but the objects of her love were few.

'A compliment from Ellison is worth a dozen from ordinary people,' her father had once said ; 'if my girl praises a thing she means it. He is a lucky fellow who gets her for a wife ; he may take my word for it that he will never repent his bargain.'

Lorraine's nature was a very different one. As a mere child she would tell people that she had a big heart, and that she loved everybody. One day, when she was still in short frocks, her governess, Madame Perier—for she and her father were then living in Paris—found her crying over her physical geography. 'Why dost thou weep, *mon enfant ?*' asked Madame tenderly ; 'is it that thy task is too difficult ?'

'Oh no, Madame,' sobbed the child, 'but I was thinking of all the millions and millions of people in the world,' and here she quoted the exact statistics ; 'how is one to pray for them all ?'

'*Ma petite*, it is not possible.' Madame was a devout Catholic, but this odd remark puzzled her, for who can fathom a child's mind ?

'Oh yes, it is,' returned Lorraine pettishly, 'and in a way one does it in church, you know. Jews, Turks, infidels, all sorts and conditions of men—that includes Chinamen, Indians, and all the poor blacks. Is it not wonderful, Madame, to think what a lot of people we shall have to love in heaven ? it quite tires me to think of it.'

When Lorraine grew up, her heart seemed to grow bigger too. Altruism was a passion with her—she was intensely human ; her sympathies grew wider and more‾discriminating, and her own troubles only taught her to feel for other women whose lives were apparently failures. Those years of intercourse with a worthless and degraded mind had happily not contaminated her. It was as though she had possessed some secret specific that was an antidote to all poisonous suggestions ; the moral leprosy of her husband's nature only filled her with pity. 'Ralph was not good,' she would say to herself, but she was sure that others were more to blame than he ; he had not had his chance, poor fellow, for she had bewildered her woman's brains over the mysterious question of heredity ; but in one sense it comforted her, for she had made up her mind that Ralph's ancestors were to blame for his vices.

If Lorraine, when she grew up and knew the world better, found it impossible to love everybody, her desire to help and comfort her fellow-sufferers had only grown more intense.

She had never had it in her power to give money, not having sufficient for her own needs ; but she gave largely of her time and strength ; and would think nothing of sitting up whole nights with a sick child to relieve the worn-out mother.

In Beaumont Street she had always begun her day by dressing the ulcerous leg of an old woman who lived in the basement, and whose rheumatic hands could not have performed the task ; and before she left she never rested until Patty Gill, a young woman living in the same house, promised to do the same kindly office.

No one but Ellison would have made that practical suggestion about the sewing and the poultry - yard on the first day of her cousin's arrival, but she had done so out of sheer kindness of heart, and Lorraine had been deeply grateful.

The one drawback to her happiness had been the fear that she would merely be the recipient of her cousin's bounty, and that there would be no work for her at Brae Farm. If Ellison would not let her help her as one sister helps another, she would not eat her bread with perfect enjoyment ; but at the mention of the sewing and poultry-yard she had smiled blissfully.

All would be well with her indeed! With two or three hundred human beings in whom she could interest herself, there was no fear that she would not find work. Highlands, although it was an earthly paradise, would have its discontented Adams and sorely-tempted Eves—human nature and human needs were the same everywhere. Where man plants his foot the seed of sorrow springs up in his path ; where the woman dwells there is often the trail of the serpent to be seen ; no earthly lot is exempt from care and the need of sympathy. Lorraine, who was essentially a ministering woman, would find her work cut out for her in Highlands, though there was little poverty and no want, and the landlords were generous and wisely tolerant of small offences.

And so, though her tired nerves needed the relief of tears, Lorraine lay down to sleep by her boy's side, a happy and grateful woman ; and Ellison, lying with wide-open eyes in her pleasant chamber of Peace, felt that quiet contentment that comes from a satisfied conscience, and from the memory of a good deed done in a right spirit. She then fell asleep sweetly, and dreamt that she was walking with Gavin in the Brae Woods, and then woke to the sunshine and singing of birds.

CHAPTER V

'The cattle are grazing,
Their heads never raising ;
There are forty feeding like one ! '
WORDSWORTH.

' But all things else about her drawn
From May-time and the cheerful dawn.'
WORDSWORTH.

LORRAINE was awake early the next morning. How was she to sleep when Tedo was sitting half-erect in his cot staring at her reproachfully, and muttering to himself in discontented murmurs ; but he smiled sweetly when she opened her eyes.

'Boy vants his socks, mammie,' he said, climbing over her bodily. 'Boy hears the coo-coos, and vants to see them'—in fact, there was no end to Boy's wants. He was so excited that Lorraine could hardly dress him, and the moment he could escape from his mother's hands he trotted into his playroom to the beloved horse, while the doves stared at him with their round yellow eyes, and bowed and cooed to each other in their dove dialect until Waif jumped up on the window-seat, and then with a rustle and a flutter of their soft grey wings they fled to the granary roof, where the pigeons were already sitting in rows.

Lorraine sat down by her open window in a perfect ecstasy at the sweet feast nature had spread for her delectation. In the garden below the white balls of the guelder roses looked like flakes of snow in the early morning sunlight, the laburnum fluttered long golden fingers, and the lilac perfumed the air. Pink and white may trees added their fragrance, and just at the end of the garden a fine horse-chestnut with pink blossoms stood alone like a stately sentinel. In the borders below her window she could see the gleaming white narcissus against a background of dark, richly-coloured wall-flowers, while the star-shaped beds of purple and yellow pansies on the lawn brought back the recollection that in her childhood the pansy had been her favourite flower, and that she had once told her father so.   How well she recalled his answer—

'Of course, Lorrie ; they are your nearest of kin—you are a heart's-ease yourself,' and after that he often called her 'his little human heart's-ease.'

In the dewy meadows the cows were feeding, and over everything lay that indescribable freshness and sweetness of a perfect spring morning that is just melting into summer, when nature is at her zenith.   Later on the grass would be burnt brown, the hedgerows and trees would lose those wonderful young tints of exquisite green that make a spring landscape so enhancing.   The painting of autumn with all its red and russet glories bears the stamp of irrepressible melancholy ; the frosty fingers with which approaching winter touches the oaks and beeches may give new colouring to the scene, but it breathes of decay and death.

Spring wears the girdle of hope ; nature then speaks only of youth and progress, and of the struggle for life.   The earth is teeming with young life ; everywhere the fresh shoots are sprouting, the strong sap is flowing freely, the footsteps of the Creator seem as though they were passing visibly over the garden of the earth, and divine lips still pronounce the approving verdict, 'and behold it is very good.'

Lorraine could have sat there contentedly for hours.   The seat she had chosen commanded a view of the gate and the approach to the farmyard, and by leaning forward a little she could even see the great black sow and her litter of pigs rooting in the clean dry straw.

Every moment there were fresh sights to interest her ; now a flock of snow-white geese came out of the farmyard with outstretched necks and garrulous hissing on their way to the big pond, a score of ducks waddled after them, and presently two cart-horses with a boy astride one of them clattered noisily down the lane ; the boy had a spray of may-blossoms in his cap, and was whistling 'O Nannie, wilt thou gang wi' me'; a dog was barking at the horse's heel ; all at once the farmyard seemed alive with sounds— cocks crowed, the pigeons and doves cooed, the lowing of imprisoned calves and the far-off bleat of lambs seemed to blend with the neighing of a young horse making overtures to his neighbours, one or two villagers on their way to the dairy passed and repassed with their great yellow jugs, chattering busily to each other.   Lorraine looked at their fresh plump faces and thought of the worn, pale women in Beaumont Street and sighed.

The pray-bell roused her at last, and as she carried Tedo down, the maids were already filing into the dining-room. Ellison merely nodded to her cousin with a friendly smile, and Lorraine seated herself silently.

The maids were just opposite to her, and as Ellison read the allotted portion Lorraine's eyes wandered now and then to the striking face of the tall parlour-maid.

The girl was singularly handsome after a most uncommon type —the pure Greek contour recalled the head of Clytie; the brown hair lay in natural waves upon the forehead, and the eyes, of a warm hazel, were certainly beautiful. Dorcas's pretty rustic face looked quite ordinary beside Ruth's. The girl was too handsome certainly for her sphere in life.

When the servants had left the room, Ellison turned to her cousin: 'Well, Lorraine, have you and Tedo slept well? You have a rested look.'

'Oh yes, thank you,' replied Lorraine brightly; 'but I have been up for hours! Tedo is an early riser. Dorcas brought me some delicious tea and bread and butter and some milk for Boy, and I have been sitting at my window very happily, it was so peaceful and beautiful; for a time the birds seemed to have it all to themselves, then the farmyard seemed to wake up. I could not help thinking what a contrast it was to Beaumont Street.'

'I want you to forget Beaumont Street for a little,' returned Ellison kindly. 'You have seen too much already of the sad side of life. We must show you a brighter side when we have finished breakfast. You must see the kitchen and dairy, and my still-room. You have no idea of the spacious territory that lies behind the red-baized door. We had outgrown the dairy, so father built a new one, and turned the old one into an apple-room. Please do not feed Bairn, Lorraine; it gets him into bad habits, and I always feed him myself. By the bye, should you like a dog of your own? Colonel Trevor has some retriever puppies; two of them are very handsome little fellows, and you could have your choice.'

'I never had a dog of my own in my life,' returned Lorraine— and her eyes sparkled with delight—'and I do so love them. Tedo would be charmed with a puppy; but are you sure that it would not be a trouble to you?'

'Not in the least—and Daniel can look after it. It must sleep in the stable—and live there too until it is older, and has left off making meals of the legs of chairs.; but you can always take it out with you. By the bye, there is a kid in the stables that will delight Tedo.'

'Tedo has been playing with his horse ever since I dressed him,' replied Lorraine; and so they chatted on happily until they had finished breakfast, and then Ellison took up her key basket and led the way to the back offices of Brae Farm.

Ellison felt a pardonable pride in her kitchen ; it was an immense room with two large windows looking out on the kitchen-garden and rows of bee-hives. There were oak presses against the walls ; the oven looked large enough to bake bread for the village ; one could see one's own face reflected in the gleaming brass and pewter ; while the huge fireplace, the freshly-scoured tables and big elbow-chairs, and the window-seat with its serge-covered cushions, gave it an air of comfort.

Lorraine was shown the small inner room where Ruth and Dorcas sat at their needlework with a pleasant view of the orchard ; and the still-room with its oak cupboards and quaintly carved presses, and bundles of sweetly-smelling herbs dangling from the ceiling.

When Ellison unlocked the press and showed her store of linen, scented with lavender, and her grocery cupboard and jam cupboard, and her stock of drugs, Lorraine's eyes opened widely and she looked at her cousin with mute reverence.

The young chatelaine might be forgiven for the egotism that prompted her to point out her little contrivances for her neighbours' benefit.

'Poor people are so thoughtless,' she said ; 'they never have anything ready for an emergency. If an accident happens, or any sudden illness, they always send up to Brae Farm for what they want. You see that store of lint and ready-made bandages, and clean soft rags ; there is constant demand for them. I have bound up a broken head already this morning, and I expect my carter, Job, round soon ; he has hurt his arm. They generally come to me to be doctored — not that I know much about it, but I have taught myself to be useful.'

'You are a happier woman than I thought, Ellison,' replied Lorraine with gentle gravity. But Ellison only smiled, and opened a deep drawer where she kept a stock of ready-made clothing.

'When Ruth and Dorcas have nothing else to do they work for the poor of South London. I generally send off a parcel once or twice a year. We do not often work for the village, as there is little real poverty amongst us. Now I must show you the scullery and wash-house just across the yard ; you can see the new buildings — I call them new, though they are fifteen years old. This is the laundry ; we wash everything at home, and Tabby Bates from the village helps us three days a week ; she does most of the ironing. Now we will go into the dairy — mind that step, Lorraine. Ah, Eunice, I see you are hard at work making up the butter.'

Lorraine looked round her in silent admiration. This was indeed an ideal dairy, the snow-white shelves with the great pans of rich yellow cream, the windows looking full upon the green orchard. Eunice, a fresh, comely-looking young woman, in her pink print dress and white bib apron, was kneading the firm yellow butter into smooth tempting rolls. She glanced at Lorraine as they entered, for all the servants were a little curious about the new inmate ; but she did not pause in her work ; she was a reliable and invaluable servant, and Lorraine often called her and Sarah Tucker her right and left hands. Tedo was growing weary and ready for his mid-day nap, so he was deposited on the couch in the sitting-room, and then, while Ellison gave her orders and attended to Job's injured arm, Lorraine wandered about the garden and orchard, and then made an exhaustive survey of the farm-building, talking to every one she encountered, and petting all the animals, until Ellison was ready to explain the poultry-yard to her, and to coach her in her new duties. The morning passed rapidly, and both of them were genuinely surprised when the gong summoned them in for luncheon.

'What shall you do with yourself this afternoon?' asked Ellison, as they sat at the table together. 'I meant to have taken you and Tedo for a drive, but Sam Brattle wants me to meet him in the big meadow ; he is full of the new fencing, and after that I have promised to sit with old Mrs. Langton, as her companion is away. I am a very busy person, as you will soon find out for yourself ; evening is generally my only leisure time.'

'I mean to be busy too,' returned Lorraine quickly. 'Please do not waste a thought on me, Ellison. Boy and I are always happy together. I shall take him out, I think. I want to cross that long meadow ; there seems a wood beyond.'

'Of course, the Brae Woods ! We drove through them yesterday ; it is a pleasant walk, but too far for Tedo. I wish Jock— the kid, I mean—were old enough to draw a little carriage. 1 think I shall get a donkey for him. I have often thought a strong young donkey would be extremely useful.'

'You must do nothing of the kind, Ellison,' returned Lorraine, quite shocked at the notion of such extravagance. 'I am used to carrying Tedo, and he really walks very nicely now ; he will be as happy as a king picking daisies and buttercups ; he has never seen any, and I shall be happier than any queen watching him. Come, my king of all the world,' lifting her boy as she spoke, 'we are going to pick up gold and silver on Nature's Tom Tiddler's ground.'

'She is very graceful,' thought Ellison, as she watched her

cousin from the window, 'she holds her head well, and walks so lightly. She is interesting, too, and I think people will take to her. I know what Gavin will say : that she is such a lady, and he will like her natural frank manner. She is much happier this morning, only every now and then I see the shadow of Beaumont Street in her eyes. Well, she has one blessing— her child. Lots are more equal than people allow, but I would not exchange with her. I have never wanted to change places with any one.'

Lorraine found that it was no easy matter to cross that long park-like meadow that lay between them and the wood that she was longing to reach. Vainly she tried to carry Tedo ; the little fellow only struggled to get down. 'Boy wants anover f'ower, mammie ; one yellow one, one pinky one'; this was his repeated cry, until Lorraine lost all patience at last, and bore him off relentlessly.

'You shall pick as many flowers as you like, darling, when we reach those trees,' and she would not set him down until they were actually in the Brae Woods.

How lovely and peaceful they looked in the afternoon light. There was no one in sight, she and Tedo and the birds had it to themselves. They sat down under the cedars to rest themselves, then followed slowly the windings of the woodland walk. Tedo's hands were full of weeds that he was perpetually dropping ; his constant refrain of 'Anover f'ower, mammie,' sounded like a far-off refrain to her thoughts, and she seemed to hear it in a dream. They had reached the gate and the lodge before Lorraine bethought herself that they had come some distance, and that baby boy would be tired.

The sound of a horse's hoof broke on her ear at this moment. A gentleman was riding towards them from the village ; he was unattended by any groom, and as he reached the gate he looked at the closed door of the lodge, and seemed about to dismount ; but Lorraine, who had her boy firmly by the hand, sprang forward, and, unlatching the gate, held it open for the rider.

The gentleman raised his hat and thanked her courteously ; then he looked at her and the boy keenly as he walked his horse through the gateway.

Lorraine had no idea that this was the owner of Brae Woods, though Colonel Trevor guessed in a moment that the young widow was Ellison's cousin. Lorraine, who was still in a sort of dream, only noticed that the man had a brown, thin face, and that he was rather distinguished-looking.

People always said this of the colonel, in spite of his leanness and brown skin; he had a fine soldierly presence, and looked especially well on horseback; but Lorraine would not have looked at him a second time, only Tedo just then broke suddenly from her grasp.

'Me wants to vide too, mammie!' he exclaimed, kicking violently as she caught hold of him. 'Boy wants to vide.'

'Put him up on my saddle, and I will hold him quite safely,' returned the stranger, much to Lorraine's surprise. 'He looks tired, and it is a good step to the Brae Farm.'

'Oh no, I could not think of troubling you; my boy is not heavy, I can easily carry him!' Lorraine was a trifle confused by this friendly overture from a perfect stranger; with all her frankness and lack of conventionality she could be dignified with the other sex.

Colonel Trevor smiled pleasantly. 'I think you had better let me have him, Mrs. Herbert,' and as Lorraine looked still more surprised at hearing her own name, he continued with an amused twinkle of his eyes, 'I see you have not identified me yet; my name is Trevor — Colonel Trevor. I live at Brae House. I knew that my cousin Ellison was expecting a visitor from London, and so I imagined at once that you were the person in question.'

'How strange; and I never guessed you were Colonel Trevor,' returned Lorraine, in a surprised tone. 'I was very dense and stupid. Are you sure that my boy will not trouble you?' and as he shook his head with another smile, she lifted Tedo up, to the boy's irrepressible delight. The flowers were all dropped now, and Tedo was shaking the reins and shouting into the mare's dainty ears, rather to Miss Alice's disgust. Lorraine tried not to feel alarmed as the mare curvetted a little; but her face was so expressive that Colonel Trevor restrained his mare. Boy's viding, mammie; look how boy vides!' exclaimed Tedo, waving his little hand. Lorraine could have covered him with kisses; the little, pale, ordinary child, as Colonel Trevor mentally appraised him, was in her eyes the very prince and pearl among children. Lorraine's cheeks flushed, the deep, still light of a mother's love came into her brown eyes as she looked up to him.

'Yes, I see you, my darling; you are very happy.' Simple words, but how eloquent were the fond low tones. Why did Colonel Trevor suddenly ask himself if Helen would have loved her boy in that fashion? It was an odd thought, but it gave him a sudden twinge; time had mercifully drawn the edges of his wound together, and it had begun to heal, only now and then a chance word reopened the old sore.

'It is too soon to ask you how you like the place,' he observed, trying to rouse from his abstraction; 'but I think you will find Brae Farm a very comfortable home. My cousin Ellison is an excellent manager; her household machinery never seems out of gear.'

'To me it is a perfect paradise,' returned Lorraine impulsively; and then she added naively, 'As I was walking in this beautiful wood just now I was half afraid that it was a dream, and that I should wake up and find myself in Camden Town again.'

Colonel Trevor gave her a quick, pitying look. He was a trained observer of men, and his penetration was rarely at fault. He had already formed a favourable opinion of the new inmate of Brae Farm: he liked her frank, unsophisticated manner. Mrs. Herbert was certainly an interesting young woman, though she had no special claims to good looks, but there was an air of refinement about her that he was not slow to notice, as she walked by his side with her light springy tread, looking up at him and her boy.

'It was too strong a contrast,' he observed quietly. 'I have only once been in Camden Town, but I have no wish to know more of it; it appeared to me to be delivered into the hands of gutter-merchants and itinerant stall-holders. It was Saturday night, I remember, and the gas was blazing, and the butchers were shouting out " Come, buy, buy, buy," and every other woman was carrying a baby and dragging another besides. It was terribly realistic, not to say squalid.'

'And I lived there for nearly five months,' she returned quietly. 'Ah, I know those Saturday nights so well: those poor, tired mothers setting out to buy their Sunday dinners; how my heart used to ache for them, and still more for the poor babies kept out of their beds until nearly midnight. It seems hard, does it not, Colonel Trevor, that some lives should be so very full of trial and care?'

'It is one of the difficult problems of life,' he replied quickly; 'but I doubt if you or I will ever solve it. I do not wish you to think me a pessimist at this early stage of our acquaintance; but I have long given up trying to answer these vexed questions. We must do what we can for other people, "help lame dogs over stiles," according to Charles Kingsley's excellent advice, and remedy all preventable evils; but even altruism can do no more.'

'Perhaps not,' sighed Lorraine, and then quickly: 'We are taking you out of your way, Colonel Trevor; those gates we have passed lead to Brae House.'

'To be sure they do !   But I am going to Brae Farm.   Do ycu notice Miss Alice, my mare I mean, is going past the gates of her own accord ?   That is because my cousin gives her sugar.   She is always eager to take that turning to the farm.'

'You are only going on Tedo's account,' returned Lorraine, smiling ; but though Colonel Trevor would not disclaim this fact, he could truthfully assure her that he and his mare were equally well pleased when an errand led them to Brae Farm.

CHAPTER VI

'Keep thy friend
Under thy own life's key.'
SHAKESPEARE.

Her eye, as soft and blue as even,
When day and night are calmly meeting,
Beams on my heart like light from Heaven,
And purifies its beating.'
KNOX.

As Lorraine and Colonel Trevor turned the corner by the farm-buildings, they came upon Ellison standing by the horse-block talking to a fair, sturdy-looking young man in a rough grey suit. She looked extremely surprised when she caught sight of the little cavalcade. Tedo called out to her at once.

'See, boy is viding, Tousin. Boy has the vhip, and vhips hard.'

'No you don't, young man,' returned the colonel, taking hand and whip into his strong grasp, 'unless you wish Miss Alice to jump that gate. Mrs. Herbert, will you take your boy, please, and then I will dismount?' And Tedo, to his evident reluctance, was delivered into his mother's tender arms.

'That must do for to-day, Sam,' observed Ellison hastily; 'we will discuss the matter more fully to-morrow. Well, Lorraine, what does this mean? You and Tedo seem good friends with my cousin.'

'Colonel Trevor has been so kind to Tedo,' replied Lorraine; 'he saw that he was tired, and he has brought him all the way from the lodge gates. I did not know who was speaking to me at first until he introduced himself—but he knew my name.'

'I recognised **you** from your cousin's description,' returned

Colonel Trevor. 'Ellison's portraits are always drawn correctly. She has a talent for seizing people's salient points ; there is nothing ambiguous or indefinite in her descriptions—he who runs may read. Ah, what did I tell you, Mrs. Herbert,' as Ellison, passing him with a quiet smile, began feeding Miss Alice with sugar from her apron pocket. Lorraine watched them with delight as the pretty creature received the dainty with her delicate lips, and then pressed her nose against Ellison's shoulder, as though to coax her for more. 'Miss Alice is getting demoralised. I believe she would follow you like a dog, Ellison ; try her when she has finished her sugar. Go towards the stable and call her.'

'Very well,' returned his cousin obediently ; and she soon found Colonel Trevor was right. The mare followed her, drooping her graceful neck and whinnying softly, until they both disappeared from sight. Then Colonel Trevor went slowly after them, and Lorraine carried her boy into the house.

He found Ellison tying up the mare herself ; then she gave her a feed of corn. Colonel Trevor watched her with amused eyes.

'What a useful woman you are,' he said, as she rejoined him. 'I believe you could saddle Miss Alice as well as feed her.'

'To be sure,' she returned composedly. 'I have harnessed Mollie before now, when I wanted the phaeton in a hurry, and I could not find Joe Brand. I should hate to be helpless. Well, Gavin, what do you think of my cousin ? I know you make up your mind at once about people, so I am not afraid to ask you.'

'I have formed a good opinion of her already,' was the reply. 'She is natural and lady-like, and she is not ashamed to say what she thinks. In that one trait she resembles you, Ellison ; but, if I do not mistake, in everything else she is your exact opposite.'

'Now, Gavin, this is absurd. You have only been a quarter of an hour in Lorraine's company, it is perfectly impossible that you could correctly diagnose her character. Why should you say that she is my opposite ?'

'My dear Ellison, simply because it is the truth. In a quarter of an hour you may find out a good deal about a person. Besides, Mrs. Herbert is not difficult to read, there is nothing occult or mysterious about her. She is an amiable young woman, who has seen a great deal of the sad side of life, and she is far too sympathetic by nature ever to try and forget it. She lives in her affections, and it is her nature to be cheerful. She walks and talks like a gentlewoman, *voila tout*.'

'Gavin, I often think you are a very clever man. If you had

asked me my opinion about Lorraine, I should have taken a week to answer you. I never let myself be prepossessed by a pleasing exterior or manners. I must find out more about people before I can heartily say I like them. Lorraine interests me, and she seems nice ; that is all I can say at present about her.'

'That is because you are cautious by nature. I am cautious too, but I can read quickly. Mrs. Herbert trusted me with her boy, but when Miss Alice pranced a little her lips were white with fear, yet she would not hurt my feelings by saying she was afraid ; I could not help noticing that. In her case you would not have been nervous ; when you trust a person your trust is so absolute that it excludes fear.'

'Yes ; but you forget. I know you, Gavin, and you were a stranger to Lorraine. My trust has grown imperceptibly for years.'

She looked up in his face as she spoke, with the slow, sweet smile that was habitual to her, and that was so pleasant to his eyes ; and he answered it by taking her hand and putting it gently on his arm.

It was almost a lover-like caress, but neither of them saw it in that light. To Ellison the idea had not yet dawned that her cousin might wish to marry her. She was so much his confidante that she knew how faithful he was to the memory of his wife, and though she had never seen Helen, she had heard so much about her from his lips that she always seemed to her like a long-lost friend of her own. In depressed moods Ellison was the only living being to whom Colonel Trevor could bring himself to speak of his wife. He liked her quiet sympathy, the absence of fuss and agitation. When he mentioned Helen to his mother she always cried, and called him her poor, dear Gavin, and pitied and fondled him till his nerves got the better of him, and he would tell himself angrily that he was a fool to speak of the past.

Marriage was not to Ellison, as it was to some women, the aim and object in life ; she gloried too much in her freedom to yield her liberty lightly. She had had her chances ; the mistress of Brae Farm was too well dowered not to possess marketable value in men's eyes ; besides which she was attractive, a fine woman, and a kind-hearted one too. Philip Earnshaw had been deeply smitten, and had left England with a sore heart because Ellison had refused him ; but though she had liked him best of all her suitors, her pity had been scant for him.

'Poor old Phil ! and you are not half sorry for him, you hard-hearted woman,' Colonel Trevor had said to her one day rather bluntly, for the proverbial little bird had carried him the news ; but Ellison had coloured angrily and held her head high.

'You have no right to know about it, Gavin. Cousin Louise ought to have known better; it is no one's business but Mr. Earnshaw's and mine.'

'And mine. You forget that all that concerns you interests me deeply.'

'No, Gavin,' she returned in a softened tone, 'I do not forget; but don't you see that it is kinder to Mr. Earnshaw that people should not know about this. He had no right to ask me; it was a great mistake. I never gave him the slightest pretext for doing so; but he chose to make himself and me exceedingly uncomfortable. Well, he is on his way to India now, so I must forgive him; but please do not mention his name to me again,' and as Ellison seemed really put out, and very unlike her tranquil self, he dropped the subject.

It might be well for some women to marry, she sometimes said when friends spoke to her on the subject; but as regards herself, a single life suited her best. She was not a submissive woman; it would be difficult for her to yield to another person's judgment unless her own entirely agreed. She preferred solitude and freedom to daily friction and argument.

Ellison was perfectly in earnest when she said this; but she had never asked herself how much of her content depended on her close friendship with her cousin; hitherto it had been warm enough and strong enough to satisfy her affectionate instincts. Gavin depended on her for sympathy, he trusted her and confided in her; his daily visits, their long talks together, were all important factors in her happiness, and as long as things remained on their present footing she was utterly and truly content.

The idea that Gavin might wish to marry again had not yet troubled her consciousness; if that day should ever come—and not she, but another woman should be his choice—how would it fare with Ellison then?

Happily no such thought disturbed Ellison's serenity; she had not yet noticed the first faint stirrings of long-dormant feelings in Gavin, and as little did she know that the thought had already occurred to him that perhaps some day he might ask Ellison to be his wife. Some day! There was no hurry for the present, things were better as they were; he was not desirous of change, and was certainly in no mood to play the lover. 'A man cannot marry twice,' he had once said, to his mother's dismay; but latterly he had varied this formula to himself: 'A man cannot love twice in the same way'; and yet as he said this, he knew there were many exceptions to this rule.

Gavin's mute caress had made Ellison very happy; when his

hand, so strong and sinewy, took hers and held it with brotherly freedom on his arm, she knew that he was moved to unusual tenderness, and she was right.

'What can a man want more when he is no longer young and the best of life is over for him?' he was saying to himself. 'Ever since I came back to England Ellison has been a comfort to me ; my need of her increases. Brae Farm and Brae House are too far apart. I should like to have her always near me, to be able to talk to her whenever I am inclined. Shall I tell her so? Will she be ready to listen to me? I know well she has no drawing towards matrimony ; but "she is a woman, and therefore to be won," as Shakespeare says, and if any one has a chance with Ellison it will be myself'; and these thoughts made Colonel Trevor so quiet and abstracted during tea, that more than once Ellison's calm blue eyes rested on his face enquiringly.

Tedo was having his tea under Dorcas's care, so Lorraine was free to enjoy hers. She was tired with her long ramble and the day's pleasure, and was content to rest without talking.

'We are all very silent,' observed Ellison at last. 'Gavin, do you know I have been expecting Muriel all day? I thought she would be sure to call on Lorraine.'

'She ought to have done so,' he returned in a vexed voice ; 'but I suppose she has forgotten all about it. I hope, Mrs. Herbert,' with a friendly glance at her, 'that you will excuse our unneighbourly behaviour ; my sister is not very strong, and sometimes is indisposed to make efforts.'

'A lame excuse, Gavin,' returned Ellison, smiling ; 'but never mind, we will not discuss Muriel. Tell Cousin Louise that I shall bring Lorraine round to see her to-morrow morning, there is no need for her to be ceremonious. In the afternoon I shall have to drive into Dorchester, Mrs. Tucker has a list of wants to be supplied.'

'Shall I drive you both over in the dog-cart?' returned Colonel Trevor. 'I am going in myself, so there is no need to take Mollie. Whitefoot wants exercise ; Stanton shall walk in and be ready to take the horse, and when you have done your business you shall meet me at the *Green Dragon*.'

Ellison looked pleased at this suggestion.

'Will this suit you, Lorraine?' she asked courteously. 'We shall go up to Brae House to luncheon, and then Colonel Trevor will drive us over to Dorchester. It is rather a charming idea ; my cousin drives so well, and Whitefoot goes much faster than Mollie.'

'But Tedo,' objected Lorraine 'I could not leave Tedo all day.'

'Dear me, I forgot all about the child,' returned Ellison, knitting her brows. 'Let me think a moment how we can arrange it. Gavin, if Mrs. Herbert sits in front with you she can easily take Tedo. Dorcas can give him his dinner and bring him up to the house before we start. Will not that solve the problem, Lorraine?'

'Yes, thank you; but,' hesitating, 'will not Tedo incommode Colonel Trevor?'

'Not unless he gets my whip, the young rascal. All right, Ellison, you and Mrs. Herbert are booked for to-morrow. Now I must go, for I have about fifty letters to write; good-bye, Mrs Herbert. Are you coming to see me off, Ellison?' But he need not have asked the question, for she had already risen from her seat.

Lorraine watched them as they walked slowly down the garden path. 'What good friends they seemed,' she said to herself; and then she leaned back in the window-seat and indulged in a delicious fit of musing until Ellison returned and took up her work, then she roused herself and began to talk.

'I like Colonel Trevor, Ellison,' she said in her frank way; 'he was so kind to Tedo, and so nice altogether. He is not young—over forty, I should say—and how the Indian suns have burnt him. He is so thin and brown, he reminds me of Don Quixote; but of course one can see he is a very clever man.'

'Yes, and he reads a great deal. He always says he had no time for reading in India—that there he was a student of men and not books. But he seems to be far better informed on most subjects than other people; we have such interesting conversations sometimes, but this afternoon he was quiet, he owned he was thinking of something.' Ellison said this quite innocently; she had not the faintest idea that she herself was the cause of his unusual abstraction.

'When he is not talking his expression is a little sad,' observed Lorraine. 'It is several years since his wife died, is it not?'

'Yes, more than eight years; but he has never quite got over it. Helen was such a beautiful creature; I have only seen her photograph, but it seemed to me that I had never seen a more lovely face, and her disposition was so sweet, too. Other people have told me that, so no wonder he has been long in getting over his trouble, poor fellow.'

Lorraine sighed; it was always a matter of grief to her that she had been unable truly to mourn her husband; she felt inclined to envy Colonel Trevor the poignancy of his regret.

'I like him all the better for being so faithful to his wife's memory,' she said softly. 'I never like people to forget. "Lord, keep their memory green." Do you remember that quaint old prayer in the Christmas story? One is tempted to say that sometimes even now.'

Ellison's smile was her only response; she seldom discussed abstract questions unless Gavin mooted them. She sewed on diligently, and Lorraine watched her until another question rose to her lips.

'Colonel Trevor has a sister, then—the Muriel you were talking about—is she nice, Ellison? is she like her brother?'

'No, indeed, you would never take them for brother and sister, she is very much younger than Colonel Trevor. Muriel is my age; there were two other sisters between them, but they died young, and Muriel's health has not been good. She is one of those people who make the most of their little ailments. She is not robust; but I sometimes fancy she is stronger than she thinks herself, and I know this is her brother's opinion. Muriel is terribly lymphatic, she hates any exertion.'

'Then you are not fond of her'—in rather a disappointed tone.

Ellison seemed surprised at this question.

'I never asked myself if I were fond of her or not,' she said, with an amused smile. 'I never put questions of that sort to myself. Muriel is nice in her way : but I have no special affection for her. I do not understand her—she always seems to me a discontented, fanciful young person. I often lose patience with her, and long to give her a good shaking. Are you shocked at me, Lorraine?—you look very grave.'

'I think it is a pity to lose patience with a person because one cannot understand them. Of course I am talking in the dark, as I do not know Miss Trevor ; but from what you say she seems to have a good deal to bear.'

'What makes you think so?' asked Ellison, rather taken aback at this remark. 'She is better off than most girls ; she has a beautiful home, plenty of money, an affectionate mother, and a brother who is as good to her as he knows how to be ; but then he is good to everybody.'

'He does everything, in short, but love her,' returned Lorraine quickly. 'Ah !' as Ellison gave her an astonished glance, 'have I made a right guess—is there no real sympathy between them?'

'Really, Lorraine, I had no idea you would be so quick. I never meant to talk about Muriel at all ; but, as we have said so much, it would be better to say a little more, for it would never do for you to think me prejudiced or unkind. Muriel and I do not hit it off, that is true, but then I could say the same of the

Mordaunt girls or Laura Holt. Girls have never been much in my line—they always exercise my patience; but Muriel is excessively trying to me, and I am not at all surprised that her brother fails to understand her. He was so many years in India that she was quite a stranger to him, and they have no sympathies in common. I believe Muriel is clever, but she keeps her knowledge to herself; but I might talk on for ever about her, though I doubt if you would comprehend matters. You must see Muriel and judge of her yourself. I am sure you will be charmed with Cousin Louise—she's a dear woman, and everybody says so.' And then Ellison laid aside her work, and Lorraine went in search of her boy. The evening passed as pleasantly as the rest of the day. Ellison had letters to write; but she brought Lorraine two or three books for her choice; the luxurious chair and reading-lamp were adjuncts to her comfort. When she raised her eyes from her page, they rested on Ellison's placid countenance with satisfaction. Ellison always dressed herself carefully, her soft grey evening silk with its dainty finishes exactly suited her. She never adopted a youthful style, flimsy textures did not suit her. When she wore her black velvet at the Brae dinner-parties, Mrs. Trevor told her son that Ellison was certainly a handsome woman.

Except in winter the blinds and curtains were never drawn over the great bay window. From her seat Lorraine could see the white moonlight streaking the lawn with silver. How peaceful it all was! In all her life had she ever known such comfort? Already she loved Ellison. Ah, if Ellison would only love her! 'She has opened her house to me; but she must open her heart too,' thought Lorraine, for her nature made imperative demands on her fellow-creatures for affection. Nothing else satisfied her—those she loved must love her in return.

CHAPTER VII

'LADY. Is she young or old?

PAGE. Neither, if right I guess; but she is fair,
For time hath laid his hand so gently on her
As he, too, had been awed.'

BAILLIE.

THE next morning when Lorraine woke she found it impossible to remain quietly in her room; so she dressed herself and Tedo, and directly they had finished their early repast she carried him out.

The dews were still heavy in the meadows, so she turned her steps in the direction of the village, leaving Brae House on her left, and passing some fenced-in fields where sheep were feeding she entered a steep, narrow lane that seemed to wind slowly under the shade of elms and beeches. Tedo was heavy, and she often had to pause and rest herself; but she was bent on seeing the village in its morning freshness and stillness, and after a somewhat weary climb she had her reward—Highlands was before her.

Yes, there were the institute and the church with the vicarage behind it, the infant school, and the long stretch of broken common, with its gorse and blackberry bushes, and the blue blackness of the firs closing in the view.

An old grey horse, a donkey, and some geese were apparently the only living objects to be seen; the sun shone on the peaked red and yellow roofs of the cottages, white roads intersected the common. Ah, they were at work in the forge, she could hear the regular clang of the hammer beating out the hissing metal, and a file of cows fresh from the milking-shed passed slowly before the open door of *The Waggon and Horses*. She had reached the main street of the village, and resting against the palings outside the blacksmith's cottage, she feasted her eyes on the charming prospect, while Tedo played beside her; then taking his hand they stood for a long time looking in at the open door of the forge, where John Drake, a fine, powerful-looking man, was shoeing a cart-horse. He glanced curiously at Lorraine as he wished her a civil good-morning, and Lorraine, true to her sociable instincts, at once commenced a conversation, and she grew so interested and took such a liking to the honest blacksmith that she forgot the time, until the clock on the school-house close by roused her.

She was late for prayers, and Ellison looked at her with reproachful eyes when she entered.

'Where have you been, Lorraine? You have been hurrying yourself, I can see that,' for Lorraine was flushed and breathless.

'You must forgive me, dear,' she returned, with a penitent kiss. 'I have been down to the village, and Tedo and I were so amused standing at the forge that I forgot all about breakfast.'

'You have been carrying Tedo all that way!' exclaimed Ellison in a shocked voice, 'and Fernleigh Lane is so steep, too!' and then she mentally resolved to speak to Sam Brattles without delay about the donkey. 'Indeed, you should not use up your strength so early in the day. You are not accustomed to these long walks.' But Lorraine only laughed and defended herself.

'You are very sensible, Ellison; but just put yourself in my place—I am like a prisoner set free and intoxicated with my freedom. It is like living some fairy tale; wandering about when the rest of the world is asleep or only just waking up, everything has a different look; one cannot describe the beauty and freshness. Those dark woods, how I long to explore them and those low hills at the back of the village!'

'All the same you are very tired, Lorraine,' returned Ellison, with practical kindness, as she poured out a cup of delicious coffee for her cousin. 'You must remember,' she continued gently, 'that though your health is good, those months of hardship and hard work have tried you a little; last night you were so tired you could scarcely hold your book. I thought every moment you would fall asleep'; and Lorraine could not deny this. She knew Ellison was right, and that insufficient food and mental trouble had told upon her constitution; her spirits were greater than her strength; it would be months, perhaps, before she would recover from the effects of those unhappy years. Sorrow stamps indelibly, and even on her healthy nature its impress would only grow fainter by degrees. Ellison's kind heart had grasped this fact, and though she had not yet learnt to love her cousin, she was sufficiently interested in her to feel troubled when she saw Lorraine's flushed, tired face and the inky shadows under her eyes.

Under the pretext of wanting some dusters hemmed, she ensconced Lorraine comfortably in the bay window after breakfast with her boy beside her, and went about her household duties, holding countless interviews in the still-room.

No one entered the sitting-room. Tedo got tired of play presently and fell asleep, and lay curled up like a puppy with his head in his mother's lap. Lorraine let him lie there, and went on with her conversation with John Drake. She was still at the forge, of course, and the hammer seemed ringing a merry tune against the anvil, 'The Men of Harlech' or 'Charlie is My Darling'; and how droll, she had never known before that cows were shod; but, of course, that was her Cockney ignorance, she would know things better when she lived in the country. But, dear me, all those cows and no cow-shoes ready! No wonder John Drake began to look bothered as he made the sparks fly; it must be distressing to any blacksmith to have a dozen cows to shoe and no shoes, and here Lorraine began to rub her eyes.

'You have had a nice long nap, and Tedo too,' observed Ellison tranquilly, 'and I hope you both feel rested. Never mind the dusters,' as Lorraine began to look ashamed, 'they made an excellent pillow for Tedo, and Dorcas will finish them this afternoon. It is time to get ready for our luncheon at Brae House; that is why I was obliged to wake you; but really it went to my heart to do it, you were sleeping so sweetly.'

'I suppose I was more tired than I knew,' returned Lorraine apologetically; 'but, oh, to think that I have slept away this lovely morning. Sonny, you must come with mother while she dresses. I will not be long, Ellison.' But though Lorraine spoke with animation she moved languidly, and in her heart she would have been better pleased to have remained quietly at home.

Lorraine's modest outfit, provided with her cousin's money, consisted of two new black dresses—a thin serge and a fine, soft cashmere. These two gowns and an old black serge formed her entire wardrobe.

She put on the new serge now, and a neat hat that she had trimmed herself; and as she glanced at herself in the glass she could not help being pleased at her own appearance. Her new gown fitted her so nicely, she thought, and the mere fact of putting on a pair of fresh unmended gloves gave her a pleasurable sensation.

She was glad, too, when she went downstairs to read approval in Ellison's eyes, and her quiet, 'You look very nice, dear,' made her blush as though she had received a compliment. Ellison was, in fact, much struck by the simplicity and propriety of her cousin's appearance. The serge dress fitted so well to the pliable curves of her figure, the white collar and cuffs relieved the blackness, and

4

though she was pale—far too pale—the coils of reddish-brown hair, so neatly and deftly arranged under her hat, was certainly a beauty.

Ellison felt that she would not be ashamed to introduce her cousin to the critical inspection of the mistress of Brae House. Lorraine was ladylike and refined, and her foreign education had given her an ease and finish of manner that she instinctively felt would make her a social success.

As they walked through the extensive shrubberies of Brae House, Ellison's active benevolence was busy on her cousin's behalf. There was a certain black silk that she had never had made up reposing on the shelf of her wardrobe ; she had no present need for it, it would make Lorraine a handsome dress when she dined at Brae House, and before they had reached the house she had decided that her cousin should have it that very evening.

Lorraine, on her side, was looking about her with admiring eyes. Brae House appeared to her a perfect mansion, she had not been prepared for such magnificence ; the extensive and beautifully kept gardens, the spacious conservatory, the handsome entrance-hall and broad staircase excited her secret wonder.

She had not guessed that Colonel Trevor was quite so rich, that he was a person of such importance, but then fine country-houses were not in her line.

In reality Brae House was a roomy, well-built modern residence It had been almost rebuilt by Colonel Trevor's father, and only a small portion of the old house remained. The stables were new, and also the conservatory, and as comfort and not splendour had been the aim, the interior was admirably fitted for the wants of a large family. As the family was at present small, the large dimensions of the living rooms, and the number of unused apartments, gave Brae House that barrack-like air of which Colonel Trevor had complained.

The front door stood open, and Ellison, without knocking or inquiry, conducted her cousin through the wide hall, with its handsome pillars and walls covered with pictures, stags' antlers, and curious weapons, and down a broad lobby.

'Mrs. Trevor is always in her morning-room until luncheon,' she explained, 'unless she is at work in the conservatory,' and she was right. In answer to her tap a melodious 'Come in' bade them enter, and a tall, handsome-looking woman rose quickly from her seat and greeted them warmly.

'This is very kind,' she said, retaining Lorraine's hand a moment. 'It is so friendly of you, Mrs. Herbert, to overlook our deficiencies in this way. Muriel or I ought to have called on you yesterday, we are such close neighbours; besides, as Ellison's connections, we should have been the first to welcome you to Highlands.'

'Never mind, Cousin Louise,' returned Ellison hastily, 'Lorraine would not wish you to stand on ceremony with her, she is just as pleased to come and see you to-day, so there is no need for excuses.'

'My dear, I have simply no excuse to offer,' returned Mrs. Trevor quaintly, 'unless you call natural indolence and procrastination excuses. I was hard at work in the conservatory all the morning, and far too lazy to move off my couch all the afternoon, so I contented myself with remarking to Muriel at luncheon that it was clearly her duty to call on Mrs. Herbert. I do not remember that she disputed the fact, only at dinner Gavin lectured us both rather severely on what he termed our want of manners. As I thought Muriel deserved the lecture, I held my tongue and let him have his say. Now, Ellison, you are laughing, you always laugh when I try to explain things properly.'

'Cousin Louise, you are so absurd. Look at Lorraine, she is laughing too; don't you see you are making things worse? We know, of course, that Muriel ought to have called, and that you were both dreadfully lazy, so you may as well leave off blaming Muriel and take your own proper share, and then perhaps we will forgive you.'

Mrs. Trevor shrugged her shoulders, and looked at Lorraine with a pleasant smile.

'Dear Ellison is a very decided person, is she not, and so outspoken. Do you always say what you mean, and do what you ought, Mrs. Herbert? I am afraid that it is not the Trevor habit. "Oh, mother, how I hate oughts"—my daughter said that to me once when she was a tiny wee child—"oughts are such nasty disagreeable things"; and, do you know, in my heart I agreed with her. Children sometimes grasp a truth wonderfully. Ellison will tell you that Muriel and I detest oughts still.'

It was impossible not to laugh, and Lorraine did so heartily, there was something so infinitely droll in Mrs. Trevor's voice. She had a bewitching smile; it was brilliant and sweet at the same time.

Lorraine was charmed with her, as Ellison knew she would be. Every one admired Mrs. Trevor; though she was over sixty and made no attempt to conceal her age, there was a *naiveté* and sprightliness of manner that made people think her much younger than she really was. More than once she had been taken for

Colonel Trevor's step-mother; they looked far more like brother and sister, people said, than mother and son; even the loss of a good husband and two lovely daughters had not sobered Mrs. Trevor, except for a time, while Colonel Trevor fully looked his age.

Ellison always said there was something Irish about her cousin Louise; her quick changes of mood, her drollery and flow of spirits, her warm heart and little tempers, her hot fits and cold fits, and casual impractical ways were rather after the Irish type; but she was always affronted if this reached her ears, and declared she was English to the backbone.

She was an affectionate mother; but her son often found her trying, and her want of depth puzzled him. She was sensitive and yet she was dense, and neither of her children guessed that her light-hearted manner often concealed deep-seated restlessness. She might laugh and make jokes and seem outwardly happy, but she never forgot her husband and children, or ceased to mourn for them. With all her frankness she was reticent on some matters. If she could have spoken to Gavin and Muriel of their father and sisters, it would have been better for her and them; Muriel would not have thought her mother shallow, and Colonel Trevor's respect would have deepened, and his masculine sense of fitness have been satisfied.

It was not surprising that Lorraine was struck with Mrs. Trevor, for she was certainly a beautiful woman—her features were fine, and, considering her age, she retained her complexion wonderfully. There was a strange picturesqueness about her—her grey hair was piled up on her head, and over it she always wore a lace lappet fastened under her chin with a small diamond brooch; it was singularly becoming to her, and the grey hair had almost the effect of powder in adding lustre to her bright, dark eyes. Envious critics called her style affected, and hinted that Mrs. Trevor was a little too anxious to keep up her reputation as a beauty, and studied her appearance too much; but she always laughed when such hints reached her.

'Every woman ought to be as handsome as nature allows her to be,' she would say. 'If I like to wear a lace lappet over my hair, no one has any right to accuse me of undue vanity. I only wish other people would follow my example—Mrs. Mountjoy, for example; she would look less scraggy and skinny if she had a comfortable piece of lace pinned under her chin. I always think of the Red Queen in "Through the Looking-Glass" when I see her; how her sharp chin would hurt one.'

'Fashion,' she would say another time, 'my dear, I set my

own fashions. Every woman over sixty ought to know how to dress herself becomingly. When any one asks my advice, which they seldom do, and then they never follow it, I say to them, " Don't tell me your age, I know you do not wish to do so ; it is criminal to be old, we all know that ; but if you are over fifty wear black. Don't let a colour come near you except in your bonnet ; good materials—silks, satins, velvets—nothing can be too rich, and lace—plenty of white, black, and soft yellowish lace about your neck and throat." Would you believe it, they all turn up their noses and walk off in disdain. " What dingy ideas, my dear Mrs. Trevor; black—perpetual mourning ! I am sorry to say our tastes differ "—all in a staccato, you know; and the poor deluded women go off to bedizen themselves in the last fashionable tint, which does not harmonise in the least with their fading complexion. Oh, I lose patience with them, they have no sense, no eye, no taste ! Don't think me conceited, Ellison, for you know I have no paltry vanity of that sort ; but if ever people called me a beautiful young woman, they shall call me a beautiful old one, if I have to wear a mob cap and drawn satin bonnet to keep up the illusion,' for on the subject of dress Mrs. Trevor could be eloquent. Ellison was after her own heart in this matter, and she often told her so, and before ten minutes were over, Ellison's sharp eyes had found out that Lorraine's appearance was giving Mrs. Trevor great satisfaction. When Colonel Trevor came into the room just before luncheon, and began to talk to Lorraine, Mrs. Trevor took the opportunity of saying, as she showed Ellison some new fancy work—

' I like your Mrs. Herbert, Ellison. She is well-bred and interesting-looking. She will be a nice companion for Muriel. Her manners are charming ; but she looks as though she wants rest and feeding up.'

' She has had too long a walk before breakfast. It exhausted her, and she has been asleep most of the morning. I am so glad you are favourably impressed, Cousin Louise, and I hope Muriel will take to her ; by the bye, where is Muriel ?' But at that moment the young lady herself entered.

CHAPTER VIII

MURIEL

'There is a great deal of unmapped country within us, which would have to be taken into account in an explanation of our gusts and storms.'—GEORGE ELIOT.

IN spite of Colonel Trevor's interesting conversation, Lorraine had more than once looked towards the door as though she were expecting some one, and a moment before Miss Trevor appeared she had said in her frank way, 'I am looking for your sister. I am so anxious to see her.'

If this speech surprised Colonel Trevor, he did not say so. 'My sister is a little erratic in her habits,' he replied quietly ; 'we often do not see her until luncheon. She has a big room in the turret where she exercises her hobbies in private. No, please do not ask me what they are '—in pretended alarm, as Lorraine looked at him in a questioning manner—' I never go in for other people's hobbies. I believe my sister is a great reader. I know she gives large orders to our local bookseller. Ah, here she comes ; and this gong reminds me that I am to take you in to luncheon.' But Lorraine did not hear the latter part of this sentence. She was looking curiously at the tall pale girl who was moving so languidly across the room.

She greeted Lorraine courteously, but with rather a chilling gravity of manner, and the young widow's bright smile and cordial hand-shake met with slight response. But Lorraine had felt the limp coldness of the girl's hand, and had drawn her own conclusions, and when Mrs. Trevor said in a reproachful voice, 'Muriel, you have one of your bad sick headaches,' she knew that she had been right.

Muriel slightly shrugged her shoulders. 'That is nothing new, mother,' she returned rather ungraciously ; ' but Gavin looks impatient ; the gong stopped quite three minutes ago,' and at this hint Colonel Trevor again offered Lorraine his arm.

Lorraine tried not to feel disappointed. She had come to Brae House warmly prejudiced in Muriel Trevor's favour, and disposed to take her part. It was evident that Ellison misunderstood her, but it was impossible not to feel a little repelled by the cold indifference of her manner ; a headache was no excuse for such utter want of graciousness. There was also a hardly-concealed touch of sarcasm in that remark about the gong ; clearly it was a hit at her brother's punctuality. As she sat exactly opposite to Lorraine during luncheon, the latter had an opportunity of studying her closely; the headache was evidently severe, for she ate nothing, and only drank some mineral water.

Lorraine never found it so difficult to take stock of anybody ; when luncheon was over she had not made up her mind whether Muriel Trevor was good-looking or absolutely plain. She would have said decidedly plain, only the features were certainly good, the mouth especially ; her hair was unbecomingly arranged, strained off the forehead, and coiled heavily behind the head ; but it was of a beautiful chestnut tint, a rich ripe brown, and was evidently abundant ; a sallow complexion, want of animation, and lack of expression were her chief defects. Very likely she suffered from the peevishness of chronic ill-health, or perhaps her temper was not naturally amiable. There was a repressed irritability of manner, a concealed antagonism that found vent in quiet little stinging speeches. Lorraine noticed this whenever Colonel Trevor spoke to her ; she could find no fault with his manner, it was perfectly pleasant, but for some reason it seemed to jar on Muriel. After a time she made no effort to join in the conversation, but sat plaiting her table-napkin with restless fingers until Mrs. Trevor gave the signal to rise from the table. Colonel Trevor went off to the stables to give some order, and his mother took Ellison to the conservatory to show her some new arrangement of ferns, and Lorraine found herself left alone with Miss Trevor. They were in the big drawing-room, which was very pleasant in this May afternoon, with the scent of jonquils and wall-flowers ; both rooms opened into the conservatory where Mrs. Trevor and Ellison were pacing up and down in the sunlight.

Miss Trevor looked at them a moment, then she said abruptly, and as though she were repeating a lesson, 'Should you care to see the conservatory, Mrs. Herbert, we can go there if you like.' Lorraine would have liked nothing better, for she was passionately fond of flowers ; but her unselfishness would not allow her to enjoy anything at another person's expense.

'I think it would be far better for us to stay here,' she returned gently. 'I shall have plenty of opportunities, I hope, of admiring those beautiful flowers; but the glare and heat would certainly make your head worse. I can see you are in severe pain, and you ate nothing at luncheon.'

A faint flush crossed Miss Trevor's face.

'You are very kind,' she said a little less coldly, 'and if you are sure you do not mind, perhaps it would be better to avoid the glare of all that glass. I am not fond of tropical heat, though my mother loves it, and spends a good deal of her time there. The conservatory is her hobby.'

'Ah, we all have our hobbies,' returned Lorraine quickly; and then she checked herself and laughed as though she were amused; 'but if any one were to ask me what mine was I should be at a loss to answer. I think my first hobby is to try and understand human nature as well as I can. I do like diving into the recesses of other people's feelings, and finding out their motives and wishes; one has such grand finds sometimes. Don't you think the study of human nature dreadfully interesting?'

Lorraine had no idea that she was going to say this, but her thoughts often came tumbling out in this impromptu fashion when she least intended it; but Miss Trevor looked as astonished as though some one had let off a rocket suddenly in her face. This was not the sort of drawing-room talk to which she had been accustomed; her mother's flow of words, though they always charmed people, were to Muriel like the babbling of some bright little rivulet that came from some bubbling spring underground and led nowhere.

'Only a flotilla of paper boats could have sailed down that sparkling little rivulet of trickling water,' thought Muriel contemptuously; but her eyes grew large and puzzled when she heard Mrs. Herbert's remark.

'Do I find the study of human nature dreadfully interesting?' she repeated slowly, as though she were revolving some insoluble problem. 'It is a study I have never attempted. I draw my idea of human nature principally from books; it is safer, I think,' as though debating with herself. 'We have the wisdom of all the ages to guide us; that is surely better than relying on our own observation.'

'I expect you are far cleverer than I,' returned Lorraine with a shake of her head. 'You are a great reader; your brother told me so before luncheon, and I know so few books.'

'My brother knows nothing at all about my tastes,' returned Muriel, her manner freezing again, and the slight illumination in her eyes fading utterly. 'I suppose he did not give you a list of my studies?'

'Oh dear no,' replied Lorraine frankly, 'he seemed quite hazy on the subject. I think his sole remark was that books were your hobby. I hope you do not consider me impertinent, Miss Trevor, but I should so like to know your especial study. There, you see, I am astride my hobby as usual. I never see any one without wanting to know their chief interest in life. Don't you see,' naively, 'every one is a piece of unmapped country. Now, that is not my own idea,' as Muriel looked impressed at this, 'I read it somewhere; wait a moment, I shall remember the passage directly; it was Sir J. Stevens said it—"Every man has in himself a continent of undiscovered character. Happy is he who acts Columbus to his own soul."'

'That is beautiful,' returned Muriel in a low voice. She had a deep, musical voice, with wonderful chords in it. People who did not like Miss Trevor always said she had a studied and rather affected manner.

It was Lorraine's turn to be electrified. She discovered that when Miss Trevor smiled she looked a different creature; no one could call her plain then; it was a pity that she smiled so seldom.

'I made a note of that passage,' she went on, 'for it struck me directly—well, that is just what I feel about people. I want to find out all their physical geography, their mountains, rivers, plains; their tastes, pursuits, interests; their little shoals and quicksands; it is frightfully, it is awfully interesting, one is always exploring, and yet there are vast regions still to explore.'

'It sounds grand, but I do not understand it,' returned Muriel with greater animation than she had shown yet. 'I have never tried to read people in that way; people mostly bore me; they are so shallow, they say the same things, and they say them over and over again; it is hot, or it is cold, they have troubles with their servants, or with their children's health; or it is politics and shooting so many head of game; ah, how they weary one! When I listen to my mother's friends all talking round her tea-table, I say—yes, that is just as the sheep jump through that big gap in the field; you know what I mean. How often I have watched them, the foolish things; one jumps, and then all the others follow; there is a rush and scurry, but what is the good of it, the grass was as good in the field they left.'

A bright humorous smile crossed Lorraine's face; after all she had been right—the girl was interesting; she could talk if she liked. If only they had not been interrupted just then; Miss Trevor was thawing; her odd unconventional speech had made an impression and created an opening; in common parlance, they were getting on as fast as a house on fire. But unfortunately the other ladies joined them, and Ellison informed her that the dog-cart was coming up the front drive, and that Dorcas and Tedo were walking up the shrubbery.

This turned Lorraine's thoughts into another channel directly: she had not seen her boy for two whole hours. She started up from her chair impulsively to meet him, when her attention was arrested by the marked displeasure of Miss Trevor's voice.

'My dear Muriel,' her mother had said, 'I am so rejoiced that your poor head is better. I was really afraid that we should be obliged to send for Dr. Howell. I was going to speak to Gavin about it, but when we heard you talking so cheerfully to Mrs. Herbert I felt quite easy. "Muriel is better, it is not one of her worst sort of headaches," I said to Ellison, "for when the pain is severe she is never able to speak or to hold up her head."'

'One is obliged to make efforts sometimes, mother,' returned Muriel in a tone that made Lorraine pause for an instant; 'my head is no better, but you forget that you left me to entertain Mrs. Herbert, and that I could not well remain silent.'

She was certainly taking ample revenge for her mother's want of tact. Quite a youthful flush crossed Mrs. Trevor's face.

'Oh, my dear child!' she exclaimed in an alarmed voice, 'do you mean that I have been remiss, and that I have been neglecting Mrs. Herbert? How could I be so thoughtless! The fact is'—turning to Lorraine—'I was so anxious to show Ellison my new fernery, and to fill her with envy, that I forgot my duties as hostess; and then I had to ask her advice about our under-housemaid—dear Ellison has so much common-sense—and the girl is not quite satisfactory, and——' but Lorraine interrupted her.

'I hope you are not intending to make excuses to me,' she said good-humouredly. 'I think it was I who was thoughtless in allowing Miss Trevor to talk to me; I can see plainly that I have done her no good. May I go out and fetch my boy? I do so want to show him to you,' but she hardly waited for Mrs. Trevor's ready permission.

'She is charming,' whispered Mrs. Trevor impressively, but both she and Ellison exchanged a glance of mutual surprise when they saw Muriel follow her.

Mrs. Trevor squeezed Ellison's arm significantly. 'I told you so,' she said, when the door had closed on her daughter, 'Muriel has taken a fancy to her; I never heard her talk to a stranger before. When Amy or Constance Mordaunt comes she is almost rude to them; little Laura Holt is quite shy of her; she never troubles herself to entertain them in the least. Her brother is always telling her so, it vexes him dreadfully to see her so indifferent to our friends ; but you heard her just now.'

'They were talking very busily, certainly,' returned Ellison. 'I think Lorraine has a happy knack of drawing people out ; but Muriel looks very ill. I suspect she has been keeping late hours ; it is really very foolish of her to neglect her health in this way.'

'It is no use speaking to her,' returned Mrs. Trevor sadly, 'you ought to know Muriel by this time. Gavin makes the same mistake, he tells her outright when he thinks she is unwise, but it does no good, and he will find it out for himself one day. He was lecturing her at breakfast-time, that is why she is put out with him. He saw the turret-room lighted up long after midnight. Muriel was so angry, I am afraid she spoke to Gavin very improperly, for, as I told her afterwards, it is Gavin's house, not ours, and that he is master here ; but I could make no impression on her. She would insist that he was not her master, and that he had no right to spy upon her little ways, and then she began on the old troublesome subject. Why could we not go to the Dower House? Gavin did not really need us ; that we were preventing him from marrying again. That is Muriel's strong point, she will insist that Gavin wants his house to himself, but I do not intend to believe her, it is all nonsense and temper on Muriel's part.'

'I am inclined to agree with you,' replied Ellison, who had often been over this ground before ; 'poor Cousin Louise, it is very hard for you. I wish Muriel would behave better to Gavin. He may be a little masterful and decided—men often are—but a sister ought to understand and make light of his little defects. Now we must really go, or Gavin will be late for dinner.'

When they went into the hall they found Tedo and Colonel Trevor playing at hide-and-seek among the pillars, and Lorraine watching them with delighted eyes. Muriel had disappeared. Tedo was captured with difficulty, and lifted on to his mother's lap, and Ellison established herself on the back seat of the dog-cart. Colonel Trevor took the reins, and they started off, Mrs. Trevor kissing her hand from the porch.

As they drove out of the gate Lorraine looked up. Yes, that must be the turret-room ; she could see a tall figure standing in the window, Muriel was evidently watching them. Lorraine waved her hand, but she could not be certain that there was any response, then she settled herself to the enjoyment of her drive.

The road to Dorchester was singularly beautiful. For nearly two miles the road skirted the Redlands woods ; the dark firs, the

broken ground—with gorse and furze—the glimpses of meadow-
lands opened up new vistas of interest every minute. Dorchester
evidently lay in a hollow, for at times there was quite a deep
descent. Now and then the road narrowed, the branches of
the trees met overhead, and the sunshine filtered pleasantly
through the green leaves. They drove at a good pace, but
Lorraine felt no uneasiness. Colonel Trevor was evidently a
practised Jehu, and he and Whitefoot understood each other.

They had just accomplished an awkward little bit of road
safely when he turned to Lorraine with a smile.

'You have good nerves, Mrs. Herbert. I should never have
dared to drive at that pace if my sister had been with me. Last
time we went into Dorchester I was obliged to let her get out
and walk.'

'I am always sorry for nervous people,' replied Lorraine simply,
'their imaginations conjure up frightful mishaps without any
adequate foundation for their fears. When I was a little girl
some one gave me the *Pilgrim's Progress*, for my Sunday afternoon
reading. I used to be so sorry for Miss Much-afraid—even in
Bunyan's time there were such things as diseased nerves.'

'I daresay,' he returned in an amused voice ; 'but I have
wholly forgotten the person you mention. There was a Mr.
Feeble-mind, I recollect.'

'Yes, and a Mr. Despondency. Ah, Bunyan was a grand
student of human nature ; even as a child I used to revel in his
descriptions.'

'I used to read the *Pilgrim's Progress* too, when I was a small
boy,' observed Colonel Trevor complacently, 'but I always liked
that fight with Apollyon best. There was such a grand picture
of the fiend — all claws and scales — that, boy-like, I gloated
over it. I think I will look it up again for the sake of the good
old times. Ah, and they were good, Mrs. Herbert ; "the thoughts
of youth are long, long thoughts," as Longfellow says ; but the
thoughts were awfully jolly, I am sure of that.'

'Gavin, I think that we had better have tea at Masterman's,'
interrupted Ellison at this moment. 'I shall order it while you
put up Whitefoot, and then we can do our shopping afterwards.'

'All right,' was the good-humoured answer. 'My business will
be done in half an hour, but I can go and have a crack with some
one at the club while you ladies do your purchases.'

It was a delightful afternoon to Lorraine. Both her companions were amused at her artless expressions of pleasure as they
sat at the little round table at Masterman's, enjoying their tea and
scones. Of her own account she began telling them about her

life at Brussels, and then of some weeks that she had once spent in the Bavarian Tyrol.

'In those days life used to be a perpetual picnic and feast,' she went on. 'When I was very tired and low in Beaumont Street I used to shut my eyes and try to imagine that I was a girl again. It was a miserable make-believe, but I think it refreshed me. I used to try so hard sometimes that I have almost smelt the roses on old Marie's stall, and could see her brown, wizened old face and dangling earrings quite plainly. Oh those roses, and the great crimson peaches, how lovely they all were ; but,' with a queer little shrug of her shoulders, 'I doubt if my dream of the fruit-market improved the flavour of weak tea and dry bread.'

Colonel Trevor gave her a quick, interested look, but said nothing. Ellison shook her head.

'Beaumont Street is an interdicted subject. You may talk as much as you like about Switzerland or the Tyrol; I love foreign descriptions ; Colonel Trevor is always furnishing me with Indian sketches—his Anglo-Indian reminiscences are wonderfully amusing. Now, really we must begin our shopping, and keep the rest of our chat for the return journey'; and as this was only sensible advice no one offered any objection, and Colonel Trevor took himself off.

Lorraine found plenty of amusement in watching Ellison make her purchases. She was an admirable business woman, she knew exactly what she wanted, and never tried to make bargains. Miss Lee was evidently well known in Dorchester ; whatever shop she entered the master always left his customer to speak to her, and, if possible, to serve her. She was very pleasant in her manners. Lorraine might think her at times a little condescending, a trifle too decided for her years, but no one is quite perfect ; and by the end of the afternoon she admired Ellison more than ever.

Tedo was tired out long before Ellison had finished her business, so she advised her cousin to sit down at Masterman's until the dogcart was ready. He was fast asleep when they fetched him, and fretted a little at being disturbed ; but he soon quieted down in his mother's arms. The return journey was slower. Ellison insisted on walking up the steep hill, and joined Colonel Trevor as he led Whitefoot. Lorraine would willingly have joined them, but she could not leave her boy, so she sat contentedly looking up the shady road, while the soft evening air played on her face.

A sudden sense of well-being, of full satisfaction made her heart swell almost painfully—could she be happier than she felt this evening? Her boy was well ; his future and hers was assured. Ellison was not one to do anything by halves. The old bad life was past and over; her poor Ralph was at rest. It was dreadful to think that she could not truly mourn for him; that was 'the worst of all; but surely it was her duty to be happy now. 'I need not doubt that God has work for me to do here,' she went on; 'if one only waits, one's work will surely come. If only Ellison will love me,' and then she smiled and sighed, and wished she could hear what they were saying; but their voices were low, and she could distinguish nothing.

The talk would have interested her. Colonel Trevor was speaking to Ellison about his sister. He was relating their disagreement at the breakfast-table, and giving her his version. He really wanted Ellison's advice and sympathy, and as usual she was very ready to give it.

'I am quite losing heart about Muriel,' he finished. 'I find it impossible to get on with her; she resents what she calls my interference; but, really, in my position and at my age, surely it cannot be wrong to offer a sister advice?'

'Certainly not,' returned Ellison decidedly; 'you are master of Brae House, Gavin, and have every right to make your own rules; Cousin Louise is always saying so. She takes your part and blames Muriel for answering you as she does.'

'It was very bad this morning,' he returned gravely. 'You know how I hate scenes; and if one cannot have one's breakfast in peace, I shall just go back to my old Indian custom and have my cup of tea in my room; bickering at breakfast spoils one's digestion for the day.'

'Muriel is ill; any one can see that. She has been sitting up over her studies and injuring her nerves. She was not in a condition to take advice this morning, and so her temper got the better of her.'

'I cannot help all that,' he returned impatiently. 'It was my duty to say what I did—that it was folly to sit over her books at midnight, and that I begged for all our sakes that she would keep better hours. Perhaps I put my foot down a little more than usual; but her manner riled me—you women can be provoking if you choose—she had no right to answer me as she did; but when my mother told her so in the kindest way, she got up and left the room.'

'Poor Gavin! Yes, I understand it all. Muriel's temper is very, very faulty. She ought to be so good to you. No, you have nothing for which to blame yourself; every man has the right to be master in his own house.'

'I am glad you think so'—looking at her tenderly. 'What a comfort it is to talk to you. I have been rather in a bad temper myself to-day.'

'You, Gavin; what nonsense! There, I had better jump up now as we are nearly at the top of the hill. You must drive as quickly as you can, or you will be too late.'

Colonel Trevor seemed in capital spirits during the remainder of the drive. As they drew up at the gate of Brae Farm, Bairn came out to welcome them. As Ellison caressed him she suddenly remembered the retriever puppies.

'Mrs. Herbert would like one of Juno's puppies,' she said. Can you spare her one, Gavin?'

'Certainly,' he returned promptly. 'Which shall I send her— Tweedledum or Tweedledee? they are both fine little fellows.'

'Oh, we will leave that to you; but he must be handsome and amiable; but I don't think I much admire your choice of names! The puppy will be re-christened, I can assure you of that.'

'Then Mrs. Herbert shall not have one at all,' was the unexpected reply. 'Mrs. Herbert, surely you would not have the bad taste to re-christen a puppy that I sent you?'

'Not if you particularly wished me to retain the name,' she returned, rather perplexed by his plaintive tone.

'No, I thought not. You are far too kind-hearted to hurt any one's feelings. I will bring down Tweedledum for you to see; he is a real beauty, and will beat Bairn into fits when he grows up; but he must be well looked after, his pedigree is most respectable, and he has not had distemper yet.'

'Lorraine, how could you be so absurd!' observed her cousin, as they walked together to the house. 'Colonel Trevor was only in fun. Fancy binding yourself to keep that ridiculous name. You ought to call him Chief or Keeper, or some suitable name; but Tweedledum!'

'It is very long, certainly. I shall have to shorten it some-how; but how very kind of Colonel Trevor to spare me one of his puppies.'

'Not at all; he wants to get rid of it. I knew that when I suggested it; but Juno's puppies are worth having, and one more dog about the Farm will not matter,' and having put things in this matter-of-fact light, Ellison went briskly into the house to prepare for the evening meal, leaving Lorraine to follow at her leisure.

CHAPTER IX

'Sow an action, reap a habit ;
  Sow a habit, reap a character ;
  Sow a character, reap a destiny ;
  Not as little as we dare, but as much as we can.'
                 BISHOP WESTCOTT.

THAT evening as they sat at their work in the bay-window, enjoy-ing the fine sunset, Lorraine began to question her cousin about the inhabitants of the vicarage.

'You have not mentioned them, Ellison,' she went on. 'You have told me so much about the Earnshaws at Price's Folly, and old Mrs. Langton at Ferncliffe, and her companion Miss Holt, and that Redlands is deserted because Sir John Chessington and Lady Chessington have gone to India for a year, but you have not spoken of the vicarage people.' But as she said this Ellison looked very grave and put down her work.

'No, but I was going to tell you, only there is so much to say about everything. There is sad trouble at the vicarage ; our poor old vicar, Mr. Yolland, has had a stroke of paralysis, and his doctor has ordered him complete rest and change for a year. They left Highlands about three weeks ago ; they are at Hastings at present, but they are going shortly to Taunton, where their only son has a living.'

'That is why the vicarage had such an uninhabited look then. I could only see one thin line of smoke from a solitary chimney, and most of the blinds were down.'

'Yes, it is to be put thoroughly into repair. There is some-thing defective about the warming apparatus, and one or two of the ceilings are down ; they expect to have workmen in for three or four months, Mrs. Yolland told me so herself. She owned it was a sad pity, as they could not house the *locum tenens;* and if he should be a married man with a family it might be very difficult for him to find lodgings near. There is only Mrs. Drake's—I believe she lets three bedrooms with the sitting - room—for they would hardly go to the *Waggon and Horses.* Tom Brattle is unmarried and does not trouble himself with lodgers ; besides, his brother Sam, my bailiff, lives with him ; and the other cottages afford very limited accommodation.'

'Is the *locum tenens* married, then ?' asked Lorraine, who was as much interested in the politics of Highlands as though she had lived there all her life.

'That is what I cannot tell you ; for at present he is a myth. One of the curates from Bramfield come over from Saturday to Monday and put up at the *Waggon and Horses;* but the churchwardens, Mr. Earnshaw and Mr. Tarrant, are in treaty with some clergyman, I believe, for the entire twelvemonth. It is very provoking altogether, for Sir John is so good-natured that he would willingly have offered Redlands, but now he has made other arrangements ; some of his friends and connections are coming down for the shooting, but until September the house will be under repair.'

Lorraine looked a little taken aback at this news. 'Oh dear, what a pity,' she said naively. 'How dreadfully you must miss your friends, Ellison.'

'Yes,' returned Ellison tranquilly. 'Lady Chessington was a very intimate friend ; I liked her best of all my neighbours ; she was a little melancholy at times ; you see they lost their youngest son about two years ago. He was such a nice boy ; he died at Rugby from the effects of a blow at football, and she has never quite recovered it, or Sir John either. Their oldest son is with his regiment in Burmah, and they have gone out to see him.'

'What an excellent plan ; nothing could be better. Why are you smiling, Ellison, in that amused way ?'

'I think you do amuse me a little,' returned her cousin quietly. 'You have only been here two days, and yet you seem as interested in all the people as though you had lived here for years. I do not think I have ever talked so much about my neighbours as I have these two days ; but I can see your curiosity is not a bit satisfied.'

'It grows with what it feeds upon, you see. Poor Lady Chessington ; of course you must love her.'

'I do not say that ; love is a rather strong word for a mere acquaintance, but we are on pleasant terms of intimacy. She used to come here very often, and I dined at Redlands every few weeks

—Sir John never liked dining alone, he is very sociable. Yes, I should miss them a good deal if I were not so busy, but I think I miss the Yollands more. He is one's clergyman, you see, and he always preached such sensible sermons, they seemed to do one good ; and then one is so sorry for poor Mrs. Yolland.'

' Yes, indeed, it must be a great trouble to her.'

' It has nearly killed her ; it is she who has always been the invalid. She had a weak chest, and never went out in the winter ; but she led such a busy life. She used to have working meetings for the South of London — one for us gentry, and one for the respectable mothers—Mrs. Drake and any of the cottagers. She gave them tea, and read to them an amusing book, and they very much enjoyed it. I half promised that I would carry it on next winter. I thought Miss Spencer, the infant-school mistress, would help me ; but I shall have you now.'

' Yes, dear, and I shall be delighted to help you. I do love mothers' meetings. I like nursing the babies and talking to the women, and I can cut out too. I have had regular lessons '; and then Ellison, in a rapid concise way, began to detail her plan. As usual, she had not spoken of it until it was fully sketched out in her own mind. I really think, Lorraine,' she went on gravely, ' that with your assistance I could have the other working-party too. I daresay Mrs. Earnshaw would have it willingly, but it is so far to walk to Price's Folly, the afternoons are so short in November. Brae Farm is more central, and I know Mrs. Yolland would like me to take it. What do you say ? Laura Holt would come, and the Mordaunts, and Muriel, and Mrs. Tarrant, and Mrs. Earnshaw—we should be eight or nine ; one of us would read to prevent gossip. I daresay Muriel or Miss Spencer would be reader.'

Lorraine cordially assented to this. She thought it an excellent idea for her cousin to gather her neighbours round her for charitable work, and commended the scheme warmly. Ellison looked pleased ; and as it was already a *fait accompli* in her mind, she made a mental resolve to send to Pryce Jones for patterns of long-cloth and flannel.

The evening passed almost too quickly, and even Ellison looked surprised when Ruth entered to set the chairs for prayers ; but as punctuality was absolute at Brae Farm, she put down her work at once. When she had dismissed her household, and gone round the place with Mrs. Tucker and Bairn, she was at liberty to dawdle and gossip as much as she liked ; and as Lorraine declared she was not tired, and that she never felt more wide-awake and averse to go to bed, they spent another half-hour looking out on the moonlight, and talking in that desultory, pleasant fashion that most women love.

The next morning Lorraine had a surprise. She was in her room getting Tedo ready for a walk when she heard the gate click, and the next moment Muriel Trevor's tall figure passed up the gravel walk.

Early visitors were very undesirable in Ellison's opinion, and no one but Muriel would have invaded the privacy of the mistress of Brae Farm at an hour when she would be making up her accounts, or interviewing her bailiff ; but Muriel's visit was to Mrs. Herbert, as she bluntly informed her, and Ellison tried not to smile as she sent a message to summon her cousin.

Muriel looked a little disappointed when Lorraine entered in her hat and jacket. ' Oh, are you going out ? ' she said abruptly. ' I thought it would be much too early ; but, of course, I would not think of detaining you this lovely morning.'

' It is a lovely morning,' agreed Lorraine cheerfully, ' and Tedo is wild to get out and pick buttercups and daisies. I was only going into the Brae Woods. Why should you not join us ? Ellison is busy '—looking at her formidable pile of account-books— ' and will be glad to have the room to herself. If you are not tired '—with a glance at Muriel's pale face—' I think the air would do you good.'

' So do I ; thank you for proposing it ' ; and Muriel's manner was quite animated. ' But before we start, Ellison, I must give you mother's message. She wants you and Mrs. Herbert to come to dinner to-morrow. There will only be Admiral and Mrs. Earnshaw and Captain Faucit—he is coming down for a couple of nights ; but mother is very anxious for you both to come.'

' We shall be delighted,' began Ellison, and then she saw an expression of embarrassment on Lorraine's face. She coloured and looked at her cousin.

' I hope you will go, Ellison,' she said meaningly ; ' but I am afraid that I must ask you to excuse me ' ; and then she added bravely, ' I have not provided myself with dinner-dresses, you know.'

' My dear Mrs. Herbert, what does that matter ? ' and Muriel seemed quite amused. ' Mother and I are very unconventional. We do not mind in the least what people wear ; do we, Ellison ? Neither of us could accept such an excuse for a moment.'

' I know what my cousin means,' returned Ellison with her usual tact. ' I gave her no time to replenish her wardrobe ; but, Lorraine, I really think for this once Mrs. Trevor will excuse my little deficiency. Am I right, Muriel ? Would not your mother be pleased to see Mrs. Herbert, even if she makes her appearance in a plain black gown ? '

' I can answer for mother,' replied Muriel so pleasantly that Ellison regarded her with secret astonishment. ' She will be delighted to see Mrs. Herbert, even in a gown of sackcloth and garland of ashes ' ; and at this they both laughed. And so it was settled ; Lorraine was too sociable by nature to need much persuasion. Vanity had lain dormant for many years, and her unhappy married life had made her rather careless of her appearance than otherwise. Until the previous day, when she had tried on her new serge gown, she had never regarded herself with such satisfaction ; and she was quite disposed to think that she would be presentable in her cashmere. They were ready now to start for their walk ; but as they left the house together Lorraine detected herself studying Miss Trevor's appearance rather critically. She had evidently no taste for dress ; everything was well-made and fitted admirably, there was no fault in the cut or style ; but the cold, quakerish grey, unadorned and without the faintest relief, only made her complexion more decidedly sallow. A darker tint, a touch of bright colour, was needed to give warmth and tone. It was a pity, Lorraine thought, that Miss Trevor should not have inherited her mother's taste ; she probably refused to be guided on such matters, and preferred her own faulty standard—and in this she was perfectly correct. Many and deep were the groans of Mrs. Trevor over dear Muriel's deplorable want of taste, and her preference for dull neutral tints. ' She is colour-blind, I believe,' she once said to Ellison in a tone of half-comic disgust, ' or she has imposed some penance on herself. Last year it was a dirty sage green, the most odious tint to blend with a sallow complexion, and she varied it with a yellowish red—a perfectly indescribable shade, something like rhubarb and magnesia with a dash of senna in it. I went on my knees metaphorically to beg her to burn that gown ; I even offered to refund the nine guineas that she had paid for it ; but she only stared at me, and said I did not understand æsthetic dress— æsthetic rubbish I call it.'

Tedo demanded ' butter-fies and day-days ' before they had reached the gate, but Lorraine was inexorable.

' No, Tedo, you must let mother carry you across the big field, and then you shall have as many buttercups as you like'; and it was pretty to see how the little fellow yielded ; evidently he was not spoilt. When Lorraine took him up in her arms, he put his arms round her neck and pressed his cheek against hers. Tedo had inherited his mother's loving disposition, and was quite as demonstrative in his way.

'How strong you are!' exclaimed Muriel enviously. 'I could not carry that child for a dozen yards without fatigue.'

'I daresay not,' returned Lorraine, smiling. 'Yes, I used to be very strong, but things have taken the strength out of me a little. I never felt so tired as I do now. Good health is indeed a blessing, Miss Trevor. I have never been thankful enough for it; one does not count up one's blessings often enough, I say that to myself sometimes. But I am afraid,' in a sympathetic voice, 'it is not a blessing that you enjoy, you seem to me very far from strong.'

'You are right,' in a low, dejected tone; 'but very few people do me so much justice. I am supposed to be fanciful and to have fads. What makes you so liberal-minded, Mrs. Herbert?'

Lorraine laughed.

'Any child could see you were suffering severely yesterday; you looked only fit to be in bed. To-day you are better, but you are still very weak and languid.'

This was such unusual treatment; there was such a delicious inflexion of real sympathy and kindness in Lorraine's tone, such evident understanding, that Muriel's starved sensibilities made instant and grateful response. No one had dealt with her wisely; her peculiar temperament needed careful management. Her mother's excessive tenderness was provoking, and only increased her irritability; her brother was far too brusque and bracing; Ellison too condescending, her good sense and robust health were almost wounding; snaffle and curb and spur, they were not for her thin-skinned and morbid nature. 'The heart knoweth its own bitterness,' said the wise man; and through the ages no words have been truer; but no one guessed how bitter the rind of life was to Muriel Trevor.

'I do not know that there is much amiss with my health,' she said presently, as they walked slowly across the Brae meadow. 'Anæmic; that is what they all say—a want of strength and vitality; it does not sound much, does it, Mrs. Herbert? There is no interesting or mysterious disease, you see; it is only "the little rift within the lute," but it is wonderful'—she paused here, and there was a deep melancholy in her voice—'it is strange how it deadens the life music.'

Never had Muriel Trevor made such a speech, even in her own home. It was Lorraine's caressing voice that had drawn it forth. Sympathy is a lever strong enough to move a world; but how often it is misapplied, or rusted for want of use.

Lorraine made no answer, but her soft brown eyes rested on Muriel's face; they were quite eloquent enough.

'It is not that I feel so ill, but that I never know what it is to feel quite well,' she went on. 'Do you know how a creaking door jars on one's nerves? Well, I am always creaking and feel jarred; the world has scant pity for nerves. One day people load you with sympathy,—you are ill, you must have every attention; but the next day they have grown a little weary,—it is want of effort then, a grievous giving way to morbid feelings.'

'Yes, yes, I know exactly what you mean, it is all too painfully true. Poor Miss Trevor, I am so sorry for you. Yes, my son, you shall walk now, you have been very good; shall we sit down on this tree-trunk to rest while he gathers us some bouquets? Be off with you, Tedo; yellow buttercups for mother, and pink and white daisies for the lady.' And Tedo went off chuckling with delight, to behead countless flowers, and carry off trophies of hot, mangled blossoms lovingly scrunched in his little hands.

It was evident that some sort of struggle was going on in Muriel's mind; she looked at her companion and seemed about to speak, and then hesitated, but finally she burst out in a curious shamefaced way:

'It is not honest to be silent; you are very very kind, but I do not deserve this pity; you would not give it if you knew how little care I take of myself; perhaps if I were wiser, and did not do many foolish things, I might have better health.'

'What things do you mean?' asked Lorraine gently; 'please tell me. Confession is good for the soul, you know.'

'It is very strange,' returned Muriel in an odd, musing tone. 'I have never owned to a living creature before that I have been in the wrong. I have known you about four-and-twenty hours, and I am talking as confidentially as though we were old friends: there is something mesmeric and uncanny in this sudden influence; humbling as it is to confess it, I should rather like to answer your question.'

'Real sympathy is always mesmeric,' replied Lorraine, 'but its influence depends entirely on its reality and depth. In spite of the fact that we are almost strangers, you are quite aware that I am sincerely interested; the whole thing—the kernel—the meaning lies in the nutshell, "Give, and it shall be given to you."'

Muriel was silent; she was conscious of an entirely new sensation; to hear a text quoted out of church on a week-day was a novelty to her experience; she was not quite sure that she liked it, and yet how true it was.

'I see what you mean,' she returned after a minute. 'Well, I will tell you one of my bad habits. I am fond of burning the midnight oil; I get interested in my studies, and I hate going to bed early. What is the good of lying awake, feeding on one's own dismal fancies? I love to feel that every one in the house is asleep, and that I am up in my turret-room under the stars. It is difficult to explain what I mean, but at no other hour do I ever have such a sense of freedom and stillness and peace ; my brain is more alive, I feel less languid and on edge. My brother has taken upon himself to lecture me pretty severely for what he terms my suicidal folly ; and as I dispute any one's right to control my movements, things are just a little strained at present. There, I have been perfectly frank for once in my life. Are you dreadfully shocked, Mrs. Herbert ? '

' I am dreadfully sorry,' returned Lorraine quietly, ' for I must be honest in my turn, and confess that I am rather inclined to take your brother's side. You are laying up trouble for yourself, Miss Trevor. Tell me one thing,—does not nature take her revenge in the mornings ? '

' Ah, you have me there ! The early morning hours are purgatorial.'

' I thought so. You do not need lectures, your conscience must tell you the truth ; you will not enjoy your stolen sweets long, they will become bitter—at least, I hope so ; you are not one to repent by halves, I am sure of that. If you would not think me hard for saying so, I feel disposed to transfer a little of my pity to your mother and brother ; but specially your mother.'

Lorraine spoke in a light jesting tone, for she was a little afraid of saying too much. But it was evident she had grazed on a sore point. Muriel coloured up.

' You think I give them plenty to bear.'

' No, indeed ; how could you imagine that I should hint such a thing—I, a perfect stranger ? But I know how mothers feel. I could not help being exceedingly touched by Mrs. Trevor's anxiety yesterday, she was so evidently concerned, she knew in a moment that you were suffering ; it made no difference to her that it might have been caused by your own fault, she only wanted to find a remedy.'

' Poor dear mother '—in a repentant tone. And then Tedo made a diversion ; he had scratched his thumb against some prickly shrub and his self-pity was excessive. He shed torrents of tears over ' mine bluggy humb,' and nothing but bandaging it with a handkerchief soothed his terror. ' Boy won't pick no more nasty fo'ers,' he said rather drowsily, for he was getting tired.

' When our pleasures tire us, they are pleasures no longer,' observed Lorraine quaintly. ' Tedo's beloved flowers have all got thorns now. What ungrateful creatures we are. I think I must go back now, for Tedo is decidedly weary. I hope you do not mind.' And Muriel reluctantly turned her steps homewards.

'I shall see you to-morrow evening,' she said, as they parted at the Lodge gates. 'Perhaps, after dinner, I might show you my den, while Gavin and Captain Faucit smoke their cigarettes.'

'That will be delightful. I shall remind you of your promise,' returned Lorraine; but as she walked swiftly, and carrying her sleeping boy, she never noticed that Muriel was standing still watching her until she was out of sight. Lorraine's arms were aching, and she was sorely tired, but her heart was swelling with tenderness. 'Poor Miss Trevor,' she thought, 'how empty her life is compared to mine.'

'She is a sweet woman,' said Muriel to herself. 'I have never met any one like her; directly she spoke to me my heart seemed to go out to her. What a smile she has! But she has made me feel uncomfortable; I wonder why?' And during the rest of the day Muriel continued to puzzle herself why had those few gentle words made her feel as though all these years she had made some terrible mistake. That night, as Colonel Trevor paced up and down in the moonlight, thinking of his dead wife in her Indian grave, no stream of lamp-light from the turret-room vexed his sense of propriety. Brae House was in darkness, and Muriel, instead of lying awake, was actually sleeping placidly like a rational woman.

CHAPTER X

'All round the room my silent servants wait,
My friends in every season, bright and dim.'
                              BARRY CORNWALL
'Away with him, away with him ; he speaks Latin.'
                              HENRY VI.

THAT afternoon, as Lorraine was watching her boy as he played in the Dovecote, there was a knock at the door, and Ellison entered with a parcel.

'I have brought you this,' she said simply, opening the paper and displaying the folds of rich black silk. 'It was a great bargain. I got it at a sale in St. Paul's Churchyard, but I could not make use of it for some time to come, and you really must have a nice dinner-dress. Mrs. Trevor and Mrs. Earnshaw are always inviting their friends. Highlands is a very sociable little place. I will drive you over to Dorchester one morning, there is an excellent dressmaker there. You will wear black silk, will you not?' looking at her doubtfully, as Lorraine did not answer—perhaps because her lips were quivering.

'Ah, Ellison, how good you are to me. Forgive me, dear'—for the tears could not be kept back—'but I am not used to such kindness. You think of everything.'

'Nonsense, how can you make so much of my little gift.' But though Ellison tried to laugh, her voice was not quite steady. Lorraine's sad little speech went to her heart. As she went downstairs she told herself that her cousin should never have cause to say that again ; undeviating thoughtful kindness should be dealt to her day by day ; her life was to be protected and happy, as far as she had power to influence it ; every want was to be supplied and every wish gratified. 'Poor Lorraine, she is very nice, and I

shall soon get fond of her,' she said to herself. 'It is so pleasant
to like people ; and I never could get fond of Letty ; but Lorraine
has a different sort of nature.'

Ellison felt all the happier as she moved about the room
arranging her flowers, the glow of benevolence seemed to warm her
own heart. The idea that her cousin must owe everything to her,
that she and her boy were already dependent on her for all their
comfort, seemed to give a stimulus and flavour to her own happiness. After all, generosity is only a refined form of selfishness ; the
donor and recipient are equally benefited ; the purse may be im-
poverished, but the heart is enriched ; it is only the niggardly and
the miser who are the losers.

Ellison would have been surprised, perhaps even a little annoyed,
if any one had told her that she was all the happier for her cousin's
society. It is to be feared that in those early days she would
have repelled such an idea with scorn ; but, nevertheless, it was a
fact, that her love of power and management was secretly gratified ;
there was larger scope for her active mind and wider interests ; it
was pleasanter, for example, to ponder over the question, what
Lorraine would like for dinner, than to order her own solitary
meal. It even gave her a better appetite to see how Lorraine
enjoyed it.

It was too soon, far too soon, to hazard an opinion, and nothing
would have induced Ellison to state one ; but she could not deny
that her cousin had admirable tact, she was so ready to fall in with
everything—to talk, or read or be silent. If Ellison were busy she
had her work or book, but she would put down her novel, even in
an engrossing part, if Ellison had anything to discuss ; and there
was never any appearance of effort in doing so. 'She is anxious to
please me, of course,' thought Ellison ; 'she is very grateful and
desirous of helping me, and I suppose I should feel the same in her
place ; but if I read her rightly she is so sympathetic that she
prefers to do what other people like. I might take a leaf out of
her book there. What an example she will be to Muriel, who is so
self-willed, and never yields to any one.'

Ellison was secretly sorry that Mrs. Trevor had issued such an
early invitation to dinner ; she was anxious for her cousin to make
a good appearance in her neighbours' eyes, and was not at all
desirous of presenting her in the light of a poor relation or a
pensioner on her bounty ; she was far too high-minded for such
ideas to be welcome.

It would have been so much nicer for Mrs. Trevor to have
waited a little, and for Lorraine to make acquaintance with everybody after the usual fashion over the tea-cups ; but Mrs. Trevor's

dinners were always stately little affairs ; people dressed smartly at them. It was all very well for Muriel to talk about sackcloth robes and garlands of ashes, but the Highlands ladies were so near London that they dressed very well indeed, and were somewhat critical on their neighbours' appearance. Muriel might take liberties with herself, but Mrs. Trevor and Mrs. Earnshaw were always turned out by their maids, as befitted two well-preserved gentlewomen who knew they had their share of good looks.

When the evening arrived Ellison looked at her cousin rather anxiously. She had put on her plainest evening gown to keep her company. It was a handsome black silk with heavy jet trimmings, and was the least becoming of her dresses ; but Lorraine thought it very stylish.

'You must put up with me, Ellison,' she said, with a comical little smile. 'I cannot do you credit this evening.' And then in a shamefaced way she put down on her cousin's lap an exquisite little spray of white flowers that Ellison had arranged with much taste.

'Thank you, dear, for your kind thought, but I must not wear flowers ; it would not be seemly in my circumstances.'

'Of course not; it was thoughtless of me,' returned Ellison, vexed at the mistake she had made, and arranging the flowers in her own dress. 'Never mind, you look very nice without them'; and she was right. Lorraine's plain black gown seemed moulded perfectly to her graceful figure, and the soft crape rouche was scarcely whiter than her slender throat ; the coils of bright auburn hair set off the small shapely head; and as Ellison watched her cross the room at Brae House, she was struck with the undefinable air of distinction which always attracted strangers.

'Your cousin has lived much abroad, she tells me,' observed Mrs. Earnshaw in the course of the evening. 'Highlands ought to give you a vote of thanks for introducing Mrs. Herbert to us ; she seems a delightful person. Just look ! you can see for yourself that the Admiral has fallen in love with her ; and as for Captain Faucit, he will go back to town a sadder and wiser man.'

Ellison laughed good-humouredly. She was unfeignedly pleased that her cousin's *debût* had been so successful ; every one seemed to like Lorraine, and to be eager to talk to her ; but more than once she had secretly marvelled at her assurance and ease of manner. There was no shyness or *gaucherie;* no consciousness that she was among strangers. Lorraine talked to every one with the same friendly interest and simplicity. It was evident that she was enjoying herself immensely ; to her sociable nature it was delightful to find herself amongst all these pleasant kindly people.

She liked them all : the small, dapper Admiral with his big white moustache and loud, decided voice; and his comely wife, with her dark, Spanish style of beauty and soft motherly ways ; Captain Faucit, a light-hearted young officer with a handsome boyish face ; and as for the Trevors, they were quite like old friends now. She chatted happily with Colonel Trevor; and Ellison noticed that he laughed more than once at her droll original speeches.

From where Lorraine sat she could see little of Muriel ; but she heard her more than once contradicting the Admiral rather flatly ; but he took her rebuffs good-humouredly, and seemed bent on teasing her. Muriel was certainly not looking her best that evening. She wore the obnoxious green gown, and had some heavily cut amber beads round her throat; the colours were ill-chosen and peculiarly unbecoming. Nevertheless, Lorraine's eyes noticed at once the beauty of her full white throat and rounded arms; they were perfectly modelled.

'With her advantages some women would have posed for a beauty,' she thought. 'She had excellent points. I have never seen a more lovely mouth, and when she lights up, her expression is full of intelligence. There is no fault to be found with her features ; it is her complexion, her want of animation, the un-healthiness, mental and physical, of her aspect that makes people call her plain. One of these days, when we know each other better, I shall tell her that it is wicked to give people such a wrong impression. Nature meant her to be beautiful, and beautiful she shall be, if I can make her so ; but she must get rid of her pet fiend, morbid fretfulness. Good old Mother Nature will allow no such intruders to mar her wholesome handiwork.'

When the ladies returned to the drawing-room Muriel tapped Lorraine lightly on the shoulder. 'Now is our opportunity,' she whispered. 'The Admiral will keep them at least half an hour while he tells his old stories. Gavin is used to them ; he generally has a nap and wakes up towards the end. Mother has her house-maid still on her mind, and only wants to talk to Ellison ; and Mrs. Earnshaw, well—tell it not in Gath—but generally she has a nap too.'

'In that case we shall not be missed, certainly,' returned Lorraine, smiling ; and they stole off together. On the first landing they paused simultaneously beside the window. The gardens of Brae were literally flooded with moonlight. The dark masses of foliage in the Brae Woods seemed only to define more sharply the alternations of light and shade. The evening was profoundly still, and an ineffable peace seemed to brood over everything ; the pathway of silver appeared to stretch away into infinite distance, and to Lorraine's fancy, dark shadows, as of veiled figures, seemed to flit under the trees ; surely on such nights spirits must be abroad, she thought, when, even to human eyes, heaven and earth seemed meeting, and wonderful ladders of light were everywhere.

'How beautiful,' she sighed ; but even as she spoke, her thoughts travelled back with curious persistence to the last moonlight she had seen in Beaumont Street. How tired she had felt that evening, for she had been sitting up the previous night with a child who had croup ; but she had stood at her attic window for a long time ; she knew by the gleam of yellow light behind the stacks of chimneys that the moon was shining, and indeed the street below was so bathed in it that she could see the gaunt form of a thin cat creep along the wall. How hungrily she had fixed her eyes on the little square patch of sky, which was all she could see from her window, until the great silver moon came into view ; it was the same moon that she had always known, just as silvery and beautiful as though it were gliding over the Lake of Geneva ; but what grimy surroundings. And now her attic was empty, and she was enjoying this exquisite transformation scene ; it was these sharp contrasts that seemed to steady and sober her. 'I must never forget,' she would say to herself at such moments ; 'I must never forget that though I am happy, other women—God help them !—are suffering as I used to suffer.'

Muriel's first words broke on her exalted mood a little sharply; when self-consciousness steps in, even a moonlight effect may be pronounced stagey and a failure.

'Don't you hate dinners, Mrs. Herbert ? How thankful I am those tiresome two hours are over. The Admiral bores one excessively ; he is terribly narrow and argumentative.'

'I thought him so amusing,' returned Lorraine. 'He is just like a little shaggy polar bear with his big white moustache and thick head of hair. I never saw such hair ; it is as fine and silky as a child's, and his face is so nice and brown, just what a sailor's ought to be. He is a dear old man—at least he is not very old ; and his wife is so handsome ; she would certainly make two Admirals, even Ellison looked quite short beside her ; but I liked to look at her ; one so seldom sees that glossy black hair in an Englishwoman.'

'Ah, there is Spanish blood in her veins. All the boys have dark hair and eyes; as old Mrs. Langton is so fond of saying, "They do not favour their father at all." They are all big, strong men, and Philip is so handsome.'

'Ellison tells me that they are all abroad.'

'Yes, Philip and Dacre are with their regiment in Burmah, it is the same regiment that Percy Chessington is in. Quentin is at a ranche in Colorado, and Howard is a middy.'

'Poor Mrs. Earnshaw; what a pity she has no daughter!' exclaimed Lorraine sympathetically.

'They had one girl, Lucia; but she died of typhoid fever when she was about fourteen. It was a great trouble, of course, and as mother has lost two daughters, she and Mrs. Earnshaw can feel for each other. They are very chummy, Mrs. Herbert; they were old schoolfellows, and suit each other down to the ground. Now, have you had your fill of moonlight, for we shall never get to the turret-room at this rate'; and Lorraine reluctantly tore herself away.

The turret-room was at the extreme end of one wing, and the corresponding turret had been fitted up with a large telescope, and was used as a sort of observatory; but Colonel Trevor had pronounced it too draughty for a sitting-room.

Muriel was evidently fond of air and light. The turret-room, although it was by no means large, had four windows, and as wall-room was scanty, and completely occupied by a well-filled book-case and fireplace, the window recesses had been utilised. A writing-table, loaded with books, stood in one; a revolving book-table and easy chair in another; a couch, with a reading lamp and low table, in the third; and the fourth window had a cushioned seat, also covered with books, large enough to hold two people, whereon slept a perfectly white Persian cat of immense size, and with the bluest eyes Lorraine ever beheld.

She knelt down to caress it at once, and the creature arched its shaggy back with a delighted purr of recognition.

'What a beautiful animal. I had no idea you had a pet: do you know, his coat reminds me of the Admiral's white hair.'

'I am afraid his name will remind you of him still more,' returned Muriel. 'Admiral Byng; he answers to his name, you see,' as the cat jumped into her lap and began rubbing himself, with an air of fondness, against her cheek and shoulder. 'You have no conception how affectionate he is; he is more like a dog than a cat; he will follow me right down to the farm, though he hates Bairn like poison, and will sit on the roof of the stable waiting for me, even if I am there for an hour or two; he goes all over the place with me, and not a dog dares to touch him; but I am always so nervous when the shooting begins, and he is never allowed to follow me then. He sleeps in my room, and has an easy chair to himself; and we are good friends—are we not, Admiral?—and I would not change you for the best dog in creation.'

'I do not pretend to be a cat-lover, but I like all animals,' replied Lorraine. 'I will not say a word of disparagement of your favourite; but I have always found the cat-nature disappointing. They are such self-centred animals; they prefer their own comfort to your society. Now, a dog is far nobler; he would prefer to follow you on the coldest day, rather than enjoy the fireside and warm rug in solitude.'

'I cannot contradict you,' replied Muriel, lifting the great cat in her arms; 'but I can only assure you that Admiral is a shining exception. He will follow me on a wet or sunny day, though it is pain and grief to him to wet his feet. It is amusing to see him stop every now and then and lift one paw and lick it gingerly, and then go on again. When he has had enough of it, he looks up in my face and mews, and then, dirty as he is, I have to carry him.'

'He is certainly a noble exception, and I respect him accordingly. But, my dear Miss Trevor, what a charming view you must have from these windows; you are "monarch of all you survey," indeed. I had no idea you could see Brae Farm, and from that further window I expect you have a view of the Woodlands Lodge ?'

'Yes, indeed, my views are richly diversified; woods, meadows, farms, and ornamental cottages; you must come up here by daylight. Let me see; Gavin is going to drive mother to Darley and Bramfield to-morrow afternoon; will you come and have tea with me ? Yes, I know Ellison asked me, but two is so much cosier than three; a three-cornered talk is not quite harmonious; you can never strike three notes in perfect unison. Do you know what I mean ? I am expressing myself awkwardly. What I would say is this; if you strike three random notes, one or other of them will be in a different key. To enjoy a real conversation two people must be in harmony; there, have I made myself plain ?'

'Perfectly so; but even here there are exceptions to the rule, and I maintain that our threefold conversation would have been quite satisfactory; still, I shall like to come. Do you have tea up here, or in the drawing-room ?'

'Whichever you like; but I think we should enjoy it more here; and then I shall tell Ford that I am particularly engaged. I have everything here,' opening a handsome carved chiffonier, where a dainty little tea-set and melon-shaped teapot reposed. 'Mother gave me these on my last birthday. She knew I should love to have a tea-set of my own; but Gavin told her she was absurd to humour my fads. Well—what is the matter now ?

as Lorraine, who had taken up a book, put it down as though it burnt her.

'Greek—do you read Greek?' in an awestruck voice, for the book was *Plato's Dialogues*—in the original.

Muriel blushed, and then tried to laugh it off.

'Why should I not read Greek? it is my favourite study. I used to read it with poor old Mr. Yolland—he was a fine scholar. We were just beginning Hebrew when he had that dreadful stroke. Oh, what a loss he is to me! He has helped me with my classical studies ever since I grew up. Mother never would let me go to Girton or Somerville as I wished, because she said I was not strong enough, and she could not spare me ; but she sees her mistake now. It would have been far better for me to mix with girls of my own age than to plod on here alone ; and now I have lost my one teacher.'

'But Mr. Yolland has only gone away for a year. A year will soon pass.'

'That is what they all say ; but I am not so sanguine. Perhaps I am disposed to take the dark view of things. I am afraid, from what Dr. Howell said, that my dear old magister is really breaking ; it is a second stroke, and I know they fear that the third might be fatal. The Vicarage was my haven of refuge ; when I was shut up with the vicar in his study working at Hebrew roots, time simply fled ; but it is dreary work drudging on alone.'

'Could not your brother help you?'—a little doubtfully.

'Gavin,' contemptuously. 'He is always telling me that his Latin and Greek have grown rusty, and that a smattering of Hindustanee and Sanscrit is all he knows. I do not quite believe him, for Helen—his wife I mean—used to tell us how clever he was at languages ; but I should be sorry to ask his help. My brother has peculiar notions ; he does not care for learned women. I made mother promise not to tell him about my lessons at the Vicarage. He has not a notion what my studies are ; I believe that he thinks I dabble in science. Now I dare not keep you any longer, or even the Admiral's stories will be over. As we go downstairs I will show you my bedroom ; it is on the floor below, but almost equally secluded ; my passion for solitude increases.'

'What a pity,' replied Lorraine in a low voice ; but Muriel either did not hear her, or chose to make no reply. Her bedroom was almost as original as her study ; the bed was hidden in a recess, and curtains of Indian silk draped the recess by day ; when they were drawn back, a curious corner window, overlooking the Darley Road, came in view. As Muriel lay in bed, she could see the children from the Lodge running with their satchels to school.

The furniture, with the exception of a massive wardrobe and foreign-looking washstand, was singularly unadapted to a bedroom. A black Indian cabinet, very finely carved, and some low book-cases to match, a writing-table, and one or two easy chairs, were the most conspicuous objects. Busts of Shakespeare and Goethe were over the fireplace, and even the toilet-table had book-slides with Browning's works; the inlaid tortoiseshell brushes that her mother had given her lay in close juxtaposition with a volume of Carlyle's *French Revolution* and a *Sartor Resartus*.

'I wonder how I ever came to have such a daughter,' Mrs Trevor had said once very plaintively to her chief confidante, Mrs. Earnshaw. 'I used to tell John so sometimes, but he always took her part; he was so proud of Muriel's cleverness. I am quite sure dear Maud and Florrie would have been very different. Darling Flo took after me; she was so proud of helping me in the conservatory, and Maud was so clever with her fingers; but Muriel and I have not a single taste in common'; and poor Mrs. Trevor sighed heavily. To this old friend of her girlhood she would at times hint at the deep unspeakable sadness that lay underneath her sprightliness of manner; perhaps no one understood her so well as Mrs. Earnshaw. The two women were strongly attached to each other; and in spite of great dissimilarity of character, their mutual sympathy never failed.

The gentlemen had already returned to the drawing-room when Muriel and Lorraine re-entered it. Colonel Trevor, who was standing beside Ellison, exchanged an amused glance with her; but Captain Faucit intercepted them at once.

'Mrs. Herbert,' he asked eagerly, 'do you think you could play this accompaniment for me? Trevor has been asking me to sing; but Miss Lee says she is no musician, and I remember I never could induce Miss Trevor to play.'

'I will try if you like,' returned Lorraine, taking the piece of music from him; 'but I must tell you frankly, Captain Faucit, that it is three years at least since I touched a piano. I used to be very fond of playing, but of course I am utterly out of practice. May I try it over first?' But though her fingers touched the keys a little uncertainly, she gained more assurance after the first few notes. Out of practice as she certainly was, her firm light touch at once conveyed the impression that she had played well.

The song was so successful and gave so much pleasure that

Captain Faucit was induced to sing again. At the conclusion of the third song Colonel Trevor came up to the piano.

'I am quite sure you sing, Mrs. Herbert,' he said persuasively, 'and I do hope you will give us the pleasure of hearing you.'

Lorraine coloured and hesitated. 'I used to sing,' she returned ; 'but my voice must have suffered from disuse, it is so many years since I tried to sing to any instrument. You must have noticed how stiffly my fingers moved when I first began to play, and it would be the same with my voice.'

'If you would only try,' he persisted. 'We are all so fond of music here, my mother especially ; but neither my sister nor I am able to afford her that pleasure.'

'If you really wish it, perhaps I could recall an old song,' returned Lorraine rather gravely. She had no morbid objection to use the voice that nature had given her. She had so often sung her boy to sleep that she knew it was still in condition ; but her piano had been carried off with the rest of the furniture, and for years she had been too sick at heart to care to sing.

Her choice must have seemed a singular one to most in the room, for she selected an old favourite of her father's, 'She wore a wreath of roses.' Her voice trembled a good deal during the first verse ; but after a little the dear old associations shut out present surroundings. They were in the old *salon* at Brussels ; the wax candles in the tarnished girandoles lighted the room dimly ; the worn red velvet couches and chairs scattered over the dark polished floor looked regal in the obscurity ; her father's grey head was distinct in the moonlight.

'Bravo, my little Lorrie, that was well sung ; you must sing it again.'

As the clear sweet voice grew stronger and fuller, Colonel Trevor left his position by the piano and stood by the window. When the song was finished, and he came forward to thank her, his face had grown strangely pale.

'My dear Mrs. Herbert, you have given us a great pleasure,' observed Mrs. Trevor, with a beaming smile. 'Your voice is delicious ; it is so true and sweet. You must sing to us often, must she not, Gavin ?' But Colonel Trevor had already made his little speech, and had left the room.

CHAPTER XI

THE THIN END OF THE WEDGE

'I am a parcel of vain strivings tied,
  By a chance band together,
    Dangling this way and that, their links
    Were made too loose and wide methinks
  For winter weather.'

THOREAU.

As soon as the Admiral and Mrs. Earnshaw had taken their leave, Ellison rose from her seat; she was only waiting until Colonel Trevor returned to the room that she might wish him good-night.

'I am going with you, of course,' he said, with a grave smile, as she held out her hand; 'and Faucit will come too; he will be glad of the walk.'

'There is no need to trouble you. Mrs. Herbert and I can protect each other,' she replied, looking at him anxiously, for his face was still a little drawn and pale.

How grieved Lorraine would have been had she known that she had just sung his wife's favourite song—though Helen Trevor had never sung it with such pathos and sweetness; but Ellison's fine tact guessed at once that this was the case, and she privately resolved to give her cousin a hint not to sing that song again.

She wished that Gavin had not insisted on escorting them to Brae Farm, for she hardly knew what to say to him. In some moods he could not bear Helen's name mentioned, and yet perfect silence might seem unkind.

It was almost a relief when he dropped behind to speak to Lorraine. She had asked some question about a creeper at the hall door, and Ellison walked on slowly with Captain Faucit; but she was rather amused when the young officer began questioning her eagerly about her cousin. How long had Mrs. Herbert lived at Highlands; he had never met her before; he had never even heard her mentioned, and yet he was always running down to Brae House ?

'My cousin has not been here a week yet. Yes, she is a great acquisition, as you say, and her voice is delightful. She has lived abroad a great deal, and in Ireland ; but since her husband's death—— But,' interrupting herself, 'were you wanting to ask me a question, Captain Faucit ?'

'I was only wondering how long ago Mrs. Herbert had lost her husband. She was not in very deep mourning, but somehow one could tell at once she was a widow. I like that sort of sensible mourning ; don't you, Miss Lee ? there is nothing gruesome or morbid about it.'

'Certainly, my cousin is not morbid. Mr. Herbert died about eighteen months ago. She has a little boy—such a nice little fellow, about three years old ; but, though I would not tell my cousin so for worlds, I am afraid he is delicate.'

Meanwhile Colonel Trevor was saying to his companion, with an impulsiveness that surprised himself afterwards : 'I did not thank you properly for singing to us. I am sure it was an effort, and we ought not to have asked you. It was a curious coincidence, was it not, that you chose my dear wife's favourite song ? '

Lorraine started—she felt suddenly hot all over.

'Oh, Colonel Trevor, I am so sorry. Why did you not stop me ? I would have sung another. I know exactly the sort of pain such a thing gives, and I am dreadfully grieved about it.'

'Why, what nonsense,' trying to turn it off. 'I ought not to have told you, but you sang it so beautifully. My poor wife could not have sung it like that ; but she was passionately fond of music, and her musical at-homes were much appreciated. Perhaps I shall not ask you to sing that song again, Mrs. Herbert, but I do hope, as my mother said just now, that we shall often have the pleasure of hearing you. By ill-luck neither my sister nor cousin has any musical proficiency. Little Miss Holt at Ferncliffe is our best performer, and sings rather nicely ; but the Mordaunts only play passably.'

'I doubt if I shall have courage to sing to you again,' returned Lorraine slowly ; 'I should dread making a second mistake.'

'You are convincing me of mine,' he said in a low voice. 'What a fool I was not to hold my tongue ; but I do not generally talk about my own concerns. I was a bit upset, you see.'

'Yes, and it was I who upset you. Well, I will not trouble you with any more repentance. You know quite well how sorry I am. Next time I sing you shall choose my songs for me, and then I shall feel safe,' turning to him with a smile.

'That is a bargain,' he returned rather abruptly; for somehow her smile rather confused him, and yet he could not have said why. Her singing had been a revelation to him; those pure, deep notes ringing through the great room were full of passionate yearning and sweetness. True, her voice was somewhat untrained; there was an unevenness of execution, and it was not always well sustained, but that was probably owing to want of practice.

He would have changed the subject, feeling that he had already said too much; but Lorraine had another explanation to make. Colonel Trevor's speech about his wife made her suddenly anxious to justify her own choice, though a moment before she had never thought of such a thing.

'I have no associations of that sort,' she said quickly. 'My husband was not at all musical, he never cared for my singing, he always said he did not know one tune from another; my father was different. I was thinking of him when I sang that song; it was the last to which he listened; that is why I love it.'

'I love it too,' returned Colonel Trevor gravely. 'I think men and women are a little different on the subject of association; women are fond of prolonging all these mournful sensations, they find the pleasure counterbalances the pain, the bitter-sweet satisfies them; but a man cannot always stand it. Some men do, but they must have a touch of the feminine instinct in their nature. I knew a man once who kept his wife's dresses hanging in her wardrobe for years. He used to look at them from time to time, but he got a bit doity over it.'

'Poor man,' replied Lorraine simply; and then she added, 'I think no two people are alike in such matters. One needs to understand a person very thoroughly before one would dare to talk on such subjects to him, you see. I am speaking of men; women have a certain freemasonry among themselves. I would venture to talk to any woman, however recent her trouble, and not fear to wound her.'

'I cannot imagine you wounding anybody, you are far too sympathetic. My cousin Ellison, too, has great tact in dealing with thin-skinned humanity; some of us, in spite of our seeming sturdiness, are wonderfully thin-skinned, and need gentle handling. By the bye, Mrs. Herbert, I congratulate you on a great victory; you have completely won my sister's heart.'

'Have I?' with an amused smile. And then she said quietly, 'Your sister's heart is worth winning, I am quite sure of that. She interests me greatly.'

Colonel Trevor seemed about to speak, and then checked himself. The moonlight and the music, and the deep sadness of waking memories, should not betray him into unguarded speech. Mrs Herbert was a stranger, and her charm of manner and womanly graces must not beguile him into a confidence that he might repent. When he next spoke it was to remark on the beauty of the night, and Muriel's name was not mentioned again.

'I need not ask you if you have had a pleasant evening, Lorraine,' observed Ellison as she lighted a candle for her cousin.

'No, indeed,' replied Lorraine, with a sigh; 'I am afraid I enjoyed myself far too much. You have no idea of my social tastes. When I find myself among nice friendly people, I am always perfectly happy. I revel in the society of my fellow-creatures. I expect I talked far too much, but I never can remember to hold my tongue till I am alone in my own room.'

'I hope not, indeed. I am quite sure that you helped Captain Faucit to enjoy himself, and then they were all so charmed with your singing. I must give you one hint, though, I am afraid that song had some painful association for Colonel Trevor.'

'Yes, I know,' returned Lorraine, knitting her brow at the recollection. 'It was his wife's favourite song, he told me so; and of course I shall never sing it again. Oh, the mistakes one makes in life! How much happier existence would be if we could read each other plainly. Please do not speak about it, it has spoiled my evening. No, I won't say that; it is too ungrateful of me.'

'How strange that he should have told her that,' thought Ellison as she prepared to go her rounds. 'Gavin is so reserved; he mentions Helen's name so rarely, even to me. Well, I am glad poor Lorraine enjoyed her evening; she was certainly a success.' But more than once before she slept, Ellison pondered with odd undefinable surprise over the thought that Gavin should have broken through his reserve with a stranger.

The next morning Lorraine began her labours in the poultry-yard; and though the work was new to her, and she had much to learn about her feathered charges, she was an apt pupil, and listened to Ellison's instructions with intelligent appreciation. The coop with the imprisoned hen clucking with visible anxiety to her brood of chickens just out of reach of the maternal care, the still more wearing labours of the speckled hen with her adopted family of ducklings, the careless provoking turkey mothers, were all sources of interest; it was a new little world, and a fussy one, but there were plenty of wholesome object-lessons to be digested.

As in life the weaker went to the wall, there was still the survival of the fittest, and the struggle of life went on. The peckings and scratchings at the dust-heap for hidden grain reminded Lorraine of the harassed workers in Beaumont Street; the loud cluck of demonstrative joy with which an egg was laid, was a faint repetition of human congratulations. Even the lordly cock, strutting at the head of his obsequious harem, might have rebuked by his gentlemanly courtesy the rough hectoring manners of the lords of creation— many of them, alas, reeling home with empty pockets to abuse their patient harassed wives.

Tedo trotted everywhere after his mother with a big basket that he laboriously filled with stones. Ellison was just ministering tenderly to a sick hen, placing her carefully in a warm hay nest, and coaxing her to eat, when a whistle reached her ear, and the next moment two fat black puppies tumbled and rolled at Lorraine's feet. Tedo dropped his basket and shouted out, 'Oh, mine 'ickle doggies !' in a voice of ecstasy.

'I have brought you the puppies, Mrs. Herbert,' observed Colonel Trevor. leaning against the lattice-work of the poultry-yard. 'The biggest and fattest is Tweedledum ; he is a finer fellow than Tweedledee, so I advise you to have him. He is a handsome little chap, isn't he, Ellison ?'

'Yes, there is no comparison,' replied Ellison, tucking in some more hay. 'Gavin, I am afraid my dear grey hen—Mrs. Muggins —is very ill. I must get John Drake to look at her if she does not get better.'

'Poor Mrs. Muggins, I am awfully sorry,' returned Colonel Trevor. 'Well, Mrs. Herbert, have you made up your mind?' But to his surprise Lorraine shook her head ; both the puppies were in her lap and Tedo was evidently trying to climb up too.

'It is so difficult to choose,' returned Lorraine, who was evidently in deep perplexity. 'Of course I know you are right. Tweedledum is very handsome, his coat is so curly and glossy ; but the other one seems to want me to take him, he looks at me so pleadingly every now and then when Tweedledum lets him be quiet. Look, Ellison !' as the puppy licked her hand with his rough, red little tongue, 'I think Tweedledee is a dear.'

'He is certainly a nice little dog,' agreed Ellison.

'Look here, Mrs. Herbert, take them both,' interrupted Colonel Trevor, 'they will make a splendid pair. And Ellison was only saying the other day that Sam Brattle wanted more dogs about the place since Rover died. It would be a pity to divide them, and they are handsome little beasts.'

'I have no objection, if you like to keep them, Lorraine,' returned Ellison good-humouredly. 'They can sleep in the out-house, and Daniel will look after them.'

But Lorraine would not hear of this, one dog was enough for any woman. She was very much obliged to Colonel Trevor, but though Tweedledum was the handsomer dog she would prefer to take Tweedledee. 'And I shall call him Tweed, it will be much handier,' she finished, hugging the puppy as she spoke.

'Mine 'ickle doggie,' persisted Tedo with peevish dignity.

'Yes, my darling, everything mother has is Tedo's, and Tedo's is mother's'; and she made him happy by putting the curly, black thing in his arms.

'Come along, Tweedledum!' exclaimed Colonel Trevor, pretending to be affronted; 'for once, good looks are in the minority. I pity your bad taste, Mrs. Herbert; though, to be candid with you, I rather suspect it will be the case of the ugly duckling, and that Tweed has the making of a good dog in him. But I must be off, as I have promised to drive Faucit into Bramfield. I have to take my mother out after luncheon.'

'Colonel Trevor looks much brighter this morning,' observed Lorraine; but Ellison was already out of ear-shot.

Gavin was evidently waiting for her to walk up the meadow-path with him; and she was never too busy to pay him this little attention. These desultory strolls were always enjoyed and appreciated by both. It was astonishing how much they always had to tell each other after even a few hours' absence.

Lorraine was in a little perplexity. Muriel had not mentioned Tedo, and she was afraid that he might be in the way. She dared not take him uninvited, and yet she was unwilling to leave him; but Ellison came to the rescue by promising to look after him.

'I have some cutting-out to do for the maids, and shall be in the dining-room until tea-time,' she said; 'so Tedo can play about and amuse himself. If visitors call, Dorcas shall look after him.' And so it was arranged; and Lorraine went off with an easy mind.

Muriel was evidently on the look-out for her; long before Lorraine reached the hall door, she was there waiting. She welcomed her with undisguised cordiality, and took her off at once to the turret-room, where a low tea-table was set out in the window overlooking the Brae Woods.

'I was so surprised to see you without your boy. Why have you not brought him?' she began. 'Oh,' as Lorraine hesitated, 'was it my fault; ought I to have specially invited him? How forgetful I am. But it must never occur again; bring him whenever you like; but this once I think I am glad to have you to myself.'

'I am afraid a child is a little disturbing, though Tedo is wonderfully good for his age. I like this room, Miss Trevor. I fancy it must be cold in winter, for it gives one the idea of being in a lighthouse, so many windows in a limited space.'

'It is cold, certainly,' admitted Muriel with some reluctance;

'and on windy nights all the witches seem to be holding Walpurgis night-revels. The shrieking and howling and wailing really affect one's nerves. I often have to wrap myself in a fur-lined cloak, and draw the hood over my head as I sit by the fire. Mother saw me once, and said I looked most weird and picturesque.'

They chatted pleasantly in this fashion over their tea. Muriel seemed like another person that afternoon, she was so animated. She asked Lorraine a question or two about her wandering, foreign life, and then grew so interested in her recital, that Lorraine was led on to tell her more and more.

'What an interesting life,' she said, when Lorraine had finished with a graphic description of Beaumont Street; 'and you have really lived it too. Forgive me, I know how much you have suffered,' as Lorraine looked at her with reproachful surprise; 'but there has been no stagnation. One can bear pain—all people have to bear it more or less at some period of their life; but stagnation implies more than pain, it is an utter dearth of interest, a lack of everything that makes life worth living; even affection stagnates if its natural flow is impeded.'

'Life without affection is certainly not life,' returned Lorraine thoughtfully, 'but we need not consider anything so abnormal. With a whole world full of human beings, we must have plenty of objects for our love.'

'Oh, you are talking in the abstract! but, please, we will leave altruism alone for this afternoon. You cannot feed famished creatures on husks; and in my present condition abstract ideas are mere husks. I want to get at the reality of things. I am interested in you, Mrs. Herbert, simply because you seem to me so human; even in this brief acquaintanceship, I can see that life means more to you than it does to other people. I want to find out your recipe: you have suffered, but your troubles have not hardened you. In your place, I should have stiffened my neck and hardened my heart into a millstone, or else I should utterly have collapsed.'

'I have no special recipe,' returned Lorraine a little sadly; 'you know there is always starlight, even when the night is blackest, only the clouds come between. The worst of it is, people talk and act as though the clouds were all. I had my child. How was I to lose faith and courage when I had to work for my boy? My dear Miss Trevor, don't you see, life is not so dreadfully complex after all. There is always some one to love, and for whom we cheerfully take up the burden of existence; no one is utterly without human ties.'

'Perhaps not; but family ties are not always strong enough to bear severe tension. I know I am talking heresy, Mrs. Herbert, but it is awfully true.   Some natures do not find happiness **in** ordinary family life.'

The deep melancholy of Muriel's tones convinced Lorraine that she was speaking of herself; and with that impulsiveness and quick intuition that was natural to her, she said gently :

'I wish that I did not understand you; but I am afraid I do, too well.   For some reason best known to yourself you are not in harmony with your environment.   That is always disastrous and fatal to true peace; but it is possible to mould oneself to one's circumstances.'

'Possible to some natures; but I am unfortunately constituted. I demand too much.'

'Oh, that is always a mistake!' but Muriel interrupted her.

'Let me talk to you a little.   If you only knew the relief it is to me to speak.   I have never met any one like you before; you seem to think of nothing but loving people and helping them; I saw that the first time we met!'

'I don't think I am at all out of the common,' returned Lorraine, smiling.   'I am a very ordinary sort of woman, and do not pretend to be better than I am   People see that I am really interested in what they are telling me, and that I am sorry for them.   There is nothing occult in the process; it is just giving out a little more freely than usual the human sympathy that many good people keep locked up in their hearts, because they are too shy to show it.   I am not shy; that is the secret!'

Muriel shook her head.   'I do not think we have got to the bottom of it.   You have not yet proved to me why I find it so much easier to talk to you than to Ellison whom I have known all my life.   Ellison and I are not on the same plane, we do **not** speak the same language.'

'You must not ask me to solve that question!' exclaimed Lorraine rather gravely; 'I am not an unprejudiced critic.   I have not known my cousin long, but I already venerate her for her goodness.   My dear Miss Trevor, have you ever known any one so unselfish?   What other woman in her position would have opened her house and heart to a perfect stranger?   It was not as though she had known me; most people would have hesitated before incurring such responsibilities.'

'I see what you mean.   Ellison is very good; my brother is always telling me so.   Ever since his return from India I have heard her praises sung daily.   But, Mrs. Herbert, you have already told me that you had met twice at least before you came to Brae Farm; you may depend upon it that Ellison found out that you were to be trusted; she is very clear-sighted, she seldom makes a mistake about people. I remember mother saying so to me, when I was disposed to think she had been a little hasty.'

A curiously sweet smile crossed Lorraine's face, but she made no response to this; but deep down in her heart she said to herself, 'She shall never find it a mistake if I can prevent it; such divine charity must bring its own blessing.'

There was a brief silence, and then Muriel said a little shyly:

'Mrs. Herbert, what would you do in my place? I have already acknowledged, though rather vaguely, I am afraid, that I am not in complete harmony with my environment. I am clothing the difficulty in grand terms, but it is really a difficulty.'

'Vagueness will not help us, I am afraid,' replied Lorraine, sensibly; 'but, Miss Trevor, at the risk of displeasing you, I am going to say something very practical. If I were in your place, my first endeavour would be to improve my health as much as possible.'

It was evident that this answer took Muriel by surprise. She coloured up and looked excessively astonished.

'It is the first duty of every one to be as well as they can,' went on Lorraine. 'Work cannot be satisfactorily done when one's physical machinery is out of gear. One feels intuitively that a healthy condition of body is somehow necessary to a healthy condition of mind. It is really awful to think how mind and body act and react on one another. I have gained my experience very painfully, I assure you.'

'Yes, yes, I feel that you are right,' with a certain impatience of tone. 'You are driving in the thin end of the wedge. I know what you want to say next, that I ought to give up my late hours; but after what I have told you it would be exacting a cruel sacrifice. You would not have the heart to rob me of those happy working hours?'

'I know it would be a sacrifice,' hesitating over her words; 'but I am quite sure you would be richly repaid for the effort. Your nerves would be stronger, your headaches less frequent, and the strain lessened. You are somehow feeding on yourself. Why should you not put my advice to the test? Give up your night studies for a time—say, three weeks or a month—and see if you do not feel a different creature. Come, you have asked my opinion, and I have not scrupled to tell you the truth. I have made myself as disagreeable as possible, and now I must go home to my boy.'

'You are leaving me just when I need you most; but there, I will think over what you say. Is it not strange, Mrs. Herbert, I am allowing you to say this to me, and yet, the other day when

Gavin said exactly the same things to me, I was as cross as possible ?'

'Perhaps the moment was not propitious,' returned Lorraine, rising as she spoke. 'We must take people at the right time, or our efforts will be thrown away. Have I been very impertinent, Miss Trevor? But when I look at those pallid cheeks and heavy eyes, I perfectly ache with the longing to do you good, if you would only let me.'

She put her hands gently on Muriel's shoulder as she spoke, and looked at her wistfully.

'You shall help me,' returned Muriel in a low voice. 'Every word you say helps me.' And then as Lorraine kissed her, in the sweet old words of Holy Writ, the soul of Muriel Trevor was knit to the woman whose gentle sympathy had gone straight to her heart.

CHAPTER XII

MOTHER AND DAUGHTER

'Knowledge of the world and of the sea is gained in tempests ; but in the eyes of the old mariner may be seen the reflection of the death he has so often braved.'—*Thoughts of a Queen.*

'A woman not understood is a woman who does not understand.'—*Ibid.*

THE next few weeks passed smoothly and happily for Lorraine. Every day deepened her attachment to Ellison and her love for her new home ; never in her life had she known such tranquil days. All her neighbours had called on her, and seemed disposed to be friendly. She had found plenty of occupation. Time only strengthened and cemented her intimacy with Muriel Trevor ; and there were few days when she and Muriel failed to meet.

Though Lorraine's affections were strongest for her cousin, she responded readily and warmly to Muriel's passionate devotion. She guessed intuitively that the girl had suffered terribly for the want of a friend to understand her. Muriel was too peculiar to invite general sympathy ; other girls of her age were repelled by her ; it had grown to be a morbid and fixed idea with her that no one needed her affection. She loved her brother ardently ; but he was never able to discover this fact on account of the constant friction between them. Her mother had never really influenced her. Muriel's fondness for her was critical and exacting. In her shallow creed it was the mother's duty to love her daughter and to bear with her, and for the daughter to take everything as a matter of course—at least she acted as though these were her tenets.

'Mother does not want me to-day ; she is quite happy alone,' was a usual formula with Muriel ; and she had actually grown to believe that this was the truth. Mrs. Trevor never took the trouble to dispute it ; she was easy and indolent of temperament, and a dull hour or two were preferable to an argument with Muriel. 'Why should the child be troubled by her depression ?' she would say to herself; 'with her weak health she had enough to bear', and she would battle bravely with despondent memories, as she sat at her embroidery; or if the task were too difficult, she would seek new cheerfulness among her beloved flowers. But if Muriel had only guessed at her mother's deep inward sadness, with what repentance she would have devoted herself to her. It is cruel to think how wilfully we blind our eyes to the needs of those who are closest to us, and how often we act upon those words that 'Evil is wrought by want of thought, as well as want of heart'; and so the tares are sown that ruin a harvest.

How bitter would have been Muriel's compunction if she had guessed how often and sorrowfully her mother thought of her dead sisters. 'Florrie would never have left me to sit alone,' she would say to herself; for Florence had been her special darling, and sometimes when Muriel was at her studies in the turret-room—when evening had closed in—Mrs. Trevor would fall into a half-waking dream in the twilight, and it would seem to her as though the sweet faces of her dead children looked pityingly on her from the shadows; nay, sometimes soft girlish hands seemed to touch her. 'Mother, are you alone ? Shall Maud and I sit and talk to you a little?' How plainly she heard the words as she started up from her doze. But she was very loyal to her daughter, and would never allow Gavin to say that Muriel neglected her; she even grew tearful if he persisted in repeating it.

'It is not as though you had other daughters,' he said one day. 'If those poor girls had lived, Muriel might have gone her own way without selfishness; but I hate to come in and find you always alone.'

'My dear boy, I am used to it,' she returned briskly. 'Your mother is not an old woman yet, I would have you remember that. Why should Muriel be pottering after me from morning to night, I should like to know, when she has her studies and——' But he interrupted her with a frown.

'A daughter's first study should be to make her mother happy: no, it is no use arguing the point—I am not to be hoodwinked. I have often spoken to Muriel on this subject, but she only quarrels with me—she disappoints me excessively.' But this unvarnished opinion of her daughter's faultiness failed to raise Mrs. Trevor's spirits. Perhaps Muriel was sometimes a little to blame, but she would rather not hear Gavin say so.

She hailed joyfully the marked improvement in Muriel's health, which was the result of Lorraine's sensible advice.

'I hope you notice the difference in your sister,' she said one day to her son. 'She has really seemed a different creature since Mrs. Herbert took her in hand. I have not heard her complain of headache for the last ten days ; and even her complexion looks clearer. Ellison was remarking on it just now. She says that now Muriel dresses her hair differently, that she has grown quite good-looking.'

'I have noticed that she is far less irritable,' he returned. 'The fact is, mother, Ellison has let me in for a thing or two. Mrs. Herbert has begged her to keep earlier hours. Why, last night it was only half-past ten when I came back from Price's Folly, and the turret-room was dark. She was half killing herself, but it was no use telling her so ; but Mrs. Herbert is a privileged person. You know what the old proverb says : " One person may steal a sheep where another may not look over the hedge." '

There was a trace of bitterness in Gavin's speech, but Mrs. Trevor hastened to soothe him.

'Yes, dear, it is very true ; but Mrs. Herbert is such a delightfully sympathetic person. She was with me a long time this morning helping me in the conservatory, and I found myself telling her all sorts of things.' But with her usual reserve, Mrs. Trevor refrained from mentioning the subject on which she had talked to Lorraine. In reality she had been speaking of her dead children ; she had pointed out a lovely creeper that had been planted on Florence's fourth birthday, and somehow Lorraine's gentle sympathy had drawn her to speak more fully.

It was an indulgence that she seldom allowed herself ; but she accused herself of selfishness when Lorraine suddenly burst into tears.

'My dear Mrs. Herbert !' she exclaimed in consternation, 'I am so ashamed of myself. I am a selfish, egotistical old woman. I have no right to inflict my troubles on other people.'

'Please do not say such things,' returned Lorraine, hurriedly drying her eyes. 'It was so foolish of me to cry ; but I do feel so sorry for you. You have gone through all this, and yet you say so little about it, and are so brave and cheerful, that no one guesses how much you have had to bear.'

'Thank you, my dear, you are very good,' returned Mrs. Trevor. 'Ah, there is Muriel coming in search of her dear Mrs. Herbert. You must not let her know that I made you cry.' And Mrs. Trevor cleared her throat, and hummed a little air as she took up the watering-pot again ; and Muriel, who was full of her own concerns, was too anxious to explain the cause of her long absence to notice anything unusual in their manner. But a few days afterwards, as they were walking from church together, Lorraine glanced back at the little group of three that were following them slowly, Mrs. Trevor and her son and Ellison, and then she said half to herself and half to Muriel :

'What strange mistakes one makes about people. When I first saw your mother I thought her one of the most cheerful women I had ever met. Such good spirits are deceptive. No one would ever guess from her manner that she had known so much trouble.'

'Ah, mother gets over things so quickly,' returned Muriel indifferently. 'Troubles do not go so deep with her as with other people. I mean,' as Lorraine seemed surprised at this speech, 'that she has a happy knack of forgetting unpleasant things.'

'Are you quite sure that she forgets?' returned Lorraine, persistently. 'Your mother has an unselfish nature. I should not be surprised if she keeps her troubles to herself on principle. Some people are strong enough to do without sympathy.'

'I do not think mother is one of them,' replied Muriel ; and then she changed the subject somewhat abruptly ; but later on she remembered Lorraine's words.

An evening or two after this, as Lorraine was walking up the Dorchester Road towards Highlands, she saw two persons standing by the gate leading to the Redlands Woods, evidently in earnest conversation. One of them was Sam Brattle, and the other, to her surprise, was Ruth, the handsome parlour-maid at Brae Farm. It was unusual for her to be out at this hour, but perhaps she had been sent on some errand. As Lorraine walked on, the girl passed her very hurriedly ; and Lorraine, who had observant eyes, noticed that her face was flushed as though she had been crying.

She mentioned it to Ellison when she reached home. 'I hope Ruth is in no trouble,' she said ; 'but I certainly fancied Sam Brattle was speaking very angrily as I passed. I thought he was such a good-tempered fellow.'

'So he is. Sam has an excellent disposition, as you know. I think most highly of him, and so does Gavin, and his opinion is worth something ; but I am afraid Ruth tries him dreadfully. She is not acting quite straightforwardly, and I begin to fear that she is playing a double game. Sam is desperately in love with her ; but though she likes him, he cannot induce her to promise that she will marry him. She keeps putting him off and making excuses, and tells him that she does not want to be engaged ; but Sam is afraid that he has a rival. The fact is, Mr. Edgar Yolland of Mansoule Farm, near Redlands, admires Ruth ; and though he is old enough to be her father, and is not at all interesting, and a widower, he is a rich man compared with poor Sam. He is a distant cousin of our poor old vicar, and calls himself a gentleman-farmer, though he is really a yeoman ; and he has a good house, and a handsome balance at the Dorchester Bank.'

Lorraine looked aghast. 'Surely, Ellison, you cannot mean that tall elderly man with grey hair and a stiff wooden figure, who sits by the organ and sings through his nose ; he is fifty-five if he is a day ; I never look at him without thinking of Noah in Tedo's Noah's ark.'

'Well, he is certainly very stiff and dry, but you are wrong about his age. Mr. Yolland is only forty-eight ; he is an old-looking man. Gavin says he has his good points. He is an excellent farmer, and very hard-working and painstaking, and he rides straight across country, for he keeps a hunter ; but report says the first Mrs. Yolland was not specially happy.'

'But it is impossible that she could think of marrying that stick of a man, a beautiful young girl like Ruth.'

'Oh, of course not,' returned Ellison rather sarcastically ; for the subject of her pretty maid's delinquencies always vexed her. 'We know no young girl ever married an old man for his money ; they are never mercenary, never alive to their own interest. What a profound observer you must be of human nature.'

'Oh, don't joke about it, it is too dreadful. Why do you not talk to Ruth ? surely you could influence her.'

'I have talked to her a score of times, but I can never bring her to book ; she is terribly slippery and evasive. I am convinced that she really cares for Sam, but her head is turned by having the attentions of a real gentleman, as she calls him. His farm is his own. The Yollands have a most respectable pedigree, and Edgar Yolland is honestly bent on marrying the girl. The vicar was very much vexed about it, but he could say nothing. The connection between them was strained, and they are not very good friends. You see, though Edgar Yolland is a gentleman in Ruth's eyes, he is simply a rich yeoman, and leads a plain, homely life ; and certainly he is not a prepossessing man.'

'And she will marry him and be miserable ever afterwards.'

. 'My dear Lorraine, Ruth will have brought her misery on herself, and in that case I should not pity her ; but I cannot help hoping that she will come to her senses before it is too late. Sam is a little injudicious ; he gets wild with jealousy, and loses his temper, and that only makes matters worse ; he should be more patient with her. Ruth is not the sort of girl to be threatened. The Brattles, with all their virtues, are thorns in my side. Do you know that Tom Brattle is making up to Eunice. I believe

7

the affair is progressing smoothly. Eunice is a perfect treasure to me, and I can ill spare her; but she will make Tom Brattle an excellent wife. I do wish Ruth would not be such a fool. If she marries Sam, Gavin has promised to let them live in that pretty cottage you have so often noticed; at present the gardener lives there, but it is far too good for him. Cousin Louise often says she would not mind living there herself.'

Lorraine could not help noticing Ruth a little narrowly after this conversation; it was soon evident to her that the girl was not happy, she was paler than usual, and moved about her work languidly. More than once Ellison spoke to her rather sharply, as though she were losing patience; but Ruth, who was devoted to her mistress, took her rebukes meekly. It was impossible not to feel interested in her; her great beauty was evidently a snare to her, and she was in danger of losing the affections of an honest, true-hearted man by her foolish dallying with the attentions of a richer suitor. Sam Brattle was a little masterful; and it was far too likely that he would soon lose heart, and in a sudden fit of despair bring the courtship to an end. In that case Ruth would certainly become the mistress of Mansoule Farm, and rue her folly ever afterwards. It was very seldom that Lorraine returned even from a short walk without imparting some information to Ellison on her return. 'My Cousin Gossip,' Ellison once playfully called her; 'but,' she added mentally, 'if only all gossip were as harmless as Lorraine's, there would be less heart-burnings and no scandal'; for Lorraine somehow had a knack of eliminating the sting from an ill-natured rejoinder; even the speeches of Miss Rebecca Potter—a sour-faced spinster who was the terror of the Darley ladies—sounded quite civil and well-meaning when translated by Lorraine.

'Poor old body,' she would say, 'she is a bundle of infirmities, mentally and bodily, and one must not judge her harshly; her bark is worse than her bite, and she is always very good to Tedo. Tedo is quite fond of her; he calls her "the ickle curly 'ooman," because of her black curls. To-day when she gave him a large piece of cake it was "nicey curly 'ooman," and she really seemed pleased.'

'Well, Lorraine, what is it this afternoon?' asked Ellison, with an amused smile, as Lorraine entered the sitting-room. 'I can see by your face that something has happened; besides, Gavin has been here.'

'Then you know it,' returned Lorraine in a disappointed tone. And I meant to surprise you.'

'Well, he certainly told me that they have settled on a *locum tenens*, and that he is coming next week. He is an Oxford man, and has had a curacy in London, near Uxbridge Road, and his name is Vincent—the Reverend Eric Vincent.'

' And is that all you know about him ?' as Ellison paused.

'Let me see—Gavin said something more; yes, that he is unmarried. He certainly said nothing about his appearance or capabilities.'

'No, of course not, for only one of the church-wardens, Mr. Tarrant, has seen him; but I can tell you more about him than that.' And as Ellison looked at her inquiringly, she continued in a triumphant tone, 'Mr. Vincent is not very well off, and has not long lost his mother; and he has a lot of young brothers and sisters.'

'How on earth did you find this out ?'

'Oh, I thought you would be interested. Well, I will tell you all about it. I was just walking up the village when I suddenly took it into my head that I would step in at the White Cottage and have a word with Mrs. Drake—you would have done the same yourself, would you not ? Well, I found the poor woman in such a fuss and pucker, she looked quite harassed, poor soul. Her first words were, did I know that the new young minister who was to do duty for the vicar had taken her rooms; and he had written to say he had four brothers and sisters, but as there were no other lodgings to be got in the Highlands they must put up with the one sitting-room. Mr. Tarrant had told him it was only a small room, but they must just make the best of it.'

'Four brothers and sisters!' ejaculated Ellison in a horrified tone; 'that pokey little parlour will not hold them. How is he to write his sermons and study ? Nay, the thing's impossible, it will drive him crazy before a week is over. I do not wonder Mrs. Drake was in a fuss.'

'I assure you she looked ready to cry over it. She had always made her lodgers so comfortable, she said; but, as her husband told her, there was no doing impossibilities. She begged me to look at the rooms, and to tell her what I thought of them : they were in such nice order, and so spotlessly clean and fresh, but of course it will be a terribly tight fit.'

'There are only two good bedrooms; the third is a mere slip of a room,' returned Ellison, whose practical mind had at once grasped the situation. 'They will be cooped up like so many chickens. I wonder how old the children are. There is one comfort that they will have Mrs. Drake to look after them ; she is such a kind-hearted, motherly woman, and she is so fond of children.'

It was soon evident to Lorraine that Ellison could talk and think of nothing but the *locum tenens*, and that her curiosity and benevolence were strangely excited. She could hardly suppress a smile when Ellison suggested that they should walk over to The Meadows the following afternoon, as it was so long since they had called on Mrs. Tarrant ; but she had the tact to suppress her amusement.

'The Meadows,' as it was called, was a comfortable red brick house, overlooking the vast park-like meadows, through which Lorraine had been driven on the first day of her arrival. The nearest house to it was Price's Folly, about half a mile off. The green seclusion of The Meadows had taken Lorraine's fancy.

The house was spacious enough to hold a large family, but the Tarrants had no children. Ellison was very partial to Mr. Tarrant. He was a big, genial man, with a never-failing fund of good humour ; but his wife was less to her taste. She was a very ordinary little person, plain-featured, and with a thick, stumpy figure, which she loved to adorn with the brightest and most crude colours. Like her husband she was good-tempered and kind-hearted ; but her benevolence was apt to degenerate in fussiness, though her intentions were good.

Ellison once remarked in a moment of confidence to Lorraine, that she often wondered why Mr. Tarrant had married his wife. 'She must always have been ordinary-looking,' she went on ; 'and she told me once that she had no money ; but they seem as happy as possible, and he is quite devoted to her.'

'There is no understanding these things,' returned Lorraine. 'She must have had some fascination for him ; probably she was in love with him, and he saw it.' And Ellison agreed that this was the probable solution of the mystery.

They would both have been honestly surprised and not a little touched if they had known that Richard Tarrant so idealised his homely little Dutch-built wife as to think her perfect. Like the renowned Vicar of Wakefield he had chosen his wife for such qualities as would wear well ; and in some respects she would have rivalled Mrs. Primrose, for she was a good-natured, notable woman.

CHAPTER XIII

> ' Like a dull actor now,
> I have forgotten my part, and I am out
> Even to a full disgrace.'
> *Coriolanus.*

THERE was no doubt of finding Mrs. Tarrant at home. She was one of those women—happily rare in these hygienic days—who take their exercise in trotting after their housemaids; a walk with her husband or a drive in the small phaeton was a treat for high-days and holidays.

'What do I want with air, my dear ?' she would say. ' I am sure our upper windows are always open, even in October. Every room in The Meadows is as sweet and fresh as possible. Richard ' —she invariably spoke of her husband as Richard—'is always teasing me to go out with him, but I tell him my feet are ready to drop off with aching with just following Jane about with the clean cretonne; girls—even the best of them—are so stupid, and Jane is such a feckless creature; she will stand talking to Timothy for half an hour together and never heeding the time.'

Mrs. Tarrant received them with her usual cordiality, and insisted on ordering up tea at once.

'Richard will be so sorry to miss you. He has gone down to the Institute with the new papers, but he will be back soon,' she said, clearing the table briskly as she spoke. There were four maids at the Meadows besides the factotum Timothy, but none of them worked harder than the mistress.

'We are so sorry to miss Mr. Tarrant,' returned Ellison, coming to the point at once, after her usual fashion. ' We wanted him to tell us about the *locum tenens;* of course we are all interested in the subject, and he is the only person who can give us information.'

'I wish he were here to tell you himself,' returned Mrs. Tarrant, who knew well in her wifely heart that Richard loved to tell his own stories, but she was just a little bit in awe of Ellison, whose quiet decision always seemed to rebuke her fussiness, and the pleasure of imparting information was a temptation, so she cleared her throat, after a moment's hesitation, and began her recital.

'Richard came home quite excited from his day in London. Directly he got into the house, while he was wiping his boots on the hall mat, he called out to me, " We have got the right man at last, Martha. Mr. Vincent seems quite up to the mark, and I have booked him for St. Jude's. I shall speak to Mrs. Drake to-morrow and secure the rooms, for he is coming next week." '

'I am glad Mr. Tarrant is satisfied. He is a very good judge of people.'

'Ah, he was more than satisfied. He says his vicar spoke most highly of Mr. Vincent, and that he seems quite grieved to part with him. But they are so poor at St. Barnabas that he cannot afford to keep two curates, and Mr. Vincent, being the junior, must be the one to leave. Richard says he is rather young to be *locum tenens*—at least he is afraid the Admiral and Colonel Trevor may say so. But he has a good degree, and is very clever ; and the vicar told Richard that he was very conscientious and hard-working, and that he was greatly beloved by the poor people.'

'Mrs. Drake informed my cousin yesterday,' interposed Ellison, 'that Mr. Vincent has some young brothers and sisters.'

'Yes, is it not extraordinary? the eldest girl is only about twelve or thirteen, and the boys are younger. He told Richard everything as they walked from the vicarage. He is not in good spirits, for his mother died recently—about three or four months ago—and he said that he was quite lost without her, and that he had not an idea what he was to do with the children ; they are only his step-brothers and sisters, you see.'

This was news even to Lorraine, although she had suspected that this might be the case. She leaned forward and asked eagerly 'if his step-father were living.'

'No, I believe not ; but I will tell you all Mr. Vincent said to Richard, for of course it is better for people to know about him. It seems his mother was left a widow while he was still an infant, and that after a few years, when he was about ten or twelve, she married again. Her second husband's name was Scott—the Rev. Algernon Scott—his own father had been an officer. Richard thinks he must have done very well by the boy, for though the living was a poor one—— Let me see, what was the name of his parish, Richard told me it began with C : was it Clacton? Dear.

dear; what a head I have! I told Richard once, soon after we were married, that I wished he had endowed me with his brains as well as his worldly goods, for I do muddle things so. Why, would you believe it, Miss Lee, I cannot really remember if Mr. Vincent's step-father is dead; and yet he must be, or they would have been all living at Clacton, or whatever place it is. Why,' interrupting herself joyfully, 'there is Richard! I knew he would be back soon.' And Ellison gave a sigh of relief as the big, fine-looking man entered the room.

'Halloa, Martha, I had no idea you had a tea-party, or I would have smartened myself a little!' he exclaimed, glancing at his dirty gaiters. 'How do you do, Mrs. Herbert? I am delighted to see you; you are beginning to look all the better for the air of Highlands.'

'Richard, my dear, what was the name of the place where Mr. Vincent's step-father lived? My head is like a sieve for names, as you know.'

'What! have you been poaching on my manors?' in rather a crestfallen tone; 'how women do love the sound of their own tongues. So you have been telling them about Mr. Vincent. Poor fellow, isn't it a sad business, Miss Lee, having all those children on his hands? Mr. Stephenson told me that he had never seen any one so cut up at losing a mother; but Mrs. Scott was a thoroughly nice woman, and he and his wife had liked her so much. Pleasant people those Stephensons. Well, Martha, aren't you going to give me any tea after my dusty walk?'

'Oh, my dear, to think that I had forgotten you; but Phebe shall make you some fresh tea, this is not fit to drink.'

'Phebe will do nothing of the kind, there is plenty of excellent tannin here,' taking up the tea-pot from his wife's reluctant hand and helping himself liberally.

'Oh, Mr. Tarrant, do tell us one thing,' pleaded Ellison interrupting this flow of playful conjugal reproach. 'Is Mr. Scott, the Rev. Algernon Scott, dead?'

'Certainly he is. Poor woman, she was unlucky to lose two good husbands. He died about three years ago, before Vincent was ordained deacon. He was very much attached to his step-father; he told me that he felt so grateful to him for the education he had given him. "I know now how he stinted himself to do it," he said, —for he is a frank, open-hearted sort of fellow. "I owe it to him and to my mother to do the best I can for those poor children." And then he questioned me very anxiously about Highlands. Was it a healthy place? The children had been ill—they had had measles lately, and were a little pulled down in consequence, and so on. But I soon convinced him that our fine air would soon pick them up.'

'I told Ellison and Mrs. Herbert, Richard, what a good young man he was.'

'Yes, I heard plenty to his credit at the vicarage. You see, I lunched there, and when I was left alone in the drawing-room with Mrs. Stephenson she quite opened her heart to me. I tell my wife that she must not be jealous, because all the ladies do that—eh, Martha?' And with a waggish look at his sturdy little wife he went on: 'She said they would all miss him so, that even in these fifteen months they had become attached to him, but that she was sure a change would be good for him; that the loss of his mother had tried him severely, she was a sweet woman, and had kept things comfortable for him; during her lifetime they had not been so badly off, she had a wealthy sister who had made her a yearly allowance; and though the house they lived in was small there was always an air of comfort about it. Mrs. Stephenson told me that this lady—she did not mention her name—had quarrelled with her nephew, and that he did not expect this allowance to be continued. Since his mother's death it had not been paid, and she had taken no notice of his letter; "so as he has little of his own," she went on, "I am afraid they will be terribly pinched, poor things, for Nora is too young to manage properly."'

'There, I knew Richard would tell you everything,' observed Mrs. Tarrant in a relieved tone; 'he has the best memory in the world—he never forgets anything. What, are you going already, Miss Lee?' for Ellison was buttoning her gloves with an air of resolution that did not escape her hostess's observation.

'Isn't it a sad story!' exclaimed Lorraine as they walked through the meadows. 'I do not remember to have heard of such a case before.'

'I wonder what Mr. Vincent has done to offend his aunt,' was Ellison's practical response to this. 'Young men have so little tact sometimes in dealing with elderly relatives. Of course she ought to do something for those children. Mrs. Tarrant said she was rich—it is this part of the story that puzzles me most.'

'I cannot help thinking of those poor, dear children,' returned Lorraine. 'I wonder who took care of them when they had measles? Poor little dears, I am afraid they must be terribly neglected.' And in this fashion they talked until they reached Brae Farm.

They found Colonel Trevor awaiting them. They had seen very little of him during the last few weeks, as he had been stay-ing with some friends in London. He had also been to Brighton and Folkestone with Captain Faucit; but Ellison, who was used to his frequent absences, took the matter very quietly; but she always welcomed him back with undisguised pleasure.

'There is Gavin,' she said, with no perceptible change of tone; but there was a brightness in her eyes as she hastened to meet him, and perhaps he held her hand a moment longer than usual.

'I have seen so little of you lately,' he said, 'that I thought I would walk down here before dinner; need we go in? it is so pleasant in the garden'; and Ellison, who generally yielded to his slightest wish, sat down willingly on the garden-seat, and made room for him beside her.

'I hope you are not going to run away, Mrs. Herbert!' he exclaimed, as she manifested no intention of joining them; but Lorraine smiled and shook her head.

'I must go to my boy; he will never let Dorcas sing him to sleep. I will come back as soon as I can leave him.'

'Mrs. Herbert looks a different creature,' he observed when she was out of hearing; 'she has gained tone and vitality; I never saw such a change in any woman. You have done a good work there, Ellison.'

'Lorraine is very happy, she is always telling me so,' replied Ellison; 'there is something childlike in her nature. I think she enjoys things more than other people do. Your mother is very fond of her, Gavin. I pretended to be quite jealous the other day.'

'And what about yourself. Has Mrs. Herbert found the way to your heart yet?'

'Oh yes'—colouring a little, for she never liked to be questioned about her feelings, only Gavin was a privileged person—'I have grown so used to Lorraine that I should not like to part with her. She seems almost like a sister to me, and she is so sweet and unselfish.'

'Yes, I am sure of that; but some one else is sweet and unselfish too; eh, Ellison?'

'I don't know about that,' with a charming blush; and then she said hastily, 'Ah, Gavin, you have no idea of all Mr. Tarrant has been telling us about Mr. Vincent this afternoon. Lorraine and I were so interested.'

It was shyness and an odd sort of reserve that made Ellison turn off Colonel Trevor's pretty speeches in this manner; she had done so more than once lately, when he had shown a disposition to be demonstrative. Colonel Trevor failed to understand himself or her just now; he was in that transition state when some crisis seemed impending. He had made up his mind during the last few weeks that it would be a good thing for himself that he should marry Ellison. When the society of a woman is necessary to a man, it is surely a desirable thing that he should make her his . wife.'

He had thought it all carefully out as he had paced the cliffs at Folkestone. His second marriage would be very different from the first; his love for his beautiful young wife had been the passionate devotion of youth; when she had died, the best part of him had died also.

Well, he had mourned for her as truly as a man could mourn, and now it remained to him to do the best he could with his life. Probably he had many years before him; a man a little over forty had a right to consider himself in his prime. During these few years Ellison had become very dear to him; their friendship for each other was unique, and did them both credit. If he could only bring himself to the point of asking her to marry him. He knew that she would make him happy. Who understood him as Ellison did? Who knew his little ways so well, or had taught herself to bear with his peculiarities as this trusty friend of his?

He had come back to Highlands two days ago with the fixed intention of asking her. They had already met once; but Ellison had had some farming business on her mind, and the mention of Sam Brattle had put courtship out of his mind. But this evening surely the Fates propitious to lovers were in his favour.

The sweetness and serenity of the June evening were so restful; the air was fragrant with the scent of lilies; Ellison's bees were returning to their hives laden with rifled spoils; Tedo's play-fellows, the doves, were still cooing on the window-sill; the pigeons were as usual strutting and pluming themselves on the red roof of the barn; the sweet, pungent smell of new-mown hay blended with other scents; it might have been at such an hour and amid such surroundings that Adam told the first love-tale to the youthful Eve. The stage was ready—the scenic decorations perfect. Even the orchestra was tuning up with good-night twitterings; it was only for the actors in the great tragedy of life to perform their parts, and yet why should Colonel Trevor be so backward in his rôle? Why should feminine gaucherie and shyness put him out? Gavin could not have answered this question. He listened silently and without any special interest as Ellison talked about the *locum tenens*. Perhaps he wondered a little that she should be so inter-ested in a perfect stranger, and being a man, he was not very much touched by her account of the children; but he heard her out with commendable patience, and asked a question or two to show that he was listening. But presently, in spite of himself, his attention wandered. The window of Good Rest overlooked their seat, and they could plainly hear Lorraine's voice singing to her boy. Gavin could even distinguish the words—it was some childish hymn or other—

> ' Every spring the sweet young flowers
>   Open bright and gay,
>   Till the chilly autumn hours
>   Wither them away ;
>   There's a land we have not seen,
>   Where the trees are always green.'

He had not heard her sing since the evening she and Ellison had dined at Brae House, and somehow the sound of her voice affected him strangely. Simple as the refrain was, the pure liquid notes were exquisitely sweet as they floated towards him.

Even Ellison paused to listen ; her cousin's singing gave her great pleasure. All at once she became conscious of her companion's mood. Gavin was inclined for silence. She dropped the thread of her talk instantly ; her fine tact was seldom at fault. Perhaps the secret of her influence with him was her wonderful adaptability to his moods.

Presently the voice ceased ; then to their surprise Lorraine herself appeared with Tedo in her arms. She had wrapped him up warmly, and meant to try the air as a soporific. She passed them with a little nod, and began pacing the long path between the clumps of tall white lilies ; but they could hear her singing softly to herself.

'Gavin !' exclaimed Ellison, rousing herself, 'you will be too late for your dinner. You had better stop and have supper with us.' And as he hesitated, she continued, 'I shall take no refusal. You have not had a meal here since my cousin came ; you were far more gracious in poor Miss Elliott's day.'

'Very well, then, I will stay, if you are sure I shall not be in the way ; but I have profound faith in Mrs. Tucker, and in Mrs. Tucker's mistress.'

'If you will excuse me, I will go in and tell Ruth to lay a place for you. By the bye, Ruth has gone to Oaklands to see her mother, but Dorcas really waits very nicely.'

Gavin made no attempt to keep her ; the hour had passed. Perhaps his humour had changed ; a man is essentially a thing of moods. As Ellison entered her house, on hospitable thoughts intent, and inwardly rejoicing that Gavin would spend the evening with them, Colonel Trevor rose from his seat and joined Lorraine. She made a sign to him to speak softly.

'Tedo has been rather fretful the last day or two,' she said ' He is not a strong child, I am sorry to say, and he is often a little ailing. You see the air has sent him off to sleep. Does he not look comfortable ?' lifting up the corner of the shawl for him to peep.

'He is far too heavy for you ; you are looking as tired as possible. Give him to me ; I will not wake him.'

Colonel Trevor spoke in a quick, authoritative voice, and Lorraine, who was a little taken by surprise, actually allowed him to take the child out of her arms. She said afterwards, laughingly, to Ellison that Colonel Trevor had a way with him that made people submit to his orders.

'He was very kind, though,' interrupting herself, as though she had been ungracious. 'He saw I was tired, and he did carry Tedo so nicely.'

Certainly Colonel Trevor understood his business. He stood still while Lorraine drew the shawl over her boy, and then he proposed that they should take a turn in the kitchen garden.

'There is no need to go in yet. It is a lovely evening, and Ellison will be back directly, and you see the boy is fast asleep.'

'But why should I burden you in this way ?' remonstrated Lorraine. 'I am sure Tedo is heavy.' But Colonel Trevor had sufficient kindness of heart not to contradict this statement. In reality he thought the little fellow too light for his age, but he would not have said so for worlds.

Some undefinable feeling made him glance compassionately at the young widow ; but Lorraine, who felt very happy that evening, misunderstood his grave, pitying look.

'Some people say that a summer's evening makes them feel sad,' she said. 'I hope you are not one of them, Colonel Trevor ? The evening sunset—oh, do you see those glorious silver clouds ?—and the scent of the lilies, and this sweet warm air, make me feel as light-hearted as a child. On such an evening all must be well with me ; that is what I say to myself.'

'Ah, I see you agree with Browning ! Not that I profess to be a student of Browning—life is not long enough, as I often tell Muriel ; but I know exactly what you want to express—

'"God's in His Heaven,
All's right with the world."'

'Yes, that is beautiful ; you have certainly understood my meaning. When my boy grows up I hope he will love the country as much as his mother does. I mean to teach him botany and natural history ; but,' interrupting herself with a laugh, 'I must first teach myself. I am always making plans about Tedo. He is to be such a good man ; so true and honourable and upright. He must never tell a falsehood if he does not wish to break my heart. Ah, you think me foolish, Colonel Trevor, but Tedo is all I have—the one treasure that I had saved out of the wreck ! How can I help setting my heart on him ?'

'Do not hold him too tightly,' was the grave response. 'I had a treasure too, and I lost it.'

Colonel Trevor never knew what made him say this. Perhaps the suppressed passion of Lorraine's tone instinctively induced him to utter this warning. It was as though some shipwrecked mariner who had lost his all were watching another toiling heavily in a frail bark. But he reproached himself a moment afterwards.

'You must not let me make you melancholy with my dour speeches,' he said apologetically, as she fixed her eyes on him without speaking, though her lips parted.

Did she understand his warning? She certainly grew a little pale. The next minute he saw her lift the shawl and kiss the arm of the slumbering boy.

'He must not be out any longer,' she said quietly. 'We are near the house. Will you kindly give him to me now?' and, without a word, he obeyed her.

'When he grows up to be a man,' he said to himself, as he turned down another path. 'Poor woman, she is storing her happiness in a very frail vessel, and I am sure that, from her manner, Ellison agrees with me. Ah, well, who knows what is for the best? Those who die young are not always to be pitied. If he were to be taken, would she still agree so joyfully to the words I quoted to her?

> ' "God's in His Heaven,
> All's right with the world." '

CHAPTER XIV

'That unlettered small-knowing soul.'
Love's Labour's Lost.

'I thank you for your voices: thank you :
Your most sweet voices.'
Coriolanus.

IN a small place the arrival of a new inhabitant is always the source of some excitement. Highlands had not yet finished discussing the attractions of Mrs. Herbert. Brae House, The Homestead, Price's Folly, and The Meadows had all vied with each other in fêting and making much of the young widow; and even old Mrs. Langton at Ferncliffe, who was a chronic invalid, and was never expected to call on her neighbours, had first sent her young companion, little Miss Holt, with her card, and had then electrified her friends by actually giving a tea-party in Mrs. Herbert's honour.

Lorraine had fallen in love with the placid, sweet-faced old lady, and before the afternoon was over they were great friends. 'You must come and see me very often, my dear,' Mrs. Langton said, as Lorraine sat beside her couch. 'I am a feeble old woman, full of infirmities, but my friends are very good to me. Mrs. Mordaunt and Mrs. Earnshaw often drop in of an afternoon to have a cup of tea with me and Laura, but no one comes so often as dear Ellison,' with a smile at her favourite.

'I shall come very often too,' was Lorraine's answer to this ; and she kept her word. The walk to Ferncliffe was a delightful one through the Brae Woods, and then across the common at the foot of Dunsford Hill ; the road winding deliciously under shady trees, between banks clothed with honeysuckle and briar roses and blackberry bushes, broken ground covered with gorse and bracken stretching into the distance. It was a favourite walk with Lorraine ; and when her pleasant chat with Mrs. Langton was over, little Miss Holt would walk back with her till they reached Dunsford Farm, where the gate led into the Brae Woods.

Every one called her little Miss Holt. She was a tiny creature ; and Lily Mordaunt, a well-grown child of twelve, was considerably taller. She had a pretty, babyish face, and very youthful manners ; but she was five-and-twenty, and had been engaged for the last six years to a sailor ; but as far as Highlands knew about it, she was not likely to be married yet. She was a distant connection of Mrs. Langton, and had lived with her ever since her father's death, and the two were much attached to each other. Little Miss Holt was a great favourite with everybody. She was a clever little body, and very good-natured and unassuming, and though her life was dull and monotonous, she always seemed perfectly content with it.

She took a great fancy to Lorraine, and would talk to her about her protracted engagement in the most confiding manner. 'You see, Mrs. Herbert,' she said cheerfully one day, ' Frank is only second officer in the P. and O. service, and of course there is no hope of our marrying yet ; but I am saving up my money to help towards the furnishing, for of course he cannot put by much. Father wished us not to get married until Frank was captain, and so we must wait ; but I have his letters, and Mrs. Langton is like a mother to me, so I ought to be happy.'

She showed his photograph to Lorraine once. Little Miss Holt's *fiancé* had a big, burly figure, and a plain face that even in the photo beamed with good nature. ' Poor Frank ; he is popular with all the crew,' sighed Laura, as she gazed proudly at the clumsy features of her lover. ' He is never out of temper with the men ; and his captain speaks so well of him. I think I am the most fortunate girl in the world.'

' She is a good little soul,' observed Ellison, when Lorraine repeated this conversation. ' Frank Sanderson is not handsome, certainly ; but he is an honest, straightforward fellow, and we were all pleased with him. Laura makes the best of things ; but Mrs. Langton is very kind to her, and I daresay she will remember her in her will, though the bulk of her fortune must go to her two nephews.'

Directly the news of the *locum tenens* was bruited abroad, there was immense excitement in Highlands ; every one called on the Tarrants ; there was a perfect stream of visitors to the Meadows, every one wanted to hear what Mr. Tarrant thought of Mr. Vincent ; and one and all held up their hands and exclaimed in horror when they heard of the four brothers and sisters.

Mrs. Mordaunt and her daughters, who lived at The Homestead, a little way down the Darley Road, were especially emphatic in their expressions of disapproval and pity.

Mrs. Mordaunt was a buxom, well-preserved widow. Report said, somewhat ill-naturedly, that she would not be averse to entering a second time into the bonds of matrimony ; but Ellison, who disliked gossip, always contradicted this flatly. Mrs. Mordaunt was a good-natured, motherly woman, she said ; not specially refined, and perhaps a little too dressy for good taste ; but she was sure she was far too sensible to think of such a thing.

Amy and Constance Mordaunt were pleasant-looking girls. They had inherited their mother's good-nature and love of finery. They had no intellectual tastes, and Muriel could not tolerate them ; but Ellison took a neighbourly interest in them—though it must be owned her manner was a little patronising. Mrs. Herbert was far more to their taste, and the Mordaunt girls would willingly have struck up a friendship with her ; but Muriel Trevor had been beforehand. Besides, in spite of Lorraine's easy temperament, she had a fine discrimination of character, and though she was gracious to all her neighbours, she soon discovered that the Homestead was not so attractive to her as Brae House and Price's Folly. Mrs. Mordaunt and her daughters were inveterate gossips ; they read little except novels and magazines, and were more intent on adorning their persons than their minds. Tennis, and dancing, and a London season were their chief interests ; and Amy and Constance Mordaunt's one aim was to persuade their mother to let the Homestead and take a flat in Hyde Park Mansions. During the summer a constant relay of guests kept the house lively ; and a succession of picnics and tennis-parties made the Homestead the rallying-point for the young people of Bramfield and Dorchester. Ellison could seldom be induced to show herself at these gatherings ; the young mistress of Brae Farm was far too important and busy a person to waste long summer afternoons playing tennis and gossiping in the Homestead garden. And from the first Lorraine seemed disposed to follow her cousin's lead ; a ramble through the Redlands pine-woods with Muriel, or a drive with Ellison, was more to her taste. One fine afternoon Lorraine had been over to Redlands with her cousin. Ruth's mother, who was a laundress, had been failing in health lately, and Ellison had been taking her some nourishing soup and jelly. Mrs. Clarke lived in a cottage overlooking the Redlands pine-woods ; it was only a little distance from the *Waggon and Horses*, and some of the fields belonging to Mansoule Farm sloped down to the cottage. From the windows one could see Mr. Yolland's big red house, and as he was Mrs. Clarke's landlord, he had met Ruth first in her mother's cottage. They had not had a pleasant visit. Mrs. Clarke was not a good-tempered woman, and, as Ellison knew, she and Ruth had never got on well together ; the mother was fretful and exacting, and the girl had a proud spirit. There had been sad scenes in the cottage until Ruth threw up the laundry work and went into service. Ellison told her cousin that Mrs. Clarke had never cared for Sam Brattle, and was always speaking against him to her daughter. She favoured her landlord, and was eager for Ruth to marry Edgar Yolland. She contrived to let him know when Ruth came home for an hour or two, and it was through her that things had gone so wrong between her and Sam Brattle. Ruth, in spite of her proud disposition, was easily influenced ; when her mother appealed to her vanity, and told her that she was handsome enough for a lady, and could hold her head as high as she chose, Ruth would succumb insensibly to the flattery. Her mother's little gibes made her discontented with her lover, and when he waylaid her on her return to Brae Farm, she would treat him with such coldness and indifference that she drove him almost mad with jealousy. On the evening Lorraine had seen them together she had goaded him until he had lost his temper. It was impossible, as Ellison well knew, that things could go on like this much longer ; and that afternoon she had spoken very plainly to Mrs. Clarke.

'All this is spoiling Ruth,' she said severely ; 'she cannot do her work properly unless she has her mind at rest. I am always finding fault with her now. She might make a valuable servant if she chose ; she is treating Sam Brattle very badly. She has allowed him to pay her attention all this time, and now she is keeping him at arm's length, and refuses to be engaged to him. I cannot help thinking that this state of things is somehow owing to you, Mrs. Clarke ; you are encouraging Ruth in her bad behaviour to Sam.'

'I don't hold with Sam Brattle,' returned Mrs. Clarke doggedly. 'The Brattles have never been to my mind. They are a bit stuck up, and think themselves better than other people. I tell my girl that she could do better for herself. Mr. Yolland is a fine figure of a man, and though he is no boy, he is equal to any young man in vigour ; and he would marry her to-morrow. He has told me so times out of mind.'

'You are a foolish, dense woman !' returned Ellison warmly ; 'and you are as wrong as possible. There is no better fellow living than Sam Brattle, and the girl who marries him will have a good and loving husband. Edgar Yolland loves no one but himself. There, I have no patience to talk to you any longer !'

'I am sure I never meant to offend you,' returned Mrs. Clarke,

8

putting her apron to her eyes. 'And you have been a good friend to my girl, as Ruth says—for though she has a stiff neck and a haughty temper, her heart is right at the bottom. Thank you for your kindness, Miss Lee; and if the soup is like the last it will do me a power of good. The housekeeper at Mansoule Farm sent me some that was not near so good; but she is a feckless sort of body, and Mr. Yolland wants to get rid of her, I hear. Well, good morning, and if you can spare Ruth for an evening next week, I will be obliged to you, Miss Lee.'

'Ruth shall come—it is her duty to come and see her mother,' returned Ellison, shortly; 'but I cannot say which evening I can spare her—we are busy just now, as you know, with the hay.'

'Well, Lorraine'—as they walked down the lane—'what do you think of Ruth's mother?' But Lorraine shook her head.

'I see where Ruth has got her beauty,' she replied. 'Mrs. Clarke has been very handsome; but there is a hard expression about her face. I never like those thin lips; but she looks ill, poor woman!'

'If I do not mistake, she is very ill, though neither she nor Ruth guesses it. She is a mean-natured woman—she thinks more of money and creature comforts than her daughter's happiness. How can any mother think that a girl could be happy with Edgar Yolland?'

'It is very sad,' assented Lorraine. And then she said, with a marked change of voice, 'Oh, do look, Ellison, at all those boxes and portmanteaus piled up before the Drakes' cottage! I do believe'—with gathering excitement—'that the *locum tenens* has arrived.'

'It certainly looks like it,' returned Ellison, insensibly quickening her pace, and they both glanced curiously towards the cottage. There was a bend in the road below the forge, and unless people had business at the forge or the cottage, or wished to make purchases or to post their letters at Brattle's, they would generally take the lower road, and avoid the steep climb to the forge; nevertheless, such is the curiosity of women, that Ellison took the upper road, which brought her directly in front of the cottage. The fact was, the heap of luggage in the tiny front garden puzzled her; it was so unlike Mrs. Drake's methodical ways with her lodgers.

They had just nodded to John Drake, who was busily shoeing a cart-horse, when two little boys in sailor suits ran out of the cottage and began swinging on the chains between the white palings.

It was a tempting, but at the same time a somewhat dangerous

amusement, as the ground sloped steeply to the road below, and
if they fell, a broken or dislocated ankle might be the result. For
young children to swing on the chains was considered very unsafe,
and mothers in Highlands had been heard to say to their little
ones, ' Now mind, Dick,' or Tom, as the case might be, ' if you lets
Sally go nigh them chains, I'll take the stick to you'; notwithstanding, little Ned Dash, swinging gleefully on the said chains with his
mouth full of butter-scotch, had been one day rudely pushed by an
envious schoolfellow and lost his balance, and was found lying in
the road below with a broken leg, and an inquisitive cow smelling
him over in a friendly fashion.

Ellison was just going up to speak to the boys, when a shrill
girlish voice called to them from the cottage.

' Hugo—Eddie, come in this moment ! Hugo, how can you be
so naughty ? ' and the next minute a girl of about twelve or
thirteen appeared in the porch holding a pretty fair-haired child
by the hand. She had a delicate, high-bred little face, but it wore
a most unchildlike expression of anxious weariness ; the plait of
soft brown hair hanging to her waist was rough and dishevelled,
and her black linen frock was crumpled and dusty ; she seemed on
the verge of tears from nervous tension and fatigue.

' Oh, Hugo, please get down '—in an imploring tone.

' My dear, do you not hear your sister calling to you ? ' observed
Ellison in her calm, authoritative voice ; ' you must not lead your
little brother into mischief, it is not safe to swing upon those
chains,' and as she spoke she quietly lifted the smaller boy from
his perilous position. They were both handsome little fellows ;
but the younger boy looked delicate, as though from recent illness ;
the eldest, Hugo, had a bold, merry expression, and his dark eyes
gleamed with fun and mischief; he was evidently a pickle, and even
Ellison's dignified rebuke did not make him look at all ashamed of
himself.

' Oh, thank you,' returned the young girl gratefully. ' I did
so beg Hugo not to play so near the edge of the road. I am so
afraid for Eddie, he always does what Hugo tells him.'

' Then Hugo ought to take better care of his little brother,'
returned Ellison ; but Lorraine made a diversion at this moment,
for with a sudden impulse she opened the little gate.

' Is that your little sister ? what a darling—may I kiss her ? I
have the dearest little boy of my own, and I do so love children.
Will you come to me, my sweet ? '

What child could have resisted those winning tones ? certainly
not Effie. A broad smile came over her face ; she fixed her blue
eyes in friendly inquiry on Lorraine, then fearlessly offered her lips.

'How old are you, my pet, and what do they call you?' inquired Lorraine, holding the chubby hand caressingly.

'Effie is six years old,' returned her sister proudly. 'We call her Effie, but her name is really Phebe. She is such a good little girl.'

'Missie, what can I do about the boxes?' asked Mrs. Drake, suddenly breaking into the conversation. 'Mr. Vincent does not seem coming back, and my master says we shall have a sharp shower directly.'

'Oh, I hope not,' in a distressed voice. 'Eric said he would not be long, and I cannot decide about the rooms until he comes. It is so difficult to know what to do; and yet the children are so tired and want their tea.'

The weary, helpless tones went to their hearts. Lorraine looked imploringly at her cousin, but Ellison's practical kindness was always ready.

'Can we help you, my dear?' she said at once. 'We are close neighbours, and I hope shall soon be good friends. We live at Brae Farm across there. I am Miss Lee—Mrs. Drake knows me very well; and this is my cousin, Mrs. Herbert, who lives with me. If I understand the difficulty rightly, you are waiting for your brother to decide on the rooms before the luggage is carried up.'

'Yes, I do so want Eric to choose,' returned the girl anxiously. 'When he went off with Mr. Tarrant, he just said that Effie and I were to have the best room—that is so like Eric, he never thinks about himself; but I have been thinking over it, and that will never do. The sitting-room is so small, it is only half the size of our old dining-room, and how am I to keep the children quiet while Eric studies and writes his sermons?'

'My dear, that is very thoughtful of you,' said Ellison, 'the idea occurred to us the other day. I know all the rooms well. Shall we go upstairs and look at them, while my cousin stays with the children? Don't you think that will be a good plan? two heads are always better than one.' And this offer was gratefully accepted, and Lorraine, seating herself on the biggest trunk, took Effie up on her lap and proceeded to tell the boys a story.

CHAPTER XV

'I would not spend another such a night,
Though 'twere to buy a world of happy days.'
King Richard III.

As Ellison followed the girl into the little dark passage, she was surprised and touched by her suddenly turning round and saying :

'How kind you are to take all this trouble, and you do not even know us ; but I am so glad that you live near. My name is Nora—Nora Scott ; but please call me Nora.'

'Very well, dear,' returned Ellison gently ; and then the next moment they stood in what Mrs. Drake proudly called her best room. It was a fair-sized room, and in spite of its low ceiling it was very pleasant ; the one window looked over the common towards Fernleigh Lane, but Brae Farm was not visible, as it lay in a hollow. The other room had the same aspect ; but it was not quite so large, and the furniture was more homely. The third room was a slip of a place with a small window overlooking the yard and the wall of the forge.

Ellison took counsel with herself for a minute, while Nora looked at her helplessly ; but at last she said in the cheerful, decided tone that always brought conviction to her listener :

'I have thought it all out, and I think you ought decidedly to give your brother the best room ; the other would do very nicely for you and Effie, and though the slip room is very small for the boys, they can manage quite well.'

'Oh, I am so glad !' exclaimed Nora joyfully ; 'that is just what I wanted to arrange, only Eric would not listen to me—he was in such a hurry and so tired, because we had been packing until late last night. Shall I go down and ask Mr. Drake to carry up Eric's portmanteaus and his box of books?—oh, there are two boxes! and they are so heavy. And where ever will he put his books?' looking round the room as she spoke.

'Wait a moment,' returned Ellison in a thoughtful tone; 'there is no such hurry. The shower seems passing off. This is really a very nice room; let us ask Mrs. Drake to push the bed against the wall, and that will give more space. Then that toilet table—if you put the glass on the drawers, you might cover the table with a dark cloth, and it will make a splendid writing-table, and there is wall-room over there for a bookcase. Your brother can use this room as his study, and he will be quiet and undisturbed. Don't you approve of my plan, Nora?'

'Yes, indeed. Oh, how clever you are! I should never have thought of anything half as nice, and Eric never will consider his own comfort; he always gives the best things to us, just as mother did. May I go down now, and send Mrs. Drake up, and you shall tell her what you mean?'

'Yes; and John Drake and Joshua may begin bringing up the boxes,' and Nora flew downstairs. When Mrs. Drake appeared, Ellison gave her a few quiet hints, which the good-hearted woman at once promised to carry out; and then Ellison, feeling that she had taken enough on herself, went in search of her cousin.

Meanwhile, as Lorraine sat over the big trunk laughing and chatting with the children, and making them forget that they were tired and hungry, she became aware of a tall young man in clerical attire hurrying up the ascent to the forge. He looked at the little group in the front garden with some astonishment; but as he raised his hat, Lorraine quietly rose from her seat.

'I hope you will not think we are intruding, Mr. Vincent,' she said, with her bright smile; 'but my cousin Miss Lee and I found your little sister in some difficulty, and we stopped to help her. The children are so tired,' she continued, with the gentle motherliness that was habitual to her, 'and they tell me that they want their tea very badly; but Mrs. Drake says that all these boxes must be carried in first.'

'They ought to have been carried in long ago,' returned the young man in a tone of vexation. 'What is Nora thinking about?' But Effie, who was a peacemaker by nature, slid a soft little hand into his.

'Nora is with the kind lady upstairs, Eric,' she said gravely. 'They are both kind ladies; but I like this one best—she has the nicest face.'

'Ah, Effie, what a little flatterer you are!' exclaimed Lorraine, bursting into a merry laugh. And then Mr. Vincent, who had seemed rather embarrassed by this speech, laughed too.

Eric Vincent was by no means handsome; but, like his young sister Nora, he had a refined, highly-bred face, and there was unmistakable intellect in the broad, thoughtful brow. His eyes were a light hazel; but their expression was gentle, and there were sensitive lines about the mouth. Young as he was, only five-and-twenty, he had a worn, harassed look that went to Lorraine's heart. Her life's experience had taught her how to read faces as well as characters, and even during those first few minutes she had detected the lines of care and sorrow on the young clergyman's face.

'Oh, Eric,' chimed in Hugo, emboldened by his big brother's presence, 'do tell Mrs. Drake to hurry up and get the tea ready. You are awfully hungry, aren't you, Eddie?'

'Yes, I am awfully hungry,' repeated Eddie solemnly.

'I am hungry too, Eric,' piped Effie, who generally completed the trio of complaints; 'but the lady was telling us such a nice story about three little bears, and the dear little cubbly one said, "Who's been a-sitting in my chair?"'

'Lorraine, are you ready?' asked a quick, decided voice, and the next moment Ellison's fair, serious face appeared in the doorway; but she also was not in the least taken aback when she saw the young clergyman.

'You are Mr. Vincent,' she said quietly, with the air of dignity that always impressed strangers. 'My cousin Mrs. Herbert and I have been making friends with your sister. My name is Lee—Miss Lee, of Brae Farm'—there was unconscious pride in her tone as Ellison said this. 'We are really your nearest neighbours.'

'I have been hearing of some of Miss Lee's good works from Mr. Tarrant,' returned Mr. Vincent, with a pleasant smile. 'That beautiful window in St. Jude's, for example, which I have just been admiring. I am greatly pleased with the church; it is small, certainly, but my church-warden tells me it is large enough for the place. He took me to the institute; that is why I have been away so long.'

'Please, Eric,' interposed Nora, 'will you ask Mr. Drake to come and help with the boxes? Mrs. Drake is waiting for them upstairs.' And this broke up the party.

'I will go and tell him,' returned Ellison. 'John Drake is an old friend of mine.' When she returned from the forge she found Lorraine slowly sauntering towards the common with Mr. Vincent and the two little boys, and Nora at the gate watching for her.

'Ah, Miss Lee,' she said eagerly, 'I begged Eric to take the boys away for a little, for I knew we should get on faster without them. Mrs. Drake says she will have the bed made in a twinkling—those were her very words; and when the boxes are up, I shall show Eric his room, and then we shall have tea.'

'That will be very nice. Now, I must say good-bye, dear; but I shall come to-morrow morning and see how you are getting on. Go to bed early, you look very tired, Nora,' and then Ellison followed the others.

They stood still and waited for her; the boys had forgotten their fatigue, and were playing hide-and-seek amongst the gorse, and Mr. Vincent walked on with the ladies until they reached Fernleigh Lane.

'I am charmed with Highlands,' he said; 'I had no idea from Mr. Tarrant's description that the village was so picturesque; those fir woods and low hills give such a fine effect. I do not think I could have done better for the children, as far as air and scenery go; but we shall be terribly cramped for room at the cottage.'

'The sitting-room is very small, certainly,' returned Ellison; 'but Mrs. Drake is such a capital manager that I really think you will be comfortable. A good landlady is such a blessing; and she is so fond of children.'

'She has none of her own, Mr. Tarrant told me.'

'No; their one child died when she was a baby; but that was many years ago. I am afraid, Mr. Vincent, that you will have to make the best of things. There are no better lodgings to be got nearer than Bramfield, and that is two miles away. You see, our lord of the manor, Sir John Chessington, and my cousin Colonel Trevor do not encourage an influx of strangers. They will not have more houses built, and there are few cottages; so of course there is no help for it.'

'No, I suppose not; and we shall muddle along somehow'—but Mr. Vincent's tone was despondent. 'If we could have had the Vicarage we should have been in clover; but Mr. Tarrant says there is no chance of that for the next five months; but we shall probably get in before winter. There is no expectation of the Yollands coming back before June.'

'No indeed; but I shall be glad for you all to be housed at the Vicarage before the winter. The cottage is terribly draughty, and in cold weather it must be difficult to keep the children warm.'

'I should imagine so. Well, I must take the boys back now. But I do not see any signs of Brae Farm; and yet you say you are our nearest neighbours.'

'Yes; we are a trifle nearer to you than Brae House; but you must go down that long winding lane and cross two or three meadows before you reach the Farm. When you are settled you must let the children come over for a long afternoon. I will send them home in our new donkey-cart, so they will not be too tired; and my cousin and I will undertake to amuse them.'

'Thank you very much. Hugo and Edmund, come and say good-bye to these kind ladies,' and then Mr. Vincent shook hands with them cordially. As they entered the lane, Ellison glanced back. Mr. Vincent had his youngest brother on his shoulder, and was climbing up the steep, broken ground manfully, with the irrepressible Hugo running beside him.

'I like Mr. Vincent,' observed Lorraine impulsively, when her cousin had called her attention to this; 'he is so good to those boys. What a fine little fellow Hugo is. If only my Tedo could be as strong and sturdy,' and Lorraine sighed; for in spite of the new donkey the warm weather was making Tedo pale and languid. He had lost appetite lately, and more than once Ellison had hinted that perhaps it might be as well that Dr. Howell should be called in; but, strange to say, Lorraine had always some excuse to offer. It was just the warm weather. She had never known June so hot. It was really more like August. The heat never suited Tedo; he always flagged a little; she noticed it last year. No, there was no need to speak to Dr. Howell. His donkey-rides and drives, and all that delicious new milk from the Alderney, would soon strengthen him; but she never noticed that Ellison made no reply to this.

Tedo was playing with the puppy, under Dorcas's supervision, when they reached home. He ran up to his mother at once, with his usual cry of delight, and as she took him up in her arms she kissed him passionately.

'Have you wanted me, darling? Has mother been too long away? You look tired and hot, my precious.'

'Boy wanted mammie dreffelly,' returned Tedo pathetically. 'Boy got tired of playing with Tweed. Boy wanted Tousin too' —his name for Ellison.

'He certainly looks very tired,' observed Ellison; and then Lorraine carried him indoors. As she sat down by the window overlooking the farmyard, Tedo rested his head contentedly against his mother's shoulder.

'Boy's quite comfy now,' he said, and then he put his arm round her neck with his customary squeeze. 'Sing to boy, mammie,' and she began one of his favourite baby songs. But for once as she sang, Lorraine's heart felt a little heavy—a vivid remembrance of Hugo's sturdy figure and bold little face came to her mind. There was no disguising the fact—her boy was delicate. There was a want of vitality about him that made her anxious. Perhaps she was wrong not to ask Dr. Howell's opinion.

If Ellison proposed it again she would not be obstinate. As these thoughts passed through her mind she lifted the little hand to her lips. It felt small and hot, and his eyes were certainly heavy.

'Are you well, darling? Is my Tedo quite well?' she asked anxiously.

'Boy is kite well,' replied Tedo drowsily. 'Sing "Ten little nigger boys," mammie. Boy doesn't want no stupid hymns,' and Lorraine obediently fulfilled his behest.

'You are a little out of spirits this evening,' observed Ellison, as they sat in the bay later. She looked at her cousin affectionately as she spoke, for she had noticed that Lorraine had answered her rather absently once or twice, as though her thoughts were elsewhere.

'No—yes—oh, I was only thinking about Tedo!' returned Lorraine, the tears starting to her eyes. 'I cannot help worrying a little over his want of strength. Somehow I fancy he is a little thinner.'

'Ah, the heat makes young children thin,' returned Ellison. 'Tedo is not a strong child, so anything pulls him down. I think you are wrong not to speak to Dr. Howell, for perhaps he only needs a tonic. Look here, I have an idea in my head. Dr. Howell is sure to be at Brae House to-morrow to see Roberts. Shall I send a note round and ask him to come on here?'

'Thank you; perhaps it would be as well,' replied Lorraine dejectedly; and Ellison concealed her surprise at this ready acquiescence.

That night was the most miserable that Lorraine had known for years. In the dark hours a perfect panic seized her. She could not sleep; she could not reason away her fears; she could not even lie still; a dozen times she kindled a light, and shading it carefully bent over her treasure; but Tedo was sleeping sweetly.

'Why have I so little faith?' she said to herself. 'Why do I fear to trust myself and my boy to my heavenly Father? Ah, well may Divine lips tell us that the flesh is weak; but then there is only One who knows how a mother's heart can suffer.'

There is no denying that imagination can inflict positive torture—that the fear of trouble may be so intense and acute that even the trouble, when it comes, will only be a little harder to bear.

Every loving soul has its Gethsemane. Has not this been said before, when, reverently be it spoken, it drinks beforehand of its cup of sorrow. In some cases it may be the prophetic instinct warns us of the coming evil, a pale reflection of the shadow that is to darken our lives seems to envelop us. Oh, the agony of such hours! Well may we pray that at such dread moments some merciful angel may be near to strengthen us, lest our human heart should break, and our human faith wax low or perish.

It was dawn before Lorraine could sleep; but though her palid look told plainly of her vigil, Ellison made no remark; she kept her real sympathy to herself. Lorraine had been fretting about Tedo; but it was kinder and wiser to take no notice. She kissed her a little more affectionately than usual, and talked quietly on ordinary topics.

But before the morning had half passed, Lorraine became her bright, hopeful self again. When Dr. Howell came, he spoke cheerfully about the boy. He was certainly not a strong child, he observed; many children of his age were a little weakly; but he would soon mend. There must be no fatigue and excitement for the present. He must be out in the air as much as possible, and lie down a good deal; and then he mentioned a few simple remedies and took his leave, and Lorraine, who was worn by her terrible night, shed tears of joy as soon as she was alone with her boy. Dr. Howell's face was a trifle graver when Ellison questioned him in the porch; but even to her he said nothing very definite.

'He is a frail little fellow, and has not much stamina; but with care and plenty of light nourishment he will do very well, as I tell his mother,' and then he began talking about the excellent hay harvest.

Dr. Howell was rather given to reserve his opinion about his patients. Unless it were absolutely necessary, he seldom took their friends into confidence. He had a strong-featured, sensible face, that kept its own counsel. His abrupt manner hid a kind heart, and in cases of real suffering or serious illness his presence was felt to be a blessing.

When Dr. Howell had left, Ellison went down to the cottage to see Nora; and on her way she met Muriel, who was anxious to know what he said about Tedo. She looked much relieved when Ellison repeated his words.

'Ah, I knew you would come!' exclaimed Lorraine gratefully, when she entered the room; 'but I have nothing but good news to tell you.'

'Is that why you have been crying?' asked Muriel gravely; and Lorraine blushed a little.

'I think I have been crying over my own ingratitude,' she said humbly. 'I am ashamed to think how I worked myself up last night. It was wicked of me; but somehow there are times when one seems to let go the helm, and we drift away anywhere. What odd creatures we are! Last night I was wading breast-high in the Slough of Despond, and now the ground is firm under my feet again. Directly Dr. Howell said there was very little the matter with Tedo, I felt life was worth having.'

Muriel looked at her as though she perfectly understood this, and then Lorraine of her own accord began speaking of other things. She told Muriel about their visit to the cottage, and described Mr. Vincent graphically, and then in her old way she began questioning Muriel about her doings. They were close friends now, and Muriel talked to her freely about most things.

They spent the rest of the morning together in the Dovecote, while Tedo sat at their feet with his bricks.

Meanwhile Ellison paid her promised visit. The little boys were evidently on the watch for her, for they rushed out of the gate the moment they saw her, and accosted her in the most friendly way.

'Nora's expecting you, Miss Lee,' observed Hugo. 'She has put the room quite tidy, hasn't she, Eddie? and we helped her.'

'Yes; we helped her a lot,' chimed in Eddie.

'Eric has gone to that queer iron room,' continued Hugo; 'but he would not take us with him. He said we talked so much that we hindered him. Do you mind boys talking, Miss Lee, when you ask us to your farm?—we mean to be quiet, don't we, Eddie?' in an insinuating voice.

'We won't speak one word,' assented Eddie.

'Dear me, what cheerful visitors I shall have. I shall feel as though I am entertaining two tame mice.'

'When do you mean to ask us?' demanded Hugo; but Nora, who had come to the gate, overheard this.

'For shame, Hugo. How can you say such things. Please come in, Miss Lee. I have been wanting you to come so much. Now run away, boys, and finish your game.' And then she led Ellison into the parlour, and ensconced her in the easy-chair.

'Well, my dear, and how have you got on?' began Ellison, with a look of approval at the slight, girlish figure before her. Nora was certainly pretty, she thought; her hair was plaited nicely, and looked smooth and glossy; 'but what has become of Effie?'

'Oh, Effie is trotting after Mrs. Drake, and pretending to help her. Mrs. Drake has taken such a fancy to Effie, and begged to have her. Oh, Miss Lee, I must tell you; Eric was so pleased with his room. He says he can write his sermons so nicely at that table, and he is going to put up the book-shelves this afternoon, and I am to help him unpack the books. He did not seem half so unhappy when he came home last night. He said you were both so kind, and it was pleasant to have such nice neighbours, and that it was such a beautiful place, and that we must try and make the best of things ; and he has promised to take us to the pine-woods after tea, and the boys are so delighted.'

'Your brother is very good to you, I am sure'; and Nora's eyes filled with tears. She was a sensitive little creature, and her many cares had made her precocious.

'I think no one is quite so good as Eric,' she said simply. 'Mother and I used often to say so. Poor mother, how she cried at the idea of leaving him. She said it was so hard for him at his age to have all us children to look after ; but Eric never let her say that. I wish I were older, and knew better how to help him ; but I am not thirteen yet, and I do make such mistakes. Grown-up people are so much happier, I think,' finished Nora, with a sigh. 'They know how to do things, and never make mistakes.'

CHAPTER XVI

'When you are not resting, work ;
When you are not ill, be well ;
When you are not miserable, be happy.'
CARLYLE.

THE cloud passed, and Lorraine recovered her customary cheerfulness. Perhaps Dr. Howell's remedies were efficacious; but
certainly Tedo seemed better. He played longer without weariness, ceased to whine fretfully if his mother left him, and took
his food more readily, and Lorraine, who felt that she had lived
through some hideous nightmare, could not make enough of her
darling. She parted from him even for an hour or two with
reluctance to fulfil her social duties; but she was inwardly
restless if anything detained her. The new donkey, Jenny, was a
great treasure, and Eric Vincent, wandering through the Oaklands
pine-woods with his little brother, often came upon the cavalcade—
Muriel Trevor with Tedo in the smart little donkey-cart, and
Lorraine walking beside them. Tedo would be shaking the reins
lustily, and shouting into Jenny's ears after his usual fashion.
'Give boy the vhip, mammie,' he would cry. 'Jenny's naughty ;
boy must vhip hard.' But Lorraine would only shake her head.
She and Jenny understood each other perfectly. Boy's 'vhips'
made no impression on Jenny's thick coat. She only shook her
long ears, and wondered placidly what curious insects were
buzzing about her. Tweedledee always made a third in the cart.
He would sit panting with his tongue out in a state of immense
excitement. The little boys were always delighted when they
came upon their friends. Since that first wonderful afternoon at
the Farm, when they had ridden on old Dobbin, and fed the
pigeons, and played hide-and-seek round the hay-stacks, they had

been frequent visitors to Brae Farm. Ellison, with her usual good nature, often invited them. Sometimes Nora and Effie would come too, and then Lorraine would give herself up to their amusement. She soon grew very fond of all the children ; but Effie remained her chief favourite ; probably because Tedo had taken such a fancy to her. ' Boy's ittle dirl,' as he called her ; but she was a sweet child, with droll, solemn little ways and speeches, and her big brother doted on her.

There was only one opinion in Highlands as to the merits of the new *locum tenens*. Tom Brattle embodied this when he said to his brother Sam after the evening service :

' I reckon the new minister is a grand success. I like that sort of solid, plain sermon—it makes a meal for a man ; and yet he is a youngish chap too.'

' Yes ; he has real grit in him,' was Sam's response to this. ' In the ministry, education has more to do with it than age. That description about Boaz's harvest-field was a fetching bit, and I could see Miss Lee was pleased with it. Mr. Vincent is clever ; but he is none too clever to talk down to the level of plain people, and that is what I like.'

Old Mrs. Langton, who seldom got to church, expressed herself much pleased with Mr. Vincent's visit.

' He is very young, my dear, to have the sole charge,' she said to Ellison, ' and I could not help telling him so. " You will excuse an old woman's plain speaking, Mr. Vincent," I said ; " but you are young to have such responsibility on your shoulders." But he answered me in such a nice, earnest way, " You cannot feel that more than I do myself, Mrs. Langton,"·he said ; " but I hope you will let me try to help you as much as I can. I see you are an invalid. I learnt a great deal from my own dear mother. She suffered for a long time before she was taken," and then he told me about her in such a simple, touching way, that I fairly cried to hear him ; but it did me good too, and I daresay he knew it would. Ah, he is young ; but he has had plenty of troubles to steady him, and I don't doubt that he will be a blessing to Highlands.'

Perhaps the Mordaunts were the only people who owned themselves somewhat disappointed in Mr. Vincent. He was so reserved, so stand-offish, the girls said, so different from other young curates that they knew. Why, Mr. Cartwright, the High Church curate from Dorchester, and Mr. Farren from Bramfield, who was Evangelical, and preached such rousing sermons that he thrilled his hearers, would come over at any time to play tennis and make themselves agreeable. Mr. Cartwright especially was a constant visitor to the Homestead ; but it was so difficult to get **Mr.**

Vincent; he was always engaged or busy, and yet he played tennis splendidly.

From the first, Mr. Vincent seemed inclined to give them a wide berth. The young ladies and their mother, with all their good looks, were not to his taste. He was too depressed and careworn, too heavily weighted by past troubles and present anxieties, to care for the gay gatherings at the Homestead, where dress and flirtations were the chief objects of interest; and he rather wondered at Mr. Cartwright's evident admiration of Constance Mordaunt. He seemed rather a good fellow, as well as a clever one, and in his eyes such infatuation seemed utterly grievous.

Colonel Trevor and Mr. Vincent had at once struck up an intimacy; and there was certainly no excuse when an invitation to dine at Brae House came to the cottage.

Mr. Vincent liked all the Trevors. He and Muriel soon got mutually interested in each other; but the hours that he spent at Brae Farm, when he fetched Nora or the boys, were more congenial to him than any others.

The society of two such women as Miss Lee and her cousin Mrs. Herbert was a great source of pleasure to him. They had been his first friends in Highlands, and he never forgot their kindness on that first evening. Colonel Trevor, who was used to a monopoly of Ellison's society, professed to be jealous when he heard of his frequent visits to Brae Farm.

'I cannot have Vincent poaching on my manors,' he said once, half seriously and half in fun. 'He has been here twice this week already. Is it you or Mrs. Herbert who encourages him?'

'How ridiculous you are, Gavin,' returned Ellison placidly. 'Why should not Lorraine and I encourage him, as you call it, when we both like him so much? I asked him to tea this afternoon, because Muriel was coming, and we wanted to talk to him about Nora.'

'About Nora?'—in an inquiring tone.

'Yes; we are so troubled about her. She is nearly thirteen, and her education has been so neglected. And yet how could it be helped?—their poor mother was a sad invalid for months before her death, and Nora had to wait on her; Mr. Vincent told us so, and of course it is not his fault. Do you know, Gavin, he teaches the little boys entirely, that is why he has so little time for tennis. When Amy Mordaunt was here the other day I could not help mentioning this, for they seem so put out with Mr. Vincent. But Amy was so absurd; she only tossed her head, and said in a huffy tone that it was odd how Mr. Vincent could always find time to call at Brae Farm.'

'There, you see, you are creating ill-will in the bosoms of the Highlands young ladies,' returned Colonel Trevor in a teasing tone. 'I am quite of Miss Amy's opinion. Mr. Vincent comes here far too often.'

'I cannot think what has come over you this afternoon,' returned Ellison, opening her eyes widely. She never could take these sort of jokes. Mr. Vincent's visits, pleasant as they were, were nothing to her; besides, she had already a suspicion that his preference was for her cousin. Lorraine's brightness and frank womanliness seemed to fascinate him. He had already told Muriel that he had never seen any one like Mrs. Herbert, and she had repeated this speech to Ellison.

'You are very perverse,' she went on; 'and there is no talking to you seriously; but I do want to tell you something that will please you. Actually Muriel of her own accord has offered to give Nora lessons. How surprised you look, Gavin. Why, you are actually frowning over my piece of good news.'

'You must let me get over my surprise first. You must recollect that I have never known Muriel make herself useful to any one before.'

'Gavin, how can you be so hard on poor Muriel. I am sure she is ever so much nicer than she used to be, and Lorraine is so fond of her. She is a different creature when she comes to us now. When I hear them laughing and talking I can scarcely believe it is the old moody Muriel.'

'Oh, she is improved, I will grant you that! She is quite civil to me now, and her health is certainly better. We have to thank Mrs. Herbert for all this; but teaching Nora Scott—well, that is a new phase!'

'It is to be a sort of Mutual Improvement Society,' returned Ellison quietly, for she knew that with all Muriel's improvement there was still a great deal of friction and soreness between the brother and sister; 'we are all to have a share. But, as I told Mr. Vincent, I hope it will not be a case of too many cooks. Muriel is to give her lessons in French and history and English literature; she is to go to her for two hours every morning. I have undertaken needlework and sums, and Lorraine is to teach her music. She will come to us for an hour or two, two or three afternoons a week, and bring Effie to play with Tedo. There is real, practical benevolence, Gavin. I hope you approve of it?'

'I approve of everything you do,' he said affectionately; 'you are the best woman I know. Wasn't Vincent properly grateful for all this?'

'I think he was a little bit upset—he did not say much at first, until the others had left the room, and then he tried to thank me. Oh yes, he is very grateful ; he said he was thinking of engaging Miss Spenser to give Nora a few lessons, for he really had no time to read with her himself ; with two sermons a week, and teaching the boys, and the schools, and the institute, and visiting, his time was fully occupied ; but I was glad to hear him say that Mrs. Drake made them very comfortable, and that, as the boys and Effie fairly lived on the common this lovely weather, their close quarters did not so much matter.'

'He really bears it very well,' returned Colonel Trevor. 'Vincent has a fine character ; very few men at his age have so much on their shoulders. We are good friends, and he speaks to me pretty plainly ; he says sometimes that it is a relief to talk over his worries with some one. He was dining with us last night, and we had a regular palaver in the smoking-room. Do you know, he has no private income ; and he and those children live upon what Mr. Yolland gives him.'

'But there is some wealthy aunt, is there not, Gavin ?'

'Oh, he was telling me all about that ; and, as it is no secret, there can be no harm in me repeating it. I did not know that you had heard of her. Her name is Bretherton—she was his mother's sister, but at least ten years older. A rich uncle had taken a fancy to her when she was a girl, and had left her a lot of money. She lives in a beautiful place in Wales. She is rather eccentric, and has an uncertain temper, and some of her ways were so odd that people said she had a bee in her bonnet ; but Vincent told me her eccentricity had arisen from a great shock when she was about five-and-twenty. She was very happily engaged, and the wedding-day was fixed ; but her lover's family had kept from her the knowledge that he had heart disease. It was thought that he was not aware himself how precarious his life was. One day as they were talking together, he suddenly put his hand to his chest and fell dead at her feet. She had brain fever after that, and had to go abroad, and her temper has always been queer since.'

'Oh, poor woman, what a story !' exclaimed Ellison.

'There are lots of such stories, I fancy,' returned Colonel Trevor. 'Many a dried-up old bachelor or weazened old maid has a sensational story in the background ; we most of us keep our private skeleton under lock and key. Happy those who have no such records in their past.'

'But how has Mr. Vincent contrived to offend his aunt ?' asked Ellison, who seldom encouraged moralising.

'Well, in this way : when he was a child she was very fond of him, he used to spend weeks at Black Nest, as it is called, playing with her cats. She has a mania for Persian cats, and keeps a small army of them. She used to load him with presents, and at last she wanted to adopt him ; but nothing would induce the boy to leave his mother. He could not endure his aunt ; for, in spite of her affection for him, she was tyrannical and uncertain, and the house was not a lively home for a boy. His mother and step-father reasoned with him ; for, though neither of them wanted to part with him, they knew how greatly it would be to his advantage, for of course, Miss Bretherton would have made him her heir ; but Vincent was not to be coerced, and he spoke his mind so plainly one day to his aunt that she never forgave him, or took notice of him again. After Mr. Scott died she had allowed her sister two hundred a year ; but this had been discontinued since her death.'

'Has not Mr. Vincent written to her and told her how he is circumstanced ? '

'Yes, for the children's sake he thought it right to do so ; but Miss Bretherton had taken no notice of his letter. I am afraid it is a bad business, and that her money will be left to charities. She seems a crabbed, narrow-minded person ; but it is hard lines for Vincent. He says himself, how is he to bring up those boys properly unless he gets a living ? Ellison, if anything happens to poor Mr. Yolland, do you think we could persuade Sir John Chessington to give Vincent St. Jude's ? He would have a good house and five hundred a year.'

'You and Mr. Tarrant might try ; but very probably Sir John will want it for one of his own nephews. But please do not discuss it, Gavin ; I should be so grieved if anything happened to our dear old vicar. Highlands is not the same place without him.'

'No, indeed ; and you are right to be loyal to your old friend ; but the last account was not reassuring. Well, as usual, I find it difficult to tear myself away ; but Tyler is coming to speak to me about the new conservatory, and I positively must go.'

'Are you really going to give in to Cousin Louise's extravagance ?' exclaimed Ellison in a reproving tone. 'You are a good son, Gavin ; you indulge your mother in all her whims, but it will cost a good deal, will it not ?'

'Yes, but I can afford it,' with a good-humoured smile ; 'and flowers are her hobby. We all have our hobbies ; yours is managing and making people comfortable. Oh, here comes Mrs. Herbert with Muriel as usual in close attendance. Upon my word, she looks positively cheerful.   I feel inclined to throw up my hat and say three cheers for Mrs. Herbert ; only I am afraid Muriel's face would wear a less becoming expression.'

'Now, Gavin, you shall not tease her ; I really begin to take Muriel's part.'   And so, laughing and jesting in the sweet evening sunshine, they parted at the little gate.

CHAPTER XVII

'Who does the best his circumstance allows,
Does well, acts nobly ; angels could no more.'
YOUNG'S *Night Thoughts.*

'May I reach that purest heaven,
Be to others the cup of strength in some great agony.'
GEORGE ELIOT.

ELLISON was right in her surmise. Mr. Vincent had left Brae Farm that afternoon, feeling as though he had acquitted himself badly ; he had made a scant response to the kindly overtures that had been made to him on his young sister's behalf, and yet all the time his heart had been full of gratitude.

It is not always easy to express one's feelings, especially if they lie deep down under the surface. Only trivial light natures bubble over into instant words ; but Eric Vincent's temperament differed from these.

His affections were strong and deep, his love for his mother had been a passion ; few mothers and sons had so entirely understood each other ; from a child Eric's devotion for her had been a sort of religion. She had been a cultivated, high-minded woman, and he had inherited her strong unselfish nature. Her death had made a blank in his life ; the loss of that perfect companionship and sympathy had changed his life into a wilderness ; her influence had permeated even his work ; he had never preached a sermon without reading it first to her ; she had helped him with his poor people, and cheered him in despondent moments ; suffering and weary as she might be, she had always welcomed him with a smile. 'How tired you look, Eric ; come and sit down and tell me what you have done to-day.' That had been her usual formula ; her ailments were all kept in the background ; and when her sufferings could no longer be concealed from his anxious eyes, it was her courage, her true Christian submission, that had braced them both to meet the impending trial.

As he walked back from the Farm, through the long leafy lane, sweet with honeysuckle and briar-roses, he was thinking of her : how happy his sweet mother would have been to know he had such kind friends near him.

The thought of his heavy responsibilities had for a time troubled the peace of her dying hours—her human mother's love had domi- nated even· her strong faith ; probably physical weakness was to blame for this ; when the bodily strength fails, dark clouds will at times sweep over the soul.

'Oh, Eric, my poor boy !' she had said once, when he had relieved the nurse and taken the night-watch on himself, 'I cannot help wishing to-night that it was God's will that I might be spared a little longer. Is it very wicked, darling, to wish this ?' looking at him wistfully.

'No, mother,' he returned gently, 'for you are wishing it not for your own, but for your children's sake. Ah ! I know yóu so well,' as she pressed his hand in mute assent ; 'you are grieving and troubling in your heart about us.'

One or two tears rolled down her wan cheeks, then a sob shook her feeble frame. 'Oh, my darling, it is so hard to leave you, and you are so good and patient, but I cannot help fretting about it. Effie is such a baby, and Nora is too young to be much help to you, and then there are the boys. Eric, you must pray that my weak faith may be strengthened, that I may feel even in this that my Heavenly Father doeth well.'

Should he ever to his dying day forget the agony of that long night ? But to his honour be it said that he put aside his own bitter trouble to comfort her in her hour of weakness, and after a time, still holding his hand, she had slept while he knelt beside the bed.

'Whatever happens to us, let her end be peace,' he prayed again and again, as he watched the calm of repose stealing over her wasted features. 'All these years she has thought of us ; but for Christ's sake let this burden of care be lifted from her last hours.' And it seemed to Eric as though, in different language, he prayed this over and over again during that vigil.

When she woke there was a strange startled look in her eyes, and then she smiled at him.

'My poor boy, have you been with me all this time ; where is nurse ? You must be worn out. Let me tell you something, and then you shall go and rest. I have had such a lovely dream. I thought it was all over, and that I was in Paradise, and that your father and my dear Richard were with me'—Richard was his step-father's name. 'They were talking so happily together—but I felt a little sad, for I was thinking about you; and then all at once they moved away, and Richard said, "He has come, as I knew He would," and some one stood there in their place. It was all shadowy and indistinct like a dream, but I could see one hand with the nail-print quite plainly, and a voice said very softly, "Are not your children mine? Daughter, where is your faith? Can I not be trusted with my own?" Oh, the reproachful sweetness of that voice as it sounded in my ears! and then I woke. Have you been praying for me, darling? for the load seems gone.' But, as he stooped to kiss her, he could only answer with his tears.

His prayer had been answered, and though his mother lingered a week or two longer there was no return of that night's anguish. She spoke of her approaching death more calmly. When the end came he was alone with her, and her last word was his name lovingly uttered.

The vicar and his wife had been very good to him. They had taken the two younger children for the first week or two, and had lightened his heavy labours as much as possible. The long illness had worn his strength, and he knew himself that some change was absolutely necessary.

The removal to a fresh scene of work had been extremely beneficial to him, and he already slept better and looked a little brighter. Kind friends had gathered round him, and seemed anxious to help him. To a man of Eric Vincent's temperament feminine sympathy is peculiarly acceptable, especially if it be applied with tact and delicacy; and from the first Ellison had stretched out a kind helpful hand to the forlorn strangers; her good sense and active benevolence told her exactly how far she might go without offending the young clergyman's sensitive pride; and Lorraine had followed implicitly in her cousin's footsteps. Their womanly finesse and management were never at fault, and it was a long time before Eric discovered how much he had to thank them for the smoothness with which daily life flowed on at the cottage; he only found it out by degrees.

Nora's lessons were successfully carried out, and her three teachers vied with each other in instilling knowledge into their docile young pupil. As Effie generally accompanied her sister to Brae House or to the Farm, the boys were left in Eric's charge. He taught them or took them with him when he went to a distant parishioner. Colonel Trevor had good-naturedly brought them a cricketing set from London, and they often played cricket for hours together on the common near the cottage, while their brother sat writing his sermon at his window, and keeping watch over them.

In the evening Nora was free to relieve him a little, and he could indulge himself with a solitary stroll after his day's labour was over, or a dinner at Brae House or Price's Folly. The boys were so happy in their free country life that even Hugo was less eager to lead his little brother into mischief. An invitation to Brae Farm was always the reward for a week's good behaviour; but idleness at lessons, or any wild escapade, such as riding Brattle's grey mare, for example, bare-backed over the common, while Eddie shouted at his heels, would immediately forfeit the treat. More than once Mrs. Drake was heard to say that she could not believe sometimes that there were four children in the cottage. 'But then the young gentlemen are always doing their lessons with Mr. Vincent,' she would say, 'or playing their cricket on the common. They are seldom indoors, except for their meals; and as for little missy, she is no trouble at all. When I am washing, she will make-believe that her doll's things are dirty. "I must have a wash too, Mrs. Drake," she says, quite solemn like, "for Rose's clothes are a shocking colour"; and then she brings her duds and rinses them out and soaps them, as she sees me doing. Mrs. Herbert caught her at it one day, and how she did laugh, to be sure.'

Eric secretly marvelled when he saw the boys coming to their meals day after day with clean hands and faces, and nicely-brushed hair, instead of rushing in dishevelled and heated after their usual fashion; but the children soon enlightened him on this point.

'Miss Lee says only cads sit down to their meals with dirty hands,' observed Hugo one day. 'She says that is one way in which gentlemen are different from cads. She was quite vexed when Eddie forgot to go upstairs, and called him a little cad. You didn't like that, did you, Eddie?'

'No; I don't like cads,' returned Eddie sturdily; 'but she called you a cad one day, Hughie,' and then Hugo grew suddenly red and changed the subject. Miss Lee had said a stinging word or two that Hugo would long remember. Sarcasm is sometimes salutary, and Hugo had winced more than once under a well-deserved stricture. Fairy Order had waved her magic wand over the cottage even from Brae Farm, and even Eddie rushed away to wash his grubby little paws when he came in from play.

Another matter puzzled Eric; but he pondered over it in heavy, masculine fashion for some time before he ventured to question Nora; but one day his curiosity got the better of him.

'Nora,' he said suddenly, when the boys had raced each other upstairs as usual, and Nora was taking the tea-caddy and jam from the corner cupboard, 'I never have buttons off my things now. I suppose the ladies at the Farm have taught you to sew them on properly?'

Nora hesitated a moment. 'Well, no, Eric, Mrs. Drake always sews on your buttons, because she does them strongly ; but I am learning to darn your socks. I learnt first on Hugo's, because Miss Lee said yours were too nice and new to spoil, and that Dorcas had better do them until I had got clever ; but I really am getting on nicely with my darning now.'

Eric gazed at her with incredulous astonishment. 'Dorcas is one of the maids at Brae Farm, is she not ?'

'Yes ; and she is so nice, and works so beautifully. She is making new wristbands for your old shirts. She and Ruth are doing them between them ; perhaps I ought not to have told you' —regarding him doubtfully ; 'but Miss Lee told Mrs. Herbert that she had no other work for the girls, and that it would be a charity to employ them ; so you see it is no trouble.'

'And the boys' things ?' in a quick, hard voice almost as though he were displeased ; but Nora knew her brother better. Eric always spoke in that voice if he were feeling anything strongly.

'Oh, we do the boys' things between us !' she replied, with an important air. 'Very often Mrs. Herbert does them ; but some-times Miss Lee helps. You see it is in this way, Eric : I have to take the boys' things to Brae Farm that Miss Lee may teach me how to mend them ; but if they are very bad—that rent in Hugo's sailor shirt, for example—Mrs. Herbert always does them ; because she says Mrs. Drake cannot possibly have time for the boys' clothes, and she rather enjoys mending. Of course it is very good-natured of her—even Miss Lee says so sometimes ; but she will have it that she likes it.'

Eric was silent. The problem was solved with a vengeance ; so the poor boys and he himself owed their freedom from rags and dis-comfort to those dear women at Brae Farm. Miss Lee had set her maids to work secretly on his behalf, and Mrs. Herbert, with gentle motherliness, kept the little lads tidy ; and it was all done under the plausible pretence of teaching Nora to work ; and Nora herself took it all as a matter of course. They were very good to her ; but then the ladies were good to every one. It was their nature to be kind—that was how Nora put it. With a child's unconscious selfishness, she accepted all their kindness, and returned it by loving them with all her warm little heart.

Eric knew well how many good things came to them from the

Farm—chickens and eggs and delicious cream and preserves; but when he thanked Miss Lee a little gravely and formally for her gifts, she always smiled and said they were for the children. 'Mrs. Herbert and I always spoil children,' she said, in this way sheltering herself and him from any awkwardness. 'One can give the children things and look after them,' she remarked to Lorraine afterwards, 'when one could not well offer them to Mr. Vincent'; and Lorraine agreed to this.

Eric was absent and thoughtful all tea-time, until the children interrupted an animated argument among themselves to appeal to him.

'I guess Eric will know,' observed Hugo; 'he knows most things, and I daresay he has made up his mind by this time. Eric, we want you to tell us which of the ladies do you like best?'

'Of whom are you talking, old fellow?' asked his brother, flushing a little at this sudden question; but he knew quite well to whom the boy was alluding.

'Why, to our ladies to be sure,' and Hugo opened his eyes wider. 'We were not speaking of Miss Trevor, though she is awfully nice too. I never knew so many nice people as there are in Highlands; they are downright splendid—aren't they, Eddie?'

'Yes, they are splendidly nice,' agreed Eddie, who never ventured to dissent from Hugo.

'I think them nice too,' chimed in Effie, with a caressing touch of her brother's coat-sleeve.

'Well, then, you are all agreed,' returned Eric quietly, lifting Effie on to his knee.

'Yes; but the boys were saying——' began Nora. 'Tell Eric what you were saying, Hugo.'

'Well, I was saying it is so funny that we all like Mrs. Herbert the best, when she never gives us anything, and Miss Lee is so awfully good to us, don't you know? She lets us ride Dobbin and Jenny, and takes us into the dairy and gives us slices of bread and cream—such thick cream; and then she so often gives us cakes and fruit—doesn't she, Eddie?'

'Yes; heaps of things.'

'Yes; and she is going to ask Joe Brand to put up a new swing in the orchard—think of that, Eric; and she has promised me a white rabbit with pink eyes for my very next birthday. Miss Lee says if Mrs. Drake does not want rabbits in her yard, that Daniel shall make a hutch for it in the kitchen garden, and then I should often see it. She thinks that will be the best plan.'

'Oh, and, Eric, Miss Lee has promised me a little guinea-pig too!' piped Eddie; 'but my birthday is not till September.'

'It strikes me, young gentlemen, that you are making yourselves pretty much at home at Brae Farm,' remarked their brother. 'Why should Miss Lee have the trouble of keeping rabbits and guinea-pigs for your amusement?'

'Oh, she loves them, and so does Mrs. Herbert; they can't have too many animals, that is what they often say.'

'And yet, in spite of all this you are so ungrateful that you like Mrs. Herbert best.'

'We can't help it, can we, Eddie?' returned Hugo, a little mystified at Eric's grave tone. 'We didn't mean to, of course, and we are dreadfully fond of Miss Lee; but then Mrs. Herbert is so awfully jolly; you can't think how jolly she is when she is alone with us.'

'Yes, and she tells us such jolly stories,' observed the faithful Eddie, who always used his brother's expressions, and seldom originated a sentiment of his own, 'fairy stories, you know, about giants.'

'And she has got such a dear face,' echoed Effie, leaning comfortably against Eric's shoulder; and some involuntary feeling made him stroke the golden head with greater tenderness.

'Yes, it is odd,' sighed Nora, regarding the tea-pot reflectively, 'the boys are always talking in this way; but do you know, Eric, I feel just the same about Mrs. Herbert. Somehow, she is so nice and comfortable, that I am always happier when she is in the room. Miss Lee is as kind as possible, and Miss Trevor too; but somehow we all save up things to tell Mrs. Herbert—don't we, Hugo? because she always understands us.'

'I don't think I care for Miss Trevor much,' returned Hugo, flinging his hair out of his eyes—one thick lock that Lorraine specially admired was always in his way. 'She is too clever for me. Why, she reads Greek and Hebrew, Eric told us so the other day; didn't you, Eric? She is a regular Blue-Stocking.'

'My dear lad, what an old-fashioned term. Do you know, Hughie, boy, Miss Trevor has actually offered to read Latin with you when I am too busy; what do you say to that?'—but Hugo only made a face of disgust, and returned pettishly that he preferred his brother's teaching.

'You are an ungrateful monkey,' replied Eric, taking him by the ear. 'There! if you have finished tea, you may as well run out. Nora, I am going to walk into Dorchester. Nicholson will not be closed, and I want some sermon paper. Get the boys to bed in good time; I shall be home by supper. Good-night, ladybird '—his pet name for Effie.

'I wish you would let us go with you, Eric; we would not

bother you,' pleaded Hugo ; but Eric shook his head.   His day's labours were over ; those evening hours were the most peaceful of the twenty-four ; he could enjoy his own company, and his own melancholy thoughts.   As he strode down the village past the *Waggon and Horses*, and down the road bordered by the Redlands Woods, he could have said with the renowned Jaques, 'It is a melancholy of mine own, compounded of many simples, extracted from many objects, and indeed, the sundry contemplation of my travels, in which my often rumination wraps me in a most humorous sadness,' but often, alas, there was no humour in the sadness.

With all his courage and unselfishness, Eric Vincent at times felt as though life were too hard for endurance ; his circumstances were abnormal, and all his love for his young brothers and sisters could not prevent his feeling them heavy responsibilities.   The narrow dimensions of the cottage fretted him ; the boys' voices jarred on his nerves, in spite of Brae influence, and Miss Lee's hints.   Nora was too young to manage, and he was far too inexperienced to direct her.   His mother had taken all domestic burdens on herself, and as far as Eric knew, everything had gone smoothly.   It worried him when Nora consulted him about the dinner, and the weekly bills were always prodigal of vexation. Eric had to appeal to Mrs. Drake at last ; and after that things went better.

'He is a dear young gentleman,' observed the good woman to Ellison one day, 'and what's more, he is a godly minister ; but he knows no more than a babe what things ought to cost, and missie is as bad.   "Do you think we can afford it, Mrs. Drake ?" she will say to me, half crying.   But there ! I do my best to help them. The boys have fine appetites, to be sure, but, as I tell Mr. Vincent, it is better to pay for bread and butter than send for the doctor ; but he do sigh so over the bills.'

'I suppose they have their butter from Brattle's,' returned Ellison.   'Brattle keeps good butter, but it is dear.   Why not send to the Farm for it as well as for the milk and eggs ?' and then a glance of great significance passed between them.

'We get butter now from the Farm ; it is a sight cheaper, Mr. Vincent,' remarked Mrs. Drake in an easy tone, as she cleared breakfast a few days later.   'It is sweet, you may depend upon it, for Eunice is a rare butter-maker, and knows her work, and you will find the difference in the bills,' which Eric certainly did. With four children butter was an important item, for the little Scots liked their butter thick and plenty of it ; but it may be doubted whether the mistress of Brae Farm made much profit.

Eric was thinking of the children's talk as he walked rapidly down the quiet road. He had listened to them and held his peace; but in his heart he knew he agreed with them. He admired Miss Lee immensely. Her calm stateliness and even temper had made an impression on him from the first, and he was strongly interested in Miss Trevor, partly on account of his growing friendship for her brother, and partly because of her unique personality. A community of tastes and pursuits created sympathy between them. He had never met any girl before who could enter into his scholarly interests and pursuits. He did not think her handsome—no one at first thought Muriel handsome; but there was something unusual about her face and style; and then she did not look happy. This roused his sympathy afresh, and before long Muriel felt as though she had a second friend.

But even at this early stage of their acquaintance there could be no denying that the young widow attracted Eric. It was quite true, as he had said to Muriel, when she was discoursing on her friend's virtues, that he had never met any one like Mrs. Herbert. In a faint, far-off way she reminded him of his mother; but Mrs. Scott, even in her son's partial eyes, lacked Mrs. Herbert's bright, sunshiny disposition. He thought, with a smile, of Nora's artless description, and especially of her words, 'We all save up things to tell Mrs. Herbert.' Somehow he had lately found himself doing the same.

Once he had apologised for it. 'Here I am bothering you again with my worries,' he had said, half laughing; 'but you are so sympathetic that we all come to you for comfort.'

He had spoken in a light, jesting tone; but to his surprise the tears came to her eyes.

'How kind of you to say that, Mr. Vincent,' she said, a little tremulously. 'That is how I want people to feel. It is such a privilege, such a wonderfully blessed privilege, to help others; don't you think so?' And of course he had agreed with her.

'They have found it out; children always do,' he said to himself, as Dorchester came in sight. 'Some natures are magnetic—they seem to give out and attract sympathy in a marvellous way. It is a gift; but Mrs. Herbert has it. Not a child in Highlands can resist her'; and then he checked a sigh and walked on.

CHAPTER XVIII

THE REDLANDS WOODS

'Behold the child, by nature's kindly law,
Pleased with a rattle, tickled with a straw ;
Some livelier plaything gives his youth delight,
A little louder, but as empty quite ;
Scarfs, garters, gold, amuse his riper stage,
And beads and prayer-books are the toys of age ;
Pleased with this bauble still, as that before,
Till tired he sleeps, and life's poor play is o'er.'

POPE'S *Essay on Man.*

HUGO'S birthday was in the following week, and, unknown to him, Joe Brand and Daniel were busily engaged in leisure hours in making a new hutch for the splendid white rabbit that Sam Brattle had procured for his mistress.

With her customary good-nature, Ellison had ordered Mrs. Tucker to make a large cake, with 'Hugo' in pink sugar on the top, and had it sent to the cottage.

Effie, who was down first, rushed up to her brother's door, in great excitement : 'Oh, do get up, Hughie !' she exclaimed ; 'you are eight years old, and that is too old to lie in bed ; and Miss Lee has sent you a real wedding-cake all covered with lovely white sugar.'

This was such startling news that no boy could be expected to dress himself under such circumstances, and the next moment two little white figures with bare, pink legs were revolving round the breakfast table in wild ecstasy, much to the astonishment of a passing rustic. Such a cake had never entered their imagination.

'Isn't it lovely, Eddie ! Don't you wish it were your birthday too ? But you shall have a big slice.'

'My birthday will be in September,' returned Eddie, with undoubting faith that equal good luck would attend him ; and then Mrs. Drake came in and scolded them soundly.

'Now you ought to know better, Master Hugo,' she said sharply, 'running about with naked feet, and all those doors open, and Master Edmund so delicate'; but Hugo only laughed, and threw back his wild lock of hair. 'And for all the world they looked like two cherubs,' as she told her husband afterwards, 'in their white night-shirts—and nothing else on'—which was rather a baffling description of cherubic attire.

It was hardly to be wondered at if the boys were slightly demoralised that morning, for never had any previous birthday, not even Eric's, known such a programme. First, they were to go up to Brae Farm and see the rabbit, and be regaled with bread and cream in the dairy; then there was to be a picnic, a real picnic, in the Redlands Woods. Miss Lee had planned the whole thing, though she was not to be of the party, as she had promised to go up to town with Mrs. Trevor. Mrs. Herbert was to take command of the expedition, and Miss Trevor was to be her lieutenant. The donkey-cart was to be packed with hampers of good things, and Dorcas was coming to help. They were to have dinner and tea in the woods, and boil a real kettle, and Eric had promised to join them in the afternoon. Colonel Trevor would have come too, but he had to go to his club, so they were obliged to do without him; but Daniel was to play cricket with them in the Redlands Meadow, for the little boys were devoted to Daniel, and Nora had promised to play too.

Never was there such a picnic—the whole menagerie was to accompany them. Hugo could not be induced to leave Humpty Dumpty, as the white rabbit was called, behind him; so it was to travel in a basket, lined with lettuce and cabbage leaves, for fear it should faint by the way. Where Mrs. Herbert went Tweedledee went too, and, in his mistress's absence, Bairn condescended to make one of the party. To every one's amusement, Muriel brought Admiral Byng, and he behaved much as Fanny Kemble's cat did, when she relates how he accompanied the family in their walks, and how, when the dogs in their gambols rolled him over, he swore at them, and, picking himself up, resumed his trot. Admiral Byng was too prudent to get into the dogs' way; he and Bairn respected each other, and were mutually stiff and tolerant; but for Tweedledee the Admiral had a vast contempt, and when the puppy approached too near, his ominous swearing filled Tweedledee with terror.

If Tedo could have had his way the doves would have come too: it was pretty to see the little fellow, with his hands stretched out, talking to them in a coaxing tone—his dear coo-coo's, as he called them; but they only leered at him out of their yellow, beady eyes, and bowed and cooed, and then spread their grey wings and fled to the granary, and Tedo moved sadly away.

Tedo had refused to ride in the cart unless his little love Effie sat beside him ; but, as Hugo wanted to drive, there was a little argument ; it ended by Lorraine carrying Tedo, and the boys driving off in triumph.

'It is Hugo's birthday, darling,' she said, as not unnaturally Tedo fretted at this usurpation of his beloved Jenny. 'We must make Hugo happy on his birthday. Look, Effie is walking beside us as good as gold, and she wanted to ride too ; but we must all give way to Hugo to-day.'

'It won't be his birthday to-morrow, Tedo,' observed Effie with solemn wisdom.

'Boy 's glad of that,' was Tedo's answer. 'Boy hates buffdays' ; but he soon forgot to be cross as he watched Admiral Byng trotting with uplifted tail after his mistress.

It was a hot July day, and Lorraine, who was weary with carrying her boy, felt with delight the refreshing shade of the pine-woods, the soft green light rested her eyes ; she put Tedo down, and he walked on contentedly, holding Effie's hand. Nora was a little ahead of them with Muriel ; the donkey-cart and Dorcas and Daniel had long vanished out of sight. Presently Admiral Byng got tired, and Muriel had to carry him, and Nora followed suit with Tweedledee ; then Tedo flagged, and Effie thought there was a funny-bone in her leg ; so the whole party were unfeignedly glad when they came to the trysting-place, and found Dorcas and Daniel unpacking the hampers, and the little boys feeding Jenny with some carrots that they had begged from Joe Brand.

It was a lovely spot, a small circular clearing in the very heart of the wood, and was known to the Brae people by the name of the Meeting-Place ; for of old picnics had always been held there. It was not very far from the keeper's lodge, and a small pile of brushwood was generally there for the use of the picnickers ; for, by the permission of the lord of the manor, good-natured Sir John Chessington, the gentry of Highlands had the right of lighting fires in the clearings to boil their kettle, and to wander about at their will. Redlands Hall lay in the meadow below, adjoining the hamlet of Redlands ; tne wood clothed the steep descent, and except at certain points the house was invisible.

At the Meeting-Place there was a break in the dense foliage which afforded a charming peep of the long sunshiny meadow, with the great red house standing against its background of dark woods. It was a view that Lorraine especially loved, and she always would have it that it reminded her of the Palace Beautiful ; she loved to sit there, with Tedo playing with the fir-cones at her feet, breathing the sweet spicy incense of the pines, and revelling in the dark solemn vistas, and soft indefinable green light that permeated the long aisles.

In their stillness and silence the Redlands Woods often seemed to her like an enchanted forest; and she was not alone in this feeling, for Muriel shared it; she loved nothing better than a solitary stroll through the pine-woods.

Luncheon was the first business of the day, and as soon as the hampers were unpacked, the little party gathered round the table-cloth, which Effie and Hugo had tastefully embellished with a border of fir-cones.

It was a curious dinner-party, for the animals were amongst the guests. Admiral Byng was soon discussing the leg of a chicken with the leisurely dignity of a well-behaved cat; Bairn was also on his best behaviour; but Tweedledee, who was young and foolish, uttered short barks of excitement at every fresh course, and whined dolefully when he was not helped first. Even Jenny left off browsing on the young bracken to thrust her rough nose over Hugo's shoulder in a search for more succulent food. Humpty Dumpty was revelling on all kinds of delicious salads in his basket; and the whole party were enjoying themselves so much that Hugo was obliged at last to roll on the ground out of sheer ecstasy, and it was at once incumbent on Eddie to roll over him.

'Oh, do sit up, boys,' exclaimed Lorraine, in pretended alarm, 'or Tedo will be doing the same, he is getting such a mimic!' But she was too late. The little fellow, excited by so many novelties, had already trotted after them, and flung himself down on the interlaced legs and arms beneath him.

'Hold tight, Tedo!' exclaimed Hugo, in a smothered voice, 'and we will roll down into the meadow.' But this was promptly checked by Lorraine.

'Take them off to play cricket, Daniel,' she said, snatching up her boy. 'Nora, you had better leave Effie with us. She and Tedo will play quietly together when those noisy boys are gone.'

Hugo was irrepressible. 'Let's pretend we are Indians on the war-trail, and on the look-out for scalps!' he exclaimed; and he uttered a wild yell as a war-cry, and flew down the wood. Eddie scrambled after him, shrieking with delight, and Daniel followed with the wickets and bats.

'Now we shall have peace,' observed Lorraine; 'and Dorcas can clear the dinner things and light the fire for tea. What a pickle Hugo is. I am afraid one of these days he will lead Eddie into mischief. Eddie never seems to have a will of his own; he is Hugo's shadow.'

'I am afraid I am not fond of boys,' returned Muriel in a fatigued voice. 'Hugo's voice has made my head ache. Girls suit me better—they are quieter and not always in perpetual motion. I am getting very fond of Nora. There is something very sweet in her disposition. She is not specially clever ; but I find her so tractable and intelligent.'

'So do I ; and Ellison says the same. We all appreciate Nora ; but I confess that I have a weakness for Hugo. He is a thorough little scamp, and I am afraid he will always be in hot water with the authorities ; but he is affectionate and generous. And then he is so good to Tedo.'

'Ah, he has found the way to your heart, then ! ' returned Muriel. 'But who could help being good to Tedo ? There are exceptions to every rule, and though he is a boy he is a darling.'

Lorraine smiled and looked at her boy. He and Effie were happily engaged in constructing a fir-cone mountain. The shouts of the children in the meadow below were still audible, but they were fast dying away. Dorcas had carried off the plates to the keeper's cottage. She would come back presently with them nicely washed, and her kettle full of sweet spring water. 'If your head aches, why do you not have a nap ? I shall be quite happy without talking.' But Muriel negatived this at once.

'Oh no, it is getting better already, and I would much rather talk to you. Somehow, though we are always together, we do not often have one of our old talks. The children are always interrupting us ; besides, you have become such a busy person.'

'My time is pretty well occupied, certainly,' replied Lorraine cheerfully. 'The poultry-yard really gives me a good deal to do, and then I have Nora's music and plenty of plain sewing, and there are other ways in which I help Ellison. You have no idea how much she does for the poor people of Bramfield. She very often asks me to go to this person, or that, with a basket of good things, and then Tedo and Jenny and I start off. I call myself her almoner ; but really the poor people are so nice to me. They often ask me to come again, though I tell them I am nearly as poor as they. I have so little to give them ; but they do not seem to mind that.'

'I think the poor people like you best, Mrs. Herbert. Ellison is very much liked and respected ; but her neighbours are just a little bit in awe of her. She tells them of their faults rather plainly.'

'And she is right in doing so'—rather warmly, for Lorraine always took up cudgels on her cousin's behalf. In her eyes Ellison was as near perfection as frail human nature allowed her to be. She often made Muriel smile by telling her quite seriously that even Ellison's faults were grand. 'I mean,' she explained, feeling her remark was somewhat Irish, 'that even her faults are not little and mean as most people's are. Certainly she is right,' she went on. 'Ellison has more moral courage than I have. I am detestably selfish, if you only knew it. I do so love saying pleasant things to people, and putting "wherret" in the background. Do you know that word, Muriel? I think it so delightfully descriptive. At Bramfield they tell you that they are in a pother or wherret, and that they are just heckled with the plague of it. Well, I am a foe to all "wherret."'

'I do not believe you, Mrs. Herbert. You have plenty of moral courage. I remember the time when you spoke pretty plainly to me.'

'Yes, and I have often wondered since at your forbearance; but, dear'—laying her hand gently on Muriel's—'I was so troubled about you, that I could not help speaking.'

'I am thankful you did,' was the low reply. 'Your words have come true, Mrs. Herbert. I certainly feel a different creature, and no longer an inanimate, useless log; but I have new interest in life now,' and Muriel's eyes were dark with feeling.

'I hope you will have many new interests,' returned Lorraine in a pointed tone; but Muriel's thoughts had travelled suddenly into a new groove.

'If only Gavin were different, and not persist in misunderstanding me,' she sighed; 'but I begin to lose heart. I am always trying to get on with him, but he never sees it; and yet he is so nice with every one else.'

'Yes, indeed; he is always so pleasant, no one can help liking Colonel Trevor, and he is so good to your mother!' Lorraine paused; this subject always puzzled her. Muriel in her confidential moments would complain bitterly of her brother's want of affection; but Lorraine could never see any outward coldness in his manner. She thought Muriel was morbid on this subject, and she was certainly wanting in tact and forbearance.

'We never do agree on any subject, and it is so tiresome,' continued Muriel. When she spoke of her brother her manner always changed and grew hard. 'He has no sympathy with my pursuits, and he is always lecturing me because I do not care for tennis, or riding, or dancing, like other girls.'

'He is so active himself, that he thinks exercise necessary for every one. Colonel Trevor is right, Muriel, it is a pity that you do not care for riding.'

'Riding makes my back ache, I have told you that before, Mrs. Herbert,' a little resentfully; 'and I am not strong enough for tennis. Gavin has no right to pronounce an opinion so authoritatively on my pursuits; if he would ask me to walk with him I should be willing to do so, but he has no desire for my companionship.'

A sudden light dawned on Lorraine. She had had a suspicion before that a great deal of Muriel's irritability and contrariety was due to jealousy; probably she felt her place in her brother's affection was usurped by Ellison.

With a sudden impulse she charged Muriel with this, and to her surprise, instead of denying it, Muriel broke into a perfect passion of tears; and then Lorraine knew that she had put her finger on the wound.

A few soothing words and a caress or two soon calmed Muriel's agitation.

'How did you find out?' she said, brushing away the tears. 'I never meant to tell you that; but it has been so hard to bear all these years. I am his only sister, since Maud and Florence died, and yet I am nothing to him.' And then, little by little, by dint of judicious coaxing and questioning, it all came out.

From her childhood Gavin had been her idol; the little sensitive child had worshipped from afar the big strong soldier brother; but, with her excessive shyness, not even her mother had guessed this.

When he went to India, his letters were eagerly looked for and perused; and when he married, her imagination centred on her unknown sister-in-law. Helen Trevor's lovely face and sweet womanly letters had won her from the first. Her death had been an awful shock, and when Gavin returned to England, wrecked in health and happiness, a worn-out, weary invalid, her one thought, her one longing had been to devote herself to him.

If, as Eric Vincent said, 'some natures are magnetic,' others seem unhappily the reverse; a shy gaucherie will often conceal a heart beating with the tenderest affection, and a total lack of expression will give a seeming coldness to the manner. Unhappily, Gavin misunderstood his young sister from the first; her shy, timid manner repelled him; he thought her cold and wanting in natural affection, because her very excess of emotion kept her silent.

He was not in a fit state to judge correctly, and Muriel's complex individuality was not easy to read; even her mother misunderstood her, and reproached her for her want of attention to poor Gavin. Muriel never defended herself, but this reproach nearly broke her heart ; she loved Gavin so dearly that she would have died for his sake, if, by doing so, she could have brought back Helen to life ; she had counted the days, and had lain awake many nights before his return, and yet she was accused of want of affection.

Muriel's faulty temper always made her harder under rebuke ; she was too proud to explain or set herself right with either of them, and so from day to day the little rift widened, and the breach grew larger.

From the first Ellison's tact and gentleness had commended her to Gavin ; disappointed in his own sister, he instinctively turned to Ellison for comfort ; and Muriel, set aside and voted peculiar, felt that she had no share in her brother's affections ; and the bitterness of discontent leavened her daily life. '

'Oh, I was so miserable until you came,' finished Muriel ; 'no one needed me—not even mother—and sometimes I was too tired and wretched to take pleasure in my beloved books. Life was a regular Sahara, and I could not find an oasis.'

'Your low spirits were a great deal owing to bad health ; you were preying upon yourself. Muriel, dear, thank you for telling me all this ; that is indeed treating me like a friend. I will not say anything more, for I see Mr. Vincent coming. I will go and meet him, and that will give you time to recover yourself' ; and Lorraine moved away.

CHAPTER XIX

COLONEL TREVOR RESOLVES TO DO IT

'How use doth breed a habit in a man!'
Two Gentlemen of Verona.

'Those friends thou hast, and their adoption tried,
Grapple them to thy soul with hoops of steel.'
Hamlet.

COLONEL TREVOR had accompanied his mother and Ellison to town.

He had an appointment to lunch with an old Indian friend at his club in St. James's Street, then he intended going on to the Army and Navy Stores in Victoria Street to make some purchases, and would meet the ladies at the station in good time, to take the last train back to Bramfield.

Mrs. Trevor and Ellison had some shopping to do at Marshall & Snelgrove's. Muriel, who was very lazy on such matters, had given her mother several commissions to execute for her; after luncheon together in Vere Street they were to part company for an hour or two. Some old friends of Ellison's, living in Portman Square, had begged her to spend the afternoon with them.

The Mervyns were very intimate friends. She had known them from childhood, and was warmly attached to them. No year ever passed without their spending a few weeks at Brae Farm, and they often invited her to share with them some delightful trip that they had planned. The previous year she had gone with them to Scotland, and some hints had been dropped lately of their going to Switzerland in August. Ellison had never been abroad with them, and she was a little excited at the prospect of an invitation. She had not seen her friends for a good many months now Miss Mervyn had been ailing, and had not paid her usual summer visit to Highlands.

She was a middle-aged woman, and delicate health and increasing deafness had determined her to eschew matrimony. Her brother was an elderly bachelor, and as they were devoted to each other, and had plenty of means, the quiet household in Portman Square was a very happy one. Ellison was much appreciated by both brother and sister, and she was always a welcome guest.

Mrs. Trevor once told her son in rather a significant tone that she thought Ellison ought to keep up such good friends.

'They are simply devoted to her, and as neither of them have married, there are no nephews or nieces to inherit Mr. Mervyn's property. He gives away a great deal in charity, and Ellison is sure he will leave most of his money to the Eye and Ear Hospital, as he always interests himself so much in it ; but in my private opinion a good slice will come to Ellison.'

'She will not need it. Ellison is not mercenary, and she has enough now for a single woman.' Colonel Trevor spoke indifferently. He always hated this sort of remark. It was Mr. Mervyn's own affair how he chose to leave his money. His father had made it in business, and had died before he had reaped any enjoyment from his hard-earned wealth.

While Ellison had tea with her friends, Mrs. Trevor was to keep an appointment she had made with a physician, an old friend of her husband's.

She had felt lately certain symptoms that gave her uneasiness. She had mentioned this casually to Ellison one day.

'Why do you not go up to Harley Street and talk to Dr. M'Callum?' Ellison had said very sensibly. 'He is a friend of yours ; it will not be like going to a stranger. It may be only a little thing that can be set right at once. In my opinion, prevention is always better than cure.'

'I hate speaking to a doctor about myself,' sighed Mrs. Trevor. 'Thank heaven, my health has been so good that I have seldom had occasion to do so ; but perhaps I had better take your advice, Ellison. Say nothing to Gavin or Muriel about it. I will go to Dr. M'Callum the first time I go to town.' And so the appointment had been made. And when Ellison had jumped into her hansom and desired the man to drive her to 11 Portman Square, Mrs. Trevor walked slowly towards Harley Street for her interview with Dr. M'Callum. If Ellison had guessed how nervous she felt, she would have offered to keep her company ; but Mrs. Trevor had made light of the whole matter. Why should she do otherwise? It was only a passing ailment. It proved how little she had had to bear, that a little pain and uneasiness should give her so much misery.

Dr. M'Callum was sure to do her good. He would probably
laugh at her for coming to him, and then she would laugh too :
but notwithstanding all these cheering prognostications, Mrs. Trevor
felt a little breathless, as though she had walked too fast, when she
entered the doctor's consulting-room. Most people under similar
circumstances know this feeling.

Colonel Trevor was the first to reach the station. He had paced
up and down for full ten minutes before he saw his mother and
Ellison hurrying down the platform. They had only just time to
seat themselves in an empty compartment before the bell rang.

'You timed that rather too neatly,' observed Gavin. 'If the
train had not been a minute late you would have lost it.'

'Oh no ; we were only talking a moment too long in the
waiting-room,' replied Ellison coolly. 'Our hansoms drove up
together, just as you were going into the station. What lots of
parcels you have, Gavin. Are there any books for Muriel among
them, I wonder ?'

'Only one ; the others are for my own use. I have had a
pleasant day. The old General was in great force, and told yarns
by the score. He is a clever old boy. How did you find the
Mervyns ? Mother, you look tired. You have been doing too
much. Where did you get your tea ?'

'You must hear my news first,' interrupted Ellison, for that
latter question was embarrassing, and must be avoided. Mrs. Trevor
had nearly made her lose the train by delaying her to give an
account of her interview with the doctor.

'Dr. M'Callum was so nice, Ellison,' she had said, with her
usual cheerfulness. 'He did not laugh at me as I expected, and
he went into things very thoroughly. But then of course doctors
must earn their two guineas. He has given me some medicine and
a few simple directions, and I am to go to him again in about three
weeks' time. I wanted to get out of it, but he was very firm. So
I suppose I must go.' And Ellison agreed to this.

'If one consults a doctor, one is bound to follow his advice,' she
said, smiling.

'Yes, I suppose so ; and I shall not be so nervous another time
but, would you believe it, Ellison, I was so breathless, and my heart
was thumping so that I could hardly speak ; and of course he saw
it—doctors see everything. He took me up to the drawing-room
to see Mrs. M'Callum, and she gave me some tea, and we had a
nice talk. Oh, my dear'—glancing at her watch—'we shall be late
for the Bramfield train !' and then they had hurried out.

'You must hear my news first,' observed Ellison, with good-
natured wilfulness. 'Your mother and the General will keep. I

have something worth telling. Mr. Mervyn and Margaret have asked me to go to Switzerland with them. They want to start in a fortnight's time, and will only be away five weeks, so I shall be back the first week in September. Is it not delightful, Gavin? I have never been to Switzerland since father took me, when I was sixteen. That is nearly twelve years ago.'

'My dear Ellison, you are not eight-and-twenty yet,' observed Mrs. Trevor, who had the old-fashioned notion that young ladies should not tell their age. Even in these enlightened days people still wish to be young. Mrs. Trevor had no such weakness on her own account, and would at all times state her age with patriarchal simplicity, but she was unwilling that Ellison and Muriel should do so. She had married so young herself, that it seemed almost terrible to her that a young woman like Ellison should tell people so glibly that she had been grown up for twelve years.

'My eight-and-twentieth birthday will be on the 10th of September,' persisted Ellison remorselessly. 'Muriel and I will soon be thirty. Why do not you congratulate me, Gavin? Don't you think it a charming plan?'

'Yes,' he returned, a little reluctantly; 'and I am sure you will enjoy it. Mervyn has been over the ground before, and will plan the best route; and then expense is no object to him—that always adds to the pleasure of a trip; so you are in luck's way.'

'I am always in luck's way,' she returned cheerfully; and indeed he had never seen her look so animated. Pleasurable anticipations had brought brightness to her eyes and colour to her cheeks. 'It is so kind of Margaret and Mr. Mervyn to wish me to go with them. I hesitated at first; it seemed almost too much to accept; but they would take no denial. Mr. Mervyn said their trip would be incomplete without me. Margaret's deafness is getting worse, Gavin. She knew that it would. Even with her trumpet she never seemed to understand what her brother was saying to me, poor dear. She is very patient over it; but it is a great trial to them both.'

'And you are going in a fortnight's time?' Gavin's voice was not quite so cheerful as usual. Ellison gave him a quick glance.

'I wish you were coming too,' she said affectionately. 'Could you not meet us somewhere accidentally—at Lausanne or Mürren—and join our party? You are so fond of Switzerland, Gavin.'

'Not this year'—shaking his head. 'Perhaps we will go some day together, you and I, and—' he paused, for as he spoke the idea suddenly struck him that perhaps there might be no need to take a third person. The thought made him flush slightly. He saw his mother looking at him, and changed the form of his sentence.

'You know I have promised to go down to Brent Park for the shooting in September, and I may perhaps go on to the Merryfields. I shall go nowhere in August.'

'That is what Muriel says,' returned his mother. 'Muriel will not hear of going anywhere this summer. She says she prefers staying quietly at home. The fact is, she is so infatuated with Mrs. Herbert, that she thinks of nothing else ; but I am sure a few weeks at Ilfracombe with the Medlicotts would have done her a world of good.'

'It is no use trying to do people good against their will,' replied her son. 'Muriel has flatly refused to join the Medlicotts, so there is no use saying any more about it.'

'Muriel is a goose,' observed Ellison ; and then Bramfield was reached, and they all got into the waggonette.

Muriel was in the drawing-room reading when they entered. She looked up at them.

'How late you are ! I have been back nearly an hour. Are you not very tired, mother ? '

'Yes ; she is tired, though she refuses to own it,' returned Gavin. 'Well, how did the picnic go off, Muriel ? Were the boys very obstreperous, or did Vincent keep them in order ? '

'Oh, they were noisy, of course—boys always are ; but they behaved very well on the whole. It has been a delightful day.' And then Gavin went off to dress for dinner, and Muriel, laying down her book, began to pace slowly up and down the conservatory. To her the best part of the day had been the walk back from Redlands with Mrs. Herbert and Mr. Vincent. The three younger children and most of the animals had been packed into the donkey-cart, and Nora and Hugo had walked beside them with Dorcas, and they had followed slowly, talking of many things, and often standing still to admire the wonderful effect of the evening light gilding some distant glade.

At the entrance to Brae Farm, Eric Vincent had carried off the happy, tired children ; and Lorraine, who was still as fresh as when she started, walked back a few steps with Muriel.

'I have been thinking over what you told me, dear, this afternoon,' she said, with her usual frankness. 'You do not mind my speaking of it again, do you ? ' Muriel shook her head. 'I know how easy it is for people to get sore about things, and then how difficult it is to judge rightly. You say that your brother constantly misunderstands you, and it may be so ; but are you sure that you do not misunderstand him sometimes ? '

After all her confidence, Muriel felt this was just a little hard She made no answer.

'I have never seen any coolness on your brother's part His manner is always as kind as possible ; of course I see what you mean about Ellison ; but once or twice I have fancied—well, never mind, let that pass'—for Lorraine felt that it would not do to put a half-formulated suspicion into words. It would not be right or in good taste to speak of such a thing to Muriel ; but now and then she had felt a little perplexed about Ellison's relation to her cousin. Was there anything between them ? she wondered. Colonel Trevor was certainly strongly attached to his cousin. When he was at home, a day never passed without his strolling down to the Farm to consult Ellison about something ; and yet the sisterly frankness of Ellison's manner seemed to contradict this surmise. Perhaps after all it was only friendship. Neither Colonel Trevor nor Ellison were quite ordinary people. Probably neither of them had any leanings towards matrimony. She had herself heard Colonel Trevor say emphatically that a man could not be in love twice, though he had softened down this statement afterwards by explaining that he was supposing a case where a man had already found his ideal. Ellison had agreed to this, for she and Gavin were thinking about Helen ; but Lorraine, who knew the world better than her cousin, had demurred. 'You must not take isolated cases, Colonel Trevor,' she had said. 'In my own experience I have known two or three people who have been devoted to their wives, and have sincerely mourned their loss, and who have seemed equally happy in their second marriage.'

'Oh yes, they are happy enough, I daresay,' he had returned, a little contemptuously, 'but if you were to question them, they would tell you that it is not the same thing. I know lots of fellows who have done it, and seem perfectly content, and I daresay their wives are happy,' but here he looked at his cousin. 'You know what I mean, Ellison ; it is not easy to explain,' and Ellison answered tranquilly that she fully understood him.

It was doubtful whether Muriel comprehended Lorraine's hint ; for she made no answer, and Lorraine went on :

'Ellison's nature seems to suit your brother. He has suffered much ; and she is very calm and strong. He is strong too ; but in trouble a man will sometimes lean on a woman. That is what I feel with Ellison. If I were in any great sorrow it would soothe me to be near her. I fancy that is how your brother feels.'

Muriel sighed heavily. 'Yes, I see what you mean. I am no comfort to him. I never have been, and it is ungenerous of me to be jealous of Ellison. I know it is dreadfully small, but I struggle against it.'

'I am sure you do, dear ; but if you would only believe that your brother cares for you. He does indeed, Muriel, and you wrong him by doubting it,' and then she had kissed her affectionately, and turned back to the Farm. She had not said much ; but those last words comforted Muriel strangely.

'Do I wrong Gavin ?' she said more than once to herself that evening. 'Can Mrs. Herbert be right when she says that he really cares for me ? I try his patience terribly at times. If I could only cure myself of this irritability ! I answer him sharply, and that puts him out, and then things get wrong altogether.'

These reflections were salutary ; but Muriel had no opportunities of making amends to her brother that evening, for as soon as he had taken his coffee, he bade them good-night and went off for a prowl. Gavin was not quite satisfied with himself. Never before in his life could he have accused himself of hesitation and difficulty in making up his mind. He had always settled his own plans and other people's with soldierly promptitude and decision, and yet his conduct to Ellison was in utter contradiction to this.

Nearly three months had elapsed since he had come to the conclusion that it would be well for him to marry Ellison ; but as yet the decisive question had not been mooted. Now and then he had dropped a word that seemed to point to his intention ; but Ellison had not seemed to notice it. There was nothing in her manner to encourage him to speak.

When a man is really in earnest there is rarely any lack of opportunity. He is ready to make his own breach and storm the citadel without much outward help. Difficulties do not daunt him. A lion in his path will not turn him. It is only the half-hearted lover who is easily deterred by circumstances.

Gavin was not exactly half-hearted, for he dearly loved his cousin ; but his love was without passion. He wished to secure the monopoly of Ellison's society, to have her near him ; but his pulses never stirred more quickly if he met her unexpectedly. And though he always parted from her with reluctance, he never found the time long until he saw her again. In plain words, he was not really in love with her, and, as far as he knew himself, he was not likely to be in love with any woman. This was why he was for ever telling himself that second love in his case was not possible.

It is lamentable what mistakes even clever resolute men will make. They will walk open-eyed and unfaltering into a snare that a weaker person would carefully avoid.

Because his visits to Brae Farm always rested and refreshed him, Gavin had come to the conclusion that Ellison was the only woman who could comfort him for Helen's loss. In every way the marriage would be suitable ; not because, as Mrs. Earnshaw said, their lands marched together, but because Ellison would make allowances for him and demand little. Tranquil, unexacting affection would satisfy them both. This made a second marriage possible to him. There would be no profound agitation to disturb him. This was how he reasoned with himself ; but if he only had known it, there was weakness in his sophistry. Ellison, with all her tranquillity, was not likely to be content with anything but absolute devotion from a husband. When the white flame of love was once kindled in her heart it would burn steadily and strongly to the end. A quiet nature can be deep, and there were depths in Ellison unknown to himself or her.

And there was another element of danger unsuspected by either. When Lorraine sang to them, as she did sometimes at Ellison's request, Gavin always felt a singular emotion. Now and then he had watched her, and told himself that Mrs. Herbert was almost beautiful. They had become great friends, and he found great pleasure in talking to her ; but with her usual tact she often left him alone with Ellison. 'He will talk about his own affairs more comfortably if I leave them,' she would say to herself. 'I am only an outsider, and Ellison will like to have him to herself.' And Ellison always appreciated this delicacy on Lorraine's part. Three people may be perfectly harmonious, but two are more confidential. Lorraine often felt it rather a sacrifice to cousinly affection to go away. Colonel Trevor's conversation interested her so much. From the first she had liked him. 'How happy Ellison must be to have such a friend,' she thought sometimes ; but there was no touch of envy in this thought. Lorraine never hoped that such happiness could be hers. 'Where has Lorraine gone ? I shall go and fetch her back and make her sing to us,' Ellison would say presently. 'You will like that, Gavin,' and then there had been a quick throb of expectation, and his tranquillity would be suddenly merged into agitated recollections of his lost happiness.

Yes ; he had been drifting on from day to day in a ridiculously aimless fashion, and now Ellison was going to leave him, the prospect of five whole weeks without her was not pleasant to him. Before, when she had been away, he had been also absent from Highlands, and so he had not missed her ; but now he had pledged himself to remain at Brae House during August, and how was he to get through the day without his usual visit to the Farm ? It was not likely that he would go and see Mrs. Herbert. Such an idea would not enter either of their heads. He would see her sometimes when she came up to Brae ; but of course daily visits were out of the question. Here he stopped to cogitate a little.

What an odd idea, he thought—fancy him sitting in the bay-window chatting to Mrs. Herbert. It would be pleasant, of course ; but then she was not his friend and cousin. She was charming, a sweet woman, but she was not Ellison ; and here he hurried on. Why should he not speak to Ellison before she left ? Why should they not be engaged properly before she went to Switzerland ? Yes, he would do it. The idea was an excellent one. He was sick of procrastination and indecision. He would speak to her, and what was more she should listen to him. He would not let her turn off his speeches as she had done lately. And then he remembered that latterly he had not found himself so much alone with her. It had not been Mrs. Herbert's fault. Mrs. Herbert was singularly ready to efface herself on all occasions. Mr. Vincent or those children had been so often in the way, or there would be callers, or urgent messages from Sam Brattle.

In summer time the Farm was a busy place, and its mistress was at every one's beck and call. He must think a minute what he would do.

They were coming up to Brae House on Wednesday to dine, and Vincent was coming too. The only other guest was Cartwright,—the Rev. Eustace Cartwright being a frequent visitor to Brae.

These summer evenings they generally strolled about the gardens, and he would easily find an opportunity of speaking a word to Ellison. He would make her understand that he had something important to say to her, and that he would come down to the Farm the next afternoon to say it. 'You must be alone. Give the servants orders that you are specially engaged, and there are to be no messages from Sam Brattle.' That is what he would say to her, and of course she would understand him, and he would find her alone and ready to listen to him, though perhaps her soft blue eyes would have a new shyness in them. And then when he had made this clear to himself, he threw away his cigar and went indoors.

CHAPTER XX

'The lady doth protest too much, methinks.'
Hamlet.

'Tender-handed stroke a nettle,
  And it stings you for your pains ;
Grasp it like a man of mettle,
  And it soft as silk remains.'
AARON HILL.

THE day after the picnic Lorraine met with a curious little adventure. She had only remarked that morning at breakfast, in a playful way, that nothing ever happened in Highlands ; and yet when evening came she had quite a sensational little tale for Ellison's ear.

Early in the afternoon she had walked over to a cottage at some distance from Highlands. A child in whom Ellison took great interest had met with a severe accident, and Lorraine had offered to carry a basket of good things to the little sufferer.

The afternoon was hot and cloudless, and the basket that Mrs. Tucker had packed was unusually heavy, and by the time Lorraine had reached the *Waggon and Horses* she wished that she had taken Ellison's advice and driven over in the donkey-cart. Tweedledee evidently shared this opinion, for he walked languidly beside her with his tongue out and his tail drooping, instead of frolicking ahead and barking at every passer-by.

A gate opposite the *Waggon and Horses* led down a broad woodland path, bordered with gorse and bracken, and Lorraine, who felt immediate relief when she reached the shade of the trees, sat down on a log to rest herself. She was still in sight of the inn. The bow-window of the principal sitting-room had a full view of the glade, and strangers who took up their quarters at the *Waggon and Horses* always spoke with delight of the charming prospect.

As Lorraine glanced in that direction she saw a little woman in grey come out of the inn and cross the road. She walked in a sprightly fashion, looking curiously about her, and Lorraine at once saw that she was a stranger to Highlands.

A new face always interested her, and she kept her place until the lady passed her. In the distance she had imagined that it was a young person ; but to her surprise the jaunty step and youthful figure belonged to quite an elderly woman. Under the broad, shady hat, tied down in gipsy fashion with a grey gossamer veil, Lorraine caught sight of a pale, worn face, and the bluest eyes she had ever seen. As Lorraine wished her a civil 'Good afternoon,' the lady gave her a keen, surprised glance, and with a slight supercilious nod passed on.

Lorraine watched her until she was out of sight, then she took up her basket again. She had never seen such a curious combination of youth and age. There was something droll and eccentric in the little lady's appearance. The unusually short skirt displayed a pair of dainty, well-shod feet. Her grey tweed jacket fitted her neat figure closely, and a mass of grey curls almost touched her eyebrows. If she had only worn a cloak instead of a jacket she would have been an excellent embodiment of Mother Hubbard.

Lorraine forgot all about her by and by ; she paid a long visit to the cottage—unpacked her basket and talked to little Susan, and then set off on her return journey, fearing that she had loitered so long that Ellison would have finished her tea.

It was still too hot to walk fast, but a faint breeze had sprung up and fanned her face deliciously; the warm scented air held the perfume of a thousand flowers ; great brown bees were hovering over some wild dainties ; the birds were voiceless, and safely hidden in leafy coverts, and only the humming of insects were audible ; now and then a gorgeous butterfly flitted past her, or a blue or grey moth.

Just as Lorraine turned up another woodland path she saw, to her surprise, the little grey lady who had passed her earlier in the afternoon; she was leaning against a gate. As Lorraine was about to walk past her, something in her attitude made her pause.

'You are in pain,' she said impulsively ; 'can I be of any assistance ? I trust that you have not sprained your ankle over one of these tree roots ?'

'No, thank you,' replied the stranger; 'it is only an old strain that sometimes troubles me ; but I shall be unable to walk until the pain passes off—even my staff will not be sufficient,' and she held out a carved ebony stick with a crutch handle. She spoke with curious abruptness and decision, but her voice was unmistakably cultured. With all her eccentricity she was evidently a gentle-woman.

'If you could only sit down,' observed Lorraine sympathetically. 'I can see by your face how much you are suffering. Do, please, take my arm, it will give you some sort of support'; but the little woman shook her head.

'You are very good, but I will not trouble you. I am used to standing alone. I have learnt by experience that the pain will pass; it is only a question of time and patience. I hurt myself rather badly some years ago. I fancy it is partly neuralgia where the old mischief was : if I had only my drops—but I was a fool to forget them—and Pritchard was another fool, too.'

The tone was decidedly irascible, but her lips were white with pain ; it was impossible for Lorraine to see any one suffering and not offer her help.

'You are staying at the *Waggon and Horses*, are you not ?' she asked anxiously. 'I think I saw you come out of the inn.' And, as the lady nodded, she went on : 'It is not five minutes' walk from here—let me fetch your medicine—you can easily tell me where to find it; the people at the inn know me. I am Mrs. Herbert from Brae Farm.'

'I was sure you were a widow the moment I saw you,' was the singular response to this. 'Herbert, aye, not one of the Herberts of Chillingford——'

'No, no—simple Mrs. Herbert ; but we are losing time, and you do look so ill. Please give me the necessary directions ; Mrs. Brent will help me.'

'Well, as you are set on playing the Good Samaritan, I will not hinder you,' was the somewhat churlish answer ; 'if you will be so good as to ask for my maid, Pritchard—she will be about the place somewhere—she will give you the drops——'

'Thank you ; that is all I wanted to know,' and Lorraine walked off quickly ; in fact, directly she was out of sight she com-menced running, and was soon in the inn passage and asking for Pritchard.

'Pritchard ? oh, you mean Miss Bretherton's maid !' exclaimed Mrs. Brent loudly. 'Here, Mrs. Pritchard, Mrs. Herbert from Brae Farm is asking for you'; and a respectable elderly woman came forward at once.

She looked a little anxious when Lorraine explained her errand. 'My mistress in pain,' she said ; 'if you will wait a moment, ma'am, I will get the drops, and be ready to come with you.'

Lorraine was about to say that there was no need for this ; but

11

on second thoughts she checked herself; the maid would know best what to do ; so she waited patiently until Pritchard returned with the remedy.   But as they hurried down the path Lorraine was asking herself what Miss Bretherton this could be ; was it possible that she could be Mr. Vincent's aunt ?   What had brought her to Highlands ?   Perhaps after all she had relented, and meant to be reconciled to him.   Lorraine was in a glow of mingled heat and curiosity and benevolence by the time she had reached Miss Bretherton.

'What an old fool you were, Pritchard, not to remind me of my drops,' was her first greeting ; but the maid, who was evidently used to her mistress's irritability, only poured out the medicine carefully.

'You have walked too far, ma'am,' she said in the affectionate reproving tone that a nurse uses to a child ; 'you would not have needed your drops if you had only taken a short stroll.   My mistress can't stand fatigue,' she went on, turning to Lorraine.   'She had a bad carriage accident, and ever since she has had a pain in her side if she walks much ; it is neuralgia, as the doctor says, but it leaves her as weak as a child afterwards.'

'Don't be a goose, Pritchard ; the drops always cure me.   Now, Mrs. Herbert, if you will kindly give me the arm you offered me before, I shall be much obliged to you, and, Pritchard, you come round the other side, and I will make an attempt to reach the inn.   I shall be forced to limp like a lame robin ; but there is no one to watch my awkward gait.   Ah, I see you are laughing at me, Mrs. Herbert.   I believe I was born to amuse people.   Not too fast, Pritchard—how am I to keep up with your great clumsy strides? I never knew such a woman for walking fast.'

Pritchard only grunted in answer, and all the way to the inn Miss Bretherton went on in the same scolding way : sometimes they walked too fast, or too slow—or the path was not wide enough, or the sun was blinding her ; and after every querulous speech she peeped round at Lorraine with a comical look that seemed to say, 'Have you ever seen such an oddity before ?'

When they entered the inn she seemed to take it as a matter of course that Lorraine should assist her up the steep stairs.   The pleasant inn parlour looked airy and inviting, with its open windows and great bowls of carnations and roses—the tea-things were on the table.   As Miss Bretherton sank down on the couch she said in the same querulous tone :

'Make the tea, Pritchard ; Mrs. Herbert is going to have a cup with me.   Take off your hat, Mrs. Herbert.   Where is the eau de cologne, Pritchard?   Ah, that dog.   I forgot him, but never mind ; It is old dogs I distrust.'

'Indeed, I cannot stay,' returned Lorraine hurriedly; 'my cousin will be expecting me; I have been out all the afternoon, and it is past five.' But Miss Bretherton took no notice of this; she had removed her hat, and was patting the mass of grey curls on her forehead with two little hands twinkling with diamond rings.

'I really must go,' continued Lorraine; but to her extreme amusement Miss Bretherton only looked at her calmly.

'You are not going, because I want to talk to you, and I have got nobody but stupid old Pritchard, and she is not amusing. Why won't you stop and have a cup of tea with me, I should like to know? I am quite respectable. My society will not contaminate you. Where is my card-case, Pritchard? Give Mrs. Herbert my card, and then she cannot say we have not been properly introduced. No, take it, Mrs. Herbert,' as Lorraine laughingly disclaimed this as unnecessary; but Miss Bretherton tossed the card by easy sleight of hand into her lap. There it lay before her: 'Miss Bretherton, Black Nest, Nefydd Madoc.'

'That is my name, and that is the name,' she went on, 'of my house; but though I live in Wales I am English to the backbone. I was not born or bred there. It was my uncle's place. He had a drop of Taffy's blood in him, and he fell in love with Nefydd Madoc. Live there he would until death mastered him. If there is a Welsh heaven, he will have made straight for it. There, now, I have shocked you. Perhaps you will condescend to drink my tea.'

Lorraine was not unwilling to stay. The fragrance of the tea was very inviting, and she was tired and thirsty, and by this time her curiosity and interest had been strongly excited, so she did as she had been hidden—removed her hat and called Tweedledee, and made him lie at her feet.

'Come, now, that is friendly,' observed her singular hostess in an approving tone. 'I knew you were a sensible woman, and the world is not over-full of them. Bring a little table for Mrs. Herbert, Pritchard. So you live or make believe to live in this little green nest of a place. What on earth do you find to do in this village of Sleepy Hollow?'

The tone was decidedly amicable, in spite of its abruptness, and Lorraine responded with her usual simple directness.

'You will be surprised to hear that I find so much to do that the day is never long enough, and my cousin often says the same. She is the mistress of Brae Farm, and I and my boy live with her. We are busy from morning to night.'

There was a singular change in Miss Bretherton's manner as Lorraine said this.

'If you have a child you are not to be pitied,' she said rather harshly. 'I thought you were a lone woman like me ; but there, I am always taking up ideas about people and finding them all wrong. I am a stupid old woman, as I often tell Pritchard.'

Lorraine looked at her kindly. Her soft brown eyes were full of feeling. 'No, I am not lonely in the way you mean. My baby boy is the joy of my life. He is such a darling !' And then feeling that she was saying too much to a stranger, she changed the subject. 'Is this your first visit to Highlands, Miss Bretherton ? I hope Mrs. Brent takes good care of you. The inn is considered very comfortable.'

'Oh, it is comfortable enough,' she returned carelessly. 'Pritchard looks after my comforts, and I am only remaining a day or two. Business, not pleasure, has brought me to Highlands. I hope you will come and see me again, Mrs. Herbert ; and you may bring that wonderful boy of yours to see me if you like. Not that I care for children ; my fondness for them has died a natural death long ago.'

She spoke with undisguised bitterness, and Lorraine understood the allusion. She was thinking, doubtless, of the nephew who had disappointed her, and repelled her affection. But Lorraine dared not mention him.

By the strangest coincidence, at this moment there was a knock at the door, and to her intense surprise Mr. Vincent entered. He looked flushed and nervous, and seemed still more discomposed when he saw Mrs. Herbert.

'Aunt Marion,' he said, in rather an agitated voice, 'why did you not let me know that you were coming to Highlands ? I have just heard from Mr. Brent that you arrived last evening, and you have been here all these hours, within a stone's throw of our cottage.'

Miss Bretherton had been evidently unprepared for this visit. At the sight of her nephew, a grey, ashen look had come over her face. Pritchard thought her mistress had turned faint, and handed her a vinaigrette ; but she pushed it angrily away.

'So you have come, Eric,' she said sharply, 'though I am not aware I sent for you ; but as you are here you had better sit down.' She took his hand coldly as she spoke. 'It is a good many years since we met, and I am not sure that I should have known you. Preaching and teaching do not seem to have agreed with you.'

'You are looking ill too, Aunt Marion,' he returned nervously. 'I heard all about that accident, and I am afraid it has told on you. She'—he evidently could not bring himself to mention his mother—'she was terribly alarmed about you.'

'Yes ; Ella was always an alarmist,' she returned unsympathetically. 'So, like a dutiful nephew, you feel anxious about your poor old aunt.' She laughed in a most unmirthful way ; but her nephew remained grave.

Lorraine rose, feeling the embarrassment of the situation. To her discomposure, Miss Bretherton objected to her going.

'Now, Mrs. Herbert,' she said crossly, 'there is not the slightest need to curtail your visit. My nephew and I have no secrets to discuss this evening.' She laid a stress on the last words. 'He has come uninvited, and you had better help me entertain him. I have not so many friends that I am anxious to part with you.'

The speech was ungracious, and in the worst possible taste, and Lorraine would have felt extremely angry on Mr. Vincent's account, only she was convinced that Miss Bretherton was in a state of nervous irritability which she was unable to control.

Mr. Vincent rose hastily. 'It is I who should go,' he said pointedly, and in a tone of strong indignation. 'Aunt Marion, I am sorry that I have intruded. I shall wait next time until you send for me.'

'Perhaps so. It will be better,' responded Miss Bretherton. 'Well, if you must go, Mrs. Herbert, good-bye.' Lorraine waited for no more ; but as she hurried out of the inn, Mr. Vincent overtook her, and they walked on in silence. Lorraine dared not trust herself to speak, she felt so much for him, and probably Mr. Vincent was trying to curb his emotion.

At last as they crossed the common she said in a low voice, 'If you only knew how sorry I am for you, and my being there made it so much worse for you.'

He turned to her at once, and she could see the tears in his eyes.

'No, I think not. You can never be in any one's way. I am sure you can never be in mine.' He paused, and then hurried on. 'You know the circumstances, Mrs. Herbert ; Colonel Trevor has told you. Is not this implacability on my aunt's part almost incredible? She is punishing a man for a child's caprice—no, caprice is not the right word'—speaking as though to himself. 'My dislike was too absolute for caprice.'

'As a child you disliked your aunt, then?' she asked, thinking that after all it would be better for him to speak out.

'Yes, I am afraid so,' he answered regretfully. 'It was horribly ungrateful of me, when she loaded me with kindness ; but she was very peculiar, and a child does not always understand. I have often been sorry to think how I must have trampled on her feelings ; but a generous-hearted woman would have condoned this long ago. When I came up just now I was full of hope that my aunt's presence at Highlands meant a general amnesty for past offences ; but you saw how I was received. She has neither forgiven me nor forgotten. No, indeed '—working himself to fresh wrath—' she means just to gratify her curiosity about us, and then go her way without lifting a single burden ; and yet she is my mother's only sister.'

Lorraine touched his arm gently. 'Mr. Vincent, it is very hard, and this evening Miss Bretherton treated you very badly. She has not forgotten, certainly ; but though she is a stranger to me, I should say that the sight of you gave her acute pain. When you entered the room she grew quite white, and I saw her hands tremble. Her visit to Highlands does not point to implacability. I think it would be wiser and kinder to reserve your judgment of her until you see her again.'

'I do not mean to see her again. Please do not look at me as though you think I am wrong ; amiability is not my strong point. I am exceedingly proud. Do you suppose in my position '—holding his head high—' that I shall permit myself to be badgered and insulted by any woman because she is my aunt ?'

Lorraine took no notice of this little outburst. She thought it was quite reasonable that Mr. Vincent should be angry.

'You certainly will not go near her again until she sends for you.'

'I shall not go if she sends for me a hundred times.'

Lorraine shook her head reprovingly.

'I am quite sure you will change your mind,' she said calmly. 'If Miss Bretherton sends for you, you will go, not for your own sake but because of the children. I know you will agree with me, Mr. Vincent, that we can do for others what we cannot bring ourselves to do for our own sake,' and then she looked at him very kindly, and bade him good-bye.

CHAPTER XXI

MOTHER HUBBARD AGAIN !

'As headstrong as an allegory on the banks of the Nile.'—(Mrs. Malaprop) SHERIDAN.

'Let us consider the reason of the case. For nothing is law that is not reason.'—SIR JOHN POWELL.

ELLISON was much interested when Lorraine narrated her interview with Miss Bretherton, and questioned her minutely on the stranger's appearance.

'I never saw any one more difficult to describe,' was Lorraine's answer. 'Miss Bretherton cannot be more than sixty, I should say ; but her face is so old ; there are fine wrinkles under her eyes and round her mouth, but her eyes are as blue and clear as a child's ; the mass of grey curls quite hide her forehead ; how I do hate a curly crop that comes too low, it robs a woman's face of all intellect. I should say she had been pretty, but bad health or bad temper, or both, have aged her ; she is certainly very eccentric.'

'So Gavin said ; he called her spiteful and cantankerous ; and by your own account she quite insulted poor Mr. Vincent. Fancy treating a clergyman as though he were a schoolboy, and she has not seen him for ten or twelve years.'

'No, it was very bad ; but, somehow, I could not help pitying her. I am sure she was suffering, and only wanted to get rid of him ; she gave me that impression ; if you only knew how I longed to get out of that room—but no,—she seemed to dread being alone with him.'

'I think you had better leave them to quarrel comfortably, and then, perhaps, there will be a chance of their making it up, a third person is so in the way' ; and, as Lorraine agreed to this, she took her walk the next day in an opposite direction, and gave the *Waggon and Horses* a wide berth.

Late in the evening, as she and Ellison were strolling across the Brae Meadow enjoying the fresh coolness of the air, a respectable-looking woman in black passed them ; to her surprise she recognised Miss Bretherton's maid, Pritchard ; she looked a little confused when Lorraine stopped to speak to her, and said something about the fineness of the weather tempting her to take a stroll. 'As I am a stranger to these parts I would make bold to ask, ma'am, if that great house yonder is Brae House ?'

'Yes, it is ; it belongs to Colonel Trevor, and Brae Farm is down there ; you see that big pond, where they are washing the cart-horses, those are the farm buildings beside it. Did Miss Bretherton send any message to me ?'

'Oh, dear no, ma'am, she did not think I should be seeing you ; my mistress has been but poorly to-day, her long walk and talking to Mr. Eric has upset her ; if she excites herself about anything she is sure to be ill afterwards, her nerves are weak, and she cannot stand it now ; she has been hoping you would call. I knew by her sitting at the window all the afternoon that she was expecting some one, though it would not have done to say so. May I say you will come to-morrow, ma'am ?'

'No, I think not ; under the circumstances it would be better not ; give Miss Bretherton my kind regards, and I hope she will soon be better' ; and Pritchard was evidently disappointed.

'I like the look of that woman,' observed Ellison, as they walked on. 'She has a trusty, reliable face ; but, you may depend upon it, she was reconnoitring Brae for some purpose ; perhaps she hoped to meet you. Miss Bretherton has taken a fancy to you' ; but Lorraine only laughed at this ; she had no great desire to see Mother Hubbard again, as she called her, though in her heart she still pitied her.

There are strange intricacies in life ; we do not know what fate has in store for us. The stranger we pass in the street, whom we regard carelessly, may become an important factor in our life's history. Little did Lorraine guess that the tiny woman in grey, whom she so playfully termed Mother Hubbard, would be a weighty influence in her life ; that, already, in that chance meeting among the furze bushes, fate was weaving the meshes of that strange web that was to draw her and Miss Bretherton together. Ah, if one's eyes could be opened to see the fine invisible web of curious coincidence and circumstance in which we are so strongly entangled, that there is no finding the way out of the maze, how greatly we should marvel. What a trifle had guided us—if we had only walked on the other side of the street, or taken another turning, or refrained from speaking, all would have been different ;

true, but these chance by-paths have been prepared for us, and an overruling Providence has ordained that we should walk in them.

Lorraine had decided to avoid Miss Bretherton, but fate had another word to say on that subject.

The next morning she and Tedo were sitting under the cedars in the Brae Woods; Jenny was browsing near them. Lorraine was making a daisy-chain for her boy, and he was standing beside her, watching her with delighted eyes, while she sang to him the doleful ballad of Cock Robin; when, all at once, she looked up from her work and saw Miss Bretherton. She was standing quite still, leaning on her ebony staff, and regarding them with a curiously fixed glance.

She gave an odd little laugh when Lorraine looked up. 'Well, Mrs. Herbert, so Pritchard tells me you have refused to have anything more to do with the sour old maid; and this is Highlands' hospitality to strangers? It is very short-sighted of you; but then good Christian people are often short-sighted; but how do you know that you might not have entertained an angel unawares? come now, answer me that.'

'If you will sit down, Miss Bretherton, I will try to do so; the ground is quite dry and warm under the cedars; I call it my cedar parlour. Tedo, my sweet, ask the lady to sit down,' and the little fellow held out his hand at once.

'So this is your boy?' observed Miss Bretherton, with the abruptness that seemed natural to her, but there was a kindly gleam in her eye; 'he is like you, Mrs. Herbert, but he looks weakly.'

'He is not a strong child,' returned Lorraine, flushing, for she never liked these remarks on her boy: 'but he is much better, every one says so, he runs about more, and does not seem so languid. Dr. Howell has done him so much good.'

'Humph! we all have our treasures in earthen vessels, I fancy,' was Miss Bretherton's singular retort. 'What's your name, my little man?'

'Theodore—the gift of God. I chose it for its derivation; my boy came to me at a very sorrowful time to comfort me; when he grows up I shall always call him Theodore, but now I call him Tedo.'

Miss Bretherton gave her a sharp glance, there was something piercing in the keen incisive look, the blue eyes grew bright and hard.

'So you've known trouble,' she said rather resentfully. 'I wonder it has not taught you more charity; you only made my acquaintance yesterday, and already you are sick to death of me, and all because I was a bit peppery with my graceless nephew!'

She spoke in such a hurt voice that Lorraine had to soothe her.

'Indeed, you must not say so. I was very sorry for Mr. Vincent, certainly. I am sure he meant so well ; we all think so highly of him ; so many men fail to practise what they preach, but Mr. Vincent sets us all an example.'

Miss Bretherton gave an angry snort.

'I daresay he is a good moral young man. I know nothing to the contrary ; his mother was a good woman, though she made the fatal mistake of marrying again. I don't hold with second marriages, Mrs. Herbert,' regarding her severely ; 'once married is enough for any woman. I have nothing to say about men, they are feckless creatures, and will just do as they like.'

'I think it is a pity to judge any one, man or woman,' returned Lorraine quietly ; 'it is no use making new commandments for people, their own conscience must guide them.'

'And yet you were ready enough to judge me,' snapped Miss Bretherton ; 'though you did not say a word, I knew you were taking Eric's part. Now, just wait a moment, and put yourself in my place. Listen to me, it sounds droll, but I am rather an uncommon person, and I have taken a liking to you ; there is something about you that reminds me of that boy's mother. I don't know where the likeness lies, for your features do not resemble her in the least ; but there is something that recalls her when she was young and in her widow's weeds, and before she took up with Scott. I never would call him my brother-in-law ; that is one of the things that made Ella so angry, but I could not bear him—a thin, starchy sort of man with his chin in the air, and a head as bald as a billiard ball.'

It was evident that Miss Bretherton enjoyed speaking her mind.

'Now my precious nephew seems to be regarded as a sort of saint down here. Brent was talking about him last night, he called him an excellent, God-fearing young man ; it savoured of cant, but he evidently meant it—so I let it pass ; but what I want to know is this,' digging her stick angrily into the ground, 'how dare he come and call on me after the way he has treated me.'

'My dear Miss Bretherton, I think I know a little about that ; he disappointed you when he was a boy, did he not, and you have not forgiven him?'

'No, nor ever shall,' with concentrated bitterness. 'Look here, Mrs. Herbert, did you not tell me the other day that that child was the joy of your life? Well, when Eric was a little fellow about his age, I set my heart at him. Heaven knows

I had not much in my life to make me happy, but I need not
trouble you with all that—suffice it to say I was lonely, rich, and
without any interest, and I just set my affections on Ella's child.
He was as beautiful as a little angel, and yet so full of monkey
tricks, and it was not a wonder that I took to him.'

'No, indeed,' and Lorraine pressed her boy closer to her. He
had grown drowsy, and was nestling to her, with his sleepy eyes
fixed on Miss Bretherton.

'When Ella made a fool of herself with Scott I offered to adopt
him, and neither of them refused me, and I took him for a time to
Black Nest. There was nothing I would not have done for that
child—he had a pony, and a dog, and a garden of his own—but
no, nothing would do, he only fretted for his mother. He stood
up and told me to my face that he would not live with me. "I
don't want all your fine things, Aunt Marion. I don't love you,
and I want to go home. If I stayed here I should get to hate you,
I know I should." There was a loving speech, and I just worshipped that boy.'

'It was very hard,' murmured Lorraine ; 'but it is impossible
not to admire his loyalty to his mother.'

'I took him back myself, and I never said another word to him.
"Your boy hates me," I said to Ella. "He is nothing to me any
longer. I never wish to see him again ; you and Scott can keep
him." And I never did see him until he walked into the inn
parlour the other day.'

'Miss Bretherton, will you listen to me now ? It was a terrible
disappointment, but surely you do not wish the man to suffer for a
child's fault. Many children are capricious in their likes and dislikes. If you had continued your kindness to him he would soon
have become ashamed of his ingratitude.'

'I never give any one a second chance,' she returned sternly.
'My nature is not forgiving ; I brood over an injury until it takes
possession of me. When I cast off the boy I did it utterly.'

Lorraine was silent. Her whole nature rebelled against this
vindictiveness.

'I am a rich woman,' she went on, 'but Eric will never have
my money. He refused my love, and he shall have none of my
wealth. I intend to send for him and tell him so.'

'Do you mean that you have come to Highlands to tell Mr.
Vincent this ? Excuse me, Miss Bretherton, if I refuse to believe
you. You could not be so hard to the son of your dead sister.'

'My sister had no right to complain of me,' she returned in the same
harsh voice, but a red flush mounted to her forehead. 'Though she
angered me by marrying Scott I allowed her two hundred a year.

'Yes, and you have withdrawn this allowance since her death, and left poor Mr. Vincent to struggle on with these four children. Do you know how poor they are? He has only his curacy, and how is he to feed and clothe and educate his young brothers and sisters? Miss Bretherton, be just, even if you will not be merciful. It could not be Mr. Vincent's fault that his mother chose to marry again.'

Something like a smile came to Miss Bretherton's lips.

'Well, I won't deny that,' in a less aggressive tone, 'and I don't say that Eric shall have nothing. If you choose to be so curious, Mrs. Herbert, I don't mind telling you that I came down to Highlands just to see with my own eyes how the land lies. I had a curiosity to see poor Ella's children.'

Lorraine felt a little relieved when she heard this, then a sudden thought made her glance at Miss Bretherton's grey tweed dress. Her only sister had not been dead more than seven or eight months, and yet she did not wear mourning ; but she was slightly confused when Miss Bretherton answered her unspoken thoughts.

'I don't hold with mourning,' she returned stifly. 'It is against my notions of Christianity. I hate saying one thing and doing another. Either we submit or we rebel ; there is nothing between. When my uncle went to his Welsh heaven, and left me Black Nest, I never wore mourning. I rather like shocking people, Mrs. Herbert, it gives me a sort of pleasure when my friends draw down their lips and say, "What a very extraordinary person Miss Bretherton is." Well, as I was saying, until you interrupted me by staring at my gown so rudely, I mean to send for Eric and have it out with him.'

'I am afraid it will be no use sending for him.'

'Eh, why not? Do you mean the young gentleman is affronted, and will refuse another interview with his affectionate aunt?'

'I do mean something of the kind. Mr. Vincent was very much hurt by the way you received him, and I fear if you do send for him that he will not come.'

'Then in that case I must call on him,' was the brisk reply. 'Will you take me to the cottage, Mrs. Herbert, to-morrow morning, or, better still, this afternoon?'

'I—come with you? Oh no, please do not ask me to do such a thing, Miss Bretherton. Why should I thrust myself into Mr. Vincent's private affairs?'

'I shall certainly not go alone,' was the cool reply. 'I would as soon play Daniel in a den of young lions. Mr. Vincent is your spiritual pastor and master. You have a right to be interested in his affairs. If you will not undertake this kindly office for a

stranger, I must just go back to Nefydd Madoc with my errand
unperformed, and then Eric will be the loser. I certainly had
some intentions of helping him, though I persist in my intention of
not making him my heir. But if you will not go with me there
is no help for it.'

'You are making it impossible for me to refuse,' retorted Lorraine in rather a displeased tone. What could this singular woman
mean? Why should she be afraid to go alone to the cottage?
She had not been too nervous to browbeat her nephew, and
humiliate him, and probably she would do so again.

To her surprise Miss Bretherton patted her on the shoulder in
a most friendly fashion.

'There, now, I knew you would be sensible, and I mean to
behave myself. I won't fly at Eric if I can help it ; but it makes
me nervous to have to hold my tongue. Well, then, we will go
this afternoon   Come and have tea with me, and we will walk
down to the cottage afterwards.'

'Very well, if you wish it,' was Lorraine's reluctant answer.
But when she went back to the farm she complained bitterly to
Ellison of her ill-luck. 'I do so hate mixing myself up in this
sort of thing,' she said. 'What will Mr. Vincent think of me?'

'He will know you cannot help yourself. It is very unpleasant
for you, Lorraine ; but I expect Miss Bretherton is really too nervous to go alone. She seems a queer mixture. I can't make her
out. I am so curious that I feel as though I must call on her. I
wonder how she would receive me?'

'I really could not say ; but I cannot help wishing that you
were in my place. I hate dancing attendance on a vindictive
Mother Hubbard.'

When Lorraine reached the inn at the hour appointed she found
Miss Bretherton sitting in state to receive her. She had changed
her travelling dress, and wore a rich black silk trimmed with
superb black lace. Her small white hands blazed with diamonds
and emeralds. She received Lorraine with great dignity, and
during tea discoursed majestically on Welsh scenery. Pritchard
waited on them silently, and her mistress did not once address
her.

Lorraine sat by the open window and looked across at the
woodland path and the fast-yellowing bracken. Before long, it
would be a mass of golden and amber tints. The village street
below her was almost empty—only a colt was feeding on a patch
of grass, and an old mastiff belonging to the *Waggon and Horses*
was sunning himself in the road. By and by the carrier's cart came
up the Dorchester Road with its mottled grey horse, and the

carrier went to the bar to refresh himself.   Presently Miss Bretherton said she would put on her bonnet, and in a few minutes returned with an airy little structure of black lace and grey wistaria, fastened jauntily on the grey curls.   The dress would have been more suitable in Hyde Park or the Botanical Gardens, but it became her, and gave her small figure quite an air of distinction.   But the pale face with its fine wrinkles was a strong contrast to the somewhat youthful cut of her garments.

'I always put on my war-paint when I am going to have a big palaver,' she said sarcastically.   'If you are ready, Mrs. Herbert, we will just step down to the cottage.'

A curious line out of *Hamlet* came into Lorraine's head as she followed Miss Bretherton down the inn stairs :

'This is miching mallecho ; it means mischief.'

CHAPTER XXII

'I will make a Star-chamber matter of it.'
The Merry Wives of Windsor.

'Je ne vous aime pas Hylas,
Je n'en saurais dire la cause,
Je sais seulement un chose ;
C'est que je ne vous aime pas.'
COMTE DE RABATIN.

TEA was not over at the cottage, and even to Lorraine's accustomed eyes the small low room, with its one window blocked up with geraniums, looked crowded, and felt terribly hot as they stood on the threshold. Nora rose from her chair with wide startled eyes, and there was a deep flush on Mr. Vincent's face as he made his way with difficulty to the door.

There was unmistakable hauteur in his look and voice as he said coldly :

'Our present quarters are rather small. Do you think you can manage to squeeze past Hugo, Aunt Marion, and take that chair? Mrs. Herbert, there is just room for you on the other side'; and as he spoke he piloted the ladies with careful courtesy, but without offering to shake hands with either of them ; but as Lorraine took her seat, she looked into the deep-set eyes a moment. The glance said very plainly, 'Please forgive me for being here, but I cannot help myself,' and then she stooped over her pet Effie, and kissed her tenderly.

Miss Bretherton's keen glance was taking in everything as she settled herself and her laces in the old easy-chair. She drew a quick breath once, as though she felt stifled. Did the memory of the cool rooms at Black Nest, and the fresh mountain breezes come to her as she looked round the mean cottage parlour? Her first remark was a querulous one.

'I wonder you have not the sense to get rid of those plants; they block out all the light and air. The room is positively unhealthy.'

'Mrs. Drake is very proud of her plants. We could not ask her to remove them,' returned Mr. Vincent stiffly. 'One must consider other people as well as oneself; in another month or so we hope to remove to the Vicarage. We shall have room to breathe then.'

'Anyhow you have not got it now,' she returned, fanning herself with nervous energy. 'Well, I suppose you are surprised to see me, Eric. As the mountain would not come to Mahomet, Mahomet decided to go to the mountain. So these are the children. What's your name, boy?'—suddenly transfixing Hugo as he stood staring at her.

'Hugo,' he returned, flinging back his unruly locks, and looking her full in the face—'Hugo Medcalf Scott. Edmund has only one name, and he is sorry for it, but I tell him it does not matter —lots of people have only one name.' Then his childish curiosity getting the better of him, 'You are our aunt, are you not?'

'I am your step-aunt,' she returned snappishly, 'and you are not like your mother a bit; Edmund is. Come here, Edmund, as you have only one name, there's a sovereign to console you. Hugo Medcalf is a Scott all over; he will help you to spend it. How old are you?'—looking at Nora severely. 'You are Honoria, are you not?' and the girl turned crimson with shyness.

'I am nearly thirteen,' she said timidly, and she edged a little nearer to her beloved Mrs. Herbert. The sudden apparition of this sharp-faced little woman, with her curt questions and severe looks, overawed the children. Eddie held his golden treasure squeezed tightly in his hot hand; but even his gratitude bordered on nervousness. Effie had taken refuge with her elder brother and refused to leave him when her aunt called her. Even the prospect of golden sovereigns would not have tempted her.

Miss Bretherton gave one of her short, dry laughs.

'I never was a favourite with children. Effie has taken a leaf out of your book, Eric. Well, if the young ones have finished their tea they might as well leave us to have our talk.'

'If you wish it, certainly,' returned Eric, with the same grand composure. 'Hugo and Eddie, go out on the common; Nora, perhaps you and Effie might join them for a little.'

'Shall we say good-bye to our aunt first?' demanded Hugo.

'Oh yes, of course!' but Hugo only stood still and stared at her.

'I wish you would tell me something first,' he said. 'Why did you give Eddie a whole sovereign just because he had one name; it makes me feel curious somehow.'

'And you are sorry you have two; is that what you mean?' returned Miss Bretherton, looking sharply at the handsome little fellow. 'Well I can only say, Hugo Medcalf, that you are not at all like your elder brother; but as you are not above asking, I am not above giving, and though Edmund is the better boy, there are two sovereigns for you.'

'Oh no, Aunt Marion, please do not give him money!' exclaimed Eric. 'Hugo has no manners, he ought not to put himself so forward'; but Miss Bretherton took no notice of this remonstrance.

'There, run away, children,' she said crossly, 'and leave us in peace. I have not even the energy to quarrel in this heat. What on earth made you come to this stifling little place?' she continued angrily; 'have you no thought for those poor children?'

'There were no other lodgings in Highlands, and the Vicarage was under repair. I could not afford to drive over from Bramfield, and beggars cannot be choosers; it is not so bad as you think, we have decent bedrooms, and the children are out on the common all day.'

'Humph! well, you have made your own bed, Eric, and you must expect to lie on it.'

'Certainly, Aunt Marion, and I am not aware that I am asking for sympathy.'

Miss Bretherton fidgeted, then she fanned herself fiercely, she was evidently putting a strong curb on herself; for some occult reason the sight of her nephew irritated her, and it cost her an immense effort to speak civilly to him.

'You are wondering that I brought Mrs. Herbert with me,' she said after a few moments. 'She did not want to come, and made a dreadful fuss about it, but I brought her as a sort of hostage for my good behaviour. Good temper is not my strong point, and I thought it might hinder quarrelling to bring a third person. There, you are more comfortable now that I have made that admission, are you not, Mrs. Herbert?'

'There is no need for Mrs. Herbert to be the least uncomfortable,' and Eric turned to her with a grave smile; 'we can never be sorry to see her here, she is far too good a friend.'

'Well, then, as the preliminaries are so pleasantly settled, we may as well go to the next stage. Eric, I was not particularly gracious to you when you were so good as to call the other afternoon, but the fact is I was a bit flurried, and it made me cross; it is never my way to apologise, and you can't teach an old dog new tricks; but whatever I feel—I am going to be civil this afternoon

12

—you and I will never be friends,' and there was a dangerous flash of the blue eyes ; 'but it is no use quarrelling.'

'It takes two to quarrel, Aunt Marion. However you may provoke me, I never intend to forget that you are my dear mother's sister.'

Eric spoke with quiet dignity, and Lorraine felt she had never admired him so much as she did that moment; but Miss Bretherton's answer took them both by surprise.

'Brent was right ; you are certainly an excellent, God-fearing young man, Eric, and I applaud your magnanimity,' she sneered slightly ; 'would that I could imitate it, but I never learned to practise meekness in my youth. Well, as you are so ready to endure with Christian patience, it is a pity not to give you something to bear. I suppose, after all that has been done and said, it will not surprise you greatly to hear that I do not intend to make you my heir.'

'I understood that long ago, Aunt Marion ; is it not a pity to say this again ? You may be quite sure that I have no expectations of any kind.'

'So much the better,' she returned ; 'but I only wanted to be sure that we understood each other. No, Eric, I am not a Christian like you. I will never leave my money to the boy who told me to my face that he hated me.'

A painful flush crossed Eric's brow.

'Aunt Marion, will you let me say something? Leave your money as you like; I am well aware that I shall not touch a penny of it ; but, all the same, I have always wanted to ask your pardon for the pain I gave you in those old days. You were too hard on my childish failings, you did not make allowances for a spoiled boy who adored his mother. I was ungrateful and treated you badly, but I have often repented.'

'Can you tell me to my face, Eric, that you did not hate me ?'

'I did not love you, certainly ; but it was a mistake on your part to force me to live with you. You bribed me, Aunt Marion, and because I was true to my childish affections you threatened me. When I think of those days at Nefydd Madoc, and those gloomy rooms at Black Nest, I do not wonder at my hating it all.'

'Very well, very well; we will not go back to that,' and there was a sombre light in Miss Bretherton's eyes. 'Your penitence has come too late, Eric ; now, let us go on, and I will tell you what I am willing to do for you.'

'You can give me nothing that I am willing to receive,' he

began haughtily, but Lorraine leant forward and whispered in his ear, 'Be patient for the children's sake—think of the children,' and the muscles of his face relaxed a little.

'Ay, she is right—think of the children, and don't be a fool, Eric. Though I don't pretend to forgive and be friends, I can't quite forget you are poor Ella's boy ; look here, I stopped that allowance, but I always meant to go on with it again. I have already settled with my lawyer that there shall be a charge of two hundred a year on my estate ; it is yours for life, and the two past quarters shall be paid up.'

'Aunt Marion, do you mean it ? But, no, how am I to take it ?' but again Lorraine's light touch warned him; 'the children,' came through her parted lips, and he checked himself; and then, in a voice of strong emotion, he went on :

'How am I to understand you ? You have been a perplexing problem to me all my life, Aunt Marion. You are contradicting yourself every moment. You tell me that we are not friends, and that you will never forgive me, and yet you are dealing generously with me. Do you know what two hundred a year means to me ?'

'I suppose it will keep you out of debt,' was the curt answer.

'I have kept out of that already,' he returned gravely ; 'but it has been hard work. I used to lie awake at night and wonder what I should do. Yesterday Hugo told me his boots were worn out, and I felt all day as it were the last straw. I am not ashamed to tell you this now.'

'Well, well, you have not much cause to thank me,' she replied ungraciously. 'It is in my power to make you a rich man, if I chose. Two hundred a year is a paltry sum after that ; but it is all you will ever get from me, Eric. There, don't interrupt me with any more virtuous observations, for I have not finished. I want to know what you mean to do with that imp of mischief, Hugo. He will be a nice handful presently. You had better send him to school.'

'He is not quite old enough for that. I think I must keep him at home for another year ; but he is certainly very troublesome. He teaches Eddie all sorts of mischief.'

'Yes ; he is a regular monkey. Did he not get two sovereigns out of me just now with his impudence ? You had better take my advice for once in your life, Eric. Choose any school you like, and leave the rest to me. I will pay his school bills, and Edmund's too, when he is old enough to go ; so for the future the two boys will be off your hands.'

'Aunt Marion ! And I am not to thank you for this !'

'I hate thanks'—still more crossly. 'Words, words, words—they mean nothing. What I am doing is for your mother's sake, not yours. I suppose I may be allowed to have some feeling for my only sister. You went to Charterhouse, did you not?'

'Yes; and my father was a Carthusian too.'

'Ah, poor Vincent, so he was! Well, Hugo Medcalf shall go there too. My lawyer will manage it. The boy must have a proper outfit, and look like a gentleman. Next spring, then, you will hear from Mr. Morgan. He will settle everything without reference to me; please to bear that in mind. I want no letters or communications of any kind. Mr. Morgan will have full instructions, and any complaints can be made to him.'

'I must accept your conditions, Aunt Marion, although they are very hard; but you shall not prevent me from thanking you. You have lifted off my heaviest burdens, and I am deeply grateful; but I should be still more so if I could hear you say that in your heart you forgive me.'

There was something very winning in Eric's manner, and few women could have resisted him. As he spoke, the same curious grey shade that Lorraine had noticed before came over Miss Bretherton's face. But there was no yielding in her voice.

'I never told a lie in my life,' she said harshly, 'and I am not going to begin now, and it would be a lie to say I forgive when I don't. I wish you no evil, Eric; but we are better apart. I am sorry to be so uncomplimentary; but under some circumstances it is best to tell the truth. Now, my business is done, and I shall just take the next train back to Nefydd Madoc.'

'Then go, and God bless you,' was Eric's answer, as he put out his hand impulsively. Miss Bretherton did not refuse it; but she made no response to the strong pressure.

'Now, then, Mrs. Herbert,' she said, adjusting her lace cape carefully, and with an imperious little nod of her head she swept out of the room.

Lorraine lingered a moment.

'You behaved nobly, Mr. Vincent,' she whispered. 'You have given me a lesson that I shall never forget. Please do not trouble. Miss Bretherton's hard words mean nothing.'

He smiled, but made no answer to that, and she hastened after Miss Bretherton. She was standing by the palings watching the two boys playing cricket; but she made no observation until they reached the inn door.

'There, I have eased my conscience!' she exclaimed, as though she were flinging off a load. 'Now I can go back to Black Nest and enjoy myself. Sit down a moment, Mrs. Herbert, it is early still, and I am not going to part with you just yet; it is not often I find a person to suit me.'

'But you look so tired, Miss Bretherton'—looking kindly at the pale worn face—'you really ought to be quiet now, and I am sure Pritchard would say so.'

'Pritchard is an old fool, and I never allow her to manage me. I am only suffering from an attack of moral indigestion—that boy has got on my nerves—he is not nearly so good-looking as he promised to be, and clerical attire does not suit him at all; he used to be far handsomer than that monkey Hugo.'

'We all think Mr. Vincent so nice-looking.'

'Well, well, think as you like—there will always be plenty of women to flatter a man, and the Highland ladies are no exception to this rule.'

Lorraine bore this in silence.

'You have all got him on a pedestal, and there he will stop; but we won't talk about Eric any more, I want to forget him—it has made me sick to hear him with his "Aunt Marion" and his smooth speeches. Why did he not get into a rage? any other young man would have done so in his place—but no, he posed as a saint—and martyr.'

Miss Bretherton was evidently working herself up again, but Lorraine took the conversation into her own hands.

'Excuse me, Miss Bretherton, but I would rather not talk about your nephew any more, we do not agree on this subject; in my opinion Mr. Vincent behaved splendidly, he was so gentle, manly, and quiet; now, I really must go.'

'Go, if you like; but you had far better stay. By the bye, when are you coming to Nefydd Madoc? you must pay me a visit there some day.'

This invitation surprised Lorraine; but she tried to laugh it off —she had no intention of being Miss Bretherton's guest.

'I could not leave my boy—and you know children do not suit you.'

'No, they are plagues—the best of them; and I always vowed that no boy should ever cross my threshold again. Well, I will think what is to be done, and if I find I can put up with it, I will write to you.'

'Yes, that will be the best plan'; but Lorraine inwardly told herself that any such invitation would be promptly refused. Mother Hubbard would not be a desirable hostess. 'Now, I must bid you good-bye, Miss Bretherton,' but her hand was detained.

'Good-bye, you are an honest woman, and I mean to see you again some day. I am not sure I can put up with the boy, but I will make a bargain with you : if you ever want a friend, or are in any trouble, just write to me, and I will do what I can for you—come, will you promise me this ? '

'Yes, indeed I will,' returned Lorraine earnestly ; and then a sudden kindly impulse made her stoop and kiss the cold soft cheek. Miss Bretherton did not speak, but Lorraine was almost sure that her lip quivered slightly ; as she walked up the road, she turned round once—Miss Bretherton was standing in the window watching her, but directly Lorraine waved her hand, she drew back, as though to avoid notice.

CHAPTER XXIII

'The pleasure of love is in loving. We are happier in the passion we feel than in that we excite.'—ROCHEFOUCAULT.

'Life, like a dome of many-coloured glass,
Stains the white radiance of eternity.'
PERCY BYSSHE SHELLEY.

THE next morning the waggonette from the inn carried away Miss Bretherton and the faithful Pritchard. Eric Vincent, coming out of the school next door to the forge, raised his hat with a grave smile in answer to the sharp little nod, which was all his aunt vouchsafed him, and then stood looking after her until the carriage had disappeared.

That evening Ellison and her cousin were to dine at Brae House, and Lorraine looked forward to the evening with unusual eagerness. She was anxious to see Mr. Vincent again, and to talk matters over with him, and secretly hoped that he would be beside her at dinner. But in this she was disappointed. The Rev. Eustace Cartwright, the High Church curate from Dorchester, took her in to dinner and sat beside her. Colonel Trevor was on the other side. Mr. Vincent came in late; but there was a peculiar brightness and animation in his glance as he shook hands with her, and, as he sat opposite to her talking to Muriel, she could not fail to see that he was in excellent spirits. He looked years younger; his face had lost a certain haggardness which had betrayed the constant pressure of anxiety. With the buoyancy of youth he seemed to have thrown off the load that had oppressed him; and Muriel, who knew nothing of what had happened, was surprised and even mystified by his unusual gaiety.

Lorraine found it impossible to hear what they were saying, as Mr. Cartwright demanded her whole attention. He was imparting to her his private views on the possible unity of Christendom, and it needed all her intelligence to comprehend him.   Colonel Trevor made no attempt to distract them.   He was rather silent, and talked little, even to Ellison.

Ellison was looking unusually handsome that evening.   The soft cream silk, trimmed with fine old lace that had belonged to her mother, set off her fair massive style.   She had pronounced the dress as far too smart for anything but a large formal dinner-party ; but Lorraine, who loved to see her at her best, had pleaded the change of fashions, and had urged her not to lay it by.   'On a hot summer's evening one can wear anything,' she had said ; 'and you really look quite lovely in it.'   And Ellison had suffered herself to be persuaded.

More than once Colonel Trevor glanced at her attentively, and thought that she had never looked so well, and there was a grave tenderness in his tone as he addressed her that more than once excited a vague surprise in Ellison's mind, but she only smiled in her tranquil way.   'Gavin was very kind,' she thought—'kinder than ever, perhaps because she was going away.'

On summer evenings it was always the custom at Brae to assemble in the great conservatory leading out of the drawing-room—coffee was always taken there—and the various cosy nooks were occupied by couples or trios.   By chance Lorraine found herself standing by Mr. Vincent.   Muriel had just left them to speak to her brother ; and Eric, who had been waiting for this opportunity, induced her to stroll with him to the fernery at the other end of the conservatory.   It was a cool, delightful little nook ; a sparkling fountain played amidst the ferns, and the delicious freshness of the green tints was peculiarly restful.   Two low hammock chairs had been placed there.   Lorraine seated herself in one and looked smilingly at her companion.

'I am so glad of this opportunity of speaking to you,' she said, with the naive frankness that always put Eric immediately at his ease.   'I have been longing to ask you if you have seen any more of Miss Bretherton ?'

'I only saw her start from the *Waggon and Horses* this morning,' he returned, a momentary cloud coming over his face.   'The waggonette passed me as I was coming out of the school.   She just nodded to me, and that was all.'   Then he added a little bitterly : 'I do not intend to delude myself, Mrs. Herbert ; my aunt is terribly consistent.   She is loading me with favours, but she will have nothing to do with me personally.'

'Do not be too sure of that,' replied Lorraine.   'It is not well to take pessimistic views, and human nature gives us odd surprises now and then. Some day Miss Bretherton may change her mind.'

'Ah, you do not know her!' he returned. 'Obstinacy is the Bretherton failing. My mother has told me some queer stories of dead and gone Brethertons. By her account they were singularly faithful in love and persistent in hate. But does it not strike you as strange and unnatural, as I said before, that my aunt should punish the man for the boy's fault? A generous nature could not go these lengths. Think of what she is doing for me,' he continued, as Lorraine looked at him sympathetically. 'I am to have a sufficient income for my own needs, and the education of the boys is assured. When I woke this morning I felt a free man, and as though some enjoyment of life were possible. Can you understand the feeling? and yet the kind word that would have enriched everything was wanting. I must take her bounty and feel myself in disgrace.'

'Oh no, you must not feel like that,' returned Lorraine earnestly. 'Remember that you are dealing with a very eccentric nature. I do not know Miss Bretherton sufficiently well to discuss her character. She is a stranger to me, but from the little I have seen—and I was a most unwilling intruder on your interview yesterday—I should say that, in spite of all her hard speeches, Miss Bretherton cares for you in her heart.'

Mr. Vincent shook his head.

'I cannot lay such flattering unction to my soul. I am afraid your kind nature misleads you. Mrs. Herbert, do not say again what you observed just now. I am thankful that you were present last evening; if I had been alone I should have found it difficult to restrain myself. I do not wish to be hard on a near relative, but I do not think that because I was a wayward, self-willed child, and behaved badly to her, that I deserved all those gibes and reproaches—at least, I am trying to do my duty now.'

'Yes, and Miss Bretherton knows it too. Mr. Vincent, it is hard, and you have much to bear. In my own mind I think it is wrong and cruel for her to disinherit you. You are her nearest of kin, and have a right to expect her to leave her money to you.'

'You are very kind to take my part, and it does me good to hear you,' returned Eric gratefully, 'but I hold a very different opinion. I think my aunt has every right to please herself in this matter, and to leave her property as she likes. It was a mere fluke that the money came to her; it is not in any sense family property; she can turn Black Nest into an asylum for idiots if she likes. I do not say that I should not be glad if the money were to come to me, but I never expect to receive another penny, and I am deeply

grateful for what she has done for me. If she would only have
given me a kind look and word I should have been more than
content. There are two ways of flinging a bone to a dog, and even
a dog has a right to his feelings.'

Lorraine was silent. It was natural, she thought, that Mr.
Vincent should be mortified and hurt by his aunt's contemptuous
repulse. His masculine pride revolted against her injustice ; and
though poverty, and not his will, consented to accept the proffered
gifts, there was a bitter flavour attached to them. She could
understand his feelings so well ; it was no use discussing a painful
subject ; it would be wiser to put it aside, at least for the present,
and when she said something to this effect he had tacitly agreed.

It was twilight now, and some coloured lamps among the foliage
gave a soft, subdued light. Ellison and Colonel Trevor passed
them at this moment on their way to the garden, and at a little
distance Muriel was standing talking to Mr. Cartwright. She had
a slightly bored expression on her face, and more than once looked
longingly towards Lorraine and her companion, as though she would
willingly have joined them. Lorraine noticed it at last.

'Miss Trevor is certainly not interesting herself properly in the
unity of Christendom,' she said in an amused tone. 'I behaved
much better at dinner. Shall we go to her rescue, Mr. Vincent?'
But this proposition evidently met with no favour.

'Cartwright is wrong to ride his hobby so perpetually,' returned
Eric calmly. 'I daresay Miss Trevor votes him a bore in her
heart, but there is no need for us to be bored too. I was just
going to propose a turn in the garden, as Trevor has set us an
example ; do come, Mrs. Herbert, it is a delicious evening.'

Lorraine rose at once with her usual good-nature ; she always
liked to do what other people wished, if possible ; and in another
moment Eric would have got his way and secured her sole company ; but the events of the previous day had unsettled him, and
he was not quite on his usual guard.

Lorraine, turning to him with her pleasant smile, was a little
startled by the grave intensity of the glance that met hers. It was
no ordinary passing admiration for a congenial companion in
Eric's deep-set eyes, and some subtle instinct put her at once on
her guard.

'I am afraid I must ask you to excuse me,' she said gently, and
yet quite naturally. 'I see Mrs. Trevor is all alone, and I have
hardly spoken to her this evening' ; and before Eric could quite
realise his disappointment, Lorraine was half across the conservatory,
leaving him sorely puzzled. Was it only her usual unselfishness,
or had she quietly repelled him? Had he in any way betrayed

himself? This was what baffled him. She had been so kind, so friendly, so sweet in her womanly sympathy; and then in a moment she had left him, and he saw her gaily chatting with Mrs. Trevor, without another thought for him.

Poor Eric, he was young enough to feel his disappointment keenly; he could so seldom get her to himself; with all her sweetness and sociability the young widow was singularly inaccessible. He did not go so far as to think himself badly treated; but he felt moody and restless, and strolled out into the dark winding walks to recover and pull himself together. 'Well, he was a fool,' he told himself savagely, as he strode down one path after another, 'but after all there was method and wisdom in his madness. How was he to help loving such a woman?' Yes— under the summer starlight he said it outright; it was that; there was no good in his disguising it from himself any longer—it was love, love, love; and there was no need to be ashamed of it. He had come to Highlands to find his fate—this sweet woman was to be the blessing or sorrow of his life. It was an assured fact, and, poor fellow, how he gloried in it. Most men of his age would have already met with some youthful divinity whom they had enshrined as their ideal, and to whom they had sworn eternal fealty. But, alas, how seldom men wed their ideal. Eric was not of the ordinary calibre; his life had been too hard-working and full of care to leave him leisure for love in idleness, and for a time his mother had sufficed him. He had not indulged in more than passing fancy until he saw Mrs. Herbert.

'How could he help himself?' he reiterated passionately, as the cool flower-scented air blew across his heated temples, and stray night-moths fluttered across his path. He had never seen any one like her. He had never asked himself if she were beautiful— he had never thought about her beauty or lack of beauty; only from the first day of their meeting a mere glance of her brown eyes had thrilled him through and through.

She was so true, so womanly, so entirely herself in every word and deed, so simple and natural and kindly, that from the first he had been at his ease with her. No—he was no fool; every one loved her—the children, and Miss Trevor, and her cousin. He wished that he knew something about her dead husband, poor fellow; how he pitied him! Fancy being married to a woman like that, and then being obliged to leave her. What a grisly enemy death must have seemed to him!

Had she cared very much for him? Strange to say, this doubt had come to him at the beginning of their acquaintance. Mrs. Herbert's calm cheerfulness was too apparent. She was certainly no broken-hearted widow, with all her best affections buried in her husband's grave ; and yet she was a woman of strong feeling. Her passionate devotion to her child proved that. He wished he could find out something about her previous life, but some delicacy prevented him from speaking to Muriel Trevor. He knew from her own lips that she had been very poor, for on the subject of her poverty she was always very frank, and she would talk perpetually of her life in Beaumont Street, and of her cousin's generosity. ' I do love to owe everything to her,' she had once said to him. ' I am not a bit proud when I care for any one. She is just a splendid guardian angel to me, and I like to feel safely tucked up under her wings. It is her nature to give, and it is my nature to receive,' she had finished, with a merry laugh at her own quaint conceit. And then she had lectured him playfully on his pride.

Eric was very happy if he had only known it—it is only youth that can be so charmingly miserable. If Werther had not committed suicide, and had allowed himself to live to hale and hearty middle age, he would have looked back on those bread-and-butter days, and his frantic admiration for the cheerful Charlotte, with something like regret. What splendid evenings of woe he had enjoyed with the nightingale. In the retrospect of years those arid desert days seem blossoming with rare roses. One can imagine the elderly and sober-minded Werther saying to himself, ' What a fool I must have been ! She was a nice creature, certainly, Lottchen ; but fancy my destroying myself on her account. Another cup of coffee, my Pauline, and then we will resume our promenade. Do you hear that youngster twanging his guitar under our Carlotta's window ? *Herz, mein Herz.* Oh, the young idiot—the dolt ; but at his age, seest thou, I should have done the same.

' The world goes up and the world goes down, and the sunshine follows the rain. From one generation to another the same old drama is enacted, and youth in its motley plays its perpetual merry jest.'

Not that it is always a jest, heaven knows—and that youth does not sometimes drink its bitter draught out of life's cup. Young hearts can ache, and some, alas ! break, and some wither and grow old before their time for want of proper nutriment. But to youth, and youth only, belong the splendid dreams that, like the rainbow, span the heavens with an arc of glory, the infinite possibilities, the fragrant pains that, like crushed rose-leaves, emit sweetness from their bruises, and which, rightly taken, form a precious spikenard for future use.

Oh, pains and penalties inseparable from youth, how impossible to understand them rightly, until the years have cleared the vision, and looking out over the world we no longer 'see men like trees walking.'

Lorraine, sitting in her snug corner talking happily to Mrs. Trevor, broke off in her sentence now and then to wonder how long Mr. Vincent would choose to absent himself. Perhaps—here her brow cleared at the thought—he had met Ellison and Colonel Trevor, and the three were pacing the long walk together.

'It was a little hard on him, but I did it for the best,' she thought, with a sort of wistful tenderness. 'Young men are so odd—they need so little encouragement. Give an inch and they take an ell. I like Mr. Vincent excessively—I would not hurt him for worlds ; but—but——' Here Lorraine, blushing a little at her own unspoken thought, interrupted herself to go on with the conversation.

CHAPTER XXIV

'The cankers of a calm world and a long peace.'—SHAKESPEARE.

' 'Tis strange, but true ; for truth is always stranger than fiction.'—BYRON.

THAT evening was destined to be an eventful one to others besides
Eric Vincent. The little drama of human life that was being
played out on the pretty stage of a 'Surrey village was steadily
advancing to its climax. But not one of the actors knew their
rôle perfectly or understood their proper part.

To Ellison, tranquil and unobservant, the stroll through the
Brae Woods in the soft summer starlight was no different from a
hundred others she had taken with Gavin. Perhaps he was more
silent than usual, or there was deeper stillness in the Woodlands.
It was a sultry evening, and Gavin had complained that there was
no air in the gardens, and had persuaded her to extend their walk
towards the Woodlands lodge. At that hour they were safe from
meeting any one, unless it were some groom or helper from the
farm on his way to the village. Ellison, wrapped in her soft fleecy
shawl, and walking with uncovered head, looked like some stately
white princess out of fairyland with her knight beside her ; for
Colonel Trevor's grey overcoat lent itself to the subdued harmony
of tones.

They had reached the gate leading to the lodge, where Gavin
had first met Lorraine, and Ellison, leaning indolently against it,
looked admiringly at the trim lodge embowered in honeysuckle
and roses. A bright radiance of lamp-light streamed from the open
window, and the doubtful fragrance of tobacco blended with the
sweetest scents ; it reminded Ellison that Gavin had not had his
usual cigarette.

As she turned to him to mention the oversight, she saw that he was leaning with one arm against the gate watching her; something in his expression gave her a curious thrill of mingled nervousness and fear.

'You have forgotten your cigarette,' she said, quickly averting her face and regarding the lodge window. An undefinable feeling made her wish that they were back in the Brae drawing-room; but even as this thought passed through her mind, a quiet hand was laid on hers, and another lightly placed on her shoulder brought her face to face with Gavin.

'Never mind the lodge,' he said with odd peremptoriness. 'It looks as it always does—picturesque and cosy. I did not wish to light my cigarette, for I have rather serious work on hand to-night. We are both of us a trifle nervous, Ellison. What makes your hand so cold, and why are you afraid to look at me? Surely you do not fear what I am going to say, that I love you?' Then a great terror suddenly took possession of Ellison's quiet soul, for she knew the dreaded moment had come, and that the crisis of her life had arrived. Other men had told her that they loved her, had patiently and persistently wooed her; but all their ardent words had not disturbed her serenity. She had sent them away, with some sadness, it is true, but no hesitation in her manner; but no such sending away was possible now.

In a moment the heaven of her still content seemed broken up with a sudden electrical storm, and her singular temperament quailed like a frightened bird, whose nest had been scorched by the lightning. A rush of unknown and agitating emotions made her breathless and white to her lips. She knew what was coming and why he had brought her here to the boundary line of his estate. He was going to ask her to be his wife; and though Helen was not forgotten, she was to be invited to fill her place.

It cannot be denied that Ellison's nature differed strangely from other women's; she shrank vaguely from the very words and looks that would have been like the elixir of life to an emotional nature. If only she could arrest those words on his lips and prevent him from saying them. How was she to explain to him that she was not yet ready; that any change in their position would be exquisitely painful to her; that it was necessary for her to become used to the idea before she could pledge herself? No thought of refusing him entered her head. Was it likely that she could refuse him anything? but if, without hurting him, she could explain—could ward off the dreaded question.

'Why are you so pale, dear?' he asked, still holding her steadily before him, and there was a hurt tone in his voice. 'Surely—you cannot really be afraid of me,'—but all the same he could read the terror in her blue eyes; the light from the lodge window made every change of expression visible to him.

'I think I am afraid,' she almost whispered. 'Gavin, do not be hurt at something I am going to say. You know I am a little odd in things, and different from other women—you have often told me so—but I want you——' And here she paused, unable to go on; the very grasp of those thin, sinewy hands was telling her mutely that he was stronger than she, and would have his way.

Her nervousness was so excessive that it made him smile, though he was a trifle. nervous himself, but he was very gentle and patient with her.

'I cannot have you look so distressed, dearest,' he said soothingly. 'Tell me what it is you want, and I will see if it be possible. You shall have your say first; will that content you?'

'You are very kind,' she returned, almost under her breath. Never, never had the stately, self-possessed Ellison looked so subdued. 'I want you not to say any more to-night, but to wait'—here her voice was scarcely audible—'until I return from Switzerland; it—it will give me time to get used to the idea.'

'You are sure that you know all I was going to say,' he asked, with a grave smile, and she bowed her head without speaking. How could she fail to know, when look and touch were so eloquent?

Colonel Trevor looked disturbed; this was plainly not what he intended; his plan had been that he and Ellison should plight their troth before she left England; but it was evident that this was not her wish.

'You are a dear woman,' he said, dropping her hands, and leaning against the gate again; 'but you are not faultless, you are disappointing me terribly to-night.'

'Am I? I am so sorry, Gavin, and I should so like to please you.'

'You could please me easily by letting me finish,' he said, looking alert and eager in a moment; but she lifted her eyes; they were full of pain and entreaty.

'I am very selfish, but will you please me in this, dear Gavin? it is only for five or six weeks.'

'Only! I don't believe you care for me in the least,' he returned almost angrily—'I mean in the way I want you to care, or you would not put me off for five or six weeks.'

'Oh yes, I do,' she replied earnestly, and then grew crimson over the admission. 'Gavin, you know I am a little odd; don't be hurt, please, but just give me my way for once.'

'Does that mean that you are never to have your own way

again ?' with a searching glance that seemed to probe her very soul , perhaps he was content with the result of his survey, for a half smile came to his lips.

'Very well,' he returned, taking her hand gently ; 'you are very wilful, most inconveniently so, but I must yield, I suppose ; but let us clearly understand each other. I am to leave you free until you return from Switzerland, and not trouble you with any worrying letters ; well, I will submit to my share of the bargain if you will faithfully promise to fulfil yours ; that is, to give me the earliest possible opportunity after your return to finish my interrupted speech ; and lastly '—and here he looked into her eyes—'to give me the answer that I am longing to hear.'

'I promise,' she replied in a low voice, but she did not look at him.

'Faithfully, Ellison !'

'Yes, faithfully—and thank you—thank you for being so patient with me !'

'I think I deserve all the thanks you choose to give me'; and then stooping over her he kissed her broad, white brow ; his touch was so gentle that it did not startle her, although she had never received a caress from him before.

'We may as well go back now,' he said, placing her hand on his arm, and very silently they walked back through the Woodlands.

Colonel Trevor was not unhappy after all, he knew that he had no cause for fear. Averse as she was to matrimony, and reluctant to give up her treasured independence, he knew in his inmost heart that he was much to her ; that the tranquil affection she had long given him would soon be quickened and stimulated ; and though the delay vexed him, he was aware that he was sure of winning her at last. Ellison might be a little cold and reserved, but she was true as steel.

Their long absence had been noticed by two people more than once. Mrs. Trevor had looked anxiously at the door leading into the garden, and Lorraine had wondered first to herself and then aloud what had become of Ellison.

When at last the truants made their appearance, and Ellison sat down beside them, each of them made their private comment. Mrs. Trevor, who was very quick-witted, saw at once that something had happened. Had they quarrelled ? Ellison certainly did not look like herself ; but no, she would never quarrel with Gavin, the thing was impossible ; had he—and here Mrs. Trevor's heart gave a quick beat of excitement—had her wish been realised, had Gavin like a sensible man asked Ellison to marry him ? She had not refused him, certainly, for her son looked far too placid for such a notion to enter her head ; very probably Ellison had asked to think over it a little ; and here Mrs. Trevor certainly grazed the truth very closely.

Meanwhile Lorraine was saying to herself :

' Something is troubling Ellison ; she has a worried expression. I never saw her look like that before. I do not think Colonel Trevor is in his usual spirits to-night either ; he was so silent at dinner. How I wish she would confide in me ; I do so long to help her, but there is no chance of that, I am afraid ; Ellison is far too strong to need sympathy ' ; and then some one proposed that Mrs. Herbert should sing, and the little group in the conservatory broke up. Colonel Trevor walked home with them as usual, but Eric Vincent made some excuse and left early ; they were rather a silent little trio, though Lorraine made a cheerful remark now and then : but as they crossed the Brae meadow, Colonel Trevor roused himself to say playfully :

' We are a very quiet party. Ellison, you remind me of the enchanted princess in the fairy tale, who was compelled to be dumb for a time. I remember she wore some shimmering gown of cloth of silver, and in this dim light all that whiteness seems to shine somehow, as though it were woven moonbeams.'

' What a picturesque idea,' returned Lorraine, with a merry laugh ; but Ellison only smiled faintly. ' Why had she bedecked herself with that bridal finery ? ' she thought, as she drew her fleecy wrap round her with a little shiver she could not control. Colonel Trevor noticed it, and asked anxiously if she were cold.

' The dews are unusually heavy to-night,' he said ; and then the lights of Brae Farm came in sight, and at the little gate they parted.

' Shall I see you again before I go ? ' asked Ellison ; she put the question with a little effort as she gave him her hand.

' I fear not,' he answered gravely ; ' you know I have to go to London to-morrow evening, and then to Chichester, and you leave early on Monday. No, we shall not meet again for some weeks, I fear.'

' Yes, I see—I hope you will have a pleasant time '—and then with a silent hand-pressure they parted ; there was nothing more to say. For the first time in her life Ellison was glad to think that there was no prospect of seeing Gavin the next day.

Lorraine followed her to her room to offer her help, but Ellison did not invite her to remain. ' Have you had a pleasant evening ? ' she asked ; ' you looked as though you were enjoying yourself. I hope you will not mind, Lorraine, but I am too tired to talk things over to-night,' and she dismissed her with a kiss.

Lorraine looked very grave as she withdrew. 'What can have gone wrong?' she said to herself. 'Surely—surely she cannot have refused him. They both look different, somehow; and she seemed so shy and silent with him. Oh, why will she not let me help her? Ellison is so self-contained, she will never ask any one's advice.' And then she kissed her boy, and her eyes suddenly filled with tears.

Lorraine could not have explained the rush of sadness that took possession of her, or why the thought came to her suddenly, that she had not had her good things like other women. The devotion of a man like Ralph Herbert had been only an unspeakable degradation; to a woman of her nature, a daily and hourly trial, a grievous burden from which only grim death could free her. She had no tender relenting memories of him; her very pity for him was bordered with contempt. For the first time it crossed her mind what it must be to be loved by a man like Colonel Trevor, a man who was at once strong and gentle and unselfish, who had no low aims, no hidden vices, and whose very faults did not detract from his real nobility; a man who was never afraid to speak the truth, and to whom crooked dealings were impossible. 'He is good as far as human frailty allows him to be,' she said to herself. 'No one can be perfect in this life; but as far as I can judge, he is worthy of her. Surely she cannot hesitate; she must know; she must surely know that the woman Colonel Trevor marries is sure to be happy'; and then she laid her cheek against her boy's soft hair. 'Tedo, my darling,' she whispered, 'if you do not grow up a good man you will break your poor mother's heart.' And then she cried a little, with some curious indefinable emotion, and knelt down and said her simple prayers; and when she arose from her knees the weight had lifted.

Meanwhile Ellison had drawn an easy-chair to the window, and was sitting looking out into the summer darkness with wide unseeing eyes. She must think things over—that was how she put it to herself.

Once, when she was a mere child, her mother had found her sitting in a dark corner with her face to the wall, and had fondly questioned her; had she been naughty, or was something troubling her darling?

'Oh no,' Ellison had replied. 'Nursie says I am very good— that she never did see such a good child—but I thought it would be nice to shut every one out, one does have such a lot of thoughts sometimes, and they are so confusing, they make my head giddy.'

Ellison's thoughts were turning her giddy now—she was simply dazed. She had never indulged much in introspection, or troubled herself about the inner workings of her mind. After the fashions of some women, psychological questions did not interest her. She had no curious instincts. It puzzled her how people cared to take a clock to pieces in order to understand its mechanism. It was sufficient for her that the clock kept good time.

Now and then Ellison felt vaguely that she was lacking in some quality which was common to ordinary natures. Why was she so content with her environment ? Other women in her position would have married long ago; but she had never felt any desire to give up her freedom. She was so happy, so entirely content. Gavin's friendship had so completely satisfied her; he was the chief element in her happiness, the nucleus of all her interest. His masculine opinions had endorsed and strengthened hers. In her opinion there was nothing missing in her life—nothing that she wished altered or improved.

The mistress of Brae Farm was a contented woman. At seven-and-twenty she looked out fearlessly and happily on life ; she never asked herself how it would be in future years ; for the present she desired no change.

But now her trusty friend had sounded the keynote that was bringing crashing discords and tremors to her tranquil mind. Gavin cared for her—more than she had guessed—he loved her well enough to wish to make her his wife, and yet, strange to say, this idea gave her more pain than pleasure.

With all her quiet matter-of-fact, Ellison was dimly conscious of unknown capacities in her nature ; of hidden depths, of which those who knew and loved her best were ignorant ; and some subtle instinct warned her that she would love and suffer with an intensity that would have surprised ordinary natures.

True, the music was dumb at present. Some instruments need a master-hand to bring out their sound and sweetness. Until Gavin spoke, Ellison was unconscious of the extent of her affection for him. Friendship is sometimes an elastic term, and includes much, and with all her good sense and cleverness Ellison was little better than a big, inexperienced child ; she had often amused Gavin by her crude and unsophisticated notions of life.

' Mrs. Herbert could tell you a thing or two, I fancy,' he had said to her once very bluntly. ' You are as innocent as one of your own field daisies' ; and this had rather oppressed her. A wise woman like Ellison objects to be told that she has no knowledge of life.

So there was sadness and dismay, but no hesitation in Ellison's mind that night. If Gavin wanted her to marry him, it was not likely that she would refuse. But oh, if he only knew what a mistake he was making, and how much better it would be to go on as they were doing, seeing each other every day.

She did not attempt to delude herself. She knew Gavin's character too well to think her old independent existence possible. Gavin would be her master and the master of Brae Farm ; with all his kindness his soldier's life had made him a disciplinarian. His wife would feel the iron curb under the velvet glove ; no doubt Helen had, though she had adored him. For the first time in her life Ellison would have to submit to the opinion of another, to wait for another's decision, and it would be no easy lesson to her.

' I wish I were more like other people,' she sighed at last. ' I ought to be so happy instead of making myself miserable. I know I have disappointed him this evening ; but how could I help it ? How is a woman to help her nature ? Dear Gavin, he was so good, so patient with me ; but if he only knew how he has spoilt things. I shall not care for Switzerland one bit now. I shall only be thinking of him, and worrying myself about things, and longing and dreading to see him again '—and here a hot blush came to her face, for all at once the five weeks seemed a weary period of absence, and her long-looked-for visit appeared in the light of an exile. ' I wish I were not going. I wish something would happen to prevent it '—and then she gave a vexed little laugh at her own inconsistency. No, it was no use trying to understand herself, she was far too upset to be reasonable. When a person was over-excited it was safer to leave all cogitation until the morning, and with this sensible reflection she went to bed, and then lay open-eyed and weary until the cheerful dawn and the faint twitter of waking birds soothed her, and she slept. But though she did not know it until long afterwards, it was a different Ellison who rose from her bed that fair summer morning.

CHAPTER XXV

'Put sadness away from you, for truly sadness is the sister of half-heartedness and bitterness.'—*Shepherd of Hermas.*

ELLISON'S behaviour during the few ensuing days that remained before her departure confirmed Lorraine in her conviction that something serious had happened that evening at Brae. Ellison was certainly very unlike herself. She was restless, *distraite*, and seemed to dread an unoccupied moment. She was incessantly roving through the house, or across the farm with her factotum Sam Brattle and the faithful Bairn, and would come back for meals with an unwontedly fagged expression on her face.

She seemed to avoid conversation, except on the most general topics, and never once mentioned the Brae people. When Lorraine begged her playfully to put aside her letters and accounts and be idle a little, she only shook her head with the excuse that she was far too busy. Yet if Lorraine left the room for ever so brief an absence, she always found her on her return sitting with her hands in her lap, and her eyes fixed on some distant object as though she were lost in thought. A sudden question at such a moment seemed to startle and annoy her, and she would answer with an impatience bordering on irritability.

One evening, when she seemed unusually restless, and was pacing aimlessly up and down the garden paths, Lorraine put down her work and joined her.

'The weather was unusually sultry, and Sam Brattle, who was rather low in his spirits just then, had indulged that morning in the most dreary prognostications.

'The weather's meaning mischief,' he had observed disconsolately. 'They were saying over at Darley that there is a storm brewing that will do a deal of harm. There has been too long a drought, and the heat of the sun is over-fierce, and when the storm comes it will be a rare one.' And Ellison could not help agreeing with him.

She made no observation when Lorraine gently slipped her hand underneath her arm and commenced keeping pace with her; and they made the round of the garden in silence.

Presently Lorraine said very quietly : 'I wish you would tell me what has been troubling you these last two days, dear—ever since we dined at Brae. I should so love to help you!'

The question seemed to startle Ellison ; a quick flush came to her face. All at once her conscience pricked her. Had she been so disagreeable that Lorraine should ask that?

'Of course I see that you are worried, and have something on your mind,' continued Lorraine impulsively. 'You are not a bit like yourself—not a bit like my dear old cheerful Ellison. There is nothing very wrong, is there, dear?'

This seemed almost to shock Ellison.

'There is nothing wrong at all,' she returned quickly. 'What can have put such a thing in your head, Lorraine?' And then her voice changed and shook a little. 'I do not like you to say that. I am not troubled—I mean,' interrupting herself, 'I ought not to be troubled, for I have no real cause for anxiety.'

'Some people are clever enough to invent their own worries,' observed her cousin cheerfully ; 'but you are no self-tormentor. Your worries are not imaginary ones.'

'I begin to think one may be mistaken about oneself, after all,' returned Ellison in a tired voice. 'Perhaps Sam Brattle is right, and there is a storm brewing. We shall feel clearer when it has passed.'

'I thought you were weather-proof,' replied Lorraine reproachfully. 'No, no, Ellison—you shall not put me off with an excuse of that kind. You may tell me in plain language to hold my tongue, if you like, and leave you in peace, and I will submit ; but no such trivial, flimsy excuse between you and me.'

Then a smile did come to Ellison's face.

'You are right, Lorraine dear,' she said penitently; 'and I will not throw dust in your eyes if I can help it. But indeed there is nothing that I can tell you. One cannot help being a little thoughtful sometimes. As Gavin says, "Life is fearfully complex."' It was curious how she hesitated as she spoke the name, as though it had suddenly become difficult to her.

Lorraine's eyes opened rather widely as she heard it, and said to herself : 'It will all come right. It is nothing after all. As poor Ralph used to say, "She is only shying at the bit."' And that night she said no more, for which forbearance Ellison was secretly grateful, though she marvelled at it.

The next day Lorraine herself felt unaccountably depressed. She had awakened so, and not all her efforts could shake it off. She spent rather a solitary day, for Ellison, who was to leave Highlands early the next morning, was very busy packing and giving her final orders to her household. Not only Sam Brattle, but Mrs. Tucker, Joe Brand, Daniel, and Eunice had their several instructions. Lorraine was to be mistress, *pro tem.*, and Mrs. Tucker and Sam were to be her chief lieutenants. 'You can always consult Cousin Louise or Gavin if you are in any difficulty,' she had remarked earlier in the day. 'We are going to such out-of-the-way places that I fear letters may be delayed a little. But you can always act safely on their advice without reference to me. It will be sure to be right.'

She had spoken a little hurriedly, sorting the papers on her table all the time; but as she was leaving the room she said, in her old matter-of-fact tone: 'Sam will not trouble you much; he knows my wishes. If he is in any perplexity he will go up to Brae House of his own accord. He is used to doing it when I am away.'

Lorraine listened and assented. Then, as Dorcas was busy helping her mistress, she went up to the Dovecote to amuse Tedo. The still intense heat was trying him and making him fretful. His unusual naughtiness added to Lorraine's discomfort. She never punished him without suffering herself; but she dared not spoil him. Her love for her child, though it verged on idolatry, never blinded her to the fact that he might possibly inherit one or other of his father's faults, and it was her constant prayer that she might see and check any such failing. Ralph had been a petted child, and the false indulgence of a doting, injudicious mother, more mindful of the outward than the inward graces of the handsome lad, had fostered dangerously the ill weeds that thrive in such soils. Lorraine knew this and took warning.

When Tedo came out of his corner, languid with crying and very contrite, Lorraine would have liked to cry herself, but she refrained as she kissed him.

'My boy is a good boy now,' she said cheerfully. And Tedo laid his curly head against her shoulder in a perfectly contented manner.

'Boy means always to be good now, for ever and ever, amen.' For this was his usual formula, his sign and treaty for the future; and for once the quaint speech did not excite a smile. On the contrary, she made a plaintive little response.

'I hope so ; it does tire poor mother dreadfully when Tedo is naughty.'

Tedo looked alarmed at this. He took his mother by the chin and looked at her anxiously. 'You won't be tired no more—there !' he announced triumphantly ; and then he went off to play with Tweedledee.

Late that evening, when Ellison came down from her room, she found Lorraine sitting in the cosy nook in rather a forlorn attitude, her hands clasped behind her head, and an unmistakable look of depression in her eyes. She did not rouse herself, but as her cousin was about to pass her, she suddenly put out one hand and drew her down beside her.

'Do sit down and be quiet a moment,' she said imploringly. 'I have not seen you all day, and to-morrow you will be gone.'

'There was so much to do,' returned Ellison apologetically, 'but I have quite finished now. Lorraine, you must be very kind to poor Bairn ; he is dreadfully low-spirited to-night. He will persist in lying on my box. I believe he means to sleep there ; that is always his way. He thinks as long as my box is there I am safe.'

'Dogs are so sagacious ! Oh yes, Tedo and I will do our best to comfort him, poor old fellow ! But, oh dear, I am dull myself to-night. I can't think what ails me. I wish you were not going, Ellison. All day long I have been wishing that ; I woke with the feeling this morning, and I cannot get rid of it. Do you believe in presentiments ?'

'I suppose I do—most people do ; but I do not call every little passing feeling of melancholy a presentiment.' And then she looked at her cousin affectionately. 'It is nice to think you will miss me, dear, and be glad to welcome me home. And you will not be dull, Lorraine. You and Muriel will be together all day. I know you both well enough for that.'

'I am afraid you are wrong there. I have had a fresh blow this evening,' returned Lorraine dejectedly. 'Muriel has just been here. The Medlicotts will take no refusal. They are very old friends of her father's, she says, and her mother seems quite hurt because she has declined to go to them ; so to satisfy them all she has promised to go on Thursday for a fortnight. She declares that she will not stay a day longer ; but one knows how difficult it is to keep one's resolutions in such cases.'

'Ilfracombe will do Muriel a world of good,' replied Ellison thoughtfully ; 'and I know Gavin will be pleased. Muriel never can be made to realise that she owes some duties to her old friends; but I am sorry on your account, Lorraine, and I don't wonder you feel dull.'

'I don't believe I am dull on Muriel's account, though I shall miss her badly; we were going to do all manner of things together. I have offered to teach Nora for an hour every morning; I have so much on my hands that I dare not undertake more; at her age it is a pity to lose even a fortnight.'

'There I agree with you'—but Lorraine interrupted her.

'There is one thing I must ask you, Ellison, before I forget it. Hugo is such a monkey, that I never dare believe his tales. I think he invents them now and then. Did you really give him and Eddie leave to sail their boat in the big pond whenever he liked?'

'Whenever he liked. Certainly not; why, they might get trampled by the cattle or horses when they come down to drink. What I told Hugo was this: that they might bring their boats early in the afternoon when things are quiet. Daniel is generally at leisure then, and can easily look after them. Hugo has strict orders from me never to go near the pond when he and Edmund are alone, and he has promised me faithfully that he never will do so; why, Lorraine, the pond is quite deep in the middle. I have told Sam that I want to have some more fencing put up in one part; but he says it will be so awkward for washing the carts and things.'

'I found Hugo very near it this afternoon, but he certainly had no boat. I fancy he was throwing stones, for the geese looked angry, and the old gander was hissing dreadfully. Hugo was a little sulky when I questioned him, and not in the best of tempers. He said Daniel was busy and his boat was broken, and his brother had not had time to mend it, and Miss Lee wouldn't mind his looking at the pond if he did not go near it, for she had told him and Eddie that they might sail their boats whenever they liked, and he made Eddie corroborate this.'

'You must just explain matters to Hugo; a little plain speaking will do him good. I hope those children will not harass you, Lorraine, they seem to have the run of the farm at all hours. I do not like to check them, for Mr. Vincent's sake, but I wish Hugo could be at school this year.'

'I begin to wish the same,' returned her cousin with a sigh; 'it is not the trouble I mind, for I love to hear the children about the place, and Effie is a darling, but Hugo teases Tedo sometimes; he is so strong and rough, and my boy is so delicate; but he is as fond as possible of Hugo, and is always wanting to play with him.'

'Tedo is getting stronger every day; Cousin Louise and I were saying so yesterday,' remarks Ellison conclusively. 'Dr. Howell's tonic suits him.' And this opinion cheered Lorraine immensely.

That speech of Colonel Trevor's had weighed on her heart very heavily, far more heavily than he could have guessed ; she had often lain awake at night thinking of it.

'Do not hold him too tightly. I had a treasure too, and I lost it.' The peculiar gravity of the voice with which he said it had affected her strangely.

Ellison went to bed early that night, for she was to start at seven ; her active day had somehow restored her balance, and she looked more like her own self as she handed the key-basket to Lorraine with a little speech she had prepared for the occasion.

'You may open every door you like, there are no Blue Beard's cupboards at Brae Farm,' she said playfully ; and Lorraine replied, with assumed gravity, that the sight of her cousin's methods and contrivances would be a liberal education in housekeeping. She was down in ample time to see Ellison enjoy her early breakfast ; but it may be doubted whether she or Bairn felt more low-spirited. When the actual moment came for saying good-bye, Bairn's tail was limp, and flapped distressfully against the ground, and there was a strained almost human look in his eyes as Ellison patted his glossy head ; but Lorraine unselfishly kept herself and her feelings in the background.

'Good-bye, Ellison darling,' she said with a semblance of cheerfulness. 'I will try and take care of everything and every-body ; have a real good time and come back and tell us all about it.'

Ellison smiled and kissed her with unusual affection, then she lifted Tedo in her arms : 'Be a good boy and take care of mother,' she said, pressing the little fellow to her heart. She had no idea how fond she was of him until that moment ; but Tedo's endearing little ways had won her heart. As the waggonette turned out of the gate she leant forward for a last glance. Lorraine was standing in the porch in the morning sunshine, her slim girlish figure in its black gown framed against the creepers ; the child and dog were still beside her ; the light breeze had brought down some white rose-leaves that fluttered on her hair, giving her a faint white halo in the distance. 'Dear Lorraine, how I have grown to love her,' thought Ellison, as she settled herself with a sigh in the corner of the waggonette.

CHAPTER XXVI

'The rank is but the guinea stamp,
The man's the gowd, for a' that.'
                                        BURNS.

'O how full of briers is this working-day world.'
                                        SHAKESPEARE.

MURIEL came down to the farm an hour or two later, and spent
most of the day there ; and as Lorraine declared that the house felt
empty and desolate without its mistress, they took their work and
sat in the Brae Woods with Tedo and the dogs.   There was no air
anywhere, but the cedars afforded them a grateful shade.   Muriel
was not in her usual spirits—the old discontented fretfulness was
apparent in her manner.   Rome was not built in a day ; and no
man or woman, however earnestly he or she may desire to amend
these faults, can root them up in a moment.

Muriel chose to pose for a martyr, because her good old friends
had been kindly peremptory and refused to let her off.   She had no
wish to leave Highlands.   She grumbled a good deal about the
length of the journey, and her dislike to what she termed 'a rabble
of young people of all ages.'   But Lorraine only smiled a little
incredulously, and assured her that she was mistaken, and that the
change would do her good ; but Muriel's next speech amused her
still more.

'You are not a bit sympathetic this morning, Mrs. Herbert.
But it is really very vexatious my going away just now.   I am
not likely to see Mr. Vincent, as Gavin is away, but I wish you
would tell him that I really am obliged to go, and that I would
not neglect Nora if I could help it.'

'But we have settled that Nora is to come to me,' returned
Lorraine, somewhat surprised at this, and then a sudden thought
made her alter her sentence.   'I shall be sure to see him !' she

exclaimed soothingly. 'Don't trouble your head about that, Muriel dear. Mr. Vincent would never accuse you of neglect, and he knows people must have a change sometimes.'

'I don't think I require change like some people,' returned Muriel rather perversely. 'Mother does. Just fancy, she has gone up to town again this hot day; she says she has some business, but of course I know it is only some little fad or other. She is coming back early; I half thought of driving into Bramfield to meet her if it gets a little cooler.'

'I would go anyway if I were you,' returned Lorraine gently. 'It would be a pleasant surprise for her,' but she thought it better to say no more. Muriel's selfishness was as transparent as a child's. She never thought to disguise it; it so seldom occurred to her to pay these little attentions to her mother.

Lorraine knew well why Mrs. Trevor had gone to town so soon again; she had offered to accompany her, but Mrs. Trevor was afraid Muriel would scent some mystery. 'I should like your society, my dear Mrs. Herbert,' she said wistfully, 'but I think it will be better for me to go alone. I ought not to be such a coward at my age,' she added, with a tremulous smile.

Muriel grew a little more cheerful as the morning wore on, and Lorraine exerted herself to make the time pass pleasantly. They had luncheon together, and then Muriel went back to Brae.

Lorraine hesitated over what she should do with herself that evening. It was no use moping indoors. A long walk and some definite errand would be far more beneficial. Mrs. Trevor had asked her to have luncheon at Brae the next day, as Muriel was to go up to town early in the afternoon to join Mr. Medlicott and his eldest daughter at the Langham, and travel down with them the following morning. 'You will be able to bid Muriel goodbye, and then we shall get a quiet chat,' Mrs. Trevor had observed. 'The house will be so dull without Ellison at first, so you must let us do all we can to cheer you up.' And Lorraine had gratefully assented.

She made up her mind at last that she would go and see Mrs. Clarke again. She rather disliked the woman than otherwise, but it was a clear matter of charity. She would take her some jelly and new-laid eggs, and the walk would do Bairn good; with a dog's unerring instinct he knew she pitied him, and he had stuck to her closely all day, even lying on her dress whenever he had a chance of doing so.

During the summer months it was Ellison's habit to allow her maids an evening walk whenever they could be spared. It was Eunice's turn this evening, she knew, so she was somewhat surprised to see her sitting quietly at her work at the open window of their sitting-room. 'Are you not going out this evening, Eunice?' she asked. 'I thought you always went out on Tuesdays?'

'Yes, ma'am; but Ruth asked me to change evenings with her this week, she had some business she was anxious to get settled, so as it was much the same to me I did not object.'

'Ruth ought to have told me so,' returned Lorraine rather gravely. 'It is necessary for me to know things in your mistress's absence.'

'I never thought for a moment that Ruth had not told you, ma'am,' returned Eunice respectfully. All the servants at Brae Farm liked Mrs. Herbert. 'She is not generally so remiss; but I fancy something was troubling her.'

'If she has gone to her mother's, it is no use my going there too,' observed Lorraine, thinking regretfully of the basket of good things that she had packed so carefully.

'I don't fancy she is bound for Redlands,' returned Eunice; 'at least she set off in an opposite direction. Ruth is a bit close about her movements, and does not care to be questioned. She saw her mother after evening church on Sunday, for we went there together. Mrs. Clarke was looking very sadly, and in a deal of pain.'

'Then in that case I had better go. You need not speak to Ruth about this, I will do so myself'; and then Lorraine set off for the village. 'If the storm would only come,' she thought, as she pushed back her hat. The strange stillness oppressed her —not a leaf stirred. The birds were silent, and took short aimless flights, as though they were uneasy. The cattle returning to the farm lowed piteously, and the few sheep in the Brae meadow had ceased to nibble dry herbage, and stood in a forlorn group huddled together.

As Lorraine passed the infant school, Mr. Vincent came out and crossed the road on his way to the low, white cottage opposite. He raised his hat and said 'Good evening,' when he saw her, but for the first time he did not stop to speak to her. Lorraine tried to fancy that he was in a hurry—perhaps some one was ill in the white house. No, he was walking slowly; then he stopped and looked back. Lorraine, who had done the same thing, felt a little foolish when he came up to her.

'Did you want to speak to me?' he asked with unusual gravity. 'They have sent for me to baptize Mrs. Glover's child; it is delicate, and they fear it may not live until the morning.'

'That is what I wanted to know, if any one were ill. I am

my cousin's almoner. What name did you say—Glover? Oh, poor Mrs. Glover! She has lost several children. I will call and see her to-morrow. Please do not let me keep you, Mr. Vincent ; that is all I wanted to know' ; and then she held out her hand.

The impending storm was affecting every one, for certainly Mr. Vincent was not himself ; and the little encounter had not tended to enliven her.

As she passed the cottage she saw Nora darning socks in the tiny front garden, with Effie playing beside her. She threw down her work with an exclamation when Lorraine passed by the gate and called her.

'What an industrious little woman you are, Nora ! But let me look at you, child. Why, you have been crying,' and Lorraine turned the pretty flushed face for a closer inspection. 'I must come in a moment and hear what the trouble is.'

'Oh, it is nothing,' returned Nora hastily ; but even as she spoke, another bright tear-drop rolled down. 'It is babyish to cry because it is hot, and Hugo is so troublesome ; but it does vex Eric so, and he said this evening that he thought I might manage the boys better.'

'Does he think you can prevent Hugo getting into mischief ?' asked Lorraine.

'No ; but he says I am always at my books, and that I do not watch them enough. But don't you see, Mrs. Herbert, it is no use watching, for Hugo won't mind me a bit. If I tell him not to do a thing, he just laughs and does it before my face. Eric was so angry with him this afternoon that he sent him to bed. Eddie is reading fairy stories to him outside the door.'

'Do you think I might go up and speak to him a moment ? Would your brother mind ?'

'Oh, dear no! Eric never minds anything you do ; he said once you always did exactly the right thing.'

'Well, I hope he will always think so,' returned Lorraine, colouring a little, but she laughed too. 'Don't cry any more, Nora dear ; you are a good little sister, and no one must blame you for Hugo's naughtiness. How beautifully you have done that darn ! I wish Ellison could see it' ; and this simple compliment cheered Nora immensely.

Eric's orders had been that no one was to go near the culprit ; but the faithful Eddie, unwilling to be separated from his playfellow, had stationed himself on a high stool by the keyhole, and was reading in a loud, sing-song, monotone voice :

'So the wicked old fairy turned quite green and danced with

rage, because Gloriana looked more beautiful than ever. Her skin was as white as milk, and her eyes shone like Sapphira's.'

'Sapphires, you duffer!' shouted an impatient voice from within. 'Hurry on, Eddie! You are so slow—I never did hear any one read so badly—and I want to get to the part about the prince and the bloodhound.'

'I am reading as fast as I can!' whined Eddie reproachfully. 'You are very unkind, Hugo, and you know there are such long words. I know it ought to be Sapphira.'

'I shall kick if you don't hurry up!' was Hugo's unfeeling remark. But here Eddie very nearly dropped his book in his surprise at seeing Mrs. Herbert smiling at him.

'That is very kind of you, Eddie,' she said, patting his hot cheek. 'I am afraid Hugo is not as grateful as he ought to be.'

'Are you going in?' asked Eddie, opening his eyes widely. 'Eric said nobody must go in.'

'I think I may,' returned Lorraine gently. But, as she opened the door, she forgave Hugo his petulance. The small, low room felt intensely hot, and Hugo, tossing on his bed, looked the picture of discomfort, his hands and face hot and grimy.

The little window was nearly closed. Lorraine propped it open, and straightened the bedclothes and cleared them of superfluous wraps; then she washed his face and hands and brushed his hair, to all of which he submitted with much astonishment. Finally she delivered her little lecture. She almost hoped she had made an impression, for he certainly listened. But when she mentioned Eric's name he frowned and tossed himself angrily.

'Eric was a tyrant! He had no right to send him to bed and treat him like a baby. He had done no harm at all. If orders were stupid there was no good in obeying them. But Eric had such a temper! He had taken him by the arm and shaken him. He would show Mrs. Herbert the bruise.'

But Lorraine declined to look at the bruise. She quietly reiterated her speech. Hugo must learn to obey. His brother was right to punish him for so daring an act of disobedience.

'I don't care,' muttered Hugo rebelliously. 'I like Eddie best of my brothers. The sovereigns were mine. You saw the old lady give them to me,' for much of the contention was caused by Miss Bretherton's unlucky gift.

Lorraine had almost forgotten about the pond until she was leaving the room, but Hugo was tired of all this moralising, which in his own mind he voted 'cheek,' and he answered in an off-hand manner:

'Oh, he knew all about that. Of course Daniel would be with

them when they sailed their boats. Eric had not mended his yet. It was all spite on Eric's part.'

'Oh, if you are going to talk in this way I shall leave you, Hugo.

And then, indeed, Hugo's conscience pricked him. She had made him so comfortable—almost cool—and had talked to him so nicely. As Lorraine rose from the bed a small brown hand clutched her dress.

'I won't talk any way you don't like, if you will only stay. But it is so horrid lying here in the daylight'; and here Hugo's voice was a little chokey.

Long years afterwards, when he was with his regiment in India, Hugo recalled that little scene. He was sitting with two or three other subalterns in the verandah of his bungalow, enjoying the moonlight, and talking and laughing with his companions. Rawlinson was telling them a droll incident of his childhood.

'I give you my word,' he was saying, 'I was one of the cheekiest little beggars you ever saw. I fairly doted on mischief.'

And then in a moment it all came before him—the little white-washed cottage room, the window that they were obliged to prop open with hair-brushes, the sloping roof of the forge across the yard, and the sweet-faced woman sitting beside him and looking at him with a kind smile. He could see the slim white hand, with the wedding-ring on it, beside his brown little paw.

'What on earth has gone wrong with Scott?' exclaimed Rawlinson, breaking off in his narrative. 'Did you see his face just now? He looked as though he had interviewed a ghost, he was so white about the gills.'

'Oh, he is a rum sort of chap,' returned a long-legged subaltern, reclining on a couple of chairs. 'He is as chummy and pleasant as you like sometimes, and then he has queer fits of silence. Go on with your tale, Jack. He will come back presently.'

But even as he spoke Hugo had disappeared into the bungalow, and they saw him no more that night.

Lorraine stayed as long as she dared, and then set off at a brisk pace for the Redlands, but it seemed as though she were fated to meet with interruptions.

As she turned off by the pine-woods she saw Sam Brattle leaning against the gate, with his eyes fixed on the ground, and a moody expression on his face. He did not appear to notice her, but a moment afterwards Lorraine heard his footsteps behind her.

'I beg your pardon, Mrs. Herbert, but I am wondering if you can tell me what has become of Ruth this evening. She appointed to meet me at the Redlands gate an hour ago. She has not stopped at home by any chance?'

'No, indeed. I am certain of that, for Eunice told me that she had gone out. But I am sorry that I cannot give you any information. I am on my way to her mother now. Perhaps I shall find her there.'

But the young bailiff shook his head.

'There is no chance of that, ma'am. I have been on the lookout for the last hour and a half, until I am fairly sick of kicking up my heels. I will wait another half-hour, and then I will turn in.' And Sam touched his hat and went back to the gate.

'Ruth is playing a dangerous game,' thought Lorraine, as she walked up the Redlands lane. 'There is a look on Sam Brattle's face to-night as though he had made up his mind to take strong measures. He is not in a pleasant temper, I am afraid. Where can Ruth be? Perhaps, after all, she has decided to avoid Sam by taking the path through the plantation. It is a steep climb, but I suppose she would not mind that. People who play a double game cannot be too nice.' Lorraine had only surmised this out of her inner consciousness. It gave her a sort of shock, therefore, when she caught sight of two people on the road before her. There was no mistaking Mr. Yolland's tall, angular figure. He was walking slowly with his hands behind him, and evidently laying down the law in rather a peremptory fashion. One or two sentences reached Lorraine's ears before they perceived her.

'You have got to do it, then, mind that. Your mother's right. There must be no more dilly-dallying. I have given you the chance of being a real lady, and dressing in silks and satins if you choose. I am not the man to stint my wife, or to let her fash herself with work. There is plenty of good hard cash in the Bramfield Bank. You can ask any one if Edgar Yolland is not a safe man. I have put it before you, my girl, and your mother has done the same, and now you must just make up your mind to fling the fellow over.'

'But it is so hard to make up my mind,' returned the girl, and then they heard Lorraine's footsteps behind them, and both of them turned. Ruth looked pale and worried, and as though she had been crying. She gave Lorraine a quick, frightened look.

There was a distant rumble of thunder. One of Lorraine's sudden impulses came to her.

'Mr. Yolland,' she said, as he raised his hat awkwardly, 'there is a storm coming on, and I want Ruth to walk back with me to the farm. I have some things for your mother,' addressing Ruth. 'Would you run on with them to the cottage, and then join me? I am sure Mr. Yolland will excuse you. It is not pleasant to be out in a storm alone,' continued Lorraine, in a perfectly natural manner that disarmed them both. Even Ruth had no idea that Lorraine had any ulterior reason. She took the basket without a word, and Mr. Yolland looked after her with a dissatisfied face. 'Now we will walk home as fast as we can,' observed Lorraine cheerfully, when Ruth had rejoined them. 'Good-evening, Mr. Yolland ; I am sorry to be taking Ruth away, but it cannot be helped.' But directly Mr. Yolland was out of sight her footsteps slackened, and then she stood still. 'Ruth,' she said, in a grave, meaning voice, 'what are you going to do? Sam Brattle is waiting for you at the Redlands gate. He has been waiting there for an hour and a half, sick at heart, and almost at the end of his patience. Do you mean to play him false for the sake of a poor creature like Mr. Yolland?'

Ruth looked at her with terrified eyes.

'Sam waiting for me? Why, I hoped he would have gone away long ago ; that he would have thought I had made a mistake. Oh, whatever shall I do!' clasping her hands in unmistakable agitation. 'I dare not see him. Sam has been so bad-tempered lately there is no managing him. He is not a bit as he used to be when we first kept company together.'

'I daresay not. You have tried him too much. Even an easy-tempered man like Sam Brattle can be roused if he feels himself badly treated ; and your conscience will tell you, Ruth, if it is treating him fairly to let Mr. Yolland speak to you as he did this evening.'

'But I could not help myself, and mother egged him on,' and then Ruth broke into a fit of sobbing. 'Oh, ma'am, I am so unhappy. I don't think any girl was so unhappy before. I do like Sam best. Only he is so short with me now, and that puts my back up, for I haven't given him the right yet to lecture me and keep me in order. And then mother says that if I marry him I shall just drive her to her grave, for she has set her heart on seeing me the mistress of Mansoule Farm. They both tempt me between them, and then I forget Sam, and fancy that I had better do it, and that I should be happier living like a lady and having my own way. And yet——' Here Ruth stopped, almost strangled with her sobs.

Lorraine put her hand on the girl's shoulder ; she had quite forgotten the impending storm ; they were still in the Redlands lane, and just round the corner poor Sam Brattle was keeping a fruitless watch for his sweetheart.

'Tell me everything,' she said kindly. 'We are two women, Ruth, and we ought to feel for each other. Let me help you ; I think I can ; sometimes an outsider sees things more clearly. It seems to me that you would not be quite so unhappy if you did not care a good deal for Sam Brattle.'

'Mother says that I do not really care for him one bit—not what she calls caring ; but I know I do. I don't mind him to be near me or touch me ; but when Mr. Yolland wanted to hold my hand this evening, it made me shiver. There are times when I most hate him, and yet he has got such a way with him that at other times I am bound to listen ; but I am sure that if it had not been for mother I never should have given him a thought.'

'Oh, how glad I am to hear you say that,' returned Lorraine joyfully. 'Ruth, what a foolish girl you are. Don't you see that it is Sam Brattle who is really your sweetheart. Mr. Yolland is nothing to you. You must marry Sam ; no other man will make you happy. Ah,' as a vivid flash made her wince, 'we are wasting time, and the storm is breaking over us.'

As they hurried round the corner, they came face to face with Sam Brattle. He stopped short, with a frown, when he saw Ruth, and then turned his back on her.

'I thought you might be a bit nervous, Mrs. Herbert,' he said, coming to her side, 'for we are going to have a rare storm ; but I did not know any one was with you. You had best take refuge in the Pattersons' cottage ; there is only the deaf old grannie at home, but you will keep dry there.' But as Sam talked he avoided glancing in Ruth's direction.

There was no time to hesitate. The next moment the heavy thunder-shower pattered down on them, and they reached the cottage panting and out of breath.

CHAPTER XXVII

'How absolute the knave is ! we must speak by the card, or equivocation
will undo us.'—SHAKESPEARE.

'Dare to be true, nothing can need a lie ;
A fault which needs it most grows two thereby.'
HERBERT, *The Church Porch.*

GRANNIE PATTERSON, or deaf Joan, as she was commonly called,
was dozing in her big beehive chair, as Sam Brattle ushered in
Lorraine and Ruth. She opened her eyes and stared at them in a
dazed fashion until Lorraine's smile reassured her.

'Ay—ay, you are kindly welcome,' she said, in the subdued
voice of extreme old age. 'Meg has gone down to Brattle's to do
her chores. Sit ye down, ma'am ; I am a bit hard of hearing,'
and then she looked at Sam Brattle's broad shoulders ; 'that be
Sam Brattle, surely. I thought I had a notion of his face. What
will ye be doing out with your sweetheart on a stormy evening
like this ?'

'I have nought to do with sweethearts,' muttered Sam sullenly,
as he turned to the window, blocked up as usual with pots of
geraniums and musks. Ruth, silent and ashamed, was eyeing
him piteously from a dark corner, while grannie rambled on to
the lady in a toothless, disconnected way from one subject to
another.

'I mind Squire Yolland's wedding seventeen years ago,' she
said, 'just as though it were yesterday. He were a fine figure
of a man then, though a bit stiff and oneasy-like, just as though his
grand clothes misfitted him. Dauncey—she was a bonnie lass, to
be sure. I mind Brattle—he be Ned Brattle I am thinking of—
coming up to me in the churchyard, "Did you ever see a bonnier
bride, Joan ? He is a dry sort of stick to match with a rosy-

cheeked maid like Dauncey Sanderson ; but he is a safe man, and one must not judge too much by outsides." Dearie me, how often I thought of that speech after, for she was not bonnie long. I never cared much for the Sandersons ; they were a hungry, grasping lot, and always looking out for the main chance. But I was main sorry for Sarah when she came crying up to my place, " I can't make out what ails our Dauncey, Joan ; she seems so cowed and changed, and has lost her sperrits. Yolland won't hear of having a doctor to her. He says she is only sulking ; but I never knew Dauncey sulk in all her born days. I have just come down from Mansoule, and my girl is sitting up in her parlour, dressed in a grand lilac silk, for they have got folks coming to tea ; but she looks far more fit to be in her bed. ' Don't notice it, mother,' she whispered, pinching my arm till I was most blue. ' Edgar is always so vexed if I am not well, and I don't want him out of temper to-night.' " Dearie me !' and Grannie's stick struck heavily against the floor, ' two years after that we were at her burying. And a fine burying it was ; but old Dr. Howell always said she ought not to have died, for she had no disease to speak of. Sarah Sanderson never held up her head after that. I was with her the night she passed away, and she was a bit muzzy and light-headed. " Joan," she said, catching hold of me, " I'm a wicked woman. Dauncey would never have wedded Edgar Yolland but for me. He is as hard as a stone, and he crushed the life out of her day by day. He broke her sperrit, and then he broke her heart ; but for him, she would be alive now." '

Grannie rambled on, well pleased to have a hearer ; but only Lorraine and Ruth would follow her. Sam Brattle was too much absorbed in his own angry thoughts to listen to old Joan's palaver. It would have been no news to him, either, for he had often heard his mother talk about poor Dauncey Yolland's premature death.

Presently Lorraine leant forward, and laid her hand impressively on Ruth's arm. ' Go to him,' she whispered. ' Make it up with him ; you may never have another opportunity. If you fall into Edgar Yolland's clutches you will be a miserable woman like Dauncey. Take warning, and be humble.' And she went softly out into the small outer kitchen, where Meg Patterson did her washing, and looked out into the steep little yard, where the rain was pouring into the empty water-butt, under which a couple of hens were sheltering themselves.

' Sam, aren't you ever going to speak or look at me again ?' asked a timid voice close beside him ; and the young bailiff, starting violently, turned round to meet a pair of soft, imploring eyes.

Ruth's face was pale and tear-stained, but never before had it worn that gentle, humble expression. 'I have treated you badly, Sam; I know that now, and Mrs. Herbert's been telling me so. I won't blame any one else for my own misdoings; but if you will look over things once and try me again, you shan't have any more reason to complain of me. I have made up my mind to that.'

Sam caught his breath, and a dusky flush came to his forehead; but his answer was more harsh than reassuring. 'You have said that to me before, and I have been a fool and hearkened; but there's limits to everything, and you won't find me so soft again. How often have I looked over things, as you call it, and made it up with you till I was sick and sore with it all? It is not that I am so angry with you, Ruth, or that I don't care for you still; but I cannot trust you. You have given the lie to me too often. Did you not promise to meet me at Redlands gate this evening?'

'Yes, Sam; but——'

'Let me finish,' in the same stern voice. 'I shall find it difficult to stomach excuses to-night. Just answer me one thing,' and here he took her hands and held them so tightly that she winced with pain; 'look me in the face, Ruth, and tell me if you have not been walking with Squire Yolland up yonder?'

'Yes, Sam, I have,' but as he dropped her hands with a look almost of despair, she caught at his arm. 'Sam, you must listen to me; it is not fair to shake me off like this. I will tell you truthfully everything that passed this evening. I have deceived you before; but I'll take my oath that I am speaking the truth to-night.'

'Go on,' he returned hoarsely, 'it may be the last opportunity you'll have to tell me anything, for I am fairly sick of sweethearting.'

'Oh, Sam,' bursting into tears, 'how can you be so cruel as to say such things to me?'

'When a man is being fooled, he is apt to turn a bit rough. Tom is a lucky fellow; he has been telling me to-night that he and Eunice are going to be cried in church soon; his courting has been as smooth as honey, and look at the life you have led me?'

'I know I have been contrary, Sam,' returned Ruth sadly, 'but I have made myself miserable as well as you. Do, do be patient a little longer, and let me tell you about this evening. I meant to meet you. I had asked Eunice to change evenings, because I wanted to make things right between us, and I hurried out long before the time, because I had some things to take mother. Just to plague Eunice, because she was so inquisitive, I took the

long way through the plantations, but I knew I had plenty of
time to spare. Mother was suffering from one of her attacks, and
I had to stay with her until she was better; Peggy Blake was
sitting with her when I first went in, but she sent her away, Sam.
I know now that she sent her with a message to Mansoule Farm,
that was just one of mother's crooked ways; she has done that
before, and then kept me with her on some excuse or other till she
had given him time to come; but I never suspected it till this
evening. She looked so bad that I was frightened to leave her,
and I thought I would explain to you how I came to be late, but
I had not shut the gate behind me before I saw Mr. Yolland
walking slowly down the road.'

'You are certain that you did not know that your mother had
sent for him?'

'No—indeed, I never thought of such a thing. Mother had
asked me to wring out some hot flannels for her to ease her pain,
and when I came back Peggy had gone. But I guessed what
she had done the moment I saw him sauntering along the road.'

'But you were glad enough to see him? Come, let us have the
truth for once, my girl.'

'No, Sam. I was not glad, I was a bit flustered-like, and hot;
when he put my hand on his arm and walked on with me I
began to feel like a poor little fly in a spider's web. He and
mother are so clever—they know my weak side; and when he
began talking about the fine furniture he had got, and how he
could make me a lady if I would only marry him, I lost my head
a little.'

'Yes, I see. Well, and so you have settled with the old stick
and his money-bags, and you are his girl—not mine? Well, I
congratulate you.'

'Don't, Sam.' And here Ruth's beautiful eyes flashed with
anger, and she gave his arm a little shake. 'You are trying to
punish me because of all the pain I have given you, but you ought
to see that I am humbling myself for once. I know I have been a
vain foolish girl, and that I thought it a fine thing to have a rich
man like Mr. Yolland to court me, but I could not bring myself to
marry him. When he put my hand on his arm I fairly shivered
at his touch, and felt as though I hated him. No, whatever mother
may say, I will never walk or talk with him again. Other folks
may be sick of sweethearting as well as yourself, Sam Brattle,
though they may not have the bad taste to say so.' And Ruth
walked away with her pretty head held high, and such a weight
at her heart. She had found out that it is not safe to play with
edged tools. The wise old adage that it was well to be off with

the old love before you are on with the new was true in her case.
The handsomest girl in Highlands was likely to lose both her
sweethearts. Lorraine was still investigating the wonders of the
backyard, where the rain still dripped and the hens still cowered
under the water-butt. Old Joan had tired of prattling to deaf
ears, and had begun to doze again, and Ruth, with an aching
heart, seated herself in one corner of the wide oak settle. But she
was taken aback when the seat was occupied beside her, and Sam's
arm drew her close.

'Supposing we try it a bit longer, Ruthie—you and I? We
have made a mighty mess of things, but maybe we shall be wiser
in future. Why should we not be cried in church as well as Tom
and Eunice? Miss Lee is willing, and I know there is a house
ready. It is not as grand as Mansoule Farm, but it is big enough
for the likes of us. Come, I am a say and seal man; there's my
hand on it. Let bygones be bygones. I will never cast it up against
you that you have been a bit flighty if you will say you'll marry
me after Michaelmas.'

'I will, if my mistress can spare me, Sam,' and then indeed
there was utter bliss in Sam Brattle's faithful heart. Lorraine
came back a few minutes later to tell them the rain had ceased,
and smiled, well pleased when she saw their faces. There was a
soft tell-tale flush on Ruth's face, and a light in her grey eyes that
had long been absent; but Sam Brattle's happiness needed the
relief of speech.

'Ruth and I have been settling matters,' he said abruptly.
'When you write to Miss Lee, will you tell her we are thinking of
having our banns put up as soon as Michaelmas is over? she will
be downright pleased to hear it, for she has been wanting me to
settle. When Eunice comes to our place, she will be glad to have
only Tom to fend for, and I will feel snugger in a house of my
own. Why are you nudging me, Ruth?' for Ruth, colouring
high, had given him sundry admonishing touches. 'Mrs. Herbert
knows all about it; there is nought to be ashamed of'; and Sam
spoke in a masterful tone.

'No indeed; and I wish you both joy. Ruth, this is good
news, and your mistress will be delighted when she hears it. Now
we must really make our way home.' And then, as grannie was
still slumbering placidly, they did not disturb her, but stepped out
into the wet fragrant garden. At the end of the village Sam
Brattle left them, and Lorraine and Ruth walked happily home.
'You will not let your mother interfere any more, Ruth?' asked
Lorraine, when they had talked a little. 'I will promise to tell
her either to-morrow or on Friday that you have settled things

with Sam Brattle; but I am afraid you will have something to bear.'

'Yes, I know, but I can bear it for Sam's sake; but I will never see Mr. Yolland again if I can help it. Oh, 1 don't deserve to be so happy, or to have Sam so kind and forgiving; but I will make up for all my misdoings. I think I have really been true to Sam all along, though I did not know it,' and Lorraine was inclined to agree with her.

The first day of Ellison's absence had not been uneventful. A moral as well as a physical thunderstorm had cleared the air—in more senses than one; and Lorraine's first letter to her cousin contained a graphic account of the 'wooing o't,' with deaf Joan in her beehive chair sleeping peacefully through it. 'I shall never see a rainy backyard and two shining hens under a water-butt, without recalling Sam Brattle's radiant face; it quite lighted up the old kitchen. I never did see a man so happy. Poor dear Ellison, you will lose two of your maids after Michaelmas.'

When Lorraine went up to Brae the next day she found Mrs. Trevor busy among her flowers as usual. She kissed Lorraine a little hurriedly, and sent her up to the turret-room.

'Muriel wants you to sit with her until luncheon,' she said. 'She is going directly afterwards, so we shall have plenty of time for our talk,' and though Lorraine rather marvelled at this quick dismissal, she put it down to Mrs. Trevor's usual unselfishness.

Muriel was not in good spirits; she had slept badly, and the old inky shadows were under her eyes, but she was unwilling to be questioned about her health.

'Oh, it is nothing,' she returned impatiently to Lorraine's kind inquiry. 'A storm generally upsets me, and I often sleep badly—my head aches, and I am a little nervous.' And then she made a great effort to talk on other subjects until the luncheon bell rang. Lorraine was thankful when luncheon was over, for she could see that Muriel and her mother were unconsciously jarring on each other. Mrs. Trevor's quick talk ranging from one subject to another irritated Muriel's nerves, and she grew more silent every moment. She rose the moment it was over, and only came back to say the carriage was at the door.

Mrs. Trevor, who was lying back on the couch as though she were tired, started up quickly. 'Oh, Muriel darling, I thought you had half an hour more to wait!' she exclaimed as the girl kissed her. Then her colour changed, and she put her hand to her side. 'Will you see her off, Mrs. Herbert?' she said, trying to speak naturally, and Lorraine nodded. She had noticed the movement once or twice before, but Muriel saw nothing unusual.

'Gavin will be back to-morrow, so mother will not be dull,' she said as she stepped into the carriage, and the next moment she had driven away.

'Muriel never noticed,' Lorraine said to herself as she went back to the morning-room ; but she was not in the least surprised when she found Mrs. Trevor lying back on the couch with her eyes closed and evidently in severe pain ; she only knelt down beside her and asked gently what she could do.

'Nothing,' replied Mrs. Trevor in a patient voice. 'I have taken my medicine, and there is nothing to be done ; it will pass directly. I shall have to get used to it.'

Lorraine made no reply, but her face grew a little grave as she went in search of a fan. She sat by her for some time silently fanning her, or from time to time bathing her temples with eau-de-cologne, and Mrs. Trevor took all her attentions gratefully.

Presently she sat up among her cushions and pushed away the fan.

'There, I am better ; you shall not fan me a moment longer. I am quite ashamed that you should see me like this, my dear Mrs. Herbert, but the pain is so bad while it lasts.'

'And you have kept it to yourself all this time,' observed Lorraine in a reproachful voice.

'Well, not exactly ; Ellison found me out one day and scolded me into going to Dr. M'Callum. I have seen him twice.' And here her voice dropped, and she looked at Lorraine a little sadly. 'I half wish I had not taken Ellison's advice, for he has not prophesied smooth things. There is so little he can do for me, and I have got to bear it, you see.'

Mrs. Trevor looked strangely wan and old at that moment. The fine face had unwonted lines on it, and there were purple shadows under the eyes and round the lips ; and though she made an effort to speak with her old sprightliness it was a pitiful failure.

'Dear friend,' whispered Lorraine in her warm-hearted way, as she passed her hand caressingly over the grey piled-up curls— they felt as soft and silky as a baby's—'tell me exactly what Dr. M'Callum said ; it is not good to keep such things to yourself.' And after a moment's hesitation Mrs. Trevor consented.

'It is such a relief to tell you this, my dear Mrs. Herbert.'

Lorraine pressed her hand mutely ; speech was difficult just then. How was she to put her pity and compassion into words ? She was very tender to any form of physical or mental suffering. The mystery of pain was at all times a complex problem to her,

At times her pity had amounted to absolute anguish, and Ellison
had once reasoned with her very seriously.

'It is not well to be too thin-skinned, Lorraine,' she had once
said. 'You talk sometimes as though you had the world on your
shoulders. You quite forget what Gavin calls the law of compen-
sation. It is his belief that people get blunted and used to
suffering.'

'Yes, I am glad you made me tell you,' went on Mrs. Trevor.
'It is terribly lonely sometimes, having to keep things to myself,
and I would not have Gavin and Muriel told just yet. Oh '—as
Lorraine was about to speak—'I know exactly what you want to
say—that I am wrong, and that Muriel ought to know! But the
child has enough to bear. Why should I trouble her?'

'Because it is a daughter's duty to stand by her mother,' returned Lorraine firmly. 'Dear Mrs. Trevor, you are making a
great mistake; I have told you so before. Muriel's nature is
peculiar. She is self-absorbed and does not see things unless they
are pointed out to her. She has never felt herself necessary
to you or her brother, and this has somehow embittered her. Let
her once feel that you are in need of her, or that she can be a
comfort to you, and you would see a different Muriel. Dear Mrs.
Trevor, I am as certain of this as I am of my own existence. You
have promised me to confide in your son; but you must do more
than that; you must give me permission to tell Muriel.'

Mrs. Trevor sighed.

'You speak strongly. I wish I knew what was best to be done.
Let me think it over; there is no hurry. Doctor M'Callum
thinks I shall go on for a long time without getting much worse,
though, of course, as he says, no one can tell this. By and by
Muriel must know.'

'Yes, when it is too late for her to retrieve a life's thoughtless-
ness! Dear Mrs. Trevor, you are taking such a one-sided view of
the case! If you would only try and put yourself in Muriel's
place, and look at things with her eyes. She is your only daughter'
—here Mrs. Trevor winced—'I mean your only living daughter.
What right have you to refuse to accept a daughter's attentions
from her, or to treat her as a child?'

'Oh, if you put it in that way,' returned Mrs. Trevor wearily
—'well, you shall do as you think best! I will not be obstinate.
I could not have kept anything from Maud and Florrie for an hour.
They would have had their arms about me, and coaxed it all out
months ago, and they would have cried their sweet eyes out whenever I had a fit of the pain! Don't I remember once, when I had
a headache, and Florrie gave up a garden party to which she had

been looking forward for a week, to sit with me and bathe my head ; and Maud wanted to stay too, and they almost quarrelled over it. There would have been no question of keeping anything from them ; they would have just found it out for themselves,' finished Mrs. Trevor, with a faint smile. The children who were gone were still living to the mother's heart.

CHAPTER XXVIII

AN ANGEL UNAWARES

'With silence only as their benediction,
   God's angels come,
Where in the shadow of a great affliction
   The soul sits dumb.'
                                    WHITTIER.

LORRAINE soon found that Ellison's absence gave her so much to do that she rarely had an unoccupied minute in the day. When her labours in the house and poultry-yard were over, she had her lessons with Nora; in the afternoon she generally sat for an hour with Mrs. Trevor. This had become a daily duty. Her evening walks were always to some cottage where sickness or trouble called for neighbourly help and sympathy. The villagers were becoming very much attached to her, and 'our Mrs. Herbert' was quite as often on their lips as 'the mistress up at Brae.' Lorraine always took pains to point out that the jelly, or new-laid eggs, or bottle of thick yellow cream, was her cousin's gift, not hers, and that she had nothing to offer but sympathy and good wishes.

'Why, bless you, we all know that,' Betty Stokes once said. 'Don't you be getting it into your head, Mrs. Herbert, that we are always wanting summat, for we are main glad to see you, empty-handed or not. Not but what the things are kindly welcome,' she went on as Lorraine unpacked her basket, 'for I never did see such cream as Miss Lee's cows yield, and a bit of her bacon is a treat as never was. But if you never brought us a thing I'd like to see you sitting there in the master's big chair; it is sort of neighbourly and cosy.' And there were others besides Betty Stokes who loved to see the young widow.

Lorraine did not see Colonel Trevor for some days; but one afternoon as she was starting for the village, she came upon him. Some workmen were putting up some new fencing in the Brae meadow, and Gavin was superintending them. When he saw Mrs. Herbert he left them, and walked on a little with her. She thought he looked unusually grave, and even a little careworn, and at once guessed the reason. His first words proved she was right.

'I am glad to have met you,' he said at once. 'I was thinking of coming down to the farm to have a talk. My mother tells me that you have been sitting with her.' And then he turned to her and said, a little abruptly, 'She does not seem quite so well to-day. I have been asking her to have Dr. M'Callum down.'

'Oh no,' returned Lorraine quickly. 'I should not propose that again if I were you, it only makes your mother nervous, and there is no need for the expense. Mrs. Trevor is really no worse than she was a week ago.'

'How are we to know that?' he returned doubtfully. 'Anyhow, I wish Dr. Howell to come regularly. I am afraid my insisting on it has upset her a bit. I don't know how it is,' he continued, in a vexed voice, 'even a sensible woman like my mother is not always reasonable. I wish you would talk to her, Mrs. Herbert. She thinks so much of what you say.'

'I don't think she will object to seeing Dr. Howell now and then,' returned Lorraine. 'On the contrary, I am sure his visits will be a comfort to her; but she would dislike the fuss of having Dr. M'Callum down. People are constituted so differently, Colonel Trevor. Your mother would not care to have her friends and neighbours know that she is ill. If you feel at all dissatisfied, why do you not go and speak to Dr. M'Callum yourself? He is an old friend of your family.'

'Perhaps I will,' he replied, as though this were a new idea to him. 'Mrs. Herbert, there is one thing I meant to ask you. Do you not think it would be well to have Muriel back? She is not all the comfort she ought to be to my mother; but I do think it must be bad for her to sit alone and think about herself. Under the circumstances it would drive most women frantic,' he finished; and his tone showed Lorraine how deeply he felt for his mother's affliction.

'Gavin is so good to me,' Mrs. Trevor said to her the next day, almost tearfully. 'Really he reminds me of his father sometimes. John was so gentle when he thought there was anything really the matter. He makes a point of my seeing Dr. Howell once or twice a week, so I suppose I must give in to him.'

Perhaps it was some relief in Ellison's absence to talk to Mrs. Herbert, for Colonel Trevor began to stroll down to the farm towards evening. Lorraine took his visits very naturally, attributing them to the right cause. The loss of his old confidante had made him restless; and with her usual good-nature Lorraine did her best for him. He never stayed long, and rarely entered the house, and their brief conversation was generally carried on in the garden or by the horse-block, where at that hour she would often be feeding her pigeons, and she was always pleased when he went away cheered. Ellison only smiled to herself when she read of these visits, and then a soft wave of colour came to her cheek. 'He will be glad to get me back,' she thought; and in her heart she knew the gladness would not be all on his side.

One afternoon things had not gone so smoothly as usual. One batch of visitors after another had called at Brae Farm, and had stayed so long that Lorraine had been unable to pay her usual visit to Mrs. Trevor, and this omission weighed heavily on her mind. She had also been obliged to send Nora away without her music lesson; and to add to her perplexities, Dorcas had a bilious attack, and Ruth had to take care of Tedo, and bring up more than one relay of freshly-brewed tea.

Lorraine tried to keep her boy with her while she entertained her visitors, but the little fellow was restless and clamoured for his play-room and rocking-horse; and he was so fretful she was obliged to let him go. 'Boy wants mine horse and a vide,' was his incessant cry; and though she was afraid Mrs. Mordaunt would think he was terribly spoiled, she dismissed him with a kiss. 'Master Tedo has gone up to the Dovecote, Ruth,' she said a moment later, when Ruth brought in some more hot scones.

As soon as the Mordaunts took their departure, Lorraine gave a quick sigh of relief; she was tired of the long, gossiping afternoon, and longing to breathe the sweet evening air. She even felt a momentary vexation when a tall shadow passed the window, and she recognised Colonel Trevor's grey tweed. He had ridden down the Stony Lane, as they called it, on his way from Darley Mill, and had stopped at the Farm as he passed.

He gave a quick glance at Lorraine's face as he shook hands.

'How tired you look, Mrs. Herbert! Have those boys been plaguing you all the afternoon?'

'What boys do you mean?' she asked, rather surprised at this. 'Yes, I do feel a little jaded. The Mordaunts have been here; Mrs. Mordaunt and Amy and Constance, and Mrs. Turner and Mrs. Earnshaw. Oh, and Laura Holt too! and it tired me rather, feeling that your mother would be expecting me.'

'Oh, you must not let my mother be a burden,' he returned. 'I saw that young scamp Hugo racing down the farmyard some time ago with Edmund at his heels, and I thought they might have been bothering you.'

'Oh no; they are always here!' And then a thought suddenly occurred to her. 'Where did you say you saw them, Colonel Trevor?' she asked anxiously, for she remembered all at once that Daniel had gone to Bramfield to see his brother, who was ill, and that at this hour Ellison had forbidden the boys to be in the farmyard.

Colonel Trevor was just going to answer, when Ruth appeared at the door with a puzzled expression upon her face.

'If you please, ma'am, I cannot find Master Tedo anywhere. I have been looking for him and calling him for the last ten minutes, so I thought he must have run down to you again.'

'Oh no; he is only hiding for fun! Have you looked in my big cupboard, Ruth? He has made himself a little cubby-house there. If you will excuse me a moment, Colonel Trevor, I will soon find him.' But as Lorraine turned towards the house they heard a frightened scream from the direction of the farmyard, and Lady Alice put back her glossy ears and strained at her bridle in alarm; even Bairn gave a hoarse bark, as though he scented mischief.

'What can that be?' exclaimed Lorraine, turning a little pale; but before she and Gavin could reach the gate where Lady Alice was still plunging, Eddie rushed up to them, his teeth chattering and his eyes wide with terror.

'Oh, do come—do come!' he screamed. 'Tedo has fallen into the pond, and Hughie can't get him out!'

Lorraine uttered a scream of uncontrollable anguish; it haunted Gavin long afterwards. Sometimes between sleeping and waking he would fancy he heard it again, and start up from his pillow. Her grey, terror-stricken face would be before him as she passed him and flew towards the pond. Quickly as he followed her he was not in time to prevent her rushing into the water. She was standing up to her waist, and in another instant would have waded up to her neck if he had not caught hold of her and drawn her back.

'Leave him to me: I shall have him in a moment!' he shouted. But he only spoke to deaf ears; even when he laid the dripping inanimate child in her arms, she only stood there with the water reaching to her waist, clasping him to her bosom as though her terror had bereft her of reason.

There was a small crowd round the pond by this time; the dogs were barking and racing in and out of the water, and Hugo, crying piteously, was being shaken by Joe Brand with no light hand.

'He promised he would only look and not move,' sobbed the

15

boy. 'I was holding him on the fence; I had tight hold, and then something cold touched my leg and startled me. It was only the old brown cow, but I jumped and let go for an instant, and Tedo fell, and it was deep, and I could not see him for a moment; and—and if he is drowned I would like to be drowned too.'

'Bring him at once to the house, Mrs. Herbert; we must lose no time.'

Gavin's clear authoritative tones roused Lorraine. There was something to be done then; the ice round her heart and brain seemed to thaw. She went to the house as quickly as her wet garments would allow her to move, followed by the weeping Ruth and Eunice. Gavin waited only to tell Joe Brand to ride off for Dr. Howell, then he bade Mrs. Tucker heat water and flannels, and followed the women upstairs.

'You must let me help,' he said quietly. 'I know all that there is to be done, and we will do it before Dr. Howell comes. Get off his wet things. Yes, that is right. Let me have that blanket to wrap him in. Now you must rub his limbs upwards, while I try to bring him to consciousness.'

Lorraine gave him no trouble; she followed his instructions, doing things as she was told with a meek obedience that went to his heart; but he could hardly trust himself to look at her. She had refused to leave the room or change her wet clothes. 'When Tedo wakes I will do it,' she said, and he could not compel her to go; he could only contrive that she should be kept doing something; but long before Dr. Howell arrived, he knew that all their efforts would be fruitless.

In vain they wrapped him in hot blankets and applied water-bottles to the little body. In vain did Gavin strive to restore the child's breathing by artificial means, or to promote circulation by rubbing his limbs; not even a feeble beat of the pulse or a single breath repaid his efforts. In his opinion life had been extinct when he first placed the boy in his mother's arms; but he dared not acknowledge this.

When Dr. Howell entered the room—Joe Brand had happily met him on his way to Brae House—the two men exchanged a look. Dr. Howell took measures into his own hands.

'You must leave me alone with the patient for a few minutes,' he said decidedly. 'Colonel Trevor may remain. He is an old soldier and will be useful. No, Mrs. Herbert'—as she turned her white, imploring face to him—'you cannot help me until you have taken off those wet clothes, then you may come back. Take her away, Mrs. Tucker.' And before Lorraine knew what had happened she was outside the door, and Mrs. Tucker led her away.

Ruth had already been rummaging in the wardrobe for some dry clothes. She had acted on a hint from Colonel Trevor, and Lorraine was at last persuaded to put them on. It was high time, for her teeth were chattering with cold ; but she refused at first to drink the cup of hot tea that Eunice brought her, until Dr. Howell took it into his own hands again.

'You must drink this, Mrs. Herbert,' he said quietly, coming to her side. 'There is good stuff in it that will keep you from taking cold, I hope. Yes, you shall go back the moment you have drunk it. There, there'—patting her on the shoulder with fatherly kindness—'it will only take you a moment.'

'Why have you left him ?' she asked indignantly. 'There is no need to trouble about me. I am strong—strong. It is my boy who is so delicate. I must go back to him. I must—I will,' for the unmoved gravity on the doctor's face frightened her.

'I will not keep you,' he returned gravely, 'but I should like to tell you something before you go back.' Then for the first time in her life fierce unreasoning terror and rebellion took possession of her soul. She put out her hands as though to keep the doctor at bay, and then put them to her ears. 'No, no—I will listen to nothing,' she said, and before he could say another word, she had walked into the next room.

'She was prepared for it. I saw by her expression that she understood me, poor woman'; and Dr. Howell winked away the moisture in his eyes. Years of practice had not hardened his kind heart, or inured him to such scenes.

When Colonel Trevor heard Lorraine's footsteps, he did not move, but put out his hand to her. He was still standing by the bed ; but all vestiges of the last hour's work had been removed. There was a straightness about the childish form and a waxen whiteness on the tiny face that told their own tale. The yellowish curls still clung damply to the temples, waiting for the mother's hand to brush them away ; but though she grasped the fatal truth, no second cry of anguish passed Lorraine's lips, the iron grip at her throat almost strangled her. She stood there by Gavin's side unconscious that he held her hand, or that Dr. Howell was speaking.

'He did not suffer, my dear Mrs. Herbert—not for an instant. Something must have stunned him, for he was not long in the water—not long enough to drown him.'

Then Lorraine startled them both.

'How did it happen ?' she asked, in the dull, level tone of one past feeling, and she looked at Gavin. She had made no attempt to touch her boy, though he lay there beside her with a solemn baby smile on his lips. One cold hand pushed back her hair as she put the question, but her eyes awed him by their still agony.

He looked at the doctor in some perplexity, but Dr. Howell motioned him to speak. 'Mrs. Herbert wishes to know; it will not hurt her. Tell her what you know yourself, Colonel.'

'No, it will not hurt me,' returned Lorraine, in the same curious inward voice, as though something were numb within her. 'Nothing will hurt me now.' And then he ventured to speak.

'It is a terrible business. They ought never to have been allowed to play near the pond. The boy ran out, none of the maids saw him; Hugo and Eddie were sailing their boats on the pond, and he begged to stay. Hugo let him climb up the fence and sit there; he says he was holding him, but something startled him and he let go, and Tedo fell into the pond. It is deep near the fence, and we think there must have been a stone, for he sank, and——'

'Yes, I understand; and there is nothing more to be done.'

'Nothing—nothing!'

'Thank you—thank you both'—and then her breath came a little quickly. 'Please let me have my way now. I must be alone with my boy.'

Again Gavin appealed for instructions, and again Dr. Howell bowed his head; and the two men went out softly together and closed the door behind them.

For a moment Lorraine did not stir, she seemed listening to the retreating footsteps. Then she looked down at her left hand, as though she wondered what that red mark across it meant, and then her tearless eyes rested on her boy; and a slow quivering of her muscles showed the enforced calm was at an end.

'Tedo, Tedo,' she whispered, and then she lay down on the bed and took the little body in her arms, and pressed her face against the soft curls. But even then she shed no tear; only her strong, convulsive sobs shook the bed.

'Do not hold him too tightly; I had a treasure too, and I lost it.' Did those words come to Lorraine as she kept her bitter vigil that night?

CHAPTER XXIX

'The living man who does not learn, is dark, dark, dark, like one walking in the night.'—*Ming Sum Pavu*, KEEN.

' Pity is the touch of God in human hearts.'—WALTER SMITH.

' I MUST go to her, Gavin. No—do not try to keep me ; in some cases it is one's duty not to think of oneself' ; and Mrs. Trevor's fine face was drawn with anxiety, and she clasped her hands nervously as she looked at her son. The moment the terrible news had reached her, she had asked for the little grey silk hood that she always wore in the garden, and he had found her tying it with tremulous fingers.

' Mother dear,' he said, sitting down beside her, ' you must not do this—you are not fit ; it would only do you harm.'

And then she had made her pitiful little protest. Three or four hours had elapsed since the fatal accident, but the servants at Brae had only just carried the news to their mistress.

' I must go, Gavin. Would you have me leave that poor thing alone, with Ellison away, and no one but servants in the house ? '

' She does not feel her loneliness,' he returned, with a quick contraction of his brows, as though some remembrance suddenly stabbed him ; ' she will not leave the child—nothing will induce her. Howell is going there now ; he says the shock has stunned her, and that she does not take things in. She is quiet and listens to everything, but he doubts whether she really understands ; the servants say it is dreadful to see her lying there fondling the child, and taking no notice of them. Howell says he shall be firm and put a stop to it ; he means to give her a sedative of some sort ; he does not like her state—she is too quiet, and she has not shed a tear.'

Gavin was walking up and down as he said this, but Mrs. Trevor only shook her head.

'How is she to cry, poor soul, when she has a ton weight just crushing her heart? Oh, I know all about it, Gavin, my dear, that is why I want to go to her. When your sisters died I hardly shed a tear for a week, but I was shedding them inwardly all the while. If I had gone on much longer I should have died—the doctors said so; but your father knew what to do, and he brought me round. John was always so clever!' She finished with a sigh, as though she were talking to herself.

Gavin felt a momentary surprise; it was so seldom that she ever mentioned his father to him; something in her tone brought him back to her side, for in those days the mother and son seemed drawn closer together.

'Poor mother, you have had your troubles!' he said, taking her hand. The many-coloured brilliants, twinkling and flashing, could not conceal that the fingers were strangely wasted.

'Yes, Gavin, but I have had my blessings, too—you must not forget that. I am not like that poor young creature yonder. I have still two of my children. My dear, you must let me have my way for once; it will be better for me than fretting through the long night. I want to sit and watch her as I should a daughter of my own, and be near her when she wakes—she must not be alone then.'

'I wonder if I dare trust you!' he returned anxiously. 'Mother, are you sure that you are honest with me, and that it will not really hurt you? Shall I ask Howell? I am going down there directly to meet him.'

'For pity's sake, no, Gavin,' she returned in alarm. 'Doctors are all very well, but one may have too much of them sometimes; besides'—with a return of her old quaintness—'I am not sure that I should obey him or you either. My boy,' she continued woefully, 'do you know what often troubles me when I sit alone? It is the thought how little I have done for other people. When one looks back over one's life and counts the blessings and the undeserved mercies, it makes one so terribly ashamed sometimes; such a strong wish comes over me to do just a little more before I have quite finished with it all.'

Gavin nodded; he could understand that; it appealed to his man's reason. If he had not done good work in his day— if he had not felt that his life had benefited his fellow-creatures, he would not have regained strength and cheerfulness. He was thoughtful by nature, and he had often secretly marvelled over the trivial aims and low ambitions of other men. No; his mother was right, and he would not keep her back. If only Ellison could be there to help them! He would have to write to her presently, and trust to good luck for the letter to reach her; there would be some delay, he feared, for the Mervyns had intended to move rapidly from place to place. Oh, if Ellison had never gone with them! But she would come back at once; she would not delay an hour, he was quite sure of that.

The thought of Ellison made him suddenly restless, and he rose. 'Well, I must leave you now, mother, but I shall be back in an hour's time and will see what is to be done'; and then he went out into the sweet, summer darkness, and walked across the dewy meadow and through the silent farmyard, and then paced patiently up and down the garden-paths until the doctor joined him.

Never since his own trouble had Gavin felt so profoundly agitated; it was not so much pity for the baby-life quenched so suddenly, though the child's engaging ways had won his heart, as an overwhelming sense of what this meant to the mother.

What had she done to deserve this bitter trial? All her life she had tried to help people and her reward was this, that a mysterious Providence—Providence—ah, it is to be feared that Gavin used another word—had taken her one treasure, her all. The widow's mite had not been proffered. What human mother would desire to lose her only child? But in Lorraine Herbert's case the furnace of affliction was heated seven-fold. Few mothers loved their little ones more intensely. Lorraine's heart had never belonged to her worthless husband, and all her wealth of affection had been poured on her child. Ordinary as he might be to others, he was priceless and precious in her eyes.

'It was so horribly unnecessary!' he said to himself, almost fiercely, as he walked down the dark garden-paths. 'If one could see any reason in slaughtering an innocent like that!' he muttered. Gavin did not mean to be profane, but from boyhood he had hated to see any weak helpless thing suffer; it absolutely tortured him to remember the young widow's face as she stood by his side looking down at her dead child. No word of complaint had crossed her lips, but he would rather that she had made any outcry than have stood in that statue-like stillness, with that look of despair in her eyes.

'How is a man to understand it?' he went on. 'How could I understand it myself, when my darling Nell cried out that she wanted to stay with me, and not go out into the dark? I was an Agnostic for months afterwards, until the old padre got hold of me, and then somehow I began to see things differently. I wish I could solve this problem,' he finished; and then the door opened and closed, and he hurried to meet the doctor.

'I am going to put up at the *Waggon and Horses* to-night,' were Dr. Howell's first words. 'I have had a hard day's work, and Brown Bess is fagged, and I am pretty well dog-tired myself.'

'You need not go as far as the *Waggon and Horses* for a bed,' returned Gavin. 'We have plenty of spare rooms at your service.'

But Dr. Howell was not to be persuaded ; he was used to his old quarters and liked them best ; he had ordered his supper in the snug room behind the bar, and he wanted to put his old slippers on and enjoy his pipe. Now and then when he was belated, or master and mare were worn out, he would turn in at the *Waggon and Horses*, and he always enjoyed this return to bachelor habits. He had a good wife who never fussed him or herself unnecessarily.

'Mollie would know all about it,' he thought, as he trudged down the lane by Gavin's side ; and then, as he thought of Mollie and his rosy-cheeked boys and girls, his face grew pitiful in the darkness.

'How is she now ?' asked Gavin suddenly.

'Mrs. Herbert, do you mean ? She was asleep, or nearly so ; I waited until the dose seemed inclined to make her drowsy. Well, we shall have tided over the night, but then I shall have reached my limits. "Canst thou minister to a mind diseased ?" I always say that to myself in such cases ; the old bard had us on the hip there. Are you going farther with me, Colonel ?'—for they had passed the gates of Brae by this time.

'Yes, I will see you through the Woodlands, and I shall be glad to have a bit of talk with you, for I never felt less inclined to turn in. I shall write to my cousin to-night. We must have her back as soon as possible.'

'Oh, she will be sure to come as soon as she hears it,' replied Dr. Howell. And then they talked a little about arrangements and various matters, until Gavin suddenly burst out again :

'Look here, doctor—I must have it out with somebody—does it not strike you that there is something horribly unnecessary in this afternoon's tragedy ? What has a woman like Mrs. Herbert done that she should be bowled over in this way ? Oh, I can't explain myself. But if one could only see the reason for such things.'

'Ah, you may well call it a tragedy,' returned the doctor. 'I have not heard of such a thing happening since the day they found little Joan Saunderson in the brook. We need not wonder Mrs. Herbert is a bit dazed with the shock. It would have tried the strongest of us. We must just give her time, and leave her to nature a bit. If she could only have the relief of a good cry, I should feel more comfortable about her.'

'I suppose grief seldom kills,' replied Gavin tentatively.

'I have never known it to do so, except in poetry or three-volume novels,' returned Dr. Howell drily. 'Though, mind you, there are cases where the heart is weak, and the vitality low, when there is no strength to bear a great trouble, and then some poor creature succumbs. But Mrs. Herbert is young and healthy, and she will have a fight for it.'

Gavin shuddered. He knew too well what such fights meant.

'If one could see the necessity for such suffering,' he said again.

The iteration seemed to strike the doctor's ears, for he looked at his companion, but it was too dark to discern his expression.

'There is one thing I mean to tell her when she is able to bear it,' he said presently, 'though just now it would be a doubtful consolation. That child's life was already doomed.'

Gavin started. 'You are quite sure of that, doctor ? '

'I was sure of it the first moment I saw him, though I thought it better to keep my knowledge to myself. I could patch him up a bit, and the warm weather, though it made him languid, arrested the course of the disease ; but he had no stamina, and the first childish ailment would have carried him off, even if——' Here the doctor paused.

'You are quite safe with me, Howell. Speak out plainly, man. It will be a relief to know what you feared.'

'Well, he was the sort of child one dreaded would have brain disease—he was weak and excitable, and I always told his mother that he could not be kept too quiet. If she had seen some children suffer as I have, she would, barring the accident, be only too thankful to lose him so painlessly. To be sure, she might have kept him another year or two, but that would only have made the parting when it came harder to bear. Depend upon it, there is not only reason but mercy in this sudden accident.'

Gavin drew a deep breath. There was consolation for him in the doctor's rough homely words.

'And there is another thing'—and here Dr. Howell's voice grew a little solemn. 'I don't know whether you have heard anything about his father—that is another bit of knowledge I kept to myself. A young brother of mine knew Ralph Herbert. He was an artist —oh, I am making no mistake, there could not be two of them. He was a handsome fellow, Gilbert said, and had a free hand ; but a more vicious, sensual reprobate never lived. He had simply no sense of honour, and told lies with a facility that would have become the old gentleman.'

'Poor woman,' was Gavin's reply to this, and again the doctor's eyes tried to peer through the darkness.

· 'You may well say that. Gilbert was perfectly horrified when he found he had a wife, though I believe he never saw Mrs. Herbert. Well, Colonel—are you following me ?—with all our sympathy for that poor woman, how is one to regret that Ralph Herbert's child should be taken ? It is against the laws of heredity to think that there would be no taint, physical or moral, in him. At best it would be an open question. Is it not better for Mrs. Herbert to be losing him now, a mere baby, than be weeping tears of shame over him later ? Oh, well, here I am at my inn, so I will be wishing you good-night.'

'Good-night, and thank you,' returned Gavin a little huskily ; and as he walked back quickly to Brae House he breathed more freely, as though he had flung off some weight that oppressed him.

He felt like a man who had lost his way in an unknown mountainous region and suddenly come to a finger-post, with familiar names inscribed on it. The doctor's blunt common-sense had thrown a new light on things. 'There is not only reason but mercy in this sudden accident.' He could almost have blessed the doctor for those words.

What a faithless traitor he had been. What if, after all, 'an angel had troubled the pool,' and pitiful, loving arms had drawn the feeble child through a second baptism of painless death. 'Those whom the gods love die young,' said the wise old heathen of yore ; but the Christian goes farther, for he knows that the little ones of the Kingdom follow the Lamb whithersoever He goeth.

When Gavin got back to the house he found his mother sitting patiently by the window, wrapped up in her old quilted satin cloak. As she looked at him questioningly he put his hand on her arm without a word, and they went slowly down to the Farm. Neither of them was in the mood for talking. The unwholesome oppression had lifted from Gavin's mind, but a sense of his own unfaithfulness and want of loyalty humbled him to the dust. Now and then his mother's feeble footsteps filled him with vague uneasiness, and he could perceive that she leant more heavily upon his arm. More than once she stopped to take breath, though she pretended it was only to look at a bright star over the roof of Brae Farm. 'The darker the night the brighter the stars,' he heard her say as though to herself. 'They are always there, even though the clouds hide them.' But he could find no response to this. On the threshold he bade her good-night, and then went back to Brae ; but it was long before he slept. And that night his thoughts were with his dead wife, and not with Ellison.

Mrs. Trevor kept vigil beside Lorraine ; by the doctor's orders, the child's crib had been removed into the Dovecote, but Lorraine, drowsy from the effects of the opiate, was unconscious of this.

She slept heavily until morning, and Mrs. Trevor dozed fitfully beside her, wrapped in her old satin cloak ; but at the first movement from the bed she was wide awake in an instant.

Before Lorraine opened her eyes she stretched out her arm involuntarily, and her fingers fluttered for a moment as they met vacancy instead of resting on the iron bar of the crib. Her brow contracted as though in vague wonder, and then the terrible truth leapt out like a sword from its scabbard. This was the moment that Mrs. Trevor's motherly heart had dreaded. As that blank look of despair came into the large brown eyes, she leant over her and said quietly :

'How glad you must be, dearest, that you called him Theodore.' The words had come suddenly to her, without premeditation.

Lorraine looked at her without speaking. She could not have uttered a word to save her life. A deadly faintness seemed to seize her, and there was a cold moisture on her forehead. She said long afterwards to Ellison that for the moment her agony was so great that she thought she was dying.

'Theodore—gift of God,' went on Mrs. Trevor, in a soothing monotone, as she took the cold hands in hers and rubbed them gently. 'A gift is sometimes given back. Your darling is safe, my poor dear ; far safer than he was in your arms ; for of such is the kingdom of Heaven.'

Still silence ; only now there was a slight quivering of the muscles of the face and throat, then one deep sigh after another seemed to relieve the labouring heart ; but though Mrs. Trevor's tears were flowing, Lorraine's eyes were dry, but presently she said :

'You are very kind. Yes, I know all about it, and you arc right. Will you go away now, please, for I must dress ?' and then she leant on her elbow with a forlorn look round the room that nearly broke Mrs. Trevor's heart. 'They have taken him away, and I cannot stay here,' and then she began to tremble all over.

'They have only moved the crib into the play-room,' returned Mrs. Trevor gently. 'There, I will open the door, and you can see it from there. If you will be good and drink some tea I will leave you to get up, but you are too weak to move just now,' and Lorraine, quieted by the view of the little crib, lay down obediently and allowed Mrs. Trevor to minister to her.

'She was so good ; she did everything I asked her,' observed Mrs. Trevor later, to her son. 'I felt as though she were my own child. She is sitting in the play-room now arranging some flowers. Tedo is looking so sweet. I never thought him pretty before. She says it soothes her to look at him. She asked if you would go up presently, Gavin. There is something she wants you to do for her.' And Colonel Trevor smothered a sigh, as he said hurriedly that he would go at once.

CHAPTER XXX

'God takes them from our hands
That seemed but made to cling ;
He sets them far away in the shade
Of His far-stretching wings.'

B. M.

COLONEL TREVOR was just taking down his straw hat from the peg
when he saw Mr. Vincent walking rapidly up the drive. As they
shook hands, Eric said in a vexed tone :

'I am so sorry that you are going out ; I wanted to speak to
you particularly, if you could spare me a few minutes.'

'My dear fellow, I will spare you half an hour if you like,'
returned Gavin good-humouredly, though, if the truth must be told,
he was chafing inwardly at the delay. 'My mother brought me
word that Mrs. Herbert wished to speak to me, but no time was
mentioned, and it is quite early. Come to the library, no one will
disturb us there.'

'I will not keep you long,' replied Eric, in a dejected tone—he
had passed a miserable night and looked wretchedly ill—'but I
must speak to some one,' and then he threw himself down in a
chair, and shaded his face from the light.

Colonel Trevor put his hand on his shoulder. 'You are upset,
Vincent, and no wonder. It is a terrible shock to us all ; but you
must not take things too much to heart; it was no fault of yours
that the accident happened.'

'I wish I could think so,' returned Eric, forcing himself to speak
calmly. 'But I ought to have kept that boy in better order.
What am I to do with him, Trevor ? Yesterday I was so angry
that I dared not touch him for fear I should have harmed him. I
give you my word, that when I was drawing the truth out of him
I had to hold my hands behind my back. Nora cried because

she said that I looked so dreadful; but at that moment I felt as
if we were all that child's murderers.'

'I daresay I should have felt the same in your place,' replied
Colonel Trevor kindly; 'but it won't do, Vincent. Pull yourself
together and look at things in a sensible light; they are bad
enough, heaven knows, without making them worse by getting
morbid over them. Hugo is the only sinner, and must bear the
penalty of his sin. I suppose a good thrashing would be best; he
richly deserves it'—and here Gavin's voice grew stern; 'by his
own confession he had his orders, and he chose to disobey them.
How dare he let that baby climb the fence. Miss Lee has forbidden the children to play in that part of the meadow, and he
knew the water was deep. I am sorry to say it, Vincent, but I
am an old soldier and believe in discipline; that boy must have a
sound caning!'

'Then you must give it to him yourself,' returned Eric, turning
very white. 'I tell you I dare not trust myself to lay a finger on
him. When I think of Mrs. Herbert and all her goodness to those
children I feel as though I hated the sight of him. Look here,
Trevor, I am not quite myself, and I cannot put things clearly, but
Hugo must be punished some other way.'

'Very well,' returned Gavin reluctantly, 'he is your brother,
not mine; but you are cruel without meaning to be so. If I
know anything of boy-nature, Hugo would rather endure a smart
caning at your hands than be sent to Coventry. He is pretty
miserable already; you may depend on that. He has had a
lesson that will last him for life. Don't shut him up in that
stifling hole where the boys sleep. I do not approve of solitary
confinement for boys.'

'He must have his meals alone. I have told Nora so. I could
not eat with him in the room. Nora may make what arrangement
she likes; she was up with him half the night; but there is one
thing I have decided—he shall go to school at Michaelmas. He
is no fit companion for Edmund, and they must be separated as
soon as possible.'

'There I think you are right; I will back you up in that; but,
Vincent, before we leave the subject, I must just say something—
don't be too hard on the boy; he deserves punishment, but it must
not be too prolonged; any signs of repentance should be encouraged.'

'He is repentant enough already,' replied Eric in a strangely-
oppressed voice. 'Did I not say that Nora was with him half the
night trying to comfort him? But what repentance will give Mrs.
Herbert back her child? We have robbed her of her happiness.
I say we, because Hugo is my flesh and blood. Look at my

position, Trevor ; it is perfectly unendurable. I am her clergy-man ; I shall have to read the service over that child ; it is my duty to offer her the consolations belonging to my office ; but I dare not go near her ; she would shrink from the very sight of me.'

'I see what you mean,' returned Colonel Trevor gravely. He thought that he had grasped the reason of the young clergyman's changed looks. His sensitive refined nature was shocked by the awful consequences of his young brother's disobedience ; but he little knew the extent of Eric's pain.

His position was as he had defined it, well-nigh unendurable ; the woman whom he secretly adored was in sorrow and dire affliction, and he dare not approach her. Others might surround her with kindly ministry and sympathy, but he, her pastor and friend, must stand aloof. Even Colonel Trevor, who was no rela-tion, was to be admitted to her presence—and here a fierce pang of jealousy made Eric's heart throb. In his youthful enthusiasm he would have been ready to lay down his life in the service of the sweet woman whom he called his liege lady, and yet his own brother had inflicted this life-long sorrow on her.

'She will loathe the very sound of our name,' he had groaned more than once during that long night. 'If one could only atone ! But the child is dead, and no such atonement is possible.'

There was very little more talk after this. Eric had said his say, but his secret wound lay too deep for masculine sympathy. Colonel Trevor's friendly words only grazed the edge of his trouble ; nevertheless, Eric was grateful for them. He went away after this, walking with hasty strides to the village, and not daring to slacken his pace or look back for fear he should see Colonel Trevor turn in the direction of Brae Farm. The thought that he would see her, speak to her, and take her hand, brought back that flood of bitter jealousy. Poor Eric ! He was so young and his life had been a hard one, and now the slow con-suming passion of hopeless love was to be added to his troubles. It was not in his nature to take the disease lightly, and yet from the first he had never deceived himself ; the young widow's frank kindness gave him no margin of hope that his affection would ever be returned.

'Poor fellow !' sighed Gavin to himself. 'He is terribly sensi-tive, but I can feel for him ; in his place I should have been ready to cut my own throat. I wonder if one dare mention his name ?' And then, as the Farm came in sight, Gavin's face grew grave and sad, and he forgot Eric in the thought of seeing Mrs. Herbert.

He knew where he should find her—in the Dovecote. Tedo's beloved playmates were in their accustomed place, peering in at the window, with their round, yellow eyes, and arching their soft grey necks as though in surprise at the unusual silence.

Lorraine had finished her work, and Tedo lay under a quilt of lovely summer flowers, and now she sat beside him, holding one tiny waxen hand between her hot palms. She looked up with dry, weary eyes at Gavin as he entered ; their heaviness, the patient oppression of her face and attitude, filled him with unutterable pity. Hardly knowing what he did he laid his hand over hers and the child's.

'Dear Mrs. Herbert, is it good for you to be here ?'

Then a vague surprise came into her eyes.

'What does it matter?' she said in a tired voice. 'Nothing can be good for me now. Of course I must be with him ; does he not look sweet? He is smiling as though the angels were talking to him. His mouth was always so lovely ; every one said so.'

Gavin could not answer ; his eyes felt suddenly hot and smarting. He had not moved away his hand, but Lorraine noticed nothing. Presently he stooped over her, and said rather unsteadily :

'You sent for me. I hope you are going to tell me that there is something I can do for you.'

It was sad to see the effort she made to concentrate her thoughts ; but he waited patiently until he saw that she had mastered the question.

'I am very stupid,' she said, putting up her hand to her head, 'but I do not seem to understand things clearly. Yes, I know now what I want. Will you take me this evening to the church-yard ? There is no one else that I can ask, and you are so kind— so kind, and my Tedo was so fond of you. He said when he grew up he meant to be a soldier like the Colonel. I must go myself and choose the place for him.'

'Do you think you are strong enough ?' he asked gently.

But she put this question by as though it did not concern her.

'It is such a pretty churchyard !' she went on. 'I remember that first evening that Ellison said she meant to be buried there ; and there is a corner with two may-trees and a laburnum ; that would just do for my little child. You will take me, will you not? I asked your mother about it, and she said you would not refuse. There is something else that I want to say to you, but everything goes out of my head.'

'Never mind, you will remember it presently, and I am in no hurry. Very well, then, I will bring round the close carriage at half-past six, if that will suit you, it is no distance, and we shall not be long.'

'Oh no, we shall not be long ! I could not stay away long. J think I shall ask Dorcas to sit beside him while I am away. I daresay you think me foolish, but I cannot have my baby left alone. I never left you more than I could help, did I, Tedo, my sweet?' and as she bent to kiss him Gavin hastily removed his hand, though Lorraine's poor confused brain hardly comprehended the action.

Gavin walked to the window, causing a fluttering of wings as the frightened doves flew off to the granary roof. The position was exquisitely painful to him. If she would only have wept and bemoaned herself, like other women. But the sight of her pale face and soft, bewildered eyes gave him positive pain.

'She ought to cry ; she must cry !' he said angrily to himself, 'Her brain is getting confused, and she can find no relief. What is a man to do in such a case ? If only Ellison were here. She ought to have a woman near her, and my mother is not fit for it.'

'Colonel Trevor'—the low voice made him start—'I know now what I wanted to say. It is something about Mr. Vincent.'

'Vincent ! Do you mean that you would like to see him ? ' asked Gavin, blundering in his surprise. But a sudden grey shade on Lorraine's face warned him that he had made a mistake.

'Oh no,' she returned faintly. 'I can see no one—I wish to see no one but you and Mrs. Trevor.'

Why did Gavin flush suddenly as Lorraine said this ?

'It is only that I wanted you to ask him not to be hard on Hugo.' She brought out the word with difficulty, and her head drooped. 'Tell him I said so.' And then she turned hastily and hid her face on the edge of the crib. And so he left her, and the doves flew back, and all through the hot afternoon they sat and cooed to the dead child ; and Lorraine, drowsy with pain, seemed to hear her boy's voice mingling with them.

At the appointed time Gavin drove to the Farm and found her quite ready for him. Lorraine wore her little black hat, and if it had not been for her sad eyes, and a certain unnatural rigidity of feature that spoke of the bitter strain, he would have noticed little difference in her. But when they entered the brougham, an action on her part startled him, for she suddenly pulled down the silk blind.

But the next moment he understood it. She could not bear the sight of the pond where her darling had met his watery grave. Never again would she stand there to see the big cart-horses come down to drink, or to watch the placid cattle standing knee-deep in the shallow water. From this day forth the broad silvery pond in moonlight and starlight would be a nightmare to her.

During the short drive she leant back with her eyes closed, but he could see by her trembling lips that she had not fainted. When he helped her to alight she staggered a little as though from weakness, and as they walked up the churchyard path he was obliged to give her his arm, but the fresh evening air seemed to revive her.

'This is the place I meant,' she said presently, pointing to a corner of the churchyard that adjoined the playground belonging to the infant school. 'It is so pretty and quiet there. No one ever passes; but the children's voices sound so cheerfully. There must be no dark gloomy trees to overshadow my Tedo. May blossoms—he was so fond of may—and the "golden curls," as he always called laburnum. Yes—that is the place. Will you tell Mr. Vincent so, and manage it for me?'

'Yes, yes—I will settle everything. Look, there is a seat. You must sit down for a moment; you are not able to stand.'

'The air is very sweet,' returned Lorraine, almost vacantly. 'You are very kind, Colonel Trevor. I am giving you so much trouble. But I have no one—no one belonging to me. Is there not somebody following us? I keep seeing a dark shadow flit round the church. Perhaps it is my fancy. I seem full of fancies to-day.'

'I will go and look,' he said, anxious to soothe her, for the dilated brightness of her eyes troubled him. But his search was brief and perfunctory. It was only fancy; for who would be taking the trouble to dog their footsteps? he said to himself. But for once Gavin was wrong. That very moment a slight boyish figure was crouching behind the buttress within reach of his hand. Hugo, wandering aimlessly about the common, had caught sight of the carriage, had guessed their errand, and had followed them.

Colonel Trevor had been right in his opinion. Hugo would rather have borne the pain of a tremendous thrashing than have endured this isolation. Eric's white face of suppressed anger the previous evening had been dreadful to him. The very way in which he had silently pointed to the door seemed to affix the mark of Cain on his brow. The poor child was half-maddened with remorse and misery, and the memory of the little limp, inert figure lifted out of the pond was so horrible that he could with difficulty prevent himself from screaming hysterically. Eric's orders had been that Edmund should in future share his room, and the little fellow was sobbing out his heart on his pillow in the adjoining room. Poor Hugo had no light, and no gleam of moonlight relieved the darkness. He could hear Eric walking up and down the passage below, and the sound was hardly reassuring. Then his door opened, and Nora, in her white night-dress, with

her pretty brown hair falling over her shoulders, had glided into
the room. She carried a candle carefully shaded, which she set
down on the washstand. Nora's eyes were swollen with crying,
but as she sat down on the bed and put her arms round him something like comfort stole into the wild suffering heart, and Hugo
broke into hoarse sobs.

'You ought not to come near me, Nora,' he gasped. 'Eric says
I am a murderer—I have murdered Tedo!'

'Oh no, no!' returned Nora, mingling her tears with his.
'No, Hughie dear, you have been very naughty—oh, dreadfully
naughty. But it is not murder. Murderers don't love the people
they kill, and you did love Tedo so. Oh dear, oh dear! We all
loved him. He was such a darling. Oh, Hughie, I don't want to
make you miserable, but why—why did you let him go near the
pond?'

'I forgot—I did indeed, Nora. I was watching Edmund's boat,
and one of the little men and the cannon had fallen into the water,
and the old drake came up and tried to swallow them. And it
was so funny, and Tedo asked to look. And then he cried—I can
hear his voice now, I have to stop my ears I hear it so plainly—
"Hughie, dear, boy vants to look. Boy vill look." And I took
him up. It was Eddie's fault. He screamed so loud, and I let go ;
and then——oh, that splash!' And here Hugo buried his face
against Nora's thin little shoulder, and clung to her.

'Do not be too hard on the boy,' Gavin had said. 'He has had
a lesson that will last him all his life.' And he was right. All his
life long Hugo would never forget those hours of boyish agony when
he first learnt the meaning of those words, 'The wages of sin is
death.' Alas, in his case, death was to the innocent.

CHAPTER XXXI

> ' What time I passed
> That day within the gate, the child arose
> And crossed Thy Threshold, and beheld Thy Face,
> O God in peace. He will not come to me,
> But I will haste across the fading hills,
> And so to Thee.'
>
> B. M., *Ezekiel and other Poems.*

WHEN Colonel Trevor returned from his unavailing search, he found Lorraine had risen from her seat. She was standing with her arms hanging loosely to her side, and her eyes fixed on the daisies. The bewilderment on her face had increased. As he came up to her she put her ungloved hand on his coat sleeve.

'How silent and dark it is. You have been gone such a long time'—he had been absent barely three minutes—'and I could not bear it. I want you to take me home ; it frightens me to stay here, and to think of what will be done here to-morrow.'

'We will go then,' he returned gently. 'I daresay Roberts will be glad not to keep the horses out any longer. You are sadly exhausted, and the dews are heavy this evening.' He hardly knew what to say, and yet he dared not be silent for a moment. He was terribly anxious about her. Something told him that she would be unable to bear the strain much longer ; the unnatural calm must be broken. He noticed the difficulty with which she dragged herself to the gate, as though her feet were weighted with lead. When they reached the carriage he had to lift her in. Neither of them noticed a little figure gliding between the tombstones, and then climbing the low wall in the dusk. As the brougham door closed Hugo swung himself up behind.

Gavin had meant to leave Mrs. Herbert the moment he saw her safely into the house, but as he was about to bid her good-night,

Lorraine felt her dress suddenly pulled and looked vaguely round, but a deadly pallor overspread her features when she saw Hugo.

The poor child was in a sad plight; his face grimy with tears and dust, but as Lorraine uttered a low irrepressible cry he flung himself on the ground at her feet—still holding her dress—convulsively.

'Oh, do let me see him, just for one moment. I want to ask him to forgive me; you may beat me, or kick me if you like, or trample on me. I know I deserve it, but I must see him, and tell him how sorry I am; I did so love him. I wish I had killed myself and not him, poor dear Tedo.'

Lorraine tried to speak—tried to release her dress; and then Gavin suddenly lifted her, as though she were a child, and carried her to the sitting-room; as he did so he could have blessed the boy, for he knew that Hugo's despairing words had broken the icy spell. As he placed her half-fainting on the couch, she hid her face in her hands, and the sound of her wild sobbing brought the frightened maids from the kitchen.

Gavin waved them peremptorily away, and whispered to Mrs. Tucker to bring wine, or some restorative; then he went up to Hugo, as he stood outside almost sick with fright, and patted him on the shoulder.

'Don't be frightened, Hugo, you have done good, not harm; no one has been able to make her cry before; don't let her see you, she will ask for you if she feels able; stay where you are for the present'; and Hugo, for once in his life, obeyed implicitly.

When Mrs. Tucker returned with the wine Gavin took it from her hand, but he made no effort to check Lorraine's tears; those deep, difficult sobs made his heart ache with pity; he was thankful when they ceased, and a passion of tears brought her relief. 'My little child,' he heard her say—'my baby, my Tedo,' over and over again. Presently when she had grown calmer, and had drunk the wine that he held to her lips, she whispered, 'Thank you so much —will you send Hugo to me a moment, he is outside still, is he not?' and Gavin at once obeyed her.

Hugo would have flung himself on his knees again, but Lorraine put out a feeble hand to stop him. 'No, Hugo, not to me. Ask God to forgive you your disobedience. As for my darling, he has forgiven long ago. In heaven there is only love and peace, love and peace.'

Her voice was very faint, as though from exhaustion.

'I cannot talk to-night, I feel too ill,' she went on. 'To-morrow—yes, to-morrow you shall see him; there, God bless you for my little angel's sake.' And as she stretched out that kind hand to the miserable child, Gavin felt as though he could have kissed the hem of her garment out of sheer worship and reverence for her goodness.

'Will you help me upstairs now, Colonel Trevor?' Gavin almost groaned as he performed this brotherly office. How lonely she was. Why had such duties devolved on him? He was nothing to her; he was already half affianced to her cousin, and yet in her sorrow it was to him she turned.

That night, as he took Hugo back to the cottage, some stern interior voice warned him of danger, bidding him walk warily for fear of hidden pit-falls.

But as Lorraine lay weeping on her bed that night, with her eyes fixed on the little crib, standing out so plainly in the moonlight, she thought more than once of Colonel Trevor's kindness.

'He is so patient with me. He has known trouble. He has lost his treasure too'; and as she lay between sleeping and waking with the tears still wet on her face, some words she had once copied for herself, came to her.

'May I reach that purest heaven—
Be to others' souls the cup of strength in some great agony.'

And then a sort of dream came to her, but it was more like a vision. She thought she was in a moonlighted garden, under some grey olive-trees, and a form she recognised was kneeling there with an outstretched cup in His hands. 'I am drinking it for thee, and wilt thou refuse it for My sake?' she seemed to hear a voice say, and as she took it fearful and trembling, she saw her boy with a dazzling halo round his baby head, smiling at her over a clump of white lilies, and in that sudden joy she awoke.

The following afternoon a pencilled note was brought to Eric. As he saw the handwriting, a dark flush came to his brow, and his hand shook as he opened it.

'Will you come to me?' it said. 'I ought to have seen you before, but I shall have him such a little while, and I wanted to be left alone with him; please forgive me my selfishness, and come now. There is something I must say to you.—LORRAINE HERBERT.'

Eric crushed up the letter in his hand with a sudden fierce impulse; then he smoothed it out and read it again. The next moment he was striding across the common. As he walked up the lane, he saw Miss Trevor coming out of the little gate; she stood still when she saw him, and they shook hands in silence.

Muriel looked pale and travel-stained. She had taken the night train, and had gone at once to the Farm.

'I have been sitting with her,' she said abruptly, but her voice was deep with emotion. 'She is quite calm, but she looks terribly ill. She told me that she was expecting you, so I said I would go across and fetch my things. I thought mother would be with her, but she says she was alone last night.'

Muriel's tone was slightly indignant, but she was not aware that Mrs. Trevor had had an attack of pain the previous evening, that prevented her leaving the house.

'I am glad you have come. Mrs. Herbert ought not to be alone, certainly,' returned Eric. His manner was constrained, and he looked ill at ease. Muriel looked at him a little wistfully. Mr. Vincent had never been so stiff and cold before. She hated herself for having such a thought, but it was there all the same. But Eric, absorbed by his own miserable sensations, was unconscious of his want of friendliness.

Miss Trevor simply bored him, and though he had at the moment no wish to seem ungracious, he left her as soon as possible. His mind was full of the impending interview. Why had Mrs. Herbert sent for him? how was he to bear himself in her presence, and in what words could he convey his sympathy?

Ruth showed him into the sitting-room. Even after these two days it had a deserted, uninhabited look; the flowers on the table were withered, and no one had carried them away; and the closed windows and blinds added to the general dreariness. Some work Lorraine had been doing that fatal afternoon as she talked to her visitor had been hastily folded together on the window-seat. Muriel found it later, and carried it away, bursting into tears as she did so. That little velvet smock with its delicate embroidery would not be needed now.

Eric stood still with his eyes fixed on the door, but he was not kept waiting long; in another minute Lorraine entered. Eric hardly dared to look at her, the very touch of her cold soft hand gave him a shock. How fearfully pale she looked; her eyes were half extinguished with weeping, but she was wonderfully calm as she walked to the window and drew up the heavy Venetian blind.

'Why have they done this?' she said, and there was a trace of irritation in her tone. 'Do they not know that he hated darkness? Will you open the window for me, Mr. Vincent? if I do not have air, I feel as though I should die,' and then she seated herself on the broad window-seat, and after a moment's hesitation, Eric seated himself opposite to her; as he did so, he noticed there was a grey thread in her glossy brown hair.

'If you had not sent for me, I should not have dared to come,' he began impulsively; 'you have not misunderstood me, Mrs. Herbert?'

'Oh no,' she returned wearily, 'there was no possibility of misunderstanding : 'it was kindness on your part that kept you away.' Her voice trembled as though she found it difficult to control it, and there was a painful quivering of the mouth ; but after a moment she gathered strength to go on.

'It is so hard not to be selfish. I feel as though I only want to think of him—people tire me so, but they mean to be kind. I wanted to speak to you about Hugo ; I saw him last night.'

Eric gazed at her in speechless consternation.

'He followed us to the churchyard, and then to the house ; he wanted our forgiveness. To-day he came again, and I took him to see my boy. It tried me ; it was very painful, but I am glad I did not refuse. It makes me almost happy to know that my little child will have helped him to be good ; that is why I sent for you, Mr. Vincent, to tell you that we have forgiven him, and that you must forgive him too.'

Eric could not master himself sufficiently to speak. She was putting them all to shame ; his silence, his suppressed agitation seemed to trouble Lorraine ; she sighed heavily, as though her self-imposed task wearied her too much.

'Promise me that you will forgive him,' she said almost imploringly ; 'he is so young, such a mere child, and he suffers so.' Then some words, from which he had preached the previous Sunday, came into the young clergyman's mind. 'Ye ought rather to forgive him and comfort him, lest perhaps such a one should be swallowed up with overmuch sorrow.' How strange that he had selected those words.

'I will try,' he returned. 'I think these two days I have almost hated him ; I could not endure to see him. Mrs. Herbert, you are a better Christian than I.' Then she shook her head.

'No, no, you must not say that, but my boy was so fond of him, Mr. Vincent. I must say one thing, and then I shall have finished. Keep Hugo near you ; be kind and patient with him. I do not think that he will give you any more trouble, but he must not be trusted with Edmund,' and then she rose from her seat and held out her hand.

'Will you forgive me ?—but I cannot stay. I am very weak, and talking tries me so, and I must keep my strength for to-morrow.'

'Please wait one moment,' he implored. 'I wanted to ask you about that. Would it pain you less if some one else were to read the service ? I could get Cartwright to come over.' But this question evidently surprised her.

'Oh no ; I should not wish that. Mr. Cartwright did not love my boy; he was quite a stranger to him. You need not have asked me that, Mr. Vincent; but I know how kindly you meant it'—and then he was obliged to let her go.

He had not promised her that he would forgive Hugo, but he knew her word would be law to him; his heart was full of bitterness to the boy, but all the same he must bring himself to tolerate him. As he walked across the common, he could see him sauntering aimlessly among the bushes like a forlorn little Esau, and he stood still and beckoned to him.

The boy approached him reluctantly.

'Did you call me, Eric?' he asked in a frightened sort of way.

'Yes, I wanted to speak to you; don't look at me as though you thought I was going to strike you. I have never yet hurt you, have I?' and Hugo shook his head. 'I want to know how you dared go near Mrs. Herbert—no, I am not asking in anger,' as Hugo began to cry, 'I only wanted to know what put it into your head to do such a thing.'

'I can't tell you if you speak in that voice,' returned Hugo piteously. 'I would rather you hit me than look at me as you do; every one hates me except Eddie, and I hate myself, but I could not have lived if she had not forgiven me'; and here, worn out with excess of emotion, Hugo flung himself on the ground in a fit of sobbing. 'Go away, Eric,' he continued passionately, 'I know you hate the sight of me, and I won't talk to you any more.'

For the first time Eric felt a little softened towards the culprit.

'Get up, Hugo,' he said peremptorily, 'and don't make a fool of yourself; don't I tell you I am not angry now? Mrs. Herbert told me that she had forgiven you, so I must do my best to forgive you too.'

Hugo looked at him as though he could not venture to believe his ears; then he left off crying, and rose slowly from the ground.

'Do you really mean this, Eric; and may Eddie sleep in my room again?'

'No,' returned his brother shortly. 'Things can't be as they were. I dare not trust Eddie to be with you.'

'Then you have not forgiven me,' returned Hugo, in a tone of such despair that Eric was touched and startled.

'Yes, Hugo, I have, at least I am trying to do so, but I cannot trust you until you have proved to me that you have learnt to obey. Eddie may play with you when Nora or I am there; but he is never to be alone with you. This is the only punishment I shall inflict. At Michaelmas you shall go to school—you will like that, Hugo—and then you will have plenty of companions.'

But Hugo, crushed and bitter, refused to be consoled by this.

'You are sending me to school because you are afraid for Eddie, and because you hate the sight of me,' he began rebelliously; and then his little heart began to heave. 'I can't bear it, Eric. I think you might trust me now; I shall never, never be naughty again.'

'Won't you, Hughie?'—and here Eric put his arm round his young brother, and there was no hardness in his voice now. 'I don't think any of us dare say that. I shall be able to trust you again some day, I am sure of that, and until then you will be brave, and try your 'hardest to be good, and—I will help you,' and he laid his hand on the curly head. That brotherly touch brought comfort to Hugo, and in his childish heart he registered a vow that Eric should never distrust him again.

Nora watched them timidly as they came in, but she never ventured to question her elder brother. 'Hugo will have his meals with us as usual,' was all Eric said, as he threw himself down in his chair. He felt terribly fagged and tired, as though he had been hard at work. Eddie, who was reading disconsolately in a corner, uttered a shrill little hurrah, and rushed out into the passage, and flung his arms round his playmate.

'You are going to have dinner with us, Hughie!' he exclaimed ecstatically, and Eric could overhear Hugo's answer.

'Yes; but we are never to sleep together again, and you won't often be allowed to play with me, Eddie. I am going away to school '—but here a howl of dismay from the faithful Eddie brought Nora out to comfort him.

The next afternoon most of the inhabitants of Highlands gathered in the churchyard. Mrs. Trevor was unable to attend; but Muriel, who had now taken up her quarters at the Farm, accompanied her brother and Lorraine.

Eric had arranged that some of the school children should carry the tiny coffin, and since early morning, he and Miss Spencer, the infant-schoolmistress, and Nora and Daniel had been busy lining the grave with ferns and wild flowers that the children had gathered. As Lorraine looked at the deep green nest with its fringe of ferns and late-blooming roses, her lip trembled a little, and there was a mist before her eyes.

The children standing in awestruck groups, the little bearers with their innocent young faces, the white frocks of the girls as they stood holding their simple posies, seemed to blend with the sweet summer sunshine, and the words of consolation that Eric Vincent was reading in a strained, trembling voice. 'I shall go to him, but he will not return to me,' Lorraine said to herself, as the children threw in their flowers one by one. She stood there so long that Gavin took her hand at last, and placing it on his arm drew her gently away. More than one person noticed the Colonel's excessive paleness as he handed the young widow into the carriage, and stood bareheaded as she drove away. 'He has a feeling heart has the Colonel,' observed Mrs. Drake to her gossips, as she wiped her eyes. 'Maybe it reminds him too closely of the day he buried his wife, eh, neighbour ? But Mr. Vincent was right when he read those words—" Man is born into trouble." It is a sorrowful world ; but we've got to live in it, and more's the pity.'

CHAPTER XXXII

HE MUST DREE HIS WEIRD TOO

'To shape the whole future is not our problem, but only faithfully a small part of it. . . . The general issue will, as it has always done, rest well with a Higher Intelligence than ours.'—CARLYLE.

'There is no steady happiness in life, save the happiness of self-forgetfulness for the sake of others.'—DEAN PAGET.

SOME one besides Mrs. Drake noticed Gavin's paleness. On his return home he had gone straight to his mother's dressing-room; and Mrs. Trevor, who was lying on her couch, looked at him rather anxiously as he stood beside her. Perhaps it was the strong sunlight, but she fancied he looked older. She had never noticed those lines before round his mouth, and his deep-set eyes were unusually melancholy.

'I am afraid all this has tried you, Gavin,' she said gently. Then he sat down beside her and the gloom deepened on his brow.

'It has not been cheerful, certainly,' he returned, with an abrupt laugh. 'But I suppose it was all in the day's work, and there was no one else to do it.' He had said those words to himself over and over again as he had walked back from the church. 'How could he help himself; there was no one else?'

'No,' she replied in a grieved voice, 'it is sad that I am such a broken reed just now. I longed so much to be there. Muriel will do her best, but she will not understand, she has not served her apprenticeship to trouble—as you and I have, Gavin, my dear —and that is why we suit Mrs. Herbert best.'

Gavin bowed his head slightly as though he agreed with her. Mrs. Herbert's frank dependence on him, her simply-expressed confidence and trust were becoming sources of embarrassment to him. Instinctively he felt that he was in a wrong position, and yet how was he to withdraw himself, or to refuse to help her—the most lonely of creatures on God's earth.

'Mother,' he said suddenly, and there was a harsh vibrating note of pain in his voice, 'I wish to heaven that Ellison would send us her address. I do not believe our telegram has reached her yet. What a horrible complication it is; if she were only here to look after Mrs. Herbert.'

'Yes, indeed,' sighed Mrs. Trevor. 'I agree with you that nothing could be more unfortunate than her absence just now. Muriel, poor child, will do her best, she is devoted to Mrs. Herbert, but she has not dear Ellison's experience. She is so helpful and strong in any emergency, and her calmness is so soothing. I miss her dreadfully, especially now when I am separated from Mrs. Herbert.'

'You do not miss her more than I do,' returned Gavin almost harshly. Something in his mother's words seemed to sting him. 'Nothing is as it should be; you are being neglected, for of course Muriel ought to be here. But how can we leave Mrs. Herbert to that loneliness? She is ill now, and I never saw any one so changed in a few days.'

Mrs. Trevor looked alarmed; in her weak state everything troubled her. 'I thought you said she was so calm, Gavin.'

'Yes, she was outwardly calm, and gave us no trouble. I think it is her nature to be unselfish, but one can see what she suffers. Muriel says the worst part is that she cannot sleep, she spends half the night sitting by her window. She does not like any one to take any notice; but, of course, one knows how this must wear her out. And then it is so difficult to make her take sufficient food.'

'Yes, I know, but you must give her time, Gavin dear. You and Muriel must not be too anxious. When the heart is sick, how is one to eat and sleep as usual? When God takes away our children we are bound to suffer; and oh, what suffering it is,' and then she looked at him with a touching little smile. 'She must dree her weird, and we must pray for her.'

'What a heart he has,' she said to herself when he had left her. 'Gavin has a noble nature, he takes after his father. How tender he is over that poor woman; that is so like John. He was so compassionate to any one in trouble. He never could do enough for them.' But Gavin would hardly have endorsed his mother's flattering opinion.

When he had eaten his solitary dinner he went out into the garden. There was a lime walk overlooking a large meadow that was a favourite resort of his. At this hour it would be deserted, and no one would be likely to invade his solitude. He had his cigarette-case in his hand, a gift from Ellison on his last birthday, but he made no attempt to light his cigarette ; a dull weight of pain had been oppressing him all day, and now he knew that he must look things bravely in the face.

What was this thing that had happened to him ?   How had it come about, and when ?   Was it not monstrous, incredible, that he should only have found it out now ?   ' Good heavens, what a fool I must have been not to have discovered it before ! ' he groaned, as he brought his hand heavily down on the fence.   ' How was I to guess that such a misfortune should come to me—to me of all men ?   Oh, Nell, Nell, why did you die and leave me, for I have made a poor business of life ever since ? '

But he must look it in the face, he was no coward, and after all it was more his misfortune than his fault. He had been good friends with Mrs. Herbert, they had been on a pleasant footing of intimacy.   Her society was congenial to him, her frankness and simplicity had always pleased him.   But he had never put her on an equality with Ellison.   When Ellison had been in the room he had often forgotten Mrs. Herbert's existence.

Why was it, then, that in her sorrow she had suddenly grown dear to him, so dear that he hardly dared to be with her, for fear he should betray his tenderness ?   Her very dependence on him added to the danger.   In a hundred touching ways she showed him how fully she trusted him.   What cruel fate had thrust this new trouble in his path ?   No, he would be honest ; he was no love-sick boy, but a sorely-tried man, who had buried his beautiful young wife long years ago, and who knew well what loneliness and pain meant.   He would not accuse himself of fault when there had been none.   His only error lay in the idea that his warm affection for Ellison would satisfy him.   That was the only mistake he had made.

Affection, friendship, admiration for Ellison's tranquil virtues , what were these compared to the passionate pulsation of his heart, when he had laid his hand over Lorraine's and her dead child's, when his love and pity had been dumb within him ?

' Yes—he loved her, loved her, loved her.'   He said it out loud, and some meek-eyed cattle feeding near him raised their heads and looked at him.   For once he would own it ; crushed, broken-hearted as she was, she was dearer to him than any other woman living.   Something in her sweetness and naive simplicity seemed to remind him of his wife.   True, she had not his Nell's beauty or her exquisite colouring, but in these last few days he had thought her almost lovely.   ' What other woman,' he said to himself,

'would have borne this trouble as she has borne it—without a
word of complaint. How can any man be near her and not love
her? No, I am not ashamed of it, I have no need to be ashamed
of anything.'

Gavin's pride and self-reliance would be a tower of strength.
He was no puny boy to shrink from suffering, but all the same he
could not close his eyes to the fact that he had made a terrible
mistake.

Lorraine Herbert was the woman he loved—the woman whom
he desired most ardently to make his wife, and yet in honour he
was already pledged to Ellison, although no formal word had
passed between them. What was that he had said to her that
evening at the gate of the Woodlands, when she had besought him
to say no more? Was it possible that she had failed to understand
him when he had kissed her brow as a sign and earnest of his
affection? Had she not promised to listen to his wooing when she
returned—promised faithfully? And could he have any doubt of
her answer? He knew in his own heart that Ellison cared for him,
far more than she knew herself; that no other man but he would
ever become her husband. And he knew, too, that this carrying
out of his unspoken pledge would be pain and grief to him; but not
for one moment did he try to escape his doom.

'He too must dree his weird,' he said to himself, with a forlorn
smile, for how could he trifle with the affections of a woman so
dear to him as Ellison? True, he would never love her as he
would have loved Lorraine—to his sorrow he knew that now—but
at least he could do his duty, and Ellison should never miss any
tenderness that was her due.

'Neither of them will ever know it,' he thought, as he paced to
and fro in the fast-gathering darkness. 'It is my own trouble, my
own pain; it will not touch them. God helping me it shall never
touch them. I shall live through it—other men have, under similar
circumstances. If only Ellison would come home, and then I could
settle it.'

Alas, there was something ominous in Gavin's feverish desire
to hurry on matters! Truthful, honourable, and upright as he
was, he was relying too much on his own strength.

Gavin was no moral coward; if he saw his duty he would try,
in the face of all obstacles, to do it. But he forgot, as even the
bravest of men will forget, that there are laws of nature that cannot
be set aside. One human being affects another; there are unspoken
influences that may set all our best efforts to restrain them at
naught. What human voice can dare to regulate the ebb and flow
of such influences, and say, 'Thus far shalt thou go and no further'?

Who can say that the tide of our passions may not engulf some other nature that has approached us too heedlessly ?

A child's hand may teach us a lesson ; the pebble flung with weak force forms the widening circles on the water ; the responsibility of our unspoken influence, of our secret wishes, lies heavy on all of us. And when Gavin in his man's pride determined to close his lips and bear his pain silently, taking no one into confidence, and making the best of his mistake, he was reckoning without two important factors—would he succeed in blinding Ellison, and how would it affect Lorraine ? But, confused by his own inward pain, Gavin did not ask himself such questions. His daily path was too full of perplexity for him to strain his vision towards imaginary troubles in the future.

When Ellison came back his course would be perfectly simple ; he must induce her to consummate their engagement, and then he must see as little as possible of Mrs. Herbert. It was clearly not possible to hold himself aloof now ; Muriel had asked him to go down early the next morning to the Farm.

'Mrs. Herbert will like to see you, and there is some business for you to settle,' she had said to him. 'We can do nothing without you, Gavin'—and then he knew he must go. No, he must not shrink from seeing her just now. She needed him too much ; and, after all—here he smiled bitterly in the darkness—what did a little more pain signify, when he had made such a mess of his life ? But not for one moment did he shut his eyes to the suffering which he knew was in store for him.

The most salient point of Colonel Trevor's character was the simple, direct straightforwardness that he brought to bear on everything. As an old sergeant in the regiment once said, 'There is nothing shoddy about the Colonel, it is all real grit and no mistake.'

The thought that in future there would be need of watchfulness over his words and actions filled him with a sense of oppression. He felt as though he were trying to breathe freely through the black vizor of mediæval armour.

There could never be complete openness and confidence between him and Ellison ; and deeply as he abhorred the idea of any mental reservation from the woman he intended to make his wife, sheer necessity would compel him to keep silence.

Again he pondered heavily over his fatal blindness, and more than once the thought crossed his mind that but for his mother's half-implied hints he would never have thought of marrying Ellison. Constant dropping wears away a stone, and his mother's little wistful speeches about his loneliness and dear Ellison's many virtues had in time done their work.

He tried to chase these thoughts away, and to summon to his aid the old dogged endurance which had carried him through his worst trouble. It was no use brooding over past mistakes, he must pull himself together and think of others, and then he lighted his cigar, and walked back to the house ; but before it was half smoked he had thrown it away.

The next day, and each succeeding day, he went down to the Farm, but so strong was the force he put on himself during the half-hour or so that he spent there that neither Muriel nor Lorraine noticed anything different in his manner.

Lorraine, indeed, withdrawn into the inner court of her great sorrow, was less observant than usual of what passed round her. In some indefinable way a sort of mist seemed between her and outward things ; but Muriel, who was less absorbed, noticed that a faint smile came to her pale lips when her brother entered the room where they were sitting.

Nothing else seemed to interest or rouse her. She would sit at her work silently, but after a few stitches the work would lie in her lap unheeded, and she would look out at the gay beds of flowers with a blank look that saw nothing.

She would sit so, while Muriel read to her, but it may be doubted how much she understood of the book. Sometimes in the middle of a sentence she would rise suddenly and go away, and then Muriel never ventured to follow her. She would find her an hour later in the Dovecote, sitting beside the crib with the tears rolling down her face, and some little garments on her lap ; she would look up at Muriel rather piteously.

'I did not mean to be rude,' she would say tremulously, 'but while you were reading I seemed to hear his voice so plainly ; and though I knew it was foolish, I felt I must come up here. I do love sitting here,' she said once, 'with all his things round me. What do you think? I was so angry with Dorcas just now ; I found her tidying the toy-cupboard. But I drove her away ; I told her she must never enter this room again. Oh, I am afraid I was very cross, for she began to cry ; but it must be my care now. Look, I have been feeding the coocoos—that is what my darling always called them. Do you see that one ? it was his favourite ; Mammy Coocoo he always called it.'

'It seems as though I can do nothing for her,' observed Muriel disconsolately, when Gavin came a little later. 'I think she likes best to be alone. Oh yes, she will come down to you ! You are the only person she cares to see, unless it is mother ; but mother has not been near us for days.'

'She is not well. Why don't you come up to the House some-

times, when Mrs. Herbert can spare you ?'   And then he paused,
and continued rather abruptly.   'We have heard from Ellison.'

'Yes, I know ; Mrs. Herbert has had a letter too.   I think it
has upset her ; she said it was so very very kind.   Did Ellison
write to you, Gavin ?'

'No,' he returned, walking to the window as he spoke ; 'the
letter was to my mother.   She is awfully shocked !   She says
nothing has ever shocked her so much in her life.   They had only
just received the news, the telegram had not reached her.   If Mrs.
Herbert has had a letter, you know, of course, about Miss Mervyn's
illness ?'

'Yes, poor woman, she has rheumatic fever.   Ellison thinks her
bed at the last inn must have been damp ; but it is impossible for
her to leave her.   They are in such a miserable little place too,
but there is no moving her at present.'

'Why did she ever go with them ?' returned Gavin irritably.
'Think of her shut up in that bare châlet in a Tyrolean valley, and
having to nurse Miss Mervyn night and day.   It will break Ellison
down, strong as she is ; but of course Mr. Mervyn will do his best
to get help.   She says they rather like the doctor; he is a sensible
sort of person, and they have heard of an English physician who is
staying at a place near, and they mean to get him over.'   But here
he broke off, as his ear caught the soft footfall outside. and the next
moment Lorraine entered.

CHAPTER XXXIII

'Patience and sorrow strove
Who should express her goodliest.'
King Lear.

'This bud of love, by summer's ripening breath,
May prove a beauteous flower when next we meet.'
Romeo and Juliet.

THE letter that Lorraine had read with such anguish that morning had been written by Ellison during one of her tedious night watches. The sad news received earlier in the day had completely unnerved her, and for some hours she had found it impossible to write a word ; but in the silence and solitude of the night some degree of calmness had returned to her. Those words of womanly sympathy and tenderness flowing straight from Ellison's good heart were treasured by Lorraine for many a long year.

'My dear, my own poor dear, if I were only not so far away from you,' she wrote ; 'to think that this awful trouble has come to you, and that I cannot take you in my arms and try to comfort you. Oh, how hard it seems !

'If I were only free, I would travel day and night to be with you ; but, Lorraine dear, how am I to leave poor Margaret ? She is in such suffering, she cannot move without agony ; and we have no one but an ignorant peasant woman to help us. Margaret is so delicate ; her heart has always been weak, and of course this makes us terribly anxious. Mr. Mervyn seems distracted ; he is one of those men who are so helpless in an emergency—so different from my cousin Gavin. There is nothing he would not do for Margaret ; but he is too nervous and incapable to be of much use in a sick-room. I have to think of everything—to give orders, and scold him into taking proper food and exercise. Ah, if you knew how heart-sick and home-sick I am—how I am longing for a sight of your dear face; but how am I to leave them! I have written fully to Cousin Louise. At least, dearest, you are not utterly alone. I hear Muriel is with you, and I know how devoted she will be, and Cousin Louise and Gavin will look after you. I must trust you to them. Promise me—promise me—for are we not like sisters, you and I?—that you will let them do their best for you. I cannot trust myself to write more to-night. When I think of that poor darling, I cannot write for tears. God comfort you, my poor Lorraine! In a day or two I will write again.' This was much of the substance of her letter.

'You will like to read it,' Lorraine said simply, as she handed the letter to Gavin. She had not shown it to Muriel. Gavin's hand shook a little as he perused it silently.

'It is just what I expected her to write,' he observed, as he replaced the letter reverently in the envelope. 'She has written all particulars to my mother; but her letter is so sad that I should not care for you to see it. Ellison feels it terribly. She tells my mother that she cannot rid herself of the thought that in some way she is responsible for the accident. One understands what she means. Ellison is not the least morbid. But the idea that that poor little fellow met his death in such a way while he was under her charge, gives her exquisite pain. "It would have been better if I had left them in Beaumont Street." That is what she said.'

Then a flush crossed Lorraine's wan face.

'No; she must not think that,' she returned in a low voice. 'Dr. Howell was talking to me yesterday. I know now that my darling could not have been long with me; that his little life was doomed. She has made his last months so happy. Oh, what a spring and summer it has been! How he loved the birds and the flowers, and those long days in the woods! When you write to Ellison you must tell her this. He was just pining away and wasting to skin and bone in Beaumont Street. Dr. Howell told me plainly that if I had kept him there he would not have been alive now. It was kind of him to tell me all this—was it not, Colonel Trevor? It makes it easier for me to bear things. I think he had not a moment's pain. Dr. Howell assures me that his little heart was so weak that the shock of the fall and the cold water must have killed him instantly. It is a comfort to know this.'

She spoke in the weak, strained voice that had become habitual to her. Her eyes looked heavy as though she had slept little. Even in this little time she had grown perceptibly thinner. As he talked to her he noticed that her wedding-ring was almost slipping from her finger. She had got into a restless habit of pushing it up and down, and it somehow fascinated him; but he averted his eyes.

'By the bye,' he said, trying to speak in his ordinary manner, 'I have brought those plans to show you. I was busy over them yesterday. I suppose Muriel told you?'

'Yes,' returned Lorraine slowly; 'and your mother wrote to me. What am I to say, Colonel Trevor?'

'I hope you will say nothing,' for he saw how her lips were quivering. 'Do you not know what a pleasure it will be to your friends? It is just what Ellison would have wished, and my mother is writing this morning to tell her about it.'

'And you will not even let me thank you. Wait a moment, Colonel Trevor, I must say something before I look at those plans that you have so kindly drawn. It does seem so wonderful. Last night when I could not sleep I could not help fretting because I had no money, and I did so long to put up a little marble cross for my darling; it broke my heart to think I could not do even that for him. And I made up my mind that when Ellison came back I would ask her to let me do without new dresses, and put the money by for this. And then as we sat at breakfast Muriel told me what you all intended to do. "It is my brother's idea, but mother and Ellison and I will all join," that is what Muriel said. No, I cannot thank you; it goes too deep for mere thanks!'

'And I may fetch my plans?' But he did not wait for her permission, and very soon they were both absorbed over the drawings. Gavin was no mean draughtsman, and his designs were skilfully and gracefully done.

'They are all beautiful, but I like this one best,' she said presently. 'I think for a child everything should be so simple; and that dove nestling under the cross is such a lovely idea.'

'Then it shall be carried out at once. And now about the inscription. His name was only Theodore—was it not? Is there any special text you have selected, or shall we wait a little?'

'I have chosen two; they are very short, so perhaps I may have both, "Suffer the little children to come unto Me," just those words, and "He shall gather the lambs with His arm," the dove and the cross will tell the rest. "Theodore Herbert, aged three years and two months." Muriel agreed with me that I could not do better.' And then as he rolled up the papers and prepared to take his leave, she looked at him wistfully. 'How kind you are to take all this trouble, and you have only known us such a few months. Sometimes at night I think how I have taken all your kindness as a matter of course, and never even thanked you.'

'One does not want to be thanked for a little civility,' returned Gavin lightly; but if Lorraine knew how her grateful look was torturing him. Why had Muriel left them together? it was just her gaucherie and want of thought, but he dared not trust himself a moment longer. But as he walked through the farmyard and long meadow he could not get her out of his thoughts. The slight, tall figure swaying a little from weakness, the pale sweet face, the thin hand with its loose wedding-ring, how pathetic it all was. But it was her eyes that tried him most. How their sadness seemed to appeal to him. 'Heaven help me, how am I to get through the next few weeks?' he said to himself. 'There seems a fatality in things; because there are not difficulties enough, there is poor Ellison eating out her heart with home-sickness and worry in that Tyrolean valley.'

'Should he go to her?' The thought came to him with a sort of shock, startling him out of his apathy. 'After all, his duty was more to her than to Lorraine. Should he speak to his mother about it and find out her opinion? She was very clear-headed, and would tell him exactly what she thought; but then as he remembered her plans for him and Ellison he wavered a little. No, she would not be impartial; her own wishes would insensibly warp her judgment. She would bid him go to Ellison and do all in her power to remove every obstacle, and for the time Mrs. Herbert would go to the wall. No, I dare not leave,' he finished, and then he drew a long breath of relief; 'my mother's state is too precarious. Yesterday I did not like the look of her. I must have M'Callum down again and hear his opinion. Ellison would be the first to tell me that I ought to remain if she knew the state my mother is in; and then in her letter she has begged us to look after Mrs. Herbert. Could anything be plainer than that sentence in my mother's letter?—"If it were not for you and Gavin and Muriel I should be utterly miserable about Lorraine; but I know what good friends you will be to her, and how tenderly you will care for her. Tell Gavin that I leave the farm and everything else in his charge. Sam Brattle must go to him for orders. Lorraine cannot look after things just now. I am writing to Mrs. Tucker and telling her the same. Poor dear Lorraine must be spared everything as much as possible.'

He quite understood why Ellison had written to his mother. It had been part of the compact that no letters were to pass between them; and though circumstances had compelled him to break the silence, and it had been his painful task to tell Ellison the

sad news, he knew well that she would not answer him directly.
'Tell Gavin how I thank him for his long kind letter, and give
him my love.' That was her sole message; but Gavin's eyes,
sharpened by love and fear, read truly between the lines.

Those weeks of absence had done much for him. Before the
first fortnight was over Ellison was already suffering pangs of
home-sickness, and even the glorious sights that surrounded
her could not console her for her exile from all she loved best,
and the thought of a certain bronzed face with deep-set eyes made
her heart beat more quickly and brought a sudden flush to her
face.

That evening at the gate of the Woodlands Ellison had reached
the crisis of her life. From the moment that Gavin's lips had
touched her brow, her old careless maidenly content and friendship
had merged into something deeper and truer, and her heart had
passed out of her own keeping for ever. Love had come to her
unsought, and certainly undesired, and had fettered even her strong
will. No girl in her teens waiting and longing for her lover chafed
more impatiently than she did at her exile. She yearned for
Gavin's presence, for the sight of his face and the sound of his
voice, as she had never yearned for mortal thing before, and at such
times the sound of music or even the sight of two rustic lovers
walking hand in hand under the pine trees brought the tears to
her eyes. How patient and gentle he had been with her that
evening, and how cowardly and unaccountably she had behaved.
Why had she feared so to listen to his wooing? What foolish
perversity and self-will compelled her to enforce these conditions
of silence? She had loved him then if she would only have
owned it, and it was her own fault that they were not engaged.

'I will never behave so foolishly again,' she said to herself
night after night as she sat thinking in her bare little bedroom.
'He is so honest and straightforward that he deserves equal openness on my part; I have treated him badly, though he will never
tell me so. Well, if I can only get back to him I will try and
make up to him for all my perversity; he shall never have reason
to complain of me again—never—never!'

Ellison beguiled many weary hours in the sick-room by dreaming happily about the future. Old Mrs. Langton was breaking
fast, and Ferncliffe would soon be empty. She knew Mrs. Trevor
and Muriel would be able to live there as they had always intended
if Gavin married again. 'There will be no need for Lorraine to
leave the Farm,' she thought; 'Gavin would never wish me to part
with her. Brae House is so near that she will not feel too lonely;
we must try and interest her as much as we can; if she could only

realise that she is helping me by looking after things she will feel better. I must not leave her just yet. Gavin is so thoughtful and unselfish that he will never ask it ; he will know how terrible this first winter will be to her. Poor Lorraine, she is so young still ; she has probably a long life before her ; if she could only marry again. It may be my fancy, but it has struck me once or twice that Mr. Vincent admires her ; he is always so eager to walk or talk with her. That evening at Brae he did not seem quite like himself. But there, I will not weave nonsensical fancies any more ' ; and Ellison took up the stout grey stocking she was knitting with a resolute air.

Down in the valley below a peasant was jodelling, a goat-herd with his goats was clambering down the rocky pass ; on the little bridge below the châlet the flaxen-haired Elsa was knitting and looking out for her lover, big burly Hans, from the mill-house yonder ; her little yellow dog Fritz barked madly at the ducks in the water. Just then long-legged Seppel came round the corner with the letter-bag slung round his neck and his oaken stick in his hand, and instantly rosy-cheeked, demure Elsa drooped her eyes and knitted furiously ; Hans and Seppel were rivals, and the fair-haired Elsa was their apple of discord, their bone of contention.

'If I speak to Long Seppel, Hans frightens me,' pouted Elsa, 'for he vows he will murder him ; he has a terrible stick loaded with lead, and swings it as he says this.'

'My Fräulein, they make my life a terror to me sometimes. I tell the Mütterchen that I shall go over the mountain to stay with Gretchen. It is dull there ; there are no cows coming home from pasture, no goats, nothing but the mines ; but one's life would be quiet, and there would be no fear of bloodshed,' and Elsa shrugged her plump shoulders, and her blue eyes looked artlessly at the gracious lady.

'Which do you prefer, Elsa ? ' asked Ellison ; the village idyll amused her much. Elsa's simple coquetry, her pride in her two brawny lovers, her little affectations and assumed terrors were as good as a play to her ; the chubby, childish face with its startled eyes and flaxen eyelashes seemed no fit subject for a tragedy. 'You cannot marry both, Elsa, you must throw the handkerchief to one.'

'Hein, who talks of marriage ? ' returned Elsa with a blush. 'Hans is my bräutigam ; we have exchanged rings ; every child in the village knows that ; but Hans ought not to be a tyrant, that is what the Mütterchen says. What is the harm of exchanging a civil word with Seppel when he wishes me good-evening ? Last night he was tired, the bags were heavy, and he sat down to rest. Look you, Fräulein, the bridge is broad enough for both, but Hans found him there, and he turned sulky and went back to the mill without giving me the kerchief he had promised, and so I cried myself to sleep.'

'Hans was in a temper! Look here, Elsa, take my advice, and when Seppel comes with the letters just go in and help your mother with the supper; last evening she was calling for you, but you were so busy with Seppel that you did not hear. Hans will be remorseful for his bad temper and will come to apologise; when he sees Seppel resting on the bridge alone, his good-humour will return; he will find you frying pancakes; well, nothing will please him more, and you will have your fine pink kerchief.'

'Seppel will be disappointed. He said he had got a fairing for me too.' But in the end Elsa took the gracious lady's advice. When Ellison came out into the balcony for a breath of air, she saw Elsa sitting on the bridge with Hans beside her cracking nuts. She had a pink silk kerchief tied loosely round her brown throat. When she saw Ellison, her white teeth parted in a merry smile.

'See, Hans, the gracious lady regards us. Is she not like a picture—with her smooth hair and her white skin, and her stately, grand figure? Listen, Hans, I will whisper it in thy ear—something tells me the gracious lady has a lover; there is a picture in her room. He has a brown face and dark, melancholy eyes, and he holds his head like a soldier, and she was looking at it once as I look at thee when thou art in a good temper'; but here the rosy lips were suddenly and effectually silenced.

'How happy they are,' thought Ellison, as she went back to her patient. 'Elsa is a coquette; but she is true to her red-haired Hans.' And then the thought came to Ellison, what if some day she should see Gavin striding up the steep little street? what if he should take her by surprise, and the rough little *char-à-banc* should set him down with his portmanteau? The mere idea made her head swim with a sort of vertigo. Well, it would be only like him. She knew exactly how he would look and what he would say. 'I have come to take care of you. Are you glad to see me, Ellison?' and there would be no doubt about her answer. The gladness would be on her face, and they would walk down to the pine woods and listen to the Angelus, and there would be no fear in her heart at all, only an intense joy that her dearest friend was beside her again.

CHAPTER XXXIV

THE CLOUDS RETURN

'Under intense grief you shut yourself up like an oyster. To force you to open your heart would be to kill you.'—CARMEN SYLVA.

'Gentleness is invincible.'—MARCUS AURELIUS.

THREE weeks had passed since Tedo's death; but Lorraine had not yet found courage to go up to Brae. In the evening she always stole out of the house, followed by the faithful Tweed, and walked through the long meadow and lane to the common on her way to the churchyard. Mr. Vincent met her more than once as he went down to open the men's evening club; but he never ventured to accost her. She would pass him hurriedly with a gently uttered 'Good-evening'; but something in her manner prevented him from addressing her. But Hugo and Edmund had no such scruples; on most evenings they would be waiting for her at the little side gate with their offerings of wild flowers.

Hugo would push his posy towards her without raising his eyes. 'They are his favourite flowers; he once said so. Will you make room for them, please?' The touch of those hot, rough little hands, and the sight of the half-withered posy, always affected Lorraine strangely.

'Thank you, Hughie,' she would say gently. 'Have you been far? You look so hot and tired.' Those few short moments as she stood there holding his hand and looking down at him with that unsteady, pitiful smile, were the sweetest in the whole day to Hugo. The boy's affectionate heart clave to his friend with a perfect passion of gratitude.

She never noticed Eddie. She forgot to take his flowers, and he cried about it; 'but she never forgets to take mine,' he said triumphantly to Nora; and wet or fine, whatever he might be doing, he always put his occupation aside to keep his tryst at the yew-tree gate.

Lorraine always hid her pain bravely; but when she left him, she would often stand still and sob quietly in a heart-broken manner. The sight of him always brought so vividly the memory of that terrible afternoon. Tweed would push his long, black nose affectionately into her hand when he heard her. The faithful creature seemed to share her sorrow. He would lie beside her patiently for hours; but his favourite resting-place was by the empty crib. If Lorraine missed him she always found him there.

Lorraine would grow calmer after she had sat by the grave a little. The silence and the gathering dusk always rested her. As she walked back in the soft summer gloaming it would seem to her sometimes as though a tiny figure walked beside her. It was a sweet fancy, but she kept it to herself; but Muriel, watching for her by the lighted window, would wonder to see the tranquil expression of her face.

'How long you have been, dear Mrs. Herbert; but you do not looked tired. Were Hugo and Eddie there as usual?'

'Yes; and Hugo had gathered some long sprays of traveller's joy. He had been all the way to Bramfield; but they were sadly withered. No, I am not tired; the walk has refreshed me,' and then she would sit down and forget to take off her hat until Muriel reminded her.

Muriel went daily to see her mother. She always brought back a good report of her. 'Mother was arranging flowers as usual,' she would say. 'She seemed so busy that I did not stay long. She sends her love, and hopes you will not trouble about her, as she and Gavin get on very well.'

This was Muriel's usual formula. Sometimes Lorraine wondered over it in a vague sort of way. If Mrs. Trevor were so well, it was strange that she never came down to the Farm. Muriel was always hinting her surprise; but neither she nor Lorraine guessed at the little daily drama that was enacted for their mutual benefit.

Muriel always went up to Brae at a certain hour, and Mrs. Trevor took care to be dressed and in her sitting-room by the time her daughter arrived. More than once she crept into the conservatory; but the effort wearied her too much. She would sit at her table turning over her silks and embroidery and pretending to work; but she put in few stitches.

If Muriel had returned ten minutes later she would have found her mother lying on the couch looking white and exhausted. 'You are not fit to be up at all, ma'am,' Collins would say, with a vexed look at the table. 'Why does not Miss Muriel stay with you a

little while the master is out ?   I shall be giving her a bit of my
mind one of these days.   Mrs. Herbert is a dear lady ; but she is
not so close as her own flesh and blood '—for Collins was an old
servant and privileged to speak her mind, and in the servants' hall
Miss Muriel's neglect of the mistress was openly canvassed.

'I hope you will do no such thing, Collins,' returned Mrs.
Trevor with quiet dignity.   'It is by my wish that my daughter
is still at the Farm ; she would come to me at once if I wanted her' ;
but Collins only pursed up her lips and shook her head incredulously.   When her mistress spoke in this tone she did not dare to
say any more, but she grumbled openly to the Colonel that
evening.

'My mistress is getting weaker,' she said dolefully, 'and being
so much alone is not good for her.   She is not one to make a fuss
about herself, and she does not tell you the half of what she goes
through ; but asking your pardon, sir, for speaking freely, I think
Miss Muriel's place is here.   There is no bringing the dead back,
but as long as the living need us they have a claim to be considered.'

Gavin looked a little startled ; but he knew that Collins was an
alarmist and took dark views occasionally.   He hoped her affection
for her mistress had made her exaggerate matters.   He got rid of
her by promising to do the best he could, and after some consideration he made up his mind to speak to Mrs. Herbert.

So the next day when he went down to the Farm and found her
as usual alone, he said rather abruptly : 'Mrs. Herbert, I am going
to ask you to do me a favour if it will not trouble you too much ;
I want you to go and see my mother.'

He saw her wince as though his words pained her, and there
was a distressed look on her face, but he went on as though he
noticed nothing.

'Collins is worrying herself about her mistress ; she is a bit of
an alarmist, but she insists that she is weaker, and that we leave
her too much alone——'   But here Lorraine interrupted him :

'I see what you mean,' she said with nervous haste, 'I have
kept Muriel too long, her mother wants her, I will tell her so to-
night ; she must go back, of course ; why did you not mention this
before, Colonel Trevor ?   I forget things so dreadfully.   Muriel has
been with me for a fortnight, has she not ?' putting up her hand to
push back her hair as though she were suddenly oppressed.

'I think it is nearer three weeks,' he returned quietly ; 'but we
need not go back to that, it was impossible for you to be alone.   I
was thinking as I walked across that Nora would be a nice little
companion for you if Muriel went home.   Vincent would spare

her, I know'; but he was sorry that he had made the proposition when he saw her turn very pale.

'No, I would rather be alone, I want no one—no one'—in a choked voice. 'Dear Muriel has been very good, but sometimes even she has troubled me. Oh, how selfish I have grown, I think of no one but myself!'

'Please do not say such things; and now will you let me finish? To-morrow I have to go to town about some lease that has fallen in, and I must see my lawyer. I could not get back until late, so I think it would be wise for me to sleep at my club. Muriel had better come back for that one night; but I should feel easier if you would pay my mother a visit too.' And then he looked at her and said gently, 'Do you think you could make the effort?'

'I ought to have made it before,' she returned in a low voice. 'Oh, how ashamed I am of myself; please do not say any more, Colonel Trevor. To think you should have to ask me this after all you have done for me. I will go to-morrow morning, and Muriel shall go later.'

'Thank you,' was all he ventured to say, but he knew that he could trust her, there would be no evading her promise; the effort, painful as it was, would do her good, but he little knew how much of Lorraine's reluctance to go to Brae lay in the thought that she would have to pass within sight of the pond.

There was another way, but it was much longer, and Lorraine knew that she was unequal to the walk; the grief that preyed on her was sapping her strength, and Dr. Howell had hinted more than once that a change would do her good.

'Her friends must not let her get into a low, moping state,' he said to Muriel; 'by and by she will need rousing, and occupation will be good for her.' But Muriel felt sorrowfully that Ellison's strong will was needed; the only person who seemed to have any influence over her was Gavin; she always tried to carry out any wish that he expressed, but for some reason best known to himself he very seldom gave his opinion. Her promise to go to Brae the next morning drove all sleep from Lorraine's eyes, a nervous dread oppressed her until daylight, but jaded and weary as she was she would not allow Muriel to dissuade her. 'I have promised,' she said tremulously, and soon after that she set out.

She was early, and Mrs. Trevor was still in her dressing-room, resting after the fatigue of her toilet. She was a little flurried when she heard Mrs. Herbert was there, but when her flush had died away Lorraine was shocked to see the change in her appearance.

Mrs. Trevor greeted her affectionately. 'How good of you to

come to me,' she kept saying over and over again, and for a little while she would talk of nothing but Lorraine's affairs and the cross, and how dear Ellison was with the idea, and how it was Gavin's thought, and how he had sat up one night until nearly three to finish his design.

'He thought nothing was good enough; but I am so glad you were pleased,' and so on. Lorraine could hardly get in a word. She sat there sad and silent thinking how she was to open Muriel's eyes to her mother's state.

It was evident that Mrs. Trevor was anxious to avoid any questioning about her own health. When Lorraine told her that Muriel was coming home she argued the point almost tearfully.

'What are you to do without her, my dear?' she said sorrowfully. 'Oh yes, I know what you are going to tell me, that nothing makes a difference, and you do not mind a little loneliness; but, my dear Mrs. Herbert, I have been through it all, and I know how one needs these outward helps. We do not always know what is good for us, and too much solitude seems to affect the nerves. I do not like the idea of Muriel leaving you, and you know that Collins takes good care of me, so I am not neglected. Gavin is a famous nurse too, and he is so kind and attentive. Oh, there is no need to have Muriel back at all!' But Lorraine was firm.

Mrs. Trevor could have said more, but she was far too loyal to her daughter. How was she to tell Mrs. Herbert that her girl failed to give her comfort? Muriel's heart had never opened to her freely; when they talked, some barrier of reserve seemed for ever between them.

Mrs. Trevor often read unspoken reproof in her daughter's grave eyes. Muriel, critical and dissatisfied, took umbrage at her mother's light speeches. 'Mother and I talk a different language,' she had once said to Lorraine; 'we look at everything in a different light; mother often calls me a pessimist because I cannot take things lightly.'

Lorraine was unwilling to argue; she saw now why Colonel Trevor had asked her to come; his mother's feeble condition had made him seriously uneasy. As she rose to take her leave, some feeling of compunction made her kiss her with greater tenderness than usual.

'Forgive me for having been so selfish; I ought to have come to you before; but I shall come every day now, and Muriel will be with you. Yes, dear, you may trust me'—for the dim, tired eyes looked at her wistfully. 'It is not right to hide things from our nearest and dearest. It is not fair to them. We must do unto others as we would they should do unto us. Don't you feel that, dear Mrs. Trevor?' But the sick woman shook her head. A mother should be able to bear anything for her children's sake—that was her creed. Muriel had enough to bear without her mother adding to her trouble.

Her visit had roused Lorraine. When Collins, who was waiting outside the door, questioned her anxiously about her mistress's condition, she answered with something like her old manner:

'She is very ill, Collins. I think Colonel Trevor is right in asking Dr. M'Callum to come down again. I am very much distressed about her. I am going back to speak very plainly to Miss Muriel. She ought not to be kept in ignorance any longer.'

'No, indeed, ma'am,' returned Collins respectfully. 'That is what I have been telling my mistress; but she will not listen to me. All her life long she has considered Miss Muriel just because she has weak health; but I don't hold with such spoiling. Miss Muriel must take her share of trouble like the rest of us, and it won't help her through the dark days that are coming to think she has never done a hand's stirring for her mother's comfort,' and here a tear rolled down Collins's hard-featured face.

'You are right,' returned Lorraine, in a low voice, and then she hurried away. She felt as though she would never forgive herself. Muriel had been absent from her mother for nearly three weeks, and it was plain even to her eyes that the disease was making rapid progress.

Muriel was sitting over her books as usual. She looked up when Lorraine entered.

'I did not expect you back just yet,' she said, as Lorraine seated herself beside her and untied her veil. 'Well, is it settled that I am to stay there to-night? I will do whatever you and mother wish; but I do hate to leave you.'

'Thank you, dear; you have been so kind. But, Muriel, it is not only for this one night. I cannot let you stay here any longer. Your mother is ill and needs you.'

Muriel raised her eyebrows. 'Mother ill?' she said incredulously. 'My dear Mrs. Herbert, what can you mean? Perhaps she is not as strong as usual; but ill——'

'Where are your eyes, Muriel?' returned her friend mournfully. 'Is it possible that you have not noticed how painfully thin she is? No, I will not blame you. Your mother has kept you in the dark purposely. Even this morning she said to me, "Do not tell Muriel that you think me looking ill. It will only worry her." That is just her one thought—to keep you from worry ; but, Muriel dear, it is not right. Your brother and Collins and I know that your mother is seriously ill.'

A flush crossed Muriel's sallow face ; her brow contracted. Lorraine's manner was making her uneasy.

'Gavin knows that mother is seriously ill, and he has not told me !' she exclaimed in a hurt voice. 'Mrs. Herbert, what does it all mean ? Mother has never been ill in her life ; she has often said so. Surely you must be mistaken. If she were ill, would not Gavin send for Dr. Howell ? But I have never heard that he has been at Brae.'

'That is because your mother did not wish you to be told ; he has called often ; and Dr. M'Callum is coming too. Muriel, try to believe me—am I likely to jest with you just now ? If ever your mother needed a daughter's tenderness and care, she needs it now. Her disease is a painful one, and there is no cure for it.'

But it seemed as though Muriel would hear no more. She rose up hastily, pushing away her books, and walked from the room. A few minutes later she re-entered in her walking dress, looking pale and determined.

'I am going now,' she said, trying to speak calmly. 'You will take care of yourself, Mrs. Herbert ?'

'Yes, yes'—and here she held the girl fast. 'Muriel, dear, I must say something before you leave me. You are right to go ; I would not keep you for worlds ; you have been here far too long ; but remember, she is very weak, she cannot bear much. You must be very gentle with her.'

'Ah, you do well to warn me !' returned Muriel bitterly. But evidently she could not trust herself to say more. Lorraine stood by the window and waved to her sadly as she hurried down the path.

'How cruel it seems. She is not prepared for it. One can see what a blow it is for her. Poor Mrs. Trevor, and poor poor Muriel,' and then, unable to bear her sorrowful thoughts or to endure the sudden solitude of the house, she put on her hat again and went down to the yew-tree gate to sit by her darling's grave.

CHAPTER XXXV

> 'Nor deem the irrevocable past
> As wholly wasted, wholly vain,
> If rising on its wrecks at last
> To something nobler we attain.'
>
> LONGFELLOW.

A WAKEFUL night of pain had exhausted Mrs. Trevor, and soon after Lorraine had left the house she began to doze. Collins darkened the chamber carefully and then sat down to her needle-work in the next room. An hour or two's sound sleep would do her mistress good, she thought, and help to shorten the long day.

Presently the sound of hasty footsteps outside made her hurry to the door, and the next moment she came face to face with Muriel.

'My mistress is asleep,' she began rather crossly; but an imperious gesture from the girl silenced her.

'Come to my room a moment, if you can leave her. I want to speak to you,' she said quickly, and Collins nodded and closed the door. She had never seen that look on her young lady's face before. For once Collins's garrulity failed her. She followed Muriel meekly to the turret-room, and stood there a little awed and alarmed. There was something ominous in the way Muriel flung open the window and tossed off her hat. Her face looked pale and hard, and there was a sombre light in her eyes. 'Collins, I want you to tell me the truth. I have been kept in the dark too long. Every one except myself seems to know that my mother is ill. I want you to tell me exactly what is the matter with her, unless you prefer me to ask Dr. Howell.'

Collins looked perturbed. The suppressed passion in Muriel's

18

voice made her uneasy. In her heart she knew the girl was right ; and yet how was she to disregard her mistress's injunctions ? Her hesitation seemed to irritate Muriel.

'I do not intend to sleep to-night until I know all that there is to know. If you will not answer me, I shall order the carriage and drive to Bramfield. Dr. Howell will be on his rounds ; but I shall follow him. It would save time and trouble if you would give me the information. There seems to be a conspiracy to keep me in the dark about my mother's state, and I will not bear it, no, not for an hour.'

The haughty inflexion in Muriel's voice, and her restrained emotion, made Collins waver.

'I would not say that if I were you, Miss Muriel,' she returned plaintively. 'There is no conspiracy. It is nought but kindness on the mistress's part. Mistaken kindness it may be ; but there, we all make mistakes sometimes. Ever since you were a mite of a child, the mistress has always tried to keep unpleasant things from you. It was just one of her loving ways. "We won't trouble Miss Muriel." Ah, how often I have heard her say that. "When things worry her, she cannot sleep, and, poor child, she has enough to bear !" She was never like that with Miss Maud or Miss Florence. She would tell Miss Maud everything that troubled her ; but she seemed to think that the wind mustn't blow on you. Times out of number have I argued with her ; but I could not make an impression. "She can do me no good, and it will only pain her to know what I suffer." Those were her words only last night. She had a terrible night, Miss Muriel, and no one knows how thankful I was when she fell asleep towards morning. Her sufferings were cruel, and I have made up my mind to tell Dr. Howell that she had better have a nurse. He has been wanting to send one in ; but we have been fending it off until now because the mistress likes me to wait on her. But I think it would be best for her comfort and my ease of mind if we had a trained nurse to help us.'

'You shall have one at once, and now please answer my question,' and of course Muriel had her way. Her strong will compelled Collins to tell her the truth, that her mistress was suffering from a painful and incurable malady ; no one had suspected it until a few months ago, and it was only lately that the insidious disease had shown itself so plainly.

'Everything has been done that could be done, Miss Muriel ; but no doctor, however clever, could cure the mistress ; the Colonel knows that. She may live for a long time yet ; there is no knowing in these cases. I nursed my own mother with it, so I know.'

'That will do, Collins, thank you.' Muriel with difficulty repressed a shudder ; this was what they had been keeping from her. When Collins left the room she leant back in her chair and closed her eyes; for a moment a sort of faintness crept over her. Her strong, energetic mother, with her light-hearted ways and pleasant social habits, to be doomed to this. 'If ever your mother needed a daughter's tenderness and care, she needs it now.' Lorraine's words seemed ringing in her ears.

She had been a bad daughter—at least a careless, selfish one—but it would not do to think of that now. She rose hastily, drank some cold water and bathed her face ; then she stole down to her mother's dressing-room so softly that Collins did not hear her.

Mrs. Trevor was still asleep, and Muriel took a seat noiselessly beside the couch.

Even in the half light, through the shaded Venetians, she could see her mother's face distinctly, and the change in it made her heart stand still for a moment: the deep hollows in the temples and the dark shadows under the eyes, the exhaustion of her attitude, and a certain wasting of the figure gave her a shock ; but as she bent over her in undisguised anxiety, Mrs. Trevor opened her eyes ; she was still confused with sleep.

'Is that you, Maud, darling ?' she said feebly.

'No, mother, it is Muriel.' And then all at once her proud stoicism deserted her, and she broke into a sudden storm of sobs. 'Oh, mother, why have you been so cruel ? but I suppose I have deserved it. I have not been good to you, not like Maud and Florrie ; and so you have kept your illness from me ; but it makes it doubly hard to bear.'

Mrs. Trevor was fully awake now ; she stretched out her thin hands appealingly to her daughter.

'Have I been cruel, darling ? I did not mean it, I was only so anxious to save you pain ; don't cry so, my poor child, come nearer to me, or how am I to comfort you there ?' Mrs. Trevor's voice had a caressing note in it, and Muriel, humbled and wretched, knelt down by the couch and laid her head in her mother's lap.

'Oh, mother, it does seem so dreadful !' she sobbed, and the hand that was stroking her hair shook a little.

'Does it, darling ? well, I have not had my share of pain, you must remember that. When your father and the dear girls were alive, I think no woman was ever so happy, every day that I lived was a joy and a feast to me ; I used to tell your father so, and it often made him smile. I used to wish you could feel the same, dearest, but your weak health seemed to deprive you of all enjoyment; that is why I never liked to trouble you about things.'

'Yes, I know, Collins has told me. It was a sad mistake, mother; you have fostered my selfishness. How could I guess that anything ailed you when you have never complained? As a daughter I have been valueless to you; Ellison and Mrs. Herbert were more to you than I; even Collins, a servant, was in your confidence.' And here Muriel, overcome with emotion, shed some more bitter tears.

Mrs. Trevor sighed, she was beginning to think she had made a mistake; she had not suspected that Muriel had such deep feeling, the girl had always been so reserved with her.

'I am afraid I have done wrong,' she returned remorsefully; 'I ought not to have kept it all to myself; don't cry, Muriel dear, try to forgive me. I did it for the best. Where my children are concerned I am very weak; I want to take their share of pain and my own too. Oh, there comes Collins to scold us! Collins, Miss Muriel is hurt with us; she thinks we have not treated her well.'

'Miss Muriel is about right there,' returned Collins a little gruffly, 'but least said is soonest mended, and it is no use nursing a grudge when one has done it for the best. Miss Muriel, my mistress must not talk too much; she has had a fine nap, and I am going to bring up her tea. Dr. Howell will be here presently, and she must not be too tired beforehand.'

'I will be as quiet as a mouse, but there is no need for Miss Muriel to leave me; my tea will have a better flavour if she will make it for me.' Mrs. Trevor spoke with her old playfulness; but when Collins had retired, she looked at her daughter fondly.

'I shall love to have you with me, Muriel dear; it has been so dull alone! I think solitude makes me fanciful. Gavin has been very good; he has often given up his evenings to me; but somehow I have always missed you. If it will not tire you too much, I shall be so glad of your company!' But Muriel dared not trust herself to speak. She kissed her mother's cheek hastily, and rose to her feet. Her heart was full. A passion of tenderness seemed to swell it almost to bursting. If she might only have time to atone for her past neglect, she would be ready to bear everything. 'God grant that she may be spared to me a little longer!' was her inward cry.

There was very little more talk between them that night. Dr. Howell came, and, seeing his patient's exhaustion, ordered her to bed without delay, and it was decided between him and Muriel that a nurse should be sent in as soon as possible.

'Collins is a very reliable person, and knows a good deal about illness,' he observed ; 'but Mrs. Trevor's condition will require trained nursing. I told the Colonel so when I was last here. You will be able to be with her as much as you wish ; but we must consider what is best for her comfort. Nurse Helena will be invaluable. She has been nursing a case for me, and will be free to-morrow.'

When Lorraine came up the next day, she found Mrs. Trevor still in bed, and Muriel sitting beside her. Directly she had greeted her friend, Muriel laid down her book and left the room, and did not re-enter it. When Lorraine's visit was over, she went in search of her, and found her sitting in the turret-room, looking dejectedly at the prospect. Admiral Byng was rubbing himself against her to attract her attention.

Lorraine put her hand on her shoulder affectionately.

'Dear Muriel, I missed you so last night and this morning ! The house felt so lonely without you ; but you are in your right place. Mrs. Trevor is so happy to have you, and I know how you must love to be here ! Your brother is not back yet, she says.'

'No, Gavin is not back ; he will come by his usual train, I expect. Mrs. Herbert, I want to tell you something. I know everything now. I made Collins tell me. I was angry, and frightened her, and in the evening I spoke to Dr. Howell.'

'That is why you have not slept. You are looking quite ill this morning ! Poor Muriel, you have sad work before you ; but you must take each day as it comes. Sleepless nights and fretting over things will do no good, and will only trouble Mrs. Trevor. She is so afraid of your breaking down !'

'I shall not break down—at least, I hope not ; but how can I sleep with this dreadful thing hanging over me ? I never knew how dear my mother was till I heard there was danger of losing her. Oh, if I had only known it before ! If I had not neglected her so cruelly ! How am I ever to be happy again ? All last night such terrible thoughts seemed crowding upon me ! All my hasty, hard speeches, and impatient ways, and how gently she bore with them all ! I thought she was so strong and light-hearted ; but I know now that she was often dull and out of spirits. Collins came up and talked to me last night. How I wished she had held her tongue ! All she said only made it worse. How could I know she had missed the girls so dreadfully, and that she was always speaking of them ! They were dear girls ; but they were never much to me. They were always together, and I was left out in the cold. It has always been like that all my life. No one has seemed to need me—not even my mother.'

'She needs you now. Dear Muriel, do let me entreat you not to undermine your own strength by dwelling on past mistakes. You have your mother still with you. She has not been taken from you without a moment's preparation. There is still time to love and cherish her.' Lorraine's voice broke, she turned hastily away, and Muriel felt a little remorseful.

When she re-entered her mother's room, Mrs. Trevor looked at her wistfully. 'Muriel, love, why did you leave us? There was no need. Mrs. Herbert and I have no secrets. I like to feel you are near me. I never want you to go away—it is so nice not to be alone any more!'

How often Muriel had to listen to such speeches! Even her mother's tenderness seemed insensibly to reproach her. Day after day as she sat by her, sometimes talking or more often silent, she learnt more and more of her mother's patience and brave endurance. How Gavin and she had misjudged her! They had thought her sprightliness and cheerfulness were owing to a shallow nature—that she took her troubles lightly ; but they had been wrong. Evening after evening she listened with dismayed pity to the history of sleepless nights spent in weeping for the husband she had idolised and the children who were so dear to her.

'It was my duty to be cheerful, and not to depress you,' she would say ; 'but it was very hard sometimes. When I woke in the morning I would say to myself, "it is all in the day's work," and then I would pull myself together and pretend a little, and after a time it grew easier. Don't you know what Shakespeare says, Muriel, "Time and the hour run through the roughest day"? I used to say that to myself over and over again.'

It was a sad and trying ordeal for Muriel ; but years afterwards she owned to a dear friend that it had been salutary discipline.

'I needed my lesson,' she said humbly. 'All my life I had lived for myself, and my mother's mistaken indulgence had only fostered my selfishness. Mrs. Herbert had been the first to warn me against morbid introspection ; but it needed the furnace of affliction to burn up the evil growth of years. For the first time in my life I forgot my own troubles. Oh, if you knew the agony of loving too late ! The thought of those wasted years, when I might have cherished and comforted the best of mothers, will give me pain until my dying day.'

With the unerring instinct of love, Mrs. Trevor once touched on this. 'Muriel,' she said one day, when she had been comparatively free from pain, and Muriel had been reading to her, 'put down your book ; your voice sounds tired, and I want to talk a little. You are spoiling the old mother dreadfully—you and Gavin. I think sometimes as I lie awake at night that no woman had two better children.'

'I daresay you are right with respect to Gavin, mother.' The sad note of pain in the girl's voice went to her mother's heart. She turned a little, and looked at her with her old beaming smile.

'Yes, I have a good son, God bless him! And I have a dear and good daughter too. Don't draw your hand away, Muriel, darling. We are not often alone together like this, and I want to tell you what a comfort you are to me! When I see your sisters—they will be so glad when I tell them that—oh, how much I shall have to tell them! I dream about it sometimes. Nurse says it is because I am so weak; but I think such dreams are sent in mercy.'

'I think so too, mother.' And Mrs. Trevor smiled and went on :

'Only last night I thought I was in some green valley. I was alone; but I could hear such beautiful singing! And presently I saw them—the girls, I mean—coming across the flowery turf. They were hand in hand, and their dresses were white, and they had wonderful red flowers in their hands.

'"Here is mother at last!"—I heard Maud say that quite plainly, and Florrie clapped her hands in the old way. "Poor dear mother—how old and tired she looks! But the good angels will take care of her!"—and then I woke. Was not that a beautiful dream?'

'Yes, dear, and no doubt it was sent to comfort you; but mother, I am so selfish. I want to keep you with me a little longer. I cannot spare you to Maud and Florence just yet.'

Mrs. Trevor looked at her wistfully.

'Thank you, darling. It is nice to hear that; but when the Master calls we are bound to go. Muriel, I want you to thank Mr. Vincent; he has been such a comfort to me all these weeks!'

'He has been a comfort to us all,' was on Muriel's lips; but some feeling restrained her from saying this. Eric had been unwearying in his attentions; he came up to Brae daily.

'He is an excellent young man,' returned Mrs. Trevor, and then she looked at her daughter a little thoughtfully. A mother's eyes are clairvoyant, and on her sick bed she had learnt to read her daughter's heart perfectly. 'He is the only man who would ever suit her,' she thought sadly. 'The love of a man like Mr. Vincent would make her a happy woman; but I am afraid he cares more for Mrs. Herbert. There is a warm friendship between him and Muriel ; but—but it is only friendship,' and then she sighed. Those clear, bright eyes of hers had read Eric Vincent's nature correctly. She knew how his strong, cultured, unselfish character, trained by adversity, was just what Muriel's fastidious, morbid nature needed to ripen and bring it to perfection.

CHAPTER XXXVI

'Ah well, for us all some sweet hope lies
Deeply buried from human eyes,
And in the hereafter angels may
Roll the stone from the grave away!'
                                        WHITTIER.

IT was well for Eric Vincent that parish work just then engrossed him and prevented him from dwelling on his private
troubles. His daily ministrations in the sick-room at Brae, and
his long talks with his friend Colonel Trevor and with Muriel,
consoled him in part for the total cessation of his visits to the
Farm.

Except in the village or at church he never saw Mrs. Herbert.
The little he heard of her was from Muriel. She told him once
that Mrs. Herbert was trying to take up her old duties again;
that she looked after the sick people at Highlands; but that if
any child was ill, she always sent Ruth in her place.

'She cannot bring herself to be with children,' Muriel added
sorrowfully; but he knew this already. Nora never dared take
Effie or Eddie to the Farm now. She always seemed so unnerved
at the sight of them. She had expressed her thankfulness openly
to Muriel when she heard Hugo had been sent to school.

'He has followed me like a shadow,' she said, brushing away
a few tears. 'I could not go to the churchyard or the village
without finding him watching for me. I used to bite my lips
and clench my hands sometimes to prevent my saying something
unkind to him; but I am thankful I never said it. It got on
my nerves at last, poor boy. It is not that I have not forgiven
him; but that it brings it all back, and I am not strong enough

to bear it.' Nevertheless Lorraine schooled herself to write a
kind letter to the little exile. Hugo burst out crying as he read
it. For months it was under his pillow at night. When he
had a bad dream he would take it out and cuddle it. 'She
says I am to be a good boy, and that I must grow up a noble
man,' he wrote once to his sole confidante Nora; 'that she trusts
me, and knows I shall never disappoint her; and I never will.
I wish you would tell Eric this, and then perhaps he will believe
in me too.'

Eric felt his banishment from the Farm acutely; but he could
not bring himself to go without an invitation; but Lorraine,
lonely and sad as she was, seemed to dread visitors above all
things.

Colonel Trevor once remonstrated with her. He thought all
these weeks of solitude would tell on her.

'Our kind neighbours feel that you are keeping them at a distance,' he said to her one day when he walked back with her from
Brae. Since his sister had left he very seldom went to the Farm;
but he always walked back with her, taking care to put himself
between her and the pond. He knew instinctively the daily
torture it gave her to pass it. 'Mrs. Earnshaw told my mother
yesterday that she feared her visit had troubled you.'

'Oh no, she was so kind to me; every one is kinder to me
than I deserve; but if you knew how it tires me to talk to people.
I never seem to have anything to say now. I have grown so
stupid; sometimes I break off in a sentence and forget what I was
going to say, and then I see people look at me, and there is silence,
and then they go away.'

'Yes, I see what you mean. I have gone through all that; but
Mrs. Herbert, if you will take my advice you will just battle with
the feeling. It is no use giving way; it only makes it worse. I
am stating my opinion rather bluntly, but I am speaking for your
own good.'

'Yes, and you are never blunt,' and then Lorraine turned to
him with a faint smile. There was a lovely dimple that he had
often admired. For one second he saw it again, but her eyes were
very sad.

'I wonder if you do understand,' she went on slowly; 'men
are so different, their life is so much more active than ours; they
do not get drowsy and stupid sitting at home brooding over troubles.
When people come to me from the outside they seem to talk a
different language. Sometimes I have an odd fancy as though I
were at one end of a dark tunnel and they at the other end somewhere in the sunshine; I can hear what they say, but somehow

the meaning is confused. Oh, it is so difficult to make any one understand who has not been through it!'

'But I have been through it, as you know well,' he returned gravely, 'that is why I cannot fail to understand you'; but he was sorry he said this when she turned to him impulsively with her eyes misty with unshed tears.

'I was very thoughtless to say that; you have suffered so much, and you are always trying to help me. Colonel Trevor, I will be good, I will try to bear with people, and not feel too impatient for them to go away. I know I have been selfish; I have wanted no one but you and Muriel;—there, I have confessed my fault and you must forgive me.'

She was evidently in earnest, for there was a sort of yearning in her deep low voice, but he answered her lightly.

He dared not let her see how her words had alarmed him; was he becoming at all necessary to her? and then he scoffed at himself for entertaining such an idea for a moment. Her very openness and simplicity disarmed his suspicions. Of course, she was glad to see him; he had been with her in her trouble and she had learnt to depend on him. 'I have been of use to her and she is grateful,' he said to himself, but nevertheless some doubt rankled in his mind; and that night he took his resolution. A few days later Ellison, sitting on her balcony overlooking the village street, received the following letter, which she read and re-read many times that night:—

MY DEAR ELLISON (it began), there are limits to everything, and it seems to me that the time has come to break this long silence that has somehow grown up between us—not by my will, you know that, dear; it was your own act—your own expressed wish that you should be left in peace; but now we have come to the end of the tether, and you will not be surprised if I tell you that my patience is at an end too.

How long are you going to be away? You left us in July and now it is October. I know how impossible it has been for you to leave your sick friend; but in your last letter to my mother you were in hopes you would soon have your marching orders.

Dear Ellison, when they come I entreat you not to lose a day —no, not an hour—in unnecessary preparation. I have no wish to alarm you, but our dear mother grows weaker every day. You know how patient she is, but I can see how she longs for your return; you have been like a daughter to her all these years, and she feels your absence a sore trial. 'Is there no letter from Ellison?': those are always her first words in the morning. What sad changes there have been in our happy valley, as you always call it; first poor Mrs. Herbert's trouble, and now the poor old vicar is gone. Vincent had a letter this morning, and came up to me at once. Muriel is writing full particulars to you. It was another stroke; Mrs. Yolland had only left him for ten minutes, but when she returned to the room he was speechless. It is a great grief to Muriel, and she was terribly upset when Vincent was here. I had to explain to him that Mr. Yolland had been her tutor, and that he and his good wife had always made so much of her. The churchwardens are writing to Sir Percy; they want me to write too and speak for Vincent; he seems a general favourite here, and the people are becoming attached to him. If Sir Percy has no one else in his mind he may offer him the living. Will you let me know how this strikes you? In my opinion he is just the man for Highlands. Our old vicar was the better scholar, but Vincent has greater energy. He gets hold of the men at the club, and there is less lounging at the *Waggon and Horses* on Saturday evenings.

Vincent being at the Vicarage will make a great difference in my life. I have got into the habit of seeing him nearly every day, and he just suits me. Muriel and I are so grateful to him for his ministrations to our mother; she often tells us that he is the greatest comfort to her, and that she forgets that he is so young; he seems older somehow and graver even to me. That terrible accident has sobered him; he has taken it so much to heart.

I fear that you will find Mrs. Herbert greatly changed; I want to prepare you for that. She is very sad and drooping, and we find it difficult to rouse her; she does her duties in a half-hearted perfunctory way, but for the present the old spring and energy has gone. My mother says we must give her time, but it seems to me as though she will never be like her old self again.

I am writing to you in my old fashion—just everything that comes into my head—the old ways are the best and sweetest! But I am keeping the real purpose of my letter to the last.

Ellison, do you remember our last walk, and what I tried to say to you at the gate of the Woodlands? My heart was very full that evening—full of unspoken love and tenderness—but you forced me to keep silence.

Dear, have you found out your mistake by this time?—for it was a mistake, was it not?—it would have been better and happier for us both if you had allowed me to finish my sentence. I want you to own this frankly. It was my intention that evening to ask you to become my wife. Our long friendship, my warm attachment, gave me a right to hope for a favourable answer; but when I found you were not ready to listen to me—that it troubled you to give up your cherished independence—I did not press my own wishes. I think you will own that I have been more patient than most men. But, as I said before, there are limits to everything— and even to this long letter—and I have made up my mind not to wait for your return, but to ask you to pledge yourself to me without any further delay. When we meet let it be on a different footing. In one sense we have been much to each other, but now the tie must be closer. I would fain believe that this absence has worked in my favour, and that you are ready now to be engaged to me. I know you will be perfectly frank with me ; indeed I deserve such frankness ! Let us thoroughly understand each other from this day forward. God bless you !—Yours,   GAVIN.

This was the letter that cost Gavin a sleepless night to write. There were sentences that he re-wrote again and again ; but he could not satisfy himself. He told himself that it was cold, unlover-like, and that it was not worthy of the dear woman whom he was asking to become his wife ; but how was he to help himself ?

Gavin's direct, straightforward nature hated shams. He would give Ellison all he could—his reverence, his honest affection, and that worship that a good man gives to the woman he honours; but he could not call her his dearest !—not yet at least !

But to Ellison that letter was simply perfect ; from beginning to end there was no single flaw in it.

At first she believed it was just an ordinary letter like the others she had received from him. He had always written to her when he had been away—long chatty letters that had given him pleasure to write, and which she had loved to receive. Were they not faithful and trusty comrades, and was he not right in saying the old ways were the best and sweetest ? 'Dear Gavin—how true he is !' she said softly, when she came to this.

But the next sentence made her heart beat more quickly, and she grew pale with sudden strong emotion. She put down the letter a moment, for the mist before her eyes seemed to blur the words. Then she took it up again and read steadily to the end.

Could any lover have written more nobly ? Every word was Gavin-like—it brought him before her. How she gloried in his simple, manly directness !

'I think you will say that I have been more patient than most men '—'My dearest, no one has ever been more patient,' she murmured, when she came to this.

'I know you will be perfectly frank with me—indeed, I deserve such frankness '—'And you shall have it, my own,' she said softly, and she pressed the paper to her lips.

Ellison soon wrote her answer; but it was very short, and to the point.

DEAR GAVIN (she wrote), you have asked me to be frank with you. You are right. Such frankness is indeed your due, and I will own to you that I made a great mistake in refusing to listen to you that evening. You have been very patient with me, my dearest—there was some attempt to erase the 'dearest,' but it had not been successful — and I behaved most foolishly. What is independence, after all, compared to the joy of being beloved? A woman has no right to let her pride and self-will stand in the way of her happiness—your noble forbearance has taught me this lesson. Dear Gavin, I will not hesitate any longer. I am perfectly willing to be engaged to you; for years your wishes have been mine. I need say no more. You have conquered—your very patience has won me. How sad everything is! Our dear old vicar—but I cannot write about that to-night—and poor suffering Cousin Louise! You will have need of all the comfort I can give you, my poor Gavin—for there are dark days in store for you. What you tell me about Lorraine is very sad. But she is so unselfish; she will not long suffer herself to droop hopelessly. I have confidence in her strength of mind. And now, dear Gavin, you will rejoice to hear that we have got our marching orders—Margaret is so much better that Dr. Strauss thinks we may safely move her. We shall travel by easy stages, and if all goes well, I shall hope to reach London by the 20th. I must sleep in Portman Square that night; but Margaret's cousin, Mrs. Garcia, will be there, so there will be no need for me to stay longer.

I have not dared tell you how home-sick I have been. I know now what exiles feel. Since Sister Rosalie came I have had too much time on my hands. I am afraid you will grumble at my looks, but these weeks of nursing would have tried the strongest woman.

I am writing this hastily, but I do not want to lose a single post.—Yours entirely and always, ELLISON.

When Gavin read this letter he sat for a long time motionless in his chair. He had burnt his boats—from henceforth no retreat was possible. His word, his honour were pledged, and from that moment he must bring himself to look on Ellison as his future wife.

If this thought brought him no joy, it was not his fault, or hers either. 'A man must do his duty under all circumstances,' he said to himself stoically; 'and no difficulty, no sense of hardship in performing it should deter him. The paths of pleasantness and peace are not for me,' he said half aloud, and then for a few moments Gavin's soul was wrapt in bitterness.

He had hastened on his own doom, and had in a sense forged his own fetters; but no one but he himself knew that his sole safety lay in doing so. Every day his position had become more perilous and fraught with danger, as every day Lorraine became dearer to him. His very manhood tempted him; he could not see her in her loneliness and helplessness without longing to shelter and protect her. 'No one understands her as I do,' he would say to himself, and there were times when he could even read her thoughts.

But it was not his own fear of self-betrayal that alone determined him to take instant action—it was some subtle undefinable change in Lorraine that roused him, and yet it was nothing tangible: a consciousness at moments of unexpected meetings that a faint colour would steal into her wan face—that those sweet pensive smiles, more sad than any tears, were for him alone—signs which first made his heart beat almost to suffocation, and then filled him with alarm; and yet such was his reverence for her that he never once asked himself how he stood with her.

'She is beginning to depend on me too much'—that was all he would allow. 'In her peculiar circumstances one is bound to protect her. Vincent stays away altogether, but with me—that is hardly possible. Ellison has entrusted me with her affairs, and I cannot shirk my duties.' Nevertheless, by degrees he had broken off his visits, and though he and Lorraine met nearly every day, their interviews were brief, and Muriel was generally with them. But Ellison was coming, and things would be placed on a right footing. Their engagement would be made public—he would take care of that.

Lorraine had been right when she said only a woman can endure to sit at home brooding over troubles. Gavin's restlessness demanded the relief of action.

Only his mother's precarious and declining state prevented him from rushing off the next day to offer his escort to Ellison. It would have done him a world of good to shake off the air of Highlands for a little, but, as he phrased it a little bitterly, he was chained to the galley-oar of duty. No, this relief had been denied him; but, at least, there was one thing that he could do; and then he got up quickly and went to his mother's room. Mrs. Trevor never left her bed now. She was lying propped up with pillows. She looked at her son with her usual loving smile as he sat down beside her, but the next moment her expression changed.

'You have something to tell me, Gavin—I can see it in your eyes. I read people's faces so quickly. Nurse is in the dressing-room,'—as he looked inquiringly towards the half-open door—'but she will not hear us. It is about Ellison—she is coming home.'

'Yes, she is coming home; the day after to-morrow they are to begin their return journey; but Miss Mervyn can only travel by easy stages, so they do not expect to reach London until the 20th. I am glad my news pleases you, mother; but that is not all I have to tell you'—and as her eyes fastened anxiously on his face, he said slowly, 'Ellison and I are engaged.'

A low sob broke from Mrs. Trevor's lips, and as he sat on the bed beside her, she suddenly flung her feeble arms round him. 'Gavin, my own dear son! Thank God for this!' she exclaimed. 'My prayer has indeed been answered. Oh, it has been so long coming, I began to think you would never make up your mind to marry—that I must give up all thoughts of dear Ellison coming here in my place. But I was too impatient. My dearest boy, you have made me so happy.'

He bent his head and kissed her. 'I knew it would give you pleasure. Ellison has always been like a daughter to you. Mother, it is not my fault that we have not been engaged three months ago; but Ellison could not make up her mind.'

'Did you ask her that evening when she and Mrs. Herbert dined here? Never mind,'—as his face clouded a little at the remembrance. 'I will not weary you about details; you shall only tell me what you like. Does Muriel know?'

'Not yet; I have come to you first. I think, under the circumstances, no one but you and Muriel must know. It would not be well to publish things during Ellison's absence; it might embarrass her. We must get used to our position before we take our friends into confidence; but you and Muriel can write to her or send messages.'

'Very well, dear. Of course, dear Ellison will be a little shy at first, and she would like a few days' quiet.'

Mrs. Trevor talked on happily. If Gavin were a little grave, a little wanting in lover-like enthusiasm, his mother thought such gravity was only becoming under the circumstances. 'He is no love-sick boy; one must not expect him to indulge in raptures,' she said to herself. 'That is why Ellison will suit him perfectly.' And when Muriel came to her later on that night, a little excited with the news, she gave vent to her joy without restraint.

'Muriel darling,' she said impulsively, 'it seems almost too good to be true. I could not help worrying a little about Gavin;

but now Ellison will make him happy, and they will both take such care of you. You will not leave them, will you, dearest ?—it would be so dull for you living alone at the Dower House.'

But Muriel refused to give any opinion on this point. 'Mother, dear,' she said imploringly, 'I have begged you so often not to trouble about the future ; there is no use making up one's mind beforehand. When the time comes I shall know what to do'; and as her mother continued to look wistfully at her, she went on hurriedly, 'Gavin and Ellison will help me to decide things.' And then Mrs. Trevor was satisfied.

'I can say my "Nunc Dimittis" now,' she said to herself that night ; and the next day she pencilled a loving little note to Ellison, which reached her in due course.

CHAPTER XXXVII

ELLISON'S RETURN HOME

'For so that I your company
May have, I ask no more ;
From which to part, it maketh my heart
As cold as any stone ;
For in my mind of all mankind
I love but you alone.'

ANONYMOUS.

ONE lovely afternoon, about a fortnight later, Ellison sat alone in a second-class compartment. In another ten minutes the train would reach Bramfield, and already her eyes had noted more than one familiar landmark. For how many weeks had she looked forward to this moment, with what heart-sick impatience and longing, bravely resisted, only she herself knew. It had been a sad trying time, but it was over now ; and as she had listened to Margaret's faltering thanks that morning, and had heard the repressed emotion in her brother's voice, she felt a satisfied consciousness of having fulfilled her duty. Nothing had tempted her to desert her post. She had brought back her charge to England, and had left her in her cousin's care ; and now she was free to return to her own dear home and to the lover who was waiting for her. Alas ! her coming back would be no unmixed pleasure. There had been sad changes during those three months of absence. How she would miss Tedo's fair little face ! And then her dear old friend Mr. Yolland had gone—and the Dark Angel was even now hovering over the roof of Brae ! Muriel's letters of late had filled her with apprehension. 'Poor mother, we shall not keep her long with us ! She suffers less, thank God ; but she grows perceptibly weaker every day.' Muriel had written this only the previous morning.

Ellison's calm, evenly-balanced nature always shrank from any strong emotion. She dreaded her first meeting with Lorraine, and had begged her not to come to the station ; but she knew Gavin would be there.

Nothing had been said about it on either side ; a sense of shyness had prevented Ellison from hinting her wish that their first meeting should take place at the Farm. She must leave him to do as he thought best.

But, as the train slackened speed, and she caught sight of his well-known figure in the brown tweed shooting-coat and gaiters, with Bairn beside him, she was conscious of a singular revulsion of feeling—an overpowering self-consciousness that made her long to hide herself. But Gavin had already seen her, and the next moment he was at the door.

Their eyes met and then he helped her out silently, only retaining her hand a moment longer than was necessary, and then Bairn jumped on her with a hoarse bark of welcome, and putting his paws on her shoulders tried to lick her face. Ellison caressed him a little nervously. She felt Gavin's deep-set eyes were watching her movements ; then she felt his hand on her arm.

'Down, old fellow—your mistress is tired. Come, dear, let me put you in the waggonette. Nicholson will look after your luggage.' The old familiar voice with its rich timbre brought a sudden blush to Ellison's face, and for the first time in her life the young mistress of Brae Farm walked out of the station without a backward glance at her belongings. Gavin helped her in, then he stood by the door talking to her quietly about the journey, until they had brought out the luggage and piled it up on the waggonette. But as he talked he scarcely looked at her—he could see how nervous and constrained she was with him, and he knew he must give her time to recover herself. He was nervous himself, and he must do the best for her and himself too—at least he had this advantage over her, that he had time to school himself and learn his rôle.

But as he placed himself opposite to her, and Bairn bounded joyously beside them, uttering jubilant barks from time to time, he leant forward and took her hand.

'You are not looking fit, dear,' he said gently. 'I am not satisfied with your looks—I am sure you are thinner.'

Then Ellison gave a nervous little laugh, and drew her hand away. There was no one near, certainly ; but Nicholson might turn round and see him holding her hand.

'I warned you beforehand,' she said, flushing as she spoke ; 'all those weeks of nursing would have tried any one. Sister Rosalie was astonished at my powers of endurance. She said it was English pluck that helped me.'

'It has taken the starch out of you, I can see that,' he returned, shaking his head; 'and no wonder, it must have been a terrible time.'

'Yes, indeed'—with a shudder—'it was so dreadful to see any one suffer as poor Margaret did, and to be without the means of alleviating her pain. How little one knows what lies before us.' And then she continued in a low voice : 'You are not looking well either, Gavin ; you have grown dreadfully thin, I noticed it at once.'

But he would not allow this for a moment. He had wanted her back, he said lightly, but there was nothing much the matter with him; things had been depressing enough, and her absence had made it worse. 'I never intend to let you go away again unless you take me with you,' he finished in a meaning tone ; and Ellison's eyelids had drooped ; every look, every word made her heart beat more quickly, and she feared that her changing colour and silence made her agitation only too perceptible to the quiet keen eyes opposite. But she need not have feared, Gavin took no advantage ; he talked on about his mother and Muriel until she became more at her ease, and began questioning him in her old manner. As they passed Brae House, he suddenly told the coachman to stop. 'I am getting out here,' he said hurriedly, as Ellison looked at him in surprise. 'It will be better for you to meet Mrs Herbert without eye-witnesses. I will see you later on,' and he laid his hand on hers for a moment—and then smiled at her and raised his hat.

She looked after him wistfully—she had scarcely spoken to him, she thought ; yes, he was thinner, she was sure of it—he looked somehow changed—graver and older—but how infinitely dearer. If Gavin had only known the rush of womanly tenderness that filled the blue eyes with tears. 'My own, my own dear Gavin,' she said to herself—and then she saw Joe Brand hurrying across the farmyard ; yes, there was the red roof of the granary, with the doves and pigeons sitting in rows, as usual, pluming themselves. The whirring and rushing of wings innumerable told Lorraine that the carriage was approaching, and she laid aside the work she had not touched, and went out into the porch. She was white to her lips, and her hands were shaking, as Ellison folded her silently in her arms ; those warm sisterly kisses were all that passed between them.

When Ellison had exchanged greetings with her household, she followed Lorraine into the sitting-room. 'Oh, how lovely it all looks !' she exclaimed, in a tone of deep content. 'My dear old room—how glad I am to get back to it !'—and then she put out her hand to her cousin, and they sat down on the window-seat together.

'You are very tired, Ellison'—Lorraine spoke in a trembling voice. 'Shall I ask Ruth to bring tea in now?'

'Thank you, dear, that will be nice'—and Lorraine hurried away to give the order. Ellison's face became very grave as soon as she was alone.

The sight of Lorraine's changed face had given her a shock; she was not ill, but she looked dwindled somehow, her face had grown smaller, and her eyes larger — their intense melancholy made Ellison's heart ache. When Lorraine returned to her seat a few minutes later, some uncontrollable impulse of pity made Ellison take the pale face tenderly between her hands and kiss it. 'Dear Lorraine, it is time that I came back to take care of you,' she said affectionately, 'there has been no one to do it in my place; but you knew how I wanted to get back to you.'

'Yes, I knew — but, Ellison, indeed every one took care of me. Muriel and dear Mrs. Trevor, and Mrs. Tucker—oh yes, and Colonel Trevor too. I have had nothing but kindness; but no one —no one could help me, really, you know. But we must not talk, talking unnerves me, and I must give you your tea, and then you shall go to your room to rest a little.'

Ellison smiled, but she made no answer, she was never less inclined for rest; it was repose enough to be back in her dearly loved home. But for Lorraine, she would have gone all over the house and farm; the horses and cows and pigs would all have been visited, and the poultry-yard and garden inspected. It cost her active nature an effort to sit there and let Lorraine wait on her and bring her her tea; but she felt instinctively that it would do Lorraine good—the only way for her to get over her trouble was to forget herself in ministering to others; but these were early days yet. As Ellison drank her tea, she felt a sort of oppression steal over her—a feeling of helplessness that was new to her—every one has had this consciousness when suddenly brought into the presence of some great trouble—a baffled, puzzled sense of impotence, as though one's very tongue were palsied. At such times the ordinary grooves of talk are impossible, and each topic seems too garish or trifling to be mentioned. The heart-break in Lorraine's sad eyes made Ellison dumb with pity; but happily speech is not the only channel of communication, and Lorraine drew immense comfort from her cousin's silent sympathy.

'She is so sorry for me that she cannot bring herself to speak,' she thought, and to Ellison's surprise and relief she began talking of her own accord of the little cross that was still unfinished.

'Colonel Trevor thinks it will be a pity to hurry it,' she said, with a shade more animation in her tone; 'he wants it to be as perfect as possible. Ah, he has been so good to me, Ellison! just as I should imagine a brother would be, if I had ever had one.'

'Gavin is always kind when people are in trouble,' returned Ellison; but she wished she could help blushing so painfully whenever she mentioned his name. She had not told Lorraine yet about her engagement; until she had seen him and realised her position a little she did not wish to tell people; it was enough that Mrs. Trevor and Muriel knew. They talked a little more about the beauty of the design, and than Lorraine checked herself, and again observed that Ellison must go and rest. 'I daresay you will like to be alone a little,' she continued, trying with unconscious pathos to put herself into Ellison's place. 'You have been away so long that you must want to look at things. The servants have been so good; I think you will find everything right. Shall I come up with you to your room, or would you prefer Dorcas?'

'I should prefer you to come, but I do not need help. I am not going to unpack, and I am quite tidy; it is only such a short journey from London,' and then they went upstairs together, hand-in-hand. But it was Lorraine's room—'Good rest'—into which Ellison turned; she walked through it, still keeping Lorraine's hand in hers, until they reached the 'Dovecote' with the little crib standing in the centre of the room, and then she stood still and looked at it. It was Lorraine's quaint fancy always to keep a cross of flowers or evergreens on the white quilt, which she kept renewed. She had fashioned it this time of late oak leaves, with shining red hips and haws, and the gleam of the berries looked well against the spotless white; the door of the toy cupboard was open, and all Tedo's playthings were arranged carefully on the wide shelves. The window overlooked the kitchen-garden, the bee-hives, and a corner of the orchard. When Ellison left home the trees had been bending under the weight of fruit, and the grass had been strewn with windfalls; now the leaves lay in piles and heaps everywhere, and through the thinned boughs she could see the Lodge roof by the Woodlands gate.

A sudden pitiful sense of the incongruity of life, of its changes and chances, made her eyes suddenly fill. 'Lorraine, dear,' she said quickly, 'don't think me unkind. I could not write, and now I find it as difficult to speak; but it is not want of feeling—you know that.'

'No, indeed. Oh, I understand you so well; there was no need for you to say that, dearest,' and, then, by a mutual impulse, the two women clasped and kissed each other, and something approaching to the warmth of comfort stole over Lorraine's bruised and crushed heart.

Ellison went to her room after that; her first act, when she found herself alone, was to scrutinise her features in the glass. Her looks had not satisfied Gavin ; but now, as she regarded herself a little anxiously, she could find nothing amiss ; perhaps she was a little thinner, a little less robust, but the fresh hue of health was on her cheek, and her eyes were as clear as a child's. The Mistress of Brae had always been a grand-looking woman, but now she had grown handsomer—Gavin told her so before the evening was out. Long before she expected him she was summoned down to him.

Lorraine had gone as usual to the churchyard, and they could meet in comfort. Ellison looked pale and nervous when she entered the room, but Gavin's lover-like greeting brought a beautiful blush to her face. 'Welcome home, dear !' he said gently, and as she seated herself, he sat down beside her, and then it seemed to Ellison as though she had nothing more to ask of life.

'Oh, stay, the moment is so fair !' Surely every true lover could say that with the aged Faust ; the cup that love fills with divine nectar seems so sweet as they quaff it. Whatever the future might bring Ellison, at that moment she was fully, utterly content.

Gavin was very quiet and tender with her, as though he guessed that she was half afraid of him, and this gentleness thrilled Ellison's very soul.

'I never thought even you could be so good to me,' she said presently ; 'but, Gavin, I wish I deserved it more. I have given you so much trouble, and have made you wait all this time ; it is dreadful to think we have lost three months out of our life, and all through my folly.'

'No, you must not say that, dear,' he returned, 'you were not ready, and I was bound to wait your time ; my liege lady had a right to my faithful service,' and then his tone changed into one of deeper feeling. 'Ellison, I never wanted you to go away. I shall never cease to be sorry that you went, but we must make the best of it,' and as her eyes expressed a faint surprise at this, he continued hurriedly : 'Things cannot be bright for us for a long time. My poor mother's state prevents that, but, at least, I shall have you near me in my trouble.'

'I shall always be near you,' she answered softly, and she took his hand as she spoke. 'Gavin, I never wish to leave you again ! Ah, you do not know how I missed you, it was not until all those miles were between us that I rightly understood my own feelings and knew what you were to me. I do not mind telling you that now'—and here her voice sank into exquisite tenderness—'now that we belong to each other.'

He drew her gently towards him and kissed her lips. How good, how loving she was to him ! How nobly true and frank in the expression of her love ! He had won her entirely, and she had given herself without stint or reserve, and in his heart he reverenced and thanked her. She was his friend and comrade. Never under any circumstances had she disappointed him, and she did not disappoint him now. Her influence was as great with him as ever. As he sat there talking to her in the soft lamplight he felt almost tranquil and at rest ; perhaps, after all, things would be well with him : when they were once married, the fever of unrest that had threatened his peace would pass away ; Ellison would be his dear and honoured wife, and time would make her dearer. It was only a delusion that he cared more for Mrs. Herbert. He would stamp out the unworthy feeling. As Shakespeare wisely said, 'A little fire is quickly trodden out, which, being suffered, rivers cannot quench.' Surely his man's strength and his sense of duty would aid him to win the victory !

Why, then, did the sound of a light footstep in the passage outside, and a low voice speaking to one of the maids, suddenly thrill him from head to foot. He could hear the question whether Colonel Trevor had gone, and Ruth's answer. A sudden fear that she would enter made him hot and then cold ; but when the footsteps passed on he felt only the chill of disappointment, and knew that he had been unconsciously expecting her all this time.

'Lorraine thinks that I shall be glad to have you to myself the first evening,' observed Ellison, and then she smiled in his face. 'Oh, Gavin, must you go now ? And you have been here such a little time !' And as he held out his watch without speaking she laughed and blushed in quite a girlish way.

'Is it so late ? I had no idea of that. Yes, of course, you must go, Gavin. I must send you away.' But there was no protracted leave-taking on Gavin's part—his quiet kiss and 'God bless you, dear,' was soon over.

Ellison would not walk to the gate with him uninvited ; but she stood at the door and watched him till he was out of sight. As he closed the little gate she waved her hand ; but Gavin was looking at a distant window, and made no response. In the candlelight he could see a slim, black figure plainly. Why was she standing there, he wondered, in the chill of the October night, looking out into the darkness ? There was something so forlorn and lonely in her attitude. 'Heaven guard and comfort her,' he muttered as he walked hastily down the farmyard and through the long meadow to Brae. It was not Ellison's fair tranquil face that haunted him ; the baffling spirit of unrest that he had vainly exorcised was beside him again, and he knew that the fight must be renewed for many a long day to come.

CHAPTER XXXVIII

> 'I feel like one
> Who treads alone
>   Some banquet hall deserted,
> Whose lights are fled,
> Whose garlands dead,
>   And all but he departed.'
>
> MOORE.

IT cost Lorraine a slight effort to deny herself the pleasure of seeing Colonel Trevor that evening ; those three months of unrestrained intercourse with him had deepened and enlarged her liking for him into a very real friendship. She had not guessed herself how much comfort his brief visits had given her, or how she had missed them of late ; and the knowledge that he was in the house made her long to hurry down to speak to him, and it was only the remembrance that Ellison might like to have him to herself that first evening that prevented her from doing so.

She had no idea how matters stood between them, and she had almost forgotten her old suspicion ; all such thoughts seemed lost in the hazy distance. In the world where Lorraine lived at present, there was neither marrying nor giving in marriage. She had forgotten that such things were ; to her life meant the hunger of a desolate heart crying after her little one, the stretching out of empty arms, all the sad martyrdom of a bereaved mother. In the world outside men still bought and sold, and made merry, and married wives ; in the cottage homes she passed she could hear the voices and laughter of the children ; but in the inner world, where she sat apart, the grey skies seemed to hover over a strange silent land, where every figure wore the garb of grief.

But that evening, as she stood at her window lost in melancholy thought, she was conscious of some added discomfort, of some new

feature of loss.   She wondered in a confused sort of way why
Ellison did not send for her, and the thought that she and Colonel
Trevor were too much engrossed to remember her existence, hardly
consoled her.

The clang of the gate gave her a little shock of disappointment.
He had gone without one word—it was strange, it was unlike him
—he was always so kind, so thoughtful ; and then she chid herself
for being so unreasonable.   Of course he had so much to tell
Ellison after her long absence ; about his mother's illness, and the
Farm ; they were such old friends, and the unrestrained intercourse
of years had sealed their intimacy.

Lorraine told herself somewhat bitterly that trouble was making
her selfish and exacting ; but in reality, strained and overtasked
and weary as she was, with the burden of a trouble too hard for
her to bear alone, she was just in that dangerous mood when
sympathy of some kind is an absolute necessity.

To her the divine right of loving and being beloved was second
nature.   While her child lived, this passionate demand had been
satisfied ; her boy's caresses had healed the degradation of her
married life, and her outraged sensibility had gradually calmed
down.   Her widow's mite ! how often had she called him that half
playfully, and yet with infinite tenderness.   Well did Lorraine
know, that of her own will she could never have yielded up her
one treasure ; but her frail ewe lamb had been taken from her at
a stroke.   To a casual observer, to one not versed in the strange
idiosyncrasies of human nature, it may seem strange that Lorraine,
broken-hearted as she was, should care for the society of Colonel
Trevor ; but the baffling instincts of a large-hearted and exuberant
nature like Lorraine's might well perplex them.   The stream that
has been dammed will seek another outlet, and fret its way over a
thousand obstacles, until it can pour its liquid riches into fresh
watercourses, fertilising the thirsty land as it flows.   And a rare
nature like Lorraine's could not live on this earth without some
object of affection.   Unknown to herself and to Ellison, her
position was one of singular peril.   The wife who had never
loved her husband, the mother who was weeping for her little one,
had been the object of tender and respectful sympathy to the most
attractive man who had ever crossed her path ; and it was little
wonder if her feelings of gratitude grew warmer with every fresh
act of thoughtfulness.   He had known sorrow too ; this was a
fresh link between them.   Lorraine during the last few weeks had
thought often and long of that Indian grave where Colonel Trevor's
wife and child lay.

She shook off the troublesome thoughts with a sigh as she went downstairs to bid Ellison good-night. 'Dear Ellison, what a shame,' she said to herself, 'to begrudge her anything on the first evening of her return.'

As she entered the room Ellison did not at once perceive her. She was lying back on her chair, with her hands clasped under her head, in an unwonted attitude of utter abandonment and comfort. The soft unbent line of her lips, and the strange brightness in her eyes, filled Lorraine with a vague surprise; she had an instinctive feeling that something had happened.

Ellison looked at her for a moment smilingly, and then stretched out her arm lazily, and drew her down beside her; but she did not at once speak.

Lorraine grew more and more puzzled.

'Ellison, dear,' she said almost timidly, 'I did not like to come down before. I thought you and Colonel Trevor would have so much to talk over—was I right?'

'Quite right,' returned Ellison dreamily. 'You are always so thoughtful, Lorraine; that is why it is so easy to live with you. You have never once been in my way—never once,' and then her manner changed and grew hesitating.

'Lorraine, dear, shall you be very much surprised if I tell you a little secret, or have you guessed it already? Gavin and I are engaged—we have been engaged a week; but, until we met, I could not realise that fact, that is why I am glad that you left us alone this evening.'

For one moment Lorraine had again the curious feeling, as though she had suddenly and unexpectedly lost something; but it was too vague and indefinite to be grasped, and the next minute she was saying hurriedly:

'I hardly know if I am surprised. Months ago, at that dinner-party, I had a sort of feeling that there was something between you, but I forgot all about it afterwards.' And then she drew a long breath, and her eyes grew sad. 'It seems a lifetime ago since then.'

'He spoke to me that evening,' returned Ellison in a low voice. 'It was my fault that we were not engaged then, but I was not ready. I think I am a little different from other women. I have never been in a hurry to marry—I have always been so satisfied with my single life that only Gavin could have persuaded me to change it.' She looked very handsome as she said this, with her head held higher, and the blood mantling into her cheeks. 'Lorraine, are you glad about this—are you going to congratulate me?'

'With all my heart, dearest'; and then Lorraine clasped her

close. 'May you be as happy as you deserve to be.' And then, in a lower tone, 'He is worthy of you. I do not fear for your happiness.'

'Nor I. Dear Lorraine, I was half afraid to tell you this. It seems so hard that I should have everything and you nothing; but Gavin and I will be so good to you. You like him, do you not, dear? You and he are great friends. You were only telling me so before he came to-night.'

'Yes, we are good friends,' and then Lorraine wondered why she found it so difficult to speak of Colonel Trevor. But again she chid herself for her selfishness. Ellison's whole nature seemed to have changed, her shy reticence had broken down under the influence of her new happiness, and she seemed to find a satisfaction in pouring into Lorraine's ears the story of Gavin's wooing and her own slowness of response.

Lorraine listened silently. Now and then the same faint surprise moved her, though she was careful not to wound Ellison by giving expression to it. How strange and baffling it all seems! How could it be possible for any woman beloved by a man like Gavin Trevor to hesitate and set up a barrier of time and distance between herself and so true a lover? For the first time Ellison's love of power, her desire for freedom and independence, appeared unwomanly and untrue to nature. What were the adjuncts of circumstances, and a few exterior advantages, when a good man— leal and trusty as Gavin Trevor—said, 'I love you and want you for my wife?' Lorraine's delicate thin face showed a momentary disdain, though she kept her lips closed. Only once she said tremulously:

'How could you fear to trust your life in his hands, knowing him all those years?'

But Ellison only laughed happily.

'You and I are very different women,' she said. 'I was never one of the soft, yielding ones. I always cared for Gavin; but even he did not find it easy to win me. But when once I am won——' She paused, and an exquisite tenderness shone in her eyes. 'Gavin knows that I shall be true to him.'

Lorraine pressed her hand, and after a few more words they parted for the night.

When Ellison lay down on her bed she told herself that she was the happiest woman in Highlands. 'My own Gavin, you know how I love you! You are satisfied with me now!' she thought, as she fell asleep.

But it was long before Lorraine could rest. A vague pain to which she could give no name, seemed to drive sleep from her eyes.

She lay open-eyed in the darkness. Now a prayer for Ellison's happiness rose to her lips, and then a petition for comfort. A sudden sense of her own poverty oppressed her. She was young— in the very prime of young womanhood—and yet what did life offer her ? The love for which she had unconsciously craved was not for her, and friendship could hardly satisfy her instincts. 'O my God ! why are women made so ?' she exclaimed with a sudden anguish of impatience, and she could find no answer to this per-plexing problem which thousands of women have tried to solve.

Some curious instinct made Lorraine avoid Colonel Trevor, and for two or three weeks after Ellison's return they did not meet. She knew the hour when he was likely to walk down to the Farm, and it was easy to prolong her evening walk so as to leave the coast clear for the lovers. She would spend solitary hours in the churchyard brooding over her past life, and trying to brace herself up to patience and endurance. But she paced up and down the yew-tree walk in the gathering dusk, her sense of desolation was almost unendurable.

But the days that were so sad and heavy to Lorraine were full of exquisite happiness to Ellison ; and even to Gavin, worn with his strange and hidden conflict, they were days of peace. Peace— that was all he asked now ; and as he sat alone with his betrothed, talking quietly of the future, and saw the lovelight in her calm blue eyes, and heard the satisfied tones of her voice, he said to himself that the past few weeks had been a dream, and that all would be well with them in the future. Certainly Ellison missed nothing. Gavin's quiet tenderness satisfied her utterly ; a more passionate and exacting attachment would have bewildered her. 'Gavin is perfect,' she once whispered to Mrs. Trevor, as she sat beside her in the short October afternoon. How bare the Brae Woods were growing ! The heaps of red and yellow leaves drifted into the hollows ; to the sick woman, they spoke of life's calm decay, and of the eternal springtime that lay before her. Very sweet and precious were those hours that she and Ellison spent together. She would talk to her of Muriel's future.

'You will be a sister to her, Ellison,' she said one day. 'Dear Muriel, she is wonderfully softened and improved. She is my greatest comfort now, after Gavin.' And again and again Ellison solemnly assured her that their home should be Muriel's too.

Lorraine still paid daily visits to Brae, but she never encountered Gavin ; more than once as he sat in his library he heard her deep low voice as she and Muriel passed the door, then a sudden flush would come to his brow as he bent over his paper ; but he made no effort to see her.

But one afternoon he came upon her unexpectedly, standing by the gate of the Woodlands—it was about three weeks after Ellison's return—he was climbing up the path that led from the long meadow, when he suddenly saw her. His first impulse was to draw back, but she had already seen him, and the faint welcoming smile he knew so well was on her lips, though she made no movement towards him. She seemed tired, and a basket full of yellow bracken and red and withered leaves was at her feet, her old black hat was pushed back, and he could see the brightness of her brown hair as it lay in waves about her temples and ears; but as he came towards her slowly he noticed that her cheek had lost its soft curves, and that her eyes looked large and sunken. They shook hands silently—Gavin was nervous, but the mere fact that he was standing beside her, and that her gown brushed his foot, filled him with a strange sense of pleasure. It was so long since he had seen that sweet sad face, alas, sweeter and dearer to him than ever; he wanted to hear her speak, and yet no words occurred to him. It was Lorraine, troubled by his unusual silence and gravity, who spoke first. ' I did not see you, and you startled me a little '— was that why she had flushed at the sight of him ? ' I have been a long way, through the Redlands Woods, and have gathered all those leaves and berries ; but the basket is so heavy.'

' Let me carry it for you,' was his quick answer ; but as he lifted it a sort of anger came into his voice. ' Why do you not take better care of yourself? Is there no one to prevent your doing these things ? Ellison cannot know how you tire yourself.'

' Those leaves are for Ellison,' she returned, a little taken aback by the sternness of this reprimand ; ' she is so fond of all these wild things. I wanted to fill her vases and surprise her. Please do not let me take you back, Colonel Trevor,'—as he did not put down the basket. ' I will leave it at the lodge and send Daniel for it this evening; it is certainly a little heavy and makes my arms ache.'

' I am going to carry it myself,' he returned in rather a dogged voice ; ' my errand was not of the slightest consequence, and you need not forbid my rendering you this slight service. Ellison is sitting with my mother and Muriel, I shall join them by and by,— and then he set down the basket and propped himself up against the gate. It was in this very spot that he had spoken to Ellison, when she had silenced him so abruptly. What if he had not considered himself bound by those few vague words—what if he had held himself as free ? but even as the thought seemed to search him, he repelled it fiercely. But as he turned to accost Lorraine he was startled to see that her eyes were full of tears.

'Do you remember?' she said tremulously, 'it was just here where we saw you first, you and Lady Alice, and I opened the gate for you.'

'Yes, I remember,' he returned, leaning towards her and regarding her fixedly.

'I can hear him now, the darling,' she continued, 'his sweet little voice, with its baby lisp, quite plainly—"boy vants a vide"—and then you took him up and I walked beside you. I was thinking of that when you startled me just now.'

'Do you ever think of anything else?' he returned almost impatiently; 'it is wrong to dwell so on the past, all these thoughts are making you thin and haggard; it is only three weeks since we met, and I can see the change in you. How are you to go on living if you will not be comforted?'

His tone, rough with suppressed feeling, made Lorraine wince. Never had he spoken to her in this way before; but this afternoon his gentle chivalry seemed to have deserted him. 'Come, the wind is cold, there is a touch of east in it, and you must not stand here any longer,' and Lorraine, a little perplexed at this peremptoriness, followed him meekly down the winding path that led to Brae. All at once a sudden thought made her grow hot and nervous. 'Colonel Trevor,' she said hurriedly; and then he stood still and waited for her to speak.

'It is very forgetful of me, but your words reminded me. I have not seen you since Ellison's return, and I have never congratulated you.'

'Oh, is that all,' he returned, trying to speak lightly as they went on together. 'In my opinion congratulations are better understood than spoken. I never was a good hand at pretty speeches.'

'But all the same, you will allow me to wish you happiness,' she said timidly, for his manner sadly perplexed her. 'After all your kindness, I can do no less'—and then her voice broke a little. 'Colonel Trevor, I do pray that you may be very happy, you and dear Ellison.'

'Thanks awfully,' he returned; but his hand shook a little, and his face looked gloomy as Lorraine looked at him. She felt vaguely dissatisfied. Was he as happy as she had imagined him to be? He had never been so wanting in geniality before; her good wishes seemed to bore him; perhaps his mother's state was making him miserable; and with her usual tact Lorraine gently changed the subject, and they chatted on indifferent topics. He carried the basket up to the door, and then to Lorraine's surprise followed her into the house.

'You will promise me to rest now,' he said persuasively, and with a return of his old manner. 'You will not bother over those weeds until you have had some tea'; and as she shook her head half-smilingly, he continued: 'It is not like you to be selfish—you ought to have some regard for your friends' feelings—if you only knew how ill you are looking.'

'I will rest,' she replied gently. How this thoughtfulness touched her; it was so long, so long, since she had heard him speak in this kind way; as she put out her hand to him she was struck afresh · by the concentrated gloom in his deep-set eyes. What was troubling him? If she could only help him—and then Lorraine sighed; the chasm between them was widening, his marriage with Ellison could not bring him nearer, and all that evening and the next day the same vague sense of loss oppressed and added to her sadness.

CHAPTER XXXIX

'The desire of the moth for the star,
    Of the night for the morrow,
The devotion to something afar
    From the sphere of our sorrow.'
                        SHELLEY.

'O fear not in a world like this,
    And thou shalt know ere long,
Know how sublime a thing it is
    To suffer and be strong.'
                        LONGFELLOW.

LORRAINE had seen little of Mr. Vincent all this time; a painful consciousness that his visits had ceased to be welcome had kept him away from the Farm.

He had called once after Ellison's return to congratulate her on her engagement, but though he knew Mrs. Herbert was in the house she had not made her appearance. The visit had been an uncomfortable one; Ellison's manner had indeed been as kind as usual and as friendly, but it had been impossible to avoid constraint, neither of them had liked to allude to the past. More than once Ellison had been on the point of saying something, and had checked herself. Mr. Vincent seemed so nervous and ill at ease that her courage failed, but in her heart she was full of sympathy for him; the old careworn look had returned, and he looked far from happy. When, at the close of his visit, he asked after Mrs. Herbert, he seemed to find some effort in speaking her name.

Lorraine came downstairs the moment he had gone, but Ellison noticed with some surprise that she never mentioned him at all. She was always very kind to Nora when she came to the Farm, but Edmund and Effie never accompanied her. Once when Ellison proposed inviting them to taste her blackberry jam, Lor-

20

raine had burst into tears and left the room; the childless woman could not yet bear the sound of young voices; with all her unselfishness her loss was too recent.

The day after her encounter with Colonel Trevor she was sitting alone, busy with some fine darning, when, to her surprise, she saw Mr. Vincent pass the window. She put down her work in some agitation, any visitor made her nervous now; but an instant's reflection reassured her. 'When he hears Ellison is out he will go away,' she said to herself, as she shrank back into the shadow of the curtain; but she was wrong, the next minute Ruth announced him.

He came in hurriedly, and there was a deprecating expression on his face as he shook hands with her. 'I hope I have not disturbed you,' he said quickly; 'perhaps I ought not to have come in. I know you do not care for visitors, but there is something I want to ask you.'

'Will you not sit down?' returned Lorraine a little stiffly. With all her effort she could not be at her ease with him; again and again she had reasoned with herself, Mr. Vincent had nothing to do with her trouble, he was utterly blameless, and yet the sight of him always disturbed her; he was Hugo's brother—and Hugo had led her boy into danger.

Mr. Vincent placed himself at some little distance. Mrs. Herbert's manner was not reassuring—and how ill she looked—her face seemed thinner and smaller every time he saw her, and her graceful figure looked more drooping; the keenness of his pity made him silent for a moment, but Lorraine looked at him inquiringly.

'Is there any one you want me to see?' she asked. 'I am always so glad to help if I can. I was at Mrs. Carson's yesterday, she was worse; but of course you know that—they would have sent for you.'

'I was there last night, and again this morning; she died two hours ago. No, there are no fresh cases that I need to trouble you about; it is only some private business on which I want your advice.'

'My advice is worth very little, I am afraid,' taking up her work again; and he could see the slight stiffening of her muscles; the old beautiful smile was not for him now; his heart ached again as he watched her. No, it was too evident she cared nothing for him; her old kindness, her cordial warm-hearted partisanship, her womanly sympathy, were things of the past; her sorrow had separated them utterly. Nevertheless, this once he must speak to her.

'It is worth a great deal to me,' he returned quickly. 'You

do not know the extent of your influence, Mrs. Herbert, or you would not put me off in that way ; let me tell you what brings me here this morning. I asked for you, and not for Miss Lee, because it was your advice that I wanted. Of course you have heard from Colonel Trevor that they have offered me the living ?'

'No,' she returned, with a manifest start ; 'we have heard nothing. Do you mean that you are to be our vicar ?' And then he saw that the idea was not a welcome one to her.

'They have asked me to remain here ; but of course I know that my friends have busied themselves on my behalf. Colonel Trevor told me that he and Mr. Earnshaw had written to Sir Percy Chessington, and also to the bishop. I heard from Sir Percy last night——'

'I must congratulate you,' observed Lorraine, but there was no warmth in her voice—but he stopped her.

'No ; not yet. I have not answered Sir Percy's letter. What would be the good of asking advice if I had already made up my mind ? Will you let me finish what I have to say ? Of course this means a great deal to me. To be sure, my aunt's unexpected liberality has lifted us out of actual penury, but even with her help we have only enough for moderate comfort. The living is worth about four hundred and fifty pounds a year, and the Vicarage is roomy and comfortable, and in excellent repair ; the field or two adjoining would enable me to keep a horse and trap without much additional expense, especially as the boys' education is assured. We would not be rich even then, but we should be able to enjoy life.'

'All your friends will be delighted to hear of your great fortune, Mr. Vincent. I think it would be well for you to write to Miss Bretherton. Surely,' looking at him in some perplexity, 'there can be no need for a moment's hesitation ; you have told me more than once how you liked Highlands, and how sorry you would be to leave.'

'That is true, and I do not take back my words. If I hesitate, it is not on my own account ; but, after all that has happened, I felt it was impossible to accept Sir Percy's offer until I had spoken to you. Mrs. Herbert, will you tell me frankly—you are always frank—will it be painful to you to see me at the Vicarage ?'

Lorraine could scarcely believe her ears ; but when she looked at him she saw he was quite in earnest. He was actually hesitat-ing to accept this good thing that had been offered to him, from a scrupulous sense of delicacy on her behalf. As he said those words, 'Will it be painful to you to see me at the Vicarage ?' his eyes had been full of a wistful sadness. She was extremely surprised and touched ; and as she answered him, the friendliness of her tone made the young man's heart beat. Lorraine had no clue to help her to interpret the real reason for Mr. Vincent's generosity : with wonderful self-abnegation, and absolutely shutting his eyes to his own interest, he was making her the arbitress of his future. In Lorraine's eyes it was the finest chivalry, and Quixotic extravagance of sentiment, but nevertheless it went to her heart. She little knew that the sacrifice she considered so noble seemed little in Eric's eyes ! He would have been ready to do far more than this to give peace of mind to the woman he loved so hopelessly—yes, hopelessly. If he had never realised this fact before, he did so to-day ; as he sat there hardly daring to look at the face he so dearly loved, he knew that he should never dare to woo her.

On her side Lorraine was profoundly touched, the tears rushed to her eyes. How good he was, and how hardly she had treated him. To Eric's surprise she stretched out her hand to him, and implored him to forgive her.

'You have so much to forgive,' she said, with a little sob. 'I have been so hard and cruel in my trouble ; it was no fault of yours that I was so unhappy, but I have treated you as though you were to blame. Why does trouble make one so wicked ? My heart has never been hard before. Mr. Vincent, you are a clergyman, you ought to know—why have you never told me that I was wrong to be so rebellious ?'

'One should not break the bruised reed,' he said nervously ; 'you must not be so hard on yourself, Mrs. Herbert. No one in their senses could have called you wicked ; your friends know you too well, you only wanted time to recover yourself.'

'No, no ; I shall never be myself again,' with a slight shudder. 'I never used to have these bitter thoughts ; even in my worst times it seemed so easy to love people ; but now, I only want to be alone and think of my boy. Mr. Vincent, I have not answered your question ; you ought not to have asked it ; bad and selfish as I have been, I am not quite so selfish as that. Please write to Sir Percy Chessington this evening.'

'You are quite sure that you mean that ?'—then again her eyes were misty with tears.

'I am sure that no one else ought to be our vicar. Mr. Vincent, please do not make me so utterly ashamed of myself, and—and let the children come as usual ; my cousin likes to have them, and I shall soon get used to it.'

'We will see about that,' he returned, taking up his hat.

But Lorraine's repentance was very real.

'If you will not give Nora my message, I shall send her a note.

Tell her she is to bring Eddie and Effie to-morrow ; I am going to write to Hugo to-night, I know that he loves letters. Will you give me the name of his house-master?'

'There is no need to put yourself to such trouble,' he replied, almost shocked at the effort she was making—her lips had turned quite white as she mentioned Hugo's name ; nevertheless, no entreaty on his part could induce her to spare herself.

'You have shown my selfishness in a true light,' she returned. 'I will give way no more ; as long as we live we owe duties to other people. If Nora does not come to-morrow I shall come down to the cottage to know the reason why '—and as she said this, he did see the ghost of a smile.

When Eric went down to Rugby, he asked Hugo to show him that letter. Hugo stared at him.

'Which do you mean ; is it a special one?' he asked. 'I have got a heap here '—and he fetched a little carved box that one of his schoolfellows had given him, and showed him seven or eight letters. The black-edged envelopes were sadly torn ; frequent reading, and perhaps tears, had defaced the neat pages : they were the treasures of Hugo's heart. Eric read them every one, sitting on Hugo's little bed ; they were a revelation to him ; those tender warning sentences were written from a wrung and sore heart, but how true and steadfast were their aim ! to lead one wild young heart to believe in goodness, and the redemption of penitence. 'Be good, dear Hugo, be obedient, and reverence those who are in authority over you. Be brave and speak the truth, and hate all lies and deception like poison '—this was the grit and moral of those letters ; he read one paragraph over again and again. 'Be true to me, Hugo, and I will be true to you. I have never hated you, my poor child ; what can have put that into your head? and please never say again that you were Tedo's murderer. Have you forgotten how he loved you—his dear Hughie? and do you suppose I could hate any one whom he loved? You once said you would do anything I wished ; I shall hold you to that. I wish you to be a brave obedient boy, of whom we can all be proud, and then you will grow up a noble man, good and brave like your brother ; promise me that you will, Hugo.' As he tied up the letters again his eyes were dim ; this was the work she set herself, to redeem and build up this wayward nature, for well did she know her influence. Years afterwards Lorraine was to reap her harvest ; when Hugo showed her his Victoria Cross, he lifted her hand to his lips. 'I was glad when they gave it me, because I knew you would be glad too, and I wanted to give pleasure to my best friend. I was thinking of you as I carried the poor fellow out of reach of fire, I never thought I should see you or England again ; and I did so want you to know that if I played the man, it was all your doing.' But Lorraine, who was looking pitifully at the empty sleeve, and the mark of the sabre-cut across his temples, was too moved to answer. Captain Scott, the hero, was her boy Hugo ; her words had come true, the brave boy had grown into the braver man.

As Eric left the Farm that afternoon he felt less unhappy than he had done since Tedo's death ; and yet for the first time he fully realised the hopelessness of his love for the young widow. She would never care for him ; he had no key to unlock the treasures of that tender womanly heart, the right password would never be his ; but, at least, he had one consolation. The barrier had been broken down between them ; again he had met those soft, friendly glances that had warmed him like sunshine, and had felt the pressure of her thin hand. She had accused herself frankly of want of generosity and kindness, and her last words to him had been almost childlike in their contrition.

'I have treated everybody as badly as possible, but I will try and make up for it. You are going to be our vicar ; you must help me to be good ; that is part of your duty.' And then she had looked up in his face with a sweet sad smile that had nearly broken his heart.

As he walked up the steep lane that led to the village he told himself that it was his part to play the man, and that any pro-longed lamentation over his disappointment would be useless and puerile.

The woman whom he loved and honoured would never consent to be his wife ; the pretty vicarage, of which he was already so proud, would be without a mistress. Well, he must learn to do without happiness, as many a better man had done ; and then by some odd transition of thought he remembered his aunt — her lonely life — and the pathetic oddities that hid a whole lifetime of pain.

How few people of his acquaintance had realised their ambitions, he wondered ; there was Miss Trevor, the merest stranger would have detected the marks of conflict and dissatisfaction with her environment ; and as this thought passed through his mind he suddenly came face to face with her.

The windings of the lane and his own thoughts had prevented him from seeing her until she was quite close to him ; but Muriel had already perceived him, and her colour was slightly heightened as they shook hands.

'I had only just retraced my steps to look for a small book I had dropped,' she began hurriedly ; then, as she caught sight of it in his hand, 'oh, thank you so much, you have found it. I was just on my way to call on Miss Spencer ; I had promised to lend it to her.'

'I was just wondering to whom the book belonged,' he returned. 'I have been over to the Farm. I wanted to speak to Mrs. Herbert. Ah ! I see you are in possession of the secret,' as Muriel's eyes began to brighten with animation.

'Yes, indeed. I was so glad to hear it. Gavin is so delighted about it ; he was quite excited when he told mother. I think all your friends are pleased, Mr. Vincent.'

'All my friends are very kind ; but you must not be too quick with your congratulations. I have not yet accepted Sir Percy's offer,' and then he told Muriel all about his interview with Mrs. Herbert.

It was not the first time he had made Miss Trevor his confidante ; they were excellent friends, and he had an immense respect for her judgment. With all her faults she was so absolutely true, and her standard of perfection was a high one. But to-day, as he talked to her, he was almost surprised by the keenness of her interest ; her colour changed, and her eyes grew misty with strong feeling, and the vibrating softness of her voice filled him with vague wonder.

'It was grand ; it was noble of you to go to her,' she said. 'I think few men would have done that ; self-interest would have prevented them. Do you see the good it has done? it has roused her by appealing to her best feelings. Mrs. Herbert is such a good woman. I am finding that out more and more ; she will never rest now until she has conquered her selfishness—for she will call it that, although we should give it another name.'

'You need not tell me that. I have found out Mrs. Herbert's virtues long ago.' Eric tried to speak lightly, but the underlying sadness was too evident.

He could not have brought himself to speak of his attachment to Mrs. Herbert to any human being ; nevertheless Muriel knew all about it. If he had consulted her she would have told him how utterly hopeless it all was. 'She will never care for you in that way,' that is what she would have said. Muriel never guessed at the reason for this sudden insight into Mr. Vincent's mind ; the characters and even the motives of her friends seemed somehow clearer to her ; she was passing through one of those crises that quicken and stimulate growth. No longer self-absorbed, she looked out upon the world—her own little world of human beings—and all at once it seemed to her that she was surrounded by a vast brotherhood and sisterhood.

In spite of her very real sorrow for her mother's declining state Muriel was happier than she ever had been; for the first time she lived, instead of dreaming away her life, and her imperious and exacting tenderness met with some adequate response. Her mother needed and leant on her. Gavin no longer repressed her; their mutual trouble and anxiety drew the brother and sister together. Lorraine's friendship had created a fresh interest in her life; but, when Muriel counted up her blessings, she was careful to omit any thought of Mr. Vincent; nevertheless, the young clergyman's influence was beginning to permeate every nook and cranny of her peculiar nature, and though she never owned her preference even to herself, his visits and their brief snatches of conversation were the chief events of the day.

Eric on his side fully appreciated Muriel's friendship, and never lost an opportunity of talking to her. They had much in common. Eric's fastidious scholarly taste was gratified by the girl's refined intelligence; her talents were certainly far above the average of ordinary women; she had read deeply, and had digested all she read. He did not think her pretty, and she had not Mrs. Herbert's fascination; but now and then the brightness of her eyes and the softness of her smile would give her a momentary beauty.

He always met her with pleasure, and on this afternoon she appeared more attractive to him than usual; there was something healing in her sympathy and appreciation. Eric was not vain by nature, but even he could not fail to feel gratified by her warm eulogium on his conduct. 'It was noble of you to go to **her.**' When she said this Eric felt himself vaguely comforted.

CHAPTER XL

'From bearing right
Our sorest burdens comes fresh strength to bear;
And some rise again towards the light,
And quit the sunless depths for upper air:
The rocks have bruised us sore; but angels' wings
Grow best from bruises, hope from anguish springs.'
C. TURNER.

THOSE dim October days that dragged so heavily for Lorraine were days of ever-deepening happiness to Ellison. She and Gavin were always together; they did nothing apart. Her daily visits to the invalid brought them constantly together; and it had grown a custom for Gavin to walk back with her, and to accompany her in her afternoon rambles round the Farm. Ellison asked his advice in everything; the young mistress of Brae Farm no longer prided herself on her sturdy independence; it was a joy to her to abdicate and divest herself of her woman's sceptre. 'The king can do no wrong,' was already a foregone conclusion, and Gavin, secretly amused and touched by his liege lady's submission, was always ready to help her to the best of his power.

In spite of his infatuation for the young widow, Gavin was not always restless and unhappy. Ellison still had the power to soothe him; in her presence he felt calm and even content. Men—even the best of them—have strangely complex natures; and it was undoubtedly true that, in spite of his passion for Mrs. Herbert, in some ways Ellison satisfied him. The ties of warm friendship that united them, the gratitude that he owed her for years of untiring sympathy, his own unselfish desire for her happiness— were all important factors in his wooing, and increased his need of her.

If Ellison had been more exacting in her demands it might have been otherwise. But the steady flame of her love was always bright and serene. Never demonstrative, her manner to her betrothed husband was full of an underlying tenderness that rarely rose to the surface, and her shy reticence permitted few caresses. No wonder, then, she satisfied the weary, passion-tossed man, and that there were times when he told himself that he had done well for his future. And another thing, the absence of all uncertainty gave him strength and confidence. He was too reasonable to cry like a spoilt child for the moon. 'The love of the moth for the star' would not have satisfied him. It was better to take the helpmeet that was near to him. In his heart he agreed with the poet that 'not enjoyment and not sorrow is our destined end or way.' To a nature like Colonel Trevor's the battle of life was likely to be a hard one.

But the fires of the volcano were only smouldering under the thin crust of the crater; the heated lava was ready to burst into flame. An old soldier like Gavin knew where the danger lay, and he avoided every occasion where he would be likely to meet Mrs. Herbert. As the weeks went on, and November winds stripped the woodlands, and the rotting leaves lay in heaps, she crossed his path less and less. Lorraine never asked herself why she avoided him. Now and then, when Ellison affectionately chid her for her absurd prudishness, she only smiled and said nothing. Ellison thought that consideration for herself and Gavin kept Lorraine away. 'There is no need,' she would urge; 'we are a steady old couple, and I feel as though I have been engaged years. We are not always talking secrets.' But Ellison pleaded in vain; some subtle instinct warned Lorraine that it was safer for her to see as little as possible of Colonel Trevor.

Early in December Mrs. Trevor grew rapidly worse; but her constitution was a good one, and it was the doctor's opinion that there would be another rally, and that she might possibly live for some weeks.

But the end came very suddenly when they least expected it. Ellison, who had spent the previous evening at Brae House, was so deceived by the temporary rally that she decided to go up to town the following morning and spend a few hours with her friend Margaret Mervyn.

'Margaret is longing to see me,' she said, as Gavin walked back with her. He had a lantern in his hand to guide them through the wintry darkness, for there was no moon. Years afterwards Ellison remembered that short walk—the bright light thrown by the lantern, and the blackness that encompassed them. Gavin had wrapped her in an old fur-lined coat of his, for the wind was piercing. 'You are making a mummy of me,' she had remon-strated laughingly ; 'my cloak is quite warm.'

But he had only laughed rather derisively.

'You must not presume on being stronger than most women. You are mortal like the rest of us.' And then he had told her not to talk, and to cover up her mouth.

Ellison obeyed him. But the winter wind might have been the softest of breezes to her, and those dark fields the Elysian meadows. Once, as she pressed closer to him, he put out his arm and drew her nearer. As he raised the lantern they seemed to walk in a path of shining light.

The same thought seemed to strike Gavin.

'Is this emblematical of our future life, Ellison ?' he said as he stopped to open the gate for her. Then in the darkness she crept closer to him and laid her cheek against his coat.

'I shall not mind any number of dark days if I only have you near me, Gavin,' she said, and her voice trembled with strong feeling. 'You are my light—you know that.'

'I know one thing—that I do not deserve you,' he returned as he kissed her brow. 'Since Helen's death you have always been my best blessing.' And then Ellison sighed happily as though her cup was filled to the brim. This is what she had wanted—to be Gavin's comforter.

Gavin had promised to drive her over to Bramfield the next morning, and, if possible, to meet her by the early afternoon train. In all outward observance and service his behaviour was perfect. He never spared himself any trouble.

'You must let me do everything for you,' he said to her more than once. 'You cannot give me greater pleasure than to let me feel that I am of some use to you.' And in those sweet early days of their engagement Ellison often invented little errands. In spite of her outward serenity she was often restless in his absence, and was glad of any trifling excuse that would bring him to the Farm.

They set out for Bramfield quite happily. Gavin spoke almost cheerfully of his mother. She had had a better night. She certainly suffered less pain. He hoped—he could not help hoping— that she would see the new year in. Ellison listened sym-pathetically, and said nothing to disturb those comfortable convictions. On her own part she had no illusions ; she felt assured that Mrs. Trevor's rally would be brief.

But little did she and Gavin guess, as they drove rapidly down the Bramfield Road, that at that moment Lorraine had sent off an urgent message for their return. A sudden collapse had taken place, and it was doubtful if she would live through the morning.

Unfortunately, the groom missed his master. The fineness of the day had tempted Gavin to drive round by Darley. There was a horse he wanted to see, and his mare was fresh ; he had left the station ten minutes before Davis reached it. The next thing was to go in search of Dr. Howell. Happily the man met him coming out of the Vicarage, and he drove off to Brae at once.

Lorraine had gone up to Brae unusually early, and without waiting to speak to Muriel, who was giving the housekeeper the orders for the day, she went up unannounced to the sick-room. The nurse had only just left the bedside, and was busy in the dressing-room, when a sudden cry from Lorraine startled her.

'Nurse, come here, Mrs. Trevor looks faint. She is trying to speak to me and cannot say a word.'

'Send for Dr. Howell and Miss Muriel,' was all the nurse said. But Lorraine read the truth in the woman's eyes. She was dying, and Colonel Trevor and Ellison were away.

She rushed down to find Muriel, and to send off that message that never reached Gavin, and then with an aching heart watched as the nurse tried vainly to revive her patient. Mrs. Trevor was sinking fast. She had looked at her daughter when she entered, and had tried to move her hand. As Muriel with a despairing cry flung herself upon the bed there was again that fruitless attempt to speak ; but Lorraine, moved to her very soul by the anguish of that helplessness, bent over them both.

'Dear Mrs. Trevor, do not try to speak ; you are too weak. You want Muriel to know how much you love her, and to wish her good-bye. There, I am guiding your hand ; it is resting on her head. If you had strength to speak you would say " God bless her," would you not ? '

A slight, scarcely perceptible, quiver passed over the dying woman's face, and showed that she understood ; but Lorraine knew instinctively that the dim eyes were searching for some one else. She stooped over her again. ' You are looking for your son. I have sent for him. He has gone out with Ellison. We hope he will be in time to bid you good-bye. I will give him your message '—and here her voice trembled. ' Oh, do not try to speak, I know quite well what you would wish to say ; you want him to have your love and blessing '—and then something like a smile came to her pallid lips. For some time she seemed unconscious, but even after Dr. Howell's entrance there was another unexpected rally. Some strong stimulant made her open her eyes with a shudder, and then she said faintly, ' Yes, tell him that ' ; and a little while afterwards, when the sinking had returned, she looked at them rather strangely.

'John,' they heard her whisper. 'John and the children'— those were her last words. Half an hour later she drew her last breath, just as the wheels of the phaeton sounded on the gravel path.

Muriel was still kneeling with her mother's hand clasped in hers, but Lorraine rose hastily and left the room ; the phaeton was still coming up the drive as she stood bare-headed in the porch.

Gavin saw her, and a prevision of evil crossed his mind. Why was she standing there waiting for him ? and then he saw how pale she was.

'My mother is worse ; let me go to her !' he exclaimed, trying to pass her ; but Lorraine's soft hand held him firmly.

'Let me speak to you first ; there is no hurry. It will be better for you to wait a little. Your dear mother has left us.' Then he stared at her incredulously.

'It is impossible,' she heard him say, and then he staggered slightly as though he were giddy, the long drive in the cold and the shock together seemed to numb him.

When Lorraine put her hand again on his arm and guided him to the library, he did not resist. His limbs seemed to totter under him. Perhaps it would be wiser to sit down for a moment before he went upstairs.

The next moment Lorraine brought him some wine.

'You must drink that,' she said with gentle firmness. 'You are cold, your teeth are chattering, and this is such a dreadful coming home. Please do not refuse it, Colonel Trevor,' as he motioned it away with some impatience. 'When I was in trouble I let you help me more than once.' Then he drank the wine and the colour returned to his lips.

'Tell me about it. When did it happen ?' he asked hoarsely. 'I have not been away more than two or three hours.'

'It was a sudden failure, a sort of collapse. She became worse almost directly you and Ellison left the house. When I went up I saw how it was, and sent Davis after you ; but you have been so long that he must have missed you.'

'I came round by Darley.' As she stood beside him a fold of her black dress brushed his knee, and unconsciously his hand closed upon it ; the touch of her gown gave him a feeling of comfort. Lorraine took no notice, and went on—

'There was only Muriel ; but she was wanting you. She could not speak until just at the last ; but we knew she was looking for you. Just before she passed away I heard her whisper, "John and the children," and such a happy look came over her face.'

'That was my father's name; she was thinking of him and the girls. Oh, if I had only been there!' and then his hand tightened on her dress. Lorraine saw the marks of his fingers afterwards. He sat still for a few more minutes, and Lorraine waited patiently beside him. When the silence had grown painful she said softly:

'Muriel is upstairs. Should you not like to see her?' And then he released her, and rose stiffly.

Later in the day, when he had transacted all necessary business, he entered the library and found Lorraine waiting for him. She had her hat and jacket on.

'Are you going away?' he asked, somewhat surprised. 'I thought you would have stopped with Muriel.'

'I thought it would be better for me to meet Ellison,' she returned quietly. 'I knew you meant to send her a note by Davis; but it seemed kinder not to let her have that long drive alone; she will be so terribly shocked when she reads the note.'

'Thank you; you are very good to have thought of that,' he said gratefully. 'But are you sure you ought to go? it is bitterly cold.'

'It cannot possibly hurt me; I am warmly wrapped up. I do not like leaving Muriel, she seems so prostrate; but nurse promised to look after her.'

'I will go up to her,' he returned; and then the brougham came round. Gavin lingered in the porch a moment, until the carriage wheels were no longer audible. A sudden memory of Lorraine, as she had stood there, came across him. How sweetly and pitifully she had looked at him; he could feel the touch of her warm soft hand as she drew him in. She had said so little; but the mere fact of her presence beside him had seemed to soothe him. How few women would have stood there not speaking to him in that silent but tender ministry. The wine he drank from her hand seemed to strengthen him, and made it possible for him to enter the chamber of death.

As he went up to the turret-room, he said, 'God bless her!' under his breath.

Muriel was lying on a couch by the fire; but she started up when she saw her brother. As he kissed her and said a kind word or two, she suddenly clung to him.

'Oh, Gavin, Gavin, how am I to bear it?'

'We must bear it together,' he said gently, sitting down beside her. 'My dear girl, why do you look at me like that? Surely it is my sorrow as well as yours?'

'Yes, of course ; but—oh, how am I to make you understand ? You have always been so good to her, you have never given her a moment of pain ; but when I think how little I ever did for her' —and here Muriel broke into choking sobs.

'My dear child,' he returned gently, 'one always reproaches oneself in such cases. Even with my darling Helen I found reason to torment myself. At such moments one's focus seems all wrong · little errors of manners, a few thoughtless words, are magnified fourfold. If I chose to be morbid I could easily accuse myself of a hundred failures.'

'Oh no, you were always so good and thoughtful ; but, Gavin, you must not try to comfort me. I was selfish. I only considered myself. I never troubled myself to think how dull she must be sitting alone ; but I know now. She has told me how much she has missed Maud and Flo.'

Gavin was silent. It was impossible to contradict this. How often he had quarrelled with Muriel because in his opinion she had neglected her mother. No ; it would do her no good to cheat her with false comfort. He wondered as he sat there, chafing her cold hands, what Mrs. Herbert would have found to say to her.

'Oh, Gavin, do say something to comfort me !' It was almost a cry, and then he put his arms round her.

'Poor child,' he said tenderly, 'you have been keeping all this to yourself ; but, indeed, there is no reason for this despair. Our dear mother would be sorely troubled if she could see you now. Granted that you were not always all that a daughter should be, has she not forgiven that long ago ? All these weeks you have been devoted to her. How often she has said to me, "Dear Muriel is such a comfort." I have heard that from her lips a dozen times.'

The fixed look of anguish in Muriel's eyes relaxed a little. During these last few weeks she had certainly striven to atone for the past. As the worn-out girl rested her aching head on Gavin's shoulder a faint comfort seemed to steal over her. She would never forgive herself, but her mother had forgiven her. Yes, after all God had been good to her ; time had been given to her. She had been allowed to minister to her dying mother, and there had been many hours of sweet converse. Gavin was right, and she ought not to abandon herself to this despair. Could she forget how tenderly her mother had provided for this hour ?

'You must not fret too much when I leave you, Muriel,' she had said once. 'Promise me, my dear child, that you will try not to be morbid. I know you so well, my darling, and how you will exaggerate things. I only want you to say to yourself, " My mother loved me dearly, and I will try to be happy for her sake." ' Often she had said something of this kind.

Yes, her mother, her sweet mother, had forgiven her ; and Gavin had forgiven her too. But for long years Muriel would carry that secret load of remorse within her heart. If one sows the wind, one must reap the whirlwind ; if tares of unkindness and selfishness mar the fair home harvest, the sheaves will be less abundant. Alas, what fruitless tears fall on many a dead face! What passionate appeals for forgiveness are poured in the deaf ears that would have rejoiced to hear them !

' If we had known,' that is what we tell ourselves ; ' if we had guessed that our beloved would have been taken from us, our words would have been kinder and less grudging ; but now there only remains an infinite remorse.'

Muriel's conscience was awake at last. Her mother's death-bed had taught her the bitterest of all lessons, that, like Esau, there may be no adequate ' room for repentance, though we seek it carefully with tears.' Others may forgive us, may speak kindly to us, may try to heal our hurt, but we do well not to forgive ourselves. Through pain we may rise, perchance, purified, to lead a nobler future that may fit us to meet our dear one again.

CHAPTER XLI

'When Time will suffer no delay,
But drives us on from day to day ;
When Duty at the cross roads stands,
And, stretching right and left her hands,
Bewildered seems.'

ANNIE MATHESON.

ELLISON was somewhat taken aback when she saw Lorraine waiting for her on the platform ; she had been looking forward to the long drive home with Gavin ; but she grew very pale as she read his note. Gavin's mother, bright genial Cousin Louise, was very dear to her ; her first words as the brougham drove off from the station door were : ' I ought not to have gone, we were both too sanguine ' ; and in a voice of deeper distress, ' all my life I shall be sorry for this, that you were there and not I.' She meant no unkindness by this speech, and Lorraine did not misunderstand her ; nevertheless she winced in the darkness ; it was not her fault that she had been obliged to take Ellison's place—that Colonel Trevor's mother had died literally in her arms—that it had been her mission to comfort and strengthen him. Ellison said no more ; most likely she felt that words were futile and inadequate at such moments. She leant back in the carriage and shed quiet tears, while Lorraine, alert and miserable, watched the dark winding of the road. Why was imagination so pitiless ? Why was she compelled to recall against her will those minutes when she had stood silently beside him in the library with that tightening grasp upon her dress ? She had had no wish to move, and yet it had given her a strange feeling of embarrassment to be so detained. If Ellison had been in her place—and then for one brief instant she seemed to picture it all ; she could see them going upstairs hand in hand, and standing

21

together by the dead woman's side. Ellison would have the right to comfort him, she—— but here Lorraine checked herself. Where were her thoughts carrying her? Was it any business of hers? She grew hot and then cold. How interminable the drive seemed to her as well as to Ellison.

Ellison went straight to Brae House, but Lorraine begged to be set down before they reached the lodge. She walked through the dark meadow, finding her way with difficulty. Once an instinctive sense of danger made her pause; in the darkness she had strayed from the path and was at the edge of the pond; another step and she would have been in the water. Ellison, preoccupied with her sad thoughts, had forgotten to warn her; all the inhabitants of the Farm carried lanterns when they crossed the Brae meadow. Lorraine shuddered as she retraced her steps; her nerves had experienced a shock, but there was no warm glow of thankfulness in her heart for a peril escaped. What if she had died the same death as her boy, would it have been so terrible after all? They would have known how it happened, that in the darkness she had stumbled into the pond; she would have been too confused to find her way out, and her heavy fur-lined cloak would have dragged her down. It was not the death she would have chosen—the icy water on a winter's evening—but was life so sweet to her that she cared to preserve it? She had good friends, but was she absolutely necessary to any human being? Perhaps Muriel would miss her most, but Ellison would have her lover to console her. Lorraine was in a strangely abnormal state, or she would not have harrowed up her feelings by imagining the tragedy; her sweet, wholesome nature had been crushed by trouble, and had not yet recovered its healthy tone; her nerves were not in order either, for a dark figure coming close to her in the lane made her scream. Dorcas, who was at the side door, ran out to her.

'It is only Bates, ma'am,' she said hurriedly, 'George Bates who works in the stables at Brae House; he ought to be ashamed of himself for startling you in this way'—raising her voice purposely—but the man took no notice, and went on. 'He knows he has no call to be loafing about our place'; and Dorcas spoke in a tone of deep resentment.

'Oh, it was Bates, was it?' returned Lorraine, with a little laugh. 'I thought it was a tipsy man, for he lurched against me, but I suppose it was the darkness,' and then she gave another little laugh strangely unmirthful—first the pond and then George Bates!

Dorcas tossed her pretty little head as she turned up the lamp and stirred the fire into a cheerful blaze. Lorraine sank down in an easy-chair and let the girl wait on her. Dorcas removed her wraps, and brought her a cup of hot coffee, and warmed her slippers.

'Dear heart, ma'am, your feet are like ice!' she exclaimed; 'and your boots are sopping wet.'

'I went a little too near the pond, Dorcas,' returned Lorraine wearily; but her tone was so matter of fact that the girl took no alarm.

'Drat that fellow,' she was saying to herself as she knelt in the firelight rubbing Lorraine's feet. All the servants at Brae Farm loved to wait on Mrs. Herbert. Poor Dorcas had some cause for her displeasure. George Bates was her *bête noir*. Two years ago he had been in Ellison's service, but she had dismissed him on account of a flagrant act of disobedience. The man had complained to Colonel Trevor, and had been so plausible in his excuses that he had been induced to take him on as a stable helper.

'He is a clever fellow, and I think Williams will find him useful,' he had said to Ellison, but she had shaken her head incredulously.

'Bates is a ne'er-do-weel,' she said decidedly. 'Oh, he is clever enough, but I am afraid you will repent your soft-heartedness, Gavin. Sam Brattle begged me more than once to dismiss him, as he and Joe Brand got on so badly together. He has given us no end of trouble; he has taken a fancy to Dorcas's rosy cheeks, and pesters the poor girl with his attentions. She will have nothing to say to him, and very rightly too, for his character is none of the best, if we are to believe Sam.'

'Give a dog a bad name and hang him; that is what all you good women do,' grumbled Gavin obstinately. 'I don't believe there is much harm about the fellow, though he does not hit Dorcas's fancy. I told him I would give him a month's trial, so I must keep my word.'

'Very well; only make him understand that he is to keep away from Brae Farm,' returned Ellison with a good-natured shrug at Gavin's perversity. She never argued with him; one day he would come round to her opinion and repent of his misplaced clemency, and then she would be magnanimous and not crow over him.

George Bates had kept his place at Brae House ever since, and Williams assured his master that he was a decent fellow and earned his wages. 'He understands horses as well as I do myself, colonel,' he answered, 'and I have never seen the stables in better order. Davis will tell you the same. He is a bit surly at times, but none of us takes any notice. I suppose most of us have our tempers.'

So George Bates kept his place; but, unfortunately for Dorcas's peace of mind, he still sneaked down to the Farm. Dorcas could not be induced to listen to him; she detested the very sight of him. 'I hope I shall do better than that, or I would sooner be a maid to the end of my days,' she would say to Mrs. Drake. 'The idea of my keeping company with a surly, ill-conditioned fellow like Bates.' But alas! Bates could not be made to take a final no. He was in grim earnest; he had good wages, he had given up drinking at the *Waggon and Horses*, he had a tidy cottage, and he was bent on having a wife; and all Dorcas's contemptuous speeches and head-tosses could not prevent him from loafing about the farmyard.

'They are all a bit skittish at first,' he said to Davis in a moment of confidence, as they smoked their pipes together in the stable-yard. 'It is just like that new mare of the Colonel's; she is a bit playful and stand-offish, but she has got no vice.'

'There I differ, Bates,' returned the groom; 'me and Williams don't hold that opinion at all. She is not exactly nasty tempered, but she is nervous, and a trifle upsets her. I hope the Colonel won't drive that mare when he goes out with Miss Lee. Williams said to me, the day Madge Wildfire came home, "She is awkward and touchy, and I don't half like the looks of her." These were Williams's very words.'

'Then Williams is a duffer, and you are another, Davis,' returned Bates crossly. 'Do you think the Colonel cannot judge a horse's temper by this time? he is no chicken, and knows a thing or two. But there—when you and Williams get a maggot in your heads there is no good contradicting you,' and Bates laid down his pipe in a dudgeon, and went into the stables to attend to the maligned animal.

'I know some one who is awkward and touchy too,' muttered Davis, with a grin. 'They are about a pair of them, Madge Wildfire and Bates,' and then he strolled off to his cottage.

Lorraine kept her own counsel and said nothing about the pond and George Bates. Ellison had quite enough to worry her just then, and was less observant than usual of her cousin's looks; it was natural that Gavin's trouble should occupy her, and she was grateful to Lorraine for discharging her household tasks, and so setting her free to be with him. Lorraine herself spent an hour or two daily with Muriel—who continued utterly prostrate—but she saw nothing of Colonel Trevor. During the funeral she remained closely shut up in the turret-room; but Ellison took her rightful place that day, and her deep mourning was more for the mother-in-law than for the cousin.

'It is a blessing the Colonel has Miss Lee to look after him, now the mistress has gone,' remarked Mrs. Crane the housekeeper to her crony, Mrs. Williams; for all the household were slightly contemptuous of Miss Muriel's fads. 'What does she want with all that book-learning and those outlandish languages, when she has not her living to get?' remarked Mrs. Williams. 'I don't hold with so much learning myself; why, Williams was only saying this morning that Miss Muriel has a good fifteen thousand of her own. She is no beauty, as he says, and is a sickly body at the best of times; but fifteen thousand is not to be despised, and many a man would be glad to have her'; and to this Mrs. Crane agreed.

In the servants' hall there was plenty of plain speaking. They had dearly loved their kindly, genial mistress; but human nature delights in every form of excitement, and the stately funeral with its long line of private carriages was felt to be a great consolation. That evening, though Mrs. Crane's eyes were red with the tears she had shed since morning, there was a subdued cheerfulness in her voice as she and Mrs. Williams discussed the probable date of the Colonel's wedding; and the opinion was general that Miss Muriel —poor, dear, young lady—would live at the Farm with Mrs. Herbert. The idea had originated with Mrs. Crane, and had been received with acclamations.

Christmas Day was spent as quietly as possible at Brae House and Brae Farm; the usual feasting was carried on in the servants' halls, but the brother and sister dined alone. Muriel had proposed that Ellison should join them; she thought the tête-à-tête dinner would be too oppressive to Gavin, but he negatived this at once. Mrs. Herbert could not be left alone; he wondered that Muriel should propose such a thing. They must get through the day as best they could. Gavin spoke with unusual irritability, but Muriel for once had tact, and held her peace.

Finally, Ellison of her own accord suggested that she and Lorraine should walk up to Brae after dinner. It would make a break in the day for Gavin; and Muriel thankfully agreed.

Lorraine pleaded to be left at home, but Ellison would not hear of this. 'If you stay at home, I shall remain too,' she replied with calm decision; and Lorraine felt herself obliged to yield.

Gavin's countenance was a little inscrutable when Muriel informed him of Ellison's thoughtfulness. 'They will come up to coffee; it will make such a nice break in the long evening,' she said; but Gavin made no reply to this. In his heart he thought even the long, monotonous evening alone with Muriel would have been more conducive to his comfort. He had not seen Mrs. Herbert for a fortnight, but he too had remembered far too vividly those silent minutes in the library.

Ellison thought Gavin more restless and out of spirits than ever that evening ; as they sat together at one end of the long, softly-lighted room, she noticed that he was unusually absent, and that more than once he answered her at random ; but her manner only grew more tender. 'My poor, dear Gavin,' she said to herself, 'Cousin Louise was right when she begged me to marry him as soon as possible' ; and then in the depths of her true, womanly heart, she vowed that no delay on her part should keep him waiting.   'If he were to ask me to marry him to-morrow I would do it,' she thought, with a sudden rush of tenderness.   But no such thought was in Gavin's mind, as he sat there beside his betrothed ; even as he talked to her, his restless glances roved to the firelit corner, where Mrs. Herbert lay back in the deep easy-chair talking to Muriel.

He was unable even to hear a word, their voices were so subdued, and from where he sat he could not see Lorraine's face ; but the graceful folds of her black drapery, and the smoothly coiled brown hair, and the line of cheek and brow were distinctly perceptible, he could even see the slender foot in its neat slipper resting on the rug.   The sight of that fair womanly presence reposing by his hearth filled him with restlessness and vague trouble ; he longed with intensity of longing to cross the room and put some question to her—that he might look in the depths of her soft, sad eyes—but he held himself by main force in his place.

'Did you hear me, Gavin ?   I was telling you about Margaret Mervyn's plan for the summer.'

'Were you, dear ?   Oh yes, I know, and I think the scheme excellent ; but she will not have you this time,' turning to her quickly.

'Oh no, Margaret will not expect that,' replied Ellison, with a sudden blush that became her well.   Margaret was going to the baths in July, but by that time she would have been Gavin's wife for months.

'You will not wait longer than Easter,' Mrs. Trevor had said to her, 'the wedding can be as quiet as you and my boy wish ; but you must marry him then'; and Ellison had promised that it should be as Gavin wished.   Gavin played his part of *fiancé* bravely that evening.   He left Mrs. Herbert's entertainment to Muriel; it was Ellison who at last gently recalled him to his duty.

'It is getting quite late, Gavin,' she said presently, 'and we shall soon be going home.   I ought not to monopolise you so completely, you have not even spoken to poor Lorraine.'

'Then I will speak to her now,' he returned slowly, rising to his feet; for the last hour he had fought with the temptation, but now Ellison had sent him from her.

Muriel gave him up her place, but he made no attempt to sit down. Lorraine looked up at him a little shyly, as he stood there with one arm resting against the mantelpiece. In her secret thoughts she had wondered more than once that he had addressed no word to her—a silent handshake on entering, and a proffered chair, and then a general remark on the wetness of the weather, this had been the extent of his conversation, and then he had left her to Muriel and seated himself beside Ellison.

It was just as it should be, and yet—as Muriel had talked on— more than once her attention had wandered; again she was standing bare-headed in the wintry wind, she could see his fixed look as he tried to pass her, and then there were those minutes in the library, he had needed her then; did he know that he was preventing her from leaving him, as he sat there silently with bowed head? there was something sacred, indescribably sacred, to Lorraine in that little scene.

Was he going to speak to her now? But at that moment Gavin turned to her abruptly, and their eyes met. 'Are you tired? you are looking very pale; but of course the day has tried you, it has tried us all. This is not a merry Christmas for any of us; but it was good of you and Ellison to come.' Then a wan smile came to Lorraine's face.

'I wanted to stay away,' she half whispered; 'but Ellison would not leave me.'

'It would have been kinder if she had,' he returned in a curiously guarded tone, and then he turned on his heel and left her wondering what he had meant by that vague speech. That night Gavin carried the lantern, and Ellison walked beside him; as the footway was narrow Lorraine followed them, but just before they came to the pond, Gavin waited for her. 'There is room on this side,' he said in a kind voice, as he shifted the lantern to his left hand, and put his right hand gently on her arm, 'please do not walk behind us any more, you as well as Ellison are under my care'; and then Lorraine knew that he had purposely placed himself and Ellison between her and the pond. It was his old kind care for her, and in the darkness the tears rushed to her eyes—how she had missed her friend! but to-night, for this moment at least, he was beside her again.

CHAPTER XLII

MADGE WILDFIRE

'And yet, because I love thee, I obtain
From that same love this vindicating grace,
To live on still in love, and yet in vain,—
To bless thee, yet renounce thee to thy face.'

ELIZABETH BARRETT BROWNING.

THE following afternoon Lorraine and her faithful escort Tweed walked rapidly up the Bramfield Road; it was hardly a day for a long country walk, the wind was intensely cold and nipping, and Sam Brattle had informed them that morning that there would be a fall of snow before night.

When Lorraine announced her intention of walking to Bramfield, Ellison had tried gently to dissuade her: 'These long solitary walks are not good for you,' she said in her sensible way; 'if they exhilarated and refreshed you, I would not say a word, but you always come back so dead tired.'

'One must be either tired or restless,' returned Lorraine rather impatiently. Ellison's kind solicitude only vexed her. 'How is she to understand?' she said to herself as she left the room; 'if one had pleasant thoughts it would be easy to sit by the fireside; but that bright, cheerful room seems to stifle me. I suffer less when I am battling with the wind, and even the greyness that Ellison thinks so dismal seems to soothe me.'

But an hour later Lorraine was forced to own that she would have been wise to have taken Ellison's advice and stayed quietly at home—the bitter wind seemed to lash her mercilessly as she toiled down the long roads; never in her life had she felt such cold, and particles of snow were already beginning to fall, Tweed's black coat was powdered with them as he stalked on bravely by his mistress's side.

Lorraine was beginning to wish herself at home—that softly-lighted room with its glowing fire and circle of easy chairs seemed unusually alluring. In another half-hour Ruth would be drawing the heavy curtains over the window, and the lamps would be lighted. It was early still, but the afternoon was unusually sombre. Lorraine was beginning to fear that the darkness would overtake her, and yet it was impossible to walk faster in the teeth of such a wind. Perhaps she was not as strong as she used to be ; her breath seemed shorter, and her legs ached terribly. Now and then she stood still to recover herself, and during one of these pauses she heard the sound of wheels coming rapidly behind her. Fearing recognition—for probably it was some one from Price's Folly — she walked on as quickly as she could, but the next moment a familiar voice arrested her.

'Mrs. Herbert, what on earth has brought you all this distance ? it is not fit for a dog to be out. Do you know that a snowstorm is coming on ?' Colonel Trevor's tone was remonstrant, almost displeased, as he checked his spirited mare and bade Bates go to her head.

'I wanted a walk, and I never thought it would be as bad as this,' she stammered ; 'but I am making all the haste I can ; please drive on, Colonel Trevor, your mare seems fidgetty' ; for Madge Wildfire was backing the phaeton on to the path in rather an alarming manner.

'She does not like standing ; keep her steady for a moment, Bates, while Mrs. Herbert gets in. Good heavens !' rather irritably, as Lorraine timidly drew back and shook her head, 'do you suppose I am going to drive on and leave you two miles from home with a snowstorm impending ?'

'I would much rather walk,' returned Lorraine, with a pleading look : she had the greatest reluctance to be driven home by Colonel Trevor. Ellison would think it so strange, and then she was a little afraid of the mare ; she did not like the way she laid back her ears and lifted her feet. 'Do let me walk,' she finished a little tamely.

'If you walk, I shall walk too,' replied Gavin, throwing down the reins with an impatient frown—women, even the best of them, could try a man's patience, he thought, for he was not in the best of tempers. Mrs. Herbert was not behaving with her usual good sense this afternoon—any child could have seen that a snowstorm was coming on, even he found the wind cruelly cutting, and how was a delicate woman to brave it with impunity ; he had no right to coerce her, but if she chose to persist in her foolhardiness he must keep her company, that was all.

Lorraine gave a little cry as she saw him prepare to spring to the ground. She had no chance of getting her own way ; his will was stronger than hers. 'Don't jump down, Colonel Trevor,' she exclaimed. 'I will do as you wish—if—if you are sure—the mare is safe.'

'She is safe enough,' he answered shortly, and then Lorraine clambered into the high phaeton ; when Gavin tucked the fur-lined rug round her, the soft warmth was very grateful to her. Tweed gave a reproachful whine, and his tail drooped disconsolately—he was left in the cold ; then Bates gave the mare her head and she started with a playful plunge or two, Tweed jumping up and barking beside her. 'Don't be afraid, Madge is only in a hurry to get to her stable,' observed Gavin, as he noticed the startled look in Lorraine's eyes. 'There is no vice in her, but, like the rest of her sex, she needs a strong hand.' And then his voice changed into reproachful tenderness as he stooped to adjust the rug more comfortably. 'Is this the way you take care of yourself, Mrs. Herbert ? have you no regard for your health ? I wonder Ellison allows you to do these mad things.'

In spite of her nervousness, an amused smile came to Lorraine's lips. 'Ellison and I have agreed to bear with each other's little idiosyncrasies,' she replied. 'Neither of us could endure control. Ellison looked at me in a shocked way when I told her I was going out. She evidently thought me crazy.'

'No wonder ; you have gone down ten per cent in my opinion. I used to think you a sensible woman, Mrs. Herbert. I never imagined you could have behaved so recklessly. Do you set no value on your health ? one has to live, you know, so one may as well grease the chariot wheels. I could not believe my eyes when I saw you just now, but of course I recognised my old friend Tweed : it was no business of mine, but I felt tremendously angry— I do still.'

'Angry with me.' Poor misguided Lorraine ! those curt, displeased sentences were sweet as the softest music to her ears ; he cared enough for her, then, to scold her for her recklessness ; never had she seen him so put out. The calm, suave Colonel Trevor was unmistakably out of temper.

'Yes, I am angry with you,' turning round with a keen, pleading glance. 'I am angry and hurt that you have so little regard for your friends, that you are trying to kill yourself. Oh, there are a hundred ways of committing suicide,' as she stared at him with wide-open eyes, 'it is not always sudden. There are slow processes—over-fatigue, cold, want of patience with your life—a cowardly refusal to endure your troubles ; oh, one can go on enumerating for ever ; but'—his voice again breaking into tender-ness—' I could never have believed that you—you could have done such things.'

The pitiless lash of the north wind was less stinging than this well-deserved rebuke. Lorraine's face grew hot. Yes, he was right, and she had done ill, her aching limbs and short breath were signs that she was using herself too hardly. 'A cowardly refusal to bear your troubles,' that was where the lash cut deepest. Gavin was speaking the truth roughly to the woman he loved, but the sight of her pinched face and blue lips as she stood by the road-side had filled him with impotent rage. He would have given ten years of his life to be able to protect and cherish her ; and honour and loyalty to his betrothed compelled him to stand apart and do nothing. His angry words were only the outcome of his hopeless love—a despairing appeal to be saved from the misery of seeing this waste of a sweet life.

What Lorraine would have answered she never knew, for at that moment the hideous braying of a lonely donkey from a field near proved too much for Madge Wildfire's nerves. The uncouth grey monster in the distance had disturbed her from a delicious vision of her warm stall and the crisp, toothsome oats that awaited her. Madge's four feet seemed in the air at once as she plunged madly across the road, and then back against a heap of flint stones. In another instant the phaeton was overturned, and Gavin, scrambling out of a deep ditch, saw to his horror that Mrs. Herbert, who had been flung into the road, was still lying motionless and inert, with Tweed licking her face.

The mare was still on her feet, and Bates, who was unhurt, had her firmly by the head, but the phaeton was on its side against the heap of stones. A cold sweat of agony broke out on Gavin's brow as he knelt down by Lorraine ; his hands shook as though with the palsy as he raised her head on his arm. How white her face looked, and her eyes were closed. Good heavens, if he had killed her ! In the anguish of that fear he lost all self-control.

' Oh, my darling, my darling ! have I killed you ? ' he exclaimed in a low but audible voice of intense emotion. ' Speak to me, Lorraine—one word—or I shall go mad. Let me see your sweet eyes, if only for an instant. Do you hear me, darling ? ' And, alas for her own peace of mind, Lorraine had heard every word. The shock had stunned her for a moment, but she had not wholly lost consciousness. She had felt Tweed's rough tongue licking her face, and had recognised Gavin's touch. ' Darling, darling ! just one word.' But how was she to answer him ? His voice thrilled through and through her as she lay there with her cheek against

his coat sleeve. The next minute she felt his lips upon her hair,
and then she tried to rise.

· 'Let me get up. I am not hurt, only stunned,' she whispered,
and his 'Thank God !' was distinctly audible to her. Gavin said no
more as he assisted her to rise, and guided her gently to a fallen
trunk. For the moment the bliss of hearing her voice, of knowing
that she was alive and unhurt, prevented him from entertaining
any embarrassing recollections.

'Sit there while I get the phaeton up,' he said in the same
moved tones ; and then he wrapped the warm rug tenderly round
her and left her.

Life was still precious to him, must always be precious as long
as she lived beside him. That instant of mutual danger had lifted
his love into a higher plane. She could never be his, his faith was
pledged to another woman ; but as long as her slender feet walked
this earth he would not refuse comfort. Loss, disappointment, was
no new thing to him—the furnace of affliction had been heated
sevenfold when he had stood in the light of the Indian moon
beside his wife's grave. Meanwhile Lorraine sat shivering and
huddled up in the fur-rug. She was still a little dizzy from the
shock. Had she been dreaming ? but no, it was far too real—those
broken sentences, the agitated tone, and the gleam of tenderness in
the deep-set eyes, had revealed the truth to Lorraine. She, and not
Ellison, was the beloved of his heart.

And then a curious thing happened ; for the same instant that
she grasped this fact she told herself that she had known it long
ago, that as surely as she was sitting there with her poor dizzy
brain whirling from the sudden revulsion, so surely did she know
with absolute certainty that they loved each other as only two such
natures can love. 'God help us both !' broke from Lorraine's pale
lips. And as she drew the fur closer a strange numbness seemed
to deaden all sensation, the snow-flakes falling round her only increased her giddiness. She felt weak, stunned, and yet intensely
alive. There was something for her to do, if she could only know
what it was. Poor Lorraine! Love the Pilgrim had met her suddenly
at the partings of the way, and had shown her His wounded side.
There was no garland of red roses in his bruised hands, and something like a thorny crown encircled his pallid brow. Suffering and
not roses, and the deep dark stain of martyred affections. The
Divine Master that she had followed all her short, troubled life
was demanding a further sacrifice.

The brown eyes grew strained and wistful as they followed
Gavin's movements. How strong and capable he looked as he put
his shoulder to the wheel. Bates was still at the mare's head, but

Gavin unassisted had moved the phaeton off the stones. He was still breathing heavily from the effort as he crossed the road.

'It is all right now,' he said, trying to speak cheerfully. 'The phaeton is uninjured; only one wheel got caught on the stone heap. Do you feel a little better? Let me help you up, for there is no time to lose; the flakes are getting thicker.'

'I am very foolish, very unreasonable,' returned Lorraine, nervously. 'Please forgive me, Colonel Trevor, but I cannot get into that phaeton again; the idea terrifies me.'

'The mare is quite quiet,' he urged. 'She will go like a lamb now. It was only that ass braying that startled her. Do you think I would expose you to any danger? Will you not trust to me this once?' with dangerous persuasiveness.

Lorraine's answer was to put her hand in his, and rise slowly from her seat, but as he stooped to assist her he saw her face. 'You will do it to please me,' he said kindly; 'but it will frighten you to death! No, you shall walk, and I will send Bates on.' And without waiting for Lorraine's answer, he threw the rug into the phaeton and told the man to drive on. 'Mrs. Herbert is too nervous to get in again,' he said coolly. 'Handle the mare carefully, Bates; she is in rather a touchy mood.' The man touched his hat and moved away.

'A pretty kettle of fish,' muttered Bates, as he drove off. 'Did ever any one hear the likes of that? I wonder what my lady up at Brae Farm would say to such goings on. It would take her down a peg or two, I warrant. "I won't have you loafing about the place, George Bates, and making love to my maids,"—as hoighty-toighty as you like. Well, here's a rum go; to think Davis should be laid up, and me taking his place, and for this to happen,' and Bates grinned ominously, for those impassioned sentences had reached his ears.

'Now let us walk on as fast as possible,' observed Gavin, as he put Lorraine's hand upon his arm—the touch of that light hand resting reluctantly on his coat sleeve seemed to thrill through him. If only the walk would not hurt her, it would be bliss to him to be alone with her; and the white, whirling snow-flakes, shutting them into a new, strange world, gave him a sort of vertigo.

'Are you sure this will not hurt you?' he said suddenly; the caressing voice made Lorraine shiver, and tingle down to her finger-ends.

'Colonel Trevor,' and then she stopped, and he could feel her hand tremble; 'oh, do not speak to me in that voice,' she burst out, 'it hurts me somehow—it seems wrong—wrong to you and me, and,' in a lower voice, 'to Ellison'; then he knew that he had betrayed himself. Good heavens! perhaps she had not lost consciousness ; she must have heard his frantic words.

'What do you mean?' he stammered ; 'how have I had the misfortune to offend you ? Lorraine, is it possible that you heard all I said ?'

'Yes,' she returned gently. 'I wish you to know that—but you have not offended me ; you were frightened, you thought I was hurt or dying, or you would never have spoken so'—and then a great sigh burst from her : how sweet, how passing sweet, death would have seemed to her at that moment.

'What can I say?' he returned hoarsely. 'I cannot take back those words. Lorraine, you have my secret, but I never meant you to know. Forgive me, dearest, or I shall never know peace again.'

'Hush, hush, for pity's sake !' she pleaded, 'there is nothing to forgive, and you are safe with me. It is not your fault. Oh I know that well ; it is a great misfortune ; a sad trouble that has come to both of us.' Then a man's fierce joy of possession seized mightily on Gavin.

'You care for me, then ?' he asked eagerly ; 'you love me, as I love you? Lorraine, my darling, let me hear that once from your lips.'

'You are wrong to ask me that,' she returned with grave tenderness ; 'it will make you no happier to know that I care. How could I help it when you were so good to me ?—hush, let me speak ; there is nothing you ought to say, nothing that I ought to hear. There has been too much said already; Colonel Trevor, you will always be a dear friend ; I shall pray daily that this may pass, and that you may love Ellison as she deserves to be loved. You will be noble, will you not? you will keep your faith to her ; you will try to make her happy ; and I—I must go away for a little while until all this grows easier.'

'Easier for you or for me, do you mean ?' holding her hands, and speaking with fierce insistence. It was growing dark, they could not see each other's faces ; they two stood alone hand in hand, and heart to heart, in a film of white snow-flakes. Lorraine made no effort to withdraw her hands from that strong grasp, but her sweet voice went out to him with a tremble in it:

'I am a weak woman, and I am very unhappy ; as you are strong, be merciful and spare me.' A world of confession was in these words—they appealed to Gavin's higher nature.

'God bless and take care of you, and help me to do the right,' he returned in a low voice ; and then very humbly, 'Lorraine, it will be no disloyalty to Ellison—will you let me kiss you once before we part ?'

For one moment there was silence, and he took it for consent and stooped over her; but very gently she put his face aside.

'No,' she said, with a sweetness of tone that even at that moment gave him exquisite pleasure. 'I must not have that kiss; it would be robbing Ellison. Let me give you something instead,' and before he could guess her intention, she had brought his hand to her lips.

'This is for the friend who was true to himself and me,' she said gently, and then she took his arm again, as though she needed support, and they walked on to Brae Farm almost in silence.

CHAPTER XLIII

'M. My fate, my fate is lonely !
J.   So it is—
      I know it is.
M. And pity breaks my heart.'
                              JEAN INGELOW:

'If thou hadst strength, 'twas heaven that strength bestowed.'
                              HOMER, *Iliad.*

ALL their life long Lorraine and Gavin Trevor remembered that walk ; but in after days they never spoke of it. That silence, so all-pervading, so pregnant with intense meaning, the mysterious whiteness of the snow-flakes, that seemed to envelop them in a softly-folding shroud, the icy coldness of the atmosphere, all lent a vagueness, a dim, nebulous obscurity to the hour at once undefinable and uncommunicable ; and yet, strange paradox of lovers, no speech could have been so lucid and explicit as that long silence.

A trifling action on Gavin's part showed that nothing escaped his notice. Lorraine had just discovered that the hand resting on his arm was growing numb with the cold, when she suddenly felt a warm, enveloping pressure. Gavin had placed his right hand over hers, and Lorraine understanding the kindly motive made no resistance.

At the little green gate they paused by mutual consent, but Gavin showed no intention of entering.

'Will you tell Ellison that I cannot come in this evening, but that I will see her to-morrow ?' he said hurriedly ; and then as Lorraine bowed her head, and mutely extended her hand, he detained it. 'Wait a moment ; I want to ask you a question. You will not go away yet ?'

'I do not know. I cannot settle things in a moment,' she returned quickly. Why had he asked her this? Did he not know that she would only feel safe when she was a hundred miles away? After the revelation this evening no human power would have kept her in Highlands. Already she had vowed to herself that she would never return until Ellison had become Gavin's wife. The question seemed futile to her; it was unnecessary, it was cruel of him to ask it. But Gavin had no selfish purport in his inquiry; he was thinking solely of her comfort; it would lie heavily on his conscience if through his recklessness she were driven away from home in this inclement weather. But he little knew the strength and tenacity that lay under Lorraine's softness.

'Promise me one thing,' he urged, as his grasp tightened insensibly, 'that you will go to no place where you cannot expect reasonable and sufficient comfort. You have had hardships enough already. I will not endure any repetition of your former life.'

Lorraine shuddered. Did he really fear that she would go back to Beaumont Street, to those hideous streets where the children played all day long in the gutter, where the shrill voices of women seemed to sound in her ears day and night? Beaumont Street without Tedo—never—never!

'I think I can promise you that,' she returned. 'Will you let me go now, Colonel Trevor?'

'You shall go in a moment; but there is one more word to say. Do nothing in a hurry; you are safe from me; you can trust me to keep out of your way as long as you remain at Highlands. I respect you too highly; I love you far too well to harass you with my presence. After to-night I shall make no attempt to speak to you, or to interfere with your future. Do you believe this?'

'I believe you implicitly.'

'And you will do nothing rashly. You will be kind to me, and take care of yourself. Lorraine—Lorraine, for God's sake promise me this!'

'I will take care of myself. Good-night, Colonel Trevor, and thank you for all your goodness'; and then she turned resolutely away. What was the use of prolonging such painful moments? Could anything lessen her misery? She loved this man, and he knew it; and the knowledge could give neither of them happiness.

The moment Lorraine rang the bell Ellison came to the door. Her fair face looked flushed and anxious.

'Oh, Lorraine dear,' she exclaimed, 'how late you are! I have been so fidgetty about you the last hour. I was so afraid

22

you had missed your way.' And then as the light showed her
Lorraine's pallid face and dishevelled appearance, she uttered a
shocked exclamation. 'What has happened? Why do you look
like this?'

'Let me come in and I will tell you,' returned Lorraine a little
breathlessly. Ellison's scrutiny made her nervous. She turned
away hastily, and entered the sitting-room. It looked just as she
had imagined it; a great log was sputtering and hissing and
diffusing tiny blue flames, the curtains were drawn, the lamps
lighted, tea was on the round table. Tweed sniffed approvingly at
the pile of muffins frizzling comfortably on the little brass tripod,
and then lay down stiffly on the rug before the fire. Lorraine
sank into the big easy-chair, and drew off her old gloves hurriedly;
she had folded them away and thrust them into her pocket before
Ellison had finished stirring the fire; she would never wear them
again, they should be sacred to her—relics to be hoarded and
treasured.

Ellison did not at once repeat the question; she unfastened her
cousin's fur cloak, and unpinned her hat. As she did so she noticed
the battered and torn brim; then she gently smoothed the dis-
bevelled hair, and brought her a cup of hot tea. 'Drink this, and
then you shall tell me; you are too numbed with cold to talk just
now. I shall ring for Dorcas to bring your slippers. I hope she
has a good fire burning in your room.'

Lorraine tried to answer, but something impeded her speech,
and the tears rushed to her eyes; she was worn out with emotion,
and Ellison's sisterly care filled her with passionate gratitude.
Ellison saw two drops rolling slowly down her cheeks, but she
took no notice. 'Could I hurt a hair of her head?' Lorraine was
saying to herself a little wildly. 'I would rather die—I would
die ten times over to spare her trouble.'

But presently, when the choking sensation had passed, she began
to speak of her own accord.

'You were right, Ellison, I ought not to have been so reckless;
but I have had my punishment. Oh how cold it was, and then it
began to snow, and my breathing got oppressed, and I could not
walk fast; that Bramfield road is so long too. I was standing still
for a moment to recover my breath when Colonel Trevor drove up in
his phaeton.' Here Ellison uttered a low exclamation, but Lorraine
went on hurriedly. 'He was driving Madge Wildfire, and Bates,
not Davis, was with him. He seemed rather vexed to see me such
a distance from home; and as the snow was beginning to fall fast,
he insisted on my getting into the phaeton.'

'Of course he did,' in a matter-of-fact tone. 'Gavin is not the man to drive on when any one is in difficulty. I daresay he gave you a good lecture on your rash behaviour.'

'Yes,' returned Lorraine, and her head drooped. 'He was rather put out, and I daresay he thought me very foolish ; but the worst was to come. Just at the corner near Brook's Farm a donkey brayed, and Madge was frightened. She plunged dreadfully, and then backed against a stone heap, and we were all thrown out. Colonel Trevor was landed in a ditch, but it was full of dead leaves, and he was not a bit hurt. I think I must have been stunned for a moment, and of course I am badly bruised ; and—and—I could not get into the phaeton again—so we walked home.'

'Why did not Gavin come in and tell me all this himself?' observed Ellison abruptly. She had turned pale at Lorraine's narration, and there was an uneasy look in her eyes. 'You are not keeping anything back from me, Lorraine? You are sure Gavin is not hurt? It is so strange'—knitting her brows; 'it is not like his usual thoughtfulness. He might have known it would have made me happier to have seen him for a minute.'

'He was cold and tired, and he wanted to see after the mare,' returned Lorraine, speaking with nervous haste. 'He is not hurt at all—as I told you, the ditch was full of dead leaves ; but he has torn his coat'—some inspiration induced Lorraine to say that. 'And he was dreadfully splashed, for the ditch was not quite dry. He told me to say that he would see you to-morrow ' ; and then Ellison's brow cleared, and she turned her attention to Lorraine.

'I shall tell Dorcas to warm your bed, and take up some hot water ; you must go to bed at once, you do not look fit to be up ; let me give you some more tea.' Lorraine did not refuse the tea, but she could eat nothing ; she was badly bruised—as she had told Ellison—and her head was beginning to ache. When she had finished her tea she went upstairs, and Ellison followed her. Lorraine would willingly have dispensed with her help, but she dared not say so ; reluctance would only have excited Ellison's suspicion. The fire burned brightly. Lorraine could not refrain from a sigh of satisfaction as she laid her head on the lavender-scented pillows. Ellison looked at her pale face anxiously ; Lorraine was certainly much thinner, she thought, as she went downstairs to write a note to Gavin.

'My dearest, why did you not come in for one moment?' she wrote, 'it would have saved me so much anxiety, and I would not have detained you. Lorraine assures me that you are not hurt, but I cannot be easy; send me one line by Daniel to tell me you are all right. I hope you will get rid of Madge Wildfire—I never trusted her — you remember I told you so, and Sam Brattle agreed with me. If you want to please me you will not drive her again.

'Dearest Gavin, do, do be more careful of yourself, you must be prudent for my sake now. Lorraine looks sadly knocked up, and has gone to bed, her bruises are very painful; I think I shall send for Dr. Howell to-morrow if she is not better—she has gone through so much that even a slight shock may be too much for her.'

An odd refrain rang in Gavin's ears as he read this note. Where had he seen the fragment?—'But he killed her down at the brook'; and then again, 'Lorraine, Lorraine, Lorée.' And 'Lorraine, Lorraine, Lorée,' seemed to haunt him persistently. Her bruises were painful, sweet soul ; but what of his, would they ever cease to ache and throb, would there be any balm of Gilead for him ?

How thankful Lorraine was when the door closed on her cousin, and she could lie there staring at the fire, and thinking out the problem of the future. 'There is only one right and one wrong,' she said wearily to herself. 'The right thing is for me to go away, and then he will come back to her and do his duty, and find peace.' And then the urgent prayer went up from her troubled heart, 'Help me to right the wrong ; to do what is just and noble, and not to think of myself'; and then again, 'it is not his fault, neither he nor I am to blame ; but from to-day, the responsibility of her happiness will rest on us both. God do so to me, and more also, if I cause her a pang of sorrow that could be avoided ; rather than that, I would shake off the dust of this dear place and never see my boy's grave again.' And strong in her pure rectitude and sense of right, Lorraine meant every word she said ; there was no specious reserve in her prayer, no cowardly wish for delay, for procrastination. From this day, from the hour of Gavin's self-betrayal, the responsibility of Ellison's peace would rest heavily upon them.

Before she sank into an exhausted sleep, Lorraine had made her plans; and though the next day she was unable to rise from her bed, and Dr. Howell had prescribed perfect rest for her, Dorcas had posted a letter in Lorraine's handwriting when she went down to the village, and it was directed to 'Miss Bretherton, Black Nest, Nefydd Madoc.'

The letter was as follows :—

DEAR MISS BRETHERTON—Do you remember what you said to me that afternoon when I bade you good-bye?—we had been to the

White Cottage together, and we were standing at the sitting-room window at the *Waggon and Horses* looking down the bracken path. 'If you ever want a friend or are in any trouble, just write to me, and I will do what I can for you ; will you promise me this?' Those were your very words; and my answer was, 'Certainly I will'; and now I am going to keep my word. I am in great trouble—my child is dead—and my heart is almost broken ; but that is not all, there are reasons why I want to leave Highlands for a little. I cannot explain, I shall never be able to explain ; but I must have change immediately. Once you asked me to visit you ; if you renew that invitation I shall not refuse. You see that I am a woman of my word, and that I believe in you.—Yours very sincerely, LORRAINE HERBERT.

'Put the letter in the post yourself, Dorcas,' Lorraine had said ; and Dorcas had done her errand so discreetly that no one guessed it. The reply came by return of post ; Lorraine was still in bed ; and her bruises still ached. Ellison placed it on the breakfast tray. '"Nefydd Madoc!" that must be from Mother Hubbard,' she said to herself. 'How surprised Lorraine will be at getting a letter from her funny old lady.' But she forgot to question Lorraine about it until Dr. Howell had paid his visit upstairs. Lorraine flushed when she saw the post-mark; she took it up languidly and looked at the angular, sprawling characters. She had mastered the contents before she touched her breakfast.

DEAR MRS. HERBERT (it began)—If I had not guessed you were a woman of your word, I would not have troubled my head about you. The world is so full of fools and idiots that it is a comfort to meet with a sensible person. It is a blessing some one believes in me. I have not made many friends during my pilgrimage of sixty-five odd years — sixty-five I was last birthday — but that stupid old Pritchard is always telling me 'a woman is only as old as she looks,' so we may as well deduct fifteen years. So your boy is dead? My dear soul, he is in the safest place, if you will only believe it. I saw in a moment that he had no constitution ; you would never have been free from anxiety about him. Which of the ministering spirits — croup or convulsions — carried him off? Ah ! they have rough disguises these good angels, but they mean well, or else so many children would not die. There is a small boy down here at the Lodge—little Llewellyn—who died this morning, and his mother, Rebecca, is fretting herself nearly sick about him. He was a red-headed, impudent little Celt ; but you would never get Rebecca to believe that. I have been talking to her for an hour, and feeding her with good broth; but her idiot of a husband only cries over her and makes her worse. And they have five other torments alive and well—but then how is a cross-grained old maid to know how a mother feels under such circumstances ? So you mean. to pay Black Nest a visit ? Well, come, then, and Pritchard and I will make you as comfortable as we can. If you are not afraid of snow-capped mountains and clear dry cold, we can promise you snug quarters, and fires that would roast an ox.

Just telegraph the day and hour of your arrival. There is a capital fast train that leaves Euston at 10.55. You must sleep in the hotel and take that; the carriage shall meet you at Croes-fford, and bring you to Nefydd Madoc. It will be a three miles' drive in the dark; but David Fechan knows the road well, and so do Moll and Brown Ben.

Your room will be ready the day after to-morrow. Betty and Beckie are busy at it already, so don't keep it waiting.—I remain, my dear Mrs. Herbert, always yours sincerely,

MARION BRETHERTON.

Lorraine replaced the letter in the envelope, but she said nothing about it when Ellison came up to wish her good-morning. Muriel found her unusually silent when she paid her daily visit. She lay and listened with an abstracted look, as Muriel unfolded her budget of news. The Vincents had moved into the Vicarage, and Edmund and Effie were staying up at Brae House. Mr. Vincent had been so grateful when she had proposed it; he and Norah were coming to dinner that evening. She had asked them chiefly on Gavin's account. He seemed so out of spirits, and it was so difficult to rouse him. 'He misses dear mother so much,' she went on, her eyes filling with tears; 'it makes my heart ache to see him walking up and down the room of an evening. I do hope Ellison will marry him as soon as possible. I told Mr. Vincent so, and he agreed with me. He said the other evening that marriage always seemed to him such a solemn thing, that he could not understand any one postponing a wedding because some relative had died. For his own part he regarded it as a sacrament. He would not think it a desecration to go from the funeral of any one he loved straight to the altar. "The pity is that people regard it from such a different standpoint," he finished.'

'I think Mr. Vincent is right,' returned Lorraine, moving her head restlessly on the pillow. 'When we are young we think far too lightly of it, and yet even Death is not more solemn—"for better, for worse"—and when it is for worse !' and Lorraine shivered as she pressed her thin hands together. Had any woman drunk the bitterness of wedded misery as she had to the very dregs ?

How all this talk wearied her ; if Muriel would only go away ; how was she to take interest in Mr. Vincent and the Vicarage ? She could think of nothing but those snow-capped mountains and of those months of exile.

·Poor daughter of Eve, she too had tasted of the forbidden fruit, and must forfeit her earthly Paradise. The angel with the flaming sword, who drove her out, was named Duty — stern, inexorable, pitiless Duty !

When Muriel at last left her, she lay with closed eyes, absorbed in the saddest reflections. Later in the afternoon, when Ellison entered, she thought she was asleep, and would have stolen gently away, only Lorraine grasped her dress. 'Why are you going away ? I am not asleep, Ellison ; sit down here'—pointing to her bed—'I have been wanting to talk to you all day.' Then, as Ellison seated herself with an unsuspecting smile, Lorraine propped herself up on the pillows, and, with hesitating speech and downcast eyes, told her of Miss Bretherton's invitation.

CHAPTER XLIV

'Could we blame him with grave words,
    Thou and I, dear, if we might ?
Thy brown eyes have looks like birds,
    Flying straightway to the light.'
                    ELIZABETH BARRETT BROWNING.

THE following evening Ellison was standing by the fire listening
to Gavin as he scraped the snow off his boots in the porch. The
snow lay deep round Brae Farm, and he had ploughed his way
with difficulty across the Brae meadow. The Woodlands looked
like a fairy forest in the pale moonlight, and the red glow of
Lorraine's fire shone in his eyes as he plodded down the lawn.

There would be no danger of meeting her this evening, the
firelight told him that ; he would be spared the deep embarrassment
of looking at her and speaking to her. He was grateful for this ;
but his anxiety about her had forced him to stop Dr. Howell that
very morning to inquire after her.

It struck him that Dr. Howell spoke in a guarded way. 'Mrs.
Herbert was suffering from nervous exhaustion ; it was a break-
down of the nerves ; the shock had only hastened matters ; it was
due to other causes, and was of long standing. She had fretted too
much about her boy ; she was extremely sensitive ; she wanted a
change. It would be good for her to go away. He had told Miss
Lee so. Those visits to the churchyard were only feeding the
mischief ; he had been obliged to interdict them. She needed
firmness and bracing ; she had given way long enough.' Gavin
pondered heavily over the doctor's curt sentences. Dr. Howell
was extremely interested in his patient ; he had taken a great deal
of notice of her since Tedo's death, and had spoken to his wife
more than once of Mrs. Herbert's pluckiness. It was no light

cause that made him veer round now, and talk of firmness and bracing.

Ellison did not go out into the porch as usual to greet Gavin. She stood quite still with one hand resting on the mantelpiece while he threw off his ulster; but as he stooped to kiss her he saw she was not looking as calm as usual. He was very quick at noticing any change of expression, and as he held her hand he asked at once what was troubling her.

'Out with it, Ellison,' he said, trying to speak cheerily. 'You have a bothered look, and confession is good for the soul.'

'I know it is,' she returned, smiling at him, for his presence and the touch of his hand soothed her. 'I have been wanting you all day, Gavin. Are you not a little later than usual? Sit down in this comfortable chair beside me while I talk to you. Oh what a comfort it is to have some one to whom one can grumble!'

'If you think that such a privilege, I am at your service to-day and every day. I like you in that black velvet, Ellison; it makes you look more queenly than ever. What a stately woman you are growing!'

'Am I? I am glad you like my new gown; but it is not velvet, you foolish fellow, it is only velveteen.' But she made a mental note that Gavin liked velveteen. She must have a real velvet in her trousseau—should it be green or dark heliotrope? either would suit her. These little feminine vanities occupied her for a moment. It was no light matter to Ellison that Gavin's taste should be pleased. Even in trifles she would be a model wife.

'Well, dear, how long are you going to keep me waiting?' he said at last as he rested his arm comfortably on the cushions of her easy-chair. Her hand with the emerald and diamond gipsy ring was already in his. 'What is the grievance, Ellison?'

'It is about Lorraine,' she returned; and then his face grew grave, and he drew back a little. 'What do you think, Gavin? she wants to go away for a long change. That odd Miss Bretherton has been writing to her, and has invited her to Nefydd Madoc. Fancy going to Nefydd Madoc this weather; but Lorraine is bent on it. I never knew her so obstinate before, and, what is worse, Dr. Howell sides with her.'

'You have talked to him, then?'

'Yes, I captured him on his way from Lorraine's room, and had it out with him this morning; but I did no good at all. I told him that Lorraine was as weak as a baby; that she had not strength to dress herself; and that she was perfectly unfit for that long cold journey; and though he seemed to agree with me he actually said it was the least of two evils. Mrs. Herbert's nervous system was seriously deranged—she had lost tone and flesh.   Highlands was not the place for her just now ; she would never regain strength until she had had change of scene.   Wales was not the best place, of course, at this season of the year ; but the dry cold of Nefydd Madoc would not hurt her ; and it would be good for her to be with strangers.   He was so positive that I had not a word to say.'

'I think you may be satisfied with his advice ; Howell is a sensible man.'

'I let him go at last.   One cannot argue with him ; he is as obstinate as a certain gentleman I know.   A word of opposition makes him put his foot down at once.   When I went upstairs I found Lorraine crying pitifully.   She wanted to go ; she felt she must go ; but she was so afraid that I should think her unkind. I had quite a piece of work with her, poor dear.   She got almost hysterical at last.   I could only quiet her by telling her that I thought she was quite right to go ; that Dr. Howell had prescribed change of scene for her ; and that it was not the least necessary to cry one's eyes out when one was going to pay a pleasant visit.   " Write and accept Miss Bretherton's invitation, and I will take you up to Euston myself," I said to her, and when I settled matters she grew calm.   Her nerves must be in a sad state, Gavin, for I never knew Lorraine give way so much before.   It made me feel quite sad to hear her sob, and say how wretched she was, and beg me over and over again to forgive her.'

Gavin's arm was still resting on her chair, but he had drawn back so that Ellison could not see his face.   He sighed heavily once or twice, but made no response.   At that moment speech was impossible.   Those tears, what did they mean ?   Was she suffering too ? Ill as she was, she was going away because she dare not trust herself in his neighbourhood, and he must let her go and make no sign.

'Is it not sad?' continued Ellison, smoothing his coat sleeve with her free hand—she had shy, loving little ways of her own.   'I shall feel so dull without Lorraine.   I have grown so fond of her during these few months.   It has been nice to have her ready to talk at all hours.   She is so gentle and unselfish that one never finds her in the way.'

'Of course you will miss her.'

'How coldly you speak, Gavin.   You are not a bit sympathetic this evening.   I do wish you liked poor dear Lorraine better.   I must say I wonder at your bad taste,' and Ellison's tone was decidedly aggrieved.

Gavin started and drew his hand away.

'Good heavens, Ellison, what can you mean ?   I have always liked Mrs. Herbert.'

'You were very good to her in her trouble. I know that, dearest; but you never seem to care to talk to her, and yet she is very intelligent and well read. It is very important to me that you should like Lorraine. By and by, when we are married'—and here Ellison blushed like a young girl—'you will see so much of her, for of course we shall always be together. I have thought of such a nice plan,' she continued—turning her long neck to look round at him. 'Why are you prowling about the room, Gavin, in that polar bear fashion? conversation is so much more comfortable when people sit down'; and at this very plain rebuke Gavin seated himself on the broad, cushioned arm of her chair, and as she leant against him he kissed the coil of brown hair that rested against his shoulder; but even as he did so in remorseful tenderness, another speech was sounding in his ears. 'No. I must not have that kiss; it would be robbing Ellison. Let me give you something else instead,' and again he felt the touch of those soft lips on his hand. With what exquisite grace and humility she had done it. 'This is for the friend who was true to himself and me.' He could hear that sad sweet voice distinctly.

Ellison smiled happily; she loved to feel that strong, protecting arm round her—gentleness and strength, those were the salient points of Gavin's character, she thought.

'What is the plan?' he asked presently.

'You are certainly not in a talking mood this evening,' she returned, laughing. 'I am sure ten minutes have elapsed since my last speech. I was only thinking how nice it would be if Lorraine were to live on here, and Muriel were to keep her company; they are such friends, and suit each other so admirably, and we could see them every day. What does your masculine wisdom say to that?'

'My masculine wisdom would prefer to think it over; it is not a bad plan'—hastily, as she looked a little disappointed; 'but would not Muriel prefer the Dower House—Ferndale I mean—when Mrs. Langton leaves it? Mrs Herbert could join her there.' Gavin had already made up his mind that Muriel must go to the Dower House. Ellison would like her house to herself; and he thought Mrs. Herbert would easily be persuaded to bear Muriel company. To live at Brae Farm—no—that would not be possible either for himself or for her.

'Ferndale!' responded Ellison in an astonished tone of voice; 'dear Gavin, why should you wish to banish poor Muriel to that distance, when Brae Farm will be standing empty?'

'Sam Brattle could live there,' he returned quickly; 'and this room and a couple of bedrooms might be kept for London friends.

Muriel always liked the idea of Ferndale ; she and the mother were going there, you know. The walk is nothing ; you could still meet every day if you wished.'

'Perhaps so, except in bad weather, and then those dripping woodlands would be hardly pleasant. You must think it over, Gavin, as you smoke your pipe this evening. I maintain that my plan is far better than yours. Brae Farm will be your property, of course, but Lorraine will be a splendid manager. I have taught her lots of things ; she is already very clever with the poultry, and Mrs. Drake will manage the new dairymaid ; it is such a bore that Ruth and Eunice have decided to be married on the same day.'

'What a hard-hearted speech, you naughty woman ; Tom Brattle was only talking about it yesterday. He took me all over the house ; it is in splendid order ; Eunice has feathered her nest nicely by taking Tom ; he is a warm man, as they call it, and Brattle's is a safe concern. Eunice will be better off than your handsome Ruth ; but Sam is getting things ship-shape at the cottage. By the bye, Ellison,' rather gravely, 'did we settle the day ? I know June is our month ; we told the dear mother so.'

'There is no need to settle the day yet,' returned Ellison with a sudden thrill in her voice ; 'it is only January now ; Lorraine will be away some weeks, but she will come back in time to help me. I think of going to the Mervyns in March to do my shopping and get my presents for Eunice and Ruth. I am going to give them their wedding dresses, and some nice table linen ; pale grey silk, rather a pearly soft grey, is to be the colour ; how handsome Ruth will look in it.'

'But they are not to be married before their mistress ?' persisted Gavin.

'No, a fortnight later ; Lorraine and I have planned that already. Surely you are not going, Gavin ?' as he rose ; but he returned a little hurriedly that he had letters to write.

The last hour had dragged heavily with Gavin, though to Ellison it had seemed only a few minutes. 'Would it be always so,' he asked himself bitterly, 'this sense of effort and oppression, these futile attempts to play the devoted lover ?' Even Ellison, happy as she was in his society, felt that something was lacking in Gavin's manner lately ; but as usual she put down his absence of mind to his recent trouble, and generously exonerated him. He had asked her to fix the day ; but her slight demur had been sufficient, and he had not repeated the request ; even as he took her in his arms and embraced her, any other woman would have missed the total absence of passion in his kiss ; it was almost the same that he gave Muriel each morning. Ellison's deeply stirred affection would have responded readily to greater urgency and warmth; more than once the thought had crossed her mind that Helen had had a different wooing, but she always checked these thoughts as disloyal to Gavin.

She knew well that the love of his youth had been given to his beautiful young wife, that she must be content with a calm esteem and affection, and with the happiness of being necessary to him. Ellison never guessed that Gavin was capable of loving again with the old passion; she could not have believed it possible. When she was his wife, she would not be ashamed of letting him know how dearly she loved him, how his very faults were dear to her because they were Gavin's faults. 'What will it matter then if I love my husband more than he loves me?' she said with warmest self-effacement. 'I know how good he will be to me, and how happy he will make me.'

Ellison sat for some time without occupying herself when Gavin had left her. She was thinking a little perplexedly over his un-expected opposition to her cherished plan, to instal Lorraine as mistress of Brae Farm; she had gone so far as to sound Muriel very cautiously, and had seen a sudden flash of joy in her eyes. 'Oh, Ellison, do you really mean it? do you think Mrs. Herbert would be glad to have me?' But Ellison had put up a warning hand.

'Hush, we must not speak too decidedly; I have not con-sulted Gavin yet; it is for our master to decide, Muriel'; and Ellison smiled blissfully. Her master—yes, he was that, she knew well—her chosen, dearly loved master, and his word was law to her.

'I should think Gavin would approve,' returned the girl thought-fully; 'he knows that Mrs. Langton will not leave for another nine months; and then Ferndale is so far away, Mrs. Herbert might be dull; and Brae Farm would be far better. I could still teach Nora, and we shall have your daily visits, dear Ellison. Please convince Gavin that it will be far far better than Ferndale.' And yet Ellison felt as she sat there that she had somehow failed in convincing him.

Gavin had not seemed to approve of the plan at all; he wanted Sam Brattle to live there, and to keep the best rooms for his friends. Strange to say, he seemed anxious to banish Muriel to the Dower House. It was not so much his words as his manner and the tone of his voice that told Ellison the idea was repugnant to him; and with all her faith in Gavin, she found herself a little perplexed. 'He might guess how I should love to have them both there,' she said to herself. 'Sam Brattle is only my servant, but Lorraine is like a sister to me'; and then the tears started to her eyes. How happy she had been in this room ; only Gavin's love could make her happier. What had she ever lacked ? All her life her lines had fallen in pleasant places. 'I have not deserved my blessings,' she said humbly, as she rose at last to see after Lorraine.

Lorraine was lying on her bed ; the red firelight shone full on her face, which was turned towards the uncurtained windows ; two feverish spots burnt on her cheeks ; her eyes were bright and looked a little sunken ; there were hollows in the temples. 'Have I left you too long alone, dear ?' asked her cousin anxiously ; 'Gavin has been here, but he did not stay as long as usual, he had business letters to write.'

'I thought I heard some one,' returned Lorraine with a restless movement. She did not tell Ellison that she had crept to the door that she might hear the sound of his voice ; she had sat for more than an hour curled up on the window seat that she might see the dark outline of his figure as he tramped through the snow ; her heart was saying good-bye to him all the time. And then she had grown hot, and then suddenly cold ; for in the whiteness she had seen him stand motionless for more than a minute, with his head raised as though he were looking up at her window ; it was impossible for him to see her, and yet Lorraine had trembled all over with apprehension.

'I thought I heard some one,' she had faltered ; and then she said hesitatingly, 'Did you—did you tell him about Nefydd Madoc ?'

She was feverishly anxious to know what he thought of her plan ; but Ellison was sorry she had put the question. Gavin had said so little, Lorraine would think he was wanting in interest.

'Of course I told him ; I never keep anything from Gavin. He seemed to think that we ought to act on Dr. Howell's advice. He has never been to Nefydd Madoc—I remember he told me so some time ago ; so he cannot judge of the place. I told him that I should take you up to Euston, and that you would probably be away some weeks.' Some weeks ! Lorraine almost wrung her thin hands under cover of her shawl. The weeks would probably be months.

'Thank you, dear,' she returned wearily ; 'I shall tell Muriel myself to-morrow.'

'Gavin will be sure to tell her to-night. How tired you are, Lorraine ; Dorcas must help you to go to bed, you have been up too long. I am going to send you up some nice slices of pheasant for your supper, and you must promise me to eat it. No, I am not bidding you good-night yet, you will not get rid of me so easily,' as Lorraine suddenly flung her arms round her neck. 'I shall come up presently and read you to sleep.'

'Dear Ellison, how good you are ; I love you—oh how I love you !' But Ellison looked a little grave as she returned the kiss. Lorraine was decidedly feverish, she thought ; she was still a little hysterical. 'She has lost her balance,' she said to herself. 'Lorraine was always emotional, but during these last few days she has been more excitable than usual. I begin to think Dr. Howell is right, and that she really wants a change.' And then Ellison, true to her practical nature, showed her affection by carving delicate slices from the breast of the pheasant. 'Tell Mrs. Herbert that I shall be dreadfully disappointed if she, does not enjoy her supper,' she said, as rosy-cheeked Dorcas carried away the tray.

CHAPTER XLV

And sometimes, by still harder fate,
The lovers meet, but meet too late.
—Thy heart is mine !—True, true ! ah, true !
—Then, love, thy hand !—Ah no ! adieu !'
                                    MATTHEW ARNOLD.

IN spite of Lorraine's ardent desire to leave a place so fraught with
peril to her, it was some time before she could carry out her resolution. She remained in her room another ten days ; and even when
she was strong enough to come down to Ellison's sitting-room for a
few hours each day, she always made an excuse to retire before
Colonel Trevor paid his evening visit. Ellison never persuaded
her to remain ; she had got it into her head that Gavin and
Lorraine failed to understand each other, and that it would be
wiser to keep them apart. Gavin's manner always became cold
and constrained when she mentioned her cousin, while Lorraine
hardly mentioned him at all. More than once Ellison had spoken
of her scheme, but Gavin had not been responsive ; once when she
had pressed him he had answered rather curtly, that he had not
changed his opinion ; he was sorry to differ from her, but he still
thought the Dower House would be best for Muriel, unless she
would prefer remaining at Brae ; and then he had added with
forced composure, 'In my opinion it would be wiser for Mrs.
Herbert to be away from the Farm. I know she has a morbid
dislike to passing the pond ; the Dower House is very retired, and
the rooms are snug and comfortable, it would be a most suitable
residence for two ladies.'

Ellison felt vexed and disappointed, more so, indeed, than she
ventured to own ; it was the first time that their wills had
clashed, and the young mistress of Brae had to fight a hard battle

with herself before she would answer pleasantly. Gavin was quite aware how he had hurt her; her flushed cheek and the impatient sparkle in her blue eyes warned him that he was putting her to a severe test, but his own peace of mind and Lorraine's also were at stake. His sense of right compelled him to be firm, he would never yield to her in this—never. Muriel should go to the Dower House or remain at Brae.

'Very well, it is for you to decide,' she answered, a little coldly; though she loved him so dearly, she blamed him in her heart for this perversity. Gavin had no right to maintain his opinions so stiffly. Brae Farm was her property; it would have been better taste to have given way to her in this.

Ellison was too proud to stoop to any entreaties; she had stated her wishes, and Gavin was simply disregarding them. He and Muriel might settle their own plans now, and she would not interfere, but all the same she was determined that she would take no steps about the Brattles; Sam should put the cottage in order for his bride, and Gavin should settle things later.

'It is for you to decide,' was all that she could bring herself to say.

'Thank you, dear. I think you may trust me to do what is best,' he returned gratefully, but he made no further attempt to bring her round to his opinion. That evening he spoke to Muriel, and she was astonished and disappointed to hear him say that he could not sanction her going to the Farm.

'I have other plans,' he said evasively. 'When we are married, Ellison and I will talk them over more fully. I think it would be best for Sam Brattle to live at the Farm, but we should retain the best rooms for our friends. The Dower House is in capital order, and the furniture perfectly good; if Mrs. Herbert will consent to live with you, I should think you would be very comfortable. You shall have the pony carriage, and the brougham and bay mare for your exclusive use, and I shall make over Davis to you—he is a steady capable fellow; and he and his wife can occupy the rooms over the coach-house.'

'Oh, Gavin, how good of you to have thought of all that,' she returned, with tears in her eyes. In her heart Muriel was excessively disappointed, though she would not have told her brother so for worlds; she was not fond of the Dower House, it was very old-fashioned, the rooms were low, and the windows small, and it was shut in and had no special view. The Farm was delightful; and only the day before, she and Ellison had planned that she should have Ellison's room 'Peace,' for no power on earth would have induced Lorraine to give up 'Good rest' and the 'Dovecote.'

23

She must resign Nora's lessons, the child could not walk all that distance ; and of course she could not expect to see half so much of Ellison. She would have to drive to church and to the village, for the walk was beyond her strength. The Dower House was a good half-mile from the Woodlands, and lay on the Darley Road ; her nearest neighbours would be the Mordaunts. Homestead was only a quarter of a mile farther, but she had no special interest in the Mordaunts.

In spite of her disappointment, Gavin had no difficulty with Muriel, she was perfectly submissive and grateful. She allowed him to fix the number of her servants, two maids and a handy man for the garden. Muriel must have a cow and a good poultry-yard, it must be stocked from the Farm. Mrs. Herbert was very clever with poultry, and the man could milk the cow. Dorcas might come to them if Ellison approved, but Mrs. Drake would still live at the Farm. Muriel got enthusiastic at last as Gavin planned it all : the brother and sister sat up quite late that night. She forgot all about the small-paned windows and the rhododendron bed that shut out the view. If only Mrs. Herbert would consent to live with her, she thought she could be very happy at the Dower House.

Muriel felt almost cheerful for the first time since her mother's death. Gavin had kissed her affectionately and thanked her warmly for falling in with his views. He remembered the cloud on Ellison's brow, and the chilly tone in which she had signified her acquiescence, with something like displeasure—but neither of them imagined what a miserable evening Ellison was spending.

It was 'the little rift within the lover's lute,' that marred the sweet harmony, the first chill breath of autumn that spoilt the downy peach-bloom of her full content. Gavin had been inconsiderate, almost unkind, and she was grievously hurt. Poor Lorraine, lying on her couch upstairs, little thought what an apple of discord she had become.

A strong, self-reliant nature like Ellison's is also strong to suffer. For the first time since her engagement she slept restlessly and rose unrefreshed. The conflict between her will and her affection had been long and obstinate, but affection had gained the mastery.

When Gavin saw her next, she met him with a sweet smile, and there was no trace of wounded feeling in her manner. As he kissed her, she whispered, 'Forgive me, dearest. I ought not to have wanted my own way so badly. If I cannot agree, I can at least hide my disagreement. You thought so yesterday, did you not ?'

'Never mind what I thought yesterday,' he said, as he put his arm round her tenderly. 'I think you now one of the sweetest of women.' Not the sweetest. Even at the moment of their reconciliation he could not tell her that ; for in word he was ever truthful, and then sitting down beside her he repeated the substance of his conversation with Muriel.

Ellison listened with downcast eyes, but she offered no objections ; only a pang crossed her as she saw how determined he was. Well, she must be content not to understand Gavin ; for she failed utterly to comprehend him. 'Muriel had better have Daisy the brown and white Alderney, she gives the best milk,' she said in a quiet matter-of-fact tone ; 'and of course she must have the black Spanish poultry, and the little speckled hen, and the bantams too, Lorraine is so fond of them ; and it is a good idea of yours, Gavin, that Dorcas should go to them ; we must try and get Mrs. Earnshaw's Jenny to be their cook, she is an excellent kitchenmaid, and cooks quite well.'

'Thanks, dear, that will be very nice.'

'But, Gavin, do you not think that Lorraine ought to be consulted without delay ?' Then Gavin shook his head.

'If you ask me, I should suggest that nothing should be said to her at present ; let her go to Nefydd Madoc and get strong ; you and Muriel could write to her there. Believe me,' as Ellison looked decidedly dubious at this, 'she is not in the state to like anything. I judge of this from what you tell me ; she is too weak to grasp things properly, and she might take a dislike to the whole scheme, and then Muriel would be disappointed.'

'If you think so, of course we had better leave it,' returned Ellison slowly ; she thought Gavin reasonable in this. In the end nothing was said to Lorraine ; and Muriel was obliged to see her depart, without knowing whether she would consent to share her home. The uncertainty tried both her and Ellison, but Gavin had proved himself their master, and his directions were fully carried out.

The day for Lorraine's departure was at last fixed for the Thirtieth of January, nearly a month after Madge Wildfire's escapade. Madge was still in the Brae stables, and Gavin still occasionally drove her. But it was understood between him and Ellison that Bates should have notice to quit. The man's manner had been rather insolent on one occasion when Colonel Trevor had found fault with him. Gavin told Ellison that he was sure he had been drinking. 'He is a clever groom, but he is shifty and quarrelsome,' he said ; 'in short, he is an awkward customer, and I shall be glad to get rid of him ; but I shall keep him a few weeks longer for my own convenience.'

Ellison privately thought this a mistake ; Gavin had done wrong in taking him at all, and it was a still greater mistake to keep him on after his insolent behaviour ; he was a perfect plague to Dorcas, and the girl seemed afraid to stir out for fear of meeting him, he was an ill-conditioned, surly fellow, and his fellow-servants were getting sick of him; but since that little disagreement with Gavin, Ellison was rather chary of giving her opinion, perhaps she recognised the futility of any argument, when Gavin had once made up his mind. Somehow since their engagement, her influence had not seemed so great with him. Gavin was altered in some way, he was not so ready to defer to her judgment, he settled things for himself in a masterful, off-hand way, and it was no longer a necessity with him to tell her every little detail of his daily life. Yes, in spite of her happiness, Ellison missed some sweet ingredient in their long twilight talks ; now and then she questioned herself, what could it be ?—what was the difference ?—did she really understand Gavin as well as she thought she did ? Could any woman really understand such a complex being as man. 'Half angel, half devil, and wholly child,' as an old Swiss Professor once described him.

Ellison with her usual thoughtfulness had made all possible arrangements for Lorraine's comfort ; she and Dorcas had done all her packing, and she had ordered rooms at the Euston Hotel ; they were to go up to London early in the afternoon, that Lorraine might have a long rest ; and she intended to give her in charge to the guard ; he would go as far as Chester. Lorraine must have her luncheon-basket and her tea ; she put aside her own fur-lined rug for Lorraine's use. Lorraine might well look on with dumb gratitude as she watched the strong, capable hands fulfil their work. It was always a pleasure to watch Ellison do anything, there was such firm decision in her movements ; busy as she might be, she was never hurried. 'Every moment has its own work,' she would say. 'There is no good crowding things in ; hurry is a proof of an undisciplined mind.'

Lorraine had no intention of seeing Colonel Trevor before she left ; they had mutually decided to avoid each other, but on the afternoon before she left, visitors had called. Mrs. Earnshaw and her son Dacre, who had just returned from Canada, had detained Lorraine downstairs beyond her usual hour. They had just gone, and she was resting for a few minutes in her chair, looking very white and weak, when Ellison entered the room, followed by Colonel Trevor.

Lorraine flushed crimson, but a screen between her and the firelight prevented Ellison from noticing her extreme nervousness. Gavin's face was rather rigid as he shook hands with her, and asked after her health.

'If Madge Wildfire is to blame for this, I shall certainly send her away,' he said abruptly ; and Ellison again felt herself a little hurt. How she had begged him to get rid of Madge, and he had only laughed at her ; but of course it was natural that Lorraine's delicacy should shock him ; and after all, no doubt the accident had caused most of the mischief. Ellison calmed down when she remembered that Lorraine had been ill a month, and that this was the first time Gavin had seen her.

To tell the truth, Gavin was so disturbed by Lorraine's fragile appearance that he could hardly bring himself to talk at all. She was terribly wasted, and the hand he had taken felt thin and hot. If he could only be alone with her for five minutes, if he could only question her ; and as though in answer to his unspoken wish, Ellison suddenly announced that old Mrs. Pierce was waiting to speak to her.

'You will entertain Gavin until I come back, will you not?' she observed cheerfully as she left the room, and Lorraine, who had risen from her chair, sat down again reluctantly. She thought it was cruel that she should be subjected to this.

Gavin hardly waited for the door to close ; he crossed the room with nervous abruptness, and stood on the rug near her ; his anxiety was too overwhelming to allow him to see how he was embarrassing her.

'Tell me,' he said quickly, almost peremptorily, 'is Madge Wildfire really to blame for your illness? I am shocked to see the change in you; if Madge is really the cause, I will have her shot at once.'

'Please do not say such things,' returned Lorraine in a trembling voice, 'how could poor Madge help being startled by that horrible bray? it quite frightened me for the moment; indeed—indeed it was not only that—Dr. Howell said so. I have not been well since—since that dreadful day,' and then she stopped, unable to say more for the sob in her throat ; but he understood her ; her strength and spirit had failed from the hour he had laid her dead child in her arms.

'Yes, yes, I know,' his voice growing dangerously tender, 'you need not tell me ; it will be good for you to be away from here, but you must not stay away too long ; if Nefydd Madoc is too cold, if it does not suit you, you must let us find you some other place.'

'It will suit me as well as any other place,' she returned.

The weary tone of indifference with which she spoke brought a mist before his eyes. He could not bear to hear her speak so, and yet what could he say? 'Lorraine—Lorraine,' he whispered huskily, 'do not speak so; you are young, and so patient and good that life must have some sweetness in reserve for you.'

. Her lip quivered, but she had no answer ready.

'Do not make things too difficult for me,' he went on.   'If you have any regard for my peace of mind, you will take care of yourself; it is the one thing you can do for me.'

Then for the first time she looked at him, and her beautiful brown eyes were full of tears.

'I will do the best I can, indeed I will.   I will promise you that.   Do you think,' her voice thrilling a little, 'that I will not do my part when you are doing yours so nobly?' and then she rose from her chair and held out her hand to him.   'Good-bye, Colonel Trevor, please forgive me, but I cannot stay; I am not strong yet—and——' Then he lifted her hand reverently to his lips, and as she turned away, she heard him say 'God bless you.'

When Ellison returned to the room a few minutes later she was surprised to see that Lorraine's seat was empty.   Gavin was warming his hands at the fire, and his back was towards her.

'Was Lorraine tired?   I had no idea you were alone,' she said, coming to his side.

'Yes, she was tired, and I thought it kinder to let her go.' Gavin spoke a little moodily.   'She looks terribly ill, Ellison; worse than I imagined.   Dr. Howell was perfectly right when he said she needed a long change,' and then with curious abruptness he changed the subject.   'Muriel asked me to bring you some patterns for the new curtains,' he said hurriedly.   'They are in my ulster pocket, I believe,' but he was rather a long time finding them, and during the rest of his visit he was strangely absent, more so than usual, Ellison thought, as she looked at him wistfully; did he not remember that she was going away for two nights? and yet he had taken leave of her without mentioning the fact; he had not even offered to drive them to the station. Ellison felt a little dull as she went back to the fireplace.   How many solitary evenings she would spend there while Lorraine was regaining strength at Nefydd Madoc.

CHAPTER XLVI

'The bleak, stern hour,
Whose severe moments
I would annihilate,
Is pass'd by others
In warmth, light, joy.'
                MATTHEW ARNOLD.

THERE are days in one's life that seem unending, when the hours drag slowly and heavily like Sisera's chariot-wheels of old—revolving and grinding in perpetual pain and monotony. Such a day came to Lorraine when she left Ellison standing on the platform at Euston that wintry morning, and sat alone in the luxurious first-class compartment, watching the grey landscape, and the frost-blackened hedges and ploughed fields fly swiftly by, while each hour her heart grew heavier and more oppressed.

Alas, each milestone only told her that she was farther away from those she loved best ; and as the day wore on, and bodily weakness increased her mental discomfort, she felt a growing horror of her approaching visit. Nefydd Madoc—Black Nest—Miss Bretherton, with her sarcastic speeches—how was she to endure it all ? The very thought of the mountains closing round her gave her a stifling sense of perpetual imprisonment ; what if her nerves should give way ; what if she should break down utterly ! when the shrill whistle sounded as they entered a tunnel ; Lorraine could have shrieked aloud with nervous tension. Later on, a dull, torpid insensibility seemed to benumb her faculties ; her warm rugs and freshly filled hot-water tin relieved the feeling of deadly cold that had been creeping over her ; a cup of steaming coffee acted as a narcotic, and she slept a little. She was still drowsy when the train stopped, and the guard informed her that they had reached Croes-fford ; the next moment the burly station-master stood at the carriage door.

'David Fechan is asking for the lady that's bound for Black Nest, Nefydd Madoc,' he said, looking inquisitively at Lorraine's pale face.

She started up at once. 'Is it Miss Bretherton's carriage? please help me to find my luggage,' and the man nodded and called up a porter. Evidently Miss Bretherton was considered a person of some importance ; half-a-dozen porters seemed to surround her in a moment. The lighted station made Lorraine feel giddy, and she was glad to take refuge in the carriage, and to sink back into the nest of warm rugs that had been provided for her comfort.

She was wide awake now, but the black darkness filled her with dismay until she got used to it a little. The moon was obscured by heavy clouds, and a wild moaning wind seemed to fill the valleys. Now and then there was a passing gleam, that showed her patches of whiteness by the roadside.

The road seemed to ascend somewhat steeply. Once, when the horses paused for a moment, she could hear the dull roar of a cataract, that only added to the weird desolation.

Lorraine never thought of that long drive without a shudder ; but in happier days it became a favourite walk with her, and she could not say enough for its beauty. The magnificent waterfalls, the luxuriant wildness of the overhanging trees, the dark solemn colour of the rocky walls, and the forms of the rugged basins into which the water rushed, the richly wooded banks of the river foaming and chafing over the huge boulders, and the glorious mountain range, gave it a loveliness that was almost sublime. How often in future days Lorraine opened the small gate and wandered down the winding path leading to the rapids, and sat on one of the rough benches in pensive enjoyment of the scene. The carriage had evidently turned off the main road, and the horses were climbing slowly a steep rough road that looked to Lorraine like a chasm of darkness. Presently they stopped, and a lantern was flashed into the carriage by a man in groom's undress, and then Lorraine saw some open gates, and a dark shrubbery path that seemed to ascend and wind for some little distance, then they turned a corner sharply. There was an open door, a gleam of ruddy firelight and lamplight, and one or two dark figures standing in the porch.

'You will be sadly tired, ma'am, with your long journey,' observed a woman's voice, and Lorraine at once recognised Pritchard waiting by the carriage to help her out. As she entered the house a tiny figure in black velvet came out of the shadow. 'My dear soul, what an age you have been,' observed Miss Bretherton in the clear, shrill tones that Lorraine remembered so well. 'I thought you and David Fechan and the horses were all buried under the snowdrift in How-Bwlch, and that we should have had to dig you out. Come to the fire, you must be starved with cold,' and Miss Bretherton's small, soft hands placed Lorraine in the curious beehive chair, loaded with eider-down cushions, that stood by the hall fire, while her sharp voice bade Pritchard and Morwyn close the door, and let Gwilym take up the luggage.

Lorraine glanced round her half fearfully. She was dazed by the light and the voices, and felt as though she were dreaming. She was in a large, square hall, wainscoted in black oak ; the place seemed full of shadows, and only one corner was fully lighted by the blazing fire of huge faggots, and some curiously-shaped lamps against the wainscot ; a tiger's skin lay before the hearth, and in a deep basket a pure white Persian cat was reposing with two kittens.

Miss Bretherton stood on the rug with her hands behind her looking at her guest, a weird, picturesque little figure with her ermine tippet and her crutch-handled stick, and her pile of fuzzy grey curls—a regal Mother Hubbard. Her eyes were as brightly blue as ever ; she had given the servants her orders in a curious medley of Welsh and English ; but after her first abrupt greeting she had said no word of welcome, only, as she watched Lorraine's face, the cloud gathered on her brow.

'Why did you not tell me how bad you were?' she said at last, 'and I would have sent Pritchard to Chester. You are no more fit to have taken the journey alone than a new-born baby. What were your people thinking about to trust you, I wonder?' her wrath evidently rising. 'Didn't I say that the world is packed with fools and knaves?'

'My cousin seemed very uneasy about me,' returned Lorraine in a feeble, deprecating voice, 'but it was impossible to send any one with me. I am better; indeed, I am better, Miss Bretherton, but the journey has tired me.'

'There is no need to tell me that,' returned Miss Bretherton impatiently. 'I have my eyesight, thank Heaven ; though I am bound to say that I should hardly have known you. We have plenty of ghosts at Black Nest, so you will find yourself in good company ; and there will be two white ladies to glide and moan about the passages and frighten the silly girls to fits.'

Lorraine tried to smile, but the tears came to her eyes instead. She was terribly ashamed of herself as they brimmed over her cheeks, but to her surprise Miss Bretherton patted her shoulder kindly.

'There, there, don't try to talk. I am a cross old woman, but my heart is not quite a millstone. Take Mrs. Herbert to her room, Pritchard, and don't leave her until she is safe in bed. Morwyn, go with them, and help them. You can send Betty to me. Let her cry if she has a mind to. Women know best what eases them, and when they are weak there is no fighting power left in them,' and then Miss Bretherton sat down in the beehive chair, and her forehead was a mass of wrinkles as she stared at the cat, who was at that moment washing her kittens in the casual upside-down fashion common to that animal. A remonstrative mew from one of the victims roused her ire.

'It is all very well for you, Winnie Fack,' she grumbled, 'to be lying at your ease and rolling those snow-balls about at your pleasure; family cares you call it—as if Puff and Pomp are not as clean as they possibly can be—only you are so absurdly proud of them. Let them be a moment while I talk to you. I hate to hear Puff squeak, it upsets my nerves; what business have you to be flaunting those babies of yours before that poor thing's eyes? could you not have the decency to hide them until she had gone? I am not pleased with you, Winnie Fack, and I will not have you jumping into my lap to make it up.' Nevertheless, she smoothed the cat's glossy coat affectionately as she spoke.

'So we have another ghost in this lively old place, Trump?' as a still larger white cat stole out of a dark corner and took up his position at her feet; 'white spirits and grey—our cheerfulness is increasing. What do you say, Trump, that you have no patience with her breaking her heart about that little pale-faced, ordinary child? Oh, but he was her only one you see; that is the droll part of mothers, they think their children beautiful; look at Rebecca Fechan—do you suppose she considered Llewellyn a tangle-headed, snub-nosed brat? not she—he had the beauty of all the angels in her eyes—cherubims were nothing to him; but you and I could not understand that.'

Miss Bretherton's voice died away into silence, and only the loud purring of the petted cats and the crackling of the logs broke the stillness; then the keen, incisive voice began again.

'Ah, you may purr with satisfaction, Winnie Fack; you have got your little ones to cuddle and wash and feed, life is not a blank to you, but it makes me sick and sorry and bitter to see the change in that poor thing; don't I remember her coming up the bracken path, with her light step, and the look of her brown eyes, and the smile that seemed to warm me through and through; and now she is hanging her head and drooping like a flower that has been broken off close to the root.'

'Oh, I don't say she's going to die, Trump; don't get that into your stupid cat head; people don't die because something in their life has gone wrong, and their heart is half broken, but it. goes against me to see that crushed look on any woman's face. Don't I know what it is to love a little child and then to lose him; I can feel the pain of it now.' And here Miss Bretherton sighed, and grasping the handle of her stick she rose stiffly and disappeared into the shadows, while Winnie Fack returned to her basket and her kittens.

Meanwhile Lorraine's tired feet had climbed the slippery oak staircase. Black Nest certainly deserved its name; most of the rooms and passages were wainscoted with shining dark oak, and the long narrow corridor leading to her room was so dimly lighted that even Betty in her white apron and pretty coquettish cap looked ghost-like round the corner.

It was a relief when a door in the darkness opened, and Lorraine found herself in a large, cheerful bedroom; even there the furniture was all of heavy dark oak, but the warm crimson curtains, the blazing fire, and some wax candles on the toilet-table gave it a cosy aspect. A comfortable-looking couch was drawn up to the fire, and a table with a reading-lamp was beside it; there were easy-chairs, some hanging shelves full of gleaming china, and a copy of the San Sisto Madonna admirably painted in oils. It was indeed a haven of rest to poor, weary Lorraine.

Pritchard, who was an autocrat in her way, sent off Morwyn and took things in her own hands, and in a short time the worn-out traveller was reposing comfortably in bed. It was only rest Lorraine wanted, and it was difficult to her to do justice to the delicately served supper that Pritchard placed before her. 'You will sleep better if you eat a morsel of this partridge, ma'am,' she said coaxingly, 'and my mistress insists on your drinking this glass of champagne.'

Lorraine took it all obediently; she had fallen into kind hands; Ellison need not fear for her comforts. If warmth and luxury and kindly hospitality could lift the burden from her oppressed heart, all would be well. She thanked Pritchard gratefully as the woman carried off the tray with a dissatisfied look. She was tired to death, but a feeling of strangeness would not permit her to close her eyes. The stillness of the house, the absence of all sounds, seemed to oppress her: ghosts—of course there were ghosts gliding along those narrow, dark passages; ghosts of dead and gone griefs, of women's hopes, of all sorts of innocent anticipations. She almost started when a light tap came to her door, and Miss Bretherton's tiny figure appeared on the threshold. Mother Hubbard had laid aside her velvet dress and ermine cape ; she wore a trailing dressing-gown of grey quilted satin, and a tiny lace hood tied over her fuzzy grey curls, her pale face had a softened and kindly expression on it, as she stood in her erect fashion beside the bed.

Lorraine put out her weak hand. 'How kind of you to come to me, Miss Bretherton. Pritchard has been so good, she has helped me so nicely, and this bed is so comfortable. But you must not let me be a trouble to you ; I am not ill, only very very tired.'

'Then you must stop there till you are rested,' was the abrupt answer. 'My dear Mrs. Herbert, if you only knew the blessing you will be to me and Pritchard, we have nothing but cats here to pet, and a human being will be such a treasure-trove. I am a woman of my word, as you know, and you and I are going to be close friends. I have been wanting you for months, and now I have got you I mean to keep you as long as I can. Black Nest is a trifle dull, until people get used to it, but it is not a prison ; do as you like, and be as happy as you can, is our motto. You shall be as free as the birds of the air, and have your own way in everything if you will only stay with me, my dear.' Was it her fancy, Lorraine wondered, or was there really a break in her voice as she said this ?

'Dear Miss Bretherton, thank you so much for saying this. Why is every one so good to me ? If you knew how little I deserve it all.'

'My dear child,' rather quaintly, 'I don't doubt your unworthiness for a moment ; don't we call ourselves miserable sinners every Sunday of our lives ? I hate folk who flaunt their virtues before one's eyes in an aggressive manner ; you and I will get on very comfortably. I am a cross-grained, vindictive old woman, but I know when a person suits me. Now I am not going to talk to you any more to-night, it is nearly ten o'clock, and we are early birds in Black Nest. Do you see that door near the big wardrobe ? I daresay you thought it was a cupboard, but it is no such thing ; most of the rooms here are oddly connected ; that door leads into Pritchard's room, and Pritchard's room opens into mine, so you need not want for company. I always sleep with one ear open, and so does Pritchard, so if the Grey Lady makes her appearance, or you have a nightmare, just call out and one of us will be with you in a twinkling. I don't believe in haunted rooms myself,' she went on, as Lorraine smiled in answer ; 'all rooms are haunted when one has lived long in them ; the country people here are superstitious ; they have got up a bogey or two out of their own imaginations. When I first came they called me the Crazy Lady up at Black Nest ; as mad as a March hare, they used to say—but, bless you, they would vouch for my sanity now ' ; and patting the bedclothes with a reassuring nod the little lady glided away.

It was long before Lorraine could compose herself to sleep, and then she had confused, troubled dreams. She thought she was walking through the Woodlands on a grey, autumnal evening, when Ellison suddenly came up to her with menacing looks. 'You are a thief—you have stolen my lover—you are an ungrateful, selfish woman !' she cried, grasping her arm ; and then she saw Colonel Trevor beckoning to her. She thought she tried to go to him, but that Ellison held her too firmly. She could hear his voice calling sadly to her from the distance, 'It is you that I love, not Ellison, why do you not come to me ?' but she had no power to answer or to move.

'My dear, you are only dreaming ; wake up, and let me settle your pillows more comfortably ' ; and Miss Bretherton raised her gently.

'Am I a thief ?' murmured Lorraine, with a drowsy sob ; 'can one be innocent and yet a thief ? how could I help loving him when he was so good to my boy ?' Then Miss Bretherton's face changed, and she shook her a little.

'My dear Mrs. Herbert, you are feverish and have the night-mare ; Pritchard often tells me I have nightmare ; drink this warm lemonade, it will refresh you.' But Lorraine's hand shook a little as she took the glass.

Was it late ? she wondered ; the room was still ruddy with fire-light, Miss Bretherton still wore her grey satin dressing-gown, but her curls had been smoothed away.

'I used not to dream so much,' she said plaintively. 'Dr. Howell says it is only weakness and nerves ; go to bed, Miss Bretherton, please, I am so sorry to have disturbed you, I shall sleep now more quietly.' But though Lorraine kept quiet, more than once that night the little grey figure glided into the room, and stood there for a minute listening to her soft breathing.

CHAPTER XLVII

'And though she be but little, she is fierce.'
                                    SHAKESPEARE.

'The will to neither strive nor cry,
The power to feel with others give !
Calm, calm me more ! nor let me die
Before I have begun to live.'
                                    MATTHEW ARNOLD.

No one seemed in the least surprised when Lorraine found herself
unable to rise the next morning. Pritchard brought her her
breakfast as a matter of course, and Betty lighted her fire. When
she pulled up the blind, Lorraine uttered an exclamation. The
faint wintry sunshine lighted up a wonderful prospect ; trees, rocks,
dark crags, and a foaming water-spout, and in the distance the
snow-capped peak of Moel-Nefydd. Raising herself on her elbow,
Lorraine could see the garden terraces merging into winding
shrubbery walks. On one side a fir wood closed in the prospect,
and, as she found out later, a rustic bridge had been thrown over
the little brawling stream that foamed and chafed night and day
among the grey boulders, until it poured itself into a dark, still
pool at the entrance of the wood. The scene was indescribably
wild and picturesque, and in winter time the sound of the ghyll
was distinctly audible as it poured down the face of the crag and
made channels for itself. Black Nest was perched on the shoulder
of a crag, and with the exception of a broad terrace-walk underneath the windows, the ground shelved steeply to the bridge,
then rose again abruptly.

'How beautiful it must be in summer time,' thought Lorraine,
and then her hostess entered. Miss Bretherton looked more like
Mother Hubbard than ever in the daylight. She wore her
ordinary morning costume, a dark red cashmere, with a velvet

tippet to match, trimmed with black fur. She had a peaked black hat perched jauntily on her grey curls, which she explained was for the birds' breakfast-table. Seeing that Lorraine looked slightly mystified, she condescended to explain that she dispensed hospitality on rather a large scale to the feathered inhabitants of Nefydd Madoc, and that it was her usual habit to give breakfast parties on a smooth bit of rock under the west wing at a certain hour in the morning.

'I go there in all weathers,' she continued ; 'the birds begin to know me now, and will pick up the corn at my feet. I have very strange visitors sometimes ; when the winter is severe a stray sea-gull will find its way to Craig-Du, and once I had a grey parrot that had escaped from the hotel at Croes-fford. No one but Morwyn ever accompanies me, the birds have got used to her too, but a stranger always scares them. I have a bell that I ring to tell them when the meal is ready,' she continued, 'but they are generally sitting in rows on the face of the rock ; now and then, if I go earlier, it is droll to hear the scurry and flapping of innumerable wings. It is rather a steep climb for an old woman, but the birds' feeding-time is the most interesting to me in the twenty-four hours.'

'Dear Miss Bretherton, how nice it all sounds. You must take me one morning instead of Morwyn,' and then Lorraine sighed and looked dejected ; 'if only I were not so weak and good for nothing.'

'Nonsense, child,' was the brisk retort. 'You will soon be as strong as ever. There is no air like Nefydd Madoc, that is what I always tell people, dry cold will hurt no one. Don't give way to low spirits ; there is nothing so wearing as worry. I am going to send you up Winnie Fack and her kittens to amuse you ; when one is weak and low there is nothing like a dumb animal—my cat-angels I call them'—and Miss Bretherton jerked her head a little more on one side, and patted her curls in the soft sunlight ; her small, thin face seemed a perfect network of wrinkles, and the baby blue of her eyes seemed almost startling by contrast.

Throughout the day she trotted in and out on a dozen different errands—to put on another pine log, to bring her some red winter berries she had found in a sheltered nook in the garden, or an egg she had beaten up with wine herself, or some books and pictures to amuse her ; she never stayed long, however much Lorraine pressed her.

'Little and often,' she said decidedly ; 'you are not fit for solitude, and you are not fit for talking either. When you have taken that egg you will have a nap.' And she was right ; Lorraine dozed most of the afternoon away. She woke refreshed, and was able to write a few lines to Ellison in the evening.

Dr. Howell had judged wisely in prescribing change for his patient. Lorraine would never have gained strength or tone at Highlands. The close neighbourhood of Brae House, the constant effort to be on her guard and to avoid any interview with Colonel Trevor, were all wearing on her nerves; the sudden transition to a place she had never seen was a healthful tonic, and even Mother Hubbard, original, keen and caustic, and yet brimming over with secret kindliness, was the best companion for her in her present state.

The next day Lorraine felt more rested, and in the afternoon she crept downstairs piloted by Pritchard. Miss Bretherton was busily engaged in tearing red flannel into breadths for children's petticoats. She looked up and nodded approvingly when she saw Lorraine; then she went on tranquilly with her business, while Pritchard settled her guest on the couch and brought her a glass screen.

'Is this the drawing-room?—what a lovely old room!' asked Lorraine, when Pritchard had left them; 'and what beautiful china, Miss Bretherton,' glancing round her with open-eyed admiration.

'We call it the China-room,' was the answer. 'There is no drawing-room at Black Nest; my great aunt Bretherton was crazy about china. There is a fortune wasted on it in this room alone; do you see that cabinet? that is all Dresden, and over yonder is the Sèvres cabinet, that on your left is old Chelsea. I don't know that I care for china myself, but it gives a nice colouring to this dark old room.'

'I think it is perfectly lovely,' replied Lorraine, and then the thought crossed her how Ellison would love this room; it was long and somewhat narrow for the length, and the ceiling was low, but the arched recesses with their quaint old cabinets teeming with treasures, the oddly-shaped tables and carved high-backed chairs, the oak settle before the fire loaded with cushions, gave it the look of an antique picture; the three high, narrow windows opened on the terrace, and a break in the shrubbery gave a view of the stream that rushed through the grounds.

'Is that work for the poor? I hope you will let me help you,' asked Lorraine presently, and Miss Bretherton graciously signified her consent.

'I don't do much sewing myself,' she observed. 'I like the tearing and cutting out best, the maids do most of the work. When you are stronger and want occupation, you shall see my

Dorcas cupboard, and help yourself. If you like I will read aloud to you while you work. I often read aloud to Pritchard. I have plenty of books, and you can take your choice, only I warn you I never read a book with a sad ending, it makes me nervous and jumpy.'

'That will be delightful,' returned Lorraine; but in spite of herself there was a sad ring in her voice. How often Ellison had read to her in the evening. A sudden pang of home-sickness seemed to turn her faint. What was Ellison doing? Ah, there was no need to ask; in imagination she could hear the clang of the little green gate, and the quick, steady footsteps on the gravel walk. It was the twilight hour when Colonel Trevor paid his daily visit. She knew well the contented look with which Ellison would lay aside her work to welcome him.

Lorraine tried to dismiss these thoughts, but Miss Bretherton's keen eyes had detected the weary droop of the lip, and the tearing of flannel ceased at once.

'I am going to ring for tea,' she said abruptly. 'Winnie Fack wants her milk, and she must not be kept waiting.' And when Morwyn entered she bade the girl close the shutters and bring lights. 'I don't hold with twilight,' she said quickly, 'it brings ghosts behind one's chair, and healthy human flesh and blood won't stand a ghost. When we are cosy I am going to read the paper to you; there is a grand debate going on in the House. And Lorraine found the debate so interesting that she first nodded and then fell into a sound sleep, while Miss Bretherton tranquilly droned on.

The China-room was mellow with lamplight, the sleeping cats lay on the black bearskin rug, the two kittens nestled close to their mother, the pine logs splintered and sputtered with spicy perfume, there was a faint smell of rose pourri and lavender. Mother Hubbard sitting bolt upright in her high-backed chair, leant her pointed chin on her hand, and perused pityingly the thin white face before her.

'It is no business of mine,' she muttered, 'and I am not going to meddle in other folks' troubles, but they have only sent her here just in time'; and then still more softly, 'Poor thing, poor thing, it is easy to read between the lines there.' And then she crept away and summoned Pritchard, and had a long confab with her.

It ended in Miss Bretherton's usual fashion.

'You are not such a fool as you look, Pritchard,' she observed with good-natured abruptness, 'and I am glad you agree with me; not that your opinion matters in the least; thank goodness I have made up my own mind about most things ever since I was a chit, and I never cared for second-hand opinions. Like most cheap finery, they won't wash. Of course it is no good asking Dr. Meredith to call—doctors are all very well in their way when there are broken bones to mend, or you want poulticing ; but there is no prescription for broken hearts that I can find out.'

'I don't know about that, ma'am,' returned Pritchard respectfully ; 'when I was a child and things went wrong, mother would say, "Take a patience powder, Molly, and put a grain of common-sense into it"—how well I remember her saying that.'

'Your mother was a sensible woman, Pritchard. I wish I could have made her acquaintance. Dear, dear, what a world it is, Rachels for ever weeping for their children.' Miss Bretherton wrinkled her forehead until her eye-brows were nearly lost in the fuzzy curls, then she said testily :

'I wish I knew how the child died ; one can never answer for those anæmic children. If he had been brought up in a cellar one would not have wondered at his washed-out appearance ; but there, if she stays here till Christmas I shall never ask her. I may be curious, but I know my manners better than that.'

'Indeed, ma'am, no one could be more considerate. Mrs. Herbert has come to the right place, as I shall make bold to tell her some day. She is a dear young lady, and it goes to my heart to see the marks of fretting on her poor face ; but you must not let it worry you too much '; and Pritchard, who adored her flighty little mistress, patted her gently, as though she were a child.

'We are a couple of old fools,' grumbled Miss Bretherton ; 'but I know who is the biggest,' and then she trotted down to the Lodge to scold Rebecca Fechan for not eating more of her good broth and jelly, and to argue and wrangle with poor disconsolate David, who had taken his child's death sadly to heart. 'Such nonsense ; why, it is flying in the face of Providence,' she grunted in an audible aside, 'when there are four hulking lads and another coming.'

'But they aren't Llewellyn,' sighed Rebecca in soft guttural English. 'My man was so fond of Llewellyn ; he was daddy's boy, and he was mine too ; and if we had a dozen sons we would miss him just as badly, David and I.'

'My dear soul, what deplorable sentiments,' and then Miss Bretherton turned red and peevish. 'If they were only girls,' she fumed ; 'but it is very inconsiderate of you, Rebecca, when you know my aversion to boys. I give you warning that I shall pack them all off to Croes-fford as soon as they are in jackets—Owen will soon be old enough to clean knives. I won't have a lot of mischievous lads hunting my poor cats and taking the wrens' nests ;

so you and David had better look out'; and then she took up her empty basket, and trotted away.

It was not to be expected that Lorraine would recover her strength quickly; but a sense of duty and sheer gratitude to her kind-hearted hostess made her struggle bravely with her depression.

She would not think; she would not succumb. As soon as it was possible to exert herself, she found occupations for every hour. Miss Bretherton pretended to grumble when she found her mending some lace for Pritchard, or sewing at some childish garment; but Lorraine refused to be idle.

Ellison was much cheered by the letters that reached her. If they had cost Lorraine an effort her cousin never knew it; she would read passages aloud to Gavin as they sat together. They were very full of description, Gavin thought. The China-room and the Oak-room, where she and Miss Bretherton took their meals, were faithfully photographed; Craig-Du, the birds' feeding-rock, and the wild, steep garden leading to the stream, and the silent pool—he could see it all. By and by came descriptions of her drives, or of her solitary strolls through the village; her first service in the little white church; and her visit to the vicarage and the venerable white-haired pastor and his homely wife.

'I begin to feel at home at Black Nest,' she wrote once; 'it is not like my own dear home, of course, but in its way it is a nest of comfort. I am becoming warmly attached to Miss Bretherton; she is very original, certainly, and her manners are decidedly brusque, but one so plainly sees the good heart beneath. No words can express her kindness to me. In her own home Mother Hubbard is a very stately little person, and the villagers round seem to respect her greatly. She is very good to them; she is always helping some one or other. If their cow dies, or they want a pony to carry their market produce, she is always ready to help them. Just now the family at the Lodge are in trouble, and we go there daily to sit with the poor mother. The other day Rebecca Fechan whispered to me to come alone, and I contrived to do so, and we had a long long talk; you see we can feel for each other, Rebecca and I. "It is a pity David and I have only boys, for the mistress dislikes them so," she confided to me; "they all run out of the cottage when they hear the rap of her stick on the door; they think she is a witch because she frowns at them and scolds them. They do say up at the house that she had once set her heart on a nephew, and that he hated her and couldn't be induced to stay with her, and so she has had a grudge against boys ever since"; and of course Rebecca is right.

'It is so odd when we walk through the village; she will smile and look pleased when the little girls drop their curtsey, and she will go into the school to hear them sing ; but if a boy crosses her path she frowns and looks away, and if one shows his face at Black Nest there is such a hubbub, and he is sent off with a good scolding. There is actually a board at the entrance of the shrub-bery written in English and Welsh—" No boys allowed to go up to the house." '

' Lorraine must be wonderfully better, or she would not write like this,' observed Ellison tranquilly as she folded up the sheet ; but Gavin made no reply. The letters were interesting, they were graphic and amusing, but they struck him as rather laboured and forced ; and how little she said about herself.

Lorraine took great pains with these letters; Ellison never guessed at the sinkings of heart with which they were written. She and Muriel wrote constantly; but their letters, brimming over with affection and interest, only added to Lorraine's pain ; and Gavin's friendly messages, sent at long intervals, always drove the blood from her face. She could not read his name without emotion —the thought of seeing him again terrified her. Nothing, nothing on earth, she vowed, should take her back to Highlands until the wedding was safely over. Ellison had promised to abide by Gavin's advice, and for some weeks Lorraine was ignorant of the arrangements that had been suggested; when at last Ellison mooted it, Lorraine was conscious of intense relief.

All this time, her chief fear had been that Ellison would expect her to live at Brae Farm. The Dower House was a mile away, and there would be no danger of daily visits from Brae. She would be free to lead her own life, and then as she re-read the letter in the solitude of her own room, she suddenly burst into tears.

It was all his doing, she knew that. She did not need Ellison to tell her that Gavin had planned it. ' He has set his heart on your keeping Muriel company in the old Dower House,' Ellison wrote. ' He thinks you will be happier there than at Brae Farm. I do hope he is right, dear ; but you know how determined Gavin is. He and Muriel have planned everything. You are to have Cowslip and the bay pony, and the pick of the poultry-yard, and Davis and Dorcas and Mrs. Earnshaw's Jenny. Directly you have signified your consent, he and Muriel are going up to town to buy carpets. You should see how happy and important Muriel looks, she gives herself all the airs of a chatelaine already. Do write and tell us what you think of this proposal. It will relieve my mind greatly if you really approve of Gavin's plan. I don't mind owning to you that I am rather disappointed about it. I had set my mind on having you at Brae Farm; you would be so close to me there, and we should have had you safely under our wing; but my lord and master says, no — that Sam Brattle must live there, and that you will be far more comfortable in the Dower House.'

'Colonel Trevor is right, and I accept his generous proposal most gratefully,' wrote Lorraine in answer to this. Grateful! how was she to express her gratitude? The thought that he had planned her future, that his care had provided her with this safe retreat, filled her with secret joy. How well he understood her. The life he had mapped out was the only possible one for her under the circumstances. Surely she would regain strength and calmness at the Dower House; merciful time would heal her deadly wound. She would find her peace in ministering to others; no life, however sad, need be empty. 'I have done the right thing,' thought Gavin, as he read those few hastily scrawled lines—'When one feels most, one can write least. Dear, dearest Ellison, if you only knew how intensely grateful I feel to you all!'

Ellison felt herself a little puzzled by Lorraine's expressions of passionate gratitude. Why should she dread the idea of living at the Farm? then she remembered what Gavin had said about the pond. Perhaps, after all, his suggestion was the wisest. The Dower House had no distressing associations connected with it. Lorraine would forget her trouble more quickly when she had nothing to remind her of it.

When Muriel proposed illuminating 'Good rest' above the pleasant room allotted for Lorraine's use, Ellison negatived it at once. 'It has not been good rest to her,' she said sadly; 'give it some other name, Muriel'; and it was finally decided to call it the Porch-room.

CHAPTER XLVIII

AN UNEXPECTED INVITATION

'For 'tis sweet to stammer one letter of the Eternal's language ; on Earth it is called Forgiveness.'—LONGFELLOW.

ONE morning, when Lorraine had been at Black Nest about three weeks, she was sitting in the roomy window-seat, busy with some sewing, when Miss Bretherton came into the room and sat down beside her.

She wore her little peaked hat, and carried her crutch-handled walking-stick ; the birds' feeding-time was just over—but her face had a restless dissatisfied expression. Lorraine, who guessed the reason, wisely held her peace. She knew that the post-bag that morning had brought a letter from Eric Vincent, but Miss Bretherton had carried it off unread.

There was unbroken silence for some minutes, and then Miss Bretherton suddenly burst forth in an aggressive voice, 'I have had a letter from my precious nephew this morning ; as usual he is posing as a saint and martyr. The good young man in the Gospels was nothing to him, he fairly bristles over with virtues ; really, Mrs. Herbert, I ought to congratulate you on your model vicar. As I said before, Highlands is a favoured parish.'

'So we all think,' returned Lorraine quietly ; 'we consider ourselves very fortunate. I suppose,' sewing with much composure, 'that Mr. Vincent has written to share his good fortune with you.'

'Yes, and to shame me with his unworldliness. There, you may read it for yourself'—and Miss Bretherton threw the letter on her lap. 'Pritchard is wanting me for some foolery or other, but I will be back to hear your opinion'; and then Mother Hubbard trotted away, and Lorraine could hear her sharp voice and quick footsteps dying away in the distance. Lorraine thought the letter very touching. In a few concise words, Eric informed his aunt that the living of Highlands had been offered him, and that they had moved into the Vicarage.

'This has made a great difference in my income,' he wrote, 'and I feel it only right to tell you this, in case you should wish to discontinue my allowance. Your kind generosity, with regard to Hugo's and Edmund's education, has so lightened my burdens that it is no longer absolutely necessary to me. True, the living is only moderate, but I have a good house, and can easily take pupils. It is only fair to tell you this, and to leave matters in your hands. I hope, dear Aunt Marion, that you will understand my motives, and that it is not any reluctance in accepting your generous gifts that has caused me to write to you. If you would only allow me to explain things to you personally, how willingly I would come to Nefydd Madoc'; and then he signed himself, 'Your ever grateful and affectionate nephew, ERIC.'

'It is just like him, just what I would have expected him to say,' observed Lorraine, when Miss Bretherton returned, and Lorraine's voice was tremulous with feeling. 'Dear Miss Bretherton, in your heart how you must admire him for this; so few people would be so scrupulously honest. I am afraid he has made a mistake about taking pupils, though ; Nora is far too young and inexperienced.'

A sarcastic expression played round Miss Bretherton's lips, but she set her chin obstinately.

'Eric is a very clever young man,' she replied in a meaning tone ; 'he knows that he will lose nothing by his honesty ; he has only done it for effect. Don't shake your head, Mrs. Herbert, you have your opinions and I have mine. I shall just write to Eric, and put the matter as briefly as possible. I will write it now, and you shall see what I say'; and Miss Bretherton marched off to her writing-table, and scrawled a few sentences with a noisy quill, then she brought the letter to Lorraine.

NEPHEW ERIC (it began), there is no use in unsettling things ; the lawyer has my instructions, and he may as well carry them out. Two hundred a year is all you have to expect from me, and Nora and Effie will each have five hundred ; as I am a rich woman, you have not much cause for thankfulness, so please spare me your expressions of gratitude.

As there is nothing that needs explanation, I will not trouble you to take this long journey—you have no love for Nefydd Madoc, I know well. I am glad you have a decent house to live in. I suppose you will stop at Highlands till they make you a dean or a bishop—lawn sleeves are very becoming. I shall keep Mrs

Herbert as long as I can, she suits me exactly.—I remain, yours truly,   MARION BRETHERTON.

Lorraine gave it back a little sadly. 'A few kind words would have enhanced the value of your gift,' she said in a tone of regret. 'I know Mr. Vincent so well; this letter will pain him so'; but her remonstrance fell on deaf ears. Miss Bretherton folded it up and placed it in the post-bag; but for the remainder of the day she was not a pleasant companion, she found fault with the maids, and was a little nipping in her answers to Lorraine; the demon of unrest seemed to have seized on her, and she was perpetually going in search of Pritchard.

'My mistress will have a bad night,' observed Pritchard later in the evening; 'she never sleeps a wink after one of Mr. Eric's letters. She has been hankering after him all her life, but she will never bring herself to own it; she has a grudge against him that makes her bitter and hard, but it is my belief that in her heart she cares as much as ever for him.' And as Lorraine shared this opinion, the two women were very soft and pitiful over Miss Bretherton's ill-humour. Lorraine had long ago given her hostess a full account of her own trouble; Miss Bretherton had listened to the history of the accident with intense and painful interest, but she never alluded to it again. They had become fast friends, and in her kindly, erratic way Miss Bretherton showed Lorraine in every possible manner that she was a welcome guest.

A few days after Eric's letter Pritchard entered Lorraine's room with an unusually solemn face. Her mistress had been ill all night, she informed her; it had been one of her usual attacks, only the pain had been more severe, and David had gone off for Dr. Meredith.

'She has taken her draught and is sleeping now,' continued Pritchard; 'when she wakes she will be as weak as an infant. Yes, you may go and look at her if you make no sound, for she is sleeping as heavily as possible'; and Lorraine crept into the next room and looked anxiously at the pallid face and dark lips. The grey curls looked damp and dishevelled from last night's agony; one thin hand was still tightly clenched on the quilt.

When Dr. Meredith came he said little, but Lorraine thought his cheerfulness was rather forced. It was a sharp attack, he said, and she would have to keep her bed for a day or two. 'Keep her warm and quiet and give her plenty of light nourishment,' he said to Pritchard. 'I shall send her the usual medicine, and we shall soon have her right again.' But when Lorraine questioned him as to the cause of the pain, he seemed on his guard at once.

It was nothing serious—at least he hoped not. Miss Bretherton might outlive them both, for the matter of that; but of course such severe pain was wearing; and a sudden chill might work serious harm.

'Miss Bretherton leads too solitary a life,' he continued. 'I am always telling her so; she ought to go away for a time and see people; she is clever and imaginative, and feeds too much on herself. A solitary life is never a healthy one. Miss Bretherton needs young life about her.' And then the busy doctor hurried off to the next case.

Lorraine saw very little of the invalid for the next two or three days. Pritchard never allowed any one to share her nursing, and as Miss Bretherton was too weak and confused by the strong opiates she had taken to bear conversation, Lorraine only went in at intervals to say a few kind words.

But one evening Miss Bretherton sent for her. She was lying back in an easy-chair looking very white and frail, but she held out her hand with her droll smile.

'Sit down, Mrs. Herbert; I have been wearying for you the last hour. I get so tired of only seeing Pritchard's face. Go downstairs and get your tea, Pritchard, and then you may go to the Lodge and have a chat with Rebecca Fechan. Mrs. Herbert will stay with me until bed-time.' And thus dismissed, Pritchard withdrew somewhat reluctantly.

'Pritchard is a good creature, but she is a bit of a tyrant, though I do not let her know that I think so; she and Dr. Meredith play into each other's hands. "You can't cure me, so you may as well let me alone, Doctor," I said to him yesterday; "I shall not die until my time comes, in spite of all your medicines"; but he only laughed and rubbed his hands. But I mean to have my way in spite of him; I am coming downstairs to-morrow. Now sit down and talk to me, I want to know what you have been doing with yourself all day.'

Lorraine began her recital. She had been to the village and made two or three new acquaintances; but as she talked on cheerfully, Miss Bretherton hardly seemed to listen—there was an absent expression in her keen blue eyes, and as soon as Lorraine had finished her narrative she said abruptly :

'I have sent for my lawyer. I am going to alter my will'; and then with a touch of wistfulness in her voice, 'I wish you would make up your mind to stay here altogether; I do not believe that Highlands suits you. Miss Trevor could live with her brother, and I need you far more than she does. Come, Mrs. Herbert; why should we not jog on comfortably together? No one has ever

suited me before.   Stay with me, and you shall be as free as one
of my birds, and after my death Black Nest shall be yours.   Why
should I not make you a rich woman if I like ?   My money is my
own.   I have done my duty to Eric, and he will not touch another
penny of my money.'

For one moment intense surprise kept Lorraine silent ; then her
face flushed with emotion, and kneeling down by the couch she
put her arms round the slight little figure.

'Dear Miss Bretherton,' she said softly, 'if you knew how I
loved you for this ; how have I ever deserved such generosity ?
This is the third home that has been offered to me, if I could only
accept it' ; and here she sighed heavily.   'But indeed I cannot
disappoint poor Muriel, I have pledged my word to her and
Ellison.   I will come and stay with you as often as you ask me ;
but it is not possible for me to do more.'

'Very well, then, we will say no more about it,' returned Miss
Bretherton decidedly ; 'you are a woman of your word, and I
respect you for it ; all the same, I mean to leave you Black Nest
on condition that you live here six months in the year, and that
you keep on my list of pensioners.   Well, what now ?' as Lorraine
shook her head decidedly.

'Dear, dearest Miss Bretherton,' she replied in a shocked voice,
'are you quite mad ?   Do you think that I would ever accept such
misplaced generosity ?   I will· never have Black Nest—never,
never—Mr. Vincent is your rightful heir.   I am nothing to you
but an attached and grateful friend ; before I would allow you to
do such an injustice I would go away to-morrow and never see
you again.   But you cannot mean it ; you would not leave this
world unreconciled to your nephew.'

'He has made his bed and must lie on it,' returned Miss
Bretherton doggedly ; 'why should I leave him Black Nest when
he has hated it all his life ?   I would sooner leave it to Nora.'

'Leave it to Nora, then, and make Mr. Vincent her guardian.
No one could find fault with you for doing that.   Nora is your
sister's child—think over it, Miss Bretherton, there is plenty of
time.   But if you want to die peacefully you will forgive Mr.
Vincent his boyish offences ; he has long ago repented of his way-
wardness to you.   Let me plead for him,' she continued earnestly ;
'he is longing to be friends with you.   Let me write to him and
tell him that he will be welcome.   There is no need to make him
your heir if you do not desire it, but you must not continue to
treat him as your enemy.   In your heart you love him dearly
Pritchard and I know that well.   Be true to yourself and him ;
and God help you to do the right thing with the wealth entrusted

to you.' And Lorraine kissed her gently on the brow and left the room.

She felt profoundly agitated, and it was a relief to sit down alone in the firelit twilight and think over things quietly.

Black Nest might have been her home, if only she had not given her word to Muriel; but it was too late now. She must not think of it again. In a few weeks she would leave her safe retreat among the Welsh mountains and take up her work again. Miss Bretherton's proposal to make her the future mistress of Black Nest only brought a smile to her lips. Such a thought could not be entertained seriously for a moment ; it was just a whimsical idea. If she should fix on Nora, well and good ; but she would say no further word on the subject. She did not see Miss Bretherton again that night, and for some days there was no further allusion to the subject. One thing was evident to Lorraine, that Miss Bertherton bore her no grudge for her plain speaking ; and to all appearance they were better friends than ever.

The next Sunday Miss Bretherton was well enough to drive to church. By some strange coincidence the sermon that morning was on the forgiveness of injuries. Lorraine, who was listening attentively, felt Miss Bretherton wince more than once. Nothing was said as they drove home ; but all that afternoon Miss Bretherton seemed uneasy and out of spirits. Later in the evening, as they sat together with Winnie Fack and her kittens basking on the rug in the firelight, Lorraine saw her look at her with strange intensity. At last she laid down her book.

'Would you like to talk a little?' she said gently. 'I am rather tired of reading myself, and I fancied you looked dull.' But Miss Bretherton's answer took her by surprise.

'I suppose you are right and the vicar is right, and I am an obstinate, cross-grained old woman. You may write and tell Eric to come here if you like, and bring Nora with him. It goes against me to forgive him ; but I suppose I shall have to do it before I take my long journey—and perhaps I have kept it up long enough ; but you had better tell him that he need not look for Black Nest, for it will never be his—"a black prison," he called it, "only fit for cats to live in."'

'But he may come, and you will welcome him kindly,' returned Lorraine, and Miss Bretherton nodded ; and before she slept that night the letter was written. Pritchard came in later to talk over things.

'I knew my mistress was coming round,' she said. 'I have had plenty of signs to tell me that her heart was softening to the poor young gentleman. She has a picture of him hidden away somewhere, and to my belief it was under her pillow all the time she was ill, though she never allowed me to get a glimpse of it. My mistress has odd whimsies sometimes ; but when she once likes a person she never changes, and she has never changed to Mr. Eric. You have told her the truth, ma'am, and it has done her a power of good. Black Nest has been a brighter place since you entered it, and my mistress has been a happier woman. God bless her, for she has had a hard time of it'; and the faithful creature wiped away a tear.

Two or three days elapsed and then Eric's letter came. It was addressed to Mrs. Herbert.

'Will you tell Aunt Marion,' he wrote, 'that I am delighted with her invitation for Nora and myself? but I cannot possibly come until next Monday, and then only for three or four days ; but Nora can stay if she wishes her to do so. You do not name any time, so I am making my own arrangements. I need not tell you that the invitation has greatly surprised me, and I cannot help suspecting that it is owing to your friendly offices ; but you know how greatly I desire to be reconciled to my sole remaining relative.'

'Mr. Vincent is coming on Monday evening,' she said quietly, 'and will bring Nora with him. He seems very much pleased with his invitation.' But Miss Bretherton only reddened a little and said nothing.

Pritchard brought Lorraine little scraps of news from time to time.

'Mr. Eric is to have his old room, ma'am,' she said one day, 'and Miss Nora is to have the blue room. My mistress is looking after everything herself. She has big fires lighted in both rooms to be sure they are aired.' And another time, 'She has been ordering in a stock of provisions from Croes-fford that would feed a garrison. It is my belief that the fatted calf will be provided for Mr. Eric.'

Miss Bretherton never opened her lips on the subject ; but early on Monday morning she asked Lorraine if she would mind driving into Croes-fford that evening to meet the travellers, and Lorraine assented cheerfully.

'There is Mrs. Herbert!' exclaimed Nora joyfully, and the next moment she threw herself into her friend's arms. Eric followed her more slowly. He looked a little flushed and excited.

'What does this mean?' he said as he shook hands with her. 'I could scarcely believe my eyes when I read your letter. Three weeks ago Aunt Marion wrote to me in the stiffest way and begged me not to come.'

'Ladies change their minds sometimes,' returned Lorraine,

smiling at him, and the young man felt a little giddy as he followed the slim, graceful figure across the station. Lorraine was holding Nora's hand. The two were whispering eagerly together.

'Dear Mrs. Herbert, how lovely it seems to see you again,' cried the girl ecstatically. 'We have all wanted you so much, haven't we, Eric?' and all the way to Nefydd Madoc she held Lorraine's hand tightly.

Eric said very little. He sat staring out in the darkness trying to recall old memories. 'What a young ass I must have been,' he muttered to himself once.

Directly the carriage stopped Miss Bretherton's tiny figure was distinctly visible. She stood in the centre of the hall, rigid and immovable, leaning on her stick. Pritchard was looming in the background.

'So you have come, Eric,' was all she said as she held out her hand to him.

'Yes, I have come. You might be sure I should do so when you sent for me,' and then Eric stooped and kissed her gently on the cheek. 'Dear Aunt Marion, if you only knew how glad I am to see Black Nest again.'

'Take them to their rooms, Pritchard,' observed Miss Bretherton a little hoarsely; 'dinner will be ready directly. Dear me, Nora, how tall you have grown; you will be a woman soon.'

'I shall soon be fourteen,' returned Nora. She was still nestling against her old friend; but as she spoke her delicate refined little face lit up with innocent pride. 'I must be a grown-up woman as soon as I can for Eric's and the children's sake.'

'She will do,' observed Miss Bretherton, half to herself, and then she sat down in the high-backed chair and stared into the fire. 'Shall I do it?' she thought; 'it is not a bad idea,' and then in the red cavernous hollow she seemed to see a boyish face with rough curly hair tossing wearily upon his pillow.

'I will not stop here, Aunt Marion. I hate it all; and I shall hate you too if I stay. I want my mother and not you. Mothers are better than anything in the world, at least mine is; and I shall break my heart if you do not let me go.'

'It hurts still when I think of it,' she muttered; 'but I have been over hard; I know that now. But to have him sleeping in his old room again,'—she sighed, and there was a mist before her eyes. The next moment she struck her stick sharply against the floor, and summoned Pritchard.

CHAPTER XLIX

NORA'S HOLIDAY HOUSE

> ''Twere all one
> That I should love a bright particular star
> And think to wed it.'
>
> SHAKESPEARE.

THE evening passed quietly. During supper Miss Bretherton treated her nephew with marked civility, as though she were entertaining some distinguished stranger whose acquaintance she was only then making, but to Nora she was perfectly friendly. Her heart seemed to open to the girl's involuntary artlessness and unconscious innocence. Her soft, wide-open glances appealed irresistibly to the lonely woman ; the very sight of Nora kneeling on the rug with the kitten in her arms brought a smile to her lips.

'Oh, auntie, how happy you must be to live in such a lovely place !' exclaimed Nora suddenly. 'Eric never told us how beautiful it was. I feel as though I could not wait until the morning to see the garden and the river, but I could hear it all so plainly from my room. Mrs. Herbert wants me to go to bed now, because she says I must be so dreadfully tired ; but I am as much awake as possible.'

'Ah, you are young, Nora ; make the most of your youth, my dear. So you think I must be happy living alone with my cat angels in my mountain nest ? Wait a moment, child, I want to ask you something,' and Miss Bretherton laid a small jewelled hand on the girl's shoulder, the diamonds and rubies and emeralds seemed a blaze of red and green light in Nora's dazzled eyes. The little pale face and pointed chin reminded her of the white witch in one of Hugo's story-books. 'Listen to me, Nora, you are a wise child, I can see that. If Black Nest were yours, your very own, would you like to live here always ? '

Nora nodded vigorously, then her face grew grave.

'I would love it, auntie ; but then I could not leave Eric,' glancing at him as he stood on the rug talking to Mrs. Herbert. Neither of them had heard Miss Bretherton's question, for she had spoken in a low voice. 'I should never care to live anywhere without Eric and the children.'

'Tut, child, Eric will be marrying some day, and then he will be glad to get rid of you,' and as Nora's face fell at this she gave her a friendly push. 'There, go off to bed, I was only joking. Of course Eric will marry, and you and Effie will have to look out for yourselves ; if only some fairy godmother were to turn up and leave you a snug home like Black Nest.'

'Would not that be delightful ?' and Nora's face flushed with excitement. 'Hugo and I often make up stories like that. If I ever had a home like Black Nest, I will tell you what I would do, auntie ; I would turn it into a Holiday house, and we would all live here in the summer, Eric should have a *locum tenens*, and fish and climb mountains and enjoy himself, and in the winter we would all live at Highlands : just fancy how splendid it would be,' and Nora's eyes sparkled.

'There, go off and dream of your Holiday house' ; and Miss Bretherton turned her cold, smooth cheek to the girl's kiss : when Nora went off chattering happily with Lorraine, Miss Bretherton rose too. 'I daresay you are tired Eric,' she said quickly. 'We are early folk at Black Nest—"Early to bed and early to rise," is our motto, so I am going to wish you good-night,' and then she nodded to him and trotted off.

Eric had an odd experience that night ; he woke up from his first sleep with a curious fancy that some one was moving about his room ; the moon was streaming full into his window, and the next moment he plainly distinguished a tiny grey figure standing at the foot of his bed.

He had never heard that Black Nest was haunted, and he was rather incredulous on the subject of ghosts. Could it possibly be his Aunt Marion ? she might be walking in her sleep, and it would never do to startle her. He lay still and watched her silently, and after a few minutes she glided to the door. He sprang out of bed to see that no harm came to her, but to his relief the gleam of a candle shone in the passage. 'It is all right, Mr. Eric,' whispered Pritchard's voice ; 'lock your door and go to sleep.' And Eric was thankful to take her advice.

As he dressed himself the next morning he determined to question Pritchard about last night's occurrence. As he left his room he met her face to face ; she stopped at once and looked at him inquiringly.

'I hope you were not much disturbed, Mr. Eric,' she said anxiously. 'When my mistress is a little excited she often walks in her sleep, it is an old habit of hers; but I am generally on the look-out and watch her until she is safe in her bed again.'

'What made her come to my room, Pritchard?' he asked curiously.

'Well, sir, that is always where she goes first; times out of number I have missed her, and found her in the north room standing by the bed; now and then I have seen her smooth the pillow as though some child lay there, and have heard her sigh as she turned away. You see, Mr. Eric, she got into the habit when you were a child and stayed at Black Nest. She never would go to her bed if you seemed at all restless or uneasy. All of us servants knew how she doted on you, and how my mistress's heart was half broken when you fretted so to go home.'

'I wonder she did not hate such an ill-conditioned little brute. I was a wretched cub in those days, Pritchard.'

'But she did not think so, Mr. Eric. She would have lain down on the ground and let you trample on her if you would only have said a kind word to her. And she treated you like a prince too. Do you remember the grey pony and the fine new saddle and bridle she bought you, and the young jackdaw that you fancied, and the white rats with pink eyes? If you opened the cupboard in your room, Mr. Eric, you would find all your old toys, not one of them missing; but then it was all no use, nothing would make you take to the place, and my poor mistress had to bear her disappointment.'

'Does she care for me still, do you think?' asked Eric in a low voice.

'As much as ever, Mr. Eric. That is why she could not rest last night with the joy of knowing you were in your old room. No one understands my mistress except David Fechan and myself; she is like one of our wild-wood nuts—they have a rough, hard shell, but when you get to the inside they have a sweet, sound kernel. There, I must not talk any longer; for I must be carrying my mistress her breakfast, she is a little weakly this morning after last night's excitement, and I have persuaded her to rest for an hour or two.'

The morning passed pleasantly to Eric, rambling about the garden and village with Mrs. Herbert and Nora. When they returned to luncheon they found Miss Bretherton busily engaged in mincing chicken for Winnie Fack. She greeted her nephew with cool civility, and then beckoned Nora to sit beside her.

'Sit down there, little girl, and tell me what you think of Black

Nest now'; and Nora, nothing loth, poured out the history of their delightful wanderings.

Mrs. Herbert had taken them everywhere—to the birds' breakfast table, and the lodge, and then to the church and the vicarage and the village. ' It is far lovelier than I thought it last night, auntie,' she finished breathlessly.

Miss Bretherton looked gratified, and during the remainder of the day she kept Nora beside her. Eric smiled a little sadly as he listened to his young sister's chatter; she seemed in no awe of her rich unknown relative. Once he saw the brown girlish head very close to the grey curls. ' Auntie, I think it is you who are our fairy godmother,' she said once. ' Eric never looks worried now when I tell him Hughie wants new boots ; he used to sigh so dreadfully, as though he had the whole world on his shoulders ; it used to make me ache to hear him. I do believe he never had enough to eat ; he would say, " Give it to the boys, growing lads are always so hungry," but I know he wanted it himself. I have seen him often, when we had finished dinner, cut himself a hunch of dry bread and eat it as he went on with his sermon.'

There was an odd flash in the blue eyes, and some of Miss Bretherton's stitches were dropped. As she picked them up her hands trembled a little. More than once that evening Eric found her keen, penetrating glance fixed on him, as though she were trying to read his very thoughts.

The next morning as he was looking over his letters, while Mrs. Herbert and Nora were putting on their hats, he heard Miss Bretherton's sharp voice call him.

' If you have nothing particular to do I want to talk to you,' she said with her usual abruptness. ' I am too rheumatic to go out myself, but if you don't mind staying with me for an hour we could have our talk, and I will tell Mrs. Herbert not to wait for you ; shall I ?' and as he assented to this in some surprise, she trotted off. When she returned she seated herself in her favourite high-backed chair, and motioned him to the settle.

She was about to speak when Eric leant forward and took her hand.

' One moment, Aunt Marion. We are friends, are we not ?' and as she reddened and tried to draw her hand away he held it fast. ' I have slept under your roof two nights, but I still feel myself a stranger. For my mother's sake—the sister whom you so deeply loved—will you not say one kind word to me ?'

' Soft speeches never come easy to me,' she said, wincing a little under his clear, candid glance. ' But I mean to be friendly, Eric. I will not deceive you. I want to be kind, and

25

to make up for my past hardness ; but I cannot—I cannot give you Black Nest.'

'My dear Aunt Marion, I do not expect it. We have settled all that long ago.'

'Nothing is settled in this world of change,' she answered wearily. 'You are very generous, Eric. If I ever called you mercenary, I never meant it for a moment. But it vexed me to see you so blameless. God forgive me for a wicked old woman, but I grudged you even your virtues ! You had done nothing really to forfeit your rights, but, all the same, I was determined not to make you my heir. Let me tell you everything. I wanted to leave Black Nest to Mrs. Herbert. I would have made her my adopted daughter, and left her a rich woman, but she refused to touch my money.'

' You could not have chosen any one more worthy,' he returned quietly. But something in his tone made her glance at him sharply. For the moment Eric was not completely master of himself. He could not hear Lorraine's name unmoved. The next moment Miss Bretherton's tiny hand rested on his shoulder. ' Eric,' she said softly, ' you care for her ' ; and as his eyes dropped as though he were abashed, she stroked his arm gently. 'My poor boy, I never dreamt of this ; if I had known it'—and then she paused and looked wistfully at him. 'Is there anything I can do, Eric ? '

'No,' he said, almost impatiently, 'there is nothing that you or any one can do. She will never care for me — never. Why did you make me speak, Aunt Marion ? I hoped no one but myself would ever guess my secret. There, let us never mention it again. She is the sweetest creature on God's earth, and the most unhappy ; but no love of mine could comfort her.'

'Eric, are you sure ? '

'Quite sure. For heaven's sake, Aunt Marion, let us talk of something else. If she would have accepted Black Nest I should have been glad. I hate to know she is poor, and living on the bounty of others. Surely you could leave her some of your money, Aunt Marion ? '

'Shall I give her your two hundred ? That would be a nice little income ! Now let me finish what I was going to say. You would never care for Black Nest as I have cared for it ; besides, it is too far away from your work, so I mean to leave it to Nora. It will be a home for her and Effie, and if you marry —don't look so shocked, Eric, there are other women in the world besides Mrs. Herbert, and you are young enough to be consoled—if you marry, my dear, Nora can make a home for the boys. I have thought over it well, and this seems the best arrangement. I will take care that Nora shall have sufficient income to keep up the place properly, and you must act as her guardian. Your share will be seven hundred a year. Will that content you, Eric ? It is not as much as you had a right to expect, but Nora is your mother's child too.'

Eric tried to answer, but his lips suddenly quivered. The good things of life were being heaped on him without measure, but the one gift he desired was as remote from him as ever. In vain he endeavoured to speak. Something like a low sob broke from him. The next moment a tender hand was laid on his head.

'Say nothing, Eric. My poor poor boy ! Do you think I do not understand ? You are good and brave, and you have fought your hard battle nobly.' And then, as her arms went round him, and he felt her motherly kiss, something like comfort stole into the young man's heart.

.That night, as Lorraine sat by her bedroom fire brushing out her long auburn hair, there was a tap at her door, and the next moment Miss Bretherton entered.

'I want to speak to you,' she began abruptly. 'You put the idea into my head, and you ought to be the first person to know that I mean to carry it out. Eric and I have settled things. Nora is to have Black Nest, and make a home for Effie and the boys, and Eric will have seven hundred a year and act as guardian. Nora is nearly out of her wits with delight, and I don't believe she will sleep for hours. She has been crying and hugging Eric for fear he is disappointed, but he has assured her that he would not have things otherwise. Nora is going to spend all her holidays with me, and Eric has promised me three weeks in September.'

'Dear Miss Bretherton, this is good news indeed. Black Nest will be a veritable nest.' But to this Miss Bretherton made no reply. She stood leaning on her ivory crutch with her eyes fixed on the fire, evidently in deep meditation. Then she said suddenly, 'Look here—I am a fool to say it, but I never could hold my tongue—Mrs. Herbert, do you know that boy cares for you ? My dear, I am an old woman, and my time will not be long. I think I should leave this world more happily if I thought you would be good to him.'

A startled look came into the brown eyes, and then Lorraine grew very pale. 'Dear friend,' she said gently, 'you must not ask me that. I like Mr. Vincent ; there is no one I respect more, but' —her delicate throat trembling a little—'I could never care for him in that way.'

'Then I will not say any more. Poor Eric ! He must just

bear his trouble. He would be dreadfully hurt if he knew that I had betrayed his secret. Ah, he was right. Do you know what he said to me ? "She is the sweetest creature on God's earth, and the most unhappy ; but no love of mine could comfort her." There, I did not mean to make you cry. You have shed tears enough, but I could have cried myself when Eric said that.'

'Why did you tell me ?' sobbed Lorraine. 'But I knew—something in his manner made me guess it. That is why I left off going to the cottage. Dear Miss Bretherton, why did I ever go to Highlands ? Nothing but mischief has come of it. If I could only stay here quietly with you. If you only knew how I dread going back.'

'As long as I live, Black Nest will be open to you,' returned Miss Bretherton, looking at her with tender compassion. 'And when I die you will find that you have not been forgotten. If I could care for you more I should do so now when I know my poor boy has set his heart on you. But he will get over it. It is not in the nature of men to spend their lives fretting after the wrong woman. He will be unhappy for a time, and then some one your very opposite will console him.'

'I hope you may be right,' returned Lorraine wearily. But when Miss Bretherton left her she wept long and bitterly. Eric Vincent's attachment infused new bitterness in her already brimming cup of sorrow. No one was happy except Ellison. 'God keep her so for all our sakes,' prayed Lorraine from her heart.

CHAPTER L

' Do not slay him who deserves alone a whipping for the fault he has done.'
—HORACE.

ALL these weeks Ellison had missed Lorraine sorely. And when two months had elapsed, and there was still no word of her return, a faint surprise, almost amounting to uneasiness, assailed her. Her wedding had been fixed for the last day of April. Colonel Trevor had indeed pleaded for an earlier date, but she had convinced him that it would be wiser to wait a little. She was now busy with preparations and the cares of her *trousseau,* and Lorraine's help and sympathy would have been a great relief. In spite of her intense and ever-deepening happiness there were moments when an undefinable sense of sadness stole over her. Gavin was strangely depressed at times ; and though Ellison put down his gravity and absence of mind to his mother's recent death, a chill sense of discomfort and oppression would creep over her sometimes during those long silent evenings.

But this vague uneasiness never troubled her when Gavin was beside her. No lover could have been more tender or considerate. Her slightest wish seemed a law to him, and he brought his masculine judgment to bear even on the colour of a gown if she needed his advice.

'Dear,' she said apologetically one evening, 'I am almost ashamed to trouble you with these details, but I want you to be satisfied with your wife's appearance.' One of her rare blushes had come to her face as she said this, and she looked at him lovingly ; and then as he pressed her closer to him without speaking, she whispered, 'All my life it will be my first thought to please you in everything.'

He had been in one of his grave moods that evening, and as

she spoke, the sadness of his eyes almost startled her. 'You must not be too good to me, Ellison,' he said in a low voice. 'I am not worthy of it; there is not a man living who is worthy of a good woman's love.'

'Nonsense, Gavin; I will not allow you to talk such heresy; but indeed I have no right to tease you with all these trifles. If only Lorraine would come home; Muriel is useless in such matters—our opinions clash on every point. Does it not seem a little strange, Gavin, that Lorraine does not speak of her return? Mr. Vincent and Nora both say that she is quite strong now, and can take long walks, and that she seems cheerful and like herself; and yet she takes no notice of all my hints.'

'Why should you hurry her?' returned Gavin, stooping to replace a faggot that had fallen on the hearth. 'It is far better for her to stay where she is. Highlands has never been the same place to her since that poor child's death. She is so unselfish that she will come at once if you tell her that you want her; but if you will take my advice, you will not let her know that.'

'Gavin, I cannot help thinking sometimes that Lorraine's absence is a relief to you'; and as Ellison said this, a dark flush came to Colonel Trevor's face.

'When Mrs. Herbert is away, I get you more to myself. Is not that a sufficient reason, dearest?' he said, with an attempt at playfulness; but he almost loathed himself as he felt the falsity of his speech. Why did she compel him to say such things? why would she not leave Mrs. Herbert alone? 'Ellison,' he continued, 'when we are married I hope you mean to be satisfied with me. I warn you beforehand, that I shall want my wife to myself.' There was a touch of peremptoriness in Gavin's tone as he said this, but Ellison only felt the sweetness of the compliment. How dearly he had loved her; well, when she was once his wife she should know that she wanted nothing earthly in comparison with his love.

Gavin took his leave soon after this. March had set in like a lamb that year, and the evening was soft and spring-like; already the crocuses were bursting into flower. As Ellison strolled with him up the farmyard, only wrapped in a soft, fleecy shawl, she noticed with delight the budding foliage; the crisp, sweet air was balmy with promise; as she parted from Gavin with a mute hand-shake, the soft serenity of her eyes struck him afresh.

'At least I shall make her happy,' he said to himself. 'My trouble is not unbearable as long as I know that.'

Ellison was unwilling to re-enter the house; the clear light, the refreshing air tempted her to stroll a little farther up the lane.

She was just in sight of the white cottages, when, to her surprise, she saw Dorcas talking to her *bête noir*, George Bates. Bates had been dismissed from Gavin's service, but he was still hanging about the place; his voice sounded angry and excited, and Dorcas was crying bitterly. When she saw her mistress she darted towards her as though for protection.

'Oh, ma'am, do send him away,' she said hysterically. 'He knows that I hate him, and that I won't believe any of his lies. He is a bad, wicked man to say such things,' and Dorcas began sobbing afresh.

'Lies do you call them ?' shouted Bates. He had evidently been drinking, and the girl's angry contempt had excited him still more. 'You need not put on these cursed airs, just because a respectable man offers to marry you. I am not like the Colonel. I have not got two sweethearts, and I only make love to one lass at a time. Turns me away from his service, does he, because I know a little too much of his goings on ?'

'Bates, if you do not at once hold your tongue and leave us, it will be the worse for you,' returned Ellison in strong indignation. 'Dorcas, you may run home'; but, as the girl obeyed her gladly, Bates, half maddened by Dorcas's repulse, only laughed derisively, and kept his place.

'You turned me away too, Miss Lee, and I will have my revenge,' he went on. 'Look here, I am telling no lies. You may ask the Colonel. Bring me face to face with him and I will say it over again. I was with them when Madge Wildfire played that trick, and Mrs. Herbert was thrown out of the phaeton, and I heard every word the Colonel said when he was kneeling on the road beside her. " My darling, my darling, have I killed you ?" I will take my oath those were his words. "Lorraine—one word. Let me see your sweet eyes." Ah, I treasured up the words in case I might find them handy. He is a grand man, the Colonel ; one sweetheart at a time is not enough for him.'

'Bates, if you do not let me pass, I will call for Joe Brand !' cried Ellison ; her blue eyes were blazing with contempt. 'Do you suppose your trumped-up story troubles me ?' And as the man, scared by that commanding voice, slunk out of her path, she walked down the lane, carrying her fair head higher than ever. Dorcas was waiting for her in the porch. The girl's eyes were red with crying, and she was trembling like a leaf.

Ellison spoke very gently to her. 'You foolish girl,' she said in a reassuring tone, 'there is nothing so dreadful after all. Bates has been drinking, and has lost his temper, but he would not have harmed you. Perhaps it would be wiser for you not to go out alone just now. I must talk to Colonel Trevor and Mr. Vincent, and see what is to be done. He is a loafing, ill-conditioned fellow, and when he has had a drop too much he is positively dangerous.'

'He had not been drinking when he followed me home last week,' returned Dorcas in a frightened tone. 'He was as sober as any man could be, and he said it then. He declared he would publish it through the village, and that he would have his revenge on the Colonel. He is just mad, because the Colonel has given him notice; and he is angry with you, ma'am, too. I told him then that I would not believe his lies.'

'Of course not.' But Ellison shivered as she spoke, as though a cold wind had passed over her. 'Come in here, Dorcas,' in a quick, peremptory voice. 'Come in, and shut the door. I want you to tell me exactly what Bates said to you the other evening, and why you are sure that he had not been drinking.'

'Because he was quite pale, and spoke in a subdued sort of sensible way. But indeed, ma'am, I could not bring myself to repeat his nasty, mischievous speeches; they are not fit for your ears.'

'You must let me be the best judge of that,' returned her mistress quietly. 'I am sorry to distress you, Dorcas, but I must get to the bottom of this. It will never do to allow Bates to spread these reports; we could have him taken up and punished.'

'If he would only go away,' sobbed Dorcas, 'for he is like a nightmare to me.' The girl was evidently reluctant to speak, but Ellison was firm and persistent. A good deal of questioning elicited a confused account of the accident, and how Bates had overheard the Colonel making love to Mrs. Herbert as she lay senseless. 'Why should he invent such things?' asked Dorcas indignantly. 'It is cruelly hard of him to say them, and every one knows what a kind master the Colonel is.'

'Yes, but we do not know how sweet revenge is to an evil mind. Bates is anxious to make mischief, and a little invention does not trouble his conscience. Dorcas, just put all this out of your head. I need not ask you not to mention it to your fellow-servants, for I know I can rely on you. You can tell them that Bates has frightened you, but nothing more. I will see what can be done to get rid of him. I think I will send a note to Colonel Trevor and ask him to come down this evening.'

'Yes, ma'am,' and Dorcas withdrew, half consoled by her mistress's calmness. 'She does not believe it, that's evident,' she said to herself as she crossed the passage.

Ellison stood by the fire a moment, knitting her white brows :

there was a puzzled expression in her eyes. A speech of Gavin's had suddenly come into her mind, and she could not banish it. 'You may depend upon it, that there is never smoke without a fire,' he had once said. 'Most lies, if patiently investigated, will be found to hold some shred of the truth.' 'There are exceptions to every rule,' she said aloud, 'for there is neither smoke nor fire here, in Bates's malicious inventions'; but there was a trace of irritation in her manner as she sat down and wrote her note :—

DEAR GAVIN—Could you possibly come down to the Farm after dinner? I want to ask your advice. Bates has been drinking and misbehaving himself; he is frightening poor little Dorcas out of her wits by his unmanly persecution. It would be a relief to talk it over with you.—Yours always, ELLISON.

There were two hours before she could expect Gavin, so she dressed herself with unusual care, and then ate her solitary supper. Ruth waited on her as usual, and Ellison spoke to her about Dorcas's fright. She was a kind and sympathetic mistress, and took a great deal of interest in her servants ; but this evening Ruth was less communicative than usual. She expressed strong indignation against that low fellow, Bates, as she called him ; but more than once when Ellison's attention was diverted, she looked at her mistress a little strangely, and even pityingly. Dorcas had suppressed the fact that she had already confided Bates's strange story to Ruth's ear, under a strict pledge of secrecy ; and Ruth, who was clever and sharp-sighted, had her own ideas on the subject. Ellison was a little restless when she returned to the sitting-room ; the whole affair had annoyed her excessively ; how dare a tipsy groom spread these infamous reports about his master. Gavin would be so angry, he would be ready to horse-whip the fellow, 'he is so chivalrous,' she said to herself ; 'for Lorraine's sake, he will have no mercy on Bates.'

It was a relief when she heard the click of the little gate, and saw Gavin's tall figure pass the window ; he only waited to throw off his overcoat, and then he came in. Ellison rose from her chair to meet him.

'Oh, Gavin, it is so good of you to come, but I hardly expected you so soon.'

'Of course I came when you wanted me,' he said, looking at her with his usual kind smile ; 'my liege lady has a right to my service. So that fool of a Bates has been kicking up a row again ; well, we must put a stop to that.'

'Yes ; and he has done more than frighten Dorcas. Gavin,

would you believe it, he has actually had the audacity to publish scandalous reports about you ?   I hate to repeat such things,' and Ellison reddened with annoyance, 'but you ought to know what he has dared to say.'

'Of course I ought to know, so you had better tell me everything from the beginning,' and Colonel Trevor drew her down beside him on the couch ; 'you look quite fierce, Ellison, as though you would like to thrash him yourself.' There was a spark of amusement in his eyes as he said this ; but at her first words it died away.

'Don't joke, Gavin.   I am afraid you will be terribly annoyed ; the wretched fellow has dared to insinuate things about you and Lorraine.   Ah, no wonder you start ! He actually had the audacity to tell me—to my face—that you made love to poor Lorraine when she lay senseless on the ground that night of the accident.   He asked me to bring him face to face with you, and he would repeat your very words.   Does he not deserve a horsewhipping, Gavin ?' and Ellison gave a musical little laugh ; 'you and Lorraine, my poor dear Lorraine, of all people.'

There was a moment's dead silence, and then Colonel Trevor sprang up from the couch and walked to the fireplace.   He had tried to echo the laugh, but no sound passed his lips.   'Good heavens !' was all he said, and he shuddered visibly.

Ellison followed him.   She was prepared for indignation, but such excessive anger alarmed her ; she put her hand caressingly on his arm.

'Don't trouble so, Gavin, it is not worth it ; Lorraine will never know of his senseless speeches, and you will find some way of making him hold his tongue.   How dare he tell these lies of his master—you of all people,' she repeated, as she looked up in his face with a trustful smile ; but the next moment she recoiled.   Why was Gavin looking at her so strangely, his face was pale, and there was an agonised expression in his eyes.   They gazed at her with dumb beseeching misery, but there was no anger, no righteous indignation in them.   A curious sensation of faintness came over her, a chill dizziness ; it was only with an effort that she could rally her energies.   'Gavin !' she exclaimed, and there was anguish now in her voice.   'You frighten me.   Why are you so strangely silent ?   How can the lies of a discharged groom affect you so strangely ?   Speak to me ; you must—you shall speak' ; and her firm grasp tightened on his arm.

'They are no lies,' he returned with a groan.   'Ellison, if you make me speak, I can only tell you the truth—not even for your sake can I tell an utter falsehood.   How can I punish a man for slanderous reports when he is stating a fact? I thought Mrs. Herbert was dead, and I knelt down by her side in the snow. In my terror I lost my self-control, and spoke as I ought not, and Bates heard me. That is all'; and Gavin smiled bitterly.

Ellison's limbs trembled under her; only that grasp of Gavin's arm gave her support; certain words were surging through her brain with hammer-like insistence as he spoke—'My darling, my darling, have I killed you? Lorraine—only one word; let me see your sweet eyes.' Then she hid her face on his shoulder with a low moan, as of one stricken to the heart. 'Gavin, tell me the whole truth,' she whispered; 'it is Lorraine, not me, whom you love.' Then he turned on her almost fiercely.

'It is cruel of you to say that. Good heavens, do you not see what I am suffering? Am I not already humiliated in your eyes? All these months I have wrestled with the temptation; but, Ellison, I can look you in the face still. If I have cared for Mrs. Herbert too much for my peace of mind, I have been absolutely true to you also; never, never, except under the provocation of that moment's terror, have I ever said one word that you would not have approved. Do you think,' laying his cold hand on hers, 'that I could be guilty of disloyalty to my promised wife? I may be weak as other men are weak, but on my soul, I have ever honoured you, and treasured the very hairs of your head as sacred to me.'

It spoke much for Ellison's trust in him, that in that hour of agony and humiliation she still clung to him. Yes, he was good, she knew that; even at that moment, when he had slain her happiness for ever, she did not wrong him by any unworthy suspicion. If he loved Lorraine, it was through no fault of his, or hers either. The misery that had overtaken them, and that had dashed the cup of joy from her lips, was dealt by the hand of Fate, and was not his doing.

'Gavin!' and she spoke with her face still hidden, 'there is one thing more you must tell me'—her voice shook, and she steadied it with difficulty—'does Lorraine know that you care? is this why she is staying away so long?'

'Yes, she knows,' he returned reluctantly; 'because in my foolish terror I betrayed myself. Do not let us speak of her, my dear one; she was like an angel of consolation sent to strengthen me in the hour of temptation; and as an angel, a saint, not as a woman, I shall ever regard her for the future. Dear, you have nothing to fear from either of us; your happiness is her first consideration, as it is mine.'

'That is all I need to ask.' And then Ellison raised her weary head. She was white to her lips; but there was a tortured look in her eyes. 'Gavin, you must go away now, I cannot talk any more. No, I am not ill, not bodily ill, but I have had a shock. Do you think'—with the saddest smile possible—'that it is a light shock to know that another woman has your love ? But I am not angry with her or you. Why should I be angry because I am unhappy ? But you must go,' pushing him from her with gentle force.

'I cannot go,' he answered, rousing up at this. 'Ellison, you must not ask me to leave you. Dear, can I not see what I have made you suffer ? How am I to go away until I have tried to staunch the wound that I have made ?' And he would have put his arms round her, but she drew away from him.

'There is no healing possible to-night,' she returned sadly. 'Gavin, if you care for me, if you honour me as you say you do, grant me this favour—let me be alone this evening. In your presence, looking at your dear face, I feel as though I can believe and realise nothing ; when you are gone, perhaps I shall be able to think.'

'Will you see me again to-morrow ? Will you let me talk to you, and make my peace ?' and he looked at her anxiously.

'To-morrow ! oh yes, why not ?' she answered, but her voice was low and weak ; she seemed like one bewildered by some terrifying vision ; then her gaze softened.

'Poor Gavin, how miserable you look ; but we cannot help it, can we ?' and then she raised her head, and kissed his forehead. How worn and weary he looked. He had suffered so much when Helen had died, and now this strange sorrow had overtaken him. 'God help us all,' she whispered ; and then she pointed with mute entreaty to the door. He dared not disobey her ; he waited for one moment to see if there were any yielding in her face ; then with bowed head he left the room.

CHAPTER LI

'I struggle towards the light—and ye,
  Once long'd-for storms of love !
If with the light ye cannot be,
  I bear that ye remove.'
                              MATTHEW ARNOLD.

THERE are hours in one's life—but thank God they are rare—when
the furnace of affliction seems heated seven-fold ; and such an hour
had come to Ellison, when the door closed upon Gavin, and she
was left alone.

Yes, he was gone, her well-beloved. The moment before he had
been standing opposite to her, with a dumb pleading for forgiveness
in his deep-set eyes, but she had sent him from her. Now the awful
silence and blankness seemed to crush her, and a choking sob broke
from her lips ; she sank down on the couch, feeling that all strength
had deserted her.

Many years afterwards, when peace had returned to her, she
said to one who loved her greatly, 'I knew then what it meant to
long for death ; life without Gavin's love seemed to me the
abomination of desolation. God forgive me my want of faith, for I
know better now ; but when the iron enters a woman's soul, as it
entered mine that day, and I saw the desire of my eyes taken
from me at a single stroke, the anguish seemed greater than I could
bear.'

And yet, though the fiery blast of disappointed love seemed to
scorch her through and through, there was no anger in her faithful
heart against the two who had wronged her. 'Gavin was not to
blame, or Lorraine either, it was Kismet, fate ; the cloudy veil that
had suddenly overshadowed them, and which had obscured her
heaven of content, had been drawn by some sorrowful angel.'

But the ordeal was a bitter one, and for some time Ellison shrank from the awful cup of suffering that was held to her lips.

Was it for this that he had taught her to love him, that he had stirred her calm nature to its very depths? She had never wished to love or marry; Gavin's friendship had completely satisfied her; but now—now—he had won her, and her tardy love burnt with the purest and most ardent flame. 'No woman, not even Lorraine, could love him better,' she said to herself as she paced the room with rapid uneven steps; 'but Lorraine must not have him, he is mine—mine—he has pledged his word, and I know him too well. Gavin, my Gavin, will never be disloyal to me.'

And again—and now her face was pallid with misery—'It was my own miserable blindness. Why was I so eager to bring them together? If I had not gone to Switzerland Lorraine would not have learnt to depend on him so utterly. Oh, I can see it all; there is no need for either of them to tell me anything; it was Gavin's good heart, his very tenderness of nature, that led him into danger. Lorraine's sorrow, her very helplessness, would appeal to him too forcibly; and then there is a charm about her—something indescribable—that would be fatal to a man like Gavin; and I, fool that I was, left him to be tempted all those months.' A heart-broken sigh escaped from her lips. 'But I will not reproach him,' she went on; 'but for this wretched man I should never have known of all this trouble: no, I cannot, I will not give him up; Gavin would not wish it, he is very proud, and he has pledged his faith to me. There are some things too hard for flesh and blood to bear; I could do anything but this; I will be patient, very very patient with him, and he will love me yet.'

And so the battle raged on, until Ellison's very soul was sick with misery. Hours had passed, and all the household was sleeping peacefully, but no rest was possible to her; rest, when she was stretched on this rack of anguish, when all her woman's kingdom was in utter chaos! 'O God, that women are made so!' was her inward cry, as it had been Lorraine's; 'that they must suffer like this.'

Once, as she paced the room restlessly, a step on the gravel-path outside her window made her shiver with sudden apprehension. She knew whose step that was; surely he was not so mad as to think she would admit him at this hour, for it was long past midnight. The next moment there was a quiet tap, and then she heard the gate close again; and as she peeped through the blind cautiously, she saw something white lying on the window ledge; but it was some minutes before she could summon up courage to open the window and take up the packet.

He had written to her. Poor Gavin, he had found it impossible to rest too. And then she sat down and opened his letter.

MY OWN DEAR ELLISON (it began)—I am writing to you to-night, because there is much that I must say to you, and much that you ought to hear ; but this evening I was too utterly abashed to speak. How is a man to defend himself when a woman looks at him as you looked at me, Ellison ? If I could have been base enough to tell you a lie, that lie would have seemed white to me at that moment. I am a guilty man, for I have suffered another woman to usurp your rightful place in my heart ; but that is the whole sum and substance of my guilt. Oh, my dear, why did you go away ? Did I not warn you that you were making a mistake ? If you had stayed, all this mischief would not have happened, for I was true to you then, absolutely and entirely true. Let me explain myself more fully—I will be perfectly frank with you ; but for that miserable fellow Bates I should have guarded my secret safely to the end, and you would not have had to suffer so cruelly. You are a proud woman, Ellison, and you have been bitterly humiliated to-night ; but if my life-long service can efface the memory of that shameful hour, you will forget it yet. My one desire, my one prayer is that you will be merciful, and suffer me to atone for the wrong I have unwittingly done you.

I cannot tell you when I began to care too much for Mrs. Herbert. I think from the first she had a singular attraction for me ; somehow at times she reminded me of my darling Nell, and yet they were not in the least alike. But I should never have succumbed to her fascinations but for the accident. You were far away, my Ellison, and I had to take your place in ministering to her ; no man with a heart could have seen any creature so utterly crushed and heart-broken, and not have tried to comfort her. I need say no more. You know me well enough to be sure that I should not weakly succumb to such a misfortune ; with the exception of those few moments, when in my terror I lost all self-mastery, I have been perfectly true to you in word and deed. Shall I tell you what she said to me that night ? 'There is nothing to forgive ; it is not your fault, it is a great misfortune, a sad trouble, that has overtaken us both,' and she was right. That is what I want to impress upon you, that it is just a trouble that we must bear together ; for you will be patient with me, Ellison, will you not, until I can pull myself together ? You will not regret your forbearance, I can promise you that ; for no wife shall be more loved and honoured. There is only one thing I must ask you to arrange, that Mrs. Herbert shall remain away until after

our marriage. Why need we embarrass ourselves unnecessarily ?
when we meet she will have taken her rightful place, as Muriel's
companion and friend. You know now, my dear one, why I did
not wish her to live at Brae Farm.

Now I will end this letter. When I see you to-morrow you
will not shrink from me again, will you ? Dear, you hardly knew
how acutely you pained me then. With all my faults I am still
your betrothed ; in a few weeks I shall be your husband.
Remember that you are very dear to me, and always will be.—
Yours now and for ever,   GAVIN.

Ah, the tears were falling now ! As she finished the letter she
buried her face in her hands and wept long and bitterly. Yes, she
was dear to him, she knew that well ; but what prospect of happiness
could there be for either of them, when this shadow lay between
them ? 'You know now why I did not wish her to live at Brae
Farm.' But was not the Dower House too near for a favoured rival ?
'God help us all, for I do not know what to do !' she cried aloud ;
but no other prayer rose to her lips that night ; yet in her dumb
anguish she had never prayed so well. Just as the day was breaking, she went to her writing-table and wrote a few hurried words.

I have read your letter, Gavin ; it is like yourself. Do you think
there is any danger of my misunderstanding you ? never—never—
I can trust you utterly. A man is not always master of his own
heart ; and, dear, though you have loved me well, you have never
loved me enough. Why did you ever think of marrying me ? That
is the one great mistake that you have made. But I am not going
to reproach you ; you are far too dear to me for that ; but I must
ask you a great favour. Do not come to me to-morrow (I ought to
say to-day, for the day is dawning), you must give me time to get
over all this. I could not speak to you with calmness, and a
scene would be abhorrent to us both. I know you will be vexed
that I say this, but I have a right to some little consideration.
You have called me proud, and you are right ; but I have never
been proud with you ; even now I am asking you most humbly to
do me this favour. Leave me alone for a day or two, and when I
have recovered my calmness I will send for you.—Yours lovingly
and sorrowfully,   ELLISON.

Ellison's will was strong, but Gavin's was equally so. When
he read these last words his face became as iron, and he muttered
between his teeth. 'No, by heaven, I will not do this thing ! She
shall see me, and I will make her listen to reason.' And as soon as
he had eaten his breakfast he went down to the Farm.

He walked into the sitting-room as usual, but the young mistress of Brae Farm was not at her bureau ; then he rang the bell, and Ruth looked at him in some surprise as he questioned her.

Her mistress had gone up to town by the early train for some shopping, she said, and she was not expected home for a day or two. No, she had not left her address ; but she supposed she had gone to Portman Square as usual. Her mistress had been very hurried, and looked far from well. She had read her letters, and then sent for Dorcas to pack her bag.

'And she left no message for me ? Perhaps there is a note somewhere.'

'No, sir ; but my mistress did say, that if you called I was to tell you that she had gone to town on business. I daresay you will hear from her by the last post.' But to this Gavin made no answer ; his brow was black with anger as he walked through the farmyard. She had gone to town to avoid an interview with him ; and he knew well that she had not taken refuge at the Mervyns'. It was no use his following her ; it was not likely that he would be able to find her. She had gone to some out-of-the-way hotel or lodging, and probably the Mervyns would not know she was even in town.

For the first time in his life he felt desperately angry with her. She had condemned him to days of misery, knowing all the time how he would chafe at her absence. She could trust him utterly, and yet treat him in this heartless way, and that after a frank and manly confession. 'My one desire, my one prayer is that you will be merciful and suffer me to atone for the wrong I have unwittingly done you,' had been his words, and he had written them out of the fulness of .his heart. In spite of his infatuation for the young widow, he did desire to do his duty to his betrothed ; no idea of shirking his engagement entered his head for a moment ; but as he walked back through the long meadow the thought of Ellison's sorrowful indignation struck chill to his heart. In spite of her letter he felt that only displeasure could have driven her to take such a decided step. She never acted from impulse, her nature was too evenly balanced for that ; but for the first time he realised that he might have difficulty with her ; at least she had found a way to punish him effectually.

Muriel felt vaguely that there was something amiss. Gavin was so silent at meals, and so very unapproachable. He was out all day, and he spent his evenings shut up in his study ; even when Mr. Vincent dined with them, he made some excuse about answering some business letters, and left his sister to entertain their guest.

Five days passed, and each morning Gavin glanced anxiously

at his letters, but no envelope bore Ellison's handwriting. At last, when a week had elapsed, he saw a tiny triangular note lying on his plate. 'Dear Gavin, will you come to me this afternoon? I shall tell Ruth to admit no one else.—Yours affectionately, ELLISON.' Nothing more; not a word of extenuation and apology. Gavin was so moody during breakfast that morning that Muriel hardly dared to accost him; he scarcely glanced at the rest of his letters, and ate and drank mechanically. All the morning he tramped about the place, finding fault with the workmen who were making some alterations in the stables. 'I wonder what has put out the Colonel,' observed one of them to the under-groom, 'he is generally as pleasant-spoken as can be; but this morning he is just ramping about the place like a bear with a sore head.' As soon as luncheon was over, he walked down to the Farm. He meant to speak plainly to Ellison, and to tell her that she had treated him badly. He would take a high hand with her; he was in that sore, touchy state when even a scene would have acted as a safety-valve. A week ago he would have humbled himself before her, and would have stooped to the most abject entreaties, but now he would stand on his rights.

There was an aggressive stiffness in his manner as he entered the sitting-room; but Ellison, who was writing at her bureau, rose at once and came quickly towards him, holding out both her hands.

'Gavin, are you very angry with me?' she said, looking him full in the face; 'are you going to tell me that I have behaved badly? Dear, you must forgive me, for I could not help running away.'

'I would not have treated you so,' he returned rather bitterly. Then she sighed heavily, and her hands fell from his. He had not offered to kiss her, and there was no attempt to take her in his arms; only as he stood looking at her with that moody displeasure in his eyes, he asked himself what the change in her could mean. She was very calm, with a sort of forced calmness that struck him as unnatural, and she looked years older, as though some blight had passed over her; but she was not ill, only a shade under her eyes spoke of broken rest.   .

'Gavin,' she said gently, 'we will have our talk now; I could not have spoken to you before, it was necessary to think over things and make up my mind; somehow,' looking at him with strange earnestness, 'even in one's worst troubles there is always light, if one waits a little and prays for it. At first I could not see the right path, something seemed to blur my vision, but I have found it now.'

'Then we will walk in it together,' he returned quickly; 'your path and mine are the same.'

'No, dear, I think not.' And then, as she rested her head on his arm, with a mute caress, he saw that her betrothal ring was not in its usual place, and his face hardened again. 'Gavin, I am not angry. I have never been angry for a moment since you told me that ; and I love you as dearly as ever, but I cannot marry you. Nothing on earth would induce me to do so.' Then, as she pressed upon him gently, he almost flung her from him.

'Ellison, you dare to tell me this to my face ! But there are two persons to make a bargain. I mean to keep you to your word. I will not allow you to jilt me.'

'Oh, Gavin, what a word !' and Ellison's face grew crimson ; but she held her fair head higher than ever. 'You are exceedingly angry, or you would not say such things to your best friend. If I loved you less—if I did not prefer your happiness before my own—should I be asking you now to give me back my freedom ?'

'I do not know. I am only certain of one thing—that you are treating me shamefully. What have I done that you should put me to such cruel humiliation ? Do you not understand that my one longing is to atone to you by a lifetime of love and service ?'

'Yes, Gavin, I understand that well. You are so good and noble that I could trust my future to you without any misgiving. As far as you are concerned, I have nothing to dread.'

'Do you mean that you distrust Mrs. Herbert, Ellison ? Do you know what you are saying ? That woman has the soul of an angel. She would bear martyrdom sooner than give you a moment of uneasiness.'

'Neither do I distrust Lorraine,' but she grew a little pale as the name passed her lips. 'Dear Gavin, it is only myself that I fear. Are you sure that you understand my nature ? I am less demonstrative than most women, and I am slow to love. Even you, Gavin,' looking at him with wistful tenderness, 'found me difficult to win ; but there is one thing I know, that the man I marry must give me his whole heart, or he could not make me happy.' Then she saw him wince, and the hard, proud expression on his face changed to one of pain.

'That went straight,' he muttered. 'You had me there, Ellison ; but surely you have generosity enough to forgive my wavering in my allegiance. If you could only read my heart, my one wish is to marry you to-morrow.'

A stifled sigh broke from her lips. He was pressing her hard, but no yielding was possible to her. She knew now that no wretchedness would equal the misery of marrying him with the shadow of another woman for ever between them. The fierce jealousy that burnt in her veins at the mere thought told her that it would be too dangerous an experiment.

If she yielded to him—if she ever consented to bear the sacred name of wife—she knew that Lorraine could never enter their house — that even the bare fact of Gavin speaking to her in ordinary civility would drive her almost to madness. 'At least I know I could not bear that,' she had said to herself more than once. But how was she to convince him? Gavin was so obstinate, so tenacious of his opinions; his idea of honour called upon him to sacrifice himself and Lorraine; no other course would seem possible to him.

'Dear, let me put on that ring again,' he whispered with insinuating gentleness; but she shook her head.

'No, Gavin, never. In my turn I must say that I will not allow you to inflict such humiliation on me. I have told you before, and I tell you again, that your one great mistake was ever asking me to marry you. Why did you, dear? We were so happy in our friendship. I was so utterly contented; but you have taught me many things, Gavin, and amongst them, that even the tenderest, truest friendship will not make a happy marriage. I am your friend still'—oh the love in her eyes as she said this—'to my dying day I will keep that title of honour, but when you marry— Lorraine, not I, must be your wife—the woman whom you love, and who loves you——' and then she left him and sat down, as some sudden weakness assailed her; and Gavin, leaning against the mantelpiece, buried his face in his hands.

What had she left him to say? Did not his conscience convict him? He knew that it was the truth, and that he had never loved her. One hair of Lorraine's head was dearer to him than all Ellison's fair comeliness; the thought of a caress from her even at this moment turned him giddy; and however he might refuse to own it, Ellison's proud, pure womanliness and utter unselfishness were saving them from a great mistake.

CHAPTER LII

'Whatever's lost, it first was won ;
We will not struggle nor impugn.
Perhaps the cup was broken here,
That Heaven's new wine might show more clear.
I praise Thee while my days go on.'
ELIZABETH BARRETT BROWNING.

ANOTHER half-hour passed, and then they parted ; but Ellison had her way—Gavin had given her back her freedom.

He had not yielded without a final protest. There had been a long and painful silence between them, and then he had placed himself beside her.

'Let us talk of it calmly and dispassionately,' he said. 'You have not looked yet at my side of the question,' and then he pointed out to her the painful position in which her refusal to carry out their engagement would place him. 'You are punishing me most unmercifully,' he went on. 'What have I done that you should condemn me to a single life ; for how could I ever bring another woman to Brae as my wife ?' but she shook her head sadly at this sophistry.

'I do not ask you to marry yet,' she said quietly. 'I know that for my sake you will wait a little. It will take time to get used to our changed position. If I dared ask another favour, Gavin, it would be that you would go away for a month or two ; it would make things easier for me ; and then when you come back you will find the old Ellison ready to welcome you.'

Then he looked at her almost indignantly.

'I am to go away and leave you to bear the brunt of everything. Do you think that likely, Ellison ?'

'I think it would be wiser,' she returned gently. 'Gavin, I have thought it all out, and there will not be anything to bear.

When you go home you must speak to Muriel; tell her every-thing, it will be safe with her; and then ask her to speak to Mrs. Earnshaw. There is no need to satisfy our neighbours' curiosity. I have broken off my engagement; that is all. Mrs. Earnshaw is a sensible woman; she will know what to say. Before Sunday all Highlands and Bramley and Dorchester will know, and there will be a nine days' wonder; but it will not affect me,' and she lifted her head a little proudly.

'You really wish me to go away?'

'Oh, if you would,' and for the first time her lip quivered; 'it would be the truest kindness, Gavin. Why do you not go to Holland as you once planned? I shall not be alone. Muriel will be at Brae.' Then he looked at her very keenly, and a smothered sigh burst from him. There was something to him almost superhuman in her calmness. Did she not remember that he had suggested the Forest of Ardennes and Holland as their wedding trip?

'Yes, I will go,' he returned slowly; 'I have no right to make things harder for you. Ellison, you are stronger than I, after all.'

'It is not that,' she answered in a low tone; but she said no more. Did he not know that his happiness and his wellbeing were her first thought? It would be better for him, as well as for her, that he should go away until things should be less strained between them. Just now the pain was too acute; neither of them could have borne to meet constantly.

Gavin had relapsed into embarrassed silence again; he dare not ask if Mrs. Herbert would return to the Farm; but Ellison answered his unspoken question of her own accord.

'I mean to see Lorraine soon,' she said by and by; 'it will be easier to talk to her than to write; but I shall beg her to remain at Nefydd Madoc for the present. You will not mind that—will you, Gavin?'

'Do you think I have a right to object to anything that you do?' he asked a little bitterly; but the sorrowful tenderness in her eyes disarmed him.

'You are so good; I know you would bear anything sooner than give me pain; but I mean to be generous too. Lorraine shall not stay away long. When I am ready for her I will tell you so, and then you shall fetch her. I mean to say this to her when we meet.'

'Ellison, you shall do nothing of the kind,' rousing up at this. 'Do you suppose that I will allow you to heap coals of fire on my head in this fashion?'

'How are you to prevent it?' with a sad smile. 'But, Gavin, dear friend, I think we have talked long enough. Now, will you forgive me if I send you away again?' And then as he saw the look of utter exhaustion on her face, he was ready to curse himself for the sorrow he had brought on her; in spite of her self-command and calmness, he knew that her heart was almost broken, and the thought was torture to him.

He took her hands between his, and pressed them in mute reverence, but he dared not venture on a caress; but to his surprise she suddenly released them, and threw her arms round his neck.

'Will you kiss me once more, Gavin?' she said with exquisite tenderness in her voice, and as he stooped over her there were tears in his eyes. Why—why could he not have loved this woman as she deserved to be loved? Why had fate been so cruelly hard? If Lorraine had not come between them he would have married her, and his friendship would have developed in time into something warmer. Even at this final moment he would have prayed her to reconsider her decision; but he knew her proud, truthful nature would never accept any compromise.

The woman's generosity had triumphed, and the sacrifice had been consummated. Two days later Colonel Trevor started for London *en route* for Greece. He was in no mood for Holland; the very idea was abhorrent to him. He had long wished to visit modern Athens, and he thought he might possibly extend his trip to Sicily, and even to Constantinople; he had an old friend living at Palermo, and he had long promised to pay him a visit.

And Ellison remained to take up her changed and marred life as best she could. It was the saddest spring she had ever known, not even her father's death had left her so utterly blank and purposeless. For the first time nature refused to sympathise with her. The budding beauties of hedge-rows and garden borders, the joyous songs of mating birds preparing their nests, the delicious trills of the thrushes and nightingales in the Woodlands only added to her numb anguish; for her, in all this wide world of living, sentient human beings, there was no mate; and God's purposes, and the meaning of life, and the mystery of pain so seemingly useless, weighed on her with a sense of doubt that was positive torture. Again and again, on balmy evenings, or in the cold serene moonlight, as she walked to and fro with her faithful Bairn, in the attempt to ease her restlessness, the same speech rose to her lips—'O God, that women are made so, that they should suffer like this!'

It was a cruel ordeal, and even Ellison's strong vitality suffered

under it, and for a few days she was obliged to give up the con-
test and own herself ill; but she did not long indulge in the
luxury of remaining in her own room.   When Muriel paid her
first visit she was sitting at her bureau as usual, looking over Sam
Brattle's accounts, and looking wretchedly pinched and worn.
Muriel could not speak.   But as Ellison looked at her with an
attempt at a smile, the girl suddenly burst into tears.

'Don't, dear Muriel,' was all Ellison said; 'we must make the
best of a bad business,' and that was all that ever passed between
them.

To Ellison's strong, reticent nature no expression of pain was a
relief; she neither craved for nor desired sympathy.   Could any
sympathy give her back her love, her lost delight, the paradise
that she had forfeited?   It was Gavin whom she wanted, and for
whom she suffered these pangs of heart-sickness; but indeed no
words could express the bitter aridity of Ellison's soul during these
first few weeks.

Lorraine felt a little puzzled.   Ellison had never written so
seldom; her letters were mere notes, and told her nothing.   She
had been to town, and was very busy; Lorraine must forgive her
long silence.   There was no mention of Gavin, no allusion to her
trousseau; a scrap of local gossip and an affectionate inquiry after
her health completed her letter.

Muriel was equally reticent.   The Dower House was now ready
for occupation, and a care-taker had been put in, and the garden was
being altered; but Muriel wrote as though she had lost all interest
in it.   'It is so stupid doing things all alone,' she wrote; 'and, as
you know, Gavin is away.'   This last clause in Muriel's letter made
her vaguely uneasy.   Why had not Ellison mentioned that Colonel
Trevor was away?   There were only five weeks to the wedding,
and it seemed a little strange that he should absent himself.   To
judge by the tone of Ellison's and Muriel's letters, things seemed
rather at a stand-still; neither of them had alluded to her protracted absence; there were no pressing entreaties for her return;
and Lorraine's uneasiness increased.

One morning she was unusually absent; she had been watching
Miss Bretherton sort out the contents of the post-bag, but there was
no letter with the Highlands post-mark on it, and she felt a keen
sense of disappointment.   It was ten days since Ellison's last hurried
letter had reached her, and she could hardly credit the fact that
there was nothing for her.

'How strange—what can it mean?' she was saying to herself,
when Morwyn entered the room with a note.

'A man from the Royal Arms Hotel, Croes-fford, has brought

this,' she said, 'and he is to take back an answer, ma'am.' But as Lorraine in some surprise took the note from the salver, a sort of shock passed through her, for she recognised Ellison's handwriting.

With a sudden sense of foreboding, for which she could not account, she tore open the note.

DEAR LORRAINE—I am at the Royal Arms Hotel, Croes-fford ; will you come down to me ? I have a great deal that I want to say to you, and I am sure Miss Bretherton will spare you to me for the remainder of the day.—Yours affectionately, ELLISON.

'I must go at once and find out what this means !' she exclaimed, rising from her seat ; but she first laid the open note on Miss Bretherton's plate. She was very pale, for an intuitive instinct told her that there was something seriously wrong.

Miss Bretherton nodded approvingly as she read the note.

'Of course you must go, my dear ; but the question is, how ? Did the man ride or drive over from Croes-fford, Morwyn ?'

'He drove a sort of high phaeton, ma'am, with a piebald horse.'

'Ask him to wait for me, and I will be ready in a moment,' replied Lorraine hurriedly ; and in an incredibly short time she returned equipped for the journey.

Miss Bretherton followed her out into the porch.

'I shall not expect you back till I see you,' she said, with a brisk nod ; 'but you had better have a sensible fly for your return journey. These March evenings are cold,' and Lorraine made a gesture of assent. 'I wonder what has gone wrong ?' she thought as she went indoors again ; 'but there, it is a stupid muddling sort of world. Why should Eric have lost his heart to her, poor fellow, when she does not care a pin about him ? It is my opinion there is some one else ; it is not only her boy that that sweet young creature is missing. Don't I know how a woman looks when she is in love ?' And in spite of her sixty-three years, Miss Bretherton sighed.

That drive seemed interminable to Lorraine ; and not even the rapid pace of the piebald mare could content her. It seemed ages before they reached the falls and heard the plash of the water upon the boulders ; they were only half-way to Croes-fford by that time, but the remainder of that lovely drive seemed like an hour in purgatory to Lorraine, struggling with a hundred half-formed fears and surmises.

At last they crossed the river, and the fine buildings of the Royal Arms, with its pleasant gardens, came in sight. At this season of the year it would be almost empty, and only a solitary waiter was in the hall. He led Lorraine down a long corridor, and then ushered her into a small but pleasant sitting-room. A bright fire was burning, and some one had evidently been sitting in the easy-chair beside it, for a book lay on the seat. When the man had gone, Lorraine took it up; it was a tiny edition of *Thomas à Kempis,* and it had Gavin's name inside. One paragraph with a pencil-mark attracted her notice—'For all men recommend patience; few, however, they are who are willing to suffer.' The next moment the sound of a footstep outside made her hurriedly close the book. Sometimes in life a door opens and all fate is changed for us, or we dread some unknown evil, and in a moment we find it is a fact; for days some dull insistent voice had been foreboding ill to her inner consciousness; something had happened—was happening—all was not well with those loved ones she had left behind. True, it was only a presentiment, but when the door opened and Ellison came quietly out from the shadows into the sunlight and stood before her there were no words needed; they only looked at each other, and Lorraine grew white to her very lips.

Then Ellison took her hand very gently. 'Lorraine, dear,' she said in tone of forced calmness, 'I cannot help it being a shock to you. I know how my sudden appearance must frighten you, but I could not bring myself to write; you **can** guess what I have to tell you.'

'Yes,' returned Lorraine, but there was despair in her eyes; 'the first look at your face has told me everything.'

'Am I so changed?' with a sad smile; 'but I was always a poor actor, Lorraine. Gavin and I have broken off our engagement; it was all my doing; he was very angry with me at first, and accused me of jilting him, but I brought him at last to own that I was right. Dearly as I loved him—as I must always love him—that was one thing I could not do even for him. I could not marry him, knowing that his heart belonged to another woman.'

A low cry burst from Lorraine, and then she hid her face in her trembling hands; but Ellison put her sisterly arms around her.

'Hush, Lorraine; there is no need for all this agitation. Thank God that for me the worst is over. There were a few terrible days, when all seemed doubt and darkness, and I suffered—ah, how I suffered! and then the light came, and I left off groping for the path, and I knew strength would be given me to do the right. Then I went home and sent for Gavin.'

'Ellison, will you let me speak?'

'Yes; but not yet. You must let me finish first.' And then in a few concise words she explained how George Bates' report had reached her.

'I did not believe him,' she went on ; 'it was Gavin's face that brought conviction to me. He is so true, Lorraine ; a lie is not possible to him, and he owned his affection for you frankly.'

'Ellison, you must hear me' ; but Ellison shook her head and went on.

'It is a great misfortune, but I have no one to blame but my-self ; I would not be engaged to him, and I went away all those weeks, and then that terrible accident happened. Lorraine, do you think that I do not understand it all—the comfort Gavin was to you, and how the love grew up in your heart almost un-consciously ? He has owned to me that you attracted him from the first ; but it has not been so with you ?'

'No,' returned Lorraine, almost inaudibly. Then she took her cousin's hands and kissed them passionately. 'God bless you for saying that—for thinking it—but it is true, true as heaven above us. It was only when he left off coming, that I began to discover how much he was to me. I think I was just a little sorry when I heard of your engagement ; it made me feel dull and out in the cold ; but I did not understand until'—and then she shivered and hid her face again. Day and night—in darkness and early dawn —those words sounded in her ears, 'My darling, my darling, have I killed you ? Open your sweet eyes and look at me.'

'You need not defend yourself,' returned Ellison softly ; 'you poor thing, do I not know all ? It is no fault of yours that this misery has come upon me. Let me say something more, Lorraine ; you know how noble Gavin is ; though he confessed to me that he loved you, he begged me with tears in his eyes to marry him. For the moment he really wished it, and if I could have brought myself to do so, he would have been so good to me. "The very hairs of your head are sacred to me ?" he actually said that. But, Lorraine, I would rather have dropped dead at his feet than have stooped to such humiliation, even for his dear sake.'

'Ellison,' and here Lorraine lifted up her pallid, tear-stained face, 'why did you ever shelter us ? I have been your curse instead of your blessing.'

'You must not say that ; this trouble has been sent for some wise purpose. Lorraine, why do you shrink from me so, as though you had been guilty of some wrong against me ? Sit down beside me and let us talk it out quietly ; we must consider the future. I will do anything for Gavin but marry him.'

'Not now, perhaps, but in a year or two's time. Dear Ellison, let me speak now. I will never come back to Highlands—never.

I am quite strong, and can work for my own living ; besides, Miss Bretherton will only be too thankful to keep me.   You shall live in peace in your beautiful home, and after a time Colonel Trevor will forget his fancy, and then he will come back to you, and you will be generous and forgive him, and consent to make him happy.'

'Never,' was Ellison's answer ; and now there was a strange flash from the blue eyes.   'Dear Lorraine, put this dream out of your head, for it will never come to pass.   Gavin will marry, of course, but it is you who can alone make him happy.   Do you know what I said to him ?   "Lorraine shall come back soon ; when I am ready for her, I will send you to fetch her."   Lorraine, when Gavin comes he will ask you to marry him ; and if my life is to know any peace you must promise me to say yes.'

CHAPTER LIII

And yet, because I love thee, I obtain
From that same love this vindicating grace,
To live on still in love, and yet in vain—
To bless thee, yet renounce thee to thy face.'
                ELIZABETH BARRETT BROWNING.

AFTER all, Lorraine did not return to Black Nest that day; in the afternoon the piebald made another journey to Nefydd Madoc, and a pencilled note begged that Morwyn would pack the few things that were necessary for the night.

'Ellison wishes me to stay here,' she wrote, 'and has promised to bring me back to-morrow. I know you will not mind, dear Miss Bretherton'; and Miss Bretherton's answer was as curt as usual.

'Please yourself, and you please me. "Welcome the coming, speed the parting guest," is the motto at Black Nest. Why do you not ask your friend to stay a week with us?—Yours affectionately, MARION BRETHERTON.'

It was Lorraine's sudden indisposition that made Ellison anxious to keep her for the night. They had been talking quietly and with greater calmness over all that had passed, when she saw Lorraine's face grow suddenly white, and the next moment her head fell forward on her breast.

It was only a passing faintness. Ellison placed her comfortably on the couch and bathed her forehead with eau de cologne, and in a few minutes the dizziness passed, and she tried to sit up; but her teeth chattered, and she looked so wan that Ellison insisted on her lying down all the afternoon.

'You are not as strong as you make out,' she said. 'You must let me take care of you to-night, and to-morrow you will be all

right.' And then she said in a low voice, 'Don't make things
worse for me; do not let me have the pain of knowing that I
have made you ill'; but Lorraine disclaimed this eagerly.

'I have had this faintness once or twice before, it is nothing;
your voice sounded a hundred miles away, and then I seemed to
hear the sea booming, and I felt you lay me down. I can write
the note now, if you will send it'; and then she had pencilled the
few words.

That day it was Lorraine who suffered; and Ellison, who had
drunk her own bitter potion to the dregs long ago, sat beside her
trying to comfort her.

More than once she repeated the same words: 'For me the
worst is over. If I live to be an old woman, I shall never suffer
such pain again; I ought to be thankful for that. When a great
sorrow comes, it seems to swallow up all minor ones.'

And presently, 'If one waits for the light, it will certainly
come, and then one must follow it closely; if only one can discern
the right path, half the difficulty is over; and unless one's eyes are
blinded by self-will, one can always see it.'

'Dear Ellison, are you sure of that?'

'I am sure of it now; I have the testimony of my own experience. One night, when I was at that hotel in Weymouth
Street, I could not sleep, and everything seemed dark and wretched.
It was like one of my old nightmares, as though I were walking
down long, endless roads that led nowhere, or traversing a sleeping
city at midnight, that seemed like the city of the dead. I was in
sore perplexity, and then all at once the words came to me, almost
as though some one had spoken them—but of course that was only
my sleepless fancy—"This is the way, walk ye in it"; and I
knew then that if I married Gavin I should be making a fearful
mistake.'

Lorraine was silent; she had exhausted her arguments, and
there was nothing more to say. Ellison's strong will baffled her
finest intentions; she left no margin for generosity. 'Dear
Ellison, if you would only see things as I see them'; but Ellison
shook her head.

'I prefer my own point of view. Ah, you think I am obstinate,
but I am only speaking the soundest common-sense. You and
Gavin have taught me a good deal, Lorraine. When you first
came to Highlands, how little I knew in comparison with you;
you were a wife, a mother, a widow, — you had seen the dark,
seamy side of life; but I was nothing but a grown-up, ignorant
child. All that is changed now,' and she sighed as she spoke.
'I know and feel what other women have known and felt before me;

and in the light of that new knowledge—and out of the very love he taught me—I say that if I married Gavin there would not be a day that I should not wish myself dead.'

'Ellison!' and Lorraine trembled; that note of passion in Ellison's voice startled her very soul.

'I must have all or none,' she went on. 'I will accept no compromise, no patched-up pretence of happiness; other women may be content with a portion of their husband's heart; other women may be satisfied with kindness and friendship and good-fellowship, with the crumbs and shreds of a spent passion, but I am not one of these. I will not pretend to be humble. I know my own value, and the worth of all I have to offer. Gavin knows it too, but he is not his own master; he respects me too much to try and coerce me in any way, and by this time he knows I am right.'

'But, Ellison,' in a timid voice, and Lorraine flushed painfully as she spoke, 'there is one thing I cannot understand; you had no scruple in accepting Colonel Trevor, and yet he had been married before.'

'I see what you mean; but that never presented any difficulty to me. Helen was my dear unknown friend; I never thought of her as a rival. Lorraine, I am sure you understand me. You know, as Gavin knows, that I am only speaking the truth in all soberness. Though I am not an imaginative woman like you and Muriel, I have my ideals, and I will not lower them. I will be true to myself and true to him, and I will not be afraid of a lonely life.'

'Oh, Ellison, if I could only be as good as you'; and then a smile came to Ellison's lips.

'You should call things by their right name—I am afraid there is more pride than goodness; but all the same, I like you to think well of me. Do you feel better now, you poor thing? Lorraine, whatever happens, remember I shall never think less of you—it is not in my nature to change; when once I care for a person, I care for ever; and you and I are like sisters.'

'You are dearer to me than any sister,' returned Lorraine with tearful earnestness. 'Ellison, how am I to say good-bye to you to-morrow? the very idea breaks my heart.'

'Give me the promise that I asked you to give me, and I will spend a week with you at Black Nest. Come, that is a bargain, Lorraine; I really mean it. I should be glad of a few days' quiet in this lovely place; but I must go back for Sam Brattle's marriage. Oh, it is all in the day's work,' as Lorraine looked at her wistfully. 'I do not mean to be soft with myself, and shrink from every little painful duty. My dear, how is one to endure life unless one doggedly does everything as it comes? Do you know what I have got into the habit of saying to myself?—

> "Come what come may,
> Time and the hour run through the roughest day."

Cousin Louise so often quoted that.'

Lorraine never knew when she gave that promise, or whether she ever gave it, but the next morning Ellison quietly announced her intention of spending the week at Nefydd Madoc. 'I am rather curious to make Mother Hubbard's acquaintance,' she said, as she cut some delicate slices of tongue and laid them on Lorraine's plate; she spoke and moved so naturally that Lorraine looked at her almost startled. No one would have guessed from Ellison's manner that she had lain awake most of the night battling with another wave of despair; but with the morning light calmness had returned to her.

They started for Nefydd Madoc early in the afternoon, and reached Black Nest by tea-time. Miss Bretherton received her new guest with great *empressement*. 'All Mrs. Herbert's friends are welcome,' she said, with old-fashioned courtesy, 'but none so welcome as the Mistress of Brae Farm'; and she made much of her.

Ellison admired everything. 'Nora's Holiday house is very much to my taste,' she observed, when Lorraine came into her room to wish her good-night. 'And Mother Hubbard herself is a stately little person; what keen eyes she has—they seem to bore one through and through.'

'I have grown to love her dearly,' replied Lorraine. 'Is it not tiresome that she will never call me anything but Mrs. Herbert? that is one of her whimsies.'

'Oh, she is as full of whims as a nut is of meat; but her heart is in the right place. Lorraine, do you think you can be content here for two or three months?' And then Ellison put her strong white hands on her shoulders and looked full at her. 'I shall want you long before that; but I think that for many reasons it will be wiser for you to stay here. Miss Bretherton will love to have you, and then the air is so bracing.'

'Of course I will stay if you wish it; Ellison, you must know that my one wish is to please you in everything; just now all places are the same to me, and I shall carry a heavy heart wherever I go.'

'Oh, that will pass,' returned Ellison hastily; and then she kissed Lorraine's cheek and gently dismissed her. It had been a long day—the days were all so terribly long now; Ellison longed for night and the darkness—when she might unbuckle her armour and think her own bitter thoughts in peace ; even Lorraine's presence was irksome to her ; her very sweetness and sadness only told her in forcible language that it was no wonder that Gavin loved her best.

But each returning day found her as calm and self-sustained as ever, and quietly ready to fall in with any little plan. There were long walks with Lorraine, and afternoon drives with Miss Bretherton ; there were desultory rambles in the garden and woods, and in the evening she would take her share of the reading aloud.

One morning, when Miss Bretherton had taken her to the birds' breakfast-table, and all the little feathered guests had partaken of Mother Hubbard's bounty, Ellison proposed that they should stroll down by the rivulet.

'There is something I want to ask you,' she continued, 'and yet my request needs explanation. Miss Bretherton, in life one sometimes plays a game of cross-purposes—the wrong couples get mixed up—and the right person somehow strays away. Lorraine and I and another person I need not name have all been taking part in that game.'

'Yes, I know,' and a significant gleam came into Miss Bretherton's keen eyes. 'Oh, you are a brave woman, Miss Lee, and my dear Mrs. Herbert is brave too, and if this world were not such a muddling place, you ought both of you to be happy.'

'There are different kinds of happiness,' returned Ellison with a sigh, 'mine and Lorraine's will not be the same. If she has more in her life than I am ever likely to have, one must remember that she has suffered more too. Think what awful depths of humiliation and sorrow her married life must have covered ; and then the loss of her only child, and she has borne it all so patiently. If any one deserves to be happy it is Lorraine.'

'Well, I won't contradict you there.'

'Of course you will not contradict me ; do I not know how you love her ? Dear Miss Bretherton, things cannot come right all at once ; a tangled skein takes time to unravel. Will you do me this one kindness ?—will you keep Lorraine until I send some one to fetch her ?—that is the favour I have to ask.'

'Then it is one that is easy to grant ; send for her when you will, summer, or autumn, or winter, and you will take away the best of my sunshine, but she shall not stay one hour longer for that.'

And then, when Ellison had left her to join Lorraine in a walk to the village, Miss Bretherton stood still for a long time leaning on the crutch handle of her stick and pondering deeply. 'She is a brave woman,' she muttered at last ; 'few would have the courage to do what she has done for that sweet young creature's sake.   It was just cutting off the right hand and plucking out the right eye. Heaven help her, it will be a weary world to her as long as her youth lasts ; but when she is old, and blessings come home to roost at Brae Farm, she will know what a peaceful heart means.'   And then Mother Hubbard trotted to the house, where Winnie Fack was awaiting her.

The next day Ellison left them.   Lorraine drove with her to the station, but on the way they said little to each other ; perhaps Ellison noticed that Lorraine's eyes were full of tears, and that every now and then she brushed them away.   Just as they reached Croes-fford and the station was in sight, Ellison laid her hand on her cousin's arm.

'Lorraine, remember you have not promised me in words, but there was a look in your eyes that told me you understood me. When the time comes, when I send him, you must be good to him for all our sakes.   Gavin must have the woman he loves, or life will be worthless to me ; for his sake—for my sake—I will not say for your own—give him the answer he wants.'   And then, as she said this in a tone of intense agitation, the two women clung to each other, and Ellison's face was wet with Lorraine's tears.

Those spring days that followed were sorrowful ones to Lorraine ; to her loving, sensitive nature the idea that she had innocently supplanted her cousin was a source of exquisite torment.   Ellison's very nobility, the absence of all reproach, the boundlessness of her generosity only added to Lorraine's compunction and regret. And there were hours when she would thankfully have given up her own hopes to restore to Ellison her lost happiness.

'If I could only undo it all and put things straight between them,' she would say to herself ; but even as she uttered the words she knew that it was too late for any such reparation.   But she suffered acutely, and it was no wonder that, as the spring merged into summer, she grew thin and pale with that ceaseless fretting.·   Miss Bretherton scolded and petted her by turns.

Lorraine tried vainly to battle with her depression ; she had many humble friends at Nefydd Madoc, and a few sick people whom she visited almost daily.   But when Muriel arrived for a long visit, she was grievously disappointed with her friend's looks.

'The mountain air has done little for Mrs. Herbert,' she wrote to Ellison ; 'she will have it that she is quite well, but she looks sadly thin and frail,' and Ellison's face grew very grave as she read this.

Muriel stayed at Black Nest for a month, and then Eric Vincent came down with Nora and Effie.   Miss Bretherton pretended to grumble when he told her that he could only stay a week.   'I will pay you a longer visit by and by, Aunt Marion,' he said to her, 'but just now my presence is needed at Highlands.' Poor Eric, it was not yet possible for him to remain in the same house with Mrs. Herbert without misery to himself.

But Nora and Effie remained behind, and Lorraine forgot her lassitude and depression as she watched Tedo's little sweetheart at her play ; very soon Effie could coax her into joining them in all sorts of delightful flower-gathering or blackberry-picking expeditions.

'Her dear Herbert,' as she called her, was soon her willing slave, for Lorraine's motherly nature could not long remain closed to any child. 'Effie was always a darling,' she said to Miss Bretherton, 'but I love her doubly because my boy was so fond of her.'

Muriel would have been happier in her mind if she could have seen Lorraine a few weeks later. How could her face fail to brighten with response when Nora hung on one arm lovingly, and Effie kissed and fondled the hand she held ?

'I do love my dear Herbert,' Effie would say ; 'is she not the beautifullest woman in the world, Nora ?' and at this childish flattery Lorraine broke into a low laugh. Effie's beautifullest woman had pale cheeks and dark tired lines round her eyes ; nevertheless Miss Bretherton and her faithful Pritchard mutually congratulated each other on the improvement in Mrs. Herbert's looks.

'She has taken a turn at last, and it is those blessed children that have done it,' observed Pritchard tearfully. 'Some women must be mothering some young creature or other, it comes natural to them, and you can see that her poor heart is just starved to death'; and Pritchard was right.

Meanwhile the mistress of Brae Farm was passing the summer days as usual, superintending her household, or going over the farm with Sam Brattle. No one ever saw her idle or unoccupied for a moment, and the work she got through between breakfast and supper would have kept two ordinary women busy, but to Ellison's strong vitality work was her only safety-valve.

After a time she went among her neighbours as usual. She was a little stately perhaps, and carried her head higher, but even her most intimate friends could not notice any perceptible difference in her. Her fair face was as serene as ever, and yet to those who loved her—to Lorraine, and to Gavin when he saw her —there was a marked change.

Gavin was at Lucca dawdling away the early autumn days when Ellison's first letter reached him. He was sitting in the loggia of the palazzo where he was staying when it was brought to him, and at the sight of the familiar handwriting the blood suffused his face.

It was one of Ellison's old letters, and every sentence breathed the old tenderness. But when he had finished it Gavin's eyes were full of tears. But the gist of the whole was in the postscript. ' Why do you stay away so long ? Surely you must have grown weary of your wanderings by this time ? Muriel is wanting her brother and Brae its master, and there is a friend at Brae Farm ready to welcome you. You know that, dear Gavin, do you not ?' It was this sentence that made him start, for he knew he had his recall. The next day he had set his face homewards, and three days later his foot was on English soil again.

He had telegraphed to Muriel, and he knew that she would carry the news to Brae Farm ; but as he drove down from the Woodlands, he looked across at the farm buildings with suppressed emotion. Would Ellison expect him that evening ; how was he to go to her as usual ? But when he reached Brae House he found the question solved for him.

Muriel welcomed him affectionately, and then she asked him if he were tired.

' Why, of course not,' he returned, evidently surprised by the question. ' You know I slept at the Grosvenor last night.'

' Then will you go down to the Farm this evening ?' she returned quickly. ' Ellison said if you were tired I was not to give you the message ; but you look as fresh as possible.'

Gavin muttered something in answer, and a moment later he left the room ; but as soon as dinner was over, he took up his hat and walked down to Brae Farm. It was best to get it over as quickly as possible, he told himself ; if one had to go up to a cannon's mouth, it was no use hanging back. Gavin was certainly no coward, but there are some things that would try any man, and the first meeting with Ellison was one of these.

. He had not expected for one moment that she would be at the gate, but as he unlatched it he saw her coming to meet him ; and the next moment both her hands were in his, and she was saying to him :

' Gavin, why have you stayed away so long ? How could you think I meant that ? I was obliged to send for you at last, and now there is something you must do for me. Gavin, I want Lorraine home. You must go to her and tell her so '; and as she said this, quietly and without faltering, he knew that she was changed indeed ; that it was not the old Ellison, but a nobler, truer, gentler Ellison who stood before him, holding his hands and looking at him with those clear-eyed glances.

CHAPTER LIV

GREEN PASTURES AND STILL WATERS

'Thou comest ! all is said without a word.
I sit beneath thy looks, as children do
In the noon-sun, with souls that tremble through
Their happy eyelids from an unaverred
Yet prodigal inward joy.'

ELIZABETH BARRETT BROWNING.

IN the garden at Black Nest there was a certain sheltered seat under a jutting crag of rock that went by the name of the Lady's Bower, and there on sultry afternoons Lorraine and her young companions would sit with their work or book until the gong summoned them to tea.

When David Bretherton built Black Nest, some of the wild moorland had been reclaimed for a garden, and had been laid out in quaint picturesque terraces.

The view from the Lady's Bower was very varied ; the terraces, gay with flowers, led down to a rustic bridge, under which a clear sparkling little stream gurgled and foamed over grey boulders. Standing on the bridge one could see now and then the silvery flash of some small fish as it rose to the surface of the water, or the gorgeous tints of the dragon-fly skimming over the pond, while the sudden splash of a water rat would invade the silence.

A little below the bridge the stream entered the wood, and on summer afternoons it was Nora's and Effie's delight to hunt for ferns and strange mosses. The river was shallow and the current small, and there was no possible risk. As Lorraine sat in the Lady's Bower, she could hear their voices plainly or see one or other of them as they emerged out on the open moorland. One afternoon they had left her as usual, but Lorraine, who had opened her book, let it lie on her lap unread, as her eyes rested on the

purple moorlands and grey boulders. Above her head hung
clusters of dark-red rowan berries, while the humming of bees
feasting on the heather honey, and the tinkling and babbling of
the rivulet, seemed to blend with all manner of musical sounds—
the soughing of the summer breeze in the tree-tops, and the
flutter of innumerable leaves ; the whirring of wings, from pewits
and grouse on the moor ; or the scurry of tiny feet as some
small furred thing ran from one hiding-place to another.   Garden
and moorland seemed alive with soft resonant music, an under-
tone of gladness seemed to pervade the deep summer stillness ;
gauzy insects and beautifully tinted butterflies quivered and danced
in the sunny ambient air ; while the spicy breath of carnations and
the sweet scents of innumerable flowers mingled with the thymy
fragrance from the herb garden, and the damp odours of hidden
mosses and water-plants.

Lorraine began to feel a drowsiness steal over her, the droning
of a wasp near her seemed magnified a hundredfold, then the
sound of a footstep on the bridge below struck sharply on her ear,
and she straightened herself and opened her eyes.   And then it
seemed to her as though she were still dreaming, as though some
illusion had crossed the threshold of her thoughts, and stood like
an actual embodiment in the sunlight ; but the next moment her
heart began to beat more violently and she grew suddenly breathless ; it was no vision ! some one in a grey tweed coat, with an
erect soldierly figure and a thin brown face, was crossing the
bridge and coming rapidly up the steps that led from one
terrace to another, and as she rose from her seat a little dizzily,
Colonel Trevor stood before her, and in his deep-set eyes there was
a gleam of intense joy.

'Lorraine,' he said in a trembling voice—and then, before she
could do more than look at him with a faint, welcoming smile, his
arms were round her, and he was holding her closely to his breast.
'My darling, my darling,' was all he said ; but the next moment
she had freed herself.

'Colonel Trevor,' she said reproachfully ; but he only smiled
at her, and drew her down beside him.

'Darling,' he said gently, 'I have brought my credentials with
me,' and he laid a letter in her lap.   'You know that writing ;
you know who has sent me to you, and why I am here.   Lorraine,
are you going to be very good to me?'

The passionate pleading in his eyes made Lorraine busy herself with
her letter ; but the words danced mistily before her, and her hand
shook so that she was obliged to put it down.   The next moment
Gavin had taken possession of both hand and letter.   'Dearest,

we will read it together by and by. You will need my inter-
pretation. But there is one thing I must know first. Lorraine,
are you still mine, as I have been yours all these weary months?
Is your heart faithful to me? Darling, surely there is no need
for any explanation? we know that we love each other. The
love that was our sorrow is now to be our joy. Lorraine,
put your dear hand in mine, and tell me that you will be my
wife.'

'But Ellison,' she whispered.

'Ellison has given you to me. Lorraine, why do you shiver
and tremble so? The time has gone by for hesitation. You are
mine already by every law, human and divine—mine, because I
am yours in body and soul—and mine, because,' and here he
stooped and looked into her eyes, 'you have already owned that
you care for me'—and then, as he said this, Lorraine hid her face
on his shoulder, and broke into a passion of tears.

Yes, he had won her; how could she resist him, who was
already so dear to her? Were not Ellison's words for ever echoing
in her ear? 'When the time comes, when I send him, you must
be good to him for all our sakes. Gavin must have the woman
he loves, or life will be worthless to me, for his sake—for my
sake—I will not say for your own—give him the answer he wants.'
But, alas for Lorraine, that answer could only be wrung from
her with bitter tears. The sweetness of love had come to her,
abundant sheaves gathered in the rich, ripe aftermath; but the
tares of sorrowful regret were hers too; it would be years before
she or Gavin either would think of Ellison's self-sacrifice and
devotion without pain.

Gavin may be forgiven if, at that moment, he forgot everything
in his passionate joy, when the woman he worshipped consented
to be his wife; but to Lorraine's unselfish nature no such forget-
fulness was possible.

He was beside her, her well-beloved; and the voice that had
been her music in many a dark hour was breathing loving words
into her ear. And she knew, and gloried in the knowledge, that
the man whom she had 'held as half divine' was hers, and
would be hers through time and eternity. And yet, Lorraine's
eyes held a deep sadness in their brown depths. 'Dear,' she
said presently, 'you must be patient with me; you must never
misunderstand me for a moment. I love you as much as any
woman should love the man she has promised to marry; but if
I do not seem as glad and happy as I ought to be, it is because
my happiness means another woman's loss; and that even in my
joy,' and then she looked at him with great sweetness, 'it troubles

me to think of Ellison'; and when she said this, Gavin's face grew also grave.

'I do not forget her,' he said in a low voice, and he thought he was speaking the truth; but how was he to remember, when the soft clinging of Lorraine's palm to his hand, and the remembered touch of her sweet lips, sent his pulses throbbing? how could he be true to his manhood, and remember Ellison at the supreme moment of his life? But as Lorraine spoke her name, he uncovered his head as though some regal presence were passing.

'Darling, I love you all the better for saying that. No, I shall never misunderstand you; that fair handwriting is far too distinct and legible,' and here he kissed her brow, and the ruddy brownness of her hair. 'All our life long, Ellison shall be our household saint, and her happiness and wellbeing shall be our mutual care. Now, love, shall we read her letter together? I must tell you honestly that I know the contents. Ellison consulted me before she wrote it.' And then, as Lorraine looked greatly mystified at this, he put it in her hand, and begged her to read it; while he strolled down to the bridge again. Perhaps he knew that she would give it better attention if he were not beside her.

Lorraine grew very pale over the letter, for Ellison begged her to marry Gavin without delay.

'When Gavin brings you back, it must be to Brae House as its mistress. He and I have both made up our minds to that,' she wrote. 'And after all, why should you keep him waiting? Gavin is not a young man, and this second engagement in a place like Highlands would be terribly embarrassing; indeed, neither he nor you could stand it, and though I am ready to do anything for Gavin's happiness and yours, I know that neither of you would regard a wedding from Brae Farm as possible or desirable. In a case like this, where there are wheels within wheels, perfect simplicity and straightforwardness will be the wisest and the best, and "doe the nexte thing" must be your motto.

'Talk matters over quietly with Gavin and Miss Bretherton. Why should you not be married from Black Nest without fuss or ceremony, and in a few weeks' time? Miss Bretherton could give you away, and she and Gavin's best man would be sufficient witnesses. I thought of this when I stood in that tiny church at Nefydd Madoc; when you and Mr. Meredith were showing me that altar-piece, I said to myself, "One day Lorraine and Gavin will take each other for man and wife, and it will be most likely in this very church." Gavin will arrange it all, and I am writing to Miss Bretherton. Dear Lorraine, you once said that you wished to please me in everything; it was one of your old pretty speeches, but I shall hold you to this.

'I am longing to see you, but I shall not welcome you unless you return as Gavin's wife. Show him this letter; he will endorse every word. The rest I can safely leave to him.'

'Well, have you read your letter?' and Gavin looked at her meaningly; but Lorraine crumpled it in her hand and rose quickly; she was very flushed, and her eyes were full of tears.

'Yes, I have read it, but I cannot talk about it now—oh, not to-day,' and here her eyes grew still more pathetic, 'surely we have happiness enough for to-day'; and perhaps the sweetness of that answer reconciled Gavin to the delay.

They went back to the house after this, and when Miss Bretherton saw them walking silently side by side, a doubtful smile crossed her lips. 'So that tangle has been unravelled,' she said to herself, 'and the right couple has got sorted'; but when she looked at her favourite, and saw the moved, humble expression on her face, and the lovelight in her eyes, her mood changed.

'Colonel Trevor,' she said abruptly, 'you are welcome. If there is one thing I love to see, it is the right man in the right place,' and the grip of her hand finished the sentence.

That night Nora made one of her old-fashioned speeches. 'I am so glad, auntie,' she whispered to Miss Bretherton, 'about what you told me just now, that our dear Mrs. Herbert is going to marry Colonel Trevor, for I can't help thinking that he likes her ever so much better than he liked Miss Lee.'

'Now, Nora, you little wiseacre, who could have put such a notion in your head?'

'Oh, I don't know, auntie, but even children notice things sometimes; besides, I am growing up now. When Miss Lee went out of the room, Colonel Trevor never seemed to mind much; but just now, when Mrs. Herbert went up to speak to Pritchard, and was away quite a long time, he never took his eyes off the door until she came back again.'

Gavin did not get his way at first; and for two or three days Lorraine could not be induced to yield to his wishes, but he brought her round at last.

'How am I ever to hold my own against two such strong wills?' she said, with an attempt at playfulness; but her lip trembled as she spoke, and he soothed her with words of grave tenderness.

Five weeks later they were married in the little grey church at Nefydd Madoc, and Miss Bretherton gave the bride away. When the ceremony was over Lorraine took leave of her friend, and she and Gavin drove to Croes-fford, *en route* for the English Lakes.

When Ellison received her cousin's first letter—from Ambleside —and saw the signature, Lorraine Trevor, she grew a little pale ; 'Thank God that it is over,' she said inwardly ; and then she resolutely set herself to bury the past in oblivion.

.   .   .   .   .

Four years later the Mistress of Brae Farm was standing at the little green gate, with her faithful Bairn beside her as usual. It was early afternoon, and the cows were still in the pastures, even the cocks and the hens were abroad rooting in distant dust-heaps, and only Tedo's beloved playmates were consorting with the pigeons on the red roof of the granary.

Ellison stood looking up the farmyard path, with one hand shading her eyes from the sun. In these four years the Mistress of Brae Farm had grown a little stouter, and a little more sedate ; and more than one person had been heard to say that Miss Lee looked older than her age. But her fair face was as placid as ever ; and there was a quiet expression in the blue eyes that spoke of a deep underlying peace. Miss Bretherton's prophecy had been verified, and blessings had come home to roost at Brae Farm. Suddenly her face brightened, as a slim graceful figure in white turned the corner by the pond, and came swiftly towards her.

Ellison unlatched the gate and hurried to meet her, and a warmer kiss than usual passed between them. 'Dear Lorraine, a thousand good wishes for your birthday, but I did not expect to see you alone. What has become of Gavin and my godson ?'

'They will be here presently. Jack is having his first riding lesson on Midge. Ellison, how sweet of you to send me that picture, it was the very thing I wanted. Gavin must have turned traitor, or you would not have guessed it. He has been hanging it in its place this morning, and now the Lady's Bower is complete.' 'And Gavin's present ?' and then Lorraine stretched out her hand and pointed mutely to a magnificent sapphire and diamond ring. 'You both spoil me,' she murmured. 'Ellison, do you know I am actually five-and-thirty to-day ? Gavin refuses to believe it. He says I grow younger every year.' And, indeed, in her white dress and black Spanish hat, Lorraine looked almost girlish. There was an animated flush on her face, and a clear sparkle in her eye, that made Ellison glance at her keenly.

'Lorraine, there is something you have to tell me. I can read good news in your face. Some one is going to be married ; oh, I was sure of it,' as Lorraine beamed and nodded, for the Mistress of Brae was an inveterate and incurable match-maker.

'Guess who it is,' but as Ellison pondered and knit her brows, Lorraine suddenly lost patience.

'No, I cannot wait, I see you have no suspicion. It is our dear Muriel. Mr. Vincent spoke to Gavin yesterday. He is so pleased about it, and congratulated Muriel so warmly. He thinks most highly of Mr. Vincent, and so do we all.'

'I am very glad,' returned Ellison slowly; 'but you have taken me completely by surprise. I had no idea that Mr. Vincent cared for her.'

'Oh, it has been coming on for a long time. They have always been great friends, but now she is absolutely necessary to him. Gavin was so gratified by the way he spoke of her; he said her high-mindedness and unworldliness had first won him, and that he had woke up to realise the rare beauty of her character.'

'Muriel is very much improved certainly,' returned Ellison, in her sedate way; 'she has grown far more womanly lately.'

'Muriel was always womanly, only she declined to move in other women's grooves; dear thing, she is wonderfully happy.' Lorraine said no more than this, but for years she had guessed and guarded Muriel's secret—she knew that all these years Muriel had cared for the young vicar far too much for her own peace of mind. 'I never expected Eric to love me, I never thought myself worthy of him,' she had said to her one close friend; 'and the wonder of it will last me my life. But it is all your doing, Lorraine,' looking at her gratefully, 'you shamed me out of my self-will and indolence, and lifted me to higher ground, and there Eric found me'; but Lorraine only laughed with tender scorn at this speech.

Ellison and Lorraine had not moved away from the gate, and the next moment a little cavalcade came in sight: first Tweedledum frolicking and barking, then a brown Shetland pony with his mane almost sweeping the ground, with a beautiful dark-eyed boy in a white sailor suit holding himself erect in the saddle. Colonel Trevor walked beside him. This was John Ellis Trevor, Ellison's godson and pet, and a baby girl was at that moment sleeping in her bassinette in the Brae nursery. It was these two children and her husband's ever-deepening love that had brought back Lorraine's youth.

'Have you told Ellison the news?' was Gavin's first question, as he lifted his boy off the pony. 'There, go to your godmother, Jack. You will make a capital horseman in time'; and the sturdy little fellow ran towards her.

'Yes, she has told me; I am very very glad, Gavin'; and

Ellison looked at him with her old kind smile. 'I suppose Mr. Vincent will be at the birthday dinner to-night?'

'Why is you glad, Cousin Ellie—Jack's glad too,' and the beautiful little face looked up at her with childish wistfulness. 'Midge was not glad when Jack whipped him; Midge does not like to be whipped, and Jack must be kind to him'; and then, as she took the boy up, two little arms squeezed her tightly round the neck. 'It is Mover's buffday,' confided Jack, 'and I gived her a picture and a big kiss, and she loved me for it. Baby gived her nothing.'

'Look at them, sweetheart,' whispered Gavin; and then the husband and wife exchanged a glance of full understanding and sympathy, as they moved slowly towards the house. Ellison was still standing in the sunlight, listening with a tender smile to her godson's prattling confidences. Gavin was right when he said Jack had two mothers; from a mere baby, Cousin Ellie had been Jack's fond and devoted slave. 'Our boy shall be yours too,' Gavin had said to her when he had gone down to the Farm to tell her of the birth of their son; and both he and Lorraine had nobly redeemed this promise.

We may leave Ellison happily standing in the sunlight, a willing victim to Jack's throttling embraces, with loving eyes watching her from the threshold of her peaceful home : for her, too, there was a goodly heritage !

In this world we see darkly, and the clearness of our vision is obscured by earthly vapours; and so to many of us it seems that the prizes of life are dealt out unequally, and that many sweet souls gather blanks and suffer loss; and in one sense it may be so, and to many of God's heroines some hard task or toilsome path in the wilderness may be assigned. But their reward is not here ; in the higher life, perchance in one of the many mansions, they shall sit down amongst the nobles at the eternal feast, and in the gladness of that day they too shall realise and

'Smile to think God's greatness flowed around our incompleteness.
Round our restlessness, His rest.'

THE END

Printed by R. & R. CLARK, LIMITED, *Edinburgh*

THE NOVELS OF
ROSA NOUCHETTE CAREY

Popular Edition.   Crown 8vo.   Blue Cloth, Gilt.   3s. 6d. each.

NELLIE'S MEMORIES.   37th Thousand.

STANDARD.—" Miss Carey has the gift of writing naturally and simply, her pathos is true and unforced, and her conversations are sprightly and sharp."

WEE WIFIE.   25th Thousand.

LADY.—" Miss Carey's novels are always welcome ; they are out of the common run, immaculately pure, and very high in tone."

BARBARA HEATHCOTE'S TRIAL.   23rd Thousand.

DAILY TELEGRAPH.—" A novel of a sort which it would be a real loss to miss."

ROBERT ORD'S ATONEMENT.   19th Thousand.

STANDARD.—"*Robert Ord's Atonement* is a delightful book, very quiet as to its story, but very strong in character, and instinctive with that delicate pathos which is the salient point of all the writings of this author."

WOOED AND MARRIED.   27th Thousand.

STANDARD.—" There is plenty of romance in the heroine's life.   But it would not be fair to tell our readers wherein that romance consists or how it ends.   Let them read the book for themselves.   We will undertake to promise that they will like it."

HERIOT'S CHOICE.   18th Thousand.

MORNING POST.—" Deserves to be extensively known and read. . . . Will doubtless find as many admirers as readers."

QUEENIE'S WHIM.   21st Thousand.

GUARDIAN.—" A thoroughly good and wholesome story."

NOT LIKE OTHER GIRLS.   24th Thousand.

PALL MALL GAZETTE.—" Like all the other stories we have had from the same gifted pen, this volume, *Not Like Other Girls*, takes a sane and healthy view of life and its concerns. . . . It is an excellent story to put in the hands of girls."
NEW YORK HOME JOURNAL.—" One of the sweetest, daintiest, and most interesting of the season's publications."

MARY ST. JOHN.   16th Thousand.

JOHN BULL.—" The story is a simple one, but told with much grace and unaffected pathos."

FOR LILIAS.   17th Thousand.

VANITY FAIR.—" A simple, earnest, and withal very interesting story ; well conceived, carefully worked out, and sympathetically told."

UNCLE MAX.   23rd Thousand.

LADY.—" So intrinsically good that the world of novel-readers ought to be genuinely grateful."

ONLY THE GOVERNESS.   23rd Thousand.

PALL MALL GAZETTE.—" This novel is for those who like stories with something of Jane Austen's power, but with more intensity of feeling than Jane Austen displayed, who are not inclined to call pathos twaddle, and who care to see life and human nature in their most beautiful form."

MACMILLAN AND CO., Ltd., LONDON.

OF

CHARLOTTE M. YONGE

Uniform Edition.   Crown 8vo.   3s. 6d. each volume.

THE HEIR OF REDCLYFFE. With Illustrations by KATE GREENAWAY.

HEARTSEASE ; or, the Brother's Wife. New Edition. With Illustrations by KATE GREENAWAY.

HOPES AND FEARS ; or, Scenes from the Life of a Spinster. With Illustrations by HERBERT GANDY.

DYNEVOR TERRACE ; or, the Clue of Life. With Illustrations by ADRIAN STOKES.

THE DAISY CHAIN ; or, Aspirations. A Family Chronicle. With Illustrations by J. P. ATKINSON.

THE TRIAL : More Links of the Daisy Chain. With Illustrations by J. P. ATKINSON.

THE PILLARS OF THE HOUSE ; or, Under Wode, under Rode. Two Vols. With Illustrations by HERBERT GANDY.

THE YOUNG STEPMOTHER ; or, a Chronicle of Mistakes. With Illustrations by MARIAN HUXLEY.

THE CLEVER WOMAN OF THE FAMILY. With Illustrations by ADRIAN STOKES.

THE THREE BRIDES. With Illustrations by ADRIAN STOKES.

MY YOUNG ALCIDES ; a Faded Photograph. With Illustrations by ADRIAN STOKES.

THE CAGED LION. With Illustrations by W. J. HENNESSY.

THE DOVE IN THE EAGLE'S NEST. With Illustrations by W. J. HENNESSY.

THE CHAPLET OF PEARLS ; or, the White and Black Ribaumont. With Illustrations by W. J. HENNESSY.

LADY HESTER; or, Ursula's Narrative; and THE DANVERS PAPERS. With Illustrations by JANE E. COOK.

MAGNUM BONUM ; or, Mother Carey's Brood. With Illustrations by W. J. HENNESSY.

LOVE AND LIFE : an Old Story in Eighteenth Century Costume. With Illustrations by W. J. HENNESSY.

UNKNOWN TO HISTORY. A Story of the Captivity of Mary of Scotland. With Illustrations by W. J. HENNESSY.

STRAY PEARLS. Memoirs of Margaret de Ribaumont Viscountess of Bellaise. With Illustrations by W. J. HENNESSY.

MACMILLAN AND CO., LTD., LONDON.

NOVELS AND TALES

OF

·CHARLOTTE M. YONGE

Uniform Edition. Crown 8vo. 3s. 6d. each volume.

THE ARMOURER'S 'PRENTICES. With Illustrations by W. J. HENNESSY.

THE TWO SIDES OF THE SHIELD. With Illustrations by W. J. HENNESSY.

NUTTIE'S FATHER. With Illustrations by W. J. HENNESSY.

SCENES AND CHARACTERS; or, Eighteen Months at Beechcroft. With Illustrations by W. J. HENNESSY.

CHANTRY HOUSE. With Illustrations by W. J. HENNESSY.

A MODERN TELEMACHUS. With Illustrations by W. J. HENNESSY.

BYWORDS. A collection of tales new and old.

BEECHCROFT AT ROCKSTONE.

MORE BYWORDS.

A REPUTED CHANGELING ; or, Three Seventh Years Two Centuries Ago.

THE LITTLE DUKE, RICHARD THE FEARLESS. With Illustrations.

THE LANCES OF LYNWOOD. With Illustrations by J. B.

THE PRINCE AND THE PAGE : A Story of the Last Crusade. With Illustrations by ADRIAN STOKES.

TWO PENNILESS PRINCESSES. With Illustrations by W. J. HENNESSY.

THAT STICK.

AN OLD WOMAN'S OUTLOOK IN A HAMPSHIRE VILLAGE.

GRISLY GRISELL ; or, The Laidly Lady of Whitburn. A Tale of the Wars of the Roses.

HENRIETTA'S WISH. Second Edition.

THE LONG VACATION.

THE RELEASE.

THE PILGRIMAGE OF THE BEN BERIAH.

THE TWO GUARDIANS ; or, Home in this World. Second Edition.

COUNTESS KATE AND THE STOKESLEY SECRET.

MODERN BROODS.

STROLLING PLAYERS. By C. M. YONGE and C. R. COLE-RIDGE.

MACMILLAN AND CO., LTD., LONDON.

MACMILLAN'S THREE-AND-SIXPENNY LIBRARY OF BOOKS BY POPULAR AUTHORS

Crown 8vo.

*T*HIS Series, which comprises over four hundred volumes in various departments of Literature, has lately received some notable additions. Prominent among these is a new and attractive edition of **The Works of Thackeray**, *issued under the editorship of Mr. Lewis Melville. It contains all the Original Illustrations, and includes a great number of scattered pieces and illustrations which have not hitherto appeared in any collected edition of the works.* **The Works of Charles Dickens**, *reprinted from the first editions, with all the Original Illustrations, and with Introductions, Biographical and Bibliographical, by Charles Dickens the Younger, and an attractive edition of* **The Novels of Charles Lever**, *illustrated by Phiz and G. Cruik-*

shank, have also a place in the Library. The attention of book buyers may be especially directed to The Border Edition of the Waverley Novels, *edited by Mr. Andrew Lang, which, with its large type and convenient form, and its copious illustrations by well-known artists, possesses features which place it in the forefront of editions now obtainable of the famous novels.* The Works of Mr. Thomas Hardy, *including the poems, have also been recently added to the Three-and-Sixpenny Library. Among other works by notable contemporary authors will be found those of* Mr. F. Marion Crawford, Rolf Boldrewood, Mr. H. G. Wells, Gertrude Atherton, Mr. Egerton Castle, Mr. A. E. W. Mason, Maarten Maartens, *and* Miss Rosa Nouchette Carey; *while among the productions of an earlier period may be mentioned the works of* Charles Kingsley, Frederick Denison Maurice, Thomas Hughes, *and* Dean Farrar; *and the novels and tales of* Charlotte M. Yonge, Mrs. Craik, *and* Mrs. Oliphant.

THE

WORKS OF THACKERAY

Reprints of the First Editions, with all the Original Illustrations, and with Facsimiles of Wrappers, etc.

Messrs. MACMILLAN & CO., Limited, beg leave to invite the attention of book buyers to the Edition of THE WORKS OF THACKERAY in their Three-and-Sixpenny Library, which, when finished, will be the Completest Edition of the Author's Works which has been placed on the market.

. The Publishers have been fortunate in securing the services of Mr. LEWIS MELVILLE, the well-known Thackeray Expert. With his assistance they have been able to include in this Edition a great number of scattered pieces from Thackeray's pen, and illustrations from his pencil which have not hitherto been contained in any collected edition of the works. Mr. Melville has read all the sheets as they passed through the press, and collated them carefully with the original editions. He has also provided Bibliographical Introductions and occasional Footnotes.

List of the Series.

VOL.

1. Vanity Fair. With 190 Illustrations.

2. The History of Pendennis. With 180 Illustrations.

3. The Newcomes. With 167 Illustrations.

4. The History of Henry Esmond.

5. The Virginians. With 148 Illustrations.

6. Barry Lyndon and Catherine. With 4 Illustrations.

7. The Paris and Irish Sketch Books. With 63 Illustrations.

THACKERAY'S WORKS—*continued.*

VOL.

8. **Christmas Books— Mrs. Perkins's** Ball: Our Street: Dr. Birch and his Young Friends: The Kickleburys on the Rhine: The Rose and the Ring. With 127 Illustrations.

9. **Burlesques: From Cornhill to Grand** Cairo: and Juvenilia. With 84 Illustrations.

10. **The Book of Snobs, and other Contri-**butions to *Punch*. With 159 Illustrations.

11. **The Yellowplush Correspondence:** Jeames's Diary: The Great Hoggarty Diamond Etc. With 47 Illustrations.

12. **Critical Papers in Literature.**

13. **Critical Papers in Art; Stubbs's Calen-**dar: Barber Cox. With 99 Illustrations.

14. **Lovel the Widower, and other Stories.** With 40 Illustrations.

15. **The Fitz-Boodle Papers (including** Men's Wives), and various Articles. 8 Illustrations.

16. **The English Humourists of the 18th** Century: The Four Georges: Etc. 45 Illustrations.

17. **Travels in London: Letters to a Young** Man about Town: and other Contributions to *Punch* (1845—1850). With 73 Illustrations.

18. **Ballads and Verses, and Miscellaneous** Contributions to *Punch*. With 78 Illustrations.

19. **A Shabby Genteel Story, and The** Adventures of Philip. With Illustrations.

MACMILLAN'S
EDITION OF THACKERAY

SOME OPINIONS OF THE PRESS

EXPOSITORY TIMES.—"An edition to do credit even to this publishing house, and not likely to be surpassed until they surpass it with a cheaper and better themselves."

WHITEHALL REVIEW.—"Never before has such a cheap and excellent edition of Thackeray been seen."

ACADEMY.—"A better one-volume edition at three shillings and sixpence could not be desired."

GRAPHIC.—"In its plain but pretty blue binding is both serviceable and attractive."

DAILY GRAPHIC.—"An excellent, cheap reprint."

PALL MALL GAZETTE.—"The size of the books is handy, paper and printing are good, and the binding, which is of blue cloth, is simple but tasteful. Altogether the publishers are to be congratulated upon a reprint which ought to be popular."

GLOBE.—"The paper is thin but good, the type used is clear to read, and the binding is neat and effective."

LADY'S PICTORIAL.—"The paper is good, the type clear and large, and the binding tasteful. Messrs. Macmillan are to be thanked for so admirable and inexpensive an edition of our great satirist."

WORLD.—"Nothing could be better than the new edition."

BLACK AND WHITE.—"The more one sees of the edition the more enamoured of it he becomes. It is so good and neat, immaculate as to print, and admirably bound."

SCOTSMAN.—"This admirable edition."

LITERARY WORLD.—"The paper and printing and general get up are everything that one could desire."

ST. JAMES'S GAZETTE.—"A clear and pretty edition."

THE

WORKS OF DICKENS

Reprints of the First Editions, with all the original Illustrations, and with Introductions, Biographical and Bibliographical, by CHARLES DICKENS the Younger.

THE PICKWICK PAPERS. With 50 Illustrations.

OLIVER TWIST. With 27 Illustrations.

NICHOLAS NICKLEBY. With 44 Illustrations.

MARTIN CHUZZLEWIT. With 41 Illustrations.

THE OLD CURIOSITY SHOP. With 97 Illustrations.

BARNABY RUDGE. With 76 Illustrations.

DOMBEY AND SON. With 40 Illustrations.

CHRISTMAS BOOKS. With 65 Illustrations.

SKETCHES BY BOZ. With 44 Illustrations.

AMERICAN NOTES AND PICTURES FROM ITALY. With 4 Illustrations.

DAVID COPPERFIELD. With 40 Illustrations.

BLEAK HOUSE. With 43 Illustrations.

LITTLE DORRIT. With 40 Illustrations.

THE LETTERS OF CHARLES DICKENS.

A TALE OF TWO CITIES. With 15 Illustrations.

GREAT EXPECTATIONS; AND HARD TIMES.

MACMILLAN'S
EDITION OF DICKENS

SOME OPINIONS OF THE PRESS

ATHENÆUM.—"Handy in form, well printed, illustrated with reproductions of the original plates, introduced with bibliographical notes by the novelist's son, and above all issued at a most moderate price, this edition will appeal successfully to a large number of readers."

SPEAKER.—"We do not think there exists a better edition."

MORNING POST.—"The edition will be highly appreciated."

SCOTSMAN.—"This reprint offers peculiar attractions. Of a handy size, in one volume, of clear, good-sized print, and with its capital comic illustrations, it is a volume to be desired."

NEWCASTLE CHRONICLE.—"The most satisfactory edition of the book that has been issued."

GLASGOW HERALD.—"None of the recent editions of Dickens can be compared with that which Messrs. Macmillan inaugurate with the ssue of *Pickwick*. . . . Printed in a large, clear type, very readable."

GLOBE.—"They have used an admirably clear type and good paper, and the binding is unexceptionable. . . . May be selected as the most desirable cheap edition of the immortal ' Papers ' that has ever been offered to the public."

MANCHESTER EXAMINER.—"Handy in form, well printed, illustrated with reduced reproductions of the original plates, introduced with bibliographical notes by the novelist's son, and above all issued at a moderate price, this edition will appeal successfully to a large number of readers."

THE QUEEN.—"A specially pleasant and convenient form in which to re-read Dickens."

THE STAR.—"This new ' Dickens Series,' with its reproductions of the original illustrations, is a joy to the possessor."

Complete in Twenty-four Volumes. Crown 8vo, tastefully bound in green cloth, gilt. Price 3s. 6d. each.

In special cloth binding, flat backs, gilt tops. Supplied in Sets only of 24 volumes. Price £4 4s.

Also an edition with all the 250 original etchings. In 24 volumes. Crown 8vo, gilt tops. Price 6s. each.

THE LARGE TYPE
BORDER EDITION OF THE
WAVERLEY NOVELS

EDITED WITH

INTRODUCTORY ESSAYS AND NOTES

BY

ANDREW LANG
SUPPLEMENTING THOSE OF THE AUTHOR.

With Two Hundred and Fifty New and Original Illustrations by Eminent Artists.

BY the kind permission of the Hon. Mrs. MAXWELL-SCOTT, of Abbotsford, the great-granddaughter of Sir WALTER, the MSS. and other material at Abbotsford were examined by Mr. ANDREW LANG during the preparation of his Introductory Essays and Notes to the Series, so that the BORDER EDITION may be said to contain all the results of the latest researches as to the composition of the Waverley Novels.

The Border Waverley

1. WAVERLEY. With 12 Illustrations by Sir H. RAEBURN, R.A., R. W. MACBETH, A.R.A., JOHN PETTIE, R.A., H. MACBETH-RAEBURN, D. HERDMAN, W. J. LEITCH, ROBERT HERDMAN, R.S.A., and J. ECKFORD LAUDER.

2. GUY MANNERING. With 10 Illustrations by J. MACWHIRTER, A.R.A., R. W. MACBETH, A.R.A., C. O. MURRAY, CLARK STANTON, R.S.A., GOURLAY STEELL, R.S.A., F. S. WALKER, R. HERDMAN, R.S.A., and J. B. MACDONALD, A.R.S.A.

3. THE ANTIQUARY. With 10 Illustrations by J. MACWHIRTER, A.R.A., SAM BOUGH, R.S.A., R. HERDMAN, R.S.A., W. M'TAGGART, A.R.S.A., J. B. MACDONALD, A.R.S.A., and A. H. TOURRIER.

4. ROB ROY. With 10 Illustrations by R. W. MACBETH, A.R.A., and SAM BOUGH, R.S.A.

5. OLD MORTALITY. With 10 Illustrations by J. MACWHIRTER, A.R.A., R. HERDMAN, R.S.A., SAM BOUGH, R.S.A., M. L. GOW, D. Y. CAMERON, LOCKHART BOGLE, and ALFRED HARTLEY.

6. THE HEART OF MIDLOTHIAN. With 10 Illustrations by Sir J. E. MILLAIS, Bart., HUGH CAMERON, R.S.A., SAM BOUGH, R.S.A., R. HERDMAN, R.S.A., and WAL. PAGET.

7. A LEGEND OF MONTROSE and THE BLACK DWARF. With 7 Illustrations by Sir GEORGE REID, P.R.S.A., GEORGE HAY, R.S.A., HORATIO MACCULLOCH, R.S.A., W. E. LOCKHART, R.S.A., H. MACBETH-RAEBURN, and T. SCOTT.

8. THE BRIDE OF LAMMERMOOR. With 8 Illustrations by Sir J. E. MILLAIS, Bart., JOHN SMART, R.S.A., SAM BOUGH, R.S.A., GEORGE HAY, R.S.A., and H. MACBETH-RAEBURN.

9. IVANHOE. With 12 Illustrations by AD. LALAUZE.

10. THE MONASTERY. With 10 Illustrations by GORDON BROWNE.

11. THE ABBOT. With 10 Illustrations by GORDON BROWNE.

The Border Waverley

12. KENILWORTH.   With 12 Illustrations by AD.
    LALAUZE.

13. THE PIRATE.   With 10 Illustrations by W. E.
    LOCKHART, R.S.A., SAM BOUGH, R.S.A., HERBERT
    DICKSEE, W. STRANG, LOCKHART BOGLE, C. J. HOLMES,
    and F. S. WALKER.

14. THE FORTUNES OF NIGEL.   With 10 Illustrations
    by JOHN PETTIE, R.A., and R. W. MACBETH, A.R.A.

15. PEVERIL OF THE PEAK.   With 15 Illustrations by
    W. Q. ORCHARDSON, R.A. JOHN PETTIE, R.A., F. DADD,
    R.I., ARTHUR HOPKINS, A.R.W.S., and S. L. WOOD.

16. QUENTIN DURWARD.   With 12 Illustrations by
    AD. LALAUZE.

17. ST. RONAN'S WELL.   With 10 Illustrations by Sir
    G. REID, P.R.S.A., R. W. MACBETH, A.R.A., W. HOLE,
    R.S.A., and A. FORESTIER.

18. REDGAUNTLET. With 12 Illustrations by Sir JAMES
    D. LINTON, P.R.I., JAMES ORROCK, R.I., SAM BOUGH,
    R.S.A., W. HOLE, R.S.A., G. HAY, R.S.A., T. SCOTT,
    A.R.S.A., W. BOUCHER, and FRANK SHORT.

19. THE BETROTHED and THE TALISMAN. With 10
    Illustrations by HERBERT DICKSEE, WAL. PAGET, and
    J LE BLANT.

20. WOODSTOCK.   With 10 Illustrations by W. HOLE.
    R.S.A.

21. THE FAIR MAID OF PERTH.   With 10 Illustrations
    by Sir G. REID, P.R.S.A., JOHN PETTIE, R.A., R. W
    MACBETH, A.R.A., and ROBERT HERDMAN, R.S.A.

22. ANNE OF GEIERSTEIN.   With 10 Illustrations by
    R. DE LOS RIOS.

23. COUNT ROBERT OF PARIS and THE SURGEON'S
    DAUGHTER.   With 10 Illustrations by W. HATHERELL,
    R I., and W. B. WOLLEN, R.I.

24. CASTLE DANGEROUS, CHRONICLES OF THE CANON-
    GATE, ETC.   With 10 Illustrations by H. MACBETH-RAE-
    BURN and G. D. ARMOUR

The Border Waverley

SOME OPINIONS OF THE PRESS

TIMES.—"It would be difficult to find in these days a more competent and sympathetic editor of Scott than his countryman, the brilliant and versatile man of letters who has undertaken the task, and if any proof were wanted either of his qualifications or of his skill and, discretion in displaying them, Mr. Lang has furnished it abundantly in his charming Introduction to 'Waverley.' The editor's own notes are judiciously sparing, but conspicuously to the point, and they are very discreetly separated from those of the author, Mr. Lang's laudable purpose being to illustrate and explain Scott, not to make the notes a pretext for displaying his own critical faculty and literary erudition. The illustrations by various competent hands are beautiful in themselves and beautifully executed, and, altogether, the 'Border Edition' of the Waverley Novels bids fair to become the classical edition of the great Scottish classic."

SPECTATOR.—"We trust that this fine edition of our greatest and most poetical of novelists will attain, if it has not already done so, the high popularity it deserves. To all Scott's lovers it is a pleasure to know that, despite the daily and weekly inrush of ephemeral fiction, the sale of his works is said by the booksellers to rank next below Tennyson's in poetry, and above that of everybody else in prose."

ATHENÆUM.—"The handsome 'Border Edition' has been brought to a successful conclusion. The publisher deserves to be complimented on the manner in which the edition has been printed and illustrated, and Mr. Lang on the way in which he has performed his portion of the work. His introductions have been tasteful and readable ; he has not overdone his part ; and, while he has supplied much useful information, he has by no means overburdened the volumes with notes."

NOTES AND QUERIES.—"This spirited and ambitious enterprise has been conducted to a safe termination, and the most ideal edition of the Waverley Novels in existence is now completed."

SATURDAY REVIEW.—"Of all the many collections of the Waverley Novels, the 'Border Edition' is incomparably the most handsome and the most desirable. . . . Type, paper, illustrations, are altogether admirable."

MAGAZINE OF ART.—"Size, type, paper, and printing, to say nothing of the excessively liberal and charming introduction of the illustrations, make this perhaps the most desirable edition of Scott ever issued on this side of the Border."

DAILY CHRONICLE.—"There is absolutely no fault to be found with it, as to paper, type, or arrangement."

THE WORKS OF
THOMAS HARDY

Collected Edition

1. TESS OF THE D'URBERVILLES.
2. FAR FROM THE MADDING CROWD.
3. THE MAYOR OF CASTERBRIDGE.
4. A PAIR OF BLUE EYES.
5. TWO ON A TOWER.
6. THE RETURN OF THE NATIVE.
7. THE WOODLANDERS.
8. JUDE THE OBSCURE.
9. THE TRUMPET-MAJOR.
10. THE HAND OF ETHELBERTA.
11. A LAODICEAN.
12. DESPERATE REMEDIES.
13. WESSEX TALES.
14. LIFE'S LITTLE IRONIES.
15. A GROUP OF NOBLE DAMES.
16. UNDER THE GREENWOOD TREE.
17. THE WELL-BELOVED.
18. WESSEX POEMS, and other Verses.
19. POEMS OF THE PAST AND THE PRESENT.

THE

WORKS OF THOMAS HARDY

SOME PRESS OPINIONS OF THE THREE-AND-SIXPENNY ISSUE

PALL MALL GAZETTE.—". . . their charming edition of the works of Thomas Hardy . . . the price asked for it . . . is absurdly cheap. . . . Any more convenient and beautiful form of presentation for these books it would be difficult to find."

ATHENÆUM.—"This edition is so comely and so moderate in price that it may well placate those who have sighed for earlier issues out of their reach. Mr. Hardy's prefaces to the volumes should not be missed, for they are models of a difficult art, whether reflective, informative, or combative."

UNIFORM EDITION OF THE
NOVELS OF CHARLES LEVER

With all the Original Illustrations.

1. HARRY LORREQUER. Illustrated by PHIZ.

2. CHARLES O'MALLEY. Illustrated by PHIZ.

3. JACK HINTON THE GUARDSMAN. Illustrated by PHIZ.

4. TOM BURKE OF OURS. Illustrated by PHIZ.

5. ARTHUR O'LEARY. Illustrated by G. CRUIKSHANK.

6. LORD KILGOBBIN. Illustrated by LUKE FILDES.

THE NOVELS OF
F. MARION CRAWFORD

MR. ISAACS: A Tale of Modern India.
ATHENÆUM.—"A work of unusual ability. . . . It fully deserves the notice it is sure to attract."

DOCTOR CLAUDIUS: A True Story.
ATHENÆUM.—"Few recent books have been so difficult to lay down when once begun."

A ROMAN SINGER.
TIMES.—"A masterpiece of narrative. . . . Unlike any other romance in English literature."

ZOROASTER.
GUARDIAN.—"An instance of the highest and noblest form of novel. . . . Alike in the originality of its conception and the power with which it is wrought out, it stands on a level that is almost entirely its own."

MARZIO'S CRUCIFIX.
TIMES.—"A subtle compound of artistic feeling, avarice, malice, and criminal renzy is this carver of silver chalices and crucifixes."

A TALE OF A LONELY PARISH.
GUARDIAN.—"The tale is written with all Mr. Crawford's skill."

PAUL PATOFF.
ST. JAMES'S GAZETTE.—"Those who neglect to read *Paul Patoff* will throw away a very pleasurable opportunity."

WITH THE IMMORTALS.
SPECTATOR.—"Cannot fail to please a reader who enjoys crisp, clear, vigorous writing, and thoughts that are alike original and suggestive."

GREIFENSTEIN.
SPECTATOR.—"Altogether, we like *Greifenstein* decidedly—so much so as to doubt whether it does not dislodge *A Roman Singer* from the place hitherto occupied by the latter as our favourite amongst Mr. Crawford's novels."

TAQUISARA: A Novel.
PALL MALL GAZETTE.—"Cannot fail to be read with interest and pleasure by all to whom clever characterisation and delicate drawing make appeal."

A ROSE OF YESTERDAY.
SPEAKER.—"There is something in *A Rose of Yesterday* which makes the book linger with a distinct aroma of its own in the reader's memory."

SANT' ILARIO.
ATHENÆUM.—"The plot is skilfully concocted, and the interest is sustained to the end. . . . A very clever piece of work."

A CIGARETTE-MAKER'S ROMANCE.
GLOBE.—"We are inclined to think this is the best of Mr. Marion Crawford's stories."

KHALED: A Tale of Arabia.
ANTI-JACOBIN.—"Mr. Crawford has written some stories more powerful, but none more attractive than this."

THE THREE FATES.
NATIONAL OBSERVER.—"Increases in strength and in interest even to the end."

THE NOVELS OF
F. MARION CRAWFORD

THE WITCH OF PRAGUE.

ACADEMY.—" Is so remarkable a book as to be certain of as wide a popularity as any of its predecessors ; it is a romance of singular daring and power."

MARION DARCHE: A Story without Comment.

ATHENÆUM.—" Readers in search of a good novel may be recommended to lose no time in making the acquaintance of Marion Darche, her devoted friends, and her one enemy."

KATHARINE LAUDERDALE.

PUNCH.—" Admirable in its simple pathos, its unforced humour, and, above all, in ts truth to human nature."

THE CHILDREN OF THE KING.

DAILY CHRONICLE.—" Mr. Crawford has not done better than *The Children of the King* for a long time. The story itself is a simple and beautiful one."

PIETRO GHISLERI.

SPEAKER.—" Mr. Marion Crawford is an artist, and a great one, and he has been brilliantly successful in a task in which ninety-nine out of every hundred writers would have failed."

DON ORSINO.

ATHENÆUM.—" *Don Orsino* is a story with many strong points, and it is told with all the spirit we have been wont to expect from its author."

CASA BRACCIO.

GUARDIAN.—" A very powerful story and a finished work of art."

ADAM JOHNSTONE'S SON.

DAILY NEWS.—" Mr. Crawford has written stories richer in incident and more powerful in intention, but we do not think that he has handled more deftly or shown a more delicate insight into tendencies that go towards making some of the more spiritual tragedies of life."

THE RALSTONS.

ATHENÆUM.—" The present instalment of what promises to be a very voluminous amily history, increasing in interest and power as it develops, turns upon the death of Robert and the disposition of his millions, which afford ample scope for the author's pleasantly ingenious talent in raising and surmounting difficulties of details."

CORLEONE: A Tale of Sicily.

PALL MALL GAZETTE.—" A splendid romance.'

VIA CRUCIS: A Romance of the Second Crusade.

GRAPHIC.—" A stirring story.'

IN THE PALACE OF THE KING: A Love Story of Old Madrid.

SPECTATOR.—" A truly thrilling tale."

CECILIA: A Story of Modern Rome.

TIMES.—" Thoroughly interesting from beginning to end. . . . Fully worthy of his reputation."
ILLUSTRATED LONDON NEWS.—" Can only enhance Mr. Crawford's reputation. . . . Admirably treated with all the subtlety, finesse, and delicacy which are characteristic of the author at his best."

MARIETTA: A Maid of Venice.

PUNCH.—" Marion Crawford is at his very best in *Marietta, A Maid of Venice.* It is a powerfully dramatic story of Venice under 'The Ten,' told in a series of picturesque scenes described in strikingly artistic word-painting, the action being carried on by well-imagined clearly-defined characters."

THE NOVELS OF
ROLF BOLDREWOOD

ROBBERY UNDER ARMS.
A STORY OF LIFE AND ADVENTURE IN THE BUSH AND IN THE GOLD-FIELDS OF AUSTRALIA.

GUARDIAN.—"A singularly spirited and stirring tale of Australian life, chiefly in the remoter settlements."

A MODERN BUCCANEER.
DAILY CHRONICLE.—"We do not forget *Robbery under Arms*, or any of its various successors, when we say that Rolf Boldrewood has never done anything so good as *A Modern Buccaneer.* It is good, too, in a manner which is for the author a new one."

THE MINER'S RIGHT.
A TALE OF THE AUSTRALIAN GOLD-FIELDS.

WORLD.—"Full of good passages, passages abounding in vivacity, in the colour and play of life. . . . The pith of the book lies in its singularly fresh and vivid pictures of the humours of the gold-fields—tragic humours enough they are, too, here and again."

THE SQUATTER'S DREAM.
FIELD.—"The details are filled in by a hand evidently well conversant with his subject, and everything is *ben trovato*, if not actually true. A perusal of these cheerfully-written pages will probably give a better idea of realities of Australian life than could be obtained from many more pretentious works."

A SYDNEY-SIDE SAXON.
GLASGOW HERALD.—"The interest never flags, and altogether *A Sydney-Side Saxon* is a really refreshing book."

A COLONIAL REFORMER.
ATHENÆUM.—"A series of natural and entertaining pictures of Australian life, which are, above all things, readable."

NEVERMORE.
OBSERVER.—"An exciting story of Ballarat in the 'fifties. Its hero, Lance Trevanion, is a character which for force of delineation has no equal in Rolf Boldrewood's previous novels."

PLAIN LIVING. A Bush Idyll.
ACADEMY.—"A hearty story, deriving charm from the odours of the bush and the bleating of incalculable sheep.'

MY RUN HOME.
ATHENÆUM.—"Rolf Boldrewood's last story is a racy volume. It has many of the best qualities of Whyte Melville, the breezy freshness and vigour of Frank Smedley, with the dash and something of the abandon of Lever. . . . His last volume is one of his best."

THE SEALSKIN CLOAK.
TIMES.—"A well-written story."

THE CROOKED STICK; or, Pollie's Probation.
ACADEMY.—"A charming picture of Australian station life."

OLD MELBOURNE MEMORIES.
NATIONAL OBSERVER.—"His book deserves to be read in England with as much appreciation as it has already gained in the country of its birth."

A ROMANCE OF CANVAS TOWN, and other Stories.
ATHENÆUM.—"The book is interesting for its obvious insight into life in the Australian bush."

WAR TO THE KNIFE; or, Tangata Maori.
ACADEMY. —"A stirring romance."

BABES IN THE BUSH.
OUTLOOK.—"A lively and picturesque story."
DAILY TELEGRAPH.—"Bristles with thrilling incident."

IN BAD COMPANY, and other Stories.
DAILY NEWS.—"The best work this popular author has done for some time."

By H. G. WELLS

THE PLATTNER STORY: and others.

TALES OF SPACE AND TIME.

THE STOLEN BACILLUS: and other Incidents.

THE INVISIBLE MAN. A Grotesque Romance. Eighth Edition.

LOVE AND MR. LEWISHAM. A Story of a very Young Couple.

WHEN THE SLEEPER WAKES.

THE FIRST MEN IN THE MOON.

TWELVE STORIES AND A DREAM.

By A. E. W. MASON

THE COURTSHIP OF MORRICE BUCKLER.

THE PHILANDERERS.

MIRANDA OF THE BALCONY.

By EGERTON CASTLE

THE BATH COMEDY.

THE PRIDE OF JENNICO. Being a Memoir of Captain Basil Jennico.

THE LIGHT OF SCARTHEY. A Romance.

"LA BELLA," AND OTHERS.

"YOUNG APRIL."

By MAARTEN MAARTENS

AN OLD MAID'S LOVE. A Dutch. Tale told in English.

THE GREATER GLORY. A Story of High Life.

MY LADY NOBODY. A Novel.

GOD'S FOOL. A Koopstad Story.

THE SIN OF JOOST AVELINGH. A Dutch Story.

HER MEMORY.

THE NOVELS OF
ROSA N. CAREY

Over Half-a-Million of these works have been printed.

47th Thousand.
NELLIE'S MEMORIES.

STANDARD.—"Miss Carey has the gift of writing naturally and simply, her pathos is true and unforced, and her conversations are sprightly and sharp."

33rd Thousand.
WEE WIFIE.

LADY—"Miss Carey's novels are always welcome; they are out of the common run, immaculately pure, and very high in tone."

29th Thousand.
BARBARA HEATHCOTE'S TRIAL.

DAILY TELEGRAPH.—"A novel ot a sort which it would be a real loss to miss."

25th Thousand.
ROBERT ORD'S ATONEMENT.

STANDARD.—"*Robert Ord's Atonement* is a delightful book, very quiet as to its story, but very strong in character, and instinct with that delicate pathos which is the salient point of all the writings of this author.".

32nd Thousand.
WOOED AND MARRIED.

STANDARD.—"There is plenty of romance in the heroine's life. But it would not be fair to tell our readers wherein that romance consists or how it ends. Let them read the book for themselves. We will undertake to promise that they will like it."

24th Thousand.
HERIOT'S CHOICE.

MORNING POST.—"Deserves to be extensively known and read. . . . Will doubtless find as many admirers as readers."

29th Thousand.
QUEENIE'S WHIM.

GUARDIAN.—"A thoroughly good and wholesome story."

35th Thousand.
NOT LIKE OTHER GIRLS.

PALL MALL GAZETTE.—"Like all the other stories we have had from the same gifted pen, this volume, *Not Like Other Girls*, takes a sane and healthy view of life and its concerns. . . . It is an excellent story to put in the hands of girls."
NEW YORK HOME JOURNAL.—"One of the sweetest, daintiest, and most interesting ot the season's publications."

24th Thousand.
MARY ST. JOHN.

JOHN BULL.—"The story is a simple one, but told with much grace and unaffected pathos."

23rd Thousand.
FOR LILIAS.

VANITY FAIR.—"A simple, earnest, and withal very interesting story; well conceived, carefully worked out, and sympathetically told."

28th Thousand.
UNCLE MAX.

LADY.—"So intrinsically good that the world of novel-readers ought to be genuinely grateful."

21st Thousand.
RUE WITH A DIFFERENCE.

BOOKMAN.—"Fresh and charming. . . . A piece of distinctly good work.

THE NOVELS OF
ROSA N. CAREY

Over Half-a-Million of these works have been printed.

34th Thousand.

ONLY THE GOVERNESS.

PALL MALL GAZETTE.—"This novel is for those who like stories with something of Jane Austen's power, but with more intensity of feeling than Jane Austen displayed, who are not inclined to call pathos twaddle, and who care to see life and human nature in their most beautiful form."

24th Thousand.

LOVER OR FRIEND?

GUARDIAN.—"The refinement of style and delicacy of thought will make *Lover or Friend?* popular with all readers who are not too deeply bitten with a desire for things improbable in their lighter literature."

21st Thousand.

BASIL LYNDHURST.

PALL MALL GAZETTE.—"We doubt whether anything has been written of late years so fresh, so pretty, so thoroughly natural and bright. The novel as a whole is charming."

22nd Thousand.

SIR GODFREY'S GRAND-DAUGHTERS.

OBSERVER.—"A capital story. The interest steadily grows, and by the time one reaches the third volume the story has become enthralling."

24th Thousand.

THE OLD, OLD STORY.

DAILY NEWS.—"Miss Carey's fluent pen has not lost its power of writing fresh and wholesome fiction."

24th Thousand.

THE MISTRESS OF BRAE FARM.

PALL MALL GAZETTE.—"Miss Carey's untiring pen loses none of its power, and her latest work is as gracefully written, as full of quiet home charm, as fresh and wholesome, so to speak, as its many predecessors."

12th Thousand.

MRS. ROMNEY and "BUT MEN MUST WORK."

PALL MALL GAZETTE.—"By no means the least attractive of the works of this charming writer."

New Impression.

OTHER PEOPLE'S LIVES.

BRADFORD OBSERVER.—"There is a quiet charm about this story which finds its way into the innermost shrines of life. The book is wholesome and good, and cannot fail to give pleasure to those who love beauty."

25th Thousand.

HERB OF GRACE.

WESTMINSTER GAZETTE.—"A clever delineator of character, possessed of a reserve of strength in a quiet, flowing style, Miss Carey never fails to please a large class of readers. *Herb of Grace* is no exception to the rule. . . ."

20th Thousand.

THE HIGHWAY OF FATE.

BOOKMAN.—"This pretty love story . . . . is charming, sparkling, and never mawkish."

19th Thousand.

A PASSAGE PERILOUS.

TIMES.—"Told with all Miss Carey's usual charm of quiet, well-bred sentiment."
OUTLOOK.—"A pretty story of English country-house life during the terribly anxious 'waiting days' of Ladysmith. The soldier's young bride is charmingly suggested and the love portions approach the idyllic."

THE NOVELS AND TALES OF

CHARLOTTE M. YONGE

THE HEIR OF REDCLYFFE. With Illustrations by KATE GREENAWAY.

HEARTSEASE ; or, the Brother's Wife. New Edition. With Illustrations by KATE GREENAWAY.

HOPES AND FEARS ; or, Scenes from the Life of a Spinster. With Illustrations by HERBERT GANDY.

DYNEVOR TERRACE ; or, the Clue of Life. With Illustrations by ADRIAN STOKES.

THE DAISY CHAIN ; or, Aspirations. A Family Chronicle With Illustrations by J. P. ATKINSON.

THE TRIAL : More Links of the Daisy Chain. With Illustrations by J. P. ATKINSON.

THE PILLARS OF THE HOUSE ; or, Under Wode, under Rode. Two Vols. With Illustrations by HERBERT GANDY.

THE YOUNG STEPMOTHER ; or, a Chronicle of Mistakes. With Illustrations by MARIAN HUXLEY.

THE CLEVER WOMAN OF THE FAMILY. With Illustrations by ADRIAN STOKES.

THE THREE BRIDES. With Illustrations by ADRIAN STOKES.

MY YOUNG ALCIDES : A Faded Photograph. With Illustrations by ADRIAN STOKES.

THE CAGED LION. With Illustrations by W. J. HENNESSY.

THE DOVE IN THE EAGLE'S NEST. With Illustrations by W. J. HENNESSY.

THE CHAPLET OF PEARLS ; or, the White and Black Ribaumont. With Illustrations by W. J. HENNESSY.

LADY HESTER ; or, Ursula's Narrative ; and THE DANVERS PAPERS. With Illustrations by JANE E. COOK.

MAGNUM BONUM ; or, Mother Carey's Brood. With Illustrations by W. J. HENNESSY.

LOVE AND LIFE : an Old Story in Eighteenth Century Costume. With Illustrations by W. J. HENNESSY.

UNKNOWN TO HISTORY. A Story of the Captivity of Mary of Scotland. With Illustrations by W. J. HENNESSY.

STRAY PEARLS. Memoirs of Margaret de Ribaumont, Viscountess of Bellaise. With Illustrations by W. J. HENNESSY.

THE NOVELS AND TALES OF
CHARLOTTE M. YONGE

THE ARMOURER'S 'PRENTICES. With Illustrations by W. J. HENNESSY.

THE TWO SIDES OF THE SHIELD. With Illustrations by W. J. HENNESSY.

NUTTIE'S FATHER. With Illustrations by W. J. HENNESSY.

SCENES AND CHARACTERS; or, Eighteen Months at Beechcroft. With Illustrations by W. J. HENNESSY.

CHANTRY HOUSE. With Illustrations by W. J. HENNESSY.

A MODERN TELEMACHUS. With Illustrations by W. HENNESSY.

BYWORDS. A collection of Tales new and old.

BEECHCROFT AT ROCKSTONE.

MORE BYWORDS.

A REPUTED CHANGELING; or, Three Seventh Years Two Centuries Ago.

THE LITTLE DUKE, RICHARD THE FEARLESS. With Illustrations.

THE LANCES OF LYNWOOD. With Illustrations by J. B.

THE PRINCE AND THE PAGE: A Story of the Last Crusade. With Illustrations by ADRIAN STOKES.

TWO PENNILESS PRINCESSES. With Illustrations by W. J. HENNESSY.

THAT STICK.

AN OLD WOMAN'S OUTLOOK IN A HAMPSHIRE VILLAGE.

GRISLY GRISELL; or, The Laidly Lady of Whitburn. A Tale of the Wars of the Roses.

HENRIETTA'S WISH. Second Edition.

THE LONG VACATION.

THE RELEASE; or, Caroline's French Kindred.

THE PILGRIMAGE OF THE BEN BERIAH.

THE TWO GUARDIANS; or, Home in this World. Second Edition.

COUNTESS KATE AND THE STOKESLEY SECRET.

MODERN BROODS; or, Developments Unlooked for.

STROLLING PLAYERS: A Harmony of Contrasts. By C. M. YONGE and C. R. COLERIDGE.

Works by Mrs. Craik

Olive: A Novel. With Illustrations by G. Bowers.
The Ogilvies: A Novel. With Illustrations.
Agatha's Husband: A Novel. With Illustrations by Walter Crane.
The Head of the Family: A Novel. With Illustrations by Walter Crane.
Two Marriages.
The Laurel Bush.
My Mother and I: a Girl's Love Story. With Illustrations.
Miss Tommy: a Mediæval Romance.
King Arthur: Not a Love Story.
About Money, and other Things.
Concerning Men, and other Papers.

Works by Mrs. Oliphant

Neighbours on the Green.
Joyce.
Kirsteen: the Story of a Scotch Family Seventy Years Ago.
A Beleaguered City: A Story of the Seen and the Unseen.
Hester: a Story of Contemporary Life.
He that Will Not when He May.
The Railway Man and his Children.
The Marriage of Elinor.
Sir Tom.
The Heir-Presmptive and the Heir-Apparent.
A Country Gentleman and his Family.
A Son of the Soil.
The Second Son.
The Wizard's Son: A Novel.
The Curate in Charge.
Lady William.   Young Musgrave.

The Works of Dean Farrar

SEEKERS AFTER GOD.   The Lives of Seneca, Epictetus, and Marcus Aurelius.

ETERNAL HOPE.   Sermons preached in Westminster Abbey.

THE FALL OF MAN : and other Sermons.

THE WITNESS OF HISTORY TO CHRIST.

THE SILENCE AND VOICES OF GOD, with other Sermons.

"IN THE DAYS OF THY YOUTH."   Sermons on Practical Subjects.

SAINTLY WORKERS.   Five Lenten Lectures.

EPHPHATHA ; or, the Amelioration of the World.

MERCY; AND JUDGMENT : a few last words on Christian Eschatology.

SERMONS & ADDRESSES DELIVERED IN AMERICA.

THE WORKS OF
Frederick Denison Maurice

SERMONS PREACHED IN LINCOLN'S INN CHAPEL. In six vols.

SERMONS PREACHED IN COUNTRY CHURCHES.

CHRISTMAS DAY : and other Sermons.

THEOLOGICAL ESSAYS.

THE PROPHETS AND KINGS OF THE OLD TESTAMENT.

THE PATRIARCHS AND LAWGIVERS OF THE OLD TESTAMENT.

THE GOSPEL OF THE KINGDOM OF HEAVEN.

THE GOSPEL OF ST. JOHN.

THE EPISTLES OF ST. JOHN.

THE FRIENDSHIP OF BOOKS : and other Lectures.

THE PRAYER BOOK AND LORD'S PRAYER.

THE DOCTRINE OF SACRIFICE.   Deduced from the Scriptures.

THE ACTS OF THE APOSTLES.

THE KINGDOM OF CHRIST ; or, Hints to a Quaker respecting the Principles, Constitution, and Ordinances of the Catholic Church.   2 vols.

THE WORKS OF

CHARLES KINGSLEY

WESTWARD HO!

HYPATIA; or, New Foes with an old Face.

TWO YEARS AGO.

ALTON LOCKE, Tailor and Poet. An Autobiography.

HEREWARD THE WAKE, "Last of the English."

YEAST: A Problem.

POEMS: including The Saint's Tragedy, Andromeda, Songs Ballads, etc.

THE WATER-BABIES: A Fairy Tale for a Land-Baby. With Illustrations by LINLEY SAMBOURNE.

THE HEROES; or, Greek Fairy Tales for my Children. With Illustrations by the Author.

GLAUCUS; or, The Wonders of the Shore. With Illustrations.

MADAME HOW AND LADY WHY; or, First Lessons in Earth Lore for Children. With Illustrations.

AT LAST. A Christmas in the West Indies. With Illustrations.

THE HERMITS.

HISTORICAL LECTURES AND ESSAYS.

PLAYS AND PURITANS, and other Historical Essays.

THE ROMAN AND THE TEUTON.

PROSE IDYLLS, New and Old.

SCIENTIFIC LECTURES AND ESSAYS.

SANITARY AND SOCIAL LECTURES AND ESSAYS.

LITERARY AND GENERAL LECTURES AND ESSAYS.

ALL SAINTS' DAY: and other Sermons.

DISCIPLINE: and other Sermons.

THE GOOD NEWS OF GOD. Sermons.

GOSPEL OF THE PENTATEUCH.

SERMONS FOR THE TIMES.

SERMONS ON NATIONAL SUBJECTS.

VILLAGE SERMONS, AND TOWN AND COUNTRY SERMONS.

THE WATER OF LIFE: and other Sermons.

WESTMINSTER SERMONS.

ENGLISH
MEN OF LETTERS

Edited by John Morley.

Arranged in 13 Volumes, each containing the Lives of three Authors.

I. **Chaucer.** By Dr. A. W. Ward. **Spenser.** By Dean Church. **Dryden.** By Prof. Saintsbury.

II. **Milton.** By Mark Pattison. **Goldsmith.** By W. Black. **Cowper.** By Goldwin Smith.

III. **Byron.** By Professor Nichol. **Shelley.** By J. A. Symonds. **Keats.** By Sidney Colvin.

IV. **Wordsworth.** By F. W. H. Myers. **Southey.** By Prof. Dowden. **Landor.** By Sidney Colvin.

V. **Charles Lamb.** By Canon Ainger. **Addison.** By W. J. Courthope. **Swift.** By Sir Leslie Stephen, K.C.B.

VI. **Scott.** By R. H. Hutton. **Burns.** By Principal Shairp. **Coleridge.** By H. D. Traill.

VII. **Hume.** By Prof. Huxley, F.R.S. **Locke.** By Thos. Fowler. **Burke.** By John Morley.

VIII. **Defoe.** By W. Minto. **Sterne.** By H. D. Traill. **Hawthorne.** By Henry James.

IX. **Fielding.** By Austin Dobson. **Thackeray.** By Anthony Trollope. **Dickens.** By Dr. A. W. Ward.

X. **Gibbon.** By J. C. Morison. **Carlyle.** By Professor Nichol. **Macaulay.** By J. C. Morison.

XI. **Sydney.** By J. A. Symonds. **De Quincey.** By Prof. Masson. **Sheridan.** By Mrs. Oliphant.

XII. **Pope.** By Sir Leslie Stephen, K.C.B. **Johnson.** By Sir Leslie Stephen, K.C.B. **Gray.** By Edmund Gosse.

XIII. **Bacon.** By Dean Church. **Bunyan.** By J. A. Froude. **Bentley.** By Sir Richard Jebb.

By GERTRUDE ATHERTON

THE CONQUEROR.
PATIENCE SPARHAWK AND HER TIMES.
AMERICAN WIVES & ENGLISH HUSBANDS.
A DAUGHTER OF THE VINE.

By J. H. SHORTHOUSE

JOHN INGLESANT: A Romance.
SIR PERCIVAL: a Story of the Past and of the Present.
THE LITTLE SCHOOLMASTER MARK.
THE COUNTESS EVE.
A TEACHER OF THE VIOLIN.
BLANCHE, LADY FALAISE.

By HUGH CONWAY

A FAMILY AFFAIR. | LIVING OR DEAD.

By W. CLARK RUSSELL

MAROONED. | A STRANGE ELOPEMENT

By Mrs. PARR

DOROTHY FOX. | LOYALTY GEORGE.
ADAM AND EVE. | ROBIN.

By ANNIE KEARY

A YORK AND A LANCASTER ROSE.
CASTLE DALY: the Story of an Irish Home thirty
    years ago.
JANET'S HOME. | OLDBURY.
A DOUBTING HEART.
THE NATIONS AROUND ISRAEL.

By E. WERNER

SUCCESS, AND HOW HE WON IT.
FICKLE FORTUNE.

By W. WARDE FOWLER

A YEAR WITH THE BIRDS. Illustrated.
TALES OF THE BIRDS. Illustrated.
MORE TALES OF THE BIRDS. Illustrated.
SUMMER STUDIES OF BIRDS AND BOOKS.

By FRANK BUCKLAND

CURIOSITIES OF NATURAL HISTORY. Illustrated. In four volumes:

FIRST SERIES—Rats, Serpents, Fishes, Frogs, Monkeys, etc.
SECOND SERIES—Fossils, Bears, Wolves, Cats, Eagles, Hedgehogs, Eels, Herrings, Whales.
THIRD SERIES—Wild Ducks, Fishing, Lions, Tigers, Foxes, Porpoises.
FOURTH SERIES—Giants, Mummies, Mermaids, Wonderful People, Salmon, etc.

By ARCHIBALD FORBES

BARRACKS, BIVOUACS, AND BATTLES.
SOUVENIRS OF SOME CONTINENTS.

By THOMAS HUGHES

TOM BROWN'S SCHOOLDAYS.
TOM BROWN AT OXFORD.
THE SCOURING OF THE WHITE HORSE.
ALFRED THE GREAT.

By MONTAGU WILLIAMS

LEAVES OF A LIFE. | LATER LEAVES.
ROUND LONDON.

By W. E. NORRIS

THIRLBY HALL.
A BACHELOR'S BLUNDER.

The Works of SHAKESPEARE

VICTORIA EDITION. In Three Volumes.
Vol. I. COMEDIES. Vol. II. HISTORIES. Vol. III. TRAGEDIES.

Works by Various Authors

Hogan, M.P.
Flitters, Tatters, and the Counsellor
The New Antigone | Memories of Father Healy
CANON ATKINSON.—**The Last of the Giant Killers**
—— **Walks, Talks, Travels, and Exploits of Two Schoolboys**
—— **Playhours and Half-Holidays; or, further Experiences of Two Schoolboys**
SIR S. BAKER.—**True Tales for my Grandsons**
R. H. BARHAM.—**The Ingoldsby Legends**
REV. R. H. D. BARHAM.—**Life of R. H. Barham**
—— **Life of Theodore Hook** [land
BLENNERHASSET AND SLEEMAN.—**Adventures in Mashona-**
SIR H. LYTTON BULWER.—**Historical Characters**
SIR H. M. DURAND.—**Helen Treveryan**
LANOE FALCONER.—**Cecilia de Noel**
W. FORBES-MITCHELL.—**Reminiscences of the Great Mutiny**
W. P. FRITH, R.A.—**My Autobiography**
REV. J. GILMORE.—**Storm Warriors**
F. GUIZOT.—**Life of Oliver Cromwell**
CUTCLIFFE HYNE.—**The "Paradise" Coal-Boat**
RICHARD JEFFERIES.—**The Dewy Morn**
HENRY KINGSLEY.—**Tales of Old Travel**
MARY LINSKILL.—**Tales of the North Riding**
S. R. LYSAGHT.—**The Marplot**
M. M'LENNAN.—**Muckle Jock, and other Stories**
LUCAS MALET.—**Mrs. Lorimer**
G. MASSON.—**A Compendious Dictionary of the French Language**
F. A. MIGNET.—**Life of Mary Queen of Scots**
MAJOR GAMBIER PARRY.—**The Story of Dick**
E. C. PRICE.—**In the Lion's Mouth**
LORD REDESDALE.—**Tales of Old Japan**
W. C. RHOADES.—**John Trevennick**
CAMILLE ROUSSET.—**Recollections of Marshal Macdonald**
HAWLEY SMART.—**Breezie Langton**
MARCHESA THEODOLI.—**Under Pressure**
ANTHONY TROLLOPE.—**The Three Clerks**
MRS. HUMPHRY WARD.—**Miss Bretherton**
CHARLES WHITEHEAD.—**Richard Savage**

THE GLOBE LIBRARY

Crown 8vo.   3s. 6d. each.

The volumes marked with an asterisk (*) are also issued in limp leather, with full gilt back and gilt edges.   5s. net each.

*Boswell's Life of Johnson.   With an Introduction by MOWBRAY MORRIS.

*Burns's Complete Works.   Edited from the best Printed and MS. Authorities, with Memoir and Glossarial Index.   By A. SMITH.

*The Works of Geoffrey Chaucer.   Edited by ALFRED W. POLLARD, H. F. HEATH, M. H. LIDDELL, and W. S. McCORMICK.

*Cowper's Poetical Works.   Edited, with Biographical Introduction and Notes by W. BENHAM, B.D.

Robinson Crusoe.   Edited after the original Edition, with a Biographical Introduction by HENRY KINGSLEY, F.R.G.S.

*Dryden's Poetical Works.   Edited, with a Memoir, Revised Texts, and Notes, by W. D. CHRISTIE, M.A.

Froissart's Chronicles.   Translated by Lord BERNERS. Edited by G. C. MACAULAY, M.A.

*Goldsmith's Miscellaneous Works.   With Biographical Introduction by Professor MASSON.

Horace.   Rendered into English Prose, with Introduction, Running Analysis, Notes, and Index.   By J. LONSDALE, M.A., and S. LEE, M.A.

Morte D'Arthur.   The Book of King Arthur, and of his Noble Knights of the Round Table.   The Original Edition of Caxton, revised for modern use.   With Introduction, Notes, and Glossary. By Sir E. STRACHEY.

*Milton's Poetical Works.   Edited, with Introduction, by Professor MASSON.

*The Diary of Samuel Pepys.   With an Introduction and Notes by G. GREGORY SMITH.

*Pope's Poetical Works.   Edited, with Notes and Introductory Memoir, by Dr. A. W. WARD.

*Sir Walter Scott's Poetical Works.   Edited, with Biographical and Critical Memoir, by Prof. F. T. PALGRAVE.   With Introduction and Notes.

*Shakespeare's Complete Works.   Edited by W. G. CLARK, M.A., and W. ALDIS WRIGHT, M.A.   With Glossary.

*Spenser's Complete Works.   Edited from the Original Editions and Manuscripts, with Glossary, by R. MORRIS, and a Memoir by J. W. HALES, M.A.   [edges.   4s. 6d.]

*Tennyson's Poetical Works.   [Also in extra cloth, gilt

Virgil.   Rendered into English Prose, with Introductions, Notes, Analysis, and Index.   By J. LONSDALE, M..A,. and S. LEE, M.A.

ILLUSTRATED
STANDARD NOVELS

Crown 8vo.   Cloth Elegant, gilt edges (Peacock Edition).
3s. 6d. each.

Also issued in ornamental cloth binding.   2s. 6d. each.

By JANE AUSTEN

With Introductions by AUSTIN DOBSON, *and Illustrations by*
HUGH THOMSON *and* C. E. BROCK.

PRIDE AND PREJUDICE.
SENSE AND SENSIBILITY.
EMMA.

MANSFIELD PARK.
NORTHANGER ABBEY,
AND PERSUASION.

By J. FENIMORE COOPER

With Illustrations by C. E. BROCK *and* H. M. BROCK.

THE LAST OF THE MOHICANS. With a General Introduction by Mowbray Morris.

THE DEERSLAYER.
THE PATHFINDER.

THE PIONEERS.
THE PRAIRIE.

By MARIA EDGEWORTH

With Introductions by ANNE THACKERAY RITCHIE, *and Illustrations by* CHRIS HAMMOND *and* CARL SCHLOESSER.

ORMOND.
CASTLE RACKRENT, AND
THE ABSENTEE.
POPULAR TALES.

HELEN.
BELINDA.
PARENT'S ASSISTANT.

By CAPTAIN MARRYAT

With Introductions by DAVID HANNAY, *and Illustrations by*
H. M. BROCK, J. AYTON SYMINGTON, FRED PEGRAM, F. H
TOWNSEND, H. R. MILLAR, *and* E. J. SULLIVAN.

JAPHET IN SEARCH OF
A FATHER.

JACOB FAITHFUL.
PETER SIMPLE.

ILLUSTRATED

STANDARD NOVELS

By CAPTAIN MARRYAT—*continued.*

MIDSHIPMAN EASY.
THE KING'S OWN.
THE PHANTOM SHIP.
SNARLEY-YOW.
POOR JACK.

THE PIRATE, AND THE
THREE CUTTERS.
MASTERMAN READY.
FRANK MILDMAY.
NEWTON FORSTER.

By THOMAS LOVE PEACOCK

With Introductions by GEORGE SAINTSBURY, *and Illustrations
by* H. R. MILLAR *and* F. H. TOWNSEND.

HEADLONG HALL, AND
NIGHTMARE ABBEY.
MAID MARIAN, AND
CROTCHET CASTLE.

GRYLL GRANGE.
MELINCOURT.
MISFORTUNES OF ELPHIN
AND RHODODAPHNE.

BY VARIOUS AUTHORS

WESTWARD HO! By CHARLES KINGSLEY. Illustrated
by C. E. Brock.

HANDY ANDY. By SAMUEL LOVER. Illustrated by
H. M. Brock. With Introduction by Charles Whibley.

TOM. CRINGLE'S LOG. By MICHAEL SCOTT. Illustrated by J. Ayton Symington. With Introduction by Mowbray Morris.

ANNALS OF THE PARISH. By JOHN GALT. Illustrated
By C. E. Brock. With Introduction by Alfred Ainger.

SYBIL, OR THE TWO NATIONS, ETC. By BENJAMIN
DISRAELI. Illustrated by F. Pegram. With Introduction by
H. D. Traill.

LAVENGRO. By GEORGE BORROW. Illustrated by
E. J. Sullivan. With Introduction by Augustine Birrell, K.C.

ADVENTURES OF HAJJI BABA OF ISPAHAN. By JAMES
MORIER. Illustrated by H. R. Millar. With Introduction by
Lord Curzon.

THE NEW CRANFORD SERIES

Crown 8vo, Cloth Elegant, Gilt Edges, 3s. 6d. per volume.

Cranford. By Mrs. GASKELL. With Preface by Anne Thackeray Ritchie and 100 Illustrations by Hugh Thomson.

The Vicar of Wakefield. With 182 Illustrations by Hugh Thomson, and Preface by Austin Dobson.

Our Village. By MARY RUSSELL MITFORD. Introduction by Anne Thackeray Ritchie, and 100 Illustrations by Hugh Thomson.

Gulliver's Travels. With Introduction by Sir Henry Craik, K.C.B., and 100 Illustrations by C. E. Brock.

The Humorous Poems of Thomas Hood. With Preface by Alfred Ainger, and 130 Illustrations by C. E. Brock.

Sheridan's The School for Scandal and The Rivals. Illustrated by E. J. Sullivan. With Introduction by A. Birrell.

Household Stories. By the Brothers GRIMM. Translated by Lucy Crane. With Pictures by Walter Crane.

Reynard the Fox. Edited by J. JACOBS. With Illustrations by W. Frank Calderon.

Coaching Days and Coaching Ways. By W. OUTRAM TRISTRAM. With Illustrations by H. Railton and Hugh Thomson.

Coridon's Song; and other Verses. With Introduction by Austin Dobson and Illustrations by Hugh Thomson.

Days with Sir Roger de Coverley. With Illustrations by Hugh Thomson.

The Fables of Æsop. Selected by JOSEPH JACOBS. Illustrated by R. Heighway.

Old Christmas. By WASHINGTON IRVING. With Illustrations by R. Caldecott.

Bracebridge Hall. With Illustrations by R. CALDECOTT.

Rip Van Winkle and the Legend of Sleepy Hollow. With 50 Illustrations and a Preface by George H. Boughton, A.R.A.

The Alhambra. With Illustrations by J. Pennell and Introduction by E. R. Pennell.

MACMILLAN & CO., LTD., LONDON.

J. PALMER, PRINTER, CAMBRIDGE.　　　20.4.06.